DAUGHTERS OF THE SUNSTONE

DAUGHTERS OF THE SUNSTONE

DARKCHILD   BLUESONG   STARSILK

Sydney J. Van Scyoc

Nelson Doubleday, Inc.
Garden City, New York

CONTENTS

DARKCHILD

For my parents, John W. and Geneva

ONE

THE BOY

The day was overcast, the sky a lowering grey. In the forest, it was a morning of fevered breezes and distant thunder. The boy's slender limbs glistened with perspiration as he slipped through the dense underbrush toward the voices. His slight body was tense, his eyes vigilant. They had accepted him now, these bristling people with their hooded eyes and their blunt husking-teeth. They treated him as they treated their own children: with offhanded brutality. So long as he jumped to his tasks when commanded and didn't get in the way of the adults, he went unmolested. But let him pause a moment in his work, let him hesitate, particularly let him question, and a heavy-handed blow caught him. Usually the blow was accompanied by the staccato grunts the boy had come to recognize as laughter.

He had never learned to share these people's laughter, any more than he had learned to enjoy the tasks they set him and the other children. He paused beneath a sour-leaf bush and gazed down at his hands, frowning. They were rough from the rock harvest. With the others he had scrabbled through tons of river pebbles yesterday, sorting out trade rocks while the riverbed was briefly dry. The tribes to the south favored the tiny nodules of crystalline grey stone while the more primitive tribes to the east and north were eager to trade for glassy blue and green stones. All were buried in deep banks of less desirable pebbles and stones. The other children's hands were covered with protective bristles. They could grub anywhere without harm. The boy's hands were not so equipped and one of his fingernails was torn back deep into the quick.

He touched it experimentally and winced. In addition to the damage he had done his hands, his arms and shoulders were stiff and his back ached. He peered up through the trees at the grumbling sky. Surely it would rain again today and flood the pebble beds.

But earlier this morning there had been unaccustomed sounds from deep in the forest: a grinding, whining drone followed by the tearing sounds of some jarring impact. After a moment's startled silence, the adults had abandoned the harvest and disappeared into the forest, not even bothering to call back threats. Later one of the men had come back to the pebble bank flashing some metal-bright device and laughing hoarsely. He had refused to let the harvesters examine his booty and finally the youths and children had given up their work and disappeared into the brush too, harking to calls from the distance.

The boy had followed, but cautiously. As he drew nearer the source of the calls, what he heard chilled him. There was a ship in the dell, fallen from the sky, a ship like those that came sometimes to trade. Nervously the boy bit at his torn nail and tried to deny the images that rushed into his mind: the flash of a metal hull, dark markings upon it; an opening port; a capsule unwinding toward him, grappling; a suited figure. He had never seen the trade vessels —none had come since he had been here—and from what the people told at night around their cookfires, no one had ever been abducted by one. Yet his mind held these stark memories and his heart pounded with them.

He gasped at a moment's sharp pain and saw he had torn his nail completely away. His finger bled. Frowning, he popped the injured finger into his mouth and sucked it.

The chilling images continued to unfold. He was in the belly of the ship, captive. It was a place of harsh lights and metallic odors, a place of smooth hard surfaces and smooth hard faces. Cold-eyed people dressed in black seized him by both arms, pinioning him to a padded table. They hardly seemed to notice his angry struggles. As he fought, one of them seized his arm and stung it with a needle. The boy's vision blurred then and a peculiar paralysis overcame him. Although his anger and fear remained as violent as before, his arms quit thrashing and his feet quit kicking. As he lost consciousness, someone lowered a metal helmet over his head. And after that came emptiness. Whatever life he had known before the ship had seized him, the metal helmet had stolen memory of it. The helmet had left him virtually nothing, not even—at first—the knowledge that he had been robbed.

Not again. It had taken him too long, a full year, to emerge from the vacuum, to begin to find himself again. For deep down in some secret place, he had managed to hide a bare scrap of identity from the helmet. He had even contrived to keep knowledge of that precious, flimsy scrap from the guide, the implacable voice that directed him now night and day, driving him to observe and classify, to question and learn—no matter what the price he paid in blows.

He knew, for instance, that he had not always lived among brutal people. He did not yet remember where he had lived before the glinting ship had taken him, but flashes of clear golden skies came to him sometimes now and other times he remembered faces that must belong to that previous life. Certainly they were nothing like the bristled faces he saw here.

He sighed, touching the memory: fair faces but with eyes so somberly violet they were like night. And hair that fell in midnight reams.

But the guide did not like it when he remembered those faces. Sharply the guide demanded that he stop and classify an unfamiliar seedling growing in the underbrush. The boy managed to retain a ghost-vision of golden skies while he crushed the seedling's tiny leaves. Their scent was tart. Quickly, hardly thinking, he made a lateral slit in the plant's tiny stem and studied it in cross-section. It was clearly related to the yellow-blooming creeper that grew on the verges of the creekbed when it rained. Deftly he stirred the soil where the tiny plant had sprouted, analyzing its organic content. A single insect clung to the underside of one leaf and he studied it minutely. No detail was too small for the guide. He insisted upon knowing everything, from the form of speech an adult male used to address his most remote female kin to the pattern of cross-hatching on the underside of a clay water pot. The guide was voracious.

He was generous too, sometimes. Since the boy had come here, the guide had given him refuge from care any number of times. The boy stood, sighing. Certainly he was tired and anxious now. If the guide would let him rest, let him crouch in the humid shadows, drop his forehead to his knees and join his brothers for just a few moments . . .

But the guide denied him. Except under the most gruelling circumstances, trancing with his brothers was a reward to be saved for night, when there was nothing left to do or see. For now, there was much to be done. The boy sighed heavily and continued through the brush. The soil was springy underfoot, the distant thunder indistinct, little more than a promise of rain.

Reaching the edge of the dell, the boy slipped forward cautiously. If the ship had the remembered markings on it, he wanted to be away quickly, before he could be taken again. He did not like this place and these people, but they were better than the emptiness the metal helmet had made of his mind.

Then he saw the ship and there were no dark markings on it. It carried a bright crest on one metal pod, a similar identification on its tubular body, and it was crumpled awkwardly between the trees. It would not fly again. And if there were crew members, they had died in the crash or had been dispatched by the people. No one appeared to defend the ship from looting.

Grunting with laughter, the people dragged crates and cartons from the fallen ship. The containers were of many sizes and shapes, but each had its own identifying markings. The boy crouched in the brush, studying the markings, memory stirring. These people did not so much as draw in the mud with sticks. But hadn't he clutched a marking instrument in his hand once, somewhere? Hadn't he made marks that had meaning upon some smooth surface? It almost seemed he could feel the instrument between his fingers now, could feel it move purposefully over the marking surface.

He frowned, absently wiping perspiration from his chin with the back of his hand. Did he know how to record meaning with quickly inscribed symbols? If not, why did he understand the concept? Why did he understand that the markings on the crates and cartons identified their contents? Quickly the boy snapped a brown pod from a nearby bush and began pulling it apart, examining it minutely, feeding sensory data to the guide. He had learned months ago that intense sensory activity served as an adequate screen for his private thoughts.

He sniffed the pulpy interior of the pod, then extracted one round black seed and crushed it on his tongue. As he relayed its sharp taste to the guide, distracting him, with his left hand he seized a small stick. He did not attempt to guide the stick consciously, but let his hand move of its own volition. It moved rapidly, leaving a series of marks in the soft soil. He flicked a second seed into his mouth and let instinct move his hand again. Then he glanced down.

His hand had not made random marks. He recognized with a quick surge of triumph that the lines and circles on the ground had meaning. Studying them with narrowed eyes, he even found certain similarities to the symbols on the broken crates. Eventually, if he could find time, he might even be able to interpret them. Somewhere in his mind he must hold the key. Otherwise, why had his hands made the marks so readily?

It was another step. If he could take enough of these steps, surely they would eventually lead him back to knowledge of the violet-eyed people whose faces he remembered. He settled back on his heels, summoning up faintly curving lips and deep eyes. There was one face in particular, the face of a woman, someone who had given him food and care—

An unexpected sound interrupted his reverie. In the dell, the people had broken into a tall carton. They pulled out brilliant skeins of silken fabric: azure, crimson, chartreuse, emerald, lilac—an entire silken rainbow. There was a single white silk too, shot with flecks of color. Chuckling, the people unrolled the skeins of fabric and slapped the luxuriant stuff against the damp morning breeze. And uncannily, as the fabric rippled, it made more than the rustling sound of fluttering cloth. It both spoke and sang in a multiplicity of alien voices.

The boy stood, drawn. It was as if the morning rainbow sang, its tones clear and yearning. The boy raised his hands to his ears, hearing color, sweet and pure and hypnotic.

The people shouted in rough delight, their hooded eyes glittering. They seized the silken lengths of fabric and slapped them against the air, making them whimper and moan and sigh. Then one man, more inventive than the others, seized a crimson length and tied it to the limb of a small tree. The silk's free end fluttered languidly in the breeze and its silken voice fell into a seductive melody. Fluttering, floating, moving like a thing alive, it sang its siren song to an increasingly enthralled people.

Quickly then the people tied the other bright swaths to the trees and drew back, superstitious awe on their heavy faces. They grunted to each other as the silks filled the dell with a symphony of voices. The breeze was damp, heavy. Yet the silks were not oppressed. Each gleaming length of fabric seemed to speak its own vivid hue, light become music.

The boy moved forward, aware of the people's panting breath and the distant mutter of thunder. The guide was not much interested in the silks, but the boy was drawn as if magnetized.

Then one of the silks, the white one, began to speak. Not in a trembling moan, not in a seductive sigh, but in a hard-edged masculine voice. The voice crackled through the dell, crisp, urgent, somehow demanding, like the restless fingers of lightning that sometimes probed the treetops. The boy halted, his jaw dropping. A shock of recognition stiffened his limbs. *The voice—*

The white silk continued its statement and somehow the other silks seemed to resent its presence. One by one their voices fell to a dissatisfied murmur. Reacting, one of the other people reached up and yanked at the white silk, muttering angrily. Another applied her nails to it, tearing at it.

The boy was stunned. *He knew the white silk's voice.* He didn't know where he had heard it or when, but it struck a chord of recognition. If he could listen to it alone, listen without the increasingly angry jibbering of the people and the sullen whine of the other silks—

Sometimes the boy found himself moving to the guide's directive without conscious decision, as if he were a creature of the guide's will, nothing more. This time it was not the guide's will but his own that launched the boy from the undergrowth. He darted across the dell and flung himself up the trunk of the tree where the white silk flapped. His fingers, damp with perspiration, tore at the knot that held the silk. Then he slipped back down the tree, gathering the silk around him, running.

The people were outraged. They surged raggedly toward him, grunting. One of the adult males, Ramar, caught him with a slicing blow to the jaw, hooded eyes staring with rage. The boy staggered, almost falling against a second indignant male. But he caught himself and managed to slip between the two, leaving them glaring at each other. Before any of the others could catch him, he had thrown himself into the brush, the white silk clinging to him, silent now.

He ran through the dense brush, across the dry riverbed, and into the trees beyond. His feet caught on runners. Low-hanging branches scratched at his face and tried to seize the white silk from him. When he paused, listening, his thin torso was slick with perspiration and he gasped raggedly for breath. But he heard no sound of pursuit. He heard only the thunder, nearer now, less indistinct.

Still panting, he secured the white silk to the trunk of a young tree. His fingers trembled as he first smoothed the slippery fabric, then released it and let it speak.

The breeze was reluctant at first. Then it caught the length of silk and lifted it and the fabric resumed its plea.

The boy recognized it for just that now. Although the voice was incisive, commanding, it pleaded with him. The boy pressed a knotted fist to either temple, trying to heighten his concentration. Had he heard the silk's language before? Were the words, the intonation familiar? Quickly he stooped and uprooted a plant specimen. He crushed its leaves and pressed them to his nose, screening his thoughts from the guide. The guide was not pleased that he had run from the dell with the silk. Almost absently the boy touched the bleeding cut Ramar had inflicted upon him when he fled. His jaw would be scarred.

That didn't matter. *Where had he heard the voice?* He was certain it had not spoken then the language it spoke now. The language it spoke now triggered no memory at all.

If only he could remember the language of the violet-eyed people. He would someday, he was sure. But now, today—

He had no time to pursue his line of thought. The indistinct mutter of thunder had become something more ominous. The sound grew, harsh, rising, until it was a wrenching scream directly overhead, as if some mammoth metal throat cried fury at him. The boy's head snapped back, and at that moment he felt himself caught in an invisible beam, his arms pinned to his sides, his eyes wide, helpless. The paralyzing ray held him for moments.

Then it passed, his eyes cleared, and he saw the ship overhead: a metal hull with familiar dark markings; a port that slowly opened; a metal capsule that descended slowly, grappling. For him. The ship had come to rob him again with its metal helmet.

His heart beat wildly and he tried to shrink back into the brush. But his knees stiffened and instead of carrying him away, his legs carried him toward where the ship lowered. The guide wanted him to go to the ship, wanted him to walk to the dry riverbed and hold up his arms, signalling to the suited man in the capsule.

He would not. He struggled against the guide's imperative. With fierce effort, he seized control of his legs. Jerkily, as if his muscles fought each other, he backed away into the trees, then turned, running, his heart pounding furiously with anger and fear. As he ran, his leg muscles writhed and cramped, trying to hold him back.

He had to remember the voice and its words. He had to save them from the helmet. Otherwise he would never know why the voice pleaded with him, why it was trapped in a length of silken fabric.

He ran through the trees knowing it was useless. Three kinds of thunder sounded in the morning forest: the helpless pounding of the boy's heart, the distant grumble of the heavens, the sharp throb of the ship's engine. The grappler caught him as he plunged down a shallow bluff near the compound where the people lived. It hooked his sparse clothing and then the suited figure jumped from the capsule and plunged toward him, something glinting in his hand. Too exhausted to struggle, the boy felt the sting of a needle. For a moment he swayed dizzily, his mouth suddenly dry, his vision blurred. As he fell, a burst of fury exploded in his mind, blinding him. It surged through his body, a last useless resistance.

The voice. The words.

The boy was unconscious. The suited man lifted him into the capsule. As the ship lifted again, rain began to fall, the drops fat and blood-warm.

TWO

KHIRA

Khira woke to the cheerful whirring of the dried rattleweed she had hung over her bed. Morning sunlight reached through her window and touched the rugged stone wall of her sleeping chamber, picking out the detail of centuries: pits, gouges, discolorations. The breeze that swept through her unshuttered window was fragrant. Beyond the palace precincts, beyond the leveed growing fields, hundreds of fruit trees were unfolding leaves and blossoms to trap sunlight and turn it to sugar. Khira's wall hangings rippled heavily, stirred by the quick breeze, and faded tapestry figures danced in the sun. It would be easy, so easy, to stretch out on her covers and let the sun warm her before she dressed and went down.

But today—

She stifled the troubling thought at the stamp of feet beneath her window. She threw off her covers and ran to the window in time to see the redmane guardian pass with her plow teams. Yvala was the guardian's name and sometimes she nodded austerely to Khira, although she ignored the other children. This morning the redmanes tossed their heads and danced with ponderous playfulness, pleased to be going to the fields. They were a Brakrathi breed, sturdy animals who stood barely waist-high to their guardian. Their stocky bodies were densely grown with shaggy grey hair and their auburn manes and tails swept the ground. With quick excitement, Khira saw that the mare with the dark forelock did not accompany the teams this morning.

Khira turned from the window, tempted to dress and run directly to the pens. Sometime since the teams had returned from the fields the evening before, the mare would have pulled out her shaggy outer coat and trampled it into a springy nest. There she must lie now, dressed only in her soft silver undercoat, coddling a newborn foal, a velvety creature with vestigal mane and questioning eyes.

Was it her own guardian ancestry, so remote, that urged her to visit the new foal? Khira sighed, putting the impulse aside. Yvala would be displeased if the mare were disturbed, even by the palace daughter. And there was a more compelling reason not to go. Khira's heart clenched and the sunny morning turned cold. Today Alzaja went to the mountain.

Today.

Khira shivered. Alzaja had charted the seasons and marked this day months ago, shortly after Darkmorning. Khira had clear memory of her sister stretched out on cushions on the throneroom floor that afternoon, the shadows of winter gathered around her, in one hand her life-scroll, wound into a tight cylinder. The throne on its dais stood over her like a dark predator and on Alzaja's shadowed face was an expression of finality, of decision.

"I've chosen my day," Alzaja said when Khira paced hesitantly across the polished floor. "The sixth day of Nindra's first spring crescent, because Nindra is my hostess and I'm the sixth daughter of the palace. I'll have perhaps five hands of days to train after spring warming. More if I go to train before the melting." The firmness of the words contrasted with the remote quality of her voice. It seemed to float in the chill air, something separate from either of them, an impersonal instrument of declaration.

Even then, with Alzaja's chosen day more than a season away, Khira felt her muscles tighten with apprehension—and a craven sense that Alzaja was abandoning her.

Alzaja was slightly built, hardly bigger at twenty-and-three than Khira at eleven, but she had been Khira's guide and caretaker through most of her years. Tiahna, their mother, was a remote figure. Sometimes she called Khira to the throne for an accounting of her time. Sometimes she advised her. But they were never alone together, because Tiahna caressed the pairing stone at her throat and spoke silently with her stone mate, Rahela, even as she talked with Khira.

Most often Tiahna was distracted by the functions of the throne. And with the coming of the cold, when the people of the stonehalls returned to wintersleep, Tiahna made the trek to the peaks to gather weak winter sunlight for spring, leaving Alzaja and Khira alone in the palace again.

Alone—yet together. Alzaja had taught Khira her first words and helped her take her first steps; had taught her running and jumping games when she was small, singing and counting games when she was older. Sometimes Alzaja took Khira to the stonehalls to play with the ruddy, white-haired children who lived there. Each time Khira returned to the palace with relief. She was a child of the palace, accustomed to its tall, stalk-grown chambers and its sparsely populated corridors. The bustle of the stonehalls was not for her. Nor was the companionship of so many children who were so much like each other, yet so different from her.

So long as she had Alzaja, she was never lonely. They were much like each other, both delicately made with auburn hair that hung straight down their shoulders and autumn-gold eyes. Sometimes Khira watched Alzaja covertly, studying the delicate bones of her wrists, the fine grain of the flesh of her forearms, and imagined that behind this primary image she saw the images of the others, the sisters she had never met: Mara, Denabar, Hedia, Kristyan, Sukiin.

Seven sisters—five of them gone now, dead on the mountain.

Today Alzaja went.

Khira laced her clothes with trembling fingers. *Today.* She wanted to dress quickly and run anywhere but to the dining hall. To the fields perhaps, to watch the redmanes draw the plows. To the canning shed, where the produce monitors would be counting containers, trying to estimate how many would be needed this year. Or to the pottery, where the wheels would be turning already, the slippery clay spattering the potters' aprons.

Today.

Khira dressed and went nowhere but the dining hall. Alzaja already sat at the table, her hair veiling her cheek. She glanced up when Khira entered and smiled when the cook's assistant appeared immediately with Khira's platter.

Today everything upon it was flesh of Alzaja's hostess. The bread was ground from grain harvested when Nindra was at her autumn fullness. The butter was churned from milk drawn at the same phase. The boiled eggs had been placed in cold storage the autumn before. And all the condiments had been gathered during Nindra's same fullness.

Today, in honor of Alzaja's challenge, every person in the valley would eat the food of Nindra's autumn fullness, even the seed monitors and the breeders, who discounted the very concept of hostess' flesh, who insisted that grains of wheat held equal nourishment whenever harvested, if ripe.

Let them choke on Nindra's bread, Khira decided, knowing she would choke on anything she ate today. With effort, she chewed a small pinch of bread and swallowed it dry. It caught in her throat and she coughed violently.

She glanced up to find Alzaja studying her. "You're pale this morning, Khira." Alzaja's voice was serene, as passionless as a dying breeze.

"I sat up the night ciphering," Khira said, although they both knew she had spent the night tossing in her bed.

"Then tonight you must sleep," Alzaja said with a smile that didn't reach her lips. Undisturbed, she turned back to her platter.

Khira studied her narrowly as she disposed of her meal. Alzaja had trained on the mountain for six hands of days, but the sun hardly seemed to have touched her. Her skin was fair, almost transparent. Through the thin flesh of her temples, Khira could see the beat of blue veins. Training had not hardened her hands, although she had honed her nails before coming down this morning. Khira frowned. Slashing-sharp nails and a bare trace of sun-darkening did not make Alzaja any more imposing than she had been before training.

"Alzaja—" But she couldn't say the rest: *Don't go! Don't leave me alone!* Perhaps if she could have said it calmly, reasonably—but just the act of biting back her plea made her head beat with emotion: fear for Alzaja; anger; dread. Even if Alzaja returned, Khira would be alone. Because if Alzaja returned, she would be changed. That was why she went to the mountain: to make her challenge and gain her barohnhood.

Alzaja read her unuttered plea and smiled palely. Pushing back her platter, she stood. "It's time for me to go now. Will you come to the orchards with me?"

Did she think Khira would relinquish her sooner? "Yes—I'll carry your pack. And your pike. Alzaja—"

"I'll carry them myself, Khira," Alzaja said with a floating smile, as if her spirit lingered somewhere outside her body, lost to its concerns. Her fingers didn't even tremble as she strapped on her pack with its single day's rations—flesh of the hostess, everything, down to the smallest bit of dried fruit—and picked up her pike. She didn't wear a hunter's leathers. Instead she wore the same bleached woolen shift she had worn to Darkmorning Evefest last autumn. Her arms were bare, as were her legs, except for her laced boots.

"You'll be cold," Khira said. "Alzaja, tonight—you'll—"

"We won't talk about it," Alzaja responded, but a bare frown marred her serenity and for a moment her fingers whitened on her pike.

Their footsteps echoed through the corridors. Spring was a quiet time in the palace, a busy time outside. They met only a pair of trimmers, who were snipping down overgrown stems of stalklamp and sweeping the glowing runners into a pile. And they met a cook's assistant, who responded to their appearance with a startled jerk and hurried away.

Once they heard a group of Arnimi nearby, discussing some project. Khira's lips tightened with distaste. She did not care to deal with the Arnimi and their cold-eyed questions today. Neither apparently did Alzaja. She quickened her pace.

They found Tiahna upon the throne, the mirrors that banked the throneroom walls focused upon her. She sat in a flush of light and the throne glowed warmly beneath her. Her skin was still blackened from the spring thawing and her eyes glowed impassively in her dark face. When Alzaja and Khira crossed the polished stone floor, she unconsciously touched the pairing stone which hung at her throat. That was her only betrayal of emotion.

"I see you have your pike, daughter," she said. "And your pack." Her voice was low, from deep in her throat.

"Yes, I'm going to the mountain now," Alzaja said, as if the entire valley didn't know. Her voice was light, clear, unaffected. "Either I will come back as tall as you or not at all."

"Come back tall then," Tiahna said huskily, the pairing stone glowing blue under her fingers. "There are valleys with empty thrones, cold places where no one lives. Let this valley be warm with the sun that touches your face." The words were ritual. Barohnas had spoken them to departing daughters for centuries. Their meaning hardly seemed to touch Tiahna.

Yet somewhere there was emotion. There had to be, unless all Tiahna's caring was directed to Rahela. Surely she felt something for Alzaja, some fear, some regret—some anger that Alzaja had to go as Tiahna once had gone.

Khira gazed at Alzaja. No one even knew what beast Tiahna had killed for her throne. She had never made a tale of it. Would Alzaja come back as much a stranger as Tiahna? As tall, as strong, as remote? And when some traveling gem master fastened a newly cut pairing stone at her neck and it took fire—but Khira did not want to think now of the loss of intimacy that would come when Alzaja found her stone mate.

"I'll bring light to the throne when I come," Alzaja responded ritually. With a nod, she turned and led way from the throneroom. Khira glanced back once. Tiahna peered impassively after them, her sun-darkened face betraying nothing. But Khira noticed that she clutched her pairing stone with tightening fingers.

It was tradition that no one of the stonehalls take leave of the palace daughter on her chosen day. And so as Alzaja and Khira left the palace and crossed the plaza to the stone avenues, the people who passed them, the runners, the stonemasons, the launderers, averted their eyes or nodded covertly. And the occasional child too young for the fields skipped past them with flushing face, lips bitten to silence.

The palace was built upon a rise at the center of the valley. Stonehalls, work buildings, and stock pens had grown up in concentric rings about it. Stone avenues stretched from it, narrowing as they neared the fields. The precious soil of the fields was carefully contained within a series of broad, interlocking stone levees. In the first days after the spring melting, thaw-water stood to the tops of the levees, making a series of drowning pools of the fields. Gradually the water seeped down until the soil could be worked.

Shading her eyes, Khira saw Yvala leading one of her teams down broad levee steps. A crew of workers followed with the plow the team would pull. In the distance, the other team was already at work in a separate leveed field. A group of Arnimi observed them from the levee, their silver suits glinting in the sun.

The tops of the levees were broad, and foot traffic from the fields passed across them to the avenues. Khira followed Alzaja across the levees, keenly aware of her sister's composure. Alzaja hardly looked where she placed her feet. Instead she peered serenely toward Terlath, as if she could already see her beast somewhere on those frozen slopes—as if she could already see him dead.

Or as if . . . But Khira dismissed the thought unconfronted. The morning was clear, the breeze warm. No one could die on a day like this one.

But on Terlath's slopes, there was snow and ice. It would be several hands of days before the first spring grass greened the mountain's stone shoulders and the herders took their sheep to pasture.

"At least the winter beasts will be weak," Khira said aloud. Perhaps the most fearsome of them would still be in wintersleep.

"No one goes to the mountain to challenge an animal who is weak."

Khira looked at Alzaja sharply. Was she really so unaffected? But Alzaja was right. The inexplicable glandular rush that brought barohnhood could not be conferred by confrontation with a beast whom winter had left weak. Quickly images of breeterlik, of rock-leopards, of snowminx flashed into Khira's mind. The snowminx were rare, elusive white shadows that prowled the winter snows. She had seen rock-leopards more often, patrolling the rocky ridges of the mountain, and she had several times seen breeterlik. They were lumbering, shaggy beasts with hot eyes and writhing belly sphincters that oozed acid. Once she had even seen a crag-charger bumping and tumbling down the slopes in its hard carapace. When it reached a level area, it took to its feet—its stubby feet set on short, retractable legs—and pounded away without seeing her. If it had sighted her, if it had charged—

But it had not. Khira shivered. The hunters took the mountain beasts with bladed pikes and with bows. Alzaja had only a simple wooden pike and her sharpened nails. But where the successful hunter brought home meat and hide and little more, Alzaja could return with the power to capture the sun's energy and store it in the sunthrone.

If . . .

They crossed the last levee and descended into the orchard lands that ringed the growing fields. Here, so near the mountain, the air was chill. The trees bloomed anyway, their petals fluttering seductively in the breeze, promising summer fruit.

"Have you ever guessed, Khira, who I named you for?" Alzaja said as they entered the trees.

Khira abandoned her thoughts with a start. "You said you would tell me," she realized. "And there was something else you said you would tell me today." For once concern had outstripped curiosity. She had completely forgotten Alzaja's promise.

Alzaja bowed her head. Sunlight passing through bright petals dyed her pale cheeks. "I've been careful to leave you with only those two promises. All the other things I've ever promised, I've fulfilled." She paused, glancing up into the trees. "It was different when Mara went."

Khira glanced sharply at her sister. Her voice was so light, so unconcerned. They might have been on their way to gather stringgrass for the cook. She tried to match Alzaja's unaffected tone. "You told me—there were things Mara never did. Things she said she would."

"Yes, so many things she promised me. Talks we would have. Scrolls she would letter for me, stories she wanted me to remember, sketches she would make. But all she left me was promises."

"She thought she would come back," Khira said uneasily.

Alzaja nodded gravely. She began to walk again, deliberately, never looking where she put her foot. "She never even considered that she might not. She was so certain, she trained for just a few days. And after she went to the peaks, the lens tenders found her pack on a rock beside the trail. She hadn't even eaten her bread. I suppose she thought she would eat it later, when she came down from the peaks."

Khira frowned. Mara had thrown her life away thoughtlessly, carelessly. Yet Alzaja was not angry, had never been. She spoke remotely, as if Mara's recklessness had not affected her at all. "Alzaja—"

"I named you from one of the early scrolls, Khira. For Khirsa. Do you remember?"

"I—" Distracted, Khira groped for memory. "She was a herder," she said uncertainly.

"Yes. In those times, there were more predators in these mountains. And the people were much more dependent upon their sheep than we are now. Each spring the young herders took their sheep to pasture and if predators came, the herders had to go against them. There was no other way. Each year herders died protecting their flocks.

"But the people had a belief then." Alzaja halted again, peering toward the flashing mirrors that beamed sunlight down the mountain. "They believed that if they saw a silverwing above the mountain, it was because one of the herders had died killing a mountain beast."

"They thought the herders actually became silverwings," Khira said, remembering the story. Frowning, she tried to concentrate her attention in the moment. There would be time later to wonder why Alzaja had not been angry at Mara, why she was not frightened now. "They—they thought the mountains had power and when the herders drew on the power to kill a predator, they were transformed."

"Yes, and transformed they lived one year in the form of a silverwing. Then they joined the web of mountain power and lived there forever. They didn't know that the sun is the source of power, not the mountains.

"But when Khirsa called on the mountain power to kill the breeterlik that had taken her ewes, she didn't change. She killed him and yet she didn't become a silverwing. And then when she started back down the mountain, she found a nest of fledgling silverwings behind a boulder—and broken shells. She learned that when you see a silverwing in the sky, it means only one thing. Somewhere there is a broken shell and a mother bird watching her fledgling fly."

Khira caught her lip in her teeth. In the story, Khirsa had been angry—angry that the people who sent her to guard the sheep had lied. Didn't Alzaja remember that?

But when had Alzaja ever been angry? Khira tried to remember a time and remembered only patience and laughter and much of the same serenity she saw in Alzaja today. Khira had always been the storming one.

"I named you for Khirsa because I wanted you to look for the truth behind whatever legend you might hear. I wanted you to know that our mother was once a palace daughter and now she is a barohna because she was strong and self-willed and went to the peaks well-trained. I wanted you to know that when you come across a killed beast, it is because someone or something has made herself stronger than the beast and has willed her life over the beast's. I wanted you to know that when people rely on powers outside themselves, or power within themselves that they haven't taken the trouble to develop—"

"Like Mara—"

"Like Mara. I wanted you to know that if you fail to prepare, your beast will have you." Her glance flickered sideways, momentarily evasive. "But Khira, there is something else. There is—"

Khira could not listen to more. "Alzaja, don't go," she pleaded, an eruption of emotion. "There will be other years. No one will say anything if you come back with me. They'll be glad. And next time, you can set your day later. You can train harder. You don't have to go today!"

"No, Khira. I have to go now," Alzaja said simply, faintly troubled. "But before I do—"

"No!" How many reasons could she name—all of them coming down to just one agonized plea? "I'll be alone."

Khira's plea seemed to stir the breeze through the trees. Leaves rattled and spring fragrance drifted heavily through the air. The twisted limbs of the orchard were thick with blossoms. Soon there would be laughing children under the trees, and this summer there would be every kind of fruit. But today there was only Khira, crying, and Alzaja, embracing her. "I have to go, Khira. Another year and I will be too old for the peaks. This is my year."

"You won't be too old!" Khira insisted. "You can set your day later next year. You can train longer and be stronger. And we'll spar during the winter. The pads Hassel made for us so we could work with the pikes—we hardly used them." Khira had laced into hers twice. They were cumbersome and scratchy. But if she had insisted Alzaja spar with her through the winter, Alzaja would already have been hardened by spring thawing.

Gently Alzaja drew Khira down to sit under the trees. "I'm not thinking of piking strength, Khira. I'm thinking of the courage it takes to leave you. Every year I have less of it. I know you will be alone and I'm sorry for it. But you're older now and you're strong. Old enough, strong enough. And I've told you everything now—except the one thing. I haven't told you about the ice and the stone."

The one secret, barely hinted at in the scrolls. How often had Khira teased Alzaja for it? How often had Alzaja evaded her? Without meaning to, Khira seized Alzaja's arm, her fingers closing tight in fresh anger. "You saved that until now just to keep me from arguing with you. You saved it—" To distract her, as she might distract a toddler from a cut finger with a piece of dried fruit. "You—"

"I saved it because this is the time when I must tell you. Now, just before I go. This is when Mara told me. I walked this far with her and we sat under the trees and after she had told me about the ice and the stone, she went up the mountain and I went back to the palace. And it was the same with the others. Sukiin told Kristyan here, Kristyan told Hedia, Hedia told Denabar—"

"Well, even if I let you tell me, I won't leave you here," Khira retorted fiercely. "I don't care what the others did. I'm going to walk to the lower pasture with you. I'm going to—"

"You will leave me here," Alzaja declared. "And there is no question of refusing to hear me. The ice and the stone come from the earliest time of the barohnas, from the days when the first barohnas learned to use the sunstone—from the time Niabi turned the fire loose and saw Lensar fall in ashes. It is always passed from elder sister to younger. When finally a sister bronzes, it passes from her to her first daughter."

"Then it's no use telling me. I have no younger sister."

"There was no younger sister when I was eleven either, Khira."

"I was expected," Khira insisted. To all her other angers she added anger that she could not break through the barrier of Alzaja's composure. "And I don't think there will be another. I'll have no one to raise. I'll be alone and I'll be the last." Miserably she recognized the tone of a spoiled child, petulant, whining. And she did not want her last hour with Alzaja to be an hour that would sour in memory. She bit her lip, her voice tearful. "Alzaja—"

"You have to know," Alzaja said. "You have to know how a barohna dies."

Khira sucked a quivering breath, caught by a numbing chill. Was that the secret of the ice and the stone? She had asked often enough when she was younger what became of the barohnas. The scrolls were full of the dying of other people—silently in wintersleep, valiantly during the warmseasons defending their stock, grimly during the brief times of trouble. But when a barohna retired to the plains, she simply strode off the story-scrolls into mystery, without ceremony, without explanation.

"I know how redmane guardians die," she said reluctantly. She and Alzaja had gone to the plain where the redmanes lived two years before at bonding time. They had visited their grandmother, Kadura, retired there with her stone mate Upala. She shuddered, the scene still vivid. First was the silence of the gathered herds, thousands of animals standing motionless under the dusken sky, dark-robed guardians watching them from every prominence. Then the moons came across the mountains and the redmanes began to pound their padded feet. They pounded until the entire plain seemed to reverberate to the beat of a single heart; pounded ever more insistently, ever more rapidly, until Khira's own heart took up the rhythm and surged with it. The blood pulsed through her body more and more quickly. Consciousness became a whining drone in her ears and she had no thoughts, only consuming awareness of the herd and of the heartbeat of the plain. She had fallen finally, when her heart beat too frenetically, had lain helpless on the shuddering ground until the bonding was done and the redmanes padded silently away, leaving their own dead behind.

Guardians had been left dead too, those too old or feeble to stand the frenzied pounding of their hearts. On their faces Khira had seen surprise and rapture. Alzaja had led Khira away by one numb arm. The first barohnas had come from guardian stock, but barohnas were not guardians. Barohnas did not die in the bonding. Did they?

Alzaja's arm tightened around Khira. "Sister, look at the blossoms," she urged softly. "See them, so bright, so happy. I've told you what the first timers thought—that the trees made blossoms to attract insects. That the insects trapped pollen on their legs and carried it from flower to flower, pollinating them."

Despite herself, Khira laughed.

"Well, that's what they thought," Alzaja said, laughing too. "Maybe it was so where they came from, before the stranding. Maybe insects flew like birds. But we know the blossoms are to please the children who come with the brushes. And before that, they are to send out perfume so the orchard monitors will know it's time to send the children. Then when the children have come with their brushes and pollinated the flowers and the fruit is started, the blossoms fall off. Because they have served their purpose.

"I've served my purpose in your life now. I'm ready to fall away. And as I do, I hope that your harvest will be sweet, Khira. But your harvest can't come until I fall away from you."

Was she to think of Alzaja as a blossom then, with glowing blue petals and velvet stamen? A blossom warming in the sun, then silently drifting to the ground, to be lost in the multitude of fallen petals that fell under the trees each year? "You aren't done, Alzaja!"

"But I will be as soon as I tell you about the ice and the stone," Alzaja said with gentle insistence. "Won't you listen peacefully, little sister?"

Khira did not miss the rebuke. "Alzaja, you know I wasn't born to a peaceful star." Not for Khira the serene Nindra or the peaceful Zan, coming and going in white silence. Adar was Khira's host, a fiery red star that came in the west, a host of beating drums, of clattering reeds, a host of militant chants from times of trouble.

But Alzaja had always known how to temper Khira's defiance, how to leash her impatience, how to turn threatened turbulence to compliance. And that was the fullest measure of Khira's loss.

Whether or not Alzaja bronzed on the mountain, their days of closeness were ending now. Khira would have to monitor her own moods, mediate her own behavior. And if she ruined these last moments, there would be no others to remember. These were the only last moments they would have before Alzaja's bronzing.

Khira closed her eyes, gathering at reserves of composure Alzaja had long tried to foster in her. "I'm ready to listen."

"Then I'm ready to talk. But what I have to tell you isn't just how a barohna finally dies. First you have to know how a barohna lives, how she becomes a living barohna."

Despite her resolve, impatience sprang to Khira's tongue. "Everyone knows that. She makes her challenge."

"She makes her challenge, yes. But there's more. If she had only to kill the hungriest beast she could find, her bronzing would lie with the beast, not with her. No, the real secret of bronzing lies in the stone."

"The sunstone?" But how could that be? No one was permitted even to touch the sunstone of the valley throne but one who was already a living barohna.

Alzaja smiled wistfully. "The stone in her heart, Khira." She touched her chest lightly with her fingertips. "That's what really happens when a palace daughter goes up the mountain and challenges her beast. She takes stone into her heart, fully and finally. She becomes hard there where she lives, hard enough to challenge the fiercest breeterlik and live, hard enough to chase a rock-leopard to its den and break its neck with her bare hands, hard enough to put herself in a crag-charger's path and find the only chink in its armor with her pike. And that's when the bronzing changes come to her.

"If she goes to the mountain with a heart that can never take stone, she may place herself in the path of the crag-charger but her pike will never find its target. It doesn't matter how hard she has trained her body if her heart stays flesh."

Confused, Khira tried to understand, tried to relate what Alzaja said to the sisters who had already gone to the mountain. "But Mara—"

"Perhaps Mara could have taken the stone. I don't know. I do know that she didn't train because she was so blindly certain that she was to be like our mother. She worshipped our mother, Khira. You've heard stories of people who took gods, people who went out of the valleys carrying stone images and never came back. Our mother was Mara's god, and Mara thought worshipping her was enough. She didn't look deeply enough. She didn't see the stone in our mother's heart, even though Denabar told her it was there. And she didn't look to her own heart. She thought she had only to walk up the mountain with her shoulders drawn back the way our mother walks, with our mother's frown on her face, and any beast would fall before her."

"And then she would go back for her pack and eat the bread she brought," Khira whispered, beginning to understand.

"Yes." Alzaja smiled again, in memory. "I wish you had known her. You would understand about her better."

"But *you* understand. You know about making—making your heart stone." For the first time since Alzaja had announced her day, Khira felt a lessening of dread. Alzaja's fate did not depend entirely upon physical prowess. There was another factor, and although Khira did not fully grasp the concept of stone, surely Alzaja did. And surely Alzaja would come down the mountain again a barohna.

A barohna. For a moment Khira frowned. But if she had to have Alzaja a barohna, so be it. Alzaja remote and impassive would still contain the germ of Alzaja as she was today, her hair floating on the breeze, her cheeks blue-stained by the sunlight that glowed through the petals of the trees. "You know," Khira said.

Alzaja sighed deeply, peering down at her crossed ankles. "Yes, I know. I know a number of things about Mara and you and our mother—and myself." For a moment she was silent, staring at her fingers, long and slender, the nails honed. "But beyond the stone lies the ice, Khira. And that's easier, I think. The stone—the stone has to be bred into you. Unless there is some small grain of it there when you are born, I don't think it will ever come, no matter how hard you train. But even that small particle won't be enough unless you strengthen it by learning and training. Even the stone can't save you if you throw your life to the beast.

"But once the stone is there, once you've lived with it there, and when it finally leaves you—when you have served your throne and your heart turns back to flesh—" She glanced down at Khira, pain shadowing her eyes for the first time. "I hate to think of you that way, hard where I'm so tender, but I feel it in you. I know the stone is in you, Khira, and I know you will serve a throne if you train properly. And I know someday your heart will turn to flesh again.

"Then you must discover how to take the ice into your heart

instead. Not immediately, I'm sure. Perhaps you will want to spend some time in the plain with the redmane guardians and your stone mate as Kadura does. Perhaps you will want to follow the herds and watch autumn sunsets. Perhaps you will bond yourself with the herds for many seasons.

"But one day it will be enough. Too many of your guardian companions will fall in the bonding and leave you standing. Then you must take the ice into your heart and end it." Seeing Khira's uncomprehending expression, she reached for her hand. "You don't understand what I'm saying, of course. You're too young. But all you have to do is remember. When the time comes and you are tired, take the ice into your heart as you once took the stone. You'll find the way.

"That's the whole secret. Stone and ice." She smiled, her gaze lingering back across the valley. "Although I will tell you this. We come from a race that has been changing for many, many centuries. When the first timers were stranded here, they were hardly fit to survive on Brakrath. But over the centuries, they changed—dozens of small changes that made them an entirely different people.

"I think the changing will continue. I think one day there will be palace daughters who can bronze at will, without going to the mountain to make a challenge. And perhaps there will be enough of them that none must live long with the stone in their hearts. Instead they can let the stone go while they are still young and live years and years with hearts of flesh before they finally take the ice."

Stone, flesh, ice. Khira's head churned with half-apprehended thoughts. They formed and dissolved so rapidly she could hardly catch their flavor. Alzaja thought she had stone in her heart. But if her heart was hard, why did she feel as if it were being squeezed to the bursting point? If she were meant to be like their mother, stern and strong, why were tears slipping down her cheeks?

And there was something else Alzaja had said, something she did not want to confront. "Please—" she begged.

Alzaja held her tight then and rocked her, stroking her hair. "You'll understand one day. I promise you will. The way will be hard, you'll be lonely, but one day you'll understand, Khira. You'll be a link in the chain of mothers and daughters."

But she was already beginning to understand something she did not want to understand. Its dimensions were becoming clearly delineated in her mind. It reached out for her awareness, reached to wound her, so deeply, so painfully—

"I have to go," Alzaja said.

No! It was coming clear, this new thought, and it was unbearable. She could not live with it, not alone. "Alzaja—"

"I have to go," Alzaja repeated, releasing her. "Sit here. This is the same place where Mara left me, where Denabar left her. Stay here until I wave to you from Borton's Cropping. Then get up and walk back to the palace, slowly, and I'll walk slowly toward the peaks. We will both walk today, Khira, at the same time.

"Think about that, Khira, only that. Think about walking. Every time you place a foot to the ground, I will too. We'll walk together." Slowly she stood. "We'll always walk together, Khira. I'll never leave you."

Yet she did. Despite the tears that burned down Khira's cheeks, despite the color that finally touched her own face, Alzaja left. She turned, took her pack and her pike, and walked away beneath the blue-blooming trees, petals brushing her hair and spiraling to the ground behind her. And Khira remained under the trees—not because she didn't want to shatter Alzaja's parting serenity, not because she didn't want to intrude her own suddenly renewed dread into their last moments, not because she had stone in her heart.

But because she knew with sudden and utter certainty that Alzaja would never come down the mountain again. And that certainty paralyzed her.

That was the terrible thing that had taken shape in her awareness: certainty. "I hate to think of you that way," Alzaja had said, "hard where I am so tender." And it was true. Despite the pain, there was a hardness in Khira that Alzaja did not have, had never had. Alzaja had other things: serenity, subtlety, grace—but there was no stone in her.

Paralyzed, Khira watched her walk up the first slopes of the mountain, her white shift bare protection against the cold. She had no inner protection either, no gritty substance, no granular core. And she recognized the lack. She had trained, but half-heartedly, hardly raising a callus on her slender hands. She had trained because it was expected, but she had known that no strength of muscle could substitute for what she lacked.

Finally, as if stunned, Khira took her feet. Alzaja turned from Borton's Cropping. She was a gash of white against that dark stone formation. Snow lay above; Tiahna's spring thawing had reached only to the Cropping. It seemed to Khira that Alzaja raised her hand and waved almost gaily before she turned again. It seemed to

Khira that she climbed more quickly, with nimble abandon, when she had looked back for the last time.

Khira walked heavily from beneath the trees, her feet like the stone Alzaja saw in her heart. Every particle of her body was weighted down by gravity. Her spirit was borne down as if it had petrified. She could not even find her anger again, and that might have comforted her.

It was mid-afternoon when she reached the palace. The sky was darkening into an early spring dusk. Khira walked down stone avenues without seeing any of those who turned to look after her. She felt old, as if she had left childhood beneath the trees, scattered there like dead petals, something to be remembered but never held again.

Tiahna sat upon the sunthrone at the focus of the dying light, her face stiller than Khira had ever seen it. When Khira entered the throneroom, Tiahna's sun-darkened hand unconsciously touched the stone pendant at her throat. But she said nothing. There were no ritual words for the moment and no one to hear them if there had been. The runners and monitors were gone. The room held only Tiahna and Khira.

"She's not coming back," Khira said finally.

Tiahna sighed heavily. "No, she will not," she said huskily. "You see that too."

"She's not coming back," Khira said again, employing every bit of her control to keep the words from ending shrilly, in tears. "I don't understand why she went when she knows she won't come back." She couldn't bear to think of Alzaja simply falling away from her life like drying petals. She could not bear to think of herself as some budding fruit that had pushed Alzaja away.

"It was time she went," Tiahna said, shifting her eyes from Khira's pleading gaze. The pairing stone glowed softly under her fingers. "She was not one to stay here as a permanent daughter. Her spirit became a woman's years ago. How long could she live in a girl's body? Yet if she had stayed much longer, she might have lost the strength to go up the mountain."

"But—but she's going to die there! She's going to let some beast kill her!" That was what she had gone for, to shed a life that had no further meaning to her. Or a life that held so much meaning that she knew she must shed it while she still had the strength.

"Or perhaps she will simply lie down in the snow and sleep there," Tiahna said softly.

Khira shuddered. She could not bear the hollow compassion in Tiahna's voice. She had never heard it there before, or anything like it. "She'll die there and you don't care!" she cried. "You don't care about her—or me—or anyone except Rahela! You're stone where everyone else lives!"

Sobbing, she ran from the throneroom, ran down empty corridors to her own bedchamber. There she threw herself on her bed and let her confusion, her inadequacy, her anger vent in strangling sobs. If that was what it meant to have stone in her heart, if it meant sitting uncaring while a daughter died, then let her have a heart as tender as Alzaja's. Let her die on Terlath as the others had and leave Tiahna alone with her glowing throne and the blue pairing stone that linked her to Rahela.

But I do care. The thought entered her mind almost impersonally. *I care.* Was it hers? And if it was her thought, why was the voice Tiahna's? And why did it go on and on, repeating the same two phrases, as she sobbed herself to sleep, tangled in her covers?

It was dark when she wakened. She jumped from her bed with a wild cry and ran to her window. Clouds hid moons and stars. Nowhere on the mountain was there sign of a white shift toiling its way upward. Nowhere was there sign of Alzaja. Emptily, Khira stumbled back to bed.

Early the next morning, Khira dragged herself from bed again. Her face was puffy, her body leaden. In the night someone—a servant?—had left a white mourning sash at the foot of her bed. She refused to touch it. Instead she sat at her window peering to the mountain until the sun stood high. She was oblivious to the breeze, to the fragrance of the orchards, to the bustle on the avenues and in the fields beyond the palace. She didn't even frown when one of the Arnimi ground cars purred beneath her window and down the stone avenue to the levees.

It was mid-morning when she picked out the glint of silver wings above the western peak of the mountain. The wings hung there, spread to the sun, then swept sharply down behind the thrusting rock of the mountain and did not appear again.

She didn't have to see the flashing wings again. She knew their message. She knew it with a hollow heart, a heart that had already hurt as much as it could and now was numb. She turned from the window and dressed, lacing her clothes with trembling fingers.

Somewhere, she told herself, tears gliding down her face unnoticed
—somewhere on the mountain was a broken shell.

Silently Khira tied the mourning sash at her waist. Alzaja would
not return.

THREE
KHIRA

Winter curled icy fingers down the mountain and across the valley. Snow flurries swept lightly upon the leaves, licking at the bare soil of the fields, melting there. The trees of the orchards were stark against the withered grasses of summer. Flowers and fruit had long since fallen.

Khira sat on Borton's Cropping, her auburn hair caught in a loose knot. As she looked across the valley, her face was as pale as winter itself, bloodless. Earlier this morning she had watched a party of lens tenders pass down the mountain, talking among themselves. A little later she had seen a last herder hurry down the slopes with her ewes and lambs. Beyond those, Khira had been alone on the mountain for three hours.

Alone with the first cold presence of winter about her. Alone with the stony ache that had preoccupied her since spring, that had come to painful focus with approaching winter. Soon would be Darkmorning, the time when the people of the stonehalls sealed their doors, scattered sleepdust, and settled into their beds for winter. They slept in families: parents, grandparents, children, aunts and cousins.

But in the palace there were no family quarters, no scatterers, no wintersleep. When the stonehalls were sealed for winter, the barohna left the palace and went to her winter throne in the peaks. Then the palace daughters were left alone to occupy themselves for long silent months in the snowbound palace.

Alone. And this year Khira was the only daughter. Her lips tightening, she opened her pack and pulled out a pouch filled with fine grey dust. Late each summer harvesters went to Terlath's western slopes, to the woody thickets where sleepleaf grew. They filled large woven bags with the fallen sleepleaves, then returned to the valley to pound the leaves to dust. On Darkmorning, when Evefest was done and the families had swaddled for winter, scatterers came to each door and sprinkled sleepdust across the floor. And the people of the halls dreamed until their bodies knew the season for sleep had passed.

Neither barohnas nor palace daughters used sleepdust—not since the time of Helsa, who had used dust and dreamed of flame. Sighing, Khira stroked the pouch. She did not have a sunstone to focus flame. Nor did she have flame to focus. She would not have until she made her challenge. Still the prohibition of generations was strong upon her and she knew she should not have taken the dust from the store closet.

But to pass the winter alone and awake in the palace, trying to harden herself against every reminder of Alzaja—

She jumped up, tucking the pouch into her pack, taking up her pike. If she dreamed of flame, if somehow it burned, it would take only the herder's cabin where she slept—and her. For the moment, with the cold upon the mountain and in her heart, neither seemed much loss.

Still she stopped and gazed down over the valley for a moment before going up the trail. Shading her eyes, she thought she could distinguish workers trafficking between the palace and the halls, preparing for Darkmorning Evefest. For a moment her stomach tightened and she thought of roasted meats, dark breads and rich confections. No one who went to wintersleep gaunt would survive the sleeping months. At Evefest everyone ate to capacity—then waited and ate more. And even though she did not take wintersleep, Khira had always joined the feasting with full appetite.

This year she would not join the feasting at all. Sharp tears came to her eyes, tears of anger. She peered down stonily, then turned and ran up the trail.

She had chosen one of the smaller herder's cabins to take her wintersleep. It sat alone overlooking a frost-killed meadow. She had come to the mountain five days ago and spent the day preparing the cabin. First she had harvested vexreed and pressed sheafs of it around the inner walls of the cabin. When the white foam from the reeds had hardened into a dense insulating layer, she had pulled down the overgrown streamers of stalklamp that clung from the ceiling of the cabin. The remaining stubs of stalklamp touched the corners with pale orange light. The lash of the wind did not penetrate the cabin at all and there were ample blankets to swaddle herself in. She had returned to the valley satisfied with her preparations.

But now she re-entered the cabin and shuddered, her hand tightening on her pack. The single room was dim, ready. But to shut herself here alone for the winter, cut off by snow from the valley, to invite the dreams the people of the halls knew . . . Quickly Khira shed her pack and paced around the cabin. She would wait for night to scatter the dust. And then she would hope that it acted as quickly on a palace daughter as on a child of the stonehalls.

She passed the midday hours restlessly. The cabin already seemed close with dreams. Twice she fled its confining walls and climbed the trail to look down over the valley. The call of the palace was strong, even with its promise of a long and lonely winter. As day passed and the sky greyed, the wind grew harsher, crying down through the rocks and crags. Khira wondered if it read her mood and echoed it.

Then she looked down and saw a white shape below her, in the rocks near the trail, and forgot all bleakness. Instinctively she froze. Snowminx were among the rarer predators of the mountain. They stood no taller than an adult human, but their teeth were savage and their claws cruel. They left their dens each year at this time, just before the snows came, to prey on the smaller creatures of the mountain as they foraged for a last meal before hibernation.

But snowminx preyed on humans as well as on small creatures. Khira stood like stone, willing her pounding heart to silence. The minx paused as it sought among the rocks and gazed toward her, its pink eyes becoming momentarily intent. Then something in the rocks caught its attention, and it sprang, white earlocks bobbing. Some small animal squealed and the minx thrashed after it. When the struggle was finished, the minx did not reappear.

Khira watched until her feet were numb. Then she picked her way down the trail, wary for sign of the minx.

By the time she reached the cabin and bolted the door, snow fell in spiraling gusts and the sky was dark with storm. Khira pulled off jacket and gloves and peered around. She was unprepared for the stark sense of confinement that came to her. Winter in the palace had always been a time for running in the corridors, with no servants to disapprove. And winter had been a time when she and Alzaja had chosen their own mealtimes, ciphered scrolls when it pleased them, sat over the gameboard for as long as they both pleased, a time when there were no set hours to the day.

Here she could only bolt the door, sprinkle dust, and dream. Suddenly her throat closed. She had dreamed before, of course, fleetingly, on summer nights. Winterdreams were different. She knew because she had listened when people of the halls recounted them. Winterdreams were filled with half-apprehended images no one ever saw waking and voices that first muttered, then were siren-shrill. Some of the people of the halls believed the Brakrath powers came into the stonehalls at Darkmorning and stayed the winter, powers as old as Terlath's cragged peaks, powers which revealed themselves to humans only when they lay drugged and helpless.

Khira shuddered. Others said winterdreams were stimulated by sleepleaf. But if the dreams came from the leaf and the leaf came from the soil, and the soil were inhabited by silent powers—

If the Brakrath powers caught her in the long night of winter and would not release her, if she could not cough sleepdust from her lungs and waken—

Or if she spent the entire winter trapped in dreams of Alzaja, if she had to part with her time and again, watch her white shift disappear up the mountainside, if she had to hear that passionless voice—*I care; I do care*—endlessly, through all her winterdreams—

With a flash of fury, Khira snatched up her pack and shook out its contents: bits of bread, dried fruit, personal implements and tools—powdered sleepleaf. The pouch was in her hand, her fingers at the ties. Enough of hesitation, enough of fear. Alzaja was gone. Khira was the eldest now, and she was stone where Alzaja had been flesh. Dreams could not wound her.

She had the pouch open, she smelled the musty tang of the leaf, when she heard the shriek. It startled her into stillness, the pouch clutched tight. The wind?

Did the wind scream like an injured thing, in terror? Without thinking, Khira was at the cabin door, peering down the mountainside.

At the lower end of the meadow were two shapes, locked. She recognized them instantly, with shock. One was the snowminx she had seen earlier near the trail. The other—

"Paki!" she cried, as if the sound of his name could save him. Paki was the foal born on Alzaja's last day—born with white film obscuring his eyes. Worse, he had stepped into a mound of sting-briar near the end of plowing time and his wounds had become infected. Faced with the choice of leaving a single foal behind for the winter or waiting until he was strong enough to make the journey to the redmane plain, Yvala had elected to leave him. If her teams were late for the bonding of the herds in the plain, the mares would have no foals next spring.

Redmanes were known for their ability to travel long distances with no guide but instinct. Apparently instinct had driven Paki to break from his winter pen and set off in search of his herd. Instead, blindly, he had blundered into the snowminx. The minx tore at him with eager claws, trying to rip through his dense winter coat to the flesh beneath.

Every three-year-old knew that to move when a snowminx was near was to invite swift-clawing death. Yet without thinking, Khira ran down the hillside, shrieking angrily at the predator. She stumbled once and sprawled, the pouch of sleepleaf still clutched in one hand. She picked herself up quickly and threw herself at the white-haired minx, bringing one booted foot up sharply against the animal's flank.

The minx spun, its pink eyes blazing. For a moment Khira looked into a face almost human, yet grown with silky white hair that hung down in curling locks. Instinctively Khira froze.

Squealing, Paki squirmed free of the minx' grasp. He backed away, stunned and uncertain of his footing, bleeding from a gash on his nose.

"Paki—" Her cry brought the minx to fury again. With a gliding hop, the animal was upon her, its breath rasping in her ear. Khira took a useless step back, throwing up one arm, the arm that should have held her pike.

Instead it held a pouch of sleepleaf.

Useless. A winter's sleep, thrown against a snowminx in killing rage.

Useless, and still she threw it. The ties were loose and grey dust scattered from the pouch in a dense cloud. The wind caught it, swirling it around the shrieking minx. The animal hesitated in confusion, giving Khira precious moments to whirl away, to race to Paki and wind her fingers into his mane. He trembled against her, his filmed eyes peering up uselessly.

"It's all right," she said in a undertone. "It's all right, Paki."

And it was. The snowminx retreated from the blinding cloud of dust, but too late. Its pink eyes were screwed tight against the sting of the dust and it coughed and choked. It drew its eyes open with

effort and peered uncertainly at Khira through the white elflocks
that wreathed its face. Slowly, stunned, it brought one clawed hand
up and raked at its scalp. Its features twisted spasmodically and its
claws caught in its white locks and pulled.

"Paki, this way," Khira said urgently, and drew the shuddering
foal past the faltering snowminx toward the cabin. The foal resisted
momentarily, then padded beside her, its sides heaving in fear.
Khira glanced back once and saw the snowminx rasping at its
white-locked skull with both clawed hands. Blood discolored its
silken hair. It swung its head from side to side, as if trying to escape
some invisible restraint.

By the time she bolted the door behind them, Khira was trembling too. The sleepleaf might have had any effect upon the minx—
or none. For a moment she sank to her knees beside Paki, pressing
her forehead into his densely furred side. His heartbeat was rapid,
tremulous.

Hers must be the same. Taking her feet, she found her pike and
went to the door. She opened it carefully, peering out and down the
stony meadow. The minx had dropped to its knees and it clutched
its head, swaying. Snow flurried around it, momentarily obscuring
it. When the flurry swept away, Khira saw that the minx was
thrashing in convulsions. Over the sound of the wind, she heard its
harsh, cawing cry.

In the end she took her pike and killed the animal to end its
agony. By then, the minx had ripped long shreds of flesh from its
scalp and lacerated its face. Khira returned to the cabin thoughtfully, wondering if anyone had ever before gone against a
snowminx with sleepdust instead of pike, wondering how many
young herders might have lived if they had known the effect of
sleepdust on the minx.

Broken shells. Terlath's rocky flanks were littered with them.
Since the beginning of human time on Brakrath, herders had
brought their ewes and lambs to the high pastures and died defending them, just as she had defended Paki.

Broken shells. Khira closed the door and Paki turned and addressed her with blind eyes. "We can't stay here now," she said
aloud. Absently she daubed his bleeding nose. The laceration was
deep. It would have to be stitched. "We'll have to go back to the
valley." Without sleepdust to slow her metabolism, she could not
survive the winter without food.

And when she woke the next morning, she knew that one night

on the mountain was enough. Her dreams were not bizarre. They did not speak to her with stone voices. There were no strange half-glimpsed images. When Paki nudged her awake, Khira was barely able to recall the content of her dreams. But they were enough. She wanted no more.

She did not want an entire winter of dreams. Better to return to the palace, loneliness and memories.

When they left the cabin, some larger predator had come for the minx' body. And snow had fallen in the night. It lay ankle deep, unbroken except for their footprints.

Paki did not accept their return to the valley with grace. Instinct still urged him to the south, to the redmane plain where his herd had gone. He fought Khira stubbornly down the trail, occasionally stopping to shrill angrily. His cry sounded keenly over the snow-bound mountainside. But no matter how intently he listened, the cry was never answered.

"Come, Paki—you have to be in your pen before dark." Tonight was Evefest, and Khira's reluctance to join the feasting was as great as Paki's reluctance to return to the valley. There were empty chairs at the barohnial table and if she attended the feast, she must sit among them. Somehow she had not felt their emptiness before, when she had Alzaja.

And tonight was the relinquishment of names. The names of all who had died during the year would be released to be used again. There would be bidding for Alzaja's name by the women who expected to deliver children in spring. Khira's hand clenched in Paki's mane. The woman who won the name would be required to change one of its letters, just as Alzaja had altered the name Khirsa giving it to Khira. Perhaps her child would be called Ilzaja or Alzada. Still it would be hard to hear her sister's name again next year and the years after.

Many things would be hard, she reminded herself. She must be hard to bear them. She must be stone.

Yet sometimes she wondered why. Without the barohnial ability to use the sunstone, the people of the halls would go hungry and would dwindle in numbers. Yet once the people of the halls had been without barohnas, before Lensar had polished the first sunstone, before Niabi had discovered its use. And the people had lived.

Why must palace daughters die to provide barohnas for the sun-throne? And why must those who lived let their hearts take stone?

As she led Paki down the mountain, Khira thought of these things. Was there an answer somewhere in the scrolls? What was now had not always been. Must it always be?

If I find the answer, Khira vowed, I will name my own first daughter for the person who lettered the scroll that gives me it.

Am I so certain I will have daughters? Pausing by the side of the trail, brushing snow from Paki's forelock, she wondered if Tiahna had been certain of her barohnhood before she attained it. Would she ever know? Tiahna's life scroll was sealed to her for so long as Tiahna lived. And Khira's certainty that she would be next barohna of the valley was a sometimes thing. It came to her at vagrant moments and evaporated just as unpredictably. If her heart had a granular core, why did she feel so much pain and uncertainty? She continued down the trail, carefully guiding the blind redmane, wondering.

Mid-afternoon darkness fell on the valley by the time they reached the pens. Despite Paki's adamant resistance, Khira found a pensman to bed him down with the ewes and lambs. "Try to forget you're a redmane until Yvala comes again," she urged him, combing his auburn mane with her fingers. She knew from the angry lift of his head that he would never forget he was a redmane.

Nor could she forget that she was a palace daughter later, when the bells sounded for Evefest. She lay on her bed, her eyes closed, trying to shut out the sound. She was angry now that she had let herself be driven down from the mountain, that she had not taken another pouch of sleepdust and made her way back, angry that palace walls closed around her for winter. There was no need for her at the barohnial table. The feasting would go on without her. Let her chair be empty—empty beside the others.

Yet when the bells sounded again, she left her bed, pulled on her woolen shift, and descended to the feastroom. As she entered and the gathered people turned to see her, she felt that the chill of winter found expression in her face. She moved toward the barohnial table without sign that she saw anyone in the room and took her chair, the one at the farthest end of the table. Tiahna already sat at the head of the table, her expression as distracted as Khira's was chill.

Khira gazed at her wordlessly and wondered if Tiahna's heart had ever been flesh. Tiahna gazed back and frowned faintly, her fingers restless at her pairing stone. Khira knew her frown from other Evefests. It had nothing to do with the feast, with the people at the tables. Tiahna's frown came when the days grew short, when storm clouds hid the sun and the lens tenders came down from the mountain. It marked the call of the peaks, where she would find sunlight even in the dead of winter.

All the smells of the feast were in the feastroom: roasting meat, fresh-baked bread, every kind of vegetable and fruit, all served steaming on huge platters. And the people who helped themselves from the platters were sleek with winter reserves, the layer of fat that would permit them to survive a season's sleep. They laughed and sang and ate of everything brought them. Then they laughed and sang again. But beneath the laughter and song was another mood. Some of them would not wake with spring. Each year there were deaths in wintersleep and none knew whose deaths they would be. So some darkness touched the feast too and made the laughter louder and more ragged.

At the barohnial table was silence. Khira stared stonily at her plate. Tiahna frowned at the scarred wood tabletop. Between them were six empty chairs and the words that had never been spoken aloud: *I do care.*

When the feasters reached first satiety, the chanters came, elder women who knew the history of Brakrath as they knew their own lives. They moved among the tables and recreated the first times for the people. As their voices rose, Khira squeezed her eyes shut and the stone walls of the hall dissolved. Instead of a people sitting to feast, she saw a great ship faltering in the sky, then breaking and falling to strand its human passengers upon a harsh mountainous world—Brakrath.

Khira sighed deeply as the chant continued. First the stranded ones looked to the mountains in fear and prayed for rescue. But after a while they felt the protecting power of the mountains and learned to live in their shadow, cultivating the scant valley soil for subsistence. And as passing generations fed themselves from valley soil, they forgot other worlds and became people of Brakrath.

And then, accepting Brakrath, they began to change. At first the alterations were small and scattered. But they spread and grew until they touched every child born, until they shaped every adult who lived within the society of the valleys. The chanting voices fell to a whispered chorus and, under the force of change, a diverse people gradually became a single new race of hardy, fair people who conserved their sparse foodstores by sleeping the winter through.

The chanted history moved quickly from that point, a montage of images. The new people spread through the valleys of Brakrath, driving rock-leopard and snowminx into the mountains. They built their stonehalls, planted their crops, and manipulated the bloodlines of their stock to meet Brakrath's demands. Ewes who had been white gave birth to brindle lambs. Soupfowl became larger and yielded more fat. A people who had gone hungry were fed.

Then in the southern plain, the people discovered the redmanes, a Brakrath species with powerful shoulders and sturdy hindquarters, and would have domesticated them. But at that point the first guardian was born from among the valley people and went to the plain to take up vigil over the redmanes. Soon other guardians were born, silent, dark women who listened to voices that bound them ever more irrevocably to the animals they tended. Centuries passed and one race became two, guardians and valley people.

More centuries passed and Dmira was born, guardian daughter who left the herds and settled among the fair people of the valleys. From her line many generations later came Niabi, who loosed the fire from the sunstone polished by her lover.

There were troubled times, there was conflict, there were periods when the people of the valleys set themselves against each other. But there were far more times when the rising race of barohnas drew the people together and gave them new prosperity. After a while, each inhabited valley held a sunthrone and each sunthrone a barohna.

Khira's fingers tightened on the arms of her chair as the elder women began their recitation of the roll of barohnas who had occupied the sunthrone of this valley. The list was long, and for every barohna there were the lesser names, those palace daughters who had gone to the mountain and not returned.

Alzaja. New courses of meat and bread were served. Puddings steamed on every table. The people ate again and licked their fingers and the chanting continued.

Alzaja. At last the time for relinquishment of names had come and women were bidding for Alzaja's name. They held up greasy fingers, too exuberant with food and drink, too driven by coming darkness, to realize they bid on a living soul.

Alzaja. Her shell was broken. The mountain had loosed her on silver wings and left her sister with heart of stone. That heart could not endure the chanting and cheer and the undercurrent of dread. Darkmorning Evefest made it feel like flesh, and this flesh was heir to agony. From the far end of the hall a woman with hair that stood around her shoulders in a snowy mass and flashing eyes called out her bid and Khira was on her feet, running through the feasters, running from the wholeness of the others when she was as broken as her sister.

No one called after her, no one followed, although she was aware of startled silence as she fled the hall. Nor did any passionless declaration touch her mind. She pounded down the dim halls—the stalklamp that grew on the stone walls had been trimmed for winter —to her room.

There were precious things there, things left her by Alzaja. She swept past them and threw herself to her bed.

And she cried. The last link was broken. Alzaja's name had been bid out. Next spring a new infant would wear it who had never known Alzaja's grace. She would grow and the name would change with her. It would take her qualities and when she relinquished it at the end of her span, the name would have taken on the connotations of her personality. The next mother who bid for it would not even associate it with the Alzaja who had walked through the orchard on her way to the mountain.

Sometime in the storm of her grief, Khira fell asleep. When she woke, there was no sign of sunlight at her windows. The shutters had been secured for winter. But she knew it was morning and she roused herself reluctantly. She was eldest daughter now and it was Darkmorning. There were small rituals to be met within the larger ritual of a people settling to wintersleep. Some of them were hers.

She did not bother to go to the dining hall. There would be no table set, no food cooked. From now until spring waking, she must make her own meals in the kitchen.

Instead she went to the plaza, where overnight snow had fallen knee deep. She looked up to the mountain and saw that clouds of snow dusted its spired peaks. Darkmorning had come more than by the calendar. It had come to the mountain and to the valley.

Shivering, Khira kept vigil in the plaza until the heavy stone doors of the stonehalls were closed and sealed. Those last people who ran through the snow to their halls had the traces of the night's feasting still on them in their rumpled clothes and sated faces. Now they looked toward the winter's dreams with eyes both expectant and fearful. When the final doors were sealed, Khira withdrew into the palace, towering metal doors closing behind her with a cold sigh. She slipped down silent halls to the throneroom, not knowing which was more to be dreaded, a winter of alien dreams or one of solitude.

Tiahna sat upon the darkly glowing throne, remote today, lonely, ageless. Khira paused to study her. Sometimes she saw in her mother the great cerebhawk of the mountain, splendid in its power and plumage, ever alert, ready to plunge. Yet one of its heads, the lesser, was held mute and powerless by the other. Today as Khira entered the throneroom, Tiahna seemed to gaze at her with the same captive alertness, the same impotent power as the lesser head of the cerebhawk.

Perhaps Tiahna did care.

Or perhaps she cared only for her growing sun-hunger and the delay of ceremony, however brief.

Khira stepped before the throne. Mother and daughter peered at each other in the silent hall. Tiahna's voice was a husky whisper. "Are the stonewarrens sealed now?" The pairing stone hung dark at her throat.

Stonewarrens: the term was archaic, a survival from the time when the people of the halls had been serfs rather than freeworkers. Khira wet her lips, suddenly nervous. Today she must play the part Alzaja had always played on Darkmorning. And although there was no one to hear, no one to see, it seemed important that she bring the same authority to the elder daughter's role that Alzaja had brought. "They are sealed," she said.

"Then the sleepdust is scattered and the people dream." Tiahna stood, her limbs long and bronze, her copper hair bound into a braided crown. The lines of her face were strong: mouth broad, eyes strongly browed, nose thrusting. Power was evident in her every feature. Yet as she paced across the throneroom, her eyes shadowed with pain. "They are dreaming, and so Alzaja lives again, for the winter."

Khira shivered involuntarily at this departure from custom. Closing her eyes, she could imagine her sister beside her now, every feature clear. "Alzaja lives with me always," she declared.

Tiahna turned an unsmiling face upon her. "Does she? And Mara—does she live with you too?"

"Mara too," Khira said with barely a pause. Many times Alzaja had applied a fingertip to a frosted window or a fogged mirror and made Mara's likeness appear. Mara's death on the mountain had become a shared event of their lives, even though Khira had never known Mara.

"Mara lives with you, yet you never saw her?" Tiahna demanded.

"Alzaja remembered her and she told me."

"And Denabar?" Tiahna demanded. "Does Denabar live with you too?"

This time Khira hesitated. Denabar had been the sister before Mara. Alzaja had tried to pass on her features, her ways, her brief legend as Mara had given them to her. But she had not been entirely successful. Khira had never been certain how much was substance, how much shadow. "She—she lives too."

Tiahna peered at Khira bleakly. "No, child. You touched Alzaja, you heard her voice, and she lives with you. But don't imagine that your other sisters live likewise. And don't imagine that when the mountain takes you, you will live with anyone but your next sister, and then only for the time she lives."

Khira stepped back, as if struck. "No," she whispered, not sure what she protested: the coming loneliness, her sisters' loss, the death her mother had so casually pronounced upon her.

Tiahna frowned, wheeling to peer impotently into the darkened mirrors which hung at intervals around the throneroom. She touched her temples, stroking pain. "Snow has banked against the lenses on the mountainside and the mirror tenders have gone to their dreams," she said in a voice hard with pain. "If I stay here longer, I will tear myself apart—and you with me."

It was the inevitable moment, the one against which Khira had steeled herself. She was resolved not to meet it weakly. Yet a plea slipped from her lips, a dry thing, powerless. "No. Please. I'll be alone."

It met the scorn it deserved. "And wasn't Alzaja alone with winter before you were born?" Tiahna demanded with a flash of dark eyes. "Are you less than your sister?"

Was she? Would she cry and beg where Alzaja had silently borne loneliness? Khira drew her slight body erect, appalled by her moment of weakness. Still her voice shook with the question that had troubled her since Alzaja's death. "When—when will you give me a sister for winter company?" It was a presumptuous question, one she had wanted often to ask but had not dared.

Anger stormed across Tiahna's face. "There will be a sister when the tide rises again in my body. And when she is born, she will not be for you or for me but for the throne."

Chastened, Khira stared down at the polished stone of the floor.

Stalklamp cast a subdued orange glow across the flaggings. From somewhere she found the final boldness to declare, "I will be for the throne."

Tiahna fixed her ageless gaze upon Khira, mercilessly evaluating. "Perhaps you will."

"I will," Khira said, this time to herself. Denabar, after all, had grasped victory in her challenge, if only in her final moments. Her body had been found on Terlath's northern face two days after she left the valley with the first changes upon it, pale flesh tinged with bronze, delicate profile sharply altered, nose and jaw no longer slight but bold. A mortally wounded crag-charger had been found nearby. If Denabar had thrust her pike deeper between its armored plates, piercing its heart, she would have returned to the valley a barohna.

Instead her pike had broken, the crag-charger had caught her with its rending claws, and the first changes had been the last. Denabar had never claimed the throne she died for.

But who was to say that Denabar was the only one of seven sisters to take stone to her heart? Who was to say that Khira could not do the same?

Suddenly the hall was cold and Khira's certainty wavered. Six sisters had preceded her and six had died. How could she hope to succeed? "If the Arnimi return while you are gone—" she ventured, trying to put away memory of her sisters. The Arnimi had gone in their ship to explore the southern mountains. Khira wished they would remain in the south for the entire winter but knew they would not. At some point they would return to their quarters in the western wing of the palace and she must see them in the halls again and hear their voices on the stairs.

"They will give you no trouble. They know that if they trespass in the stonehalls while the people sleep, I will close their quarters and forbid them the valley." Tiahna strode back to her throne. The black stone glowed darkly at her touch. "Now go while I empty the throne. And don't watch as I leave the valley. I won't carry tears in my memory as I hunt the sun up the mountain."

They had returned to ritual and there were words for this moment. Recognizing the inevitability of separation, Khira said them. "May you find it bright on the peaks."

"May I bring back its light tenfold to make spring for the people of the valley," Tiahna responded, and waited for Khira to withdraw.

Slipping from the throneroom, Khira ran to her chamber. The only light came from glowing stalklamp stems. Khira had refused to let the servants trim them when they groomed the halls and chambers for winter. They groped up the stone wall, clawed suckers holding the succulent stems in place. A single jagged leaf had unfolded from one stem.

Khira knew now why she had refused to have the stems trimmed. Biting her lip, she snapped off the single offending leaf. She must have light this winter, not shadow. She would have light on every wall, light on the ceiling, light growing across the floor. With a strangled sob, she drew water from the melter tap and drenched the stone pots that held the stalklamp roots.

She must have light, if nothing else this winter. And she would not cry. She was elder daughter now and there was stone in her heart, however sparse and fine the grains.

She kept that vow less than five minutes. Winter began with tears and snow.

FOUR
KHIRA

The first days of winter were the most wrenching. Palace corridors were peopled with ghosts, familiar forms that never quite materialized. Khira slipped between them, wanting to reach out to them, expecting them to speak. But when she turned her head, they dissolved into shadow. Alzaja, Tiahna, the Arnimi commander, servants, monitors, cooks—they all seemed no farther than an arm's span. Yet when she reached, she touched nothing. Each day as she checked the boilers, Khira listened anxiously for the sound of footsteps behind her in the deserted corridors. Sometimes she slipped into the throneroom, hoping to find someone she knew in the sun mirrors. She found only herself.

Occasionally she ventured as far as the sealed door that led to the west wing. But the Arnimi had left no trace of themselves in the stone corridor outside their quarters, not even a musk to prove they were as human as they claimed. Often she climbed the watchtower and looked out over the snow. Terlath was a forbidding white presence in the distance, low-hanging clouds hiding its steep spires. The stonehalls had become white-blanketed mounds and the palace itself was lost in deep drifts. Only towering ventilation chimneys and the tower itself marked the presence of life in the valley.

At no time did she anticipate the sharp terror that was to come. Loneliness was terror enough.

Four hands of days, three five-fingered, one three-fingered, decorated her chamber wall when sound broke the night. By then she had almost accepted her solitary existence, letting it lead her back to a child's state she had thought she left behind. She spent much of her time playing scatter-hop in the deserted corridors, tossing her sharp-edged marker stones with a defiant clatter, then hopping be-

tween them on one bare foot, trying neither to scatter the stones
nor to step on them. Sometimes at the end of the game, her bare
feet bled and she strapped her boots back on with a certain sour
satisfaction. Other days she played the board games Alzaja had
taught her. Some days she simply patrolled the halls, mentally peo-
pling them with servants and monitors, putting these shades
through their usual paces, now making them double-step, now
freezing them in awkward postures.

And each day after she had tended the boilers that warmed the
few rooms she used, she assiduously watered stalk pots throughout
the palace. Alzaja had taught her to leave the pots dry through the
winter, but this year Khira flooded the roots, forcing the luminous
growth, then trained the tender new stalks into bright patterns. Her
bedchamber became luxuriant. It shimmered with light, like the
inside of a precious gem. Khira liked to lie in bed and imagine
herself a quarri, a mischievous being of infinitesimal size, secreted
within a faceted glowstone like Tiahna wore when the Council of
Bronze met in the great hall.

She was so hidden, bounded by the wafer-thin walls of the imagined gemstone, when the screaming voice came. One moment she
was alone in chill silence. The next she was at the vortex of a
terrible storm of sound, a harsh, rending scream. She burst the
walls of the glowstone with a sharply indrawn breath and found
herself lying taut in her bed, her blankets kicked away reflexively,
her eyes wide and staring.

The sound continued, shrieking, grinding, unbearable. She
caught another breath, desperately. Her first coherent thought was
that one of the great mountain beasts, a crag-charger, a breeterlik, a
rock-leopard, had broken into the palace. But she quickly recognized that the shrieking whine was a metallic cry. Arnimi ships,
just before they settled to ground, bellowed and screamed like this.
Some of their instruments and devices also emitted squallings and
bleatings of an inhuman nature.

She expelled her breath with effort and drew another, pulling
herself up into a knot, knees to chest. Were the Arnimi returning?
So soon? But the continued shriek was much louder than the voice
of their ships.

And a moment later an alien energy entered the chamber. Khira
sensed rather than saw it. It prickled along her spinal column and
raised the hair on her arms, making her teeth clench involuntarily.
For long minutes she had the sense of being paralyzed at the center

of some unaccountable radiation, some binding but unseen light. She was distantly aware of a curious grunting, her own labored breath.

Then the sensation was gone, and she was alone with the brilliant orange glow of overgrown stalklamp—and her own fear. Her entire body was racked by a shuddering spasm. Her teeth clattered wildly. And still, she realized, the terrible scream continued.

She cowered until shame drove her from the bed and into the hall. What palace daughter could tolerate this intrusion without challenge?

The metal-throated scream was a thing alive throughout the palace. She ran from chamber to chamber, trying to find its source—in vain. Her clattering teeth and her pattering feet were the only other sounds in the empty palace.

Twice again, as she ran through the halls, the unseen shaft of energy briefly caught her, held her, then released her.

She reached the throneroom and flattened herself against the stone wall, peering up into the darkened sun mirrors set around the walls. Briefly the shrieking cry grew deeper, more intense, making the surfaces of the mirrors shimmer. Then, as Khira sidled toward the throne, thinking to find some surcease there, the sound began to retreat. Within minutes it was gone and Khira was alone with a silence deeper than any she had ever known. It seemed to close over her, a deep well of utter stillness. The only sound was the harsh measure of her breath and the continued chattering of her teeth.

Finally, stiffly, feeling infinitely small, she slipped from the throneroom and first walked, then ran down the corridor. If the source of the sound lay within the palace, she would find it and confront it. Otherwise it would hold mastery over her even in its absence.

The sound did not return as she searched palace halls and chambers. Nor did the invisible beam. But she knew as she forced herself to dare each empty room and then to return defeated to her own chambers that those terrible moments had left their permanent mark. If she could confront the source of her terror, if she could assess its dimensions—but she could not. Nowhere in the palace was there anything that had not been there before.

Nowhere that she thought to search. She did not remember the watchtower. And it was not until late the next morning that she heard the insistent *chink-chink-chink* at its barred door.

She was a ghost in the halls that day, frightened, ashamed of her fright, cold. She neither cast her hopping stones nor sat at the inlaid gameboard. Instead she drifted from place to place, stopping in shadowed corners to listen, to watch.

She had passed several hours in anxious patrol when she heard a distant sound, as if stone struck stone. She froze, her eyes large, her breath caught. The sound was irregular, faint. *Chink. Chink-chink. Chink.* Khira threw off her first paralyzing fear with something close to fierce joy and set off down the hall. Resolution, no matter what its nature, must be better than the haunted, waiting silence that hung over her this morning.

Quickly she traced the sound to the barred stone door that led to the watchtower—the one place she had not searched the night before. She halted short of the door, the hair at the back of her neck rising. Who could summon from the tower in the dead of winter, with the door into the palace barred and the observation dome sealed with heavy glasstone? Khira's eyes sought the stalk-lit hallway to either side of the door and found nothing. She tried to swallow back a sharp rise of panic and choked instead. The sound stimulated a fresh flurry of tapping from the other side of the door.

Khira's first instinct was to run away as quickly as her feet would carry her, to never come near this end of the palace again. Ashamed, she squeezed shut her eyes and bit her lip. Alzaja had gone to Terlath's rugged peaks for her beast carrying only a pike and a day's ration of food, gone in the tradition of palace daughters through the centuries. How could Khira do less than step forward and rap softly at the stone door with a single white knuckle?

The answering clatter was sharp. *Chink-chink! Chink-chink-chink!* Khira fell back, trying to gather fresh courage from the shadows of the corridor. Then, trembling, she fell to her knees and probed the hairline crack at the bottom of the door. She detected a razor-thin edge of cold air. She jumped to her feet, frowning. The glasstone panes of the watchwindows were securely caulked and the double doors at the top of the staircase were as tightly fitted as these. But the chill at her fingertips was unmistakable, as unmistakable as the renewed tapping from the other side of the door.

Alzaja, she told herself, would have unbarred the door immediately. Finally, with trembling hands, she forced herself to lift the bar.

The door swung open of its own weight and Khira's eyes widened. Whatever she had expected, it was not the slight, dark boy dressed in grey who hunched on the lower step. He clutched a fragment of glasstone in one bare hand and peered up at her with eyes as deep as mountain pools—but darker, much darker, and in some way empty. He shivered perceptibly in the cold well of the staircase.

Khira stared at him, at his inappropriate clothing, then peered up the dim stairwell. "You broke the view-window." Her accusing tone surprised her. But she was angry: angry that he trespassed here, angry that he had reduced her to trembling fright, angry that the inexplicability of his presence stirred still deeper fears in her.

Slowly the boy took his feet. His body was sparse, his limbs slender. He met her accusing gaze with a faint, anxious frown and mumbled something that sounded almost like an apology, but with a questioning inflection.

"And the upper doors," she added vengefully. "You broke down the upper doors too, didn't you?"

This time he attempted no hesitant apology, no reply at all. He simply regarded her with bleak eyes, rubbing his chilled fingers together.

Why wasn't he as frightened as she? He seemed only to be cold, and certainly that was no mystery. The suit he wore was pitifully thin. With exaggerated anger, Khira swept past him and ran up the stairs. She found the double doors at the top thrown open, undamaged. She bit her lip. Apparently she had forgotten to bar them the last time she had used the tower.

But she certainly was not responsible for the shattered glasstone that littered the floor, nor for the scorched patch on the stone floor. She peered up at the broken panes, then gazed out over the greylit winterscape. Snow lay deep over the stonehalls and the palace, and Terlath was little more than a looming shape lost in cloud. An oddly dished area marked the frozen white sheet which overlay the main plaza. From the gleaming solidity of the crust, it appeared the snow had melted, then refrozen. Narrowing her eyes, Khira distinguished two similar frozen concavities in the distance.

She turned to find the interloper at the top of the stair. He had come silently and his dark-eyed gaze was unreadable, at once steady and empty. Staring at him, chilled, she tried to find some way to bring the encounter into the realm of the familiar, the everyday.

He was only a child. Taking the offensive, she addressed him as one. "All the glasstone is good for now is hopping stones. If you plan to come down with me, you can carry your share." Bending, she gathered the transparent grey shards. When he did not join her, she said sharply, "Well?" This time he complied, copying her action, still watching her without expression.

So his behavior could be manipulated. As she led the way down the stairs, her mind worked furiously. Why had he come? From where? Were his intentions hostile? How hostile could be the intentions of a shivering boy in a thin suit? Her first thought was to bar him from any significant room of the palace: the throneroom, her mother's bedchamber, the pantries and kitchens. Let him see only corridors and lesser chambers. But her second thought, feeling his steady gaze on her back, was to cow him with the scope and importance of the palace. If somehow his intent were hostile, if he had force to back it, there was no one she could call on. But if the spaciousness and grandeur of the palace itself intimidated him—

Accordingly, reaching the bottom of the staircase, she led him directly to the throneroom. Passing through the towering arches, she stepped aside silently to permit him full view of the carved black throne upon its high dais.

If for her the room with its arches, mirrors, polished flagstones and dark throne was invested with power, for him it was not. He stared at the black throne expressionlessly, then turned like an automaton to gaze around the room. He seemed untouched by the stalk-lit walls, by the darkened mirrors. He still held his hands stiffly before him cradling jagged shards of glasstone.

She bit back an angry scowl. She had never seen his like. Children of the halls were sturdy and fair with ruddy cheeks, thick white hair, deep chests and the palest of blue eyes. Palace daughters were like herself, slight, pale, with auburn hair and amber eyes. And the redmane daughters of the southern plain—

This child resembled none of these. He was as slight as she, if a little taller, and there was a haunted gauntness to him. His hair, cut just below the ears, was black and his eyes were so dark she could barely distinguish the iris from the pupil. Frowning, she assayed him feature by feature: neatly formed ears that lay back against his skull, thin lips, narrow, well-defined nose, finely arched eyebrows as dark as his hair, high forehead, hands as slim as her own but much darker. The nails, by contrast, were pink. His skin was slightly rougher than her own and darkly bronzed. He had two visible flaws: a long pink scar on his jaw and one fingernail that looked as if it had recently been torn back.

She felt a superstitious thrill. How had he come to the tower in the dead of winter? And his bronze skin—had he earned it or was it simply his natural pigmentation? Pushing up her sleeve, she stared at her own milk-white skin. Silently the dark child copied her motion, placing his arm against hers. He studied their contrasting complexions impassively.

Despite everything the Arnimi had told her about the people who inhabited other worlds, she could only gaze at his dark arm with perplexed awe. On Brakrath, males never bronzed. The barohnial line ran exclusively from mother to daughter. Indeed a barohna was incapable of bearing sons to full term; Tiahna had aborted five male children. And any children Khira's father may have sired in the stonehalls—she had no way of knowing if she had half-siblings; no palace daughter inquired after her father's identity and no barohnial mother volunteered the information—would never bronze. They were stonehall stock, just as she and her sisters had been barohnial.

Yet this boy stood beside her in flesh of bronze, studying her with eyes as black as the stone of her mother's throne. Threatened by the mystery of him, she pushed her sleeve down. "I know you came in a ship," she said sharply. "I've heard ships before."

His pupils narrowed minutely at the displeasure in her tone. One corner of his mouth twitched.

He had come in a ship, but there was no ship now. And how large must the ship have been to create the metallic scream that had terrorized her? She remembered her cowering fear with mortification. "You can't do this," she challenged abruptly, thrusting out one hand, closing it around jagged shards of glasstone. When she opened the hand, palm and fingers were speckled with blood.

A flicker of his dark brows betrayed emotion. He tongued his lips and deliberately closed the fingers of his right hand. His fingers were still white with cold. And still numb too, she decided scornfully. But quick pain quivered across his thin face and his hand jerked open, spilling the stones. He peered up at Khira, wary of her reaction.

"So you want to play scatter-hop," she mocked him softly. It rankled that he had come secretly in the night, terrorizing her. It rankled that he had tapped insistently at the tower door while she cowered on the other side, afraid to slide the bar. It rankled that he didn't shiver with the cold that was still upon him. Quickly she threw her own shards across the floor and bent to unfasten her boots. "There are two ways to play scatter-hop: the child's way, with boots on your feet, and the midling's way. Are you still a child?"

He hesitated momentarily, then released his second handful of shards. Mimicking her actions, he touched open his boots—how smooth they were; how strangely they fastened—and stripped the thin stockings off his narrow feet. His feet were as dark as his hands and face, but heavily callused. He peered up at her for instruction.

Her eyes sparked with malice. She pulled her hair back into a loose knot. "Watch!" Then she hopped across the field of shards on one bare foot, trying neither to scatter the stones nor to cut her foot on them. The stones had fallen too closely, but when she felt their sharp edges cut her foot, she bit the inside of her cheek and continued until she had crossed the floor. Then she ran a quarter circle around the scatter of shards and hopped through them again on the other foot. When she finished, both feet marked the floor with blood. She counted the dark spots with satisfaction. "Well?"

He gazed at her bleeding feet, then looked up at her.

"Yes, it's your turn!"

He nodded, more in acknowledgement of her anger than in acquiescence. With an almost audible sigh, he raised his right foot and hopped through the scattered stones. His first two jumps were successful. With the third, he miscalculated and landed heavily on a large shard. He gasped and peered at her, warily.

"Go on!" she urged, ashamed of the hot blood that rushed to her cheeks. Alzaja would never have permitted this. It was childish. But Alzaja was not here. "Finish!"

He ducked his head and continued, dark stains marking his course. When he emerged from the scatter, he put his foot down gingerly, his lip quivering. Without looking at her for instruction, he made a quarter circle and changed feet.

He had almost completed his second course when he stumbled. He uttered a wordless cry as he fell across the jagged stones. Khira stepped forward, then stopped herself. He lay for moments as if stunned. When he picked himself up, not looking at her, he bled from half a dozen deep cuts. But he pushed himself to his feet and finished the course, moving with painful deliberation. Then he stepped away from the scattered shards trembling visibly, his face ashen beneath its bronze pigment. He peered at her as if expecting rebuke.

Khira was immediately repentant. She was monitor of her own behavior now, and she had failed in her duty. Quickly she pushed him down on a stone bench to examine his injuries. He quivered at her touch. "Stay here. I'll get ointment from the supply locker."

Returning, she smoothed ointment on his cuts and dabbed his damaged garment with a damp cloth. Then she peered up into his face, feeling the weight of responsibility. However he had come here, whatever his purpose, he was alone in a strange place. And she was the only person he could turn to. "Aren't you hungry?" she wondered.

When he did not answer, she touched her lips and patted her stomach, raising her brows in question.

He bit his lip, as if afraid to respond. Then, hesitantly, he imitated her gestures, watching closely for her reaction.

"Hun-gry," she said again, enunciating clearly. She repeated the word twice, touching lips and stomach again, and watched him intently. It suddenly seemed very important that he respond.

When he finally did, his voice was low, his enunciation alien. "Hun-gry."

A single word, the first she had heard in sixteen days, and she abandoned all reservation. *"Hungry!"* She jumped to her feet elated. Through some miracle the long days of silence were broken. She no longer needed to reach out to ghosts in shadowed corridors. She had a companion. As she led way down the hall, she prattled inanely, the words spilling from her eagerly. "There's a fire in the kitchen, you know, in the smallest stove. I've kept it fed. And we can take anything we want from the pantry. There's bread, cheese, there's even roasting fowl in the ice locker." She had someone to talk to, someone to talk to her through the long frozen months ahead.

The kitchen was a cavernous place, its great feast-stoves cold now, its dozen pantries silent. Khira lit fuel lamps. When she hung them, the interloper's eyes darted around the shadowy cupboards and his nostrils quivered. For a moment both emptiness and wariness were gone from his eyes. He stepped quickly toward the pantry where fragrant loaves of spring bread were stored for spring waking. He brought himself up short at the pantry door, turning alertly for her reaction, licking his lips nervously.

Did he think she would starve him? "It's all right. I always eat some of the spring bread while the people sleep." She fetched one of the heavy loaves and cut into it. The bread was rich with dried fruits, groundnuts and the eggs of soupfowl. She hacked off a generous slice and offered it to him.

He hesitated momentarily, then snatched the bread and retreated to the shadowy nook beside the warm stove. He hunkered down there, wolfing the bread almost without chewing.

He was starved. Quickly she cut him a second slice. He accepted it without hesitation. As he ate, he peered up from the shadows, his eyes momentarily like live coals. But before he could finish the second slice, he drew a shuddering breath and his eyelids fluttered shut. The last scrap of bread fell from his fingers as his head dropped to his knees.

Alarmed, Khira knelt beside him, monitoring the regular rise and fall of his chest. He seemed simply to have fallen abruptly into the deep sleep of exhaustion. But if this were more than that, if he were somehow, inexplicably, falling into wintersleep . . .

She frowned. The Arnimi had told her that the Brakrathi were the only human strain that employed wintersleep. And even if the intruder came from some unreported human subgroup, certainly there was no trace of sleepdust in the kitchen.

Still she was troubled. If he fell into true wintersleep, he would never waken. Although sleepdust slowed the metabolism to a crawl, greatly lessening the amount of body fuel required to survive a snowbound winter, even the sturdiest people of the halls woke weak and depleted in the spring. And the intruder had no saving cushion of body fat. None at all.

Khira's fingers clenched as she fought an overpowering urge to seize him and shake him awake. He had already spoken one word of Brakrathi. She would teach him her entire language. She would teach him the games Alzaja had taught her, the songs, the chants. She would teach him to cipher the scrolls stored in the alcove behind the throne. She would teach him everything.

If he woke.

And he would people the winter for her. She would have someone to talk with, someone to share her meals—someone to consider when Adar flared bright in the winter sky and her temper rose red and ragged. She stood, addressing stone walls, and vowed that this year she would forever master Adar's warlike influence—if the intruder woke.

Then, driven by a sudden furious need for activity, she fetched blankets and heaped them over him. She peered down at him a moment before hurrying away again. The bedchamber next to hers stood vacant. Working quickly, still repeating promises under her breath, she made up the bed and assembled all the things he might like to have near: woven hangings, braided chains of rattleweed, tiny carved figurines, an inlaid gameboard, the best from her own collection of stream-polished stones. Some were possessions of her own relegated to storage when she had inherited Alzaja's treasures.

Momentarily her jaw tightened. Perhaps he would not be impressed. There was something troubling about his lack of responsiveness, about the dark vacancy of his eyes. Only food seemed to fully stir his interest. Perhaps if he had been starved, she would have to use his hunger to draw him out. But in any case, he would sleep here and between sleepings, she would teach him to talk to her. Softening, she hurried to rearrange the new growth of stalk-lamp stems across the stone walls.

Finally, driven by the remnant of anxiety, she returned to the watchtower. The sky was sullen. The dimpled areas she had noticed earlier remained crusted with ice. The wind blew harsh through the shattered pane. Nothing had changed.

She had no doubt he had come from a skyship. The scream that accompanied his arrival had been unmistakably similar to the sound of Arnimi ships landing. But certainly he was no Arnimi.

Did the Arnimi even pass through a child state? She tried to imagine those balding personages as infants, as children—pot-bellied boys and girls with receding hairlines and bulging eyes. She laughed aloud. Yet every Arnimi she had questioned insisted that once he or she had been a child.

Finally, thoughtfully, she went down, barring the double doors at the top of the stairs and the single tall door at the bottom. When she reached the kitchen again, her new companion stood at the counter hacking off chunks of spring bread. He started at the sound of her voice, dropping the knife, his eyes startled.

Her laugh was like a handful of crystals, too-bright, clattering. "If you keep on eating like that, I'm going to call you breeterlik. Hungry breeterlik," she declared, drunk with relief. The stones had honored her vow. He had not fallen into wintersleep.

He relaxed slightly and in an evident effort to please her said indistinctly, "Hungry."

"Breeterlik!" Her voice was shrill. She was not to be alone.

By evening she had renamed him Darkchild. The next day she taught him her proper name and despite the disturbing emptiness deep in his eyes and the sometimes slack set of his features, winter was brighter in the deserted palace for a while. It almost seemed Adar would not storm from winter skies this one year. Khira had promised.

FIVE

THE BOY

T he boy came to the palace empty in every way, empty of thought, of preconception, of memory. He came from circumstances he could not remember to circumstances he could not comprehend. He came without weapon or word. He came—somehow—to be sitting on cold stone steps facing a tall door and when he rapped, there was no answer.

Then there was an answer and the boy found himself in the palace, as empty as he had been before the door opened, except that the girl fed him. And with food in his stomach, he realized that although time began abruptly on the cold steps, it did not end either there or in the room where he ate. It stretched ahead into other hours and places. That much hunger and satiation told him, though he could not have said how.

Indeed time did stretch ahead and the boy found it came not only in units of hours but in units of days, a continuity of days. During the first few of those days the boy had little awareness of anything beyond the cold, the girl and the demands of his internal guide, that omniscient presence that instructed him in everything he did. He woke each day in a chill, lofty chamber hung with things that rattled and things that were bright with color. His environment included the bed he lay upon, stone walls and ceiling overgrown with a bright gridwork of glowing stems, two tightly shuttered window-apertures, and an array of articles displayed upon the walls and upon a wooden chest.

Each morning upon waking he lay quietly waiting for his guide to direct him. When his guide was ready, the boy pulled on his boots and made a slow round of the chamber, examining its contents. He touched nubby hangings, polished stones, tiny figurines and dried plant material, and the characteristics of all these were methodically transmitted to that portion of his brain that stored data. After the first few days, the ritual was repetitious. But the boy's brain was empty and it was to be filled in the manner of the guide's choosing. The boy understood this and acquiesced. His guide's will was his will.

One of the first things the guide chose to file in the boy's brain was the girl's language. And she was eager to teach him.

The first night they met, the boy was confused and thought there were many girls in the palace. When the heavy door that confined him opened, the girl who stared at him was a frightened girl. A few moments later, at the top of the stair, he was confronted by an angry girl instead. She was quickly displaced by a girl who was both angry and frightened. He left the tower with that girl and went to a cavernous room with arches, mirrors and polished flagstones. The girl he met there made him hurt himself, but almost immediately another girl appeared to soothe him and feed him.

In appearance the girls were identical: slight and fair with amber eyes and auburn hair. Finally he grasped the symmetry of the situation and was immediately less tense. There was only one girl, just as he was one boy directed by one guide.

When he left the sleeping chamber each morning, the girl met him in the hall and began repeating the words of her language for him. "Tile, Dark-child—tile. This is a floor tile." Usually she caught his arm to be sure she had his attention and pointed to the things she named. Then she held his arm tight and continued pointing—"Say it: floor tile. *Floor tile.*"—until he echoed the sounds she had used. It took him several hours on the first morning to realize that the sounds she made were associated with the objects she indicated. His mind was very empty. But once he understood the relation, he learned quickly.

There were walls, doors, floors and ceilings; beds, tables, cushions and chairs; spring bread, meltwater, roasting fowl and eggs; gameboards, markers, mirrors and throne. And many other things. He learned the sound for them all. He learned the sound for the things he and the girl did together too: running, jumping, walking, clapping. "I'm smiling, Darkchild. See—look: *smiling.*" Although he never tested her, he thought the girl would not let him eat if he did not learn, and he was hungry. He felt as if he had been starved.

Perhaps it helped that he had no words of his own for any of the things to be found here. If he did not use the language she taught him, he could not speak at all. And his guide wanted him to speak because there were questions to be asked. The boy felt their pressure at the back of his mind. The tension they created was uncomfortable.

The girl didn't seem to appreciate just how quickly he learned her language. Perhaps she had never taught anyone before.

But there was more than language to be learned. The palace was cavernous and many-chambered. In each room there were things to be examined and classified. The boy moved to that chore automatically during his first days in the palace, touching, smelling, tasting, stroking, weighing, manipulating. At times he paused to puzzle over what he learned, over the relationship of texture and aroma, form and weight. Other times the process of exploration seemed to go on without his conscious attention, as if his senses and his hands knew their work and proceeded unassisted.

There were other facets of himself too, he realized vaguely, that worked unassisted. Sometimes he found his face moving into expressions that mirrored the girl's mood even though he did not share it. Sometimes his head nodded at something she said even though it did not interest him. Often he followed her quietly in activities from which he really wanted to withdraw. She was very fond of board games. They spent hours each day bent over the large inlaid board moving carved pieces according to obscure rules. The boy wanted to explore instead, but his guide instructed him to play. It was important to please the girl.

Later undoubtedly there would be other people who must be pleased. The boy gave it no more than passing thought. It was apparent his body knew its job and would perform appropriately. His guide saw to that. Although his guide had no perceptible external influence, although he could not manipulate the world except through the boy, as far as the boy was concerned, his guide was omniscient and omnipotent. He was a force to be obeyed without question.

There were some things in the palace the boy liked better than others. At first he liked to be in the kitchen because bread and the warm stove were there. But soon the kitchen offered more than creature comfort. In some unnameable way, it seemed to offer memory. Each day the boy went to the kitchen and explored the long shelves of preserved goods. Then he tapped inside the cold box where roasting fowls were kept in frozen blocks and examined drawers of utensils and containers and implements. From all these things, he drew a sense of life extending into the past as well as the future. The boy liked to caress the wooden handles of the knives and draw upon the presence of the people he imagined had used them. The big boiling pots that hung on the wall hooks were dented and pitted. He liked to place them on the cold stoves and imagine he heard the scrape of carved spoons against their sides and the happy bubbling of things thick and savory. These sensory echoes were his only clue to some personal existence spanning the time before he found himself on the watchtower steps.

The spices and herbs quickly became his special pleasure. They were stored in dozens of small bottles of uniform size and shape. The bottles lined an entire shelf, their contents fragrant, pungent, musty, bitter, sweet. After he had discovered their pleasures, the boy never went to the spice shelf unless he had time to open each container in turn and sample its contents. Most of the spices were stored in ground form but a few of the bottles held loose dried leaves and five held seeds.

He found it satisfying to arrange and rearrange the bottles on their shelf according to their contents. After a few days, he elaborated a set order for the bottles, one that seemed to provide a progression from the mildest spices through the strongest, with those in each range of intensity ordered according to the nature of their taste: sweet, sour, bitter, and so forth. Entering the kitchen, he would carry all the bottles from the shelf to the long cutting table. He liked the table because it showed the scars of many years' use. He could finger its wounds and hear the thump of cleavers, perhaps not here in the palace but elsewhere—in some place he could not even remember. Once the spices were arrayed in a long line, he sampled them at his leisure, one by one, sometimes randomly, sometimes in predetermined order. Then he set them back into place on the shelf jar by jar, arranging them fastidiously.

At first his guide urged him to work in the kitchen. Then his work there was done and the guide grew impatient. There was much to be learned in the palace and the boy was wasting time. When his guide first objected to the extended samplings from the spice shelf, the boy let himself be separated from this most satisfying activity. For a while he came to the spice shelf only once a day to sample and sort the bottles.

But one day he made a startling discovery. He found that if he worked at the spices and herbs very intently, saturating his senses, his guide became too occupied filing the resultant sensory data to direct the boy away from the activity. Apparently the guide could not combine certain activities, and the boy had discovered one activity, sensory filing, that overrode others. The boy experimented over the next few days and found that certain herbs were the most distracting to his guide. There was a complexity to their bouquet that completely overwhelmed the guide. If the boy alternated tasting and smelling from those bottles with sampling from other, less distracting bottles, he could work unhindered.

This realization gave the boy his first intimation of identity and purpose separate from those of his guide. He began to observe the girl closely and soon he wondered why he had a guide when she seemed to have none. She seemed to do as she pleased with no internal direction at all.

At this point, the boy experienced an initial stirring of resistance to his guide. But he was uncomfortably aware of his dependence upon the guide. For soon after coming to the palace, the boy had learned that deep within the wasteland of his mind lay a place of warmth and welcome. That was the trancing room, and within the trancing room lived his brothers.

Had the trancing room been a physical reality somewhere? Had he met there with his brothers before coming to the palace? He didn't know. He could remember nothing. Now the trancing room was a place within his mind. Whenever the boy was tired or confused, he yearned to be there, yet only the guide could open the door. Each evening the boy placed himself at the trancing-room door by resting his forehead on his knees and taking a series of slow, deep breaths. But he knew that if he incurred his guide's displeasure, if his guide chose not to let him trance, he would find himself breathing very quickly instead and the door would not open. He would be left bitter and cold and alone. Completely alone.

It was upon such a bitter occasion—the first—that the boy realized the girl was alone too. He had lingered too long in the kitchen that afternoon, exploring drawers of utensils, resisting his guide's instruction that he play board games with the girl. She had come for him twice, she had pleaded with him, and he had pretended not to see or hear her. The first time she had gone away with an anxious frown, the second time with angry tears. Both times the boy had continued his inventory of the kitchen drawers with no pang of remorse.

But that night when he retired to the corner of the throneroom where he tranced, his guide refused him the trance-room. The boy placed his forehead upon his knees and worked to make his breath slow and steady. Instead he found himself breathing so rapidly he became dizzy. He raised his head and peered around blankly, then dropped his head again. This time he regulated his respiration with painstaking care—and heard his breath huffing rapidly, grunting in his chest. His heart began to hammer and when he jumped up, he swayed dizzily, nauseated.

He gave it up finally and sat shivering and wakeful, staring emptily into the dark mirrors that hung at intervals around the walls. The palace was cold by night and he was hungry for the comfort of his brothers' company, hungry for the sound of their voices, the warmth of their faces. He wondered about them, bleakly. Had he been with them before he came here? Where? Would he return to them someday? Although he entered the trancing room each evening, when he returned he could never remember clearly what he and his brothers did there, what was said among them. Nor could he remember their faces, but he knew they must be much like his.

Sighing, he gazed into the dark mirrors. The only face he saw was his own.

The chill of his loneliness was heavy when the girl approached and knelt before him, her auburn hair falling between them. Her face was shadowed and she touched his shoulder tentatively. "You're going to sleep again, aren't you?" she demanded with the blend of diffidence and hurt anger she sometimes used. "Every night after we eat, you sit here and go to sleep. You never talk to me at night."

The boy peered up at her with some surprise. It had never occurred to him that she noticed his body sitting here while he tranced. There were traces of tears at the corners of her eyes. That, combined with her plaintive anger, touched him. Apparently she felt much the way he felt tonight: lonely, angry, helpless. "I talked to you today," he said finally, not certain it was the right thing to say.

"You talked to me this morning. This afternoon when I came to get you for games, you wouldn't hear me. You pretended I wasn't there." She wiped angrily at her eyes.

"I—I was busy," he said lamely, wondering how he had turned her away twice with no compunction. She had let him explore all morning, and the games were important to her.

"You always talk to me in the morning," she went on. "But at night you sit here with your forehead on your knees and your face cold. It doesn't matter how hard I shake you, I can't wake you. You always leave me alone at night."

"You shake me?" The suggestion startled him. He was never aware of her presence when he tranced. She was always in her own chamber when he returned from the trancing room and walked through the cold halls to his bed. He had never even wondered how she spent the evenings.

"I shake you until your teeth rattle," she said with bleak relish. "And I bring you food, but you never take it. Here—" She produced a rich chunk of fruitbread from a folded square of cloth. "At least you're awake tonight. Eat it."

Touched, he wet his lips with the tip of his tongue.

Something blazed in her eyes when he took the bread: hurt flashing through fresh tears. "You could offer me half," she said with a tearful sting.

And he felt her loneliness. He gazed into her pleading eyes, and before her anger could win through again, he broke the chunk of bread and held half of it for her. She was alone in the palace and she hadn't even brothers to trance with. The sisters she spoke of were dead and mourned. She had only him.

She accepted bread from him, but with lingering wariness. That night they played the board games he had refused to play that afternoon and he enjoyed playing because it helped her forget her loneliness. That in turn helped him forget the trancing-room door that had refused to open. Late in the night they walked the cold corridors together, and before they parted, their hands touched and clung. The boy went to bed with the warmth of her fingers still on him.

This, he realized, was a warmth he could touch any evening. He did not have to wait for the guide to open a mental door for him. And afterward, if he spent the evening with the girl instead of in the trancing room, he could remember what had passed, what had been said.

Was he disloyal to his brothers? He lay in bed wondering. Perhaps if he could remember their faces, if he could recall whether they had ever met outside the trancing room—but no memory came to him and finally he slept.

From that night, he became aware of an increasing tension between himself and his guide. It was necessary for the boy to please the girl. But his guide did not consider it necessary for him to find pleasure in pleasing her. Pleasure was supposed to be granted only by the guide.

It made the guide uneasy when the boy ran through the halls with the girl laughing just because the running and laughing felt good. It made the guide uneasy when the boy and girl bent together ciphering scrolls and the boy enjoyed the warmth of her body near his. It made the guide uneasy when the boy smiled at the girl just because he liked to do it.

Yet the boy continued to steal pleasure from the girl's company, even when he knew his guide would refuse him the trance-room afterward. The trance-room had simply become much less important to him. Sometimes he went for days without thinking of his brothers.

In fact, the boy had entered a period of testing which he would have considered impossible earlier. During the day, he enjoyed the girl's company and ignored his guide's discomfiture. But sometimes he woke in the night and was frightened. Who was he to try to direct his own course of behavior? The girl at least had a name—Khira. As far as he knew, he had none. Or if he did, he could not recall it, no matter how hard he tried. And sometimes he tried very hard.

Ciphering scrolls soon became one of his favorite pastimes. The scrolls were stored in an alcove behind the throne and were made of fine-grained skins laced with inked symbols. The boy especially enjoyed sitting beside Khira on cold evenings tracing the symbols with one fingertip and repeating their meaning after her.

The scrolls related the story of Khira's world, Brakrath. Khira's people had come to Brakrath a hundred centuries or more before—he tried to deal with that span of time in terms of the few days of life he remembered and was dizzied by it—and not by intention. They had been outward bound for another destination when their ship had failed and stranded them here.

They had found Brakrath cold and hostile. For centuries they fought to survive its winter storms and short summers while they waited for rescue. But rescue did not come and after a while they forgot to wait and began to adapt to Brakrath. The scrolls told of the changes they underwent and of the people who underwent them. They told of people who learned to fatten for winter and to sleep through the entire snowseason in sealed halls. They told of people who learned to heed the voices of Brakrath's mountains and of other people who were drawn to the distant plains. They told of the great herds of redmanes that were found in the plains and of the women who became their guardians. They told of other women, daughters of the redmane guardians, who unleashed from blocks of black stone quarried in the mountains capabilities never before dreamed of. Khira was descended from these women, the barohnas of Brakrath.

Khira was never angry or sad when she ciphered from the scrolls. Her fingers flew over the inked symbols and her voice rang. Absorbed, she seemed not to appreciate just how quickly the boy learned to cipher the scrolls with her. Almost certainly she had never taught anyone before.

Often after they finished ciphering, they sat talking for hours. Khira told the boy of the people of the valley, of her sisters, of the mountains she loved and the plains she sometimes visited. She told him of the festivals and feasts that ushered in Darkmorning, the first day of winter, when the halls were sealed and sleepdust scattered. She told him of the lambs that were born when the sheep woke from wintersleep. She told him of spring days when teams of redmanes came to the valley with their guardians to plow the fields. She told him the entire saga of her sisters, and in the telling they seemed to live again.

She seldom spoke of her mother. He had no memory of a mother to make him wonder why.

The boy had nothing no tell Khira in return, in fact. He had no people, no world, no memories. He had nothing but the unremembered faces of his brothers. Sometimes she paused in her tales and flicked a question at him—"Do the children gather summer fruit where you come from? Or do they leave it for the adults to bring in?"—and he couldn't answer. He had never smelled a feast cooking, had never minded animals at pasture, had never watched a field planted to grain. Or if he had, something had happened to his memory of those things.

Instead of memories, he had the guide. He became increasingly restive under the guide's domination. Why should he yield when Khira yielded to no one? And yet at times resistance was useless. If the guide considered the situation merited, he could speak through the boy's mouth without the boy's consent, could use the boy's arms and legs as if the boy himself had no claim upon them.

The boy had been in the palace for five hands of days when he learned that Khira had neglected to mention a very important matter to him. One morning they stood in the watchtower gazing across the gleaming snow that covered the valley. His eyes narrowing, he traced the outlines of the palace in the drifted snow—and realized with surprise that a certain barred door far from the wing of the palace he and Khira used did not lead outside but into another wing.

Somehow, he realized with a sudden sinking, he had missed knowing of the existence of an entire wing of the palace.

He was not prepared for the abruptness or intensity of his guide's anger. Recognizing the oversight, his guide uttered a harsh epithet in a language the boy did not recognize and seized control of his feet, driving him down the stairs. Involuntarily the boy was propelled through the warren of corridors to the closed door that led to the unexplored wing.

"Where does this go?" he had asked Khira when he first encountered the barred door.

"Nowhere," she had said, and led him away.

He had been directed to learn everything, and he had failed. He should have known from the quick drop of her eyes, from the tight line of her lips, that this was not simply another door to the exterior of the palace. It was different from other doors. It was of a different metal, smoother, lighter, newer. Even the hinges that held it were different. Driven by his guide's displeasure, he tested the door with his fingertips, with his knuckles, finally with his entire body. When the door refused to budge, his breath came in a frustrated hiss.

Khira had run down the stairs after him. She watched wide-eyed, frightened, as he fought the door. Finally he stepped back. "This door—" His guide's anger choked him. He could barely speak.

"It leads to the Arnimi wing," Khira said with obvious reluctance. "It's sealed. We can't open it until they return from the southern mountains."

He spun back to the door, his eyes flashing with the guide's anger. But it was useless to batter at the door. It would not yield. "The Arnimi?" he demanded.

"Yes. This is their wing. The Council of Bronze gave them permission to make permanent quarters here—in our valley."

And who *were* the Arnimi? his guide demanded. His voice was harsh, driven by his guide's anger. "You never told me anyone lived here but your own people. Who are the Arnimi? Where do they come from?" Were they even Brakrathi?

She retreated from his anger, her slight features grim. "They—they come from Arnim. It's on the other side of the galaxy. They've lived there since Earthexodus—since people left Earth to live in the stars. They changed Arnim to make it like Earth. They altered its climate and turned the ground over to Earth-plants. It's still like Earth there."

"They're—the Arnimi are humans? Like us?" Some of his guide's anger ebbed at this revelation.

A tight frown contracted her eyebrows. "They're human—but not human like we are."

Why was she so reluctant to tell him about the Arnimi? As she answered each question, her lips contracted back into a tight line. "How many of them live here? In the palace?"

Her fist clenched and she walked away from him, her voice distant. "There were twenty when they first came. More of them have come since, so now there are fifty-two. They're—they're making a study of Brakrath."

Was that what angered her? That they studied Brakrath? "Why? What do they want here?"

She essayed a resentful shrug. "They're compiling a history of all the human races and what's become of them since Earthexodus. They have—they have three questions they're trying to answer. They want to know if every new world shapes the people who settle it into some unique form. They want to know if humans can adapt to any world that doesn't destroy them in the first few generations. And they want to know if there's some common characteristic that we always retain, something that never changes, no matter where we settle or how."

"And they're trying to answer those questions here?"

"They're trying to answer them everywhere. They're studying worlds all over the galaxy, dozens of worlds. But they're especially interested in Brakrath because no one knew we were here for so long. We haven't traded with other worlds and we haven't fought with them. We haven't been influenced by anything but Brakrath since the stranding."

"And the Arnimi—they've been here how long?"

"The first ones came fourteen years ago and they'll be here another ten or more. The Council of Bronze gave them permission to stay as long as they want so long as none of them leave Brakrath or send information back to Arnim until their study is completed."

The boy felt his forehead pucker in a tight frown. As he listened to Khira's explanation, he was aware of his guide's reactions as if they were his own. His guide was angry that an entire people existed here without his knowledge. Why hadn't he been told about them? He was worried too. Were their purposes the same as his own? Would they be hostile? Would they try to sabotage him? What should he expect of them?

The guide struggled under the concentrated stress of uncertainty. The boy stepped away from the metal door, aware of an unexpected shifting within his mind. It was as if . . . He shook his head, trying to clear it. He felt as he sometimes felt just before the door to the trancing room opened—remote, detached, drifting.

And then a door did open, but it was not the trancing room door. It was another door, one he hadn't known existed. His mouth opened on a strangled exclamation. For a moment the door stood wide and it was as if a dazzling array of codified information flashed into the boy's awareness, blazing alive too rapidly, too vividly for him to do more than reel back from it, stunned. "What—"

Did he expect an answer? He received none. Swiftly his guide disappeared, blotting out the door behind himself.

His guide had entered the secret room. Without comment or instruction, his guide had slipped into a hidden place where information was stored and closed the access, leaving the boy suddenly alone.

He had never been alone before. At first he did not even recognize the strange, echoing sensation for what it was: emptiness. The boy swayed dizzily, probing his temples with his fingertips. There was another door in his mind. His guide knew how to open it, how to enter. Did *he* have access too? Could he follow?

Did he want to follow? He was aware of Khira staring at him. "You—" he stammered. "Khira—" Was this the freedom Khira knew all the time? This absence of a directing presence? The boy peered down the stalklit corridor, momentarily disoriented. I can do anything I want, he realized with wonder. Anything.

But what did he want to do?

Khira was clutching his sleeve, her face parchment. "Dark-child—"

What *did* he want? It surprised him a little. He wanted to learn. During his days in the palace, he had worked at mastering Khira's language, at cataloguing the contents of every room of the palace because the guide had so directed him. Now, with the guide gone, he found that he simply wanted to learn different things.

He wanted to know everything about the Arnimi, for instance: how they looked, how they talked, what customs they practiced, what crafts they engaged in, how they structured their kinships. If there were artifacts, he wanted to touch them. If there were scrolls, he wanted to cipher them.

"Khira—" Where were the words for everything he wanted to know?

"Darkchild—are you sick?"

He shook his head, questions choking him. *"No.* No—I want to know about the Arnimi. I want to know—" Everything.

Khira touched her lips with the tip of her tongue, troubled. "I—I can draw you likenesses of them," she offered.

That was good for a beginning. She had drawn him likenesses of her sisters, each stroke careful and loving. "Yes," he said eagerly.

This time she did not fetch an unmarked scroll and ink. Instead, quickly, she led him down a long-unused corridor to a chamber that hadn't been swept for years. Dust lay thick on the floor. Stalk-lamp covered ceiling and walls in a dense tangle, creating a garish light. Entering, Khira glanced back at the boy tensely, then knelt. Her forefinger moved through the dense dust and the caricature of a human appeared.

The boy crouched eagerly. The man she drew had narrow hunched shoulders and a pendulous belly. His eyes were prominent, staring, and his lips were bunched in a frown. "They're bad," he said immediately.

Khira shrugged. "No."

"But you—"

"I hate them," she said with a cold hiss. "They want to know everything. They leave nothing private. They go to the stonewarrens when the people are awake and measure them. Not just how tall they are but how large their heads are, how long their legs are, how wide their toes are. They put needles in people and draw out blood and feed it into their machines." She glared at him, scowling with grievance. "They carry meters on their belts and point them at us. They tramp through the fields poking sticks into the ground. Four years ago they tried to butcher a redmane and cut into its brain. Now the redmane guardians don't let them come to the plain anymore. One of them even tried to follow my mother to her winter throne one year. He wanted to meter her when the sun was dim, to study the activity of her brain."

"But I—I want to know things too," he reminded her. "I look at things and ask you questions." There were dozens of questions he wanted to ask her now about the Arnimi.

Frowning, she stubbed out the dust-portrait. "You eat with me," she said shortly. "Techni-Verra is the only Arnimi who has ever eaten with me—and Commander Bullens put her on penalty for it."

That made the difference? He followed her from the chamber, knowing it did not. Perhaps the difference lay in his manner, in the fact that his guide insisted he please her. "Khira—" Then he stiffened, pressing his fingertips to his temples, drawing a rebellious breath. A sense of change—his guide had returned.

And the boy wanted to fight. He wanted to fight for the inviolability of his thoughts, of his mind. Yet how? He pressed his temples, trying to drive the guide away by sheer physical pressure.

The room—did it have a physical site in his brain? Was his perception that information was stored there correct? Could his guide enter it anytime, or only in times of stress? Khira turned with a questioning gaze. He was aware of the rigidity of his muscles, of the perspiration that suddenly stained his suit. Trembling, she drew his hands from his temples.

Who was the guide? The question popped into his mind and he was shocked at its audacity. "Khira—"

But she didn't have the answers to his questions. And his guide restrained him from asking more about the Arnimi. It was obvious Khira did not want to talk about them—and his guide had other sources of information.

The boy frowned. Earlier his guide had uttered an epithet in a language the boy did not know. Now the boy wondered what language it had been—and what language the guide had used to direct him before Khira had taught him (them?) Brakrathi. Did he and the guide have a language of their own? How many others did they share it with? Or did it exist only to serve the two of them? It angered the boy that he did not know, could not remember.

The room where the guide had gone—were there memories hidden there that once had belonged to the boy? Khira had memories. Surely the boy had them too: places he had seen, people he had known, experiences he had undergone. Perhaps he even remembered a time when his guide had not been with him, when he had been free. If he could find his way alone to the place where the guide had gone, if he could find the key and unlock the knowledge there, if he could find a way to purge the guide from his mind—

Without thinking, the boy snapped off a stem of stalklamp and slit it with his thumbnail. He studied the internal structure of the stem intently, then touched tongue to the bitter sap, screening his thoughts from his guide. The place where his guide had gone, where information was stored . . . But he had no idea how to find that place.

Yet he could not forget one question: *who was the guide?* As the day passed, he moved through the palace distractedly, overwhelming his guide with sensory data as a screen for his own thoughts. The effort yielded nothing but a growing sense of futility. His consciousness seemed to be a single small room, with closed doors at every side. Some must lead to his past, some must hold memories of a time when he had had no guide. But he could not even sit quietly and probe his thoughts. He had to keep moving, touching, smelling, tasting.

Doors . . . His guide was becoming increasingly restive under the barrage of sensory information. The boy moved to the kitchen, to the spice jars, vaguely aware of Khira following him anxiously from place to place.

There was only one door the boy knew how to open, the door to the trancing room. And his guide had final control of that door. Who controlled the other doors, the doors out of this narrow band of awareness? The boy sighed heavily, tired and confused.

That evening he sat in a corner of the throneroom after the evening meal, waiting for Khira to come down from her chamber. He had reached that point of exhaustion where his thoughts had neither substance nor direction. His head hurt and his shoulders ached. He sat on a down cushion, his head resting against the polished stone wall, his eyelids heavy. He had questioned all afternoon and he had found no answers. None at all.

When he first heard his brother's voice, he sighed with relief and let his eyelids fall shut. In the trancing room at least he would not be tired, nor would he be confused. He would be warm in his brothers' company. With another deep sigh, he slowed his respiration, reaching for forgetfulness.

Then his eyes sprang open. *He heard his brothers laughing and he had not summoned them.* He stared around the empty throneroom. Even though his eyes were open, his brothers' voices were still with him. Confounded, he let his eyes slip shut again—and saw the trancing room door. It stood open. He recognized his brothers' faces through the blaze of light that always warmed the trancing room. They were smiling, beckoning him, all those faces so like his own. Some were young, little more than infants. Others were older. Some were men already, smiling men, laughing men—calling him.

He shook his head in confusion. Calling him—*they were calling him by name.* He listened intently, trying to grasp the name they called him. But he couldn't piece its separate syllables into a whole.

They knew his name—it was their name too. And their voices— He stepped toward the door, reaching out for them.

Before he could enter, Khira bent over him. He hadn't even heard her approach. "Darkchild?"

Darkchild. But that wasn't the name. Moaning, he fought Khira's intrusive voice. The door was so near. His brothers . . .

Khira's voice was clearer now, anxious. "Darkchild!"

Something of her distress cut through his dazzled consciousness. The door was open; his brothers were calling him; their faces— *Why was the door open now?* He had not put his forehead to his knees. He had not regulated his breathing. Why did his guide offer him the trancing room now?

To reward him? When his guide was angry at being screened?

The boy drew a deep, sighing breath and forced his eyelids open. His head had fallen forward. His chin rested on his chest. He lifted it as if it were a great weight. He could still hear his brothers' voices calling his name.

His elusive name . . .

Khira's eyes were pleading. "I thought we were going to play magic squares, Darkchild."

Desperately he fought off the trancing room spell. "My name—" He spoke faintly over the retreating murmur of his brothers' voices.

She touched his shoulder, troubled. "I don't know your name— not your real name."

Neither did he. His brothers' voices had faded. They were barely audible. The boy looked up at Khira. "He thought he could distract me," he said slowly, testing the truth of the perception. "He thought he could open one door and make me forget the other." His guide had attempted to play the same game with him that he had played with his guide.

But it had failed. Even as the boy peered up into Khira's uncomprehending eyes, the trancing room door closed, shutting off his brothers' light. The boy sighed deeply. The light was gone and he had become a shadow—excluded by his own will.

Khira had named him correctly. He was a shadow child, a dark child. Exhaustion gripped him, sudden, total. "I'm tired," he said. When had he been this tired before?

Khira took his hand. Her sympathy was direct, tinged with worry. "I'm sorry."

The boy looked up at her. His brothers had been his comfort, his solace. To give them up was unthinkable. But to let his guide use them against him, to maintain dominion over him, was unthinkable too. If Khira hadn't called him back, he would have stepped into the trancing room and his guide's trap. In her loneliness she had pulled him back.

He must be lonely too, he realized. He must give up the comfort of his brothers' company if he was to find the answers to his questions and fill the emptiness someone or something had made of his mind. Sighing, he spoke with great effort. "Do you want to play magic squares?" He could not think while he played. But so long as he was actively occupied, the guide could not lure him into the trancing room.

"Will you?"

"Yes. I will." He rose stiffly and moved to the inlaid board, forcing himself to set the carved pieces into place. He had learned a lot today. Not so long ago he had considered his guide omniscient and omnipotent and had granted him complete dominion over his will. Now he claimed his own will, however painfully.

And in the claiming, he had become the person Khira had already christened him—Darkchild, child of shadow.

SIX

KHIRA

Two nights after Darkchild discovered the west wing, Khira was wakened by a shrieking metallic cry that jarred through the silent palace. She struggled up from sleep and lay with every muscle clenched, tensely expecting the sound to expand into the terrible metallic scream that had brought Darkchild. Instead the sound was quickly muffled and became the cry of the Arnimi ship as it plunged through drifts of snow to settle on the western plaza.

Khira's racketing pulse had hardly returned to normal when Darkchild materialized in her doorway, his face grey. "That—what was that?"

Khira made no attempt to purge resentment from her tone. "The Arnimi ship. They've returned from the southern mountains." And tomorrow they would walk the palace with their meters, tapping and testing and talking among themselves. Techni-Verra might speak to her, might even take time to ask after her winter's occupation. But the others—if they spoke, it would be to probe, to question. It would be with no care for her, only for whatever information they might elicit from her.

She smiled grimly. Precious little that would be. She had offered Techni-Verra bread and the Arnimi woman had accepted. She would offer none of the others anything.

Darkchild peered at her uncertainly, sensitive to her anger. "They've come back to stay?"

Khira sat, one hand clutching her coverlet. "They won't leave until thawing." And even if you had not come and given me company, she added silently, with sour satisfaction, I would have gone the entire winter without speaking to them. I would have been alone here—except perhaps for Techni-Verra.

"Adar is rising," she said without thinking. Yet the observation was not an irrelevancy. Although she seldom thought about the red star's winter appearance, she kept an internal calendar, and tonight the belligerent surge was in her blood. Quickly she jumped from her bed. "Let's go to the tower."

Darkchild stepped back, surprised at her sudden change of mood. "Now?"

"Yes, and you'll see my host." Watching Darkchild during the first days after he emerged from the watchtower had been like watching a living intelligence emerge from shadow. At first he had been like a person brain-injured: remote, vacant-eyed, slack. Although he moved through the palace touching and evaluating whatever came within range of his senses, he seemed barely conscious of the totality of his surroundings. It was as if he were one of the Arnimi's data-gathering instruments bound up in human flesh. And when Khira worked with him he seemed so little aware of her as a living person that she might have been stone.

Yet he learned, and as she added fingers to the hands on her wall, he changed. His smile became less vacant, his explorations less groping. More and more often, willed intelligence moved behind his eyes. Recently he had given up his evening time of retreat. He played board games with her now instead. And these past days, his eyes often flashed with some covert defiance, some half-hidden rebellion.

Yet through all the changes, one thing persisted: his curiosity. And he had *not* seen Adar.

Nor did she for some minutes when they reached the tower. The wind whipped frosted fingers through the broken window, piling the floor with snow. Khira hugged her down jacket tight and peered into the clouded sky. She knew her star was there. She could hear his drums and the clatter of reeds in her blood, Adar's warcall.

Darkchild was more interested in the shadowed concavity that marked the western plaza of the palace. He held himself stiffly, staring at the dark place where the Arnimi ship had settled, as if at an enemy.

His gaze was black. Adar's was red, and finally heavy clouds shifted and Adar's pinpoint light burned through. Khira clutched Darkchild's hand. "There! There is Adar!" He was a gleaming red light in a misted collar of orange, burning down at them. "Now you see why my feast table is empty."

Darkchild followed her pointing finger, distracted at first. When he found the red star with its misty nimbus, he peered at it with deepening interest. "Because nothing is harvested now," he said slowly. "Your star comes too late. There is nothing to be brought in from the fields now."

"Yes. And no one to bring it. Adar comes only in winter—in the war months."

"But there are no wars. You told me that."

"There are no wars now. In the early days of the barohnas, there were. And this is when raiders came, late enough that the people were sleeping, early enough that most of the winter was still ahead. They never came when there was a barohna in the valley. They took the halls first and they slept for a while. Then they woke and ate and went to lie in ambush for the barohna." Khira should have shuddered as she recounted the brief history of violence that had marked the first centuries of the barohnas. But when the host-markers had been spread for her infant hands, she had reached for the red stone. And in taking it, she had surrendered some of the tenderness of her sisters, moon and blue-star daughters.

War and barrenness. She held Darkchild's hand tighter, until it warmed in hers. Every year on her feast day, there was fasting in the valley. Yet somehow hunger had fed her and the drums of Adar warmed her. She turned to Darkchild, staring at his intent profile. If he were offered the stones, if he took a host, which body might it be?

Darkchild's eyes held the war-star for a moment longer, then returned to the dark concavity on the western plaza. Khira dismissed her moment's speculation. The barohnas had sprung from the women of the halls, and so female infants of the halls took hosts just as did female infants of the palace. But males were never offered choosing stones. They were soil-bound. The sky and its energies touched their realm but did not comprise it.

"Khira—"

She didn't even have to hear his question. "Yes. Tomorrow we will go to the Arnimi wing." Let him see the Arnimi. Let him examine their instruments and appliances. Let him ask them his questions. In the end, he would like them no better than she did.

Still she delayed their visit until the middle of the next morning and approached the western wing with distaste. She had not taken time to train the stalklamp that grew in the remote regions of the palace. As they neared the Arnimi quarters, glowing stems hung in slack streamers. The sealed door to the west wing stood tall and immobile. Normally when the Arnimi were in residence, it opened automatically at Khira's approach. Today, to her surprise, it did not.

She halted and stared up its imposing expanse, puzzled. Then, aware of Darkchild rigid beside her, his gaze flickering tensely from her to the door, she tapped lightly.

A metallic throat cleared somewhere nearby. "Goodwinter, heiress. I see you have acquired a companion."

Startled, she stepped back. Sometime since the Arnimi had returned in the middle of the night, they had recessed a small grill into the door. Beside it was a tiny lens. She peered into the lens, her face tightening into a frown. It was like the Arnimi to suddenly speak to her through the door instead of opening it. "Yes, my friend is with me," she said sharply, waiting for the door to open.

Still it did not move. "How long has this friend been with you, heiress?"

The query, despite its metallic tone, betrayed something sharper than polite interest. "Long enough," she said with asperity. She did not like to be questioned as they might question a child of their own race, condescendingly, through a closed door. "We have come to see the rock samples you brought from the southern mountains."

She heard muttered voices beyond the door. She rapped again, beginning to be angry. Even less than she liked being addressed as a child did she like being barred from a portion of her own palace. "I'm waiting," she prompted.

More muttering, then a whining electronic sound and the door slowly opened.

Khira and Darkchild caught their breath simultaneously. Now instead of a metal door, they faced a shimmering screen of light, beyond which stood two Arnimi. Both Arnimi gazed at Darkchild, their lips bunched severely, their prominent grey eyes cold. One was male—Commander Bullens—and one was female, but to Khira they were almost identical in appearance: potbellied, with greying hair that receded from their high foreheads and hung to their shoulders in thin streamers. Even the characteristic Arnimi expression was identical: remote, chill, disapproving.

"What is this?" Khira demanded, more angry than before. "What have you hung in this doorway?"

"This is a privacy screen, heiress," Commander Bullens informed her. "We saw the shattered watchtower window when we landed and we found your guest's prints on our door. The screen will protect our quarters from unauthorized visitors. If you are eager to see our samples—and you have never been eager before—you may step through the screen. Your companion may not."

"Your companion may wait in the corridor," the female Arnimi said. Although both wore translator buttons at their belts, they had learned to speak Brakrathi without aid. Now, however, Commander Bullens placed his button against his throat. As he subvocalized, the button spoke his words in a tongue Khira did not recognize.

Darkchild clutched Khira's arm spasmodically. He rose to the balls of his feet, his lips parting in shock, his pupils contracting.

The Arnimi spoke again, and this time the alien words held clear warning. Khira stared from the haughty Arnimi to Darkchild, startled by the flush that stained his bronze cheeks. "You have his language in your bank," she realized in surprise, wheeling back to the Arnimi.

"Yes. I told him in his brother-language that while the heiress may enter our quarters and do what she pleases—even though she has never been so interested in entering before—we have guarded the portal against the Rauthimage. He may not enter."

"Rauthimage?" The word was unfamiliar.

"He is the image of Rauth." It was a clarification that clarified nothing. Again the Arnimi placed his button to his throat and subvocalized. This time the alien words were harsh, challenging.

Darkchild dropped Khira's arm. Muscles bunched beneath his thin coverall and his face twisted fiercely. With a quick sideways glance at Khira, he lunged forward, one hand extended.

Whatever invisible force guarded the door became briefly visible, limning Darkchild's slender body in blue light. Serpents of light seemed to snap at his coverall and his bare head. Then Darkchild was propelled backward, to slam against the rough stone wall, his face blanched, his dark eyes staring.

Khira was torn between anger and concern. She ran to Darkchild. "Are you hurt?"

Pain and bitterness mingled in his gaze as he peered at the Arnimi who had blocked his passage. Muttering something in the same language the Arnimi had used, he stood away from the wall and retreated down the corridor, shoulders set. He seemed oblivious to Khira's concern.

She turned back to the Arnimi, her words stinging. "I am heiress here and I invited my friend to enter this wing with me. He was under my protection."

The two regarded her, unintimidated. "Then you would do well to recall your protection. You are a child who has taken a Rauthimage for a friend," Commander Bullens said coldly.

His arrogance made Khira flush with anger. "I am a child who has taken another child for a friend. I am also the palace daughter in my mother's palace."

"Yes, and it is regrettable your mother is not here to deal with the Rauthimage."

Khira felt her gorge rise giddily. "You have already classified him when you have just met him? How do you know he is anything more than a stranded traveler? If you want to use a word in conversation with me, define it or I will consider it nonsense."

She had intended to sting them into anger to match her own. However they consulted silently with an exchanged glance, coldly unconcerned. The female Arnimi said, "We found his prints on our door this morning and we classified them immediately against data in our banks. If you would care to come into our quarters, we will show you tapes containing an exact description of your friend and a number of other verifications of his identity."

Khira touched her lips with a tongue suddenly dry. She could not shake their stony self-possession. And she knew the Arnimi had honed the science of classifying and identifying persons, plants and objects to a degree that confounded even Tiahna. "You—why would you carry identifying data on a stray child in your banks?"

"Because he is not a child; rather he is a child but beyond that, more importantly, he is a Rauthimage. Bring us a sample of his hair; we will show you spectroscopic readouts proving we have already classified samples of his hair. Bring us his fingerprints; we will show you we already have them on file. Bring us a scrap of fingernail, a flake of skin; we will prove that we have already analyzed identical samples and carry the data in our bank to permit exact identification." The Arnimi offered an arrogant grimace. Apparently it was intended as a smile. "We have already satisfied your mother that no two separate persons have identical structures. Even the set of identical twins she brought us were distinguishable in a dozen ways. Isn't that correct?"

Khira refused to concede the point. "You've told me yourself we're a small group of people. There are billions of people on other worlds. Out of all of them—"

"There is no duplication there either, not among people who have not been imaged from a prototype—as your friend has been and as we can prove from our data tapes."

Khira's fists clenched, the nails digging her palms. If they knew where Darkchild had come from, why he had been abandoned half-starved in the tower—But Adar was risen and anger overrode any softer approach. "If you have identification on Darkchild on your tapes, you came to our wing last night and took samples to create it. You came to my personal wing without permission while I slept. You—"

The Arnimi shook their heads. "We have not left our own wing. We carry Rauth tracings in our databanks as a matter of course. Every ship of our flag carries them."

And there was the flaw in their argument. "You're lying!" she flared. "Darkchild is no older than I am. You have been here since before he was born. How could you have tracings in your databanks when he was born several years after you left Arnim?"

She had finally nettled Commander Bullens. He flicked the lank hair off his collar. "We do not lie and we do not argue with children, even imperial children," he said frostily. "We have identifying information on the Rauthimage and if you ask reasonably we will permit you to examine it. If you want our advice, that will be yours too."

Why had Tiahna ever permitted him to quarter his people in the palace? Why had the Council of Bronze allowed the Arnimi to stay on Brakrath at all? "What would that be?"

Commander Bullens laid a proprietary hand on his paunch. "It is very simple, heiress: lead your image-friend to the nearest exterior door, open it, and send him out into the snow. Then seal the door behind him."

She could not believe what he said. Khira stared at him incredulously, for a moment even anger forgotten. "Put him into the snow —to die?"

The Arnimi shrugged, betraying the barest trace of pettishness. "You will only have terminated an image, one of hundreds."

What did he mean? That there were hundreds of Darkchild? Or that there were hundreds of people to whom the ill-defined term Rauthimage could be applied? And what was the meaning of the term? He refused to make it clear. "Hundreds?"

"There are hundreds of Rauthimages scattered through the galaxy. Each one has separate life and awareness—to a degree. But you cannot be said to kill an individual human when you terminate a Rauthimage. It will be simplest for you and for your mother if you disallow whatever individuality you see in this particular Rauthimage and dispose of him."

Khira stared up into his chill face, repelled by his words, by everything about him. At the same time, she felt the first whisper of fear. "And if I don't—don't put him into the snow to die?"

The Arnimi shrugged. "Then he will live."

"You—you won't kill him yourself?" She could guard him of course, but she was one and the Arnimi were fifty-two. She could not stay awake all winter.

This time it was the female who shrugged. Grotesquely, she ran a coquettish hand through her receding locks. "He is no threat to us. We will protect our wing against his entry simply because we do not want him here. It is up to you to protect the rest of the palace."

Protect? "And if I don't?" Were they saying that Darkchild was a threat to her, even in some unspecified way to the palace itself? "He has been here twenty-seven days and he has harmed nothing."

"Physically he will not harm you. But there is a threat, and if you do not care to put him into the snow yourself, we will discuss him with your mother when she returns. She will understand the threat clearly. I think she will take the wise course."

Khira's eyes sparked with rekindling anger. "I will understand the threat well enough myself if you tell me what it is—if there *is* a threat. If it is not simply a lie. And if you ask me, I will tell you which I think is the case."

A glint of malice flashed in Commander Bullens' eyes. "We have discussed enough with you already, heiress. On Arnim we would not have confided any of this to a child. If you want to enter and see the samples we brought back with us, you may do so now."

Khira bit back a dozen intemperate replies before she said, fiercely, "At this moment I never want to enter your quarters again. However your quarters are a part of my mother's palace and I will enter whenever I feel ready."

"Come when you wish then. The portal is not guarded against you." He pressed a button mounted on his control belt, and the shimmering screen of light melted. With a nod, he touched another button and the tall metal door swung shut.

Khira stared up at the expanse of metal, her face set with anger. How could Darkchild be a threat to the palace—or to her? And how could he live by the hundreds all across the galaxy? He was flesh as she was flesh, blood as she was blood. When he was hungry, he ate. When he was tired, he slept. She had seen him cry and she had heard him laugh.

Yet Commander Bullens called him a threat and would not tell her why.

And how did they know so much about him? How could identifying material have been placed in their databanks before Darkchild had ever been born? Commander Bullens had evaded her on that point, retreating into huffiness. Khira paced slowly down the corridor. Had they at any time denied that he was a child, no older than herself?

They had not.

Darkchild crouched in a doorway near the end of the corridor. At her approach, he stood stiffly, his eyes blazing with the same anger that animated Khira. Khira hesitated. She had never seen him angry before. It seemed an alien expression, as if someone or something had taken possession of his features. Yet there was wariness in him too, much like she had seen in his early days in the palace. She caught his arm. "He spoke your language—what did he say to you?"

Mutely Darkchild shook his head, pulling back from her.

"You're not afraid of me!" she said sharply, clinging to his arm. "Whatever he said—"

He answered with a single guttural syllable she did not know. His face twisting, he broke from her grasp and ran down the hall.

For a moment, anger urged her after him. But perplexity held her back. Rauthimage . . . If he would answer her questions . . . But she had long since learned it was useless to ask them. He never gave her more than a dark, unknowing stare or a helpless gesture. And now this single word from his own language. She mouthed it silently.

One word. She knew one word of his language. Probably the first word any child learned to use: no.

She did not pursue him. However she found him a short time later in a corner of the throneroom, his head resting on his drawn-up knees, his eyes closed. She dropped to her knees beside him, frowning. If he retreated now . . . But his respiration was rapid and his face hot. An angry grimace disfigured his features, as if he fought the impulse to retreat.

Impatience overcame her. Khira pressed her fingers into his arm.

"Darkchild—what did Commander Bullens say to you? Did he tell you he wants me to put you outside?"

Darkchild shook his head, his eyes squeezed shut, perspiration on his upper lip. His breath came in a harsh grunt.

Khira bristled. If no one would tell her anything, if everyone excluded her, the Arnimi, Darkchild himself . . . Her muscles tightening, she called upon Adar, upon the reservoir of gritty anger he inspired in her. Her grip tightened on Darkchild's arm. "I can't help you if you won't tell me what Bullens said! *What did he tell you?*"

With a strangled sob, Darkchild raised his head from his knees and let it fall back against the stone wall. The motion seemed to require great effort. "The door—" he said in a harsh whisper, his eyes still squeezed shut, his entire face wet with perspiration.

Khira's anger dissolved instantly. "The door—it hurt you! It hurt you when you tried to step through." How could she have forgotten the light-serpents that had snapped at him, then repelled him. Quickly she examined him. But there were no scorch marks on his skin or on his coverall. "Darkchild—"

He caught his breath in a second choking sob and forced his eyes open. They were drowned in tears, half-focused. He spoke rapidly, indistinctly. "He wants me to step through the door. The door—he wants me to go so he can open the other door. He needs to know—" Suddenly he clutched Khira's wrists, his fingers digging into her flesh painfully. *"He wants me to go through the door."*

Dread squeezed her heart. Was he delirious? If the Arnimi privacy screen had burned him—but he had talked about doors the night after he had discovered the west wing too, before he had challenged the privacy screen. "Darkchild—"

He was struggling to his feet, muttering incoherently. She stepped back helplessly as he staggered across the throneroom.

He left the throneroom at an awkward gait, stumbling, lurching, falling against the corridor wall. Khira followed him down stalklit corridors. His thin coverall writhed as if the muscles beneath it were in spasm, as if he fought himself. He made his way to the kitchen and fell against the spice cupboard. His hands shook violently as he opened the cupboard and seized half a dozen small bottles, staggering toward the chopping table with them.

His entire body shuddered as he wrenched open the first jar and inhaled deeply. Khira grimaced. Hathlo was a particularly pungent herb gathered from Terlath's eastern slope just before Darkmorning. The cooks seldom used more than a tiny pinch in a large kettle of broth. Darkchild shook a mound of the dark leaves into his palm and tipped it into his mouth.

"Darkchild—" She had seen him use hathlo before, in small quantities. But to use so much—

His face twisted as he choked down the herb. His arm jerked spasmodically and flung the jar across the stone floor. Resisting his twisting muscles, he squeezed his eyes shut and groped for a second jar. This time his hand shattered the jar on the stone floor before he could wrench off the lid. His eyes flew open. He stared blankly at the broken jar, dark flecks of hathlo on his lips. Struggling against rebellious spasms, he reached for the jar of milo, a sweet yellow powder used in cakes and puddings.

Adar was no host for this occasion. Khira could find no anger to help her. She found only panic. Her hands shaking, she took the milo jar from Darkchild and shook the powder into his palm. He licked it up hungrily, coughing on the dry powder. She ran to the melt-tap and fetched water. He gulped it down, hiccoughing now, tears running down his cheeks. But he continued through the jars, feeding desperately, choking, crying.

And finally he was calm. He stepped back from the table, wiping his eyes with a shaking hand. "The door is closed."

Khira's hands trembled. What door? she wanted to demand. And who wanted him to step through it? But this was not the time to challenge his composure. He turned shakily to the task of re-arranging the spice jars on their shelf. She stood frozen, watching him, remembering all the times she had seen him at this task. Had he been confronted with a door each time?

When the last jar was in place, he turned back to her with a faint frown. "Can we eat now?"

Her stomach clenched rebelliously. "Yes," she said faintly.

Nodding, distracted, Darkchild took a loaf from the pantry and cut it. Khira accepted a thick slice but could not choke it down. Darkchild found his mouth too dry for bread too, although he drank three mugs of water.

She stared at him, at his ashen profile. He was a Rauthimage, and when Tiahna returned, Commander Bullens would inform her of the fact. Would Tiahna accept Bullens' warning? Khira's nails dug her palms. Why should Tiahna hesitate over the fate of a cast-away child when she had seen each of her own daughters go to die on Terlath? And bade them farewell with nothing more than a nod from her throne?

With a moan of pain, Khira threw down her bread and ran from the kitchen. She slipped down stalklit halls to the throneroom. There she sat cross-legged on the edge of the dais, staring into winter-dead mirrors. She seemed to see images of Darkchild there, starved and empty-eyed as he had been when he first came. She had fed him, given him shelter, taught him her language. And she had defended him against Commander Bullens. How could she consider him a threat?

Her hands fisted in her lap. How could he harm anyone when he was torn against himself? When he muttered about doors and gulped down herbs and spices in some bizarre exorcising ritual? Was that the nature of a Rauthimage, to struggle against himself?

Did she care? For the first time since Alzaja's death, she had a companion—one who was not steeped in barohnial tradition. When Darkchild looked at her, he saw not myth and tradition, not lineage and the potential of transforming power, but simply a child as slight as himself and as lonely, gifted with nothing more than an occasional fit of temper. He did not see a child who would either die on Terlath or accede to the throne. He saw simply—Khira.

Only Alzaja had seen that before, and Alzaja was dead. Slowly tears began to course down Khira's face. She wiped at them furiously, angry with her own weakness, angry with her fear. For the first time in all her years, she dreaded spring and her mother's return. And though she might go to the watchtower night after night, how could Adar arm her against something she could not understand?

Darkchild was a Rauthimage and there was no one to tell her what that meant to either of them.

SEVEN

THE GUIDE

Thirty days after the full inception of his mission, the guide found himself stymied, his instructions ignored, his directions rejected, his imperatives contravened. When he spoke, he spoke to the wind. If the boy did not fight him, he ignored him—or worse, screened his thoughts and activities behind sensory data. And when the guide offered the reward that should have insured the boy's obedience, the boy spurned him.

The guide could not fail. Failure was not acceptable. The guide had no alternative but to fulfill the contract by which he had been empowered:

To guide the boy in strange places.

To keep his body safe and fed.

To prompt him to inquire and explore.

To urge him to learn and know.

To divert him from knowledge which was interior.

To direct him to knowledge which was exterior.

To codify those facts and impressions the boy gathered.

To store and preserve them to meet the terms of the contract.

It should have been simple. The boy was naturally curious. He was also intelligent, observant and at first he had been docile.

Now he was docile no more. He had discovered routeways past the guide's vigilance and he used them. He had realized that his brothers were used as a distracting influence and he refused to meet them. He had learned there was information the guide kept from him and he sought it.

The guide was baffled. There were guidelines for the boy's behavior, but the guide had increasing difficulty enforcing them. The boy was strong where he should have been weak, rebellious where he should have been meek, autonomous where he should have been dependent. And uncomfortably the guide knew that for all his troublesome behavior, the boy was still relatively quiescent. He had only begun to test his strength.

The guide's only recourse was to claim the boy's body and use it directly to meet the terms of the contract. Over the past few days, since the Arnimi's return, he had done just that on a number of occasions. He had done it despite the boy's increasingly desperate resistance. Yet he had been given no instructions for implementing that action on other than a temporary basis. It was assumed that the necessity for permanent intervention would never arise, that the boy would remain pliant. Certainly the mastery of the boy's body was an exhausting effort.

The girl now . . . The guide mused. He could not pace a lonely path upon some stone floor while he thought. He had no physical presence, at least not at this time. His being was expressed within a framework of non-dimensional space. He was bounded by his thoughts, defined by them. And he thought about the girl a lot.

She was the boy's prime source of information. She dedicated hours to him every day, teaching him, coaching him, answering his questions. Despite her occasional impatience, she seemed to take pleasure in the activity and in the boy's company. Yet there were things she had not told the boy.

The Arnimi, for instance. Again the guide mused. The girl had not told the boy about the Arnimi, and his own reference material about them had been difficult to access. He had had to rummage dangerous moments for it and then it had been so incomplete as to be deceiving. He should have known before he encountered the arrogant Bullens, should have known before he challenged the Arnimi force curtain, that the Arnimi would be inimical to him. And the insult the Arnimi had addressed to him in his brother-language —the guide seethed. Apparently he was a threat to the Arnimi, a trespasser on territory they had reserved for their own exploitation.

After his first encounter with the Arnimi, the guide realized it was more vital than ever that the boy please Khira. His very life could depend upon her when the barohna returned. Yet that created a dilemma for the guide. It was Khira who had lured the boy from his brothers' orbit, Khira who drove an ever-widening wedge between the boy and his guide. It was Khira who gave the boy strength, who encouraged him. The guide found himself dependent upon the very person who was wresting the boy's loyalties from him.

The guide was torn. And he felt very much alone. He was silent audience to every conversation the boy had with Khira. Yet none of her warmth touched him. While the boy and Khira laughed and talked, while they ate and played, the guide was cold and solitary in a non-existent space. These past days, out of frustration, he sometimes seized control of the boy's body and tried to take his place with Khira. But Khira recognized the change and drew back from the guide uneasily and he remained as isolated as before.

Sometimes the guide fought the boy for control of his body anyway and used it to propel himself around the palace. He always ended the experience in anger. Things that were fresh and bright to the boy turned cold and dull when the guide motivated the boy's body. Tastes and scents grew insipid, colors dull, textures bland. Somehow only the boy could bring alive the magic of the palace and the guide did not understand why that should be.

He also did not understand how he could experience anger and loneliness when his functions were limited to fulfilling the contract. But he did, more and more.

Certainly he experienced anger on the fifth day after the Arnimi's return. Various of the Arnimi had emerged from their quarters on each of the previous days and performed a ritual metering of the palace's public chambers. The guide had watched them silently from room to room, grimly determined not to be cowed by them. They were an unattractive people. The guide found their thin, greying locks offensive, their wobbling potbellies distasteful. The arrogance in their chill grey eyes was most grating of all. They seemed to be mocking him for his humiliation on that first day, every one of them. And although they pretended to ignore the boy, when they spoke among themselves it was in their own tongue rather than in Brakrathi. Afterward Khira told the boy they had never committed such discourtesy in her presence before. Certainly her own stony silence when addressed by Commander Bullens was a discourtesy as deliberate—and as grave.

On the fifth day after their return, a female Arnimi appeared in the throneroom as the boy and Khira sat on the dais ciphering scrolls. She was the youngest Arnimi the guide had seen and with her dark hair and deep-set eyes, she was less unattractive than the older Arnimi. Even the characteristic abdominal fat deposit was only in its incipient stage.

The boy glanced up warily when she entered the room. He had conceived a dislike of the Arnimi entirely separate from the guide's dislike. But the Arnimi did not address him. She smiled at Khira instead and indicated the instrument she carried. "I'm sure you remember how this instrument works, Khira," she said.

The guide recognized Khira's resistance to the Arnimi's overture in the stiffening of her shoulders. She had not spoken directly to an Arnimi since the day after their return. But she had told the boy once that she considered one Arnimi—Techni-Verra—her friend, and apparently this was that Arnimi. Because now Khira said grudgingly, "I remember."

The Arnimi nodded, ignoring Khira's reluctance. "Well, it slipped out of my hand this morning. The case didn't shatter, but I'd like to test my instrument to be certain it is working properly. Will you help me?"

Khira eyed the instrument, her lips tightening in suspicion. "You can test it on your own people."

"Yes, of course I could do that," Verra responded without offense. "But I want to test the instrument's entire range, and for that I need someone who is not an Arnimi." Turning, she finally acknowledged the boy's presence with a direct glance. "It's too bad I left my translator in my quarters. Your friend could help me test the meter too."

The guide was stung. The Arnimi claimed to know who he was. Did this one think then that he required more than thirty days to learn a language as simple as Brakrathi? Impulsively the guide seized the boy's tongue. "You don't need a translator to talk to me. I speak Brakrathi as well as you."

The Arnimi's brows rose in exaggerated surprise. "You do? Then you have worked hard this winter."

She dared condescend to him. "Khira has worked hard to teach me," he said with a rush of scorn. "She has answered every question I have asked her." His challenge was clear. Would Khira have done as much for an Arnimi? For any Arnimi?

Never.

"And you have understood all her answers?" The Arnimi touched her hair in a coquettish gesture. A second flick of her brows made her expression sceptical.

Stung, the guide fought the resistance in the boy's jaws. "I understand everything that is presented to me!"

The Arnimi woman nodded, becoming thoughtful. "Yes, that is

characteristic of Rauthimages, their ability to assimilate information quickly and completely. You understand what you are, of course; that you are a Rauthimage."

Without glancing down at the meter in her hand, Techni-Verra had activated it, setting its tiny needle aflicker across its printed dial. Drawn, the guide moved the boy's body nearer. "I know my name," he said sharply, peering at the printed dial. When he spoke, the tiny needle danced nervously between ranges of printed numbers.

The Arnimi noted its movement before saying, "Then I would like to know it too." The needle flickered lightly in response to her words.

The guide caught the slight movement with narrowing pupils. Curiosity was the boy's province, but the guide found it moved in him too. And there was challenge in the Arnimi's query. Did she think his name had been kept from him? "I am Iahnerre Trigonne Rauth-Seven," he said, drawing himself erect. Again the needle swung wildly. The guide felt the boy struggling to assert himself. He squelched the effort with impatience. "What is this instrument?"

"You're probably not interested in its technical name," Verra said. "I call it simply a response evaluator. It's very sensitive to the electrical responses within the human nervous system. The needle's movement tells me if a person is speaking the truth as he knows it —or lying."

The guide narrowed his eyes. Again the needle had flickered lightly in response to her words, while it had swung wildly both times he spoke. "Then who is lying—you or me?"

The Arnimi laughed at his challenge. "Neither of us, actually. There are certain differences within our nervous systems that cause us to give different readings even though we are both telling the truth. If I were to ask Khira a question, the needle would stand completely still when she responded—if she answered truthfully. And I've found that I can't use my instrument in the presence of Khira's mother at all. Her field makes the readings meaningless. Isn't that correct, Khira?"

Khira frowned at the boy, obviously troubled by the change in him. She responded to Verra's question distractedly. "Yes, you've shown us that."

The needle stood completely still at her words. Techni-Verra shrugged lightly. "I believe my instrument is working quite properly." She directed a smile at the guide. "So you are an IT-7. Can you tell me how many IT-7 brothers you have?"

The very casualness of her tone made him stiffen. Belatedly the guide recognized his error and flushed with emotion: fear, anger, confusion. He should never have spoken to the Arnimi. Hadn't his encounter with Bullens shown him clearly that they were inimical to him? And certainly he should never have spoken out in the presence of Khira—*and the boy*. Oh yes—*the boy*. He had been listening. And now the guide had been tricked into giving the boy his name—the one bit of information that might have had the most potency in keeping the boy under control.

Iahnerre Trigonne Rauth-Seven. He had uttered the precious syllables arrogantly, forgetting the boy's hunger for possession of those same syllables. He had almost drawn the boy into the trancing room several times by offering him his name. Now he would never have that potent enticement to offer again. He had let the Arnimi make a fool of him.

Techni-Verra misinterpreted his silence. "So you miss your brothers," she said. "Well you might. But I'm sure you've been taught to connect back into the consciousness of Rauth when you need support." When he still did not respond—*how had she tricked him so easily? why hadn't he been alert?*—she turned to Khira. "Isn't that true? Doesn't he leave you sometimes to trance with his brothers?"

Khira glanced from the boy's taut face—taut with the guide's consternation—to the instrument in the Arnimi's hand, obviously torn between loyalty and her own need to know. "I don't watch him every moment," she said noncommittally.

The needle remained completely still.

"And you don't betray him either," Verra concluded. "Well, it's a lonely life being a daughter of the palace. Your sisters are spread from you in time and you have no way of linking back to them. Of course for that matter, your friend doesn't actually link to his brothers, but the illusion is there and that's some comfort. Wouldn't you welcome a link, even an illusory one, now that Alzaja is gone?"

"A link?" The question erased the troubled frown from Khira's face, replaced it with stark emotion. *Alzaja, Mara, Denabar, Hedia, Kristyan, Sukiin*—she recited the names like a litany sometimes, when she was troubled, trying to conjure up something of her sisters' presence. He could see the names on her lips now.

"But then of course you might find yourself burdened with a guide, as your friend is," Verra continued.

Khira purged the litany of names from her lips. She darted a glance at the boy, then back to Verra. "Darkchild has no one but me."

The Arnimi shook her head. "You're his only flesh and blood companion, yes. But he has inner direction—an internal force termed a guide. Whatever he says, whatever he does, however he responds—even down to the fact that he is standing here listening to me tell you this—all his activities are in direct obedience to his guide. Never mind that there is no one you or I can see. Your friend is very much aware of his guide. His guide's instructions are buried so deeply in his mind, embedded so completely, in fact, that your friend doesn't even realize that the voice that instructs him is not a living entity at all but a programmed response of his own mind, just as the link with his brothers is a programmed response."

Fear, anger, confusion—if the guide had suffered them before, now they choked him. He drew the boy's body up tight, fighting down an angry flush of blood to his cheeks. That she could speak of him as a programmed response, that she could call him *no more than a part of the boy himself*—

That she could call him that *in the boy's presence*—

And the boy was listening. There was no mistaking that. The guide had commanded control of the boy's motor muscles, but there was no provision for cutting off the boy's sensory awareness without luring him into the trancing room.

At least the guide knew of no such provision. The guide raged. Why had the contract been implemented so clumsily? He had been told that the assignment would be simple, that the boy would be totally subordinate. He had been told he had only to follow rudimentary guidelines. Instead the assignment was turning into a nightmare of complexity.

There was another betrayal too. He had been told that he would be the rational, directing force, that he would go about his duties without suffering emotion or attachment. What were fear, anger and confusion if not emotion?

Both the Arnimi woman and Khira were staring at him. The boy wanted to speak to them. The guide fought him, making his lips stiff. And at the same time the boy blocked the guide from speech. The guide clutched at their throat, choking. He had to take the boy away from the Arnimi before she gave him more destructive information. With a dry croak, he forced the boy around and brought him to a staggering half-run.

He ran painfully, awkwardly, muscles knotting and cramping in resistance. The guide could feel the boy fighting to hold him back, grappling for control of the body. Once the boy turned and looked back at Khira and the Arnimi, pleading.

The guide would not yield. He dragged the boy unwilling from the throneroom and down the corridor to the watchtower stairs. Perilously he staggered up the stairs, groping at the wall for support. When he reached the tower, he threw the boy's body down against the wall and forced his head to his drawn-up knees, oblivious of the cold. The desperate heaving of the boy's chest was his own, pained, spastic.

Grimly the guide worked to slow the boy's respiration and draw the pounding blood from his head. Gradually the boy's struggles weakened and he sat with face cold and still, breath slow and regular.

If the boy's brothers were illusion, then the guide was master of illusion. He released the brothers' voices into the boy's consciousness, from the cry of the youngest infant brother to the reassuring murmur of the elder brothers. When the boy's attention was fixed, the guide slowly brought the trancing room door into visibility. Light spilled from it, and within hung the faces of the boy's brothers, brilliantly lit. Yet there was a swirling, misty quality to the air of the trancing room that diffused detail. The boy's brothers smiled out at him, beckoning, their features bright but indistinct.

At some level, the boy still fought. A moan escaped him. The guide disregarded it, spinning out his illusion, playing it against the boy's trapped awareness.

Then without warning his own awareness quaked. He felt the boy's head snapped sharply back against the wall, felt pain in his shoulder, quailed under the angry lash of Khira's voice. His eyes flew open. She bent over him, shaking him angrily. Her lips were a taut slash, her cheeks hotly flushed. Her eyes blazed.

Anger. He was dependent upon Khira and she was angry. Hurriedly the guide abandoned the trancing room illusion, letting the brothers' voices die. He worked the boy's lips stiffly. "Khira—" Her name did not come hard. The boy was struggling to call it too.

She was not appeased. Adar burned from her eyes, bright for war. "Do you know how many times I've asked you questions and you've pretended you could tell me nothing? And then an Arnimi comes to the throneroom with an instrument in her hand and you talk to her. Now you're going to talk to me too."

"No!" The guide and the boy fought to utter the same word. It emerged a dry husk. "No! I—I can't. I can't—"

"But you can," Khira retorted immediately. Her fingers dug deeper into his shoulder. "You talked to Techni-Verra. You told her your name. Now you're going to tell me the things I want to know. You're going to tell me where you came from. You're going to tell me why you were left in the tower. You're going to tell me what you want here. You're—"

"No!" The guide spoke alone this time, in furious indignation. "The Arnimi tricked me!"

Khira matched his anger. "Yes—she tricked you because she knows all about you. She knows where you came from, who your people are. She knows how you got here, why you came. She knows all about you—and she's never done anything for you."

He had to please her. "And you have done everything," the guide said with forced humility.

"Yes! I've done everything! I've fed you and given you blankets and taught you to speak and cipher. But you ignore my questions and answer hers. And you've changed since the Arnimi came. I talk to you and your face changes, your voice changes, everything about you changes. You're—I don't like you when you change. I don't like you when you're stiff. I don't like you when you're like an Arnimi!"

"I—"

"You're like an Arnimi! You're like one now! You're looking at me like an Arnimi, like you want something from me and when you have it, you won't even see me anymore."

The boy responded to the pain behind her anger and his hand came up in a pleading gesture. The guide snatched it down in panic and tried to make his voice appeasing. "Khira—"

She refused to be appeased. "You—how many times have you done this? How many times have you gone to someone and used them like an Arnimi?"

That she could compare him to the arrogant Bullens, to the deceitful Techni-Verra—But the boy broke through the guide's guard. "Khira—I can't tell you—I can't—even if I knew, I—"

Khira's pupils narrowed, recognizing the change in him. But her anger remained caustic. "Why? Because your guide won't let you talk to me? And tell me this—if your guide guides you, who guides him?"

The guide felt the boy grasping desperately for an answer. "I—don't know. I—"

Fiercely the guide snatched for control. The boy was eager to please Khira. But he could not be trusted to do so without betraying vital information. The guide crushed the boy's windpipe with tightening cords of muscle and the boy's voice became a strangled sob. "He's angry! He won't let me talk! Khira—"

Khira seized his arm, hardened to his distress. "Well, I can talk, and this is what I have to tell you, Iahnerre Rauth-Seven. If you won't answer my questions, I'm going to go downstairs and bar the door on you. If you won't talk to me, I'll leave you here to freeze."

"No!"

"I will." Her eyes were fire and stone at once. They brimmed with her anger. "If you won't talk to me like you talked to Verra, I'll send servants for your corpse next spring."

Frantically the boy leapt free of the guide's control. "You wouldn't!" His hands were clenched, white. "You wouldn't! You've done everything for me, Khira. You've taught me Brakrathi. You've shown me everything in the palace. You've taught me about the plants and animals that grow outside. You've told me about the mountains. When the snow thaws, I have to go there. I have to climb the mountains. And your people—"

Khira drew back from him, her face set. "And after all my lessons, you haven't learned what I am? I'm the imperial daughter of this palace and I have stone in my heart. Yes—my heart is rock. It's hard and cold. If you're still here when my mother returns, the Arnimi will tell her about you. They'll tell her what they've told me and everything else too; they won't tell me more because they consider it demeaning to talk to a child. But when they tell my mother, she will have you taken to the mountain to die. She'll do that and never care. What makes you think I'm softer than she is?"

"Be—because you are."

"I'm not. I'm hard where other people are soft, and if you won't answer my questions, I'll lock you here and never look back."

Her words carried a gritty conviction. The boy's mouth opened in appeal, but the guide was caught in a frenzy of sheer panic. *She meant it; she would lock him here to freeze and never care. He was no more than an Arnimi to her.* A sharp spasm of fear cut off the boy's words. The boy pressed himself against the rough stone wall, his eyes glazing as repeated muscle spasms closed off his breath. The guide drew up the boy's knees and pressed his forehead against them in instinctive retreat.

Khira uttered a fierce cry and shook the boy until his head snapped back against the stone wall. "If you leave me now—if you leave me, I won't come back! I won't come back until the snow thaws!"

The threat hardly touched the guide. He did not even notice the tears in her eyes. His panic seized the boy's throat and choked consciousness from them both. As if from a great distance, an unfamiliar voice spoke to him. It spoke in a droning voice. *Tell her nothing.* The message was repeated, and a hypnotic force uncoiled in his mind, dulling it. *Tell her nothing. Tell her nothing.*

Yes, he must tell her nothing. Because nothing he told her would be right. She could not be appeased and she must not be informed. She had succored the boy but she despised the guide. There was no way to please her now without betraying himself to her.

And the questions she had asked him—if he was the trainer, who had trained him? Who had placed him in authority over the boy? Who had sent them both here? He had answers. But behind those answers, was there meaning—or deception?

Why did he wonder? Why did he doubt—if there were no cause for doubt?

Tell her nothing, tell her nothing, tell her nothing. Desperately the guide threw aside doubt and clung to the voice. It was his lifeline. It would save him when nothing would. He had only to tell her nothing. *Nothing.* And that was easy, so easy, with his head sagging back to his knees, with awareness slipping away on the tide of repeated command.

Tell her nothing. The boy's head lolled loosely against his knees as he lost consciousness.

EIGHT
KHIRA

Khira's anger still rang in the chill tower as she ran down the stone steps and bolted the lower door behind her. But what rang in her heart was hurt and bewilderment. How had Darkchild slipped away from her? She had taught and tutored him from his first day in the palace, she had fed him and given him a warm place to sleep, she had coaxed him free of whatever it was that shadowed him—she had made him her own.

Yet these past days he had undone her making. He had become a stranger to her. All too often he spoke in a changed voice, he looked at her with hard eyes, he pressed her with questions she did not want to answer. Before the Arnimi had come, he would have recognized that she did not want to answer them. Now he was frequently insensitive to her reluctance.

Yet each time she reached a peak of irritation, he slipped back into his old manner and she could not lash out. She could only put aside her anger and wonder at the change in him.

Was this what it meant to be a Rauthimage? Was he some soulless being? Like the mythical benar that lived high in the mountains and rolled down the slopes each spring in invisible avalanche, moaning and crying for lost memories? Certainly Darkchild's memories seemed lost.

They had seemed lost—until today, when he had arrogantly pronounced his name for the Arnimi.

And Khira—she had told him she was stone, hard where other people were soft. But was she? If so, why did his behavior wound her? How could he touch her feelings if they were guarded by a rocky core? If she was stone, why were there tears on her face?

She wiped at them angrily and ran through palace halls, deaf to the echo of her feet. If he would not answer her questions, if he would not show her the courtesy he showed an Arnimi, why should she care if he froze? What was he to her?

She was just stone enough to run to the throneroom and hide herself behind the throne until her heart stopped racing. Then she began to sob. What did it matter that Darkchild didn't answer her questions? Was that the price of her friendship, words he didn't want to give? The Arnimi knew where he came from, who his people were. Techni-Verra had tricked him into telling her his name. But Khira knew the sound of his laughter, the touch of his hand. And where did friendship lie but there, in warmth?

She was weakening. Smothering her tears, she pulled a scroll from the alcove and tried to concentrate on it. If she had not intended her threat, she should never have uttered it. To release him now would be to admit defeat. She ran her fingers down the scroll, trying to distract herself. Darkchild was nothing to her, a boy from nowhere, torn against himself. He was not even whole.

But her eyes would not focus on the scroll. The symbols swam before her, meaningless. She was not stone where Darkchild was concerned. She was butter. Melting, she threw down the scroll and ran back to the watchtower, ran up the stalklit stairs, burst through the upper door.

Darkchild lay on his side on the stone floor, his face grey, one hand outflung. His eyes were open and staring, but he made no sign when she threw herself across him and pressed her ear to his chest. She listened, breathless. His heart beat to a faltering rhythm.

Her own heart quivered with panic. Why was he like this? He had retreated often enough, sitting with his forehead on his knees and his face cold. But she had never found him unconscious on the floor. She rolled him to his back, seized his shoulders and shook him. "Darkchild! *Darkchild!*" When he did not respond, she slapped first his cold cheeks, then his wrists. "Iahnerre!" The name was alien, but if it would call him back . . . "Iahnerre!"

He shuddered and squeezed his staring eyes shut. Khira released him, thinking he was about to waken. But his facial muscles relaxed and he lay completely still again. Sobbing, she pressed her ear to his chest. His heartbeat had become barely perceptible.

She couldn't have destroyed him by shutting him in the cold tower for less than an hour! He had stayed here overnight when he first came. But if she left him here much longer, even the faint throb of his heart might cease. She jumped up, her heart clenching in panic. There was no one she could go to, no one to help her—

Except the Arnimi. She bit her lip, hesitating, then ran to the stairs. If she could carry him down, get him to his bed—

It was hopeless. She was no larger than he and the stairs were steep.

There was no one but the Arnimi. She pounded down the stairs and ran through the halls to their door. It opened and she plunged through the protective screen and peered around urgently.

Three Arnimi approached, one of them Techni-Verra. Choking back panic, Khira summoned as much authority as she could master. "My friend is sick in the tower. I want two people to carry him to his bedchamber." Her voice sounded reedy, thin.

The senior Arnimi's response was aggravatingly deliberate. "The Rauthimage is ill?"

Throttling her anger, Khira turned to Verra. "He's unconscious and there's snow on the floor. We can carry him down, the two of us. He isn't heavy." Wasn't it Verra's fault she had locked him in the tower in the first place?

Verra hesitated, glancing at her superiors. "He isn't in trance with his brothers, heiress?"

Desperately Khira seized her arm. "He's unconscious. I can barely hear his heart." Why had she played for even a moment at ruthlessness? Why hadn't she simply accepted him as he was, with all his inconsistencies?

Verra's superiors eyed her coldly, but her hesitation was brief. "I can see that you are concerned. Tomer, I will return to the conference as soon as possible. If necessary, I'll call back for Medi-Torrens." Quickly she followed Khira.

"Will your medical officer treat Darkchild?" Khira demanded as the metal door closed behind them.

"It probably won't be necessary, heiress. Rauthimages are bred hardy."

Bred. Khira's lips tightened. "Here we breed animals," she snapped. "We have other terms for human generation."

Verra frowned faintly. "I am aware that you do, Khira. But in some places, under some circumstances, these things are different."

And why should Khira be angry with Verra over the fact? When Darkchild was dying in the tower? Fighting to tame her indignation, Khira led the way.

Darkchild lay as she had left him, on his back, eyes closed, arms reaching for nothing. Verra bent over him quickly. She tapped his eyelids and pressed his scalp, then stood. "I think we must get him downstairs to his bed and warm him," she decided. "I'll carry his shoulders. You take his feet."

"He—he isn't—"

"I think he will recover when he is warm."

Khira bobbed her head in relief. They inched down the steep stairs tread by tread. When they reached the bottom, Verra assumed Darkchild's full weight while Khira bolted the lower door and led the way to his quarters.

Verra catalogued the furnishings Khira had provided Darkchild with a slight elevation of her brows. "You have made him comfortable here." Carefully she laid Darkchild on the bed and examined him again, listening at his chest, lifting each eyelid in turn, lightly slapping his pallid cheeks. She frowned, unconsciously coquetting at her hair. "From what I've read of Rauthimages, I would guess he has been overstressed."

Khira stared at her in puzzled dismay. Did Verra mean he would not recover at all? "I locked him in the tower," she said hesitantly, "but for just a few minutes."

"You did? Why?"

Khira's face colored. "He answered your questions and then wouldn't answer mine."

"Ah." Verra's brows rose. "You questioned him then, after you left me. Harshly?"

Khira was instantly defensive. "He's asked me hundreds of questions since he came here and I've answered them all, no matter how he asked them." And since the Arnimi had come, the manner of his asking had often rankled.

"I know you have taken pains with him. That much is apparent in how quickly he has learned here. But a Rauthimage is not trained to give information—only to gather it. And a Rauthimage is provided with protective programming to prevent him from violating his training. Can you imagine any better protection against a loose tongue than falling unconscious?"

Khira peered up at Verra with dawning incredulousness. "You mean he can't answer even simple questions? If I ask him where he was born, how he was raised—" But she had asked him those questions. She had tossed them at him at unexpected moments, trying to catch him off guard. He had not answered, but neither had he fallen unconscious.

Verra shook her head. "The harm isn't entirely in the asking, heiress. There are times when it's easy to turn a question aside. Imagine that one of my fellow officers and I decided to have information from you which you knew we should not have. If we approached you separately, whom would you find it harder to resist— my fellow or me?"

"You," Khira said promptly.

"Yes, because you and I have something together that you have with none of the others. We haven't spent a lot of time together, but we have shared bread and kindness."

"And the others are as cold as the glacier," Khira said with venom.

"Exactly. Or so it seems to you. To them—because my science is a softer one, because I was trained differently, because I come from a rural province and was reared within a family while they were raised in nurseries—I seem to be the deviant one. I suffer a dangerous lack of objectivity. I let myself read things into charts and graphs that cannot be proven mathematically or in any other way. If your mother had not insisted that every Arnimi who comes here remain until our evaluation is completed, Commander Bullens would have sent me back to Arnim long ago.

"But your friend has never exchanged kindness with me. He refused my questions easily once he realized I had tricked him— because he had no bond with me. But he does have a bond with you, a deep one. If you questioned him, if you questioned him ruthlessly—"

Khira winced. "Yes. I did."

"Then you placed him in an extremely stressful position. On one hand, I'm sure he wanted to answer you because you are his friend; on the other, his guide could not permit him to answer. It is against his programming. Ultimately his programming took the choice out of his hands and he fell unconscious."

"So I'll never know anything about him," Khira said bitterly.

"You'll know enough when the barohna returns," Verra pointed out. "Commander Bullens will tell her far more than he told you. And I have observed that she regards you as less of a child than my people do."

Khira's clenched muscles relaxed. That much was true; Tiahna would not keep information from her. But if this were information she would regret having . . .

Verra bent over the bed again and laid the back of her hand

against Darkchild's ashen face. "He is warmer. Let him sleep for a few hours. If he doesn't waken normally then, come for me again. But I think he will recover with no problem."

"And if he needs care from your medical officer—"

Verra sighed. "Then I will try to prevail upon Torrens to come. But I hope that won't be necessary. And if I don't return to quarters for conference now, I will be on penalty for the next three clock-days."

Anxiously Khira watched her out the door. Then she ran after her. "Wait!"

"Yes?"

"At least tell me—how long will he be here? Will he leave before —before very long?"

"I have no way of knowing, heiress. That apparently depends upon the contract."

"The—contract?"

"Heiress, I can't tell you more. The information must come through your mother."

And perhaps it would be information she would forever regret having. Khira let Verra go and returned to Darkchild's chamber, her mind teeming with questions. Where had Darkchild come from? Why had he been subjected to training, to programming? Could he be freed of his guide, of his illusory brothers? Her shoulders sagging, Khira sat on the side of his bed, occasionally touching his hand. No matter what the provocation, she vowed, she would never question him again. Never.

Darkchild recovered slowly from his somnambulent state and for hours that day lay staring at the wall, bleak-eyed and unresponding. Khira watched over his recovery anxiously. It was two days before he began to eat again, three before he left his room. For a full hand of days, he spoke to Khira in cautious monosyllables when he spoke at all. And she was aware that he studied her with silent wariness when she was not looking.

But at last he did recover, although he no longer asked questions. He leashed his curiosity just as Khira leashed hers. The effort created an atmosphere of constraint between them. They bent over the gameboard day after day in silence, tense with the effort not to trespass upon each other. Sometimes Darkchild went exploring the palace alone, trying to answer his own questions, and Khira did not see him for most of a day. Occasionally they experienced a brief revival of mindless conviviality, running through the corridors shouting and laughing until they were exhausted. But even then, as they caught their breath, Khira would look up to find Darkchild gazing at her intently, anxiously.

She watched him too, at odd moments. Since their encounter in the tower, he seemed to have settled into a condition of internal truce. He always spoke in his own voice, never in the harsh demanding voice he had employed sometimes after the Arnimi returned. He seldom moved with the stiff, awkward gait she had seen during the same period. But the effort of maintaining inner truce apparently cost him vitality. He moved at everything more slowly, as if he deliberately held himself back.

When Khira had drawn eighty days on her chamber wall, it was time to open the shutters high in the vault of the throneroom. Khira did so reluctantly. Despite the strain between herself and Darkchild, she cherished their winter isolation. She couldn't guess what spring would bring for either of them.

For three days after opening the shutters, she watched the throneroom mirrors and saw no sign. On the fourth day they flashed once and on the fifth they flashed three times. On the sixth day the light came in a steady beam that bathed the dark throne for minutes. When the light died, the throne briefly continued to glow and Khira retreated to her chamber, evading Darkchild's silent question. He had read the scrolls. He knew that the flashing of the mirrors meant the end of winter. There was nothing she could tell him.

That night they stood side by side in the watchtower, looking out over the frozen valley, neither of them speaking. Snow was mounded on the stone floor beneath the shattered window and chill wind reached into the tower. Yet Khira thought she felt the first balm of spring in the air and the clear night sky revealed a universe of stars.

"You came from one of them," Khira said finally. "You came from one of the stars, didn't you?"

Darkchild stiffened. Silently he turned and left the tower.

Khira's hands clenched into fists. It was the first question she had asked him since he had recovered and he had walked away from it. If Adar had still been in the winter sky, she would have felt anger.

But Adar was gone and she felt only emptiness.

Five days later they sat together over the gameboard when there was an insistent rapping at the heavy metal doors that led to the central plaza. Darkchild's head snapped erect, his eyes dark with quick fear.

"It's the servants," Khira reassured him, and ran to unbolt the door.

Five of the palace caretakers had wakened and tunneled through the snow from their stonehall. Normally sturdy people, they were gaunt now from wintersleep, their eyes hollow, their hands gnarled. They nodded to her gravely. "We will begin to clear the plaza now, heiress," Palus, eldest of the group, governor of his hall, told her formally. "We feel the energy. The barohna comes down the mountain."

"She comes," Khira acknowledged. She felt the energy too, crackling through her nervous system. It had moved her through the palace with increasing restlessness the past three days. "Dig."

Darkchild materialized beside her when she closed the door. His gaze was intent. "Your mother will be here soon."

"In a few days." She was surprised at the bleakness of the words. She and Alzaja had always celebrated when the flashing of the mirrors signalled that Tiahna had melted the snow from the relay lenses stationed upon Terlath's snowbound slopes.

Sensitive to her mood, Darkchild kept silence as Khira retreated to the throneroom. She stood at the center of its great emptiness, peering up at the vaulted ceiling, at the dark mirrors and dull throne. Winter had delivered the silent palace into her custody for seventeen hands of days. Now spring was about to snatch it away.

She turned. Darkchild peered at her with an intensity she had not seen for many days. She sighed. What did it matter if she relented, if she answered the questions she saw struggling just beneath the surface of his self-control? There were many things the scrolls did not explicate. If they had only a few days left together, why thwart each other?

"We can watch them dig from the tower," she said, suddenly eager to escape mirrors that had begun to beam sunlight again and throne that answered with its own dark glow. Surrendering to the spiking energy that signalled her mother's return, she ran from the throneroom and through echoing corridors. Catching her mood, Darkchild ran after her.

They went to the tower to watch each morning for three days. Each day Terlath's rugged silhouette grew more distinct through the dissipating mists of winter. And each day more gaunt people appeared with shovels and barrows to excavate the deep-drifted plaza. They worked with monotonous strokes, moving to the imperative of the approaching barohna.

At first, when Darkchild realized that Khira was receptive to his questions again, he voiced them hesitantly, rationing himself, testing her reaction. But on the second day after the appearance of the servants, he already monitored the activity in the plaza when Khira reached the tower. He turned slowly. "Khira—why do they dig back the snow if your mother can melt it when she comes?"

Khira approached the window reluctantly. Tiahna was nearer today and the energy played restlessly through Khira's nervous system, making her fingers twitch and her toes tingle. Her voice seemed flat, overcontrolled. "It's custom for the people to gather in the plaza to greet her when she comes."

He seemed not to notice her tension. "She looks for them there? She will be angry if they don't come to watch her return?"

Khira shrugged. "They're always there when she comes."

"But if the servants rebelled," he probed, watching intently for her response, "if they didn't want to dig snow when she could easily melt it herself, if they—"

She frowned, unable to fathom the direction and intent of his question. "They *do* want to dig the snow. They want to see her," she said sharply. "When the barohna is near, everyone gathers on the plaza and the families stand in pyramids. They pile the lighter members of the family, the children, the smaller women, on the shoulders of the men and the sturdier women. Every family wants to be the first to see her."

"Because they worship her?"

Was he baiting her? "Do you think my mother is a stone image to be carried from valley to valley? They are eager to see her—that's all. Everyone is eager to see her. She takes the snow from the fields and soon there will be fruit and crops." She hugged herself, trying to control her rising irritability.

He studied her intently. "Khira—there are so many things I haven't asked you. In the first scrolls after the barohnas discovered the sunstone, the people did worship them. And the barohnas ruled the valleys. But in the later scrolls—"

"The people became serfs when the barohnas found the sunstone —yes. But that changed centuries ago. Now the people are freeworkers. And my mother is simply barohna of this valley."

"But she sits on a throne."

Khira frowned. He seemed to be trying to fit information into some preconceived framework. Perhaps where he came from there were still rulers and serfs.

"She links to the sunstone of the throne—and of the bathing slab in the plaza. She draws the sun's energy and invests it in the stone. Then she discharges it to melt the snow. If she didn't concentrate the sun's energy at this time of year, it would be wasted on the mountainsides and spring would come late to the valley. There wouldn't be time to grow enough crops to feed all the people."

"But she directs the people in their work—like a ruler," Darkchild persisted.

Far on the mountain, a single mirror flashed. A tremor passed through Khira's body. "She—my mother is the brain and the people are the arms and legs. Together they are the body. The body can't live unless the brain directs and the limbs work. The people choose the governors and jurises to govern them in their halls, but my mother selects the people who will oversee the work teams in the fields. She picks those who understand her directions best."

"But even in the halls—"

"She makes no decision concerning the halls unless the juris sends people to her. Then she sits to hear them."

"She settles disputes, you mean."

A second mirror winked brightly in the distance and prickling energy surged through Khira. She turned from the view window, her voice crackling. "Disputes are for stock animals, not for Brakrathi."

Darkchild's pupils narrowed minutely. "You disputed the Arnimi."

Khira colored. "I've watched here long enough," she snapped, pushing past him to the stairs. Sharp spikes of energy danced through her nervous system. Later in the season she would harden to them. She would hardly notice them. But today they made her nerves quiver. And she had no tolerance for questions. She wanted only to run down the stairs—to run through the palace until she was too tired to think. Then she wanted to cry until she could cry no more. At all cost, she wanted to quench thought.

Darkchild ran down the stairs after her and caught her arm. "Khira—"

She twisted away from him with a flash of anger, throwing herself against the corridor wall, her body unconsciously arching into a posture of defense.

Darkchild stepped back, his eyes widening. A long moment passed before he said, "Khira, you're—you're afraid today."

Angry blood flowed to Khira's cheeks. She was afraid—and he didn't know why? "I wouldn't be afraid if it weren't for you!" she snapped. "Soon my mother will be here and the Arnimi will tell her what they told me—to put you into the snow to die. How do you expect me to feel?"

His finely arched brows drew into a tight frown. He wet his lips with the tip of his tongue, thoughtfully. "Why do you care? Why do you care what happens to me?" The query was more curious than probing.

Why indeed? Because he had made a lonely winter short? Because she had taught him to speak much as she might have taught an infant? Because she had knelt hours beside his bed while he lay unconscious? Why did one human care for another? "Wouldn't you care? If I were the one to be put into the snow?" she demanded bitterly.

His lips parted. He said slowly, as if discovering something he had not known before, "I would. Yes, I would care."

"Well, I care too!" Before he could see her tears, she broke free again. She ran down empty corridors, blinded by tears, dimly aware that this time he did not follow.

She cared because he had won his way past the stone in her heart to the flesh. She cared because even the scars of Alzaja's death had not hardened her where she lived. Pain had not come once and put an end to her vulnerability. Instead it had heightened her to new vulnerability.

She pounded through echoing halls until her legs ached, until her mind was numbed. Then she ran to her room and threw herself against the pillows of her bed, sobbing. Winter ended as it had begun, with snow and tears.

NINE

DARKCHILD

It was early morning, and the upper halls of the palace held a spectral emptiness, as if the stones waited in hollow silence for the barohna. Darkchild moved along the corridor at a deliberate pace. This sedate gait was one of the tricks he had mastered since Khira had locked the guide in the watchtower. The experience had stirred the guide to a state of chronic anxiety—and frightened, he was amenable to compromise. Darkchild had learned that so long as he did not agitate the guide by darting through the palace impulsively, moving too quickly for the guide to anticipate his direction or intent, so long as he did not screen his thoughts from the guide, so long as he refrained from worrying at questions that made the guide anxious, he could go where he pleased, studying what interested him, ignoring what did not.

On the whole, the equilibrium they had struck served Darkchild well. But sometimes compromise was unsatisfactory, and today was one of those times. Darkchild paused in the corridor outside the printing room. He had been there often these past days, slipping between the tables where during the warmseasons printers inscribed scrolls. It was as if hidden memory drew him here. Whenever he thought of the printing room, of parchment, pens and ink, his fingers contracted involuntarily, as if tightening on the shaft of a pen. And his breath quickened, creating an impatient flutter in his throat. He thought he knew what this meant: that he had taken pen in hand somewhere before . . . and his hand was impatient to scribe again, to form inked figures that would tell stories only his fingers remembered.

Those stories were exactly what the guide did not want to think about. Frowning, ignoring the guide's discomfiture, Darkchild pushed open the door and stepped into the printing room. The room was cold and smelled of soured ink. Darkchild paused, sampling the distinctive odor. Then, deliberately, he moved across the room. On each long table was a selection of scrolls to be copied. Some of the older scrolls were so brittle Darkchild hardly dared touch them. Others were soft and pliant. Carefully he unrolled a scroll he had not examined before.

It was a tale from early times, a story of sheep that strayed and a herder who searched for them and found a beast like no one had seen before bathing in a mountain pool. Darkchild caressed the parchment, as if he could touch the herder's time with probing fingertips. The early scrolls made him hungry for the world beyond the palace. Mountains, meadows, plains—he had never tasted water fresh-drawn from a valley spring. He had never climbed a slope and looked back over diked fields. And he had a strong sensory curiosity. He wanted to record the texture of every kind of stone with his fingertips. He wanted to see Terlath through all its seasonal moods. The quality of daylight was important to him. And the rush of storm clouds across the valley, the pattern of rain and snow—he had a hunger for them all. Hundreds of experiences awaited him beyond the palace, and each would tell him something about the people who lived here, who they had been, how they had become as they were.

But he had a more immediate hunger: to snatch up a pen, dip it in ink, and let his hand have free rein across clean parchment. However when he reached for a pen, his hands clenched into claws and he jumped back involuntarily, a sharp rise of panic in his throat—the guide's panic.

Darkchild frowned, reluctantly averting his eyes from the pens. It was the same each time he came here. And each time he found that much as he wanted to scribe, he wanted more to preserve the balance he had struck with the guide.

Still he lingered for a while, skirting the tables, occasionally examining a scroll, hoping the guide would be soothed by his desultory activity. There were other things in the palace that seemed to promise memory too: certain utensils in the kitchen, the silk mourning sash Khira had shown him once, a crudely carved pebble he had found on the floor behind the wardrobe in his room. And twice recently thunder had sounded from the mountains and he had found himself crouching and peering behind himself—for something he could not name.

But none of these things promised so much as the pens and ink, and those he could not even touch without disturbing the guide. Finally, dissatisfied, he left the printing room.

A short while later he sat at the gameboard with Khira when a group of workers appeared under the great arch at the entrance to the throneroom. Darkchild glanced up with quick interest. The scrolls told of a sturdy people who had survived on Brakrath against great odds. But the people he had watched clearing the plaza had appeared uniformly gaunt, their shoulders bent, their white hair ragged. And now, seen more closely, they looked no hardier.

One of them, a woman, stepped forward, inclining her head stiffly. "Heiress, Palus sent us to trim the stalk. It has overgrown."

Khira looked up with an irritable frown. "Yes, I watered the pots. I wanted light."

"Now the barohna brings light," the woman said without rebuke and withdrew. The others followed.

Darkchild stood, drawn. He had barely had time to catalogue their appearance: the coarseness of their clothing, the crumpled quality of their flesh, the arthritic stiffness of their limbs. And none had so much as glanced at him. "Didn't they see me?"

Khira slumped back against her cushions, glancing up irritably. "Of course they saw you."

"But none of them said anything."

"What would they say?" Khira's hands tightened on the edge of the playing board. "They have the manners of Brakrathi, not Arnimi."

And it was mannerly not to see a stranger? Darkchild frowned. Khira was tense today, distracted. She moved her gamepieces clumsily, as if she were a learner. And she spoke to him either absently or sharply. He knew he should stay with her, but he was drawn to the people he had glimpsed so briefly. "They won't mind if I watch?"

Khira shrugged, and he jumped from his cushions and ran after the workers.

They had fetched ladders, trimmers and a cart from the store room. They began their work in the corridor nearest the throneroom. At first they seemed constrained by Darkchild's presence, carefully avoiding his curious eyes, never glancing directly at him. But after a time they forgot him and moved to their work without self-consciousness. There was a musty smell about them, clinging to their clothing, to their hair, and their voices were hoarse, as if from a winter's disuse. They worked stiffly, slowly, and talked little. Yet Darkchild observed that there was no confusion among them. Each moved to his or her chore readily, without stepping in the way of anyone else. When one had cut down the overgrown stalks, another stood ready to sweep the stems into the dump-cart and another to wheel the filled cart away.

After watching the cutting and sweeping for a while, Darkchild followed the carter and found that the glowing stalks were emptied in a barren, windowless room beyond the kitchen. When the carter turned from dumping his load and found Darkchild standing in the doorway, he rolled his cart to a halt and gazed fixedly past Darkchild's left shoulder.

Darkchild glanced behind himself uneasily, then stared up at the carter. "Will the stalks rot here?"

The carter inclined his head quizzically, as if harking to some faint sound, but said nothing.

Darkchild bit his lip, puzzled. The carter waited—but for what? Some ordinary courtesy that Darkchild didn't know how to render? Guessing, he said, "My name is Darkchild. Did you—did you bring the stalks here to rot?"

At that the man honored Darkchild's presence with a direct glance. His eyes were grey and sharply alert in his crumpled face, as if winter had tried to quench them and failed. "I'm Rabbus from the seventh hall of Tiahna's valley." He nodded with careful formality. "I bring the stalks here to make root so we will have more for the pots."

Darkchild's eyebrows rose in surprise. He glanced past the carter to where the stalks lay on the bare floor. "But there's nothing here for them to grow in—Rabbus."

Rabbus inclined his head. "Then perhaps they require nothing. Do you intend to stand aside and let me pass, Darkchild from nowhere, when you've told me your hall?"

Darkchild flushed, stepping aside quickly. "I'm—my hall is here. In the palace."

"A warm hall with sound beams." The comment was ceremonial. Briskly Rabbus wheeled his cart into the corridor.

Darkchild ran after him, encouraged. "Rabbus—why didn't you speak to me at first? Before I told you my name?"

Rabbus' matted brows rose in feigned surprise. "Would you speak to a shadow on the wall, Darkchild?"

"No," Darkchild said quickly. "But I'd roll my cart past it without stopping—if I really thought it was a shadow."

Rabbus inclined his head, his eyes glinting in appreciation. "Ah, but there are shadows and shadows. If you suspect the shadow might eventually give you name and hall, it is inconsiderate to injure it. It is as well to be considerate—don't you think, Darkchild?"

"It—yes."

"And if you are considerate and there are people working, it is good not to tax them with questions," Rabbus went on with a sideward glance. "Because if you are considerate, you know there are times when people like to answer questions and times when they do not."

Darkchild nodded, rebuked—not so much for the few questions he had asked as for all the others he had intended to ask. "But you won't mind if I watch—without talking?"

"I'll tell my mates you're not a shadow and none will mind."

They did not, but neither did Rabbus' mates talk among themselves as they worked. As the day went on and they trimmed corridor after corridor, Darkchild was increasingly tantalized by the unstudied efficiency of their work. He watched silently, doggedly testing unspoken questions against their silence.

At midafternoon the workers left the palace without explanation, silently putting down their tools in the middle of a half-trimmed corridor and going without word. Puzzled, Darkchild followed them to the plaza door. Rabbus turned and lifted a single finger in parting salute.

Disappointed, Darkchild went to find Khira. But her chamber door was closed, and when he called she did not answer.

Nor did she join him in the kitchen for the evening meal. He ate uneasily, puzzled at the behavior of the workers, wondering if he had hurt Khira by leaving her alone to watch them. There were things, he began to realize, that he had not gathered from the scrolls—a host of cues and nuances that he would have to gather in person instead.

It was dusk when he discovered Khira's chamber door open and found her at the window of a nearby chamber. She had removed the shutters and night air chilled the very stones of the room. She stood unmoving, her hands clenched at her sides, and from her expression Darkchild thought she was angry because he had left her—until he reached the window and saw the people gathered on the plaza below. They stood silently, men, women and children, peering toward the mountain, shadowed now by dusk. It took him a moment to understand, and then his heart leaped. "Your mother's coming!"

Khira stood like stone, pale and graven. "She's coming. We'll see her light in the night."

Quickly Darkchild's eyes flicked toward the cloud-veiled mountain, toward the gathering darkness there. Khira had sketched her mother for him, tall, bronzed, sunlight her captive. She would come wearing a sunstone circlet at either wrist, and each wristlet would glow with winter sunlight gathered at her mountain retreat. "Will we have to wait long?"

He was surprised to see a tear slip down Khira's cheek. "Yes," she said, making the word bitter. "As long as we wait for dawn."

Darkchild frowned. "Khira—" But something in her face told him it wasn't the time to talk.

And even the sight of her distress did not quench his eagerness. He leaned out the window, his arms resting on the cold stone casement.

Dusk passed into darkness and for a time the sky cleared and stars were visible. Then clouds came again and hours passed. Through them all, the people on the plaza were silent, Khira motionless. Darkchild watched with barely flagging eagerness, occasionally stamping life into his feet or chafing his hands, refusing to let the cold dull him.

It was near dawn when he distinguished a cloudy glow far in the distance, barely perceptible through the last mists of night. As he watched, the light grew more distinct and moved toward him, gliding slowly through the dark. He caught a ragged breath. "Khira—look!"

The light drifted down the lowermost flank of the mountain, a ghostly nimbus, yesterday's sunlight cast against today's pre-dawn darkness. No limb of the barohna showed from within the drifting cloud of light. There was only a gash of brilliance at its center, featureless, floating. But as Darkchild watched, he could imagine Tiahna striding over tumbled rock, striding toward the palace she had deserted months before.

When Darkchild turned from the window, he was surprised to find his lips stiff, his tongue dry. "Khira, can we—can we watch from here? When she comes to the palace?" Did Tiahna expect Khira to wait in the plaza with the others?

Khira lidded her eyes, her face silver-pale. "We always watch from here." A whisper.

Darkchild felt a momentary pang. "Khira—you don't have to be afraid. Not for me." Because that was why she had been angry earlier, why tears shone on her cheeks. She was afraid her mother would listen to the Arnimi and put him into the snow.

She turned, the cold light of dawn silvering her tears. "How can you say that? When Commander Bullens talks to her, when he tells her about you—"

"Khira—"

She shook her head, refusing to let him speak. "When Commander Bullens talks to her and she calls you and questions you—what can you tell her?"

For a moment he was caught by the plea in her eyes. For a moment he wanted to tell her he would find answers for Tiahna if she questioned him. But he bit the lie from his tongue. "I—can't tell her anything, Khira."

Her eyes narrowed in pain. "Darkchild—" She caught his hands, clutching them. "Darkchild, if you could just tell her—if you could just tell her the things you couldn't tell me—I locked you in the tower, but you knew I would come back. My mother won't. If she sends you to the snow, she won't call you back. She—she's never exiled anyone. And she's never turned anyone to ash. But she could do it. If you could just tell her—"

What? Briefly Khira's fear infected Darkchild. Tell Tiahna that sometimes when he heard thunder he was afraid? That he thought there were stories in him that he didn't know how to tell? That there were doors in his mind he could find no way to open? "Khira, I—I don't know anything to tell." Desperately he groped for words to explain his helplessness. *He* does. *He* knows things—or where to find them. But I don't."

Her hands tightened on his, bruising. "*He?*"

Darkchild caught his breath, surprised he had told her so much. "The guide."

"The guide?" She frowned. "Your guide? The one who tells you what to do?"

But he couldn't explain. "I can't tell you. Khira—I can't tell you about him. And I can't tell her either."

She pleaded silently a moment longer, then dropped his hands in quick hopelessness. She turned back to the window, her lips trembling. "You can't tell her anything. And she's in the orchards now."

He glanced out the window and saw that all across the plaza families had grouped themselves in pyramids, lighter members standing on the shoulders of the sturdier. Momentarily his throat closed. But he had waited a cold night to see Tiahna. With will he drove Khira's fears from mind.

The gliding light passed through the skeletal orchards, across the diked fields. At last Terlath's jagged peaks were limned with dawn and Tiahna herself was visible, tall, bronze, striding toward the palace. A child cried out below and dozens joined her.

"Tiahna comes!"

"The barohna!"

"Warm days! Warm days!"

Darkchild leaned out the window, caught. Even from here, he felt the heat and power of Tiahna's presence. Her features were stern, strong, and her hair fell rough to her shoulders, torn ragged by the winds of the mountain. She wore a woolen shift that might once have been white. Now it was stained and torn and there were streaks of blood at its hem.

Tiahna did not acknowledge the people as she moved across the plaza. She clutched the pairing stone at her throat, and occasionally it surged with light. The glow of the sunstone circlets at her wrists was constant, as if winter sun fought the dawn-darkness of spring.

Tiahna's bathing stone was located at the center of the plaza, oblong, black, dull. Tiahna approached and touched it almost absently with the fingertips of one hand while the pairing stone glowed in the other. The sunstone circlets at her wrists blazed, then dulled, and the bathing stone glowed briefly with diffuse light. Bowing her head, Tiahna closed her eyes and stretched herself full-length upon the stone.

She lay motionless for a long period, eyes shut, face stern. People tumbled from their pyramids and total silence fell across the plaza. Then the sun peered over the shoulder of the mountain, pale, morning-hazed. Tiahna's eyes opened and she tipped her head forward sharply to direct her gaze to the rising sun.

Darkchild felt an involuntary tremor, as if he were about to see something that should be secret. "Should—should we watch?"

Khira's answer was barely audible. "We always watch."

He watched. The sun hovered upon the horizon, diffusing energy across mountain and valley alike, across sterile rocky slopes and fields waiting for cultivation, across pasture land and waste land. Then Tiahna caught its orb in her suddenly blazing eyes and drew the energy it diffused to her, concentrating it into a single intense beam.

The beam quivered from sun to glowing eyes, quickly becoming so finely concentrated that it exactly matched the aperture of Tiahna's distended pupils. Mountainside and palace fell into darkness. Even the plaza became jet with blackness.

Darkchild thrust one hand before him and could not see it. All he could see was the concentrated energy that linked sun and barohna. Silently she drew it through her distended pupils and invested it in the black stone slab upon which she lay. The slab began to glow, until it became an ill-defined white radiance at the center of the plaza, Tiahna's form a shadow upon it.

Although he could not see the people, Darkchild knew they had drawn back from the bathing stone. He turned and tried to penetrate the darkness of the chamber. He could feel Khira's arm against his, could hear her irregular breath, but he could not see her. "Khira—"

She clutched his arm, her fingers cold. "Darkchild, if your eyes burn, don't look at the stone."

"But I can't see anything else." There was only the blazing sunstone—and darkness.

Her fingers tightened. "Darkchild—the stone can blind you. Look toward the edge of the plaza."

Reluctantly he obeyed, but only when the blaze of the bathing stone seemed to fill his consciousness, blocking out every other image. For a long time after he turned away, he saw the glare of the stone as clearly as if he still gazed at it.

As the sun slid up the sky, Tiahna's head moved to maintain direct visual contact. The cold in the room where Darkchild and Khira watched became profound, even when the sun hung at the crest of the heavens, a pale yellow disk. Solitary, immobile, it continued its path down the darkened sky. Tiahna arched back upon the stone slab, her eyes tracking its motion.

At last the sun slipped behind the western mountain. Tiahna lidded her eyes and dusk came diffusely to the valley. The sunset sky was briefly rosy, then fell into hues of violet and indigo.

Slowly the people stirred from the plaza, stiff, silent. Khira continued to stare down, her shoulders rigid. Below Tiahna lay motionless, her woolen shift falling from her in ashes, the flesh beneath dully gleaming. Staring at her, Darkchild felt that she was stone upon stone, that she had never been flesh, that she had never walked, had never done the things other women did. But as he watched, the stone at her throat glowed and her hand moved to clasp it.

He turned to Khira and for a moment was frightened by her pallor. Her face hung like an ashen moon in the dim chamber. "She —will she sleep there tonight? On the stone?"

She spoke bleakly. "She'll lie on the bathing stone until day after tomorrow. Then she'll carry the energy to the fields to melt the snow. That will take three days more."

"And we'll watch here every day?"

"And burn?" She turned and stalklamp cast shadowless light into the hollows of her eyes, haunting them. "No one watches while she finishes drawing the sun and spreading the heat."

He drew back. "Not even from the tower?"

"No—*no.* If you look before she comes to the throneroom a hand from now and strikes the gong, if you go to the tower to watch—"

"What?" His voice was husky.

"You'll burn as fine as the ash of her shift."

His heart bumped once, softly jarring his ribcage. "Khira— there's nothing in the scrolls about that."

"Not in the scrolls you've seen. But there are hidden scrolls. Alzaja ciphered them with me the winter before she left, some of them. That's how the sentence of death was carried out in the troubled times. The people who were condemned came to the plaza on the second day of spring and stood to watch the concentration. And they were turned to ash. If you look, you can see where they stood. When the troubled times were past, black flaggings were put down there."

Darkchild shuddered involuntarily. He had seen the black flaggings from the tower window when the workers shoveled away the snow. "I won't watch," he assured her. "And Khira—I won't leave you."

Instead of being reassured, she drew away from him, her eyes suddenly glinting. "You say that. But you'll leave me if she sends you."

"No—"

"You will. You'll leave me just like Alzaja did. You'll promise to be with me—and you'll go." Choking, suddenly sobbing, she pushed past him.

Surprised, he ran after her. But when she reached her chamber, she slammed shut her door, leaving him helpless outside. Twice he knocked. Once he took the knob in hand. But he did not turn it. Instead, after a while, he withdrew, the sound of her sobbing still with him.

Alzaja had left her and now she thought he would too. Slowly, troubled, he went to his own room. It seemed as he had left it the morning before, bright with overgrown streamers of stalklamp. There were cushions scattered on his bed, small artifacts waiting on the bureau for him to touch them. Yet today Tiahna lay on the stone in the plaza.

And in a hand of days, when she came to the throneroom and sounded the gong? Frowning, Darkchild paced his chamber. He had no fear at the prospect of meeting Tiahna. Instead he felt anticipation. To stand near enough to study the texture of her dark skin, to feel the heat of the sun radiating from her sunstone wristlets, to listen for the sun's power in her voice . . . He was eager for Tiahna to come to the throneroom, eager to see the throne catch her light and burn with it.

But Khira knew Tiahna and Khira was afraid. Pensive, Darkchild walked the stone floor. It was long before he slipped into his bed, longer still before he slept. Twin images came to him as he dreamed: Tiahna dark against the glowing stone and Khira graven pale at the window. For the first time, dreaming, he felt something that might be fear—fear that he would leave Khira despite his every promise—and he moaned in his sleep.

TEN

KHIRA

T he next day the palace seemed caught in vacuum. Its stalklit halls were silent, the very stones like living creatures, their tongues muted in anticipation. Stems of stalklamp took life, dipping down into the chill silence. Khira woke with the memory of harsh words and slipped from her bed to find Darkchild.

She found him in the corridor that led to the plaza, peering up at the tall stone doors at the end of the corridor, at the glare of concentrated sunlight that poured through the narrow scissure between door panels and casement. Khira stopped in the shadows, breath held, and gazed at his intent profile. She was hardly aware that her hands tightened and her lips drew hard.

He felt her gaze and turned, his glance briefly wary. "It's much hotter today." He seemed to test the words against her mood.

She nodded, unconsciously loosening clenched muscles. "We can't come to this side of the palace at all tomorrow. We'll have to stay in one of the other wings until she goes to the fields."

Darkchild's brows arched. "And the day after—when she goes to the fields?"

"Then it will be cold again. Almost like winter—for three days." But without the sense of unstructured time stretching ahead. Instead there would be—*should have been*—sharp anticipation of the freedom of the warmseasons. Biting her lip, Khira turned away. If they had only five days and she ruined them with her anger, the memory would be forever gall. "And after that it will be spring and I'll show you the valley," she said quickly, as if she could convince herself with the words. But she was aware that he studied her, weighing the strained tone of her voice against the promise of her words. And the effort of keeping back tears was painful.

The next five days passed slowly, as if they were caught up in some ceremonial ordeal, able neither to escape it nor to hasten its conclusion. Whenever Khira felt the rise of anger, of fear, of the tearful sense of impending desertion, she quickly damped it. But she knew Darkchild heard more than she said, saw more than she let her face tell, and sometimes his silence was more than she could bear.

By night she slept uneasily. Once she dreamed vividly of Tiahna. In her dream, she saw Tiahna slip from the glowing bathing stone and cross the plaza. As she approached the fields, banks of snow and ice melted before her and frost-hard soil turned to mud. Although Khira had never witnessed the spring melting, she visualized it in minute detail. And she woke with a cry of pain when Tiahna's radiant cloud touched a small animal and turned it to ash —a small animal with eyes she knew, intent eyes, questioning eyes.

The next day Khira was silent, knowing that beyond palace walls Tiahna moved as in her dream.

Finally on the sixth day she and Darkchild waited in her chamber for the sound of the gong. When it rang, Khira took the shutters from her window with trembling hands. Instead of snow, mud and water stood in the valley. The air was clouded with moisture and Terlath was lost in steamy clouds. Darkchild drew a disbelieving breath.

"It's time for the sharing," Khira said, turning from the window. And an emptiness far more disturbing than fear took hold of her, a protective numbness so profound her own words seemed distant. "Come."

By the time they reached the throneroom, it was crowded with people from the halls, pale, cold, crumpled. Tiahna sat upon the softly glowing throne, her eyes hooded, her flesh burned black. She had not taken time to trim the singed strands from her hair or to wash mud from her feet. Her hands lay motionless on the arms of the throne and the pairing stone hung dark at her throat.

Darkchild halted, and Khira's heart hurt when she saw how he looked at Tiahna—breathlessly, as if she were a myth taken flesh. "We sit to the left of the throne," she said, drawing him through the crowd to the dais. The sunstone throne radiated warmth, but Darkchild seemed not to notice. He perched on the edge of the dais, peering up at Tiahna with parted lips.

At a gesture from Tiahna, Palus struck the gong again. Without instruction, the people formed a line that wound through the throneroom and into the corridor. When Tiahna raised her hand again, the line began to move, each person coming before the throne and pausing, hands folded, to stand briefly in the warmth of the sunstone. Through the ceremonial sharing, the untended mirrors flashed intermittently, making the throne pulse with light. Tiahna sat unmoving except for the occasional flicker of an eyelid. Darkchild stared up at her in breathless silence, every pore open to her presence.

It was mid-afternoon when the sharing was done and Tiahna closed her eyes again. Darkchild shot a wordless question at Khira. She shook her head, her stomach suddenly leaden, her shoulders and arms weak. It was time to stand, to speak . . .

Before she could do either, the abrupt clatter of boots announced the arrival of four Arnimi. Darting a glance at her mother, Khira caught the slight tightening of Tiahna's lips before she opened her eyes.

"Goodsummer, Barohna," Commander Bullens said, stepping forward with stiff ceremony. He had groomed carefully for his audience with Tiahna. His lank grey hair was combed back smoothly from the crown of his head and he had plucked his brows and underscored his prominent eyes with a thick-pencilled black line.

"Goodsummer, Commander." Tiahna's voice was husky with disuse. "I trust you found our mountains of interest again this winter."

A sharp pang brought Khira to her feet. "Mother—" But Tiahna silenced her with a raised hand.

And Commander Bullens spoke as if she had said nothing. "We find everything on Brakrath worthy of study, Barohna: your mountains, your palace, the persons of your people." He permitted a small, chill smile to touch his lips. "We hope the Council of Bronze will kindly grant us another year's extension to continue our studies."

Absently Tiahna's fingers rose to the stone at her throat. "The Council has granted you an extension every year since your arrival, Commander."

His smile grew and became smug. "Yes, and this year we are in a position to return some favor for your continued hospitality." He glanced covertly at Darkchild. "While we studied in the mountains this winter, while your palace was deep beneath the snow—"

"Mother—"

Tiahna stirred restively. "Speak plainly, Commander. My intelligence is as sound as it was last fall."

Bullens tossed lank hair off his collar, glancing irritably at Khira. "Very well. While you were gone, a ship of the Rauthfleet came and deposited an image here—the image your daughter has brought with her today."

Khira saw a ripple of tension tighten Darkchild's face. Her eyes flashed. "He is not an image," she said angrily. "He is my companion and he has a name: Darkchild. And nothing the Arnimi tell you about him is true!"

For the first time Tiahna looked directly upon Darkchild. Her impassive gaze brought him to his feet, stiffly, his lips parted. Tiahna frowned, clasping the stone at her throat. "So he is not one of yours, Commander Bullens?"

Bullens colored. "You know we brought no personnel for creche and training facilities. This is a Rauthimage."

Tiahna continued to gaze at Darkchild. "You will have to define the term, Commander. I see a male child, of the same age as my daughter. He is not one of my people nor apparently one of yours. Whose child is he then?"

Bullens stroked back his smoothly brushed hair, recomposing himself. "Properly no one's, Barohna. His predecessors had their origin in a cell specimen taken illegally from a man named Birnam Rauth one hundred and thirty years ago. His creators are the Benderzic, a ship race—a human strain that has never taken a world of its own. They inhabit a constellation of mother ships orbiting a small yellow sun in the vicinity of Betelgeuse. At the time they proclaimed autonomy, their gene pool was too limited to assure normal offspring over a period of generations. They chose a specialized form of reproduction to overcome that limitation: imaging.

"A cell scraping is taken from the parent, male or female, put through a series of procedures, and an offspring is grown from each separate cell. Some are implanted into human uteri. Others are grown entirely in the laboratory, as in the case of the Rauthimage —although it is not properly an offspring of the Benderzic but a tool."

Displeasure passed briefly over Tiahna's features. "You have told me a number of incredible things in the years of our acquaintance, Commander."

Bullens smiled, a chill baring of teeth. "I'm telling you nothing incredible now, Barohna. Consider. Each human body cell contains the genetic information required to reproduce the characteristics of the original. It is only a matter of stimulating a single selected cell to reproduce and then of stimulating the multiplying mass of cells to differentiate and take on the various specialized functions of the human body. The image you see here is one of hundreds identically grown, programmed, then dropped throughout this galaxy and others by the Rauthfleet."

Tiahna inclined her head, her singed hair falling over her sun-blackened shoulders. "I assume then that the Rauthfleet is an entire fleet operated by this child's—siblings?"

"No, Barohna. The Rauthimages have no hand in Rauthfleet operations. The fleet is simply a group of ships given over to producing, programming and distributing Rauthimages—a lucrative operation. It contributes considerably to the Benderzic's ability to maintain autonomy." His thin lips quirked in an arrogant smile. "Of course I advised your daughter immediately upon finding a Rauthimage here."

Khira surged forward angrily. "Mother—"

Tiahna raised one hand. "You advised her—how, Commander?"

"I told her to escort the Rauthimage to the door and lock him outside to freeze. She chose to ignore my advice—as you can see—and so now it is up to you to dispose of the image."

Tiahna's gaze returned to Darkchild, lingering until the blood ran from his face. "Is there some particular reason I should dispose of him, Commander Bullens?"

Khira knew Tiahna's moods, knew that her disinterested tone hid anger. And her anger, Khira realized with quick elation, was not directed at Darkchild. It was directed at Commander Bullens as he postured in his dress uniform, stroking at his lank hair. *She despises you as much as I do,* Khira mocked him silently, pleased.

But Bullens was insensitive to Tiahna's mood. "In the first place he exists without the consent of Birnam Rauth, the man from whom he was imaged. The cells from which he derives were taken illegally and by force. He has no right to independent existence under the circumstances."

"Birnam Rauth himself has demanded that the images be destroyed?"

"Birnam Rauth is a hundred and twenty years dead, Barohna." Momentarily Bullens lidded his eyes. "He was a resourceful man but careless of his safety. The Benderzic have had to program considerably more caution into his images."

"But before he died, he requested the termination of these images?" Tiahna persisted.

Bullens was scornful. "Apparently he never recognized the gravity of the offense. But my people recognize it and are repelled by it —as I am sure you are. And there is a more immediate reason for disposing of him: the threat he poses to your people."

"Ah—and what is the nature of that threat, Commander?"

He flicked at his hair. "Your isolation from the mainstream of human civilization has given you false confidence, Barohna. You are not invulnerable."

"No one is invulnerable. I am far less vulnerable than most."

"And your people are far more vulnerable than many," he said smoothly, as if the evaluation pleased him. "This image has one purpose here—one only. That is to learn everything possible about Brakrath, its resources, its people and culture—and to relay what he has learned to the Benderzic."

Tiahna's fingers curled around her pairing stone. For a moment its light glowed from between her fingers. When she spoke, her voice was husky, intimate. "In other words, his purposes here are the same as yours—to learn about us and to communicate to others what you have learned."

Bullens frowned faintly. "His goals and purposes are entirely different from ours, as different as his origins. We have come to analyze your world and your way of life for scholarly purposes."

"And he?"

The single female Arnimi stepped forward, her uniform stiff, her bearing stiffer. "Barohna, you think you see a child here, an ordinary human child. But no, this is a data-gathering instrument, nothing more—a tool. Birnam Rauth was an explorer, a man who flirted at the very edges of human civilization. He had very special qualities of mind: resourcefulness, a probing curiosity, and a particular ability to form data into patterns. This image possesses those qualities and in addition he has been programmed in various ways to increase his utility to the Benderzic.

"He appears harmless to you. Many hosts even find him appealing. But if you permit him to live, he will study your resources, your customs, your weaknesses and limitations. He will learn about your land, your mountains. He will learn what grows here, what minerals are available to be extracted. He will learn how you can be overthrown and how your people can be welded into a slave labor force. He will learn everything you permit him to learn.

"Then the Benderzic will send a ship for him and draw what information he has gathered from him and place it in databanks very similar to our own. They will sell that information to the highest bidder."

Khira drew a shivering breath. She recognized Tiahna's mood now, her scorn for Bullens and his arrogance. But if she believed the female Arnimi—*if what the woman said were true*—

Fiercely Khira turned on the Arnimi. "Let them come for him! We won't let them have him!"

Bullens reacted with a cold flash of irritation. "Then they will take him by force."

"If they can find him! He doesn't have to stay here. There are mountains—and hundreds of valleys. He can hide anywhere. We—"

The female Arnimi tossed her head emphatically. "Heiress, you could bleach his hair white, put blue lenses in his eyes, make his skin as fair as your own, and the Benderzic would find him. There is a small unit embedded deep in his heart muscle. They can pick out its signal from the stratosphere of your planet and home on it with great precision."

"Then we'll remove it!"

"And kill him in the process. The device contains a minute amount of extremely potent poison—which it will release into his bloodstream at the slightest trauma to the heart muscle. No, they will find him easily."

"And thereafter," Bullens said, "he will disgorge every bit of data he has accumulated for sale to whomever will pay most to exploit Brakrath. No matter if he swears he will say nothing. He has no control over the process by which the Benderzic program their databanks directly from his brain tissue."

Distractedly Khira noted Darkchild's rigidity, his pallor. She glared at Bullens, groping for some definitive argument. "That's not true! No one would send a child to spy! No one—"

Tiahna silenced her. "Yes, Commander. Why would anyone send a child to gather information he can hardly be expected to understand?"

"But who learns more readily than a child?" the female Arnimi countered. "The younger the child, the greater the ability to assimilate language and cultural nuances. And the less ready his hosts to dispose of him. Virtually all human cultures conserve human young. The surprising thing is that they've sent a Rauthimage as old as this one. He has obviously had previous assignments. But he will have no memory of those. And he needn't understand the information he gathers. He need merely record the raw data to be transferred to the Benderzic databanks and interpreted there."

Tiahna nodded, dismissing the Arnimi's argument. "In any case, there is little here to be exploited."

"There is a great deal to be exploited," Bullens said immediately. "I can show you reams of data about the mineral content of the mountains to the south. Your own Terlath has deposits valuable enough to make export mining extremely profitable. And we have documented dozens of unique plant specimens. I can project commercially feasible uses for many of them.

"On the other hand, you have no military strength and you have a potential slave labor force numbering into the hundreds of thousands. A winter strike, when the barohnas are in their mountain retreats and the people are in wintersleep, would meet virtually no resistance."

Khira chilled. But Tiahna remained aloof from Commander Bullens' arguments.

"And in addition to the conventional resources, Barohna, there is the sunstone. Perhaps you don't appreciate the value of a block of stone no larger than your throne which can absorb sufficient energy to melt the snow from a valley this size—or to raze entire mountain ranges. Because I appreciate very well that you use only a tenth of the capacity of your stones."

Tiahna considered him with remote impassivity. "I use only a hundredth of the capacity of my stones, if that. Only what is necessary to maintain a valley this size. And I have capabilities you haven't guessed at, Commander. But I stress the personal pronoun: *I* use the stones. There are just four hundred living barohnas on Brakrath. Without us the stones are useless."

"To your people, yes. To mine perhaps. But there are commercial combines that would gamble on finding ways to use the sunstone. The Benderzic may not have sent the image here on speculation, you know. They may have a sponsor for his services, some group that already suspects Brakrath is worth its attention."

For the first time Tiahna brought the full force of her attention to bear on the Arnimi, studying him from deep-set eyes, her voice falling to a husky whisper. "It seems you know enough to endanger Brakrath yourself, Commander."

Bullens flushed. "We do not deal in information."

"Yet you plan to disseminate the information you gather."

"To responsible scientists and scholars, yes. But never for gain. We will not sell a scrap of information."

Tiahna's long fingers tapped a measured beat upon the arms of the throne. "And none of your responsible scientists or scholars will sell a scrap of information either? Despite the value you ascribe to data about Brakrath?"

Bullens' prominent eyes bulged with quick anger. He tossed the hair off his collar with a flick of his head. "People of the caliber of those who will be privy to our study do not deal commercially in information."

Khira smiled with savage pleasure at his discomfiture. *Yes, she despises you.*

"I see." Tiahna's fingers drummed. She leaned forward, her hair falling across her scorched shoulders. "Of course you are my only source of information about the behavior of all those peoples beyond Brakrath. I have no one else to consult."

Bullens' voice crackled with impatience. "Then you must take my word, Barohna, that if you permit the Rauthimage to live, you place your sovereignty at peril."

"And if I permit you and your colleagues to live?"

For a moment Bullens seemed not to understand. Then his florid face drained. "We have enjoyed your hospitality for fourteen years."

"Yes." Tiahna leaned back, pleasure playing lightly at her lips. Khira could see it there. "Yet you understand me so poorly that you don't know if I'm threatening you or toying with you. You don't know if the Council is permitting you to amass a fund of information which only we will see, or if we intend to let you return to Arnim one day."

Bullens' lips seemed stiff. "The Council has permitted us to augment our research staff from Arnim three times in the past ten years."

"We have permitted you to bring in fresh personnel, yes. Under the terms of agreement, however, you have not been permitted to send personnel or data back to Arnim. You don't know, do you, if you are our guests or our prisoners? You have always asked if you could stay, never if you could leave." She smiled faintly. "This winter a breeterlik wandered into my mountain quarters looking for prey. You know the breeterlik, Commander. You have hand weapons that could destroy it despite its size—if you kept your wits. I didn't need a weapon. I drew energy from my wrist-stones and the breeterlik fell in ashes.

"I can render this boy ash in a fraction of a second. Within the same quarter moment I can do the same to you and your companions. Why shouldn't my daughter have a companion until I can give her another sibling?"

Commander Bullens gathered at visibly dissolving stores of nerve. "Barohna, this is no companion. This is not even a human. He is the image of a man who died over a century ago. And his training has made him a creature of conditioned reflexes, nothing more. He appears to respond to the stimulus of the moment, but actually he responds only to the instruction of his guide."

"As you respond to the instruction of your superior on Arnim? Even though you have not seen him for fourteen years?"

Bullens' features tightened into grimness. "There are two ways to prevent this image from betraying you. You can wipe his deep brain centers and leave him a vegetable, if you have that ability—or you can dispose of him entirely."

Again a shadowed smile lingered on Tiahna's lips. "I hope you will remember that you prescribed the suitable measures for dealing with a guest who has become unwelcome." She raised one hand in a dismissing gesture. "We'll talk again, Commander."

The four Arnimi seemed not to comprehend. They stood frozen at the center of the polished floor.

Tiahna repeated her dismissal. Lips seaming, Bullens wheeled and stamped from the throneroom. His companions followed, stricken. The clatter of boots turned their recessional into flight.

Their discomposure was fuel to Khira's flame. Her eyes flashed with triumph. "Darkchild can stay then!"

Sighing, Tiahna leaned back against the polished throne, closing her eyes. Absently she caressed her pairing stone. "Did I say that, daughter?"

"You said—" Khira surrendered her elation reluctantly. "You said—"

"I asked the Arnimi why my daughter should not have a companion until she has a sibling to occupy her."

"Then—Darkchild will be my companion," Khira declared. "The things the Arnimi said about him—"

"They are to be considered."

"No! They're lies! They told you lies!" The words emerged shrilly, unconvincingly—because Khira had observed Darkchild's curiosity herself, his determination to master the Brakrathi language, the searching questions he asked.

"Perhaps they did," Tiahna said. "Even so, I will have to know much more about your friend before I decide whether he can stay." Slowly her deep-set eyes opened and rested upon Darkchild. He gazed into them as if held in spell.

"I'll tell you everything you need to know about him!"

"And how do you know what questions I intend to ask him, child?"

"I—I know everything important. He's—he's told me everything."

"I doubt that he's told you what I need to know." Tiahna sighed, deeply, and clasped her pairing stone. When it dulled, she said, "Rahela needs me now. Bring your friend to me tomorrow at first gong, after I have slept. I will talk with him then." She lidded her eyes, dismissing them.

Khira caught Darkchild's hand and drew him away, hardly noticing his stunned gaze. Tiahna would question him at first gong. Twelve hours until she found he could not answer her questions—would never answer them.

And then? Khira had never seen her mother ash so much as a stingmadder. But Tiahna had bid Alzaja a tearless farewell—and five daughters before her. And Darkchild was nothing to her.

A spy instrument. If she were to believe the Arnimi, Darkchild was nothing more than a data-gathering instrument, dropped by a soulless people to determine if Brakrath was a ready victim for exploitation. Khira halted in the corridor beyond the throneroom, trying to order her thoughts. But they eluded her, lashing out chaotically in every direction.

"Khira—" Darkchild's voice was thick.

She drew breath in a half-sob. "I have to think. I have to . . . Go to your room and I'll—I'll come there later. When I've had time to think." She could not imagine the depravity of a people who lived by exploiting others. How did they structure their private lives? Did sister fight sister for food and trinkets? Were Benderzic young trained to subordinate each other to the greed of the strongest? Or did the women who governed them see that their venality was directed entirely outward?

"Khira—"

She gazed at him distractedly. At least he was not one of them. He was their victim instead. His very flesh had been taken by force from Birnam Rauth. And his mind, deliberately programmed—

"Please—I'll come to your room later."

He honored her distress with a silent nod and slipped away. She turned back down the corridor, her mind racing. If only he could lie when Tiahna questioned him—

If only he could lie . . .

Khira frowned, her thoughts turning in a new direction. Why hadn't the Benderzic simply programmed him to lie? Then he could have told her any tale he pleased about his people and his origins. And tomorrow he could tell Tiahna the same tale: that he was a stranded traveler, separated from his people by accident; that someone who wished his family ill had abducted him and abandoned him here; that he was a student sent to study Brakrath ways; that—

But he could tell Tiahna none of those things. He had not been taught to lie. Caught in her thoughts, Khira paced the corridor. She looked up in surprise when Techni-Verra spoke; she had not heard the Arnimi woman's approach. "Khira—were you in the throne-room when Commander Bullens spoke with your mother?"

"I was there. Verra—"

"He says your mother threatened to hold us here indefinitely—to terminate us if we try to leave. He's going to message Arnim command immediately."

Terminate. It was like Bullens to use a word that had neither flesh nor blood. "She was toying with him," Khira said impatiently. It surprised her that Verra didn't understand that. "He tried to tell her the Council of Bronze couldn't protect Brakrath. And he tried to tell her Darkchild was nothing but an image—something you see in a mirror." Insubstantial, without independent life.

Was he only that, a shadow cast on a reflective surface? She could not believe it. No more than she could long believe he was only a data-gathering instrument.

"It's—it's only a term, heiress," Verra said, distracted. "A translation. There are any number of words we could use if you spoke Arnimi. But Commander Bullens is very upset. He wants us to leave immediately. He's going to call for fire-support ships from the nearest CoSignators."

Khira shook her head, rejecting Verra's digression. "Verra—why can't Darkchild lie to my mother when she questions him tomorrow? If he could tell her he's never heard of the Benderzic, if he could tell her—"

Verra ran a splayed hand through her hair, disarranging it. "Child, we're talking at cross-purposes. The threat your mother made Commander Bullens—"

Khira flung out her arms in frustration. "Verra, she was toying. She was angry. If you had spoken to her instead of Commander Bullens, she would have said nothing. And he won't be able to reach his command anyway. That was part of the agreement with the Council, that no messages be sent off-planet unless they're monitored by a member of the Council. That's why all your message-casters had to be turned over to the Council when your group was given permission to quarter here."

"Yes, yes, of course. But Khira, Commander Bullens didn't turn over all the casters. He kept one, a small unit."

Again Khira was surprised by Verra's ignorance. "I know. Alzaja showed it to me three winters ago."

Verra became very still. "She—she couldn't have. We told no one about it. It looks—like another kind of instrument entirely."

"Yes, a weather instrument. Don't you remember Commander Bullens let Alzaja use your databank keyboard and screen the winter she was learning to read your language?" Alzaja's interest in Arnimi was an enthusiasm Khira had never shared. "She was screening inventory lists and she learned that one of your weather instruments was really a message-caster."

Verra's face was suddenly ashen. "She—"

"She told my mother of course."

"The barohna knows we have a message-caster in our quarters?"

"She knows it's there. But it hasn't been useful for three years." Khira suppressed a momentary pang at Verra's distress. "Some of its components were very delicate."

"Yes," Verra said softly. "They were. Very delicate."

Impulsively Khira seized her arm. "Verra, my mother won't hurt you. She was toying with Commander Bullens—because he's arrogant. But she's going to talk with Darkchild tomorrow, and if he can't lie to her, if he can't tell her he's a lost traveler, that he's never heard of the Benderzic—Verra, why can't he tell her that? Why didn't the Benderzic teach him to lie?"

Verra finally seemed to focus upon Khira's concern. She clasped Khira's hand, shaking her head. "Khira, sometimes I think we take the information in our databanks too literally. We've told you what the Benderzic intend when they produce a Rauthimage. They intend to send out a child who presents the semblance of a human but performs with the precision and predictability of a machine. Certainly that child should be able to lie to your mother, to you and to me—effortlessly. A lie should have no meaning to him.

"But the Benderzic are working with human flesh. And from what I've learned of Birnam Rauth, he was a man who trusted his life to his own senses and resources and little else. Certainly not an easy man to subdue, even at the level of a single cell. Your friend probably shouldn't have slipped into stress-state under less than physical torture. He shouldn't have cared enough for you to reach that level of distress—if his programming were fully effective."

Yet he had. Khira groped to clarify her thoughts. "Then—a Rauthimage shouldn't care for anyone?"

"I doubt a properly programmed Rauthimage cares for anything but his guide and his brothers. But there is something else we haven't considered, heiress. A Rauthimage is first sent out at a very young age—before his fourth birthday. He is most valuable when he is very young—when his mental capacities are fully plastic. The major part of his programming is completed before that age. Your friend has had at least seven years then to outgrow his programming. And the programming—even the refresher programming the Benderzic impose between missions—is suited to a much younger child than your friend. If the Rauthfleet retrieved Darkchild from his last assignment and dropped him again without realizing that his programming had partially failed, that he was outgrowing it—"

"Then he wouldn't be as Commander Bullens says! He would be—"

"We don't know how he would be," Verra cautioned her. "All we know is that he wouldn't be as the Benderzic intended him."

Khira's pulse sang with momentary elation. It died almost immediately. "But tomorrow then, when my mother calls us—" What Verra said accounted for the difference between Darkchild as Khira knew him and the person Commander Bullens insisted he should be. But what help would that be when Tiahna questioned him?

Little.

None.

Verra felt her distress and responded to it. "Khira, perhaps you're letting yourself be frightened unnecessarily too."

"I—" Dumbly Khira shook her head. "I don't know." Perhaps after Tiahna had rested, she would accept Khira's word that Dark-

child offered no threat. Or perhaps when he could not answer her
questions, Tiahna would simply dismiss him until another time.

Perhaps. It seemed unlikely.

But if they left the palace before Tiahna could question Darkchild—

The snow was melted from the valley now. The fields were ponds
of mud. But she and Darkchild could run along the tops of the
levees until they reached solid ground.

And then run where? To the mountain, where snow still lay deep
and predators were waking hungry from wintersleep? Khira was
surprised to find she clutched Verra's arm. She squeezed it urgently.
"Verra, she won't harm you. I promise it." Then she turned and
ran.

Her feet clattered down the corridor, up the tower stairs. Cloud
hung dense over the valley, shrouding the mountains. Even
Terlath's lower slopes were lost. The air would be unstable for days,
cold air masses from the mountainside rushing down into the valley, warm air from the valley rising to form towering clouds. There
would be storms; thunder would bring avalanches grumbling down
the mountainside.

But they would not have to climb far to reach the tunnel that led
to Mingele's valley, deserted for almost three centuries now, since
Mingele's last daughter had died without bronzing and Mingele's
powers had waned. The snow would be as deep in Mingele's valley
as on the mountain. There was no barohna to bring early spring.
But they would have Mingele's palace for shelter and game for
food. They would be safe there for a time.

Perhaps a time was all they needed. If Khira could tutor Darkchild to claim to be something other than a Rauthimage—

For the first time since she had locked Darkchild into the tower
so many hands ago, Khira found hope. She had taught him to
speak, to cipher, to play board games. Now she must take him to
Mingele's valley and teach him to lie. Quickly she slammed down
the tower stairs and ran to the kitchen to pack supplies. Her heart
hammered with elation, counterpoint to her running footsteps.

ELEVEN

THE GUIDE

The guide fought his way from dreams of ice and fire, perspiring, and pushed himself erect in bed. Beyond the palace thunder rolled, the voice of the mountain. Stiffly, troubled, the guide left his bed and unshuttered his window. Below, the plaza was deserted under the occasional trembling brilliance of lightning. Cloudy mists closed around the darkened bathing stone and the smell of night was the smell of wet soil. Somewhere a solitary cock celebrated some remembered dawn.

Remembered. The guide turned from the window and stared bleakly across the room. For Darkchild thunder carried the promise of memory. It brought alien images into his dreams and made him toss and strain for them. But the guide knew he must not be permitted to touch them. There was not just memory in Darkchild's dreams—there was loss and aching pain. More pain than Darkchild could bear if he came upon it at the wrong moment.

The guide retreated from the window, bleakly whispering the terms of the contract by which he was empowered:

To guide the boy in strange places.

To keep his body safe and fed.

To prompt him to inquire and explore.

To urge him to learn and know.

To divert him from knowledge which was interior.

To—

The guide started as his door swung open and Khira hurried into the room. For a heart-stopping moment he thought Darkchild's dreams had summoned her.

But she was urgent with some other concern. "Darkchild?"

The wardrobe and bureau cast shadows along the far walls of the chamber. Instinctively the guide edged toward them, speaking with Darkchild's voice. "I couldn't sleep."

Khira frowned, momentarily distracted by the tension in his voice. But her own concern was uppermost. "I packed supplies for us and took heavy clothes from the storeroom," she said hurriedly. "They're downstairs in the kitchen."

The guide understood at once. She intended to take Darkchild from the valley rather than permit Tiahna to question him. "We're leaving."

"Yes. And we have to be out of the valley by dawn." She turned toward the door, then turned back when he did not immediately follow. "Darkchild, we have to go now, before anyone wakes."

Yes. Before they could be stopped and brought back to the palace. Still he hesitated. *To guide the boy in strange places; to keep his body safe and fed* . . . He was charged with these duties. And beyond the palace were beasts and perils.

But within the palace was Tiahna. Softly the guide shuddered, remembering her deep eyes and the power she held. She slept tonight, but tomorrow she would send for Darkchild and question him.

Unconsciously the guide's hand rose to his throat. Darkchild could not lie, and the guide knew that if he faced Tiahna in Darkchild's place, he would not be able to speak at all. His windpipe would close and he would fall unconscious. Panic squeezed a premature beat from his heart. Why *had* the Benderzic sent him out without the protection of a lying tongue? It seemed such a simple defense, to glibly tell Tiahna some tale of a fallen ship and lost people.

Tensely he stepped from the shadows. "I have to put on my boots. I'll meet you in the kitchen."

Khira studied him for a moment, frowning, then hurried away.

The guide didn't notice until he tried to close his boots that his hands shook. He clenched his fists and stared at them with a rising sense of helplessness. All the things he had been promised: that he would not be troubled by fear, by uncertainty—not only were they untrue; when he tried to remember the person who had promised him, shadow fell across his memory and he could not see. If he was to believe the Arnimi, his masters were the Benderzic—but he could not remember their faces.

And he *was* troubled by fear and uncertainty. Since the day Khira had locked him in the tower, they had been his constant companions. It was hard to believe his former arrogance. Now he saw danger in every corner, heard threat in every sound. Even Khira frightened him when she frowned, when she spoke sharply—frightened him so much he was afraid to answer her. That he left to Darkchild, because Darkchild at least knew how to please her.

But now the guide realized, sitting on the edge of his bed, that he had left too much to Darkchild. For hands of days—out of fright, out of anxiety—he had permitted Darkchild to go where he pleased, to touch and sample and question at will. He had interfered only in moments of sharpest panic. He had abdicated all responsibility, conscious not of the contract and his obligation to enforce it, but of his own fear.

With will, the guide stood. If he could think of fear as a tool, a warning, surely he could master it. And by that measure, uncertainty was a tool too, a sign that he must give more thought to his activities, that he must not let events sweep him along. That he must meet his responsibilities.

Now, tonight—there was thunder, and thunder moved Darkchild to reach for images that hovered just beyond the brink of consciousness. The guide must forestall that seeking, even if it meant mastering Darkchild and going with Khira himself. Even if it meant facing her anger and scorn. Because she had made it clear in the days after the Arnimi came that she despised him.

Quickly, before his resolve could slip away, the guide left his chamber and hurried down the corridor toward the kitchen. All he had to do, he told himself over the anxious thump of his heart, was go with her as Darkchild would go, answer her as Darkchild would answer her. If he were careful, perhaps she would not even notice, in the dark.

But for a moment, when he stepped into the kitchen and she turned and glanced sharply in his direction, he wavered. She would know him immediately from his stiff gait, from the timbre of his voice, from a dozen other clues.

Even so, better Khira's anger than Tiahna's fire. "I had trouble fastening my boots," he excused himself, trying to keep the harsh note from his voice.

She nodded distractedly. "Here—try on these leggings. If they don't fit, I'll have to go back to the store room." She frowned at the bulging packs. "Everything else is packed."

The leggings fit and within a short time they slipped from the palace, each carrying a pack and a bundle. The guide stayed well behind Khira, hoping she would not notice how awkwardly he moved.

On the plaza, the night air was at once steamy and chill, as if the heat Tiahna had brought to the valley struggled to repel the intruding cold of the mountains. They ran across the plaza and Khira seemed not to notice that the guide moved stiffly. But when they climbed the broad steps that led to the tops of the leveed fields, he forgot himself. He peered into the turbid water that stood in the fields. And stopped. Slowly his tongue circled his lips, wetting them. "It's—deep."

She turned, surprised. "It's over our heads," she said with a shrug. "You're not afraid?"

Wasn't he? His fists clenched at his sides and he struggled to subordinate his fear. The levee tops were broad and smoothly paved. Even though he didn't have Darkchild's easy coordination, why think he would fall into the water?

That reassurance didn't wipe the perspiration from his lip, didn't make his feet any less reluctant to move.

Khira gazed back at him with rising irritation. "It'll be just as deep an hour from now," she reminded him sharply.

Yes. He could not stand here until the water sank. Reluctantly he forced himself to follow Khira. But he ran painfully, conscious of each footfall.

When they left the last levee, his knees weakened with momentary relief. But now they were in the orchards, running through skeletal trees, their feet sinking in mud. And what might live in the mud he was afraid to think. Once as he ran after Khira he tripped, stifling a frightened cry. Khira turned back and helped him up without reproach.

The air grew colder, and near dawn they reached Terlath's lower slopes. There they stopped to pull on quilted jackets and leggings. Khira stuffed her hair into a fur-lined cap and the guide chafed trembling hands before pulling on thick mittens. Harsh winter winds swept down the mountainside, pushing beneath the warm, steamy air of the valley and raising it in dense clouds. The sound of thunder was closer, sharper, and lightning flashed in sheets across the clouded sky.

Memories. The guide put them back and climbed the snowy slopes after Khira, plunging through snowdrifts and over fresh rockfalls. She moved as if she were made for the mountain. He moved gracelessly, constantly stumbling, frightened. After a while they reached a great glasstone lens set in a supporting frame that swiveled to beam sunlight down the mountain and concentrate it upon the throneroom mirrors. They rested there for a while, thunder grumbling on all sides. The guide hugged his bruised knees until he realized that Khira studied him, faintly frowning. Anxiously he forced his body into a more relaxed posture, but he suspected she had already seen what he had wanted to conceal. When she got to her feet and continued up the slopes, she went without speaking.

At last she raised one hand, calling a halt. "There, ahead—" She pushed at a straggling strand of hair and gazed narrowly back at him. "There beyond the cleft in the rocks—there's a tunnel leading to Mingele's valley. We can shelter in the palace there." Her lips hardened and she studied him more closely. "But there may be rock-leopard in the tunnel. They sleep there sometimes in the winter."

Rock-leopard. The words scoured his nerves. He knew about rock-leopards from the scrolls. They dragged prey to their dens live and devoured it by bits over many hands of days. Sometimes they kept partially eaten prey captive for an entire season, kicking up barricades of rock to contain it while they hunted the mountainside for fresh tidbits. The guide couldn't contain the blood that drained from his face, couldn't keep the shrill panic from his voice. "We can't go in there!"

Khira's lips twisted in a scornful grimace. "If there is a leopard, he'll be sleeping. All we have to do is slip past without waking him —if you can do that. You've kicked enough rock down the mountain to wake a hundred leopards this morning."

And Darkchild wouldn't have stumbled once. Unconsciously the guide wiped at his eyes. "Is there stalklamp? In the tunnel?" The demand was brittle with fear. But if he could at least see whatever beast they met—

Khira's smile was small, satisfied. "A few strands at either end. The main part of the tunnel is completely dark at this time of year."

He shrank. But this was no time to hesitate, wounded by her scorn. She turned and moved up the trail, challenging him by the careless set of her shoulders. Tensely he followed, fear singing in his nervous system. Perspiration broke out on his upper lip. As she entered the tunnel, he tried to gauge how much time he would have for flight if a leopard rose from the dark and attacked them.

In the end there was no leopard in the tunnel. They burrowed through drifted snow into a chill darkness that smelled of damp stone and stagnant water. The tunnel was broad enough for two to walk abreast, tall enough that neither had to bend. The floor was worn smooth from the traffic of centuries. Near the inception of the tunnel, occasional tendrils of stalklamp clung to the tunnel roof, offering anemic illumination.

The guide crept along the wall of the tunnel after Khira, his nerves quivering. Loose rock littered the floor and in places there were animal droppings. He felt them underfoot. Disoriented, the guide clutched at the rough walls for reassurance.

The tunnel twisted twice. At each bend, the guide paused and listened. Each time he heard nothing but his own breath and Khira's. Each time, following Khira, he found nothing but a further stretch of empty tunnel.

The guide's nerves ebbed abruptly when they reached the far end of the tunnel. He collapsed against the rock wall, breathing hard against the whine in his ears.

Khira had already begun digging at the drifted snow that blocked the end of the tunnel. She turned on him with a scornful flash. "Well? Do you expect me to do all the work?"

Stung, ashamed, he joined her, working awkwardly, and after a while the last of the drifted snow fell away and they looked down over Mingele's valley. It lay deep in snow, the empty palace girdled in white, its watchtower blind. Tall breathing chimneys marked the sites of the deserted stonehalls. Occasionally a brief stretch of levee was visible, breaking the layer of frozen white that covered the dead valley. The air was clear and biting.

And there was no thunder.

For a moment, looking down over the snowbound valley, tasting the crisp silence of the mountainside, the guide felt a sharp sense of elation. He could walk here and leave footprints where no one had left footprints before. He could shout and there would be no ear to hear. He—

He stiffened as sunlight caught the strangely carved stone mounted at the peak of the watchtower below. The stone was large, darkly translucent, and for some reason sight of it made his mouth go dry. "Khira—there at the top of the watchtower—"

She shrugged off his agitation irritably. "An eyestone. The barohnas used them during the troubled times to watch the valleys. No one uses them now."

Then why did he have the feeling that the stone watched him?

Khira returned to the tunnel, warming her nose and mouth in her mittened hands. The guide remained outside, trying to recapture the first sharp ecstasy of freedom. Instead he found only a sense of threat.

When he turned back to the tunnel, Khira crouched on the floor, her pack open. His pack lay kicked against the wall beyond her. She looked up, and it seemed to him that she deliberately challenged him to step past her to retrieve it.

"I'm hungry," he said, aggrieved.

Her pupils narrowed at the harsh tone of his voice. "Then eat." But she made no move to let him pass. Glancing down, he saw that her pike lay on the tunnel floor at his feet. Angrily he snatched it up. "I'll hunt for my dinner."

Khira jumped to her feet, her face flushing. "With my pike? For what?"

"Brownfowl. They nest under the snow. I'll have those." If she would not feed him, he would feed himself.

Her eyes glinted, challenging. "You don't know anything about hunting brownfowl."

But he did. "I know to look for a place where three hollow reeds stick up through a deep drift. The nest will be there. I know to kick the snow back and strike for the largest fowl—the drake. I know to leave the hen with the eggs so there will be young at hatching time."

Khira's voice crackled with scorn. "You know what you've read from the scrolls! You've never used a pike in your life. And predators hunt this valley. There are no people to drive them away. You don't even know how to tell if they're nearby."

He was stung. "Do you think I won't notice prints in the snow?"

"You won't—if it snowed last night and a minx has been waiting behind a boulder for three days. They wait that long at this time of year, you know. And if you move when there is a minx nearby—"

She didn't have to tell him. He knew from the scrolls of the snowminx' killing fury. His gaze dropped. *Make fear a tool*, he reminded himself.

A tool this time to keep him from doing something foolish out of wounded pride. He was charged with keeping the boy safe—even at sacrifice to his own pride. Silently he dropped Khira's pike. "I want my pack," he said in a harsh undertone. "I'll eat from my pack."

She glared at him disbelievingly, then hurled the pack at him, her teeth clenching in an angry grimace. "Take it! And eat at the other end of the tunnel!"

He turned without defending himself. But he didn't retreat to the other end of the tunnel. He ate a dozen meters from her, choking dry bread down a dry throat. Then, although it was only midday, he slumped against the cavern wall and fell into exhausted sleep.

It was dark beyond the cavern mouth when Khira shook him awake, her fingers digging into his shoulders, her voice pounding shrilly at him. With a frightened gasp, he pulled himself to a sitting position, trying to escape her gripping fingers. Instead they tightened. By the stalklamp that clung sparsely to the cavern ceiling, he saw wild anger in her eyes and tears on her cheeks.

"You're not Darkchild! *You're not Darkchild!*"

The guide's heart shuddered and the blood left his face. The way she loomed over him, the way she held him . . . "Khira—"

"I thought you were Darkchild, and I didn't understand why— why you were acting that way. The way you acted all day. And then I dreamed. I dreamed about you, about the way you acted after the Arnimi came back to the palace. I dreamed about your voice and the way you walk—the way you kept falling down today. I dreamed you fell down and when you got up, you got up twice. You were two!" Fiercely she pushed him back against the wall, releasing him with a violent shove.

The guide raised one hand, imploring. If only she would listen; if only she would understand. "Khira—I'm—*I keep Darkchild safe.* I guard him. I—"

Her lips twisted. "You keep him safe—by falling down? By stumbling every time you put one boot in front of the other?"

"I—" How to explain his clumsiness when he didn't understand it himself? Darkchild moved easily, surely, and without fear. But something seemed to bind the guide's muscles, making his entire body rigid and ungainly. It bound even his throat, so that his voice came harshly. "Khira—"

"You're the guide!" She leaned near him, her eyes blazing. "You're the one he tried to tell me about. The one who knows things! *You're not even Darkchild!*"

So she hadn't known. She hadn't guessed until now. He slumped back against the wall, his muscles feeling as if they had been pounded. "I'm not."

His admission quieted her for a moment. She drew back and

slapped angrily at her tears. "I don't understand," she said finally, like a child lost.

He sighed. He didn't understand either. Why should they be two in one body, one anxious and frightened, the other unafraid? One holding back, the other pushing ahead? Because the Benderzic had made them thus? Because the Benderzic had given him fear to guard Darkchild with? Because there was no other way to control and protect?

"I don't understand," she said again, with new force, her eyes suddenly dry and angry. "But I know one thing. Darkchild promised not to leave me." Her lips tightened. "That's what he told me —that he wouldn't leave me."

How could he answer her? He couldn't tell her about thunder and dreams, about his contract, about responsibilities too long neglected.

What would Darkchild tell her? The guide peered up at her hopelessly. Khira, when he leaves you, he wanted to say, whenever Darkchild has to leave you, I won't. I won't leave you alone. The words and the emotion he found in them moved him strangely and he wondered at his feelings. Why should he care that she was angry and hurt? There was nothing in the contract about her.

Still it mattered. "Khira—"

"He promised not to leave me," she said with finality. Quickly she took her feet and strode away into the darkness of the tunnel.

Her hurt touched him, ached in him. He wanted to go after her, to reassure her. But he knew the only reassurance she wanted was Darkchild.

And he could not give her Darkchild. Because when he finally slept again, curled uncomfortably against the stone wall, his dreams were of thunder: the thunder of storm in some damp jungle, the thunder of a ship in the sky, the thunder of Darkchild's heart. And all through his dreams, he felt Darkchild groping for images he must never grasp: violet eyes and midnight hair, a silk that sang in the sun, golden skies.

Darkchild was searching for things he must not find. And when the guide woke, he knew that he too had reached for something he must not have. He had reached for Khira; he had cared for her. And he must not. He could not fulfill the contract by caring.

He must not care for anyone or anything.

Still it mattered that the next morning Khira would not meet his eyes, would not speak. She ate silently, as if she were alone. And when the guide followed her from the tunnel, she did not look back. She walked as if she were the only person on the mountain.

Her rejection was a physical pain. It ached the same way his bruised knees ached, the same way his strained thighs hurt. But he followed silently, making no effort to reconcile her. He knew he must not.

Morning sunlight glinted off the snow crust that covered mountain and valley. Everywhere were signs of game. Hollow reeds poking above the snow created breathing chimneys for nests of brownfowl. A series of icy potholes marked the spot where dens of heapers slept. Coveys of early-hatching groundrunners squawked and scattered at his approach. Twice Khira froze and the guide saw signs of snowminx in the snow. He stood utterly still, not breathing, listening with bristling hair for the slithering approach of Terlath's eeriest predator.

Both times they passed without seeing the minx that had left its sign.

It was midday when they reached Mingele's valley. The guide peered uneasily up at the eyestone on the peak of the watchtower. But today it did not seem to look back.

He followed Khira across the valley with a hollow sadness. If he were Darkchild, he would absorb every new sight and sound eagerly. He would run with Khira across the snow and they would laugh together.

Instead they walked separately, silently, until they reached the deep-drifted plaza of Mingele's palace. Breathing chimneys stood like giant straws, ringing the palace. The watchtower cast its shadow across the snow.

They shed their packs and Khira threw herself down in the snow to catch her breath. Dully the guide explored the perimeters of the plaza. Mingele's palace was centuries older than Tiahna's, built in an era when the climate had been briefly milder and crops had grown lush. Assured of a rich harvest, the people had lavished time and skill upon the palace. Windowed turrets grew from its four corners, rivaling the watchtower. Carved forms were set into stone recesses at intervals around the exterior walls, native forms alternating with forms that had accompanied the stranded humans. A snowminx stood half-crouched, razor claws raised. A stone ewe grazed at non-existent grass. A bellowing breeterlik reared on its hind legs, stomach sphincter gaping. Its neighbor was the legendary horse, driven from the valleys during an early famine period. Then came the cerebhawk, poised ready to fly, its opposing heads glaring at each other in frozen anger.

Poised . . .

The guide experienced a momentary twinge of apprehension, transitory, unexplained. Frowning, he returned to where Khira rested and stretched out in the snow. When he closed his eyes, he was for a moment keenly aware of the ache of his muscles. Then weariness anesthetized him and he drowsed.

He woke at Khira's sharp exclamation and sat instantly. Khira was on her knees, peering tensely around the plaza. She turned on him wildly and for the first time that day spoke to him. "Darkchild—there's something—*something*—don't you feel it? In the air?"

At the sharp panic in her voice, the guide jumped up and without thinking scooped up her pike. Was there a crackling sense of electricity in the air? And did the eyestone watch again, from its high tower?

"Darkchild—" Turning, Khira had found the focus of her fear and stared up at it, her lips parting in disbelief. "The cerebhawk—"

The guide gazed up, his pulse pounding. Slowly the stone bird moved, its dominant head turning on its extended neck. The bird peered around, then flexed its wings. Every motion was deliberate, as if the bird were testing the responses of an unfamiliar body. The dominant head drew back and swept the plaza with an angry stare, while the secondary head remained locked in position, helpless, its eyes glittering bleakly. Then, abruptly, the dominant head shot forward and the stone bird uttered a strident cry.

Khira struggled to her feet, one hand flying to her throat. "I thought it was a legend. I thought it was just a story people told—"

Dreadfully the stone bird glared at them, shrieking again. The sound tore at the air.

The *warm* air, warm and crackling, as if an unseen web of energy had fallen across the plaza. Khira and the guide were caught in it, trapped. All around them ice and snow began to melt. The guide stared, open-mouthed, fear chattering through his nervous system, his fingers and toes tingling with it.

With a third tearing cry, the bird launched itself from its perch. The guide knew that if it were a bird of flesh, it should have mahogany and white markings. It did not. Instead it was grey—even its claws, which should have been black. The stone bird swooped across the plaza, one head still locked helplessly into position, the other extended, stone eyes staring, beak parted.

Finally Khira found words. They came weakly, dry husks of sound. "It's my mother. The legend—she can make stone live."

The pike fell from the guide's clenched fingers and color ran from his face. *Tiahna*. There was a legend in the scrolls—he had not read it, but he had seen reference to it—that a barohna had the power to invest herself in stone, to make it move like a living creature, to make it leap, run, scream, cry.

Kill.

"I never believed it," Khira whispered.

Nor had he taken it for more than a legend. But now the legend flew at them, death in its eyes. And they faced it helplessly. The guide wanted to run, to hide. But his muscles were locked in shock.

Struggling against paralysis, Khira bent and retrieved the pike the guide had dropped. The terrible energy of Tiahna's presence snarled and crackled around them, rendering everything unreal: the empty plaza, the melting ice crust, the carved figures, immobile in their niches.

"Mother, no! I made him come with me! I made him run away!" Her voice came in shrill bursts. "The Arnimi told you lies! *Mother*—"

The guide felt his intestines coil with fear. Him—*she had come for him*. She was going to tear him with stone claws. As he stared up, the hawk snapped its stone beak. Its cry was deafening, harsh.

Khira dropped to her knees, the pike falling from her fingers again. As the guide watched helplessly, Khira tried to shape her babbling plea into coherent words, words to save Darkchild by. But her throat closed as the great hawk swooped near and she did not even scream.

A moment later she shrieked with pain. For the hawk flew not at Darkchild but at Khira, dragging its stone claws across her cheek, then swooping up again and soaring away. Khira clasped her bare hand to the bloody wound, unbelieving. The guide stared at her with the same mute disbelief.

Tiahna had not come for him. She had come for Khira.

Why? There was no time to wonder. The hawk passed again, this time snatching at Khira's hair, tugging tufts of it bloody from her scalp. For a moment the hawk hung before them on beating wings, glaring at Khira with eyes the guide knew, Tiahna's eyes. Then the hawk soared away.

"Khira—"

She turned numbly, staring at him with fixed pupils. "She—she's—"

The guide's heart hardly seemed to beat. He stood like a carved figure, rigid, cold, helpless, as the hawk returned, wings spread, head thrust, beak ready to tear. Returned—*for Khira.*

In his fear the guide had forgotten Darkchild. And if the guide could not move, Darkchild could. Bending, he snatched up the pike Khira had dropped and raised it. Startled, the guide struggled silently with Darkchild's renegade muscles, making them writhe and cramp.

Run! The guide broadcast the shrill warning to every muscle. *Run!* Tiahna would have Khira. How could he stop her? But she could not have them both at once, and that meant he had bare moments to race across the plaza and hide himself.

Darkchild fought the guide, rejecting his directive. The screaming hawk burst upon them savagely. With knotting muscles Darkchild threw himself between Khira and the bird, raised the pike and loosed it.

Incredibly the pike placed home in the ghostly grey beast. The bird hung in midair, a shriek frozen in its throat. Then, with a choked cry, it plummeted to the plaza, wings drawn tight in agony, and sank through the melting crust. Steam boiled up furiously, shrouding the place where it had fallen.

Instantly the air of the plaza was cold again. The momentum of his thrust had slammed Darkchild to his knees. His arm sank to his side. When he stood again, when he turned, he looked at Khira with pain in his eyes.

Numbly Khira stepped forward and peered down through the icy crust. The stone hawk had melted its way to the surface of the plaza. It lay there unbroken, the pike buried in its chest. Khira's face twisted. "Mother—" She turned back to Darkchild. "The legend—no one ever killed a barohna when she was stone."

The guide seized at Darkchild's feet, trying to spur them to flight. He succeeded only in taking a single stumbling step back.

Grief, anger, pain—they passed across Khira's face in swift succession. Then both she and the guide realized the air had warmed again. They spun.

High above them the carved snowminx stirred to life. It tossed its stone head, stiff ringlets sweeping across its shoulders. From its throat, Tiahna spoke. "I told you I must know more about your companion, Khira, before I could decide whether he could stay."

Khira faced the stone figure, trembling. "Yes," she whispered. "You told me. Mother—"

"Now I know more. You may stay, Rauth-Seven."

It took the guide a moment to realize he had been reprieved. Then he set aside Darkchild's quick surge of elation for the trembling weakness of relief.

"Go to your redmane cousins for the warmseasons, daughter. Take your companion and teach him whatever he wants to know. We have no need for secrets. Leave when your grandmother tells you and come back to the palace for winter."

Khira nodded. Her words seemed dry, as if her mouth were packed with wool. "Yes. We'll—go."

"Goodsummer then, daughter. Travel well." The snowminx became immobile again.

With Tiahna's going, a cold wind swept down into the valley. The guide looked down and saw that his boots had sunk into the melting crust of the snow. As he watched, the crust froze again, imprisoning his feet.

Laughing giddily with relief, Khira freed her feet from the crust. The stone hawk lay at the bottom of a deep well in the snow. Khira slipped down the frozen well to retrieve her pike. But when she touched its haft, she drew away quickly and scrambled back to where the guide waited. "It's—it's stone! My pike has turned to stone."

The guide peered down the ice well and shuddered. He had felt the pike's smooth wooden haft in Darkchild's hand just minutes before. Tiahna had made stone live and now she had made wood stone.

He could not escape another thought. If Darkchild had accepted his command, if he had run, would they both be ash now? Was that what had decided Tiahna—that Darkchild had defended Khira?

Stricken, the guide drew to the back of Darkchild's mind. He had been charged with keeping Darkchild safe. But if Darkchild had yielded to his instruction, if he had run—

The contract—its terms seemed so clear. To guide Darkchild, to keep him safe, to urge him to explore and learn. But how could the guide know what course of action would protect and what endanger when he could not see beyond the moment and his own fears?

He had been told he would be coolly rational, a safeguard against Darkchild's recklessness. Then where was his own safeguard?

He had none. This time, only Darkchild's recklessness had saved them.

Preoccupied, the guide did not notice that Khira peered at Darkchild narrowly in recognition and held her hand to him. He did not notice that Darkchild and Khira clambered away together across the freezing crust. They pushed at heavy palace doors and stepped into an entryway harsh with the light of long-untrimmed stalklamp. The smell of winter was heavy in the deserted palace. Long corridors were deep in dust. Somewhere a small animal squealed and fled.

That might have been him—squealing, running, crying. Tiahna had told Khira to take Darkchild to the redmane guardians for the warmseasons, but the guide wanted only to retreat to some dark place and hide.

Yet where Darkchild went, he must go. What dangers Darkchild faced, he must face. And without the rewards that were Darkchild's: Khira's hand in his, the warmth of her smile. They were together. He was alone.

TWELVE
KHIRA

From Mingele's valley they traveled ten days through snow-frosted mountains and steaming valleys. Sometimes they heard rockslides in the distance, sometimes the sharp crack of thunder. Shy mountain creatures ran across their trail and they saw frequent signs of predators. During those ten days came many hours Khira cherished—hours when she showed Darkchild her world and saw it freshly through his eyes. His was an eager curiosity. He wanted to know every sign in the snow, wanted to touch every exposed rock and twig. Khira indulged him. There was no hurry to reach the plain.

But interspersed with the good hours were the others, when Darkchild hardly seemed to see the trail before his feet. Times when his eyes gazed inward, times when what he saw hurt. He was especially withdrawn in the mornings when he woke—from what dreams?

She wondered about his dreams sometimes, crouched over a quickly kindled cookfire, turning foraged foodstuffs and staples from her pack into a morning meal. Too often Darkchild joined her silently, eyes averted, hardly aware of her presence.

And sometimes, when he had been particularly troubled, she found she served food to the guide instead of Darkchild. There was no mistaking the guide once he raised eyes to hers. His gaze was flinching, frightened, yet in some way pleading. She might have been touched by it—if his very presence hadn't turned her first brittle-cold, then hotly angry. She could never see him without remembering her dream: Darkchild clumsy on the steep trail, crying out, falling; then, before she could reach him, some shadow of him pushing itself up from the ground—and as the shadow walked away, a second shadow rising to follow the first.

How could he be two and still, at any time, be wholly one? And the other—the guide—who was he but a creature of the Benderzic? Darkchild shared his body with an entity who was stuff of his exploiters. And that must diminish him in a dozen small ways—ways that might someday take him away from her.

He was two, and she must not let the one win her with pleading eyes. She must shrink him with silence and scorn.

Silence and scorn. She honed them to perfection as they traveled through the mountains. She learned when silence would drive the guide away and she learned when scorn would do it. She even learned which of his fears were the greatest and played on them. Shamelessly, since one of his fears was that she would be injured. Another was that she would abandon him. And was that so different from her own fear that Darkchild would leave her?

She examined that thought only once, and it made her so uncomfortable she put it from her mind.

At the end of ten days, with the sun scarlet in a dusk-violet sky, they finally reached a rocky cropping overlooking the plain. Red rock and winter-bitten grasses stretched below them, broken by stunted trees and bare-limb bushes. The sun seemed enormous, as if it might consume the plain. Yet the air was bitter-chill.

Khira looked silently over the plain, stirred. The redmane guardians who had been her remotest ancestresses had patrolled these dark rocks and desolate trees for tens of centuries, watching for breeders come to steal redmanes. They patrolled still, silent in their umber capes—not because breeders often came these days but because the guardians had become a plains people. And now for a summer Khira would be a daughter of the plains too, wading streams with guardian daughters and clinging to the backs of redmane foals.

Darkchild crawled to the edge of the rocky ledge and peered across the plain intently. "We'll have to walk another day before we see the herds," Khira told him, her fist clenching on the strangely carved pike they had brought from Mingele's palace.

He turned, his eyes bright with anticipation. "And the redmane guardians—"

"They'll be with the herds. The plowing teams won't leave for the valleys for at least another hand of days." She gazed across the plain. The wind was sharp on the mountain by night. On the plain, it would be just as bitter and there would be little shelter. "We'll have to shelter here tonight and cross the plain tomorrow. My grandmother and Upala make their kefri in a guardian campment near the northern rim of the plain. We can reach their kefri in a day and a half." She was not surprised to find herself suddenly eager to see her grandmother again, and Upala, Kadura's stone mate.

She turned and peered back up the mountainside. Dusk already cast shadows behind the rocks and made the air grey. She climbed back the way they had come and found a cove of boulders. "We can sleep here."

Darkchild scrambled after her to inspect the rocky cove. "I saw nesting signs back the way we came. I'll bring something for the cookfire."

"Yes." He had made himself a hunter these ten days. Giving him the pike, she crept into the rocky cove and sat down, resting her head against the rocks. Without intending, she fell asleep.

When she woke, the sky was dark. She sat, momentarily disoriented, groping for her pike. But Darkchild had taken it. And he hadn't returned. Alarmed, she crawled from shelter and peered around. Nindra rode low on the horizon, amber in a starred sky. Gazing into the darkness, Khira distinguished only the shadows of the mountainside and, below, the darkness of the plain.

But somewhere something moved. She heard it and caught her breath. "Darkchild?"

He spoke from nearby, whispering. "Khira—someone's coming."

She turned quickly, peering around until she found him in the shadow of a boulder, tensely alert, his eyes gleaming. A string of fresh-killed brownfowl hung from one shoulder. "Where?"

"Up the trail from the plain—there." He inclined his head.

"A guardian," she guessed, but it could be a renegade breeder scouting the way for a stealing party. She slipped forward, peering down the dark mountainside.

After a moment she distinguished a single figure moving in the rocks below, head bowed, limbs lost in the folds of a dark cape. As if summoned by Khira's gaze, the figure paused, raising its head. "Kadura!" Khira cried and ran down the trail.

She threw herself into her grandmother's arms and was enveloped in the black cape Kadura wore. Then she stepped back and peered up into her grandmother's face. "Mother's mother—" But the words died in her throat. She drew back involuntarily.

She had never found age in Kadura's face before, only strength and the promise of compassion. But tonight there was pain in her eyes and her face was visibly thinner, lined. And there was something in her eyes . . . Without thinking, Khira glanced down. Beneath Kadura's cape, a white scarf bound her waist, its ends hanging to her knees.

"Upala—" Khira said with sinking heart.

Kadura's shadowed face contracted and she touched the mourning sash. "Yes. We lost good friends among the guardians last warmseason, and her heart suffered. I found her dead beside me at the end of wintersleep."

Upala . . . gone. For a moment Khira was stricken, then sharply alarmed. "But you—you're not ill?" Quickly she took Kadura's hands. They were as strong as ever, but the veins stood more prominently, and the skin felt dry and loose.

"I'm well, daughter's daughter," Kadura assured her. "But I'm too much alone. Ice is forming where it should not. I'm pleased you've come."

"And I've brought a friend," Khira said quickly.

"Yes, Nezra's stone brought us that message. That you were bringing a child from elsewhere who wants to know how we live." Kadura peered up the mountain, her brows drawn in a faint frown. "Do you suppose he intends his pike for my heart, child?"

Startled, Khira turned and peered up the trail. It was no longer Darkchild who stood on the rocky cropping. Instead the guide hunched there, pike raised. Indignation seized Khira. Angrily she launched herself up the trail. Catching the guide's arm, she spun him around, blind to the quick fear in his eyes. "Would you pike my grandmother?"

He shrank, licking dry lips. "How—how could I tell who it was? In the dark? She came without calling—she pulled you under her cloak. She—she could be anyone!"

"Well, she isn't! She's my mother's mother and she's come to take us to the herds. But she can go back and leave us here if she wants. Or we can both go and leave *you.*"

The guide's face twisted in panic. *"You wouldn't!* Khira—"

"Wouldn't I?" Khira seized the pike and tapped the string of fowl he carried forgotten in one hand. Her anger was not calculated; it was genuine. "I could leave you and you'd starve in a day. You don't know how to pike these—you don't even know how to pluck them for roasting. Do you?" She refused to be touched by the trembling fear in his face. "Do you?"

Kadura had followed Khira up the trail, tall and silent in her dark cape. Now she spoke. "Do you always abuse your friend, Khira?"

Khira spun, bristling at the rebuke. "This isn't my friend!" She snatched at the string of fowl, and the guide jumped back, letting them fall. "I'll pluck these myself," she said, directing a fiery glance at him. "Maybe by the time they're ready for roasting, someone will build a fire. If anyone here knows how." She stalked away, leaving the guide gazing up empty-handed at Kadura.

Khira set to the plucking with a fury, hardly aware that the guide had slipped away to gather moss and twigs for the fire. After a moment Kadura joined Khira and Khira found herself uncomfortable in her silent presence. Was it judging? Stern? Khira's anger turned sour in her mouth. She glanced up at Kadura, expecting some further rebuke for her temper. But Kadura looked at her from shadowed eyes and said only, "You've had a loss too since I saw you last, Khira."

For a moment Khira did not know what she meant. Then her eyes fell to Kadura's mourning sash and she said in surprise, "Alzaja is gone." It was long since she had thought of her sister. The summer they had spent with Kadura and Upala seemed a lifetime ago, although it had been just three years before. Her eyes narrowed, trying to penetrate the shadows that fell upon Kadura's face. "Did you know—"

"Did I know she wouldn't succeed in her challenge?" Darkchild had returned to the rocky cove—Khira knew instantly it was him and not the guide—and had begun building a fire. Kadura watched as he worked, her face shadowed, her voice remote. "I guessed it, of course. Alzaja was tender—in ways I'm sure she explained to you before she went."

"She told me about—about the ice and the stone," Khira said with frowning reluctance. She had put those things behind her when she left the valley and she was not eager to take them up again now. She had enough to concern her with Darkchild.

Kadura nodded, her eyes lingering on Darkchild's intent face as he worked over the fire, striking the spark, kindling it to life, blowing carefully on the fledgling flame. "The boy who was here a few minutes ago was not your friend. This boy is, I think."

Unexpectedly Khira flushed. "He—is."

"And the other?" Kadura probed. She threw back her hood and shook down her hair. It was dark, sparsely streaked with white. It fell heavily across her shoulders, making her seem like some dark-maned plains legend, wise in her age. Her face, shorn of shadow, had the barohnial strength Khira remembered.

"The other—the other was his guide." Stubbornly Khira gazed at the ground. If Kadura wanted to know more than that—

But Kadura only nodded and continued to watch Darkchild as he spitted the birds and roasted them. He did not glance up at her until the birds were browned, and then it was her sash that drew his attention.

They ate, Kadura silent, Darkchild flirting glances at the white sash that gleamed beneath her cape, Khira tensely poised. When the cookfire flickered into nervous embers and they had thrown the bones of the roasted fowl aside, Kadura turned her attention fully to Darkchild. "No one has told me your name, Khira's friend."

He wrenched his gaze from her sash and met her eyes with a moment's flinching wariness. His voice was husky. "I'm named for the shadows: Darkchild."

"Ah. Then the shadows have eyes—do they not, Darkchild? Bright eyes?" Kadura stroked her scarf.

Darkchild dropped his gaze, flushing.

"No, no, I'm not rebuking you. I like to think about names, about how they define the people who carry them. Tonight you are a child looking out of the dark—but you see everything around you, no matter how shadowed. So you make your own light, and perhaps one day you will have to change your name. Is that permitted among your people?"

He raised his head warily, trying to read her gaze. "I—I don't know. It isn't among yours."

"No, but then our names seldom have any particular meaning. I've wondered sometimes—" For a moment she seemed to recede into her thoughts. "I've wondered if having a name with meaning molds the person who carries it. Upala, my stone mate, was one of the few whose name described something other than herself. And in my mind, she came to resemble the stone her name described. But did she become as the stone because she carried its name—or because that was her nature, no matter how she was named?"

"She was named for a stone?" Khira said, surprised.

Kadura nodded, fingering her mourning sash. "The upala was a milky white stone the first timers carried when they were stranded.

You'll read of them in the very earliest scrolls. When you gazed into the upala, deep inside you saw fire of every color. The gem masters never faceted it. They simply polished it to bring out the fire."

Khira frowned. "I've never seen a stone like that."

"Because they no longer exist. They were fragile and they crumbled. Upala was like that to me—a still surface that hid fire. I had to look deeply, but when I did, I saw the fire. Not to be touched— only to be glimpsed, and then only if I looked closely."

"And now she has crumbled," Darkchild said, and Khira glanced at him sharply.

Kadura nodded, gathering her hair, pulling the hood over it. Her face retreated into shadow again. Her voice fell to a husky thread. "She has crumbled, but she's left me memories, Darkchild. I remember the day I took my pairing stone from the gem master and put it on my neck. I felt Upala's fingers in my mind for the first time that day, but it seemed to me I had waited all my years for her cool touch in my mind." Her eyes studied Khira, but they seemed distant, as if they saw herself instead, younger. "You'll know that touch one day, Khira. And when it comes, you'll realize how alone you have been."

Khira recoiled, glancing quickly at Darkchild. "I'm not alone."

Sighing, Kadura returned from a distance. "You have your friend, of course. And I'm an old woman who needs to sleep before we walk tomorrow."

An old woman. Khira watched her grandmother as they crossed the plain the next day. Her stride was still firm, her shoulders steady. Khira knew she would never be old in the withered, helpless way of valley women. But there were long times when she walked blindly, absorbed in some reverie, hardly aware of Khira and Darkchild. And by daylight the strength in her face seemed eroded by loss.

Yet whenever one of them spoke to her, she made the long journey back and answered with attention. Sometimes it seemed to Khira that she regarded Darkchild with special thought as the morning wore on, as if she were heeding him with some sense Khira did not possess. And he seemed aware of her attention and walked silently beside her, his eyes lingering on her sash.

When they stopped for their midday meal, Kadura said, "We may see stray 'manes from the herds this afternoon. Stay near me, Darkchild, until they accept you. The plow teams have seen people from the valleys, but most of the herd 'manes have never seen a human male."

Darkchild had been studying the ground, absently drawing one forefinger through the dirt. He glanced up in quick surprise. "There are no men in the plain at all?"

For a moment Kadura studied the lines he had made in the dirt. "No. None."

"But the guardians bear children. Khira's told me that."

Kadura smiled faintly. "There are men in the valleys, Darkchild. When a guardian wants to bear a child, she must go there for a time."

"Then—if her child is male?"

For a moment Kadura's eyes lingered on him regretfully. "No guardian ever bears a male infant to term, any more than a barohna ever does so. We have no sons here, Darkchild—only daughters." Deliberately Kadura slid back her hood and shook her hair over her shoulders. "The Arnimi outworlders tell us there are human cultures where no woman considers herself complete until she has a son. Have you heard of places like that, Darkchild?"

"I—I don't know," Darkchild said in confusion. When she said nothing more, he touched his lips with his tongue and finally, in hurried confidence, said, "I have brothers."

"Ah." Kadura drew her fingers through her hair, holding the dark strands to the breeze, calculating the effect of her words. "But no sisters, Darkchild?"

"No." Softly. Tentatively.

"Still perhaps you know of people where some women have only daughters and think of sons."

Khira squirmed resentfully. There were things in this conversation she did not understand: the patterns Darkchild's finger made in the dirt, the calculation in Kadura's words. Somehow they excluded her much as Tiahna excluded her when she paused in conversation to touch her pairing stone. "He has no people," she said sharply. "He's a Rauthimage."

Darkchild glanced at her uncomfortably. When Kadura did not respond to Khira's comment, he wet his lips with the tip of his tongue again. "The silk you wear—may I touch it?"

Khira jumped up, clutching his arm. But Kadura gestured her aside. "Of course you may. There are tens of these in the memory house near our kefri. I chose white because Upala was named for a white stone."

He nodded, touching the scarf carefully. His fingers tensed, and Khira thought he would bunch the scarf. But he did not. He only permitted himself to stroke it lightly, once, then drew back. When he sat again, his finger did not return to its absent marking. Instead his fists lay clenched on his legs.

Kadura spoke softly. "You may touch the others when we reach the campment if you want."

Darkchild nodded, but Khira noticed that he had averted his eyes from the scarf and stared intently at the ground, his jaw muscles clenching.

Khira's fists knotted too, but with a different tension. She wanted to protest—but protest what? That Kadura said things to Darkchild that she could not understand? That Kadura seemed instinctively to know Darkchild at some level where Khira did not? "I want to see the 'manes," Khira said abruptly. She flung her pack over her shoulder and hurried away, fleeing some vagrant thought that hurt.

When Kadura and Darkchild followed, it was at a distance. Khira turned several times as she ran ahead of them, but she could not tell whether they talked or whether they walked together silently.

It was an hour before Khira joined them again. The three of them walked together without speaking, Darkchild's manner silent, distracted—as if Kadura's presence directed his attention inward. Khira frowned uncomfortably, feeling that some communication had passed between them that excluded her.

Kadura touched her arm lightly. "Tomorrow we will reach the campment, daughter's daughter. Then you and Darkchild can ride the 'manes and wade in the streams and do summer things with the guardian daughters."

Khira bristled. Was she a child, to be appeased with a child's pleasures when her intimacy with Darkchild had been compromised in some way she did not understand? "I have other plans," she said stiffly.

Kadura regarded her with a thoughtful frown. "Does it disturb you so much that I study your friend?"

Khira scowled. "Study him all you want!" she snapped, wondering at her spite. It was like some harsh new jealousy, disturbing in its intensity. "Study his guide too, and tell me what you learn." Without waiting for a reply, she ran ahead again.

They ate from their packs that night, building a fire to brew drinks. Again Darkchild drew sparks from the tinder and breathed the fire alive. Then he slipped back into the reverie that had gripped him earlier in the day. Though neither he nor Kadura spoke, Khira scowled into the fire, her hands tight on her mug, and felt alone.

Alone . . . Absently she remembered what Kadura had said of Upala's first coming, of cool fingers of thought joining hers. Her own stone mate would find Khira's thoughts an angry chaos—so angry perhaps she would withdraw and never return.

She looked up to find Kadura studying her. "You'll have your companion back, granddaughter."

As if she had traced the line of Khira's thoughts simply by studying her face! "How do you know I want him?" Khira demanded bitterly. "I was alone for months after Alzaja and I did well enough."

"Ah. Then why have those months left a mark on your face, Khira?"

Involuntarily Khira touched her face. "You—you see nothing there."

"I see a great deal," Kadura rebuked her. "You're how old? Twelve? You had your day just a few days ago, didn't you?"

"I—I didn't observe it." In fact she had forgotten her day until now.

"Even unobserved, it made you twelve. But do you know how many years I've lived? Over two hundred. In that time I've given birth to a dozen daughters, raised them and saw two bronze and ten die. I brought early spring to my valley more years than I care to remember. I worked the stones—the sunstone, the eyestone and the pairing stone.

"I took a stone mate and we lived almost a century in each other's thoughts. Then when your mother bronzed and my heart turned flesh again, Upala and I knew a period of hardship that neither of us ever forgot. Upala's only surviving daughter was a child of six, years from bronzing, and suddenly because I had lost the power of the stones, Upala was alone in her thoughts—and she lost the power too. It went right out of her heart.

"She left her valley—she had no choice—and came to the plain with me. And for years we lived here while the valley she had nurtured grew cold and barren. Each year the crops were smaller, the people fewer. Some left, some died—everything she had spent her life for slipped away. We were together, but the pain was between us every day.

"Her daughter made her challenge at her first majority, when she was thirteen, and died—and there was more pain between us. It was eleven years before Melora, Tandara's second daughter to bronze, came to take the throne and restore the people. Eleven years before our own good years could begin.

"Do you wonder that after all I've known I can read things in your face that you think are hidden? I see the loss you had when Alzaja died, the joy you had when your friend came. And I see all the fears and angers you've had with him in the interval—including those you have now."

Khira's muscles pulled tight. How could Kadura see so much when she hardly seemed to look? "Then what do you see in Darkchild's face? Or can you read that?"

"I can, granddaughter." Kadura glanced at Darkchild. He had removed himself from them and peered into the fire, lost in thought. "You consider him two people and so does he. But he is one with a divided awareness—one person divided from himself. As your friend Darkchild, he is shut into one room of his life, unable to find doors into the others—rooms he knows must exist because he hears sounds from beyond the walls. There are certain things that make him feel he is about to find those doors. My scarf is one. He thinks he might open doors with my scarf.

"But the guide is afraid that if Darkchild opens doors, he will find things behind them that will hurt more than being divided and alone. And so when Darkchild reaches for those doors, the guide holds them ever more firmly shut. The guide is even trying to keep his own feelings shut against you—but the harder he tries, the less he succeeds." Kadura smiled, the lines of her face falling into repose. "That's what I see in your friend, Khira."

"He talked to you!" Khira exclaimed, nettled.

"Very little."

"Then how do you know any of that?" If he hadn't said things to Kadura he had denied her, if he hadn't openly shared his thoughts . . .

"Perhaps you're too angry to understand me, Khira. I need very few words from other people to know them. Very few indeed. Often I need no words at all."

Khira stared at Kadura, suddenly frightened by the serenity that had come to her lined face. Great coldness gripped her. "You've learned to move among minds," she said, stricken. There were whispers among the people that certain barohnas who had left their stones could exercise that power. Khira had never given the rumor credence.

Kadura pulled up the hood of her cape, shadowing her face from Khira. "You could call it that, granddaughter. I think of it as bridging—reaching from the loneliness of my mind to the loneliness of another's. When Upala and I could no longer enter each other's minds through the pairing stones, we found we must communicate in other ways. Because we knew each other so well, we found it easy to read small signs in each other: an inclination of the head, a passing frown, any small gesture. We learned to read both the thought and the feeling behind these. Soon it was hardly necessary for us to speak to each other.

"Later we learned that others shared the same unspoken language. We learned to read what they said to us with their bodies and we learned to read what time and experience had recorded in their faces. Perhaps we read far beyond that—it's hard for me to set boundaries between myself and another and then to calculate how far within those boundaries I've penetrated.

"If you want to call this moving among minds, then I do it. I can't help doing it, anymore than you can help seeing the prints of a breeterlik in the snow or storm clouds in the sky. It's become so customary I hardly realize now that I do it."

Khira stood, tense, angry at Kadura's revelation. When Darkchild looked up, she demanded, "How do you like that? How do you like being read like a scroll? How do you like my grandmother knowing what's in your mind from what she sees on your face?"

Darkchild frowned faintly, troubled. "Does it disturb you?"

"Don't quiz me! I want to know how *you* feel!"

He glanced covertly at Kadura and sighed. "I—I don't mind it."

Not only did he not mind, she saw. He was comforted—comforted to have Kadura see into him and speak to what was there. Slowly Khira sank back down beside the fire. If he was comforted, why should she be angry? Because she could not share the intimacy of his mind as Kadura could? Because what the two of them shared excluded her? Or because she did not want to admit that Kadura could read her as clearly as she could read Darkchild?

No, she did not want her thoughts bare to anyone—because of their very pettiness. There was no order to her thoughts and no serenity. They were colored with angers and jealousies that she would hide even from herself if she could.

She bit her lip, peering up into Kadura's shadowed eyes. Not

only were her thoughts filled with pettiness. She had spoken to
Kadura with the greatest rudeness, doubting her, challenging her,
all but accusing her. And Kadura had answered with nothing but
patience. "My grandmother—" she pleaded. There was much to
forgive. If Kadura could forgive at least some of it—

"I always forgive the young, Khira," Kadura said from the shadows of her hood. "At your age, I was much the same—full of
energies and needs and what I considered pettinesses. Over the
years other things gradually took their place. That is the natural
order of life. Age never comes before youth."

But did youth have to be thoughtless? Rude?

"No," Kadura said. "Youth is the time to learn not to be
thoughtless. To grow in spirit as you grow in body. And if you wish
to grow, you can begin with your friend."

"Darkchild?"

Slowly Kadura shook her head. "The other—the one you despise. Or think you despise. You have some tenderness for him too.
You can begin growing by examining that tenderness, by fostering
it. Your friend has trouble within himself. If you support him, even
that aspect of him you like least, you will strengthen him to deal
with his inner difficulty."

"And if I—if I do that—then Darkchild won't leave me again?"

Kadura sighed. "Granddaughter, I can't promise you that. But if
you can bring yourself to support both aspects of your friend, to
tolerate him when he speaks to you as the guide just as you do
when he speaks to you as Darkchild—if you can bring yourself to
care for him whichever face he presents—certainly the support will
make him stronger."

Khira drew back from the fire, shrinking from Kadura's suggestion. Care for the guide? When his very presence meant Darkchild
had left her? Her fists tightened and the muscles of her arms
cramped. "I'll never care for him! I can't!"

"You feel that way now," Kadura said. "You may always feel
that way if you permit it. But I think you are old enough to begin to
manage your feelings, to begin to master them."

"No. No, mother's mother—" How could she care for the guide
when she felt angry at the very sight of him?

"It is really very simple," Kadura answered her. "Now when you
see him you feel confused and angry and you lash out. You address
your anger to him. The first thing you must do is refuse to behave

in an angry way. You must learn to put on the face you want him to see—the accepting face.

"That seems hard. But after a time it will no longer be just a face. You will no longer be making a pretense. Eventually the act becomes the reality, Khira. If you behave in an accepting manner toward the guide, soon you will accept him."

"No—"

"Yes, even the guide, Khira."

Khira recognized the finality in Kadura's words and argued no more. But as she settled for the night, she had to stifle a rebellious desire to disavow everything Kadura had said. Darkchild and the guide were two—and she could never learn to care for the guide. If she had her wish, she would never see him again.

Never.

Khira lay awake long after Kadura wrapped herself in her cape and closed her eyes. The fire died to embers and Darkchild curled near it. Dimly Khira realized that he was wakeful too.

If only he could answer her questions. If only he could tell her where he went when the guide appeared, what he did; if only he could describe the state of his awareness then—

At last she stirred and sat. "Darkchild—" But it was the guide who gazed at her across the embers.

Her anger came so quickly it took her breath. *The guide!* He made anger flare in her like fire in dry leaves. And Kadura wanted her to control the fire? Biting her tongue, Khira jumped up and backed from the embers, backed into darkness. She stumbled from the fire in anger and confusion, finally throwing herself down beside a boulder a distance away. The night was bitter cold but she hardly noticed.

Manage her feelings? Master them? Put on a face that was a lie in the hope that even her feelings would become a lie? Khira wanted to run back to where Kadura lay, to throw herself into her grandmother's arms and tell her that she could do none of these things.

But she did not. She huddled against the boulder until her anger ebbed, leaving only a gritty residue of shame. Then she returned to the fire and lay down again, wide-eyed, sleepless, making herself promises she could never hope to meet.

THIRTEEN
KADURA

Kadura felt the dream as if it were her own, as if she had become transparent and it passed through her.

It was daylight and the boy walked a white-pebbled path beneath trees that wept silver leaves. He was younger than she knew him, slighter, and he moved along the path with stomach-knotting tension. Far ahead he heard voices. Singing? Calling? No—laughing. Hearing them, he felt the familiar leap of joy—and then turned rigid. The dream seldom went past this point: the path, the voices, the reaching. Beyond these lay only anger and loss as the dream was snatched away.

But tonight—Kadura frowned: was it because of something she had said? was it because she had let the boy touch her sash?—he continued down the path. The images continued to form before him: the branching of ways, one fork leading to the dancing glade, the other to the hamlet. He chose the second fork, and when the dream still was not snatched from him, his heart began to pound against his ribs, making his breath short. If he could move quickly enough, if he could run, perhaps he could reach the edge of the hamlet before the dream vanished. Perhaps—

Afraid to hope, he forced the dream to flow ahead. It carried him quickly through the nesting bushes where bluerunners chuckled, past the first and second kneeling posts—he paused, but only momentarily, to press his forehead against the polished stone pillars—past the public ponds where the untempled must sow their seed. By then the voices were clearer and he stood at the edge of the hamlet. It was a place of rambling, airy structures, roofless houses sheltered by the bending trees that stood around them. When it rained, the people felt a light, cooling mist through the leaves. When the sun shone, its light fell dappled everywhere.

He paused, hardly daring to breathe. It was so fragile, this dream, and so full of longing. He had reached for it so many times. If it vanished now—

But it did not. It remained. With an eager rush, he ran down the path. When he reached the house where the family lived, when he passed through its open door, an entire montage of faces and scenes came to him so quickly he could scarcely sort them.

His dream was a reunion, a return to people he had almost forgotten he had lost. He rejoined them with tearful eagerness: the violet-eyed woman who knelt beside him as he took pen in hand and made his first marks upon a thick block of yellow bond, the girls who sang in the next room, the men who talked outside while silver leaves whispered.

He had been nowhere, hungry and frightened and alone, his mind an emptiness. Then the woman had found him and suddenly he had a home and sisters, three of them. They wore robes of sunset colors and they chattered happily, each word clear and singing, while he struggled simply to make himself understood. But he was the one the woman bent to each day after he had bathed. He was the one she taught to use pen and paper.

Because he was the one whose presence gave the family license to kneel in the sky-roofed temple with the other families. No family could kneel there until there was a son to sign the family names in the yellowing pages of the register. And until he had come—how? from where? and why had his mind been so empty?—there had been no son for this family.

Now he was the son.

Came the day—in the way of dreams it came swiftly, before its time—when he could form the characters of each name properly. Then the entire family walked beneath the arched span of the temple with proud shoulders and knelt to hear the wind singing through the strings of the godsvoice.

While they listened to the voice of the templed god, the women and the girls combed out their midnight hair with their fingers and let the god speak through those strands too. No man was permitted long hair, so no man could ever hear the godsvoice in that intimate way. But once the godsvoice had spoken through the hair of the woman and her daughters, the seeds they cast on the family pond would sprout in plenty and in the brown mud the sweetest bulbs would multiply more rapidly than they could feast on them. They would never have to cast seed in the public ponds again and they would never again be hungry.

Godsvoice—the woman had told him how it was created, by finely drawn strands of metal stretched tight and raised to the wind. She had told him how the godsvoice worked too, how it touched the people in a secret way that made their prayers powerful and their wishes accessible. Their first wish, of course, was that their pond feed them well. Their second—

The boy moaned, suddenly hearing something else in his dream —not the woman's voice, not the godsvoice, but another metal voice. It came first as a deep, droning sound in the distance. Then it was nearer, a tearing metallic scream.

Abruptly the fabric of the dream tore. The boy sat with a sharp cry, clutching his bedding, struggling for breath. *The droning, the scream—and something in the sky, a shape he could not distinguish* . . . For a few moments, the remnant of the dream clung in his mind, making him tremble with terror. Beyond the terror was something worse, something he could not bear. He shuddered and abruptly, as if a door had been closed, the dream vanished. No shred of it remained, visual or aural. There was only fear.

Fear so intense Kadura had to will herself shut against it, before the undisciplined rush of blood damaged her heart.

The boy's cry had wakened Khira. She sat in confusion. "Darkchild?"

He stared at her numbly, as if he looked beyond her into emptiness. "I—I had a dream."

Khira dismissed her waking confusion quickly. "A nightmare? Darkchild—what did you dream?"

As yesterday, Kadura was touched by the depth of Khira's concern. Time had passed since the summer Khira had run the plain with the guardian daughters and Alzaja had watched and secretly wondered if she would ever settle from her wildness.

"What did you dream?" Khira pressed when Darkchild did not answer.

He shook his head. "I don't remember. I thought—I thought it was good. But—"

Yes, a joyous dream that had ended in terror. And now he remembered nothing. He had only the dregs: fear. He turned to Kadura, and for a moment she saw herself with his eyes: the spent power of her presence, the face set so long in its folds and creases that it told nothing of her present thoughts, and her eyes—eyes that saw, relieving him of the necessity of words. "Kadura—"

"Yes, Darkchild. You need to get away for a while. It will be light soon. Walk until then. Khira—"

"I'll go with him."

"Yes." Kadura watched them into the greyness and then continued to sit, her hood sheltering her face against morning chill. So strange to deal with fears and passions after the silence of winter. So strange to feel the rush of youth in her thoughts, keen and clear and aching. She wondered, for a moment, if her heart still had the elasticity to meet what she found in these two. The first ice had touched her heart when Upala died and it gave her pain now, as she waited for Darkchild and Khira to return.

Troubled, Kadura rose and began gathering sticks and moss for the morning fire.

Khira and the boy returned as she had instructed them, Darkchild calmer but distracted, still reaching for lost images. They traveled soon after dawn. The plain was desolate in the cold shadows of morning. Only an occasional gnarled tree broke its brown monotony. Within an hour they met a solitary redmane, an elderly buck with faded mane and fat haunches. He accepted the boy readily and carried both Khira and the boy without protest. Later, when they met a small herd, Khira and the boy selected younger mounts. Soon they rode as heedlessly as if there had been no dream of metal voices.

Kadura's mood lightened as the sun warmed the plain. They reached the campment at midday: caped guardians silent at the doors of their mud-walled kefris, bright-haired guardian daughters running through the sparse, early spring grass, redmanes grazing, and for Kadura the welcome shelter of her own kefri. She pushed aside the stretched skin that served as her door, pleased to return to her own fireside.

But Khira was restless and soon took the boy with her to visit favored spots. It was near night when they returned, wind-bitten and hungry, smelling of dust and redmanes. "Mother's mother, there's a teaching tonight. Can we go with you?" Khira demanded when she pushed through the door.

The boy paused behind her, touching the coarse netting that covered the sloping interior walls of the kefri, studying the lamps in their brackets and the soft mats arranged around the firepit. Then he turned to Kadura and raised his brows experimentally. *Will the guardians let me come to the teaching?* In his mind was the image of the tall silent women he had seen that afternoon, their faces shadowed and forbidding.

Kadura nodded to his silent question. "We will go to the teaching together, Khira, if you can keep your eyes open."

Khira laughed sharply, throwing herself down by the firepit. The wind and the company of the guardian daughters had burnished her spirits. "I won't sleep. Mother's mother—"

"Yes?" In the boy's mind, carefully framed, was another silent question. *If I can talk to you this way, why does Khira ask you aloud, Kadura?* Kadura smiled, declining the question although she was pleased he had realized he could address her directly without speaking.

Khira frowned impatiently. "Mother's mother—if Darkchild sits for the teaching—"

Kadura finished the groping thought for her. "If he were to listen as the guardian daughters listen for as many years as they listen, I think he would learn the same things they learn."

"Just as I would learn, if I stayed here?"

"Just as you would learn if you stayed and listened in the proper way. Not with your ears, but with the soles of your feet, with the palms of your hands, with the marrow of your bones." She was aware of the dampening effect her words had on Khira, who was a creature of sight and sound. At the same time she felt the boy's heightened excitement. He had left his morning fear behind. The afternoon had left him eager for everything the plain had to offer. "But first you must eat and then you must put on the nightcloaks I took from the storehouse for you. Otherwise you will take chill."

They left the kefri when Nindra rose and walked through the campment with the others, the guardians silent in their heavy nightcloaks, their daughters laughing and running, auburn hair like silk on the night breeze. The teaching place was an area of hard-pounded soil beyond the campment. It was grassless in every direction and sloped gently to a shallow basin filled with spring water.

"We sit here, at the top of the slope," Kadura instructed Darkchild. "The guardians and their daughters sit nearer the pond."

And they learn about the redmanes by listening with their bodies? They learn—?

"I can't tell you what they learn, Darkchild. The ways of the redmanes aren't the ways of people. Each person who learns here learns something different."

And that's why the guardians are so silent, he rushed ahead eagerly. *Because they listen to the redmanes. They don't have to talk with each other when they're lonely. They hear the animals.*

"You've learned a lot today. A guardian can train herself to pick out the footfall of an individual animal within its herd—and from a great distance. She can monitor the rhythm of its heart, the surge of its blood. If that animal becomes alarmed or angry, the guardian will know. A guardian can even tell which mares are carrying live foals and which dead—and when they will deliver."

His eyes darkened in excitement. *They bridge to the redmanes like you bridge to me.*

Kadura nodded, aware that Khira was struggling to hold back possessive anger. "A little like that—yes."

But they don't bridge to each other?

"No—and I'm surprised you haven't noticed that Khira is uncomfortable when you speak to me without talking."

A quick narrowing of his pupils marked his discomfiture. "Khira—" But Khira averted her eyes, frowning, and refused to respond to his apology.

Then it was time for the teaching. The time was marked, as always, by the arrival of the first redmane at the spring. The elderly buck who earlier had carried Darkchild and Khira appeared from the dark and approached the water. His mane hung ragged and the coarse hair of his tail was tangled. But by Nindra's light, his haunches seemed more powerful than fat and he ignored the wind that tore at his dense coat.

He stood for a while beside the spring, gazing up at the assembled guardians and daughters. When the last restless daughter settled quietly in her mother's shadow, the buck lowered his head to drink.

"We place our palms to the ground now," Kadura instructed Darkchild. "And our feet."

"But my boots—" Darkchild gazed at the buck in fascination.

"He's different tonight, isn't he? And your boots won't hinder you if you make yourself still—very still everywhere, in your mind, in your body."

If I reach out to him—

"No, don't reach out. Make yourself empty—totally empty—and wait. And don't expect anything tonight. This is your first teaching. You don't yet know how to listen with your body." But she realized, as he placed his hands lightly on the packed earth, that to some extent he did know. Listening with more than ears was inbred in him.

The buck raised his head from drinking and peered at the girls and women who sat so still, so empty. Kadura sighed, letting the world slip away, letting the buck's heartbeat enter her. There was pain in one of his legs, an irritation of the joint, and deep in his abdomen a blood vessel had become twisted and the blood did not pass as readily as it should. But he felt the rising of spring throughout his body and he raised his head and shrilled.

Kadura withdrew her consciousness from him, making herself empty again as the mare padded to the spring to join him. She was even older than he, but her body held memory of a younger time, of bondings and matings and foals, and she moved with pondersome grace. She grunted in answer to the buck, then bent her head to drink. She was the oldest mare of her herd and she carried the knowledge of their kind in the very tissues of her body, carried it like a compendium of redmane wisdom. She knew where to look for the tenderest grass whatever the season, knew how to find water even in the driest days of summer, knew how a foal should look and smell in the first moments after birth, knew everything a redmane must know to live.

Behind her gathered others, younger, stronger, restless. They waited as she drank, their heads lowered, their ears soft flaps lost in coarse fur, their eyes empty as they opened themselves to her. Teachings had happened on the plain long before the first guardian had come. At the springs and at the streams, redmanes had always gathered on moonlit nights and stood in the presence of age to learn.

Kadura let her breath sigh away. Sometimes the cares and responsibilities she had put down so many years ago still burdened her: decisions made, mates chosen, daughters sent to die. When she emptied herself of all those things and let the secrets of the redmanes enter, she became ageless. She joined the dust of the plain, and in dust there was no weariness and no pain, no loss, ever.

Dust.

Take care, my herd. Pondwater smells different when stingmadders nest in the rocks. It smells this way . . . this way . . . and when it smells so you must not drink or you will surely be stung.

Beware, my herd. There are places on the plain where you must not walk. Corrosives have been dissolved from the underlayers and have come to the surface and your pads will burn. When you near such a place, you will know it immediately by the dusty shimmer in the air, a shimmer that will look to you . . . this way.

Mind me, mares. There are years when you must not foal. In those years, the egg has formed improperly and to conceive would be to misconceive. You will know that is the case by the tightness in your abdomen when your mate approaches you. It will feel to you . . . this way . . .

Listen, foals. Near the end of summer, you must eat certain barks and leaves to balance the nutrients you have taken from the fresh grasses. At those times, there will be a sensation at the back of your throat that will feel to you . . . this way . . .

So the teaching went. The buck had wisdom too and the younger animals received it from him, as did the guardians and their daughters. As the teaching went on and the second moon rose, Kadura saw that Khira had curled down in to her nightcloak and fallen asleep. The boy sat with hands and feet flat to the ground, the day's excitement still vividly in his mind despite his effort to empty himself.

"Child, this way," Kadura instructed him. "Close your eyes as I do and with each breath, let one thought leave you. Let it slip away on your breath, until all are gone."

Everything?

"Yes, everything. You must let your mind become completely empty."

He sighed, lidding his eyes, letting his head fall forward. He attuned his breathing to Kadura's, inhaling deeply, extending his exhalations. Slowly Kadura felt the level of his thoughts sinking. His body relaxed until his forehead rested against his knees.

Doors. They formed dimly in his mind. His body tensed again and his hands clenched.

"Let the doors go," Kadura instructed. "If you want to learn, you must empty yourself of everything, even those."

He wanted to learn. He attuned his breathing to hers again, and with each sighing exhalation, the doors became fainter. Unconsciously he opened his hands and pressed them to the soil. His face had become pale, his mind barren.

He was empty.

Empty—and then his consciousness filled with light, faces, fear. Kadura recoiled, feeling the panic-surge of blood to her heart. Swift-riding images filled the boy's carefully emptied mind. He was in a place of metal walls. He lay on a metal table, restrained by straps. Cold-eyed people stood over him. They wore black and their eyes were the grey of the metal walls. They spoke incomprehensibly among themselves, their voices muffled. Helpless on the table, the boy had fresh memory of the sting of a needle. It numbed him, removing him from the people who surrounded him. Even if his arms were free, he could not reach those people.

But they could reach him, effortlessly. He struggled to keep his eyes open, fought to plead with them in the only language he knew, even though it was not a language they would understand.

They would understand it soon enough, because now the metal helmet hung over his head, its needles ready to pierce his scalp and steal his thoughts. Desperately he fought the straps. Relentlessly the helmet drifted toward him. With terrible effort, as its needles touched his scalp, he drew a deep breath and released it in a scream.

Kadura shuddered, clutching her chest, and the boy jumped to his feet, startled from his trance by his own scream. He stared down at her wildly, his lips working. Then, his body stiff, every movement forced, he turned and ran from the teaching place.

Kadura tried to fend away the clenching pain in her chest. Had he screamed aloud or had it been a remembered cry that had stiffened them both? Khira had not stirred, nor did the guardians or their daughters turn to peer. The teaching continued.

No matter which the nature of the cry. The boy should not be alone and she had no strength to follow him. His cry had driven fresh swords of ice into her heart. "Khira—" She hardly had breath for words. "Khira—your friend needs you."

Khira blinked owlishly, struggling to wakefulness. "Darkchild?"

"Your friend—be with him. He went back toward the campment."

It took Khira moments longer to waken. Then she said, "I'll take him to the kefri," and was gone.

Kadura remained at the teaching place until the pain in her chest eased. Then she stood and slowly made her way back to the campment, even less certain than before that her heart had the strength to meet what she found in the boy. There was a great coldness in her chest.

Khira and the boy huddled on opposite sides of the firepit, silent, still buried in their nightcloaks. Kadura paused at the door, armoring herself against their tension—the boy's pain, Khira's anger. When she stepped into the kefri, she went first to the boy. "You must take off your cloak when you sit by the fire. If you perspire too heavily, you'll take chill."

Instead of obeying, he stared up at her with trapped eyes and hunched tighter into the garment. She read his dilemma clearly in his face. She was the one who had tricked him into letting the doors dissolve. She was the one who had prompted the emptiness into which the Benderzic had come. She was the one he must guard against.

Yet she was also the one who understood. She understood the darkness that lay behind him—in its fullest extent.

Sighing, Kadura sat beside him. "Yes—too well. I understand too well what you're trying to protect yourself against." Because she had caught not just the horror of the helmet but the deeper nuances of what had happened to him, of how he had been used against the people who had fed him and given him comfort.

He gazed up at her tensely and she read conflict in his eyes. He should say nothing to her. But the terror was heavy upon him, and if he could not dissolve it in words—

"Not me—*him,*" he said, clutching her hand. "I have to protect *him.*"

Darkchild. Kadura touched his cloaked shoulder, trying to reach past the fear that sundered him. "Child, you are him. You are Darkchild." Was he ready to hear it?

"No," he said. "I am his guide. I'm the one who keeps him safe. I'm the one who keeps the doors closed."

"But do you want to live behind closed doors? I think you've lived behind those doors long enough. You aren't responsible for the use the Benderzic made of you. If you can accept what has happened—"

"*No!*"

Kadura drew back involuntarily, willing her heart not to contract at the despair behind the single word. It was easy for her to see what he must do; hard for him to do it. Even as she studiously dismissed tension from her shoulders and upper arms, she watched him set himself at a distance from his own emotion. Memory became grey, feeling diffuse.

She clasped his shoulder again, trying to draw him back. "Child, what do you achieve by erecting these barriers? What do you accomplish by putting your fear so far from you? You—"

"I have no fear," he said in a harsh voice, forcing the words through clenched teeth. Perspiration glittered on his forehead. *"He's* afraid—Darkchild's afraid. I'm not."

Khira had listened impatiently. Now she threw off her night-cloak and leaned toward the fire, her eyes glinting. "Darkchild isn't afraid of anything. You're the one who's afraid!"

The boy stared across the fire at her, wounded by her scorn, and Kadura felt fresh conflict in him. He wanted to reach out to Khira, to make her care for him as she cared for Darkchild. But he was afraid of the emotion she evoked in him, afraid of all the other emotions it could call to life.

"You're afraid of your own shadow," Khira hissed with fresh scorn.

The boy cringed; and for Kadura it was enough. "Khira, go to the shelf and take down the powdered terris root. Then bring me mugs and water. You both need sleep more than you need argument."

Khira turned on Kadura, forgetting all her promises in a flash of temper. "He *is* afraid!" she snapped. "Just look at him! He was shaking when I found him—and mumbling to himself. He—"

"Child." Kadura spoke with such chilling authority that Khira drew back, paling. "Child, this is your friend and he needs you. Won't you accept him?"

Briefly Khira's eyes flashed, and angry rejection reeled through her mind. Accept the guide? What was he but the Benderzic's creature? Certainly he was Darkchild's enemy—and hers. He—

"No, he is simply one aspect of your friend," Kadura said. "He is the aspect that guards the past—but he wants to touch the present too. He wants to reach out to you. And the other aspect of your friend—Darkchild—is searching for the past the guide guards. If your friend can't touch what he reaches for in both his aspects, he may always be as he is now—divided."

Khira sank back to her heels, bowing her head as if Kadura's words were physical blows. "If I can't accept him—if I can't accept the guide—"

"But you can. You are strong."

She had chosen the right words. Khira's temper and uncertainty deserted her. She sighed, peering across the fire. The guide sat stiffly hunched, guarded. But he could not hide the pleading in his eyes. "I'll try," Khira said finally.

"You will succeed," Kadura assured her. "And now the terris

root, Khira." Her heart was stabbed with ice again. The pain would not ease until she saw them both sleeping.

Over the next hands of days, some sense of serenity returned to her kefri. The boy continued to reach, the guide tentatively seeking Khira's company by day, Darkchild dreaming by night, waking to find his dreams gone. Sometimes he followed Kadura as she went to her morning chores and addressed her silently. *Kadura, you know what I dream. If you would tell me—*

She refused him every time. "You hide the dreams from yourself, Darkchild. When you're ready, you will find them."

No, the guide hides them. If you will help me find them—

"Child, we each choose our own path. When you are ready to remember, you will put your feet to that path and you will remember." When he might be ready for that new path, she could not guess. Khira worked at accepting the guide, but she was often tight-lipped and strained in his presence. And no matter how carefully Kadura guarded herself, Darkchild's dreams frequently brought her awake, perspiration clinging to her body and wetting her hair. Some nights she silently left the kefri and went to the memory house to sleep.

It was there Nezra found her one morning three hands after Khira and the boy had arrived in the plain. Kadura woke and found the failed barohna standing over her, her mottled stone clutched in one withered hand.

Kadura sat, chilling. Three centuries before Nezra had taken her bronzing prey prematurely. She had gone to the mountains a willful child of ten and returned not a barohna but something other, something never before known on Brakrath. She had the stature of a child, the face of a barohna, and just one gift. Although the gem masters had polished sunstones for her, she had never learned to invest them with light. Instead she had gone to the mountains again and found a stone of her own, dark, discolored, untouched by any hands but her own. With it she found messages in the air and, when the mood moved her, delivered them to the appropriate parties.

Kadura looked into Nezra's withered face and read nothing. Nor had she ever been able to read anything there beyond the fleeting expression of the moment. "Is there something?" she said.

Nezra's hair was fair and silken, shining incongruously against her withered cheek. Unconsciously she touched it with one clawed hand. "There is something," she said, looking down at Kadura with indifference.

"Then what is it, Nezra?" A message from Tiahna? Some notice from the Council of Bronze? It was many hands before the Council was due to convene, but if there were some unforeseen eventuality—

Deliberately Nezra turned away. "Someone comes," she said, and left the memory house.

Kadura's hands slackened on her bedding. Go after her and demand to know who was coming? But Nezra would not tell her. She knew that from the indifference of her gaze. Time and circumstance had created a unique perversity within Nezra. Sometimes she carried her messages in good fellowship, sometimes indifferently, sometimes with malice. Whatever her mood, she delivered them as it pleased her.

Today it pleased her to say simply, "Someone comes."

Stiffly Kadura stood and unfolded her bedding. She was troubled as she went to her morning chores and she felt warning jabs in her heart and a coldness that ran to her very fingertips.

Khira and the boy rode to the pinnacles that day with a group of guardian daughters. They returned late in the afternoon and Kadura saw immediately that the boy was bleeding. She stood from the firepit to tend him, but Khira went to the medicine jars herself and found bandages for his injured leg.

See what happens when I try to make friends of myself? Darkchild chided Kadura as Khira cleaned his scrapes and cuts and applied an herb dressing. *I let the guide climb the pinnacles and he fell and left me with the pain. I had to ride all the way back with it.*

"Was it a bad fall?"

Khira frowned over the herb jar. "He wouldn't have hurt himself at all if he had relaxed when he felt himself falling. But he stiffened."

"And you were kind afterward, just as you were patient before," Kadura said. "You *are* strong."

"The guide just doesn't know how to fall."

Kadura nodded, as pleased with Khira's off-handed acceptance as with Darkchild's good-humored rebuke.

It was dusk by the time they finished their evening meal. "Will you come to tonight's teaching?" Kadura asked.

As usual, the boy exchanged a glance with Khira and Khira said, "We'll come." She would sleep, Kadura knew, and the boy would sit stiffly, watching but afraid to participate.

So it might have been. They reached the teaching grounds as

Nindra rose and the first redmanes gathered. Although summer had come and grasses grew deep on the plain, the night breeze was still chill. And as soon as she sat, Kadura felt a ripple of apprehension. The redmanes were restless, passing the same news among themselves, silently, that Nezra had brought to the memory house: *Someone comes.*

Kadura touched the soil and emptied herself. It was a woman who came, she found, and the woman was not a guardian. She came from the direction of the mountains, her face lost in the folds of a cape. She came slowly, heart-sore.

That was all Kadura found in the redmanes. The woman's face, her identity, were not significant to them.

The eldest redmanes approached the water to drink and then looked up at the gathered women. The younger redmanes moved restlessly behind them, ready for the teaching. It did not begin.

My herd, a woman comes.

My foals, she comes now.

Kadura gazed into the darkness, distinguishing motion from the small grove of trees west of the teaching place. The woman, whoever she might be, was there, hesitating in the shadow of the trees. Then she stepped into the moonlight and Kadura knew her immediately.

She was a barohna, her white shift stained, her dark hair wind-torn. She moved to the edge of the pond with eyes downcast, one hand clasping the pairing stone at her throat. The redmanes moved aside, and the barohna's reflection fell on the water. She was a woman shorn of the sun. Nor did her pairing stone glow between her fingers.

Kadura's hand clenched over her heart, trying to press away pain. She read everything that had happened from the woman's face even as the woman snapped the chain that held her pairing stone and threw the stone into the pond.

The water rippled and the gathered guardians sighed collectively. The barohna raised her head. Her voice trembled against the wind. "The sun has gone from my stones and the stone from my heart. I have come to live my quiet years among you."

Kadura turned to see the blood drain from Khira's face. She stood slowly. Her features seemed carved from ice, they were so pale, so immobile. The boy jumped to his feet, shocked by Khira's reaction. "She—Khira, who is she?"

Khira's eyes were huge with shadow. "Rahela—my mother's stone mate. She's turned flesh and left my mother alone."

The boy licked dry lips, trying to understand. "She—"

"I have to train." Khira's voice was flat.

"But—*why?*" This was Rahela, who made Tiahna's stone glow? She'd left her throne? The boy did not understand.

"I have to train," Khira repeated, this time with a note of hysteria. Turning blindly, she fled the teaching ground, fled the women who turned to look after her, testing her with their eyes.

The boy hesitated, not even able to formulate a silent question for Kadura. Then he turned and ran after Khira. When their footsteps faded, Kadura let her head fall to her breast, the icy pain in her heart greater than any she had known. She drew a fluttering breath and as she expelled it, she let her resistance to the swiftly proliferating ice crystals ebb away. There was pain in the ice, pain as the jagged crystals gouged the tender flesh of her heart, but eventually the cold would bring her numbness and peace. Then she would not have to think of Khira called so young to meet her beast.

FOURTEEN
KHIRA

"*The sun has gone from my stones and the stone from my heart.*"

Khira stumbled from the teaching ground, blind to everything but the afterimage of Rahela at the pond. Shock had driven her blood to some deep place and left her entire body cold. Numbly she pushed back the nightcloak and extended her arms. They were grey. Like stone.

Every part of her was stone. She wanted only to stand, a graven monument to this moment. But she had to have her pike. And her pack, with clothes and supplies. She had to have those things to train. She stared down at her empty hands, the fingers pale, stiffly clenched. Would they always be this way, cold and useless? How could she strike if she could not close fingers around the haft of her pike?

How could she find her beast if her legs would not carry her?

She was dimly aware of Darkchild calling behind her. She did not turn. He belonged to another time, a time before Rahela had committed her pairing stone to the water. A time when the sun-throne had waited in the distant future.

Now it shadowed her life, darkening her eyes so she could hardly see.

"Khira—*please!*"

The plea in his voice touched through her shock. She stopped and turned, stiffly. Darkchild had thrown aside his nightcloak and wore only the grey suit Timar had tailored for him when they first came to the plain. Moonlight glinted upon his face and glanced from his eyes. Perplexity sat upon him like pain. "Khira—I don't understand. That woman—"

"Rahela."

"Your mother's stone mate—why is she here?"

Khira shook her head dumbly, trying to dismiss the dull pounding that filled her head—the rush of slow-pulsing blood through petrified veins. "She's lost the power of the stones. Her daughter—Lihwa must have bronzed." Impatient Lihwa—but no one had expected her to go this year. She still had a sister to raise, a child of four.

"She—Rahela's not a barohna anymore?"

"She's a barohna without stone. Like my grandmother. Like Upala. And she's left my mother alone. My mother has no one now."

Darkchild's pupils narrowed in quick comprehension. "She threw her pairing stone into the water because she can't use it anymore. And now that your mother is alone—"

Briefly an image of Tiahna flashed to mind. How would she look without the sun in her eyes? With the sunthrone dull behind her? "Her heart will turn flesh too. She will have to leave the valley."

"When?"

"Whenever her heart turns. Now—or hands from now. If it turns before I bronze—" Then the valley would taste the slow death of prolonged winter: scant crops, dying stock, debilitating cold.

"But you can't go now. You're too young. What you told me—about Nezra—"

Khira shuddered. "I'll go on the day of my first majority."

"On your birthday? Next spring?"

"Yes." Her whisper stood between them, thready, and she quivered with sudden cold, realizing that all of her had turned to stone but one vital organ: her heart. That had begun to ache with what she saw ahead: the hardship, the loneliness, and finally the challenge. "I have to go, Darkchild. I have to go to the mountain in the spring. And I have to go there now to train." She peered up at him, begging him to understand.

He studied her from a great stillness. She could see that he wanted to protest. But at last he took her hand and held it between his, warming it. "Yes. I'll help you."

And suddenly she wasn't stone at all. Suddenly she was weak, her blood rushing a dizzy course through her head. With the blood came tears and panic—and shame. Alzaja had gone in serenity—would she go in fear? She caught at Darkchild's arm, pleading.

"Darkchild, if the guardians come from the pond now—if they come—"

He held her, hiding her face against his shoulder. "I won't let them see you cry," he promised.

Her relief that he understood made her tears come that much faster.

They left the campment at dawn the next day with packs on their backs and pikes in their hands. Kadura watched from the door of her kefri, her cloak tucked around her as if to hide a mortal frailty. When they reached the edge of the campment, Khira turned to look back, knowing it was not the campment she left behind but childhood. She would never again run through the coarse grass with guardian daughters. If she one day rode a redmane again, it would not be for sport. And if she ever returned to the plain, she would not sleep through the teaching. She would listen and begin to learn.

They reached the mountains two days later, tired and dusty, and sheltered the night in the same rocky cove where they had slept before. Khira lay awake as the moons progressed across the sky, listening to the wind in the rocks, to Darkchild's sleeping breath, to the anxious throbbing of her heart. Tomorrow they would weave targets and fashion other training devices. They would cut staffs for sparring. And they would run, but not as they had run together before, in play. This time they would run to harden her legs and strengthen her wind.

Khira tried to distance herself from fear by listing all the things she must do in training: all the things Alzaja had not done because she knew they would never be enough; all the things Mara had not done because she hadn't thought them necessary; all the things Denabar had done—and had almost won the throne by doing.

Still her fear was not quieted. *Heart, be stone. Flesh, be fearless.* Sliding deep into her bedding, she whispered long verses from the earliest scrolls. Her voice rasped in her throat. But that was not the way past fear either. The verses only emphasized how little had changed since the first palace daughter had gone to make her challenge. These many centuries later breeterlik still slept in deep caverns, fouling the air with the stench of meat that rotted between their teeth. Crag-chargers still tumbled down mountainside in horny armor and stingmadders still slipped along the surfaces of quiet ponds. Snowminx still crept like white shadows.

Palace daughters still trained.

Hand, be sure. Eye, be vigilant.

Finally she slept, restlessly. When she woke the next morning, it was not to train. She fought from sleep as if from a smothering blanket, perspiring. Darkchild bent over her anxiously. "You were crying, Khira. In your sleep. And your face—" He tested her flushed cheeks with measuring fingertips.

Fever. She had tried to be strong, but this morning the fear that burned in her spirit burned in her body too. She pushed aside her cloak and sat. Dizziness forced her down again. "I have a fever." She would not train today.

Nor did she train for many days. Later Darkchild found a small cavern higher on the mountain and helped her to it. Then he searched for the herbs she directed him to find and brew. Those did not help. The fever persisted, a physical manifestation of her weakness. Alzaja had been wrong. Her heart was not stone. It was flesh and the flesh was failing.

She dreamed in her fever, dreamed for most of many nights and days. She often woke to find Darkchild sitting beside her, trying to hide his worry. Or she woke to find the guide bending over her, pressing her hand, silently pleading for her to be well.

One? In her dreams Darkchild and the guide melded and become one person manifested in two personalities. In her dreams she even recognized why the guide was awkward, why his voice was harsh. He was afraid too and fear drew his muscles tight, binding his joints. Fear stiffened his throat and made his voice grate.

He was afraid. She was afraid. Beasts came to her in her dreams and she struggled against them until her bedding was soaked with perspiration. When the beasts did not come, Tiahna did, her pairing stone dull, the sunstone circlets dead at her wrists. Then Khira fought to throw off sleep, driven by a growing sense of urgency. She must go to the valley. She must go to the people. If she did not, they would die.

But each time she tried to go, the beasts were upon her again.

The beasts . . . Tiahna . . . the valley . . .

Finally on the seventh night of her illness, the fever receded and she lay weakly in her bedding. Darkchild sat against the cavern wall, sleeping with his forehead resting against his knees. She studied his profile, the clean line of forehead, nose and chin, seeing him with a new clarity. He was the one who had taken the stone from her heart. He was the one who had made her flesh. She had let herself care for him as she had not cared for anyone else—even Alzaja—and in her caring, she had lost her gritty substance.

Weakly she stood and groped to the mouth of the cavern. The night was clear, the stars white. If she could see Adar instead of these serene points of light, if she could fill her eyes with his war-fires—

But she would not hear the rattle of Adar's drums tonight. She would not feel his anger rise in her, expunging fear and shame. This was not Adar's season.

I'll never go to my beast, she realized, except to die. I've given Darkchild the stone from my heart. Now nothing can make me strong.

She turned back to the cavern. She was relieved that Darkchild did not stir as she slipped back into her bedding.

They left the cavern the next day, traveling slowly through the mountains. As they went, they fashioned staffs for sparring and wove targets for striking. But when Khira trained, she did so reluctantly, with no heart. Darkchild pressed her gently, he watched anxiously when she withdrew from activity, he hunted and cooked for her. At night, she knew, he often watched while she slept. He thought her reticence, her reluctance, were remnants of illness. She did not know how to tell him otherwise.

They traveled through the mountains for five days. On the morning of the sixth, Khira woke at a sound from beyond the cave where they slept. As she reached for her pike, her heart hammering, a shadow fell across the mouth of the cave. Carefully Khira slipped from her bedding and touched Darkchild's shoulder. His eyes slid open, the pupils glistening in the dim light. She held a finger to her lips and indicated the cave's entrance.

Before he could slip from his bedding, Nezra stepped into the cave.

Slowly Khira lowered her pike, the hair prickling at the back of her neck. Nezra's child's body was lost in a black cloak, but her silken hair hung free on her shoulders. She carried a walking stick in one withered hand, clutching it like a sparring staff.

"My mother—" Khira said without thinking. Had Tiahna already lost command of the stones?

Nezra's pale eyes glinted child-bright and malicious in her withered barohna's face. "Tiahna requests that you come to the palace immediately to celebrate midsummer. The people ask to see you."

"She—" Was that all? Had Nezra come just for that? And was it midsummer already? So soon?

"You will meet the Arnimi at midday in the northernmost meadow of Ladana's valley, below. They will take you to the palace in their aircar."

"The—the Arnimi are still in my mother's valley?" Khira was surprised to find she had not thought of Verra and Commander Bullens since she had left the palace.

Nezra lowered her stick and thumped the ground with it. "Is there some reason they would not be?"

"No." She had never taken Tiahna's threats against the Arnimi for more than a moment's temper. "Nezra—"

"I have no time," Nezra said with a second impatient thump of her stick. "Midsummer comes to the plain too and my redmane waits for me. Join the Arnimi below."

"And if I don't go?" Khira demanded, stung by Nezra's arbitrary manner.

Nezra peered at her from unwinking eyes. "Is there some reason you should not?"

Khira shuddered. Something dark looked from Nezra's pupils, something not at all human. It made her think of a stingmadder resting on the surface of a pond, waiting. "I'll be in the meadow."

Nezra nodded, drawing lids over the threat in her eyes. Swirling her cape, she vanished. For a giddy moment, Khira wondered if her feet had even left prints in the dirt.

Prints there were, and when Khira went to the cave mouth, she saw a black shape tramping down the mountainside, golden hair gleaming. Seen from behind, Nezra might have been a palace daughter in her mother's cloak—a child born three centuries before to an unkind destiny.

"You don't want to go to the midsummer festival?" Darkchild asked softly.

Khira turned back to the cave, refusing to meet his gaze. "I'll go." The words were hollow. She would go and the people would know when they saw her that their valley was lost. Lost for the lack in her heart. Lost because there was fear where there should have been courage.

They descended silently. When they reached Ladana's valley, it was midday and the Arnimi aircar waited. Khira approached silently, too preoccupied to notice that Darkchild hung back momentarily before following her.

The aircar rose across the mountains. Khira stared down on rocky spires and jutting formations, letting the grumble of the car's rotors relieve her of thought. Had she been less preoccupied, she would have seen that Darkchild sat stiffly erect, his jaws clenched, his hands gripping the arms of his seat.

Soon they passed over Terlath's dark spires and the valley lay below, green fields and bright orchards. Sunlight shone in broad beams from the lenses on the mountainside and converged on the throneroom mirrors. Khira saw with relief that there was no sign of dereliction in the valley.

But when the aircar landed, the people who had gathered on the plaza were silent in their bright festival robes. Khira shrank in her seat, not wanting to face them.

Silence and watching eyes—no one could miss the shadow that lay across the people as Khira disembarked from the aircar. She felt unreal under the gaze of so many eyes. Shrinking, she picked out Letra, the weaving mistress, in a gown that shimmered with centuries of embroidery. "Letra, are you well?"

The weaving mistress inclined her head, her pale eyes studying Khira, evaluating her in every detail. "As well as ever, daughter."

"And my mother is well?" Again Khira managed to keep her voice from trembling.

Again the weaving mistress inclined her head without lowering her gaze. "Well but lonely. She waits in the throneroom to see you. We all wait, daughter."

And now you see. You see that I am not the daughter you thought I was. You see that I am lacking in the very thing you require: heart. "I will go to her," Khira's lips said, completing the exchange of their own volition.

With Darkchild, she descended from the ship and crossed the plaza, conscious of each person who watched. Did Tiahna feel this shrinking loneliness when she returned from her winter throne each spring? The weight of so many eyes—Khira wanted to hide. These were her people and they were strong. But if the throne stood vacant, not one of them could command the stones and bring warmth to the valley.

Nor could she. If she had guessed that in the mountains, she knew it now. As she crossed the plaza, there was nothing but flesh beneath her ribs, aching flesh. She clutched Darkchild's hand.

The great iron doors of the palace cried open for her. The stones of the entry hall were oppressive. She had never noticed how dark they were, how crusted with centuries. Even the clinging glow of stalklamp could not brighten them.

She hardly saw the people who stepped aside to let her enter the throneroom. Light, color, motion—the throneroom was hung with banners, thronged with dancers. But she saw only the blazing throne and the swords of light that stabbed down from the throne-room mirrors to inflame it. She halted, letting her breath seep away. To sit there, to grasp the sun's bright blade and turn it to her people's use—

But she could not. Could not.

Tiahna stood. Her summerfest gown was black, embroidered with sun-emblems that struck light as she stepped forward. Her strength remained visible in the blaze of the throne and in the fire of her sunstone wristlets. But the pairing stone hung dull at her throat and her eyes were like Kadura's now, looking back rather than ahead.

Had she already begun to enter minds? If so, in Khira's mind she would find the lost wraiths of anger, drowned in fear. In Khira's mind she would find the same darkness that soon would consume the valley.

Tiahna's voice was husky. "Goodsummer, daughter. We are gathered for the midsummer dancing of the tides. Bring your friend; join me."

The flagged floor seemed to stretch for spans beneath Khira's feet as gowned dancers parted to let her pass. Walking among them, Khira could feel their tension. Where the people on the plaza had been silently vigilant, the dancers were eager and perspiring. It was time to call up the tides, and nothing mattered more today.

Without word, Khira took her place beside the throne, drawing Darkchild down beside her. Tiahna seated herself and raised her hand to the dancers. They were paired, woman and man, their dance gowns rich with centuries of embroidery. Many were pairs who had produced a child together that spring. Others were pairs chosen to produce a child the next spring. As they began to dance to the soft thump of drums, the year's infants were carried into the throneroom in the arms of their paternal grandfathers. Each child was wrapped in an investiture robe woven centuries before and embellished with the embroidered devices of every generation since.

The dance was as old as the gowns of the dancers, older. It began with a stamping of sandaled feet, with a clapping of hands, with a solemn turning and bowing and nodding. Each gesture was a styl-

ized promise to the infants in arms and to the community, a vow of
guidance and care.

As the dance continued, the stamping grew heavier, the clapping
faster, the turning and bowing and nodding more emphatic. Gradually the dance became a promise of the dancers not to the infants
but to each other, man to woman, woman to man. Tonight when
woodsmoke fires burned on the plaza and all who had been selected
gathered there, the tides would rise, those sweet inner tides, and
man and woman would yield to them in the fullness of joy.

The tides would rise, and their response would be of more than
the body. It would be a response of the spirit, calling up the un-
joined elements of the child who was to be conceived that night,
urging them to union. Flesh would yield, fluids would flow, and the
child would feel the call of the parents, the call to life. Sperm and
egg would make their separate magic and two halves would become
one whole.

We call you, spirit, the dancers whispered, clapping. *We call you,
child. You bring us together. We bring you to union. Come, use us as
your tools. Come, make yourself of us.*

We call you child, the dancers chanted, clapping. *We have a name
for you. We have a name with grace and strength and intelligence.
Come—make yourself of us.*

*We call you, child. We have a robe for you. It is embroidered with
the thread of centuries. You will be one strand of that thread. Beyond
you will be others. Come!*

The dance continued, and the valley itself called. The mountains
called. There were paths to be walked, ground to be tilled. There
were garments to be woven, songs to be sung. Later there would be
other children to be summoned to conception.

The drums gave the call its heartbeat. The dancers spun and
clapped and chanted, perspiration staining their embroidered gowns.
Without thinking, Khira turned to Tiahna. She had turned each
year, looking for some sign that the tide rose in Tiahna too.

Foolish to study Tiahna's impassive profile this year. She was
Tiahna's last daughter. Perhaps next year there would not even be a
dance. Perhaps next year—

Khira felt Darkchild's hand on her arm. At the back of the
throneroom, the elder women had come with torches. Tiahna
stood. At a gesture, the men who held the ropes to the throneroom
mirrors turned the mirrors. Swords of sunlight were immediately
sheathed in darkness. Only the throne gave light—and the torches.

The torchwomen strode through the dancers, the light of fire shining from their sweated faces. "We call you, we call you!" The dancers chanted louder and louder, until they were shouting, until the throneroom echoed with their cry to the tides.

"We call you!"

Khira closed her hand over Darkchild's as the dancers reached the peak of frenzy. Abruptly the dancing pairs shouted once and stopped mid-stride. The drums fell to silence, as if the heartbeat of the palace had ceased. The torch bearers pounded their feet on the floor, making their own ululating cry as they ran to the perimeter of the throneroom where vessels of water waited. They plunged their torches into the vessels. Flame died in the roar of steam.

As the steam dissipated into the throneroom, shrouding the throne, Juris Fenilis stepped before the dais. "Torch and vessel— join tonight as your parents joined before you, as others have always joined. Go!"

The mirrors remained dark as the people left the throneroom. Tiahna sat in silence, dark against the captive sunlight of the throne, until everyone had gone. Then she turned to Khira and studied her impassively. "This is your last year to take midsummer feast with the children, daughter."

Khira shrank against Darkchild. "There will be no other," she whispered. She had not expected Tiahna to be so direct.

"Next year," Tiahna continued, as if she had not heard, "you will feast with the women. You will drink the ovulants and if the tides are right, the year after there will be a new daughter in the palace."

Disbelief brought Khira to her feet. Could Tiahna look at her with clear eyes and not see the truth? "Next year I'll be dead—or in exile in the mountains!"

Tiahna accepted her outburst with faint surprise. Unconsciously she clasped the dulled stone at her throat. "I don't believe you will be either dead or living in the mountains next midsummer, daughter. I believe you will sit here on my throne while I celebrate midsummer in the plain with Rahela." For a moment her gaze touched Darkchild. "Your friend, I expect, will be here beside you."

Couldn't she see? *Wouldn't* she see? "I'll never take the throne!" Khira cried, pain and rising anger mingling in her voice. "If I were fit to command the stones, my heart would be ready. I would be ready to train!"

Again Tiahna expressed faint surprise. "Most certainly you are ready to train, daughter."

"For what? To die?" The vehemence of her response surprised her. Faced with Tiahna's bland insistence, Khira felt muscles draw tight that had grown slack. Had Adar come into the heavens out of season? "If I go to my challenge like this—afraid—I'll never come back."

Tiahna's brows rose. "So you are afraid, Khira." It was more statement than question.

Khira stared up at her, wanting to deny it. But surely the truth was apparent. "Yes!" Angrily.

Tiahna stood and paced across the dais, her gown rustling. When she turned back, her customary impassivity had fallen away. For the first time she spoke to Khira as to an equal—as to a younger friend who was also sister and daughter. "You're the only daughter ever to tell me that, Khira. You're the only one strong enough to voice your fear."

"I'm—" Khira's mind turned blank. Strong enough to voice fear? If only she were strong enough to hide it!

"Khira, you think the stone is gone from you. No—I'm not moving in your mind. I'm simply reading your face. You've studied your heart so closely you no longer see its nature. You see confusion. You see fear. Pain. Caring that gives you as much pain as joy. You see such a conflicting range of emotions in yourself that you can no longer distinguish one important element—courage. And so you think you are weak."

"I am!" Khira admitted, a whisper. Tears stung her eyes.

"Yes. You are as weak as I was when I began my training. That weak, Khira."

"No."

"Yes. You are as weak as your father. I've watched for him in you for twelve years now and today I see him. Today I see your father as he was before he went to the mountains that last time. No, I won't tell you his name and I won't tell you the name of the valley where he was born. He made his valley his home for a short time before he went to find new veins in the mountains."

Khira caught her breath, unbelieving. Surely no barohna ever told her daughter even this much of her father. "He was a gem master," she realized.

"Yes, and I trust he found some stone that pleased him when he left here. I've always hoped that for him, that he held it in his hand when the avalanche caught him." She turned to address Darkchild, who peered up at her with darkly questioning eyes. "A barohna does not choose her mate in the way the women of the halls do, Rauth-Seven. In the halls, the families confer and study genealogies and when they make a selection of mates, it is the culmination of a long thoughtful process. At midsummer the proper tides rise and the contractants conceive. If the selection has been a good one, there are healthy offspring and the contractants enjoy the mating through many years.

"A barohna pursues no such course. She moves through the months of the year watching for a man who will make her tides rise. Sometimes she finds him at Midsummer Fest, and then she goes to him and dances with him. Other times she finds him when she least expects—as she walks the fields, as she talks with her people. A man who has never been of interest to her before suddenly becomes so and she arranges to meet with him.

"And sometimes she is alone on the mountain when she meets a lone lens tender or a herder—or a gem master."

Darkchild spoke hesitantly. "Gem masters—are the only men sensitive to stones."

"Yes. They are the only men who have feeling for the stones that a barohna can use. Lensar was the first gem master—though since he was the first, he did not call himself that. And he did not live to see how the sunstones he found and polished were ultimately used."

Darkchild nodded. "Because when Niabi learned how to release the sun from the stones, she turned him to ash."

"Yes—you've studied the scrolls. Niabi had no way of knowing what she could do with the stones until she had done it—and then it was too late. Lensar was dead." Tiahna turned back to Khira. "Your father came to the valley to bring me a pairing stone to replace one that had chipped. When he placed it on my neck, when his hands touched me, I wished it could take me into his mind instead of Rahela's. He had many of the strengths and sensitivities of a woman, and when the avalanche caught him, I knew it. I felt it through the pairing stone he had polished for me. If he had lived, he intended to polish an eyestone and wear it at his neck as I wore the pairing stone. He intended to wear it wherever he went."

"So you could see what he saw," Khira said softly.

"Yes. I would have accompanied him on all his travels that way. I would have gone everywhere with him, seen everything he saw.

And if he had come back to the valley midsummer next, I would have danced with him and you would have had younger sisters."

But he had not returned, and the tide had never risen for Tiahna again. "But I'm still afraid," Khira said.

"I've been afraid for most of my life, Khira."

"You?"

"Yes, afraid of every event of my life. Afraid I would fail in my training and then in my challenge. Afraid I would fail on the throne. Then afraid I would never bear daughters, afraid the daughters I did bear would never bronze—afraid Nezra would not find you and bring you to midsummer.

"The test is not in the absence of fear, Khira. The test is in acknowledging fear and living beyond it."

"Yes." The sighing word was Darkchild's. Tiahna acknowledged it with a nod, then turned back to Khira—waiting.

There were centuries behind her waiting—and all the stones of Brakrath. To Khira's surprise, she felt fear and inadequacy ebb away to be replaced by quiet certainty. Her father had lived by the stones and died by them. Tiahna had lived by the stones too.

Now it was her time. Without thinking, she raised one hand to her breast. It clenched there, clutching at the stone that was suddenly in her heart again. Not the stone of harshness, of uncaringness. Tiahna was not harsh and uncaring, although she had often seemed so in her loneliness. Nor need Khira be harsh and uncaring to take the throne. "I'm ready to begin training," she said.

Tiahna returned to her throne, silhouetting herself against its captive fire. "Yes, you are ready. But not tonight. Tonight there is a feast to be eaten. And then I would like you to return to the plain for the bonding of the herds. Your grandmother is not well—I have that message. If this is her last bonding, I would like you to be with her.

"Then you may train."

Yes, she would use pike and targets. She would spar with staffs. She would run and do all the things necessary to build her body. But her heart required nothing. It was whole again. She caught Darkchild's hand and felt the strength of the stones between them.

She was whole.

FIFTEEN

DARKCHILD

Kadura was not well. Dark-child saw that immediately when they reached her kefri. She waited near the door, wrapped in her nightcloak despite the afternoon heat. There were new lines in her face, as if the flesh had fallen, and there was a shadow upon her eyes. But what it might hide—

Khira seemed not to notice. She ran to Kadura eagerly. "We haven't missed the bonding, have we?"

The old woman embraced Khira, then studied her closely, looking deep. Khira wore her auburn hair knotted loosely over one ear, and her skin had taken a healthy sun patina. There was no mistaking her buoyancy or her new confidence. "The herds haven't gathered yet. You've had a good journey, daughter's daughter."

"Yes—I've begun training. I've trained for ten days now in the mountains."

"You've begun well. I see that in your face." Kadura turned to Darkchild, the shadow upon her eyes deepening. "And your friend —Darkchild, have you helped her?"

"When I could," he said, passing off the question hurriedly. "Kadura—" *Kadura, why do you look this way: ill?*

But she nodded away his unspoken question and led Khira into the kefri. This was not the time to talk about the change he saw in her.

This was the time to undertake a new phase of Khira's training: night stalks. They made the first that night, leaving the campment at sunset, taking only their pikes and a few bars of dried fruit. "I want to go to the grove beyond the pinnacles," Khira explained as they passed the deserted teaching ground. "Whispreys come there sometimes in the summer—and nightcallers. And sometimes a whitemane comes from the forest beyond the plain."

"A whitemane?" Darkchild responded distractedly, still wondering about the change in Kadura. If she would not tell him what made her ill—and if what he had heard about the bonding were true—

"They're—" Khira halted, listening. Then she shook her head. "Nothing. Some people think they're a form of redmane. Other people think they're descended from animals that came with the first timers—horses. Guardians go to the forest sometimes to try to learn their ways, but no one has ever found their teaching grounds. So no one knows how they live. If we could stalk one and find their teaching ground—"

"We wouldn't learn anything," he reminded her. Certainly neither of them had learned the ways of the redmanes that summer. He always sat stiff, cold and guarded through the teachings, while Khira slept.

She sighed, surrendering her moment's enthusiasm. "Someday I'll learn to listen."

Except for the browsing redmanes, the plains were sparsely populated. There were occasional groundfowl, chortling sleepily from nests deep in dense clumps of grass. Khira paused at every sign, listening intently. Then she studied the ground for droppings and for the scratching tracks the fowl left in the soil.

But there was not much cunning to be gained in tracking groundfowl. Soon the moons rose and found Khira and Darkchild making a steady pace toward the pinnacles. Occasionally they passed a solitary redmane or a buck and mares.

Several times they skirted guardian campments and passed places where groups of redmanes and guardians gathered around pools or streams. Darkchild guarded himself against the urge to stop, to try to fathom the animals' silent communication.

Sometimes riding, sometimes walking, they reached the pinnacles in the middle hours of evening. The sterile rock peaks cast bizarre shadows upon the plain, and by moonlight Darkchild could believe their legend: that once a party of breeders had come to abduct the most ancient mare of all the redmanes as she stood teaching at the pond, and that upon lashing their ropes to her neck, the seven breeders and their five helpers were turned to stone. There was frozen agony in the craggy rocks, as if they were caught in a timeless scream. By moonlight there were eyes too, staring from deep-shadowed crevices.

And tonight an ancient redmane stood teaching at the pond, younger redmanes gathered near. Darkchild followed Khira with stiff reluctance, feeling the cold of the summer night for the first time. Nindra and Zan rode upon the surface of the pond in silver silence. No redmane moved.

Listen, my herd—

Darkchild could not listen. With choking panic, he ran, not even looking back.

He stopped, breathless, when the pinnacles were faceless crags in the distance. *Doors*—when he emptied himself to the redmanes, he saw doors. He wanted to move past them, into the dreams that still troubled his nights. But the doors were guarded by dragons. Shaking, he wiped cold sweat from his face. If he could capture a fragment of his dreams, a scrap—a color, a face—

Khira had caught up with him and studied him anxiously. "I couldn't stay there," he said shakily. "I saw their faces in the crags —the breeders—"

She accepted that explanation and they rested for a few minutes, then continued their stalk.

As they neared the grove, Khira walked with silent stealth, watching and listening. A crushed leaf, a fallen feather—she must be alert for every sign now. She had come to pit her cunning against the most elusive creatures of the plain—not to take them for meat, but to sharpen her instincts and her senses in stalking them.

Darkchild let her walk ahead, let her search for the faint signs marking the passage of prey. Even so, he was first to see the wisp of grey fur caught in the coarse grass near the edge of the trees. "Khira—"

Khira turned and quickly saw the direction of his gaze. "Whisprey." Her lips formed the syllables silently.

There was no second wisp of fur, but as they slipped through the trees, they found other signs: the faint track of small feet, a shredded seed pod, raw dirt where the animal had scratched for insects. The trees of the grove were tall but widely spaced. Darkchild and Khira passed through an intricate gridwork of moonlight and shadow, searching.

Then Khira halted, raising her hand for silence. Darkchild peered around. A small shape crouched at the base of a nearby tree. Its pear-shaped body was lightly furred and soft with fat. Its feet were tiny and man-like, with pink-nailed toes. There were two small arms with man-like hands. But there was no neck and no distinct head. Instead there was a cluster of tiny oval eyes near the rounded peak of the body. As Darkchild studied the creature, it peered back at him, lidding and unlidding its many eyes with confusing rapidity.

Carefully Khira eased herself to the ground. She moved her head from side to side, closing first one eye, then the other. In response the whisprey rocked too, its eyes flickering even more rapidly than before. When the animal quieted again, Khira reached into her pack for a fruit bar.

The whisprey considered the offering with much blinking of eyes. Then it edged forward, and from the palms of its pink-nailed hands came a buzzing whisper. The creature accepted the fruit bar and the whispering rose to a whining peak. Quickly the whisprey tore the bar into two pieces and closed one hand around each section.

After a moment its hands opened and it began to rock from foot to foot, whispering again, this time with a note of demand. Darkchild edged forward. There was a stickiness in the palms of the creature's hands—nothing more. And still the whispering petition continued, rising to an angry buzz when Khira did not offer a second fruit bar. "No more," she said, closing her pack.

Film appeared immediately upon the whisprey's clustered eyes. It stood utterly still, clenching its small hands until even the residual stickiness was absorbed. Then, abruptly, it stood and ran, fat and waddling, comical.

However comical the creature, it was much harder to track this time. It left scant trace on the dry-thatched ground: an occasional fallen hair, a drop of spittle, a barely perceptible disturbance of the fallen leaves that matted the ground. It took all Khira's concentration and skill to follow its trail.

Then they spotted the plump creature crouched beneath another tree, waiting. Again it peered up with rapidly blinking eyes, again it begged a fruit bar and absorbed it. Again it retreated in indignation when refused further offering.

The third time the whisprey was still more difficult to track. Darkchild and Khira wandered through the trees with little clue until the animal showed itself and buzzed for its reward.

The fourth time they found the animal, the clues that led through the grove were so tenuous Darkchild was not certain the animal they found was the same animal they had been tracking.

But the animal agitated to be fed almost immediately and this time vanished without being verbally refused a second offering.

"I don't think we'll find him again," Khira said.

They searched anyway, studying the ground minutely for traces. Several times they crossed their own trail and followed it a distance before branching away again.

They had passed under the same hollow-trunked tree three times, its feathery leaves brushing their hair, when Darkchild glanced up and saw a faintly glistening shadow in the distance. He froze as the shadow slipped from sight, knowing that in the grove were black shadows and grey shadows, but none the color of moonlight. "Khira—there—"

She looked in time to see the shadow reappear. It stood poised among the trees, a dewy white form with graceful neck and slender legs. It seemed to watch them from the center of a great stillness. "A whitemane," Khira whispered, moving forward slowly. "If we don't move too quickly—"

The animal watched with quivering alertness as they crept toward it. With each deliberate step, Darkchild distinguished more detail: long narrow head with pricked ears and flared nostrils; eyes that glinted pink by moonlight; a silken white mane; powerful shoulders and hindquarters supported by delicately formed legs. The whitemane peered at them across the shadowed grove, a creature of grace and strength.

It was also a creature of easy frights. It tossed its glistening mane nervously as they approached and danced backward through the trees. They halted until the animal forgot its fright, then inched forward again. This time the animal rose to its hind legs, pawing the air with anxious hooves. Darkchild caught his breath, afraid the animal would overbalance and fall. But it sank to fours again and danced away into the trees, uttering a shrill cry, its hooves striking the densely thatched soil with barely a sound.

The whitemane's trail was not difficult to follow. It led to the far edge of the grove—and beyond, to the north. Darkchild and Khira stood at the edge of the trees and Darkchild was torn between feelings of privilege that he had glimpsed the elusive white creature at all and sharp feelings of loss.

"It's gone back to the forest," Khira said finally. "We frightened it away."

"How far is the forest?" If they could reach there before daylight, if he could see the whitemane by moonlight again, enchanted . . .

"We wouldn't reach the trees until afternoon, unless we found redmanes to ride. And if we stayed more than a day or two, we might miss the bonding."

The bonding: the gathering of the herds of the plain to select mates for the coming year and to cull their numbers. Darkchild felt a moment's uneasiness, the return of a question he had silently nursed as they made their way back to the plain after the midsummer feasting. *Kadura* . . . But this was not the time for that question, and he put it aside. "We'll have to go back to the campment," he agreed reluctantly.

They encountered the whisprey again as they made their way back through the grove. It hissed and buzzed and finally shrilled angrily when they did not stop. By silent agreement, they stalked no more that night but walked back across the plain. The ancient mare still taught beneath the pinnacles and the moons still made the plain silver-bright. But a white shadow stood between Darkchild and his surroundings. He could not forget the whitemane's alert grace.

Each time they passed a guardian campment, Darkchild noticed that there were more redmanes than he had seen earlier. Many were dusty with travel and they moved restlessly among the other, quieter animals, stallions nudging mares, mares rubbing against stallions in silent inquiry.

"The herds are gathering," Khira explained, frowning distractedly.

Kadura—he must talk to Kadura tomorrow.

But Kadura left the kefri before he woke next morning. And when he dressed and ate and went asking for her, no one could give him word. He searched with rising anxiety. The herds were gathering. Everywhere were dusty, tired animals. He studied them covertly. They walked heavily on padded feet, their coats dense, dull, grey. Their manes hung tangled and rust-red across stocky shoulders. They scarcely raised their heads as he passed.

He had caught only isolated glimpses of the whitemane in the trees, but he could imagine how it would look moving aloof and pale among these heavyset animals, how it would bend its long neck to graze, how it would pause, raising its head, gazing around with quivering alertness, ears pricked. How anyone could think the whitemane related to the redmanes . . .

Kadura still had not returned to the kefri late that afternoon. There was only Khira, stirring a pot of soup, ladling some for him. "Tonight is the night of veils at the teaching ground. Will you come?"

"Veils?" There were so many customs he had not heard about.

"The oldest guardians, the ones who think they may not come back from the bonding, wear veils tonight and join in the teaching."

Darkchild shuddered. That would answer his question, if he went to the teaching and Kadura sat veiled beside the pond. But to have his answer that way, to see Kadura's face shadowed as if death already fell across it—

"I'll stay here," he said shortly.

He kept vigil in the kefri while Khira went alone to the teaching. Despite his rising anxiety, the warmth of the kefri and fatigue made him drowsy. He lay down and without intending it went to sleep.

It was much later when he woke. The fire had died to embers and Khira and Kadura had returned and gone to bed. Darkchild sat, looking at Kadura's shadowed face and aching with hollow uncertainty.

Tomorrow. Tomorrow he would ask her: *Kadura, I know that guardians die in the bonding. The old, the unfit, the tired—they fall then. Khira has told me that. But no one has told me—do barohnas fall in the bonding too?*

You look old now and tired—so much older, so much more tired than when we first came to the plain. Will you die when the herds gather?

Kadura stirred, the light of the single hanging lantern falling across her face, making a death-mask of it. Darkchild squeezed his eyes shut and burrowed into his bedding.

The next morning there was the sound of many padding feet in the campment. Redmanes passed in weary numbers, heads bowed, flanks dusty. Darkchild stood at the door of Kadura's kefri watching. There were dark-cloaked shapes among the animals, guardians walking silently with the migrating herds. And there were bright-haired figures—guardian daughters, laughing and making a game of the pilgrimage.

Again Kadura had slipped from the kefri before Darkchild woke, but this time she returned at mid-morning. She was wrapped loosely in her heavy nightcloak, and the shadow upon her eyes had darkened. "We go with the herds this afternoon, Darkchild," she said without preface. "The bonding will begin at tomorrow moon-

rise. You will be the first male to see the bonding in many centuries
—very many."

He peered up at her, stricken dumb by the darkness in her eyes.
Kadura—

At the last moment, afraid, he tried to call back his silent question. But he had rehearsed it too often. It came of itself.

Her response surprised him. She smiled, her eyes clearing. "No,
child, barohnas never die in the bonding. There is something in us
so enduring we must will it dead before it can die. But we lose our
guardian friends in the bonding and sometimes we realize then it is
time to take the ice and follow."

Again he could not hold back his question. *Kadura—this year
will you take the ice?* Without her stone mate, without the oldest of
her friends, without health, how long would she choose to live?

Kadura sighed, her eyes sinking into shadow again. "Do I look
so old to you—and so ill?"

*You look older than you did just hands ago, when we first came
here. You look like something hurts you.* That was the shadow in her
eyes—pain.

She nodded, completely shadowed now. "There are many things
to hurt a person like myself, Darkchild. The loss of my mate, the
loss of friends—but so many other things too. Imagine yourself
moving among minds as I do. Imagine all the things you might see
and feel—and wish you had not."

The burden of everyone's pain. The ache of everyone's loss, and
all of it as immediate as if it were her own. Without thinking, he
reached for her hand. It was unexpectedly fragile, as if the bones
had turned dry and brittle beneath the weathered skin. *That's why
barohnas finally take the ice,* he guessed. *Because they learn to read
more and more in other people until someday they read too much.*

"Someday . . ." she agreed, a dry whisper, and stepped past
him into the kefri.

They left that afternoon, walking eastward. Padding redmanes
surrounded them in every direction, walking with weary purpose,
heads lowered. No one rode. They walked together, women, children and animals. As they walked, Darkchild held himself stiffly
aloof, clutching his pike. Something in the migration made him feel
that a great teaching was taking place on the plain, that every
animal was silently speaking to the consciousness of every other.

Although he tried, he could not entirely close himself to the teaching. It was too pervasive. The very soil of the plain pounded with it, like an earthen heart. It reached him through every sense.

He dreamed that night, a confusion of dark images. Terror moved scarlet in his dreams; despair stalked them, black. He saw everything through the screen of those dark colors: faces, structures, trees, paths. He woke half a dozen times, trembling. Each time Kadura watched him from her blankets, her face grey. He didn't try to speak.

The last time he woke, Kadura had gone. Khira bent over him, concerned. "You—you shouted."

"A dream," he muttered hoarsely and turned away to darker dreams still.

Late the next afternoon they stood on a promontory overlooking the bonding ground. Below them redmanes stretched as far as the eye could see, a massed assemblage of thousands. Upon reaching their destination, the animals had thrown off their plodding weariness. From below came calls and shrills, piercing, excited. Although the massed animals gave the appearance of a solid field of grey, individual animals moved constantly, shrilling at each other, rubbing necks, chewing manes in greeting and courtship.

Darkchild looked down upon them as if upon a nightmare. He had not brought a single concrete image from his night's dreams into consciousness, no more than ever. But he remembered the colors of his dreams and he remembered terror. And somehow the redmanes were responsible for his recalling that much.

"They've already begun pairing," Khira said, and he watched reluctantly. Pairs of redmanes rose on their hind legs, jabbing the air with padded feet, tossing their tangled manes. Foals darted among the courting pairs in noisy excitement, stirring the red dust of the bonding ground into obscuring clouds.

Uneasily Darkchild gazed around. Caped and hooded, guardians lined the promontories that commanded the plain. He had never before been so aware of their silence. Tonight it was a watching silence, a waiting silence. He caught his lower lip in his teeth. There were perhaps sixty barohnas among the guardians, and they waited too, in silence as deep.

Darkchild and Khira sat atop a boulder until sunset. With dusk an acrid odor rose from the plain, a musk that drove the redmanes to shrilling excitement. Darkchild sucked at the cold evening air, his hands gnarled into fists. More than once Khira glanced at him in concern but said nothing.

Finally, with darkness, the plain became still. Courting bucks and mares fell to fours and stood motionless. Even the foals ceased their running and shrilling. Darkchild stirred uneasily as thousands of animals became as stone. After a while the silence was complete —and terrible from so many animals. Darkchild turned to Khira. She had grown rigid, hardly seeming to breathe.

Then Nindra appeared over the crest of the horizon, her silver face looming silently in the dark sky. She had never been so luminous, so large. She cast a glimmering radiance over the redmanes, a blessing of silver light. The animals raised their heads, suddenly shrilling and tossing their heads again, loping and cantering around the plain, necks arched, padded feet kicking.

As Darkchild watched in growing astonishment they played teasing games, charging each other, darting away. Some danced on their hind legs, flailing the air with their manes.

And with the silver shadow of the moon upon them—

"The whitemane!" Darkchild whispered. "You can see the whitemane in them." Before, they had been stocky and grey, without spirit. Now there was beauty in them: grace, swiftness, joy. As he watched, the plodding bodies, the tangled manes, the heavy feet became guises quickly tossed aside. Whitemanes courted and danced in the spell of Nindra's light.

"Khira—they're like whitemanes!"

Khira seemed not to hear. And Kadura stood like stone, her eyes hard, black, lusterless. Her face had become a petrified mass, deeply fissured, only the harshest edges weathered smooth.

Darkchild turned back to the dance of redmanes. Then Zan's silver rim appeared above the horizon and the redmanes were suddenly still again. They stood in frozen silence until the second silver circlet completely cleared the horizon. Darkchild waited in poised tension. *Dance!* he wanted to cry. *Dance, whitemane!*

But when both moons glided up the black sky, the animals did not dance again. Instead they uttered a long quivering sigh and began slowly to stamp their padded feet.

They stamped in unison, heads lowered, as if they listened to the sound of their own feet. At first the beat was slow, a gentle pounding that reverberated across the plain like the beat of an earthen heart. Shivering, Darkchild drew up his feet from contact with the soil. If he could make the boulder an island, a place where nothing could touch him, if he could look out upon the thousands of animals, yet isolate himself . . .

The stamping grew stronger, more emphatic, gradually accelerating. Gazing around, Darkchild could see that the guardians had spread their feet, bracing themselves against the softly vibrating earth. He shuddered, trying to shut out the reverberation that reached him even as he sat on the boulder, feet pulled up.

Khira clasped his arm for a moment, then released it, sliding down from the boulder. When her feet touched ground, she spread them as the guardians did. Darkchild stared down at her in frightened fascination. Khira was invulnerable to the teaching. She always slept when the elder mare taught at the pond. But now the slow heavy rise of her chest told him her heart had slowed to meet the beat of the plain.

The redmanes pounded the ground harder, faster. Darkchild held his breath, refusing to empty himself, refusing to make room within himself for the spell the redmanes cast.

But were they redmanes? As the mesmeric pounding continued, it seemed to him he saw the whitemane dancing among them again, throwing its silken mane as it raised delicate hooves to strike the earth. Its neck arched, it pounded the earth in the same rhythm as the redmanes—heavier, faster, ever more emphatic. Its hooves clipped at the ground, striking a sharp repetitious note.

Later he could not remember when he slipped down from the boulder to stand beside Khira. Could not remember when he spread his feet. Could not remember when he let the pounding of feet and hooves become the pounding of his own heart. But Zan had not risen far above the horizon when Darkchild's will seeped away and his heart's rhythm altered to meet the rhythm of the bonding.

The pounding of thousands of feet went on and soon all were one: redmanes and guardians, soil, mountains and moons. They bonded.

One. The feet pounded and barriers fell. The feet pounded and doors were splintered. The feet pounded and all the memories the guide had hidden were revealed.

Memories: the violet-eyed people who had found the boy in the forest, hungry and alone, and fed him. The woman who had bent to him, teaching him to scribe symbols that would admit the family to the temple where the godsvoice sang. Then the long, good years, the godsvoice strumming for them and the family pond yielding all the good things that were to be desired: tender bulbs, delicately flavored stems, rich seeds and pods.

Memories: his sisters' hair combed out between their fingers to catch the godsvoice. Only women and girls could hear the godsvoice in that special, intimate way. But sometimes—yes, sometimes he imagined he heard a thin, high singing too. And then he wondered if his prayers too might be made more powerful, if his desires might become manifest.

Because beyond the silver forest and the people who were his family there lay still earlier memories: plain people in plain clothes. People with dirt under their nails and the smell of the soil on them. They were scattered thin across their rich world and peace was their wish. The plenty in the soil and in the mountains, the rich, fine things that could be made of the elemental stuff of their world —not for them. They had no desire to mine their world and make themselves wealthy. They were few and their simplicity was special to them. In physical austerity, they believed, lay the source of spiritual riches.

The plain people: they found him—so small a child to be crying and alone—and fed him on plain foods and love. They filled his emptiness and helped him grow, until one day—

Darkchild gasped, trying to force his way out of the trap of memory. But there was no escaping. He could not build back the doors. They were shattered. How could he refashion barriers of a handful of splinters?

Two peoples had cared for him. Two peoples had taken him in and fed him. Two peoples had fostered his growth, had formed him in the ways of love. Without them he could never have learned to care for Khira. They had taken an empty, hungry child and made him human.

And both times had come the droning in the sky. Both times had come the screaming ship. Both time grapplers had reached down for him and taken him to where the Benderzic helmet waited.

Then the helmet had stripped his mind of all the detail stored there and used that detail to strip the peoples who had cared for him of their very way of life.

Yes. He knew that now—now that the doors were gone. That was what the guide had been hiding from him. He had been used against the people who fed him like a tool of destruction. He had been sent among them to record in infinite detail their resources, their defenses, their weaknesses, their ways. Then what he had learned had been codified and analyzed and exploiters had taken the processed information and used it for their own ends.

He didn't have to be told what they had done then. He could guess. They had come to the silver forest in ugly ships and stripped the very tongue from the temple—from every temple. They had muted the godsvoice, for the metal that sang in its taut strands was exceedingly precious in trade. Then they had brought in blasters and loaders and haulers and taken away all the ore from which the metal of the godsvoice was refined.

The exploiters had taken every smallest part of that essential metal—he didn't have to be told; he knew—and left the gentle people to starve. What else could they do, with their temples silent and the women stripped of the mystical power that lived in the presence of the godsvoice? If by some chance the people took straggling crops from the public ponds after that, surely the poisons excreted by their own festering spirits soon made their souls bloated and gangrenous.

And the plain people—he could guess the terrible things that happened to them when factories and refineries rose in their farmlands and trade ships came and gaudy people of every race bought and sold in hurriedly constructed marketplaces. They had retreated to the stonedeserts, surely, and there their simple austerity had become hard-bitten poverty. And while a chosen austerity had made them strong, exile and poverty could only weaken the fibers that held them together in love.

Darkchild shuddered. Dead, the two peoples who had befriended him. Dead at his hand as surely as if he had been a Benderzic or an exploiter. Dead because they had not murdered the strange child they found hungry on their hands but had succored him.

And the people of Brakrath? Khira? Tiahna? Kadura? Darkchild trembled, cold sweat standing on his face. The redmanes' feet pounded faster, ever faster, making his thoughts whine by dizzily.

The Benderzic ship would come again, droning, screaming. The grappler would come again. The helmet would slide over his head again and the Benderzic would learn of the sunstone and the barohnas and of a people who slept for many hands while the snow lay deep in their valleys. And then—

Then the exploiters. He could not guess who they might be or how they would turn the sunstone to their ends. But they would come and they would destroy.

Blindly he turned his head, trying to grasp reality through the ever-accelerating fury of thoughts and images. Below, padded feet pounded faster and faster, until the beat of every heart was swift and violent. Darkchild's blood raced dizzily, singing in his ears. Guardians stood braced against the frenzy and guardians lay fallen in the dirt. Below, redmanes had begun to fall too, those whose hearts were too weak to sustain the pounding fury of the bonding.

And Kadura—Darkchild stared and hardly knew her. Her face was the grey of stone. Her eyes hardly seemed flesh. They stared at him in stark agony as her body swayed. Her hands, he saw, were clenched on the folds of her cloak, bloodless.

But she had told him barohnas never fell in the bonding. She had told him she must will her death. She had told him—

She had told him of the pain she took from the minds around her. Now, he realized, it was his pain that made stone of her. It was his pain that made her rock on her feet, as if she would fall and shatter.

And before—so much suddenly became clear—before *he* was the one who had made her old and ill. He had come to the plain with Khira and brought the poison of hidden memories with him. The guide had protected him against memory—but Kadura saw everything. She had read his memories, she had read his dreams, and they had hurt her so much she faltered in her will to live.

What had he ever loved that he had not destroyed? The people of the silver forest, the plain people—and now he would destroy Kadura and Khira too, one with pain, the other with unwilling treachery. With terrible effort—feet pounded and his blood whined —he pressed his hands to his ears, ground his fists against his eyes. He could not quench the gouting rush of memory.

Colored stones, singing scarves, a strangely familiar voice pleading with him in a jungle clearing—he had destroyed another people too. He—flesh of Birnam Rauth, creature of the Benderzic. The Arnimi commander was right. He was not human. He was a killing-tool.

A tool—but a unique tool, one that could at least choose its own obliteration. On the plain more redmanes had been culled by the heart-stopping frenzy. On the promontory another guardian fell, her body slowly sinking until she lay lifeless, her face hidden from the watching moons by the hood of her umber cape.

He could fall too. Already the singing of his blood had become a buzzing, the buzzing a whine. His heart beat a useless frenzy against his ribs, robbing him of breath. He choked on rising bile.

He could fall if he gave himself totally to the bonding. He could fall and never hurt anyone again.

He could fall and at last he did, his knees bending, his body slumping against the throbbing soil. He felt its roughness against his cheek and made a pledge upon the soil of Brakrath: he would not rise again; he would not kill again.

The last thing he saw as his senses faded was Khira's face, moon-misted, staring. He did not know if she really bent over him or if he just wished it. But as she drew nearer he repeated his pledge and released himself into the oblivion of her eyes.

SIXTEEN
THE GUIDE

The guide left the kefri on the tenth night after the bonding, slipping away silently while Khira and Kadura slept. He didn't take pack or supplies. He took only Darkchild's pike—and that only because his hand felt naked without it. He had never learned to use the pike properly, only to carry it.

Nor had he learned to ride properly, but when he reached the edge of the campment, he summoned a redmane, a staid mare well past breeding age, and climbed to its back. The animal's gait was wandering and uneven. But if he fell, there was no one to see. The plain was empty tonight, its barren sweep mirroring his own emptiness.

Gone—Darkchild was gone. In the ten days since the bonding, the guide had sent mental feelers in every direction. Everything Darkchild had experienced on Brakrath was meticulously recorded in the brain they had shared: the smell of spices in the palace kitchen, the texture of stone beneath his fingertips, the sound of the whitemane's hooves on the floor of the grove. Even now, ten days after Darkchild's death, every detail was fresh. But Darkchild himself was gone.

The guide sighed. Even the body they had shared felt different now: stiffer, thicker. Now that he was alone, his hands were perpetually cold, his lips and tongue dry and thick. Food had lost its taste and when he spoke, his voice grated.

And Khira—bleakly the guide clung to the redmane's neck. Better if Khira had openly rejected him. Instead she treated him with elaborate kindness—and she watched. He felt her eyes on his face a hundred times a day, watching for Darkchild there. She listened for Darkchild in his voice.

Gone. Darkchild was gone. And now, if he had the courage to let himself go too, if he had the courage to let ice form in the living cells of his heart, as an aging barohna might . . .

When he neared the pinnacles, the guide slid off the redmane's back. There was no teaching tonight. There were no redmanes at the pond. This was the season when redmanes roamed and mated. The guide walked stiffly until he stood at pond's edge. Zan lay upon the water's surface, white, crater-marked, shining.

A single step and another face lay on the pond too: dark, with thin lips, a narrow, well-defined nose, finely arched brows—and empty eyes. The guide stood for a time gazing at his own reflection before he realized that his lips were moving, that he was whispering a teaching of his own:

I am empowered to guide the boy in strange places.

To keep his body safe and fed.

To prompt him to inquire and explore.

To urge him to learn and know.

To divert him from knowledge which is interior.

To direct him to knowledge which is exterior.

To codify those facts and impressions which the boy gathers.

To store and preserve them to meet the terms of the contract.

It had seemed so simple in the beginning. The terms of the contract were clear. And if he had been properly prepared, if he had been as devoid of feeling as the Benderzic had intended, his duties would have been simple. He would have guided the boy without compunction. He would have used Khira and cast her easily aside. When the ship came, he would have returned the boy to the helmet without hesitation.

Now?

Now, he realized numbly, he could still return the boy to the helmet. The required data was there, carefully stored, waiting for analysis and classification.

But so were doubt, indecision, regret—and thwarted caring. What would the helmet make of those?

Sighing, he summoned up courage to do what he must: invite the cold into his heart. He left the pondside and walked to the place where the spires rose so abruptly from the floor of the plain. He stared emptily at the cragged rocks. Then he lowered himself to the ground and sat with his knees drawn up, arms encircling them. He stared into the empty plain for a time before he lowered his head to his knees, letting the cold of night, the cold of the plain, penetrate him. He thought of cold things: mountain snow, winter wind, fear —helpless fear.

He thought of those things and after a while he became so cold his thoughts froze and awareness slipped away. With distant relief, he let it go.

It was daylight when he thawed to life, unwillingly, pain in every muscle. He opened his eyes reluctantly, not sure what had wakened him, and stared blankly at the ground, at the tall shadow that lay at his feet. It was a long, painful time before he raised his head. "Kadura."

She looked down from the folds of her cape, the strength of stone in her face. "Did you think it would be so easy, child?"

Easy? Tears stung the guide's eyes and filled his throat. "I'm taking the ice," he choked. "Like you, Kadura." And it had not been easy.

"But I'm not taking the ice," she said, kneeling before him. "I've put the ice out of my heart. You said something the day we left for the bonding. You told me you thought barohnas took the ice when they had taken too much loneliness, too much pain, from others. Do you remember?"

He shook his head stiffly. "I didn't say that. Darkchild—"

"You said it and I thought about it when we carried you back from the bonding. No one has ever brought as much fear and pain among us as you have. I can't believe you came to us without purpose. I think you came to test us and to teach us. You came to show us—to show me—that we must learn to erect barriers against what we find in others.

"We think ourselves strong, but I see now that we must be stronger. Those of us who have mastered the stones remember times that are only tales to the people of the halls. Their legends are our memories. What they read from the scrolls we know in the cells of our bodies. The past lives in us—we carry it into the future.

"And Brakrath's future is in the crucible now. The Arnimi are among us. One day there will be other humans here—and non-humans as well. The time is past when those of us who can bring past and future together can permit ourselves to take the ice and die. The time is past when we can let ourselves grow tired and then take the easy way from our weariness.

"You tested me ten nights ago, child, and I thought I would fall. I thought I would be the first barohna ever to fall in the bonding.

"But I did not fall. I walked away from the bonding and from all the pain of your memories. You provided me a tempering fire and now my blade is more resilient than ever it was before. I won't let it be broken when my people may soon need it.

"Child, you must be resilient too."

He stared up at her. He had hardly noticed, in his self-absorption, that the shadow was gone from her eyes. Her face still fell in creases, but there was no longer weakness there. Kadura no longer looked like a woman old and ill. She looked like a woman seasoned and strong again, a source of stability for her people, a foundation.

"Darkchild—" He caught his lip between his teeth, fighting back tears. Where had the blessed, numbing cold gone? She held his hands in hers and drove it away. "It was Darkchild!"

"You are Darkchild."

"No." He peered up into her eyes, pleading. "No!" *If I were Darkchild, I would be with Khira now, helping her train. But I can't spar with her—I'm too clumsy. I can't ride with her—if I try to keep up with her, I fall. She's tried to teach me to strike at targets but my pike flies wide.*

Now she wants me to go to the mountains with her. If I go, I'll only hinder her. I was weak, I let the doors fall, and Darkchild is dead. If I go with Khira, I'll fail her too.

"But you aren't weak, child," Kadura said, his hands still captive in hers. "You're afraid—so afraid you have set one part of yourself completely aside. Of course you feel diminished.

"But you can reach for that part of yourself. You can take back all the things that are yours."

"No." He didn't want to hear. He was responsible for what had happened to Darkchild. He would not be responsible for whatever might happen to Khira too. He pulled his hands from Kadura's, struggling to his feet.

He had been sitting too long. His feet cramped, his legs were barely able to hold him. Fighting weak muscles, he turned and stumbled away, fleeing the old woman and the weight she would place on him.

None of it—he would have none of it. He would have the ice and he would have peace.

His heart fluttered as he fled the pinnacles. He looked back only once. Kadura remained where he had left her, black-caped, immobile. She might have been stone—a thirteenth pinnacle. He cried with relief that she did not follow. How many times could he wrench himself away from her strength and stability?

He did not want to go to the grove. Darkchild had left behind carefully stored memories of the grove, of the whisprey and of the white-shadowed whitemane. But where else could he lose himself in cold shadow at mid-morning?

Painfully he made way toward the tall trees. The grove was an alien place by daylight, the trees broadly spaced, sunlight striping the ground with shadow. The soil was soft and moist underfoot. Occasionally he saw phalanxes of insects marching from hive to hive bearing unidentifiable objects. He saw no sign of whisprey, heard nothing that might have been a nightcaller.

But then it was not night. It was day, and when he sat at the base of a towering tree, in the deepest shadow he could find, and closed his eyes, he could summon no night-chill. He thought of cold things and his body remained warm. He imagined a network of crystals forming jagged and white in his heart—but his pulse continued its steady throb.

At last, thinking of the things Kadura had said to him, thinking of what she wanted of him, he put his head on his knees and cried.

He dozed fitfully through much of the day, his arms wrapped around his drawn-up knees. It was not until night that he woke and began to draw the cold into himself again. Moonlight was like silver crystals spilled out across the sky, then pounded into smooth metallic sheets. He had only to stare up long enough and the sheets broke into crystalline form again.

He let the dancing crystals dazzle him, let them carry him away from the grove, back into some deep place where brother-voices spoke. And the brother-faces—if he gazed steadily into the crystalline light, it turned warm and golden and deep inside it he could see the brother-faces. How many times Darkchild had reached for those and come away with no clear concept of their beckoning features.

Now the guide reached for them. He wanted to lose himself in them, to become another diffuse image among the many, smiling and empty, without awareness. An image had no responsibility, no care. An image could never fail anyone. Certainly an image had no life to dash away on shores of ice.

An image did not hear his name spoken in a voice he had not wanted to hear again. "Iahnn! Iahnn!"

It was Khira's voice, using the name she had given him since the bonding. He pushed out a trembling breath and tried to lose himself among the brother-faces.

No use. "Iahnn! I saw the whitemane. It was standing beside you. Iahnn—don't you want to track it?"

The whitemane? He raised his head, bewildered.

"Iahnn! Look—you can see its prints."

No. But he looked anyway, peering down at the soft soil. There was the unmistakable mark of a hoof—and another beside it.

Chill moved along his spine. The whitemane had stood beside him, so close he might have touched it. The elusive creature that had enthralled Darkchild had come to him as he sat unseeing.

Now it was gone. But it had left its prints. Slowly, reluctantly, the guide raised eyes to Khira's. She was watching him intently, as if she expected something profound of him.

As if, he realized with a sharp rise of bitterness, she expected Darkchild to resurrect himself to follow the whitemane. As if she thought this was the stimulus that would finally call him up.

The guide caught his breath in an angry sob. She had called *his* name—the name she had given *him*—but she wanted Darkchild to answer. That was all she wanted from him. Never mind that she treated him tenderly, as she would treat someone she tried to cherish from the grip of illness. It was only Darkchild she wanted to raise from this particular sickbed.

Stiffly the guide stood, setting his jaw against angry tears. "Leave me alone," he said. His voice was at its harshest.

Khira flinched. "Iahnn—"

"I didn't ask you to follow me. I don't want you to follow me. I don't want to see you again." Because she did not want to see him. Never mind her tolerance, her patience—they were for Darkchild, not for him. *"I don't want to see you again!"*

He stumbled crazily as he fled, his legs cramping. She called after him, she ran after him, but she didn't know the right things to say. When finally she caught her foot on a protruding root and fell with a cry, he didn't turn back. He ran through the grove and across the plain blindly. It was true—he never wanted to see her again. It hurt too much that she did not want him, and it hurt too much that if he went back to her, he would fail her.

He ran until his lungs burned and a cramping pain in his side brought him to his knees. As he gulped raggedly for breath, he stared blindly at the crescent-shaped indentations in the soil before him.

Hoof prints—running blindly, he had followed the whitemane's trail. When he could walk again, he pushed himself up and stumbled on, blindly again, wondering.

Again he followed the whitemane's trail without intending it. Sweat poured from his face, his heart labored, his eyes refused to sort images. But whenever he stopped and his eyes cleared, the whitemane's trail lay before him in the dirt. Finally he threw himself down, trembling with fatigue. Why follow the whitemane? The animal meant nothing to him.

Only to Darkchild.

Still he kept to the animal's trail. Finally he accepted the fact that he was tracking the whitemane—just as Darkchild would have done.

And Khira was tracking him. He glimpsed her a dozen times as he stumbled across the plain. She made no attempt to overtake him. Nor did she call out. She simply limped a distance behind him, a lonely figure.

As lonely as he.

By late afternoon he was exhausted and hungry. He stopped several times to gather berries and once he used the tip of his pike to dig edible roots. They were crisp with moisture.

Dusk came and soon he tracked the whitemane by moonlight, glancing up frequently, as if he expected to see the animal before him. As early evening wore on, the vegetation on the plain grew denser. Thorny thickets appeared and sometimes small stands of trees smudged the landscape. Peering intently ahead, the guide saw a larger smudge on the horizon—the forest. His heart thumped against his ribs, a beat of anticipation. He hurried ahead, walking less stiffly.

As in the grove, the trees of the forest were widely spaced, the ground shadow-laced underfoot. There had been rain recently, and the soil was soft and damp. A woodsy musk hung in the trees, a forest perfume that seemed to promise mystery. The guide walked among the tall trees with his pike clutched tight, walked alertly, on the balls of his feet. He hardly noticed that Khira followed just paces behind him now, as watchful as he. There was something here, something in the trees . . . He peered down at the hoofprints in the damp humus, wondering where they led—wondering why he followed.

He followed until he reached a small clearing where grass grew, moon-silvered, and the ground curved in a shallow bowl. Sighing, he sat down to rest and soon curled in the grass, dozing. He heard

Khira step through the trees, felt the warmth of her body as she curled next to him, but he was too tired to confront her.

He woke to her warning touch. He opened his eyes, drawing a cautious breath.

The whitemane stood on the other side of the small clearing, and for the first time he saw it distinctly. The silky texture of its mane, the glistening white hairs of its coat, the pink transparency of its eyes—he stared in awe. The whitemane held its head alertly poised, ears pricked. Its lips were pulled back to reveal strong white teeth.

A distillation of moonlight? An hallucination? Or a living animal, studying him with a curiosity as keen as his own?

Khira's hand tightened on his arm. "Iahnn—do you hear? That sound—I think the whitemanes are bonding. Somewhere in the trees."

He listened. The sound grumbled almost subliminally through the soil. He felt it in his teeth more than he heard it. But as he listened, it became louder—sharper.

Droning. It was not the sound of bonding, not the sound of thunder. The guide's throat was suddenly dry. He took his feet.

No, not a bonding—except of himself with the Benderzic helmet, the metal helmet come to take Darkchild's carefully stored memories and convert them to objective information.

Information about Brakrath. About the stones that stored the sun's energy and the women who controlled the stones. Information about the barohnas' weaknesses and strengths, about the customs and habits of their people. Information about the resources of the mountains and valleys.

Information to be bid away to whoever would pay most richly for it.

Information to destroy a culture by, to make dead a people who had struggled for centuries to live.

The Benderzic had come. The droning of their ship was unmistakable now, sharp, high, ominous. And the guide couldn't move. He stood as frozen as the whitemane.

"What is it?" Khira's nails drove hard into the guide's arm. "Iahnn—what is it?"

He couldn't answer. He was caught helpless in the web of destiny. This was the moment preordained from the time Darkchild had found himself on the tower steps. It had always waited for him. And he knew too well what came next: the flash of a metal hull by moonlight, dark markings upon it; an opening port; a capsule reaching down, metal grapplers engaged; a suited figure stepping from the capsule; the glint of a needle—

He had forgotten the paralyzing beam that came before anything else. It moved across the clearing before the shrieking ship appeared. At the last moment the whitemane panicked and reared to its hind legs, slashing the air with delicate hooves. The beam caught it that way, its powerfully muscled body helpless, its dancing hooves frozen in midair.

Then the beam caught Khira. The expression of shock on her face became a mask, staring. The guide hardly noticed when the beam froze him. Shock and anticipation had already made him helpless.

The contract—this was the moment the contract had directed him toward. This was the culmination of its terms. This was its ultimate end: to see him loaded aboard the Benderzic ship without struggle, data ready for extraction and use.

A tool—He was even more a tool than Darkchild had been. He was the tool the Benderzic had used against Darkchild, to hide the truth from him, to keep him ignorant and docile.

He was—

"Darkchild!" Khira raised her pike as the beam released her and the port opened.

"No!" the guide cried, frightened by the protective anger that glinted in her eyes. "They have weapons. Khira—they have blazers." He remembered now. He had seen the Benderzic turn fire against the damp vegetation of the last world they had taken him from, just for sport. He remembered how wet leaves had curled and blackened, how moss-grown trees had blossomed with clouds of damp smoke.

It was familiar now: the capsule reaching down on its hinged metal arm, grapplers working. He was supposed to aid the retrieval process by stepping forward and letting metal fingers catch in his clothing. Inside the capsule was one suited figure, at the port another—expecting him to cooperate, without question or hesitation. The guide stared hopelessly at Khira. If she slipped away into the trees, if she did not anger the Benderzic—

Because he remembered more about the Benderzic now. He remembered so much he had forgotten. There was fury in them—laughing fury. They spent too much time in ships' holds, biting back all the things they could not direct against each other. How could they survive in close quarters if they set darts of jealousy and anger flying there?

So they set them flying other places—and laughed.

Now the figure in the capsule threw back its head and the guide cringed. He had forgotten how wet Benderzic lips were, how moist Benderzic eyes. He had forgotten the way their brows grew low over their eyes. That much was clearly visible by moonlight.

He turned. "Khira—" His voice caught. He had run from her today. He had told her he never wanted to see her again. But he had not thought of saying goodbye to her this way, with a Benderzic mocking them both and grapplers reaching. "Khira—run! They don't want you. Run!"

She stared at him, momentarily uncomprehending. Then her mouth tightened. "No."

"Khira—" He glanced up urgently. The second Benderzic crouched in the shadowed port.

"Darkchild—how many are there? Just two?"

It was his turn to stare. Her first anger had turned to calculation. Her eyes narrowed with it, and that frightened him more than her anger. "Two—in this ship. But this is only the retriever, Khira. There are others on the carrier ship. Khira—" There were so many things he wanted to tell her, things he had never dared: how bright sunlight looked on her hair in the mornings; how well she walked, boldly yet lightly at once; how kindly she had treated him even when she looked for Darkchild in his face.

How he wanted to cry at leaving her—and at being used against her.

Yes—he would be used against her and against Kadura, against Tiahna, against all the people who had been kind. *Again.*

Used. Without warning, a change came in his throat, as if the muscle tone changed, as if the tension on his vocal chords altered. *"Two,"* he said. The word shocked him because he said it in Darkchild's voice.

Her eyes glinted up at him with triumph. "Then if we can get them out of the ship—"

And take them with pikes, two hand-flung weapons against blazer-armed Benderzic? The guide waited for the thought to shrivel him.

It did not. Because the alternative was not just his death in the helmet, a spiritual surrender, but Khira's death and the death of Brakrath. Without thinking he caught her hand and pulled her with him from the clearing, evading the grapplers. Get the Benderzic out of the ship? "They want to come out," he said, remembering more about them. The Benderzic liked to crush soil under their boots. They were a ship-people, with laughing scorn for the web of life that constituted the environments cherished by others. A thought struck the guide and he glanced back toward the clearing, alarmed. The whitemane—

But the animal had fled without harm.

And the capsule was opening. The first Benderzic was stepping out, putting his boots down heavily, as if he relished the death of land-borne microorganisms beneath them. His voice was heavy with scorn. "Rauth-Seven, you are called."

With a shock, the guide recognized the brother-language. For a moment he experienced a sense of giddiness, as if some part of him prepared to step forward—called. He conquered the impulse easily, almost without thought. If he could answer in the brother-tongue, lashing out with withering words—

But the tongue had deserted him. And his bravado was fading. How could he think of going against the Benderzic? Although Darkchild was a skilled hunter, the guide had never so much as brought down a groundfowl with his pike. "Khira, you have to run," he said in a low voice, hurried. "They have blazers—there are two of them—and I can't help you." He held out his pike uselessly, pleading.

She stared at his stiff arm, at the extended weapon. She stared so hard that he stared too, then caught a sharp breath. He didn't hold the pike in a gesture of surrender. He held it in strike position, raised, ready to fly.

And he held it in Darkchild's hand. There was no mistaking that. His own hand had never closed so lightly, so cleanly around the haft of a pike. Nor had his arm ever risen so smoothly, the muscles like bands of elastic. Slowly, stunned, he looked up and watched the second Benderzic slide down a cable and drop to the moonlit clearing.

"You can help me!" Khira said and laughed sharply, a challenge.

The guide stared in frozen horror as she darted to the clearing and faced the Benderzic. They grinned, pleased by the game she offered, their wet lips curled with pleasure. She turned back once to the guide, moonlight glinting on her hair, challenge bright in her eyes.

The Benderzic unsheathed their blazers, ready to sting her, ready to torment her with a dozen little burnings before they dispatched her and took their prey. The guide had no choice. He joined her at the edge of the clearing—not stiffly, not jerkily, but boldly, with a smooth stretching and contracting of muscles.

Darkchild's muscles.

"What is this, Rauth-Seven?" the first Benderzic mocked, snapping off a beam of fire at the ground, making the damp grass sizzle. "Deserted your brothers for a dirt-witch?" He made a second patch of grass steam at Khira's toes. "Your brothers call you, Rauth-Seven. They wait for you in a place where your boots will make a decent sound when you walk." The Benderzic stamped the ground. "What kind of sound is that for a walking man? There's no ring to dirt, Rauth-Seven. And this dirt-witch—" He raised his blazer, tiny muscles contracting beneath his eyes as his finger closed on the fire pin.

For a moment the guide thought he would watch, helpless, unable to move. But Darkchild's muscles tautened as the Benderzic darted flame at Khira. And Darkchild's hatred moved in his blood. With a scalding cry, the guide raised the pike and sent it slamming across the clearing. Sent it slamming not just at the Benderzic who touched Khira's shift with fire, who burned the pale flesh of her leg, but at every Benderzic who had ever come to laugh and destroy.

Khira cried with pain. The Benderzic staggered, his blazer dropping as he clutched at the pike buried in his chest. His mouth sagged in surprise and then filled with blood, a dying tide. His eyes glazed. He fell slowly, in stages, and the ground did not ring at his impact.

"Darkchild!"

The second Benderzic crouched, laughter dying in his throat, and flashed fire across the clearing. The guide dodged aside at Khira's shrieked warning, feeling heat on his face. He caught Khira's hand, pulling her into the trees. He threw her to the ground to smother the fire that ate a bright hole in her shift. "Your leg—"

"He shot at you!"

That surprised her? His mind worked rapidly, sorting possibilities. Few of them promised hope. "Can you run?"

"He shot at you—Darkchild, he doesn't want to kill you! He—"

He caught her hand again, pulling her to her feet. Behind them the second Benderzic had gone mad with his blazer. Fire ate at the trees and bit at the damp soil, raising clouds of smoke and steam. "All he needs is my brain," the guide said through gritted teeth.

"But alive," Khira insisted, staring up at him in disbelief. "He—"

"He needs me alive long enough to use the helmet. No longer." The helmet would extract the data Darkchild had stored in a matter of moments. And in extremis, the data would be available for minutes after his heart stopped beating. Brain activity would continue at the necessary level for that long.

Oh yes, he remembered a lot now. The Benderzic had no ultimate need for him alive. His conditioning had failed and he was past the age of greatest usefulness. The guide choked on a bitter laugh. He was too old to be the Benderzic's tool now. He was a child no longer; there was a dead man in the clearing to prove it.

They ran. The Benderzic shouted hoarsely, and when Darkchild turned he saw that the trees blazed reluctantly behind them. Thick smoke stung his throat, making him cough. Nearby he heard rustling sounds of alarm. A dark animal shape flashed through the trees, fleeing the smoke.

The whitemane? But the shape was too slight, too dark. Distracted, the guide stumbled over a fallen limb. He caught himself, his lungs burning, the Benderzic's angry shouts in his ears.

The Benderzic continued to direct his blazer at the trees, raising clouds of damp smoke. The guide and Khira ran, coughing, stumbling, gagging. Numbly the guide was aware of forest creatures running with them, silently, invisible in the dense smoke. The woods were damp. If he could fell the Benderzic, the fire would smother itself.

"Khira—your pike—" The guide fell against a heavily mossed tree, fighting for breath. "Your pike—"

She looked at him dumbly, her face streaked, then peered back into the dense smoke. Although her face was set, a carved mask, her eyes seemed to take fire from the burning trees. She turned back to the guide and he saw a stoniness in her he had never seen before, a hard strength that would not be denied. Adar burned in her eyes. Deliberately she raised her pike, the muscles of her calves stretching, pulling her to tiptoe.

The Benderzic plunged through the trees and halted, glaring. He didn't laugh now and he didn't cough, despite the smoke. His eyes rolled with anger and his wet lips were dry and cracked. Perspiration stood like melted wax on his face. "You—image!" He made the word obscene. Then he saw Khira, saw the same thing in her eyes that the guide had seen. Momentarily he faltered, letting the blazer waver in his hand.

Adar flared in Khira's eyes and it seemed to the guide that she raised her pike with taunting deliberation, to the sound of drums. It seemed to him that her every muscle and tendon did its job with mocking slowness. It seemed to the guide that she made the Benderzic wait an eternity for his death.

Then the pike rode the air with blinding swiftness, just as the Benderzic's flame reached out. Without thinking, the guide leapt aside, pulling Khira with him. The matted leaves where they had stood blazed damply.

The Benderzic fell as the first Benderzic had fallen, slowly, the pike quivering in his chest. Again the soil did not ring with his impact.

Two Benderzic—dead with their faces pressed to living soil rather than to ship's metal. Both damned, in their way.

Khira stared at the dead Benderzic, Adar's brightness dying from her eyes. Unconsciously she raised one hand to her face. Smoke swirled around her, wreathing her as it would a figure of stone.

The guide was first to recover from shock. He seized Khira's hand and pulled her away from the dead Benderzic, leaving flames to lick unenthusiastically at the body. They stumbled through the thinning smoke, the guide trying to understand what had happened to him. When first the Benderzic had come, he had been stiff and afraid—and then, inexplicably, he had been neither. First he had stood helpless, ready to throw down his pike—and instead he had killed with it.

And now—he shook his head, trying to clear it. Something had happened to him and something continued to happen. Because so many things were coming alive as he ran. Memories: the savory taste of roast fowl, the smell of rain in the mountains, the bright color in Khira's cheeks when she walked against the wind. None of these were his memories. They were Darkchild's—yet they were suddenly vivid and alive.

He frowned, coughing. Darkchild's courage, Darkchild's memories—Darkchild's awareness. Confused, the guide felt it stir and waken in him, as if the Benderzic's death had terminated some long estrangement. He had called upon Darkchild's courage. He had called upon Darkchild's physical prowess. And now he felt himself caught up in Darkchild's rousing consciousness.

As if it were his own. Dizzily, he fought a sharp rise of panic. If he was afraid and daring, if he was curious and frightened, if he was strong and weak—all at once, all within himself—if there were no partitions, no barriers—if there were no doors—if he could touch the past and reach for the future, all at once—

That should have been release. That should have been freedom. But if his consciousness and Darkchild's co-mingled, if he could use freely all the gifts that had been Darkchild's exclusively, if he could not extricate himself from the resurrecting network of Darkchild's memory—and he could not. He tried to shut back the flow of images and failed. They continued to pound at him, color, sound, event, emotion. If he could not retreat from them—*who was he?*

Who was he if he halted in the moonlit forest, fire dying damply behind him, and found he could not say his own name? Who was he if he could not look down at his hands and name them either as Darkchild's or the guide's? Who was he if he touched his face and knew that it was his—*his*—but could not identify by name the person who bore its features?

He drew a shuddering breath and his heart raced with panic. What was happening to him? He was no longer the guide, but neither was he Darkchild. Before he had been afraid—either of the past or of the future—but at least he had known his own name. Now he did not. Incredibly—*he did not.* Neither of the names he had used fit him.

Nameless, he bit his lip, squeezing his eyes shut. He tried desperately to partition himself—tried to separate guide from Darkchild. But something had happened since the second Benderzic had died. He could not extricate the awareness of the guide from the consciousness of Darkchild.

Kadura had told him he was one. He had insisted he was two. Now, suddenly, he was—neither. And his confusion was overwhelming.

Behind, the dampness of the forest slowly stifled the Benderzic's flames. The boy threw himself down in damp leaves, trembling, lost. Unconsciously he drew up his knees and dropped his forehead to rest upon them. He was hardly aware of Khira beside him.

"Darkchild—"

The boy raised his head, shaking his head dumbly, unable to speak. Whose voice would he hear if he did?

"Darkchild—" Deliberately, reluctantly, Khira moved from the shadows where she stood and knelt before him, moonlight full on her face. "Darkchild—I think it was too soon."

Too soon? Uncomprehending the boy stared at her. It was moments before he realized what he saw, and then he did not believe it. The pigmentation of her skin could not have changed so quickly. The bone structure of her face could not have altered in minutes. And her eyes—

They were deep now, dark by moonlight. They held the same ageless power he had seen in Tiahna's eyes—and the same helplessness, as if Khira found herself shaped by forces she could not control—forces she must live by nevertheless.

"Khira—your face—" Forgetting his own dilemma, he reached out, cupping her chin in both his hands. Slowly, disbelieving, he explored the contours of her features. Her chin, the line of her jaw, the pressure of her cheekbones against the visibly darkening flesh—

"Darkchild, if I took my prey too soon—" She held out her hands—her changing hands—to him in appeal. "Darkchild, if it was too soon, I'll be like Nezra."

Nezra, the failed barohna, trapped in a half-changed body, her powers perverse and unaccountable. The boy felt his hands tremble. Khira had taken the Benderzic with her pike months before her first majority. She had taken him with all the stony deliberation she should have directed against her bronzing prey. She had taken him as if he *were* her prey—and now the first marks of a barohna were upon her.

The boy set aside his own pain and confusion and cradled her face in his hands. Tears gleamed in her shadowed eyes and spilled down her face. They were like acid on his fingers. *Too soon?*

SEVENTEEN
KHIRA

Neither of them had intended to sleep. But at some point Khira curled against Darkchild and they slept, heavily, exhausted.

It was morning when Khira woke, alone. The sun reached through the trees and stung hazily at her eyelids. The faint smell of smoke clung to her shift and to her hair. She roused herself slowly and lay for a moment in the warm hollow of leaves, unwilling to confront the thoughts that came with waking.

She had taken a human for bronzing prey. No barohna had done that before. Indeed no Brakrathi within her knowledge had deliberately taken human life, and she should have felt diminished. She should have begun preparing to offer herself on the plaza on the second day of the next spring concentration.

But she had only to close her eyes to hear the Benderzic's mocking laughter, to see the glint of his eyes by moonlight, and she felt no regret. He had shown less respect for Darkchild than a hunter for an animal caught in his snare. And that had made the Benderzic himself less than human. That had made him a predator to be exterminated.

Khira sat, putting the Benderzic's death behind her. The pike was thrown. Now she had the present to consider. Frowning, she stretched her hands before her. They had changed. The flesh was darker, the fingers longer, the tips blunt instead of tapered. But they were not the hands of a barohna. They were too delicate, the texture of the skin too fine. And when she stood, she was little taller than the day before, although her legs were darker, their muscular structure more clearly defined.

Perhaps her delayed physical transformation was significant; perhaps not. It was her inward sense of herself that troubled her, the feeling that the stone had come fully into her heart for a few instants—and had immediately deserted her when the Benderzic lay dead. Certainly she did not feel it now. She felt only the ache of stiff muscles and a yawning sense of uncertainty.

She turned at a sound from the trees. Darkchild stood in the shadow. When he stepped forward, her chest tightened. There was something in his gaze—a tentativeness, a moment's apprehensive wariness—she had seen before, but in the guide's eyes. And this was Darkchild. She knew him from the easy way he moved, from the way his brows arched in question. "Did you see the whitemane?"

Darkchild's voice—but with a hint of the guide in the inflection. And something more too, something she didn't recognize at all. Khira frowned, puzzled. "No. I just woke."

He nodded and stepped from the trees, his pack thrown over one arm. "He was watching from the trees when I woke. I followed him as far as the retriever ship." He glanced at her, the guide's tentative eyes momentarily looking from beneath Darkchild's arched brows. "It set down and burned. There wasn't much left except the hull. I salvaged two blazers and a stunner, but the stunner has no pack." Squatting, he tumbled the three weapons to the ground. "Have you thought about where we want to meet them?"

"Them?" Blankly.

"The Benderzic—from the carrier ship."

Her lips turned cold. The three Benderzic weapons seemed to absorb light, creating a small darkness at her feet. "They'll come down?" Somehow in her self-occupation, she had set aside thoughts of the carrier and its contingent.

He frowned at her preoccupation. "They'll come, Khira. I don't know if they'll send another retriever first or if the carrier itself will come. But they'll be here." His eyes held hers, searching, troubled. "Khira, if we separate now—if we go different ways—"

She chilled. If they separated, she could go to the campment, to the mountains, wherever she pleased, and the Benderzic would not interfere. They had no interest in her separate from him. "No," she said.

Still he held her gaze. "I thought of leaving you," he said. "This morning I thought of following the whitemane and not coming back."

"But you came."

He nodded, looking down at the ground, saying nothing. After a while he stood, sighing, and slipped the three Benderzic weapons back into his pack. "Will you come with me if I track the whitemane now?"

Again the deep-biting chill. "Yes." Did it matter where they met the Benderzic? If the strength she had felt when she raised her pike against the Benderzic was to return, it would come whenever she went.

And if it was not to return?

Then she would be like Nezra for however long she lived, caught in a half-matured body, her command of the stones perverse and unpredictable. The valley would grow cold and even Darkchild would eventually turn away from her bitterness.

No—and this time the chill was bone-gripping. If the strength did not return, they would be two children against the Benderzic carrier ship and the blazers he had brought from the shuttle would do nothing to even the odds.

If the strength did not return, the Benderzic would take Darkchild and she would not live to become like Nezra. She would not live to repel anyone with her bitterness.

She bit back those thoughts, helpless against them. Darkchild studied her with a detachment she had never felt in him before, gauging her anguish with more pity than concern, as if he had withdrawn from her even though he had invited her to join him in tracking the whitemane.

Troubled, she followed him into the trees. As they walked, almost peripherally, around the obscuring mass of her other concerns, she wondered about the change she saw in him today. He was clearly Darkchild, returned from whatever limbo he had occupied since the bonding. The easy way he slipped among the trees told her that. But there was a remnant of the guide in him, an occasional brief awkwardness, a moment's uncertainty. And there was something entirely new in him too, something she could not fathom. She could only see its outward manifestation in the detachment of his gaze, in the repressive set of his lips. He held some secret from her and it created a distance between them.

The whitemane's trail was clear in the deep leaves. It led them far into the forest, through the area where the Benderzic had set his fires and beyond. There were places in the forest where the trees grew close, towering up like living spires, their trunks darkly mossed, their sparse leaves breaking sunlight into dancing tatters.

There were other places where the ground sloped gently and there were no trees at all but only lush vines.

There were still other places where springs bubbled up from rocky outcroppings and tall grasses grew. It seemed to Khira that there was a special stillness near the springs, as if only the voice of the water would be heard there and sometimes the answering call of the wind in the trees.

It was beside one such spring that they sat down to fashion pikes of stout limbs cut from hardwood trees. It was beside another that they sat to eat their midday meal from their packs. And it was beside another, late in the afternoon, with the sun reaching horizontally through the trees to cast its halo around them, that they found the whitemane.

He stood beside the spring, his head raised, one leg flexed, the hoof resting on a mossed boulder. Nearby, in the grass, his mate lay curled protectively around their foal.

Darkchild's fingers closed on Khira's arm. The whitemanes regarded them steadily from eyes that were pink transparencies, the pupils scarlet pinpoints. The setting sun cast a rosy light upon the three animals, making their smooth coats gleam.

The very directness of the animals' gaze was disconcerting. So was Darkchild's utter stillness, his concentrated awareness. Khira caught his hand. "Darkchild?" Somehow he was slipping from her. He met the animals' gaze and she felt as if he were caught up in a teaching that could never include her, as if he were losing himself in it. *"Darkchild!"*

He shook his head, freeing himself from her claim. Wordlessly he slipped his hand from hers and stepped forward. The whitemanes did not tense or shy at his approach. They continued to gaze at him, the rosy dazzle of the setting sun in their eyes. Silently Darkchild approached them, knelt and placed his hand on the foal's brow, touching the silken hairs gently. He knelt there for minutes and only the voice of the water broke the silence. Then he stood and stepped back.

When finally he took Khira's hand again, she felt the foal's warmth still on his fingers. Darkchild's voice was husky. "He has my mark now."

Khira looked back to the whitemanes, uncomprehending. Then she caught her breath in surprise and incomprehension. The mark of Darkchild's fingers lay like a shadow on the foal's brow. As she watched the mark darkened, until the foal carried a flame-shaped black blaze where Darkchild had touched it.

"How—how did you—"

Darkchild shook his head. "I don't know. I don't know why I put my mark on him. I don't know how. But I think—I think he'll wait for me. Even if I don't come back." His eyes narrowed and he gazed past the whitemanes into the forest. "There are others—other whitemanes. I don't want to bring the Benderzic here."

Khira followed his gaze into the trees, trying to see what he saw. If there were other whitemanes nearby, they had hidden themselves well. Perhaps instead they were scattered over many spans of forest, gathered in small groups around dozens of small springs.

If I had touched the foal instead—But she bit back the thought. She would never have thought to place her hand on its brow. It was not her the whitemane had stood over in the clearing. She had never felt the compulsion Darkchild felt to follow the whitemane. Certainly she had not seen whitemanes at the bonding. Her presence here was incidental.

She understood that if she understood nothing else. She turned back to Darkchild and found he had slipped back to some inner place where she could not follow.

Where? Why? As they turned back through the trees, she thought more about the distance he had set between them than about the whitemanes, the Benderzic, or the lack in herself.

They returned the way they had come, walking until the moons rose. Then they made their bed in the leaves, each wrapped separately against the night chill. Khira lay awake for a long while, wanting Darkchild's warmth against her. But when she turned to him, he stared at her blankly from moon-silvered eyes. There was no invitation there for her.

Was he repelled by the change in her? Was that why he made himself a stranger? Or was it the change in him that created the distance? Khira fell asleep reluctantly, alone.

They emerged from the forest early the next morning, speaking little. The emptiness of the plain was absolute. No breeze stirred the occasional tree. No redmane offered companionship. Even the swarming insects had taken to their burrows. Khira walked with head bowed, trying to feel something new in the touch of sunlight on her shoulders. If only she could find heart-wholeness, if only she could find certainty . . .

But how to recapture the wholeness she had felt at Tiahna's

throne? How to find certainty when Darkchild hardly spoke to her all morning, when he gazed past her at nothing and walked toward that nothing as to the distant mountains—steadily, silently, with a frown of concentration.

They reached the pinnacles late that afternoon and by silent agreement made camp there for the night. Darkchild fell asleep early, curled in the protective shadow of the craggy spires. Khira lay beside him, feeling curiously suspended, as if the world had fallen into unreality around her and only moonlight were real.

Finally, when she could not sleep, she threw off her cloak and stood. She had avoided the pond earlier, afraid to glimpse her reflection. Now she was drawn there. She knelt beside the quiet water, eyes closed, and let her breath ebb away, let her will seep after it.

Slowly she opened her eyes and gazed upon herself in the moon-silvered water. One hand rose, touching her face. She was dark now where she had been fair and her hair hung copper upon her shoulders. From the vestigal features of childhood a new face had emerged, the eyes deeper, shadowed, the nose longer, broader, the mouth wide and unsmiling. There was new strength in her jaw, new prominence in her cheekbones. Even her eyebrows had darkened and become bolder.

It was a stranger's face—but not yet a barohna's.

No. These were only the first changes. She looked now as Denabar must have looked when they carried her down from the mountain. But Denabar had lived only seconds after taking her bronzing prey. For Khira it had been two days. Her head dropped and reality flowed back, weighting her like a stone.

The next morning, Darkchild sat watching her when she woke. She felt his scrutiny for moments before she opened her eyes, but she was not prepared for the sadness she saw in his face. She sat, her heart closing in painful spasm. "Darkchild—"

"I'm going to stay here," he said, as remotely as if he were reading from a scroll. "The Benderzic will find me here. I want you to go back to the campment."

"Without you?"

He sighed and placed a hand over his eyes. "Khira, you can't do anything for me here. If you go back—"

"No!"

"Khira—"

She could never be as remote as he. *"I won't,"* she hissed, making an icy thread of her voice. "I won't go back to the campment unless you go."

He shook his head. "I won't go to the campment. I won't bring the Benderzic there."

"Then I won't go either."

She had the pleasure of seeing a moment's helplessness in his eyes then. She had the pleasure of seeing quick tears. He quenched them with a shaking hand, stood, and walked away, his shoulders stiff.

She saw little of him that day. He climbed among the pinnacles, making his way up the steepest of the craggy spires. He didn't climb as they had climbed with the guardian daughters, for sport. He climbed with silent concentration, deliberately picking his way up the jagged and treacherous faces of the three tallest spires, Upquir, Falsett, and Principe. There were places in the pinnacles where a fall would do little physical injury beyond scrapes and bruises. There were other spires from which a fall would inevitably be fatal: Upquir, Falsett and Principe.

Khira watched, her nerves leaping with tension. He knew how to fall, she reminded herself—loosely, unresisting. But even that would not save him if he fell from the tallest spires.

In any case, he did not fall. He returned to the pond at dusk, his face streaked, his hands bleeding. Jagged rocks had ripped his suit and scarred his boots. He ate without a word. Khira could find no emotion in his face: sadness, regret, anger.

Nor did she find any change in her own face when she knelt beside the pond again at moonrise. Darkchild made his bed at a distance from hers that night, curling up with his back to her, his face lost in shadow. Khira lay wrapped tight in her cloak, her heart empty.

They were waiting for the Benderzic and the night was a trap, set to spring. A snare waiting to close—not on the Benderzic but upon them. She stared up into the stars, watching for some light moving among them that should not be there. She studied the moons, expecting the shadow of the Benderzic to fall across their bright faces. She and Darkchild were prey to the Benderzic—not formidable prey but totally vulnerable prey. They had no defense beyond their pikes and the two blazers Darkchild carried in his pack. When the carrier came, the Benderzic it brought would be wary—as the first two Benderzic had not been. And they would be many.

Khira sat, fighting against a sudden sense that the breath was being squeezed from her chest. The emptiness of the plain called her. Her feet knew the path to the campment, to Kadura's kefri, and her senses knew the comfort of settling beside the embers of Kadura's fire with all the friendly smells and sounds of the campment around her. And Kadura, silent but understanding.

Yes, understanding that she had run away and left Darkchild to face the Benderzic alone. Fighting tears, Khira got up and walked silently to the pond. She knelt and peered at her reflection, trying to make a friend of her altered face, trying to establish some familiarity with it.

She sat until she was stiff, until her hands were numb with cold. Then she rose to return to her bedding. Self-absorbed, she did not notice at first that Darkchild no longer lay asleep. She glanced at his empty bedding without registering his absence.

Then chill moved into her heart. He was gone, leaving not even a print on the hard soil or a hint of warmth in his blankets. Wildly she peered around. She wanted to call his name but the irrational fear that the sound of her voice would betray them to the Benderzic stopped her. Unspoken, his name formed an obstruction in her throat.

She searched the rocks at the base of the pinnacles, probing shadows for some clue to his presence. At last she looked up and saw him far above, silhouetted against the stars. He clung precariously from the tallest spire—Upquir, the master breeder. The craggy peak reared against the stars, and Khira felt the malevolence of the petrified breeder, caught so many centuries before in his quest for the eldest of the redmanes and turned to stone. Tonight, glinting from his dark face, she saw eyes—vengeful eyes. Upquir had only to shrug, to bend, to stoop his steep, stony shoulders, and Darkchild would fall to his death.

Darkchild. But she could not call his name around the obstruction in her throat. And she could not see his face. It was too distant, shadowed.

But now, beyond the spires of the pinnacles, she saw the alien light she had watched for earlier in the sky. It was winking and red and it passed among familiar constellations like the blinking eye of death. It moved, steadily, inexorably, growing nearer, until the body of the ship it announced slowly blotted out the surrounding stars. As she watched, the Benderzic ship created a larger and larger darkness in the sky, a strangely empty darkness, a growing shadow.

The snare was closing, its jaws moving slowly shut, and she stood paralyzed. She could not call out, she could not run. She could only watch as the Benderzic carrier ate the familiar stars. At last the ship was a visible presence over the plain, a dully glinting metal form that hung so silently above the ground that she could not believe she saw it there in all its massive presence. It moved, pondersomely, until its shadow made dark the ground at her feet. Nindra and Zan cast down their silver light futilely, creating no more than a pale halo around the perimeter of its obscuring metal body.

Then the ship moved silently away and settled to the ground beyond the pond. With the return of moonlight, Khira felt suddenly exposed. She watched, still caught in silent paralysis, as multi-colored lights appeared from recessed wells and illuminated the area around the ship, dimming the moon's light.

She expected the metal hatch to open with some groan of sound, some metal protest. Instead it slid aside silently, creating a rectangular darkness in the flank of the ship. A metal ramp appeared and slid smoothly into place.

Darkchild. She tried again to call his name and could not. She could scarcely breathe around the mass in her throat.

Three Benderzic appeared upon the metal ramp, black-uniformed, with gleaming metal at their wrists, at their necks, at their waists. They were much like the Benderzic of the forest landing, short-limbed, compactly built, with thick dark hair, wet lips and rolling eyes. But they were not laughing. They were not mocking. They were stiff with vigilance.

She stepped back involuntarily as the multi-colored lights winked out and the Benderzic and their ship sank into the relative darkness of moonlight. It took Khira's eyes a moment to adapt. Then she saw that the Benderzic still stood stiffly upon the ramp, gazing up at the pinnacles.

Up . . . *Darkchild!* He clung from Upquir's precipitous peak, his face white by moonlight. Khira stared up at him and could almost feel the shuddering breath in his throat, the soft jarring of his heartbeat, the cramping tension of his muscles. He was so far from her—not just because of the physical distance that separated them but because he had moved away from her in spirit.

The three Benderzic who stood upon the ramp did not speak. But the ship did, in a carefully modulated tone. "Rauth-Seven, you are called," it announced.

And gazing up, Khira suddenly knew what was in Darkchild's mind. She knew why he had insisted upon meeting the Benderzic here. She knew why he hung so high upon Upquir's face. She knew why he had drawn away from her.

The Benderzic had come to return him to the helmet, but they didn't care if they returned him as living flesh or simply as brain tissue, briefly electric with residual life, then darkening into death. All they wanted of him was the information he had stored in the cells of his brain.

And he would not let them have that information. He would not permit them to take either him or his dying brain.

He had climbed Upquir and he knew how to fall. He knew how to release himself to the jagged rocks below in such a way that his skull would be crushed and his brain turned to a useless bloody smear.

He had calculated his victory over the Benderzic. The prime element in that victory was his own death.

"Rauth-Seven, your brothers call you to join them," the ship's amplified voice reminded him. "The door stands open and your brothers are gathered. Your brothers wait, Rauth-Seven."

As Khira watched, the ship's interior took a warm golden light. The light had a misty quality, as if a golden haze circulated within the ship, spilling lightly from the open hatch, enveloping the three black-clad Benderzic.

Then came the voices, not in chorus, but speaking out randomly, calling. Voices of men, voices of boys, voices of small children. They spoke a coaxing language, a summoning tongue. Their message, she knew, must be the same as the Benderzic's: Darkchild was called.

Called to the warm light, called to the beckoning voices. Hardly breathing, she peered up to where he clung to the rock of Upquir. Did the golden light tempt him? The voices? She could not read his expression. The distance between them was too great. But she could see that his face was white and strained.

Then, as if her vision had become telescopic, reaching out to bring in detail she could not normally distinguish, she saw Darkchild's fingers loosen, surrendering their grip on the rock. And suddenly the obstruction in her throat filled her chest instead, crowding aside her lungs, squeezing the breath from her in a loud pant. Her ribs cracked loudly.

No, not her ribs. It was the stone of the pinnacles—of Upquir, of

Falsett, of all the others—that cracked loudly and began to heave and grind and tumble and fall. Khira stood with open mouth as the pinnacles shook apart in sudden fury, stone from stone, and boiled in the air. For a moment it looked as if the stones might simply hang in midair, suspended. Then it looked as if they were fashioning themselves into a giant hand that reached to cradle Darkchild as he fell.

Numbly Khira turned to stare at the Benderzic. How had they done this—sundered the pinnacles and robbed Darkchild of his victory? But the Benderzic were as startled as she. They retreated toward the hatch of their ship, their faces twisting with panic, their rolling eyes for once frozen and still—bulging with shock.

As they watched, a stone hand did form from the sundered rocks of the pinnacles. It formed beneath Darkchild's falling body and lowered him gently toward the ground even as the rubble that boiled all around him whipped through the air and pounded toward the Benderzic ship. Driven by invisible force, the stones caught the retreating Benderzic and knocked them from their feet. The Benderzic screamed and the stones pounded, raising a haze of blood from their quickly battered bodies.

With the blood came further fury. Khira felt it as if it were her own. Felt it as if she were sister to the stones that hammered against the metal hull of the Benderzic ship, sister to the stones that hurled themselves through the open hatch and raised cries of fear and sounds of pounding destruction from the interior of the ship.

Khira felt as if she were the stones, as if they had become an extension of her will—as if she flew with them into the carrier and sought out the black-uniformed Benderzic wherever they tried to hide and pounded them to limp, bleeding masses. She felt as if she were the stones that rattled and thumped at all the shining equipment of the ship, smashing and shattering. She felt as if she were the stones that destroyed everything in their path.

Everything except the four empty children who sat silent in one compartment of the ship and watched the destruction with vacant eyes. Them the stones did not touch.

Strange how she smelled the perfume of the orchards as the stones rattled and pounded. Strange how she glimpsed Alzaja through the hail of rocks, walking serene and pale up the mountain. Strange how she heard Alzaja's voice.

Strange how she heard herself sob with concentrated fury. Darkchild had tried to leave her as Alzaja had left her. He had tried to leave her and the stones of the pinnacles had borne him safely to earth and flung themselves at his enemies.

Now Khira stood in the rubble of the Benderzic ship staring at the destruction and tears ran down her cheeks. The obstruction in her throat, the mass in her chest, had shrunk and become nothing more than her heart. Shattered glass lay at her feet. Nearby, beneath a mound of rock, lay a dead Benderzic. His blood spattered the ravaged metal wall.

"Khira?" It was a voice from somewhere far away, from a place she could never visit again—a place of innocence. "Khira?"

She shook her head, the tears burning her face. There was blood on the stones and there was stone in her heart. She felt it there now. It lay heavily in her chest even as she felt all the changes come to her body that had not come before. She gazed down numbly and watched her fingers grow. She felt her hair fall ever more heavily upon her shoulders. She touched her face and knew that it was a barohna's face now.

It was the face of a barohna who, under the threat of loss, had made stone live and used the living stone to kill. It was the face of a barohna who had done these things almost without knowing she did them.

"Khira—these are my brothers."

The empty children. She turned to Darkchild and saw that he had led them to where she stood. They looked up at her emptily. They were slight, their eyes so dark she could barely distinguish iris from pupil. Their black hair was cut just below the ears and their thin lips were encased in grey garments. As they gazed at her, she expected to see their brows arch in question.

But they were too empty to question her, even silently. They simply stared.

She sighed heavily, putting aside the burden of guilt. These were Darkchild's brothers, but they were not even children, not now. The Benderzic had made tools of them, just as they had once made a tool of Darkchild. And in the making the Benderzic had surrendered their own humanity.

She was a barohna who had made stone live and used the living stone to destroy evil. "These are your brothers," she acknowledged huskily. Then she stepped past him to the hatch of the ruined ship.

Where once the pinnacles had stood there was only rubble now. But the pond was undisturbed, its surface clear. Khira walked to it and gazed down at her reflection: at the strength of her limbs, at the power of her features. While the stones flew, she had become as tall as Tiahna and as strong. There was the same mystery in her eyes, the same impassivity upon her face—the same stone in her heart. Not the stone of harshness, but the stone of strength and caring.

Slowly she raised her head. Darkchild stood behind her, still ashen with residual shock, his empty brothers gazing vacantly after him. From the starred sky Nindra looked down with silver serenity.

We'll always walk together. Khira frowned. Those were the words Alzaja had said before she walked to meet her beast. And those were the words Khira had heard her say again as the stones flew against the Benderzic. Khira raised her head and for a moment saw the blue of sunlight falling through orchard blossoms.

Then she turned back to Darkchild. If she had changed suddenly, in the flight of stones, he had changed slowly over the past days. He had breached the barriers that divided him and become one, and that one was more than the sum of the two.

Even so, he looked at her with reticence and white-lipped awe. "You're a barohna now," he said, holding himself back from her, as if he were afraid of violating some new boundary her barohnhood set between them.

"Yes," she said. She was taller than he and she was a woman. But he was no longer a child either. He had seen things no child saw and done things no child did. He was a man and he knew the nature of her heart. And now that they were both changed, they must learn to know themselves again—and each other. Silently she held her hand to him, dissolving whatever boundary change had created between them. They left the ruined pinnacles together and led the four empty boys back in the direction of the campment.

We'll always walk together. Alzaja's words, but Khira used them herself now, and with some measure of Alzaja's certainty.

EPILOGUE

Yet he would leave her one day, he or his son or his son's son. He would go.

Because he had heard his brothers' voices from the Benderzic ship. He had heard them young and old and they had roused the last fragment of his lost memory: the white swath pleading with him in an alien tongue in a jungle clearing.

The voice it used had been familiar to him even then. Now he knew why. It had been his own voice as it would sound when he was grown. And when he had brought up from memory the words of the swath's plea, the Arnimi had translated them for him. They were spoken in a language used in Birnam Rauth's time, in the years of his unsolved disappearance, and their message was simple.

"I am held here, I don't know how. They keep me bound and they feed me strange substances. I can't speak, but the thoughts that leave me go somewhere. Somewhere, and I think they are recorded. If you hear them, come for me. Let me go. Set me free.

"My name is Birnam Rauth and my thoughts are recorded. If you hear them, come for me.

"Come for me."

BLUESONG

For Ruth and Van

ONE
KEVA

It was morning and mist rose from the slow-running stream, cloaking the streambank where Keva walked. In the distance she heard the hiss of geysers. Nearer, topweeds eddied gently upon the water's surface, yellow throats closed against the heaviness of dawn.

Keva shivered, not from the cold but from the dreams she had left behind in Oki's hut. Fire—she had dreamed fire again, a diffuse brightness rimmed on all sides by jagged mountain peaks. As she watched, it overflowed the basin of mountains and lapped against the sky, rising higher and higher until its smouldering heat pervaded all her dreams. She had wakened with her lungs burning and her cheeks flushed. Wakened with the feeling she was about to see something she did not want to see, something so frightening, so confusing . . . Shaking, she had pulled on her clothes and stumbled from the hut, leaving Oki and Lekki still asleep.

The sense of a burning sky was so real it was upon her still, despite the mist and the running water. Keva pulled her padded jacket close, hot and cold at once. Why did she dream of fire in the mountains when Oki said she had never seen the mountains that lay to the north? Par sat on the streambank sometimes with children at his feet and told tales of women who lived in the mountains and drew the sun's fire as easily as Oki drew water from the warmstream. He called them barohnas, and he had many stories of the barohnas and the people they ruled because at one time the warmstream people had lived in the mountains too.

Although Keva was too old now to sit at Par's feet, his stories had been much in her mind these past days. She had accepted them with no question when she was young, but recently some sense of incompleteness had begun to disturb her, as if Par had drawn his tales short of the truth. Was that why she dreamed of fire so often? Because she was worrying at the details of Par's tales? Or did she dream of fire because she *had* seen the mountains—when she rode behind the bearded man? Because she did know something of fire? Something she had put aside? Something she did not want to examine?

Keva glanced around, almost expecting Oki to appear in her nightcloak with denials. Oki said she had never seen fire in the mountains or heard the strange, grinding rumble that sometimes woke her sobbing from her sleep. Oki said she had never ridden a white steed with blowing mane and heard a bluesong that had no words. Oki said there had been no bearded man. Oki said Keva had always lived beside the warmstream, daughter of weeders lost one day when the bottomweeds, their stems unfurled to take the sun, had snarled shut at the approach of storm and dragged their vessel to the bottom.

Keva frowned, walking deeper into the mist. What Oki told her was more plausible than the notion that she had come from the mountains. Yet there was something inconsistent in Oki's manner. Why, if she were only telling Keva's story as it had happened, did her heavy features become so rigid when Keva questioned her? And however hard she tried, Keva could not summon memory of her parents. She could not remember their touch, the smell of their clothes, or the sound of their voices, not even here, where the mist eroded the boundary between past and present.

Yet she remembered the bearded man clearly, the dark of his eyes, the restless way he looked and moved. He was a roaming man, a searching man, and for a while she had searched with him.

Or she had dreamed she searched with him.

Keva tugged at the sleeves of her jacket, trying to warm her fingers. No, she didn't believe she had dreamed the bearded man, no matter what Oki said. Moving softly, Keva crept to the water's edge and peered at her reflection. She was tall and slender. Even haloed by obscuring mist, her hair was the color of night, hanging straight and smooth to her shoulders. Her eyes were at once bright and dark, her brows finely arched. Her lips and nose were cleanly made, and her hands were narrow, with nails that showed pink against her bronze skin.

All this told her the bearded man was no dream. None of the fisher-people looked as she did. Their brows were thicker, their bodies heavier, their hair rougher. And none were so dark, like a shadow upon the water. The only person like herself was the bearded man.

If he were a fantasy why had she created him in her own image, down to the finest detail?

And the bluesong—she could call back scraps of it sometimes, when the sun was bright. It came to her as clearly as if it sang in the trees, a high, wordless yearning. Yet actually the song had come from a blue silk sash the man wore at his waist when he rode.

A silk that sang? That was more fanciful than any tale Par had ever told. Yet she remembered its voice. Puzzled, Keva walked upstream to the rocky place where the geysers played. She watched them, lost in thought, until the sun rose and the bottomweeds sent their thick stems slashing through the water's surface. Turbulence lashed at the streambank and the topweeds opened reluctant throats.

Sighing, Keva turned back toward the fisher village, leaving the streambank to walk among the trees. Their trunks were broad and mossed. Morning shadow pooled dark and cold at their bases. Even her footsteps were lost in their silence.

Preoccupied, she did not realize she had disturbed Oki at her cache until she heard Oki's surprised grunt and looked up to see her back hastily from the base of a hollow tree. Keva halted, startled by her foster-mother's damp consternation.

Oki scrubbed her stained hands on her loose trousers, her heavy shoulders hunched defensively. "Tip leaves from the newest fire-growth," she said quickly. "There's nothing here but tip leaves for medicine."

Keva's brows rose. Did Oki think she would disturb her cache? When the smallest fisher-child knew she must never disturb a private cache without permission? "I didn't see anything," she said.

Oki's heavy head bobbed involuntarily. "Fire-growth," she repeated, stepping away from the hollow tree. For a moment she stared at Keva with damp anxiety, as if she expected to be questioned. Then she scrubbed perspiration from her face and said sharply, "You left without laying the fire under the boiling pot this morning. Have you gathered wood?"

Keva hesitated. Laying the fire was her foster-sister's chore, but Lekki had probably gone hunting bark-beetles with her friends and forgotten. And Keva was anxious to escape Oki's challenging gaze.

"I'll gather the wood now," she said quickly, turning back through the trees.

She had already laid the fire and filled the pot when Oki returned to the firepit, still scrubbing her hands against her trousers. Grunting, Oki sorted briskly through the fibers piled nearby. Silently they set to work boiling and pounding fibers to be woven into cloth. Keva fell to the rhythm of the work, briefly forgetting the things that puzzled her.

At midday the bottomweeds stretched erect, straining toward the sun, and the weedfishers launched their vessels into the stream. Soon they were calling across the water, diving after the edible roots and bulbs that grew in the mud at the bottom of the stream. Teal, tallest of the young weedfishers, splashed and called more loudly than the others, his bragging smile inviting Keva to admire his prowess.

She did not respond. She was of an age now to pull moss from the trees and sew a mattress to share with Teal. Others her age had already sewn their first mattresses, but the warm days of spring roused no desire in Keva to do so.

I don't have moss thoughts because moss burns when there is fire.

Moss burns. Keva shivered as the image of fire smouldered in her mind. *Fire.* "Oki—" she said impulsively.

Oki turned from the pounding stone, warily.

"Oki—I dreamed about the burning in the mountains again last night."

Oki's face stiffened, the heavy plane of cheek and jaw turning rigid. "You dream too much," she said shortly.

Keva shook her head, refusing the rebuff. Instinctively she knew everything was related: her dreams, the bearded man, the bluesong. And Oki could tell her about them if she would. Keva was sure of it. "Oki—tell me about the women in the mountains. The barohnas."

Stiffly Oki stood, her face grim. "There is nothing for you to know about those women."

If there were nothing, why did Oki always respond to questioning with such prickly anger? "I have to know," Keva insisted. "What they look like, how they live—Oki, tell me." The stories Par told the children had the taste of fantasy, of tales passed through so many generations of storytellers they had lost all but the barest flavor of truth. But there were other stories—stories passed among the adults, and Oki knew them. Keva was certain of it. Otherwise why did perspiration stand on Oki's stiff face, just as it had when Keva surprised her at her cache? *"Tell me."*

Oki's jaw clenched, a stubborn resistance. "What they look like?" she demanded roughly. "They look nothing like you or me. They look more like the women who come from the plain with the herds in summer. Dark and tall—Par has told you that. How they live? They live in mountain ways, and if you were meant to know those ways, you wouldn't be a daughter of warmstream weed-fishers. We live here where the barohnas never come because we want to know nothing about them and their mountain ways."

"But you know something," Keva argued. "The weedfishers came from the mountain valleys once. Par told me they used to live there with the mountain people, in stone halls." Surely that much of what Par said was true. The rest, the stories of barohnas lifting heavy boulders and making them dance in the air, the stories of stone eyes that saw long distances—tales, surely; only tales.

Oki's hands bunched on her trousers, kneading the coarse fabric. Her mouth twisted bitterly. "The weedfishers lived in the mountains—yes—before they were weedfishers. And they left because they would not live there any longer. There were things happening in the mountains that should never happen when people live together."

"Things—are they still happening?"

"Now?" Oki's face darkened. "What does it matter if they're happening now? Our people left the mountain valleys so many generations ago we don't count them. We were pale white-haired people when we left, like the serfs who slave for the barohnas. We *were* serfs then, and now we're free people—with no look of the stonewarrens upon us. We've changed that much.

"But the barohnas haven't changed. No matter what the plains women tell us when they come with their herds, they haven't. Perhaps they don't use their fire to burn their serfs now. Perhaps they don't make war from valley to valley. But today is only one moment in time. So long as the barohnas can draw fire from the sun, they will burn again—and we will stay here where they never come."

Keva's eyes narrowed. Challenged, Oki was suddenly willing to talk. "But Par never—"

"Par never tells the children the ugly things," Oki said bitterly. "He's like a child himself—lost in pretty tales. So you grow up ignorant. You've never heard about serfs turned to ash in their fields and children blinded because the barohnas decided to make war on one another. No storyteller will tell you those things when he can weave a pretty story of palaces and orchards and children with hair the color of mist."

Reluctantly Keva nodded. Par's tales had been that: pretty. And if he had not told the children about the burnings—her mind raced quickly ahead—what other things had he expunged from his tales? What bitter things? Because if there were no bitter things, why did she always wake in pounding terror when she dreamed of fire in the mountains? And the bearded man—were there ugly things to be told about him too? About the people he came from?

What people could he have come from? Keva pressed her temples and her thoughts took an instinctive leap. "He's one of them," she realized aloud. "Par told us the barohnas are dark and tall, and the man I rode with was dark and tall. He was their kin." And since he *was* dark, not fair, he was not serf but master—an ugly thing in itself, if what Oki said were true. If the barohnas used their fire not just to warm the valleys and thaw the ground for planting but as a weapon.

And if she had been riding with him, traveling in his care, under his guardianship—

Oki's heavy face contracted. "There was no bearded man. Your father was a weedfisher. Your mother built her hut upstream of mine when I lived in the southern village and I was there to tie the cord when you were born. They went on the water one day—"

"No." Keva rejected the familiar litany. The story of her birth and her parents' death meant no more now than it ever had. She could not remember her parents and she could not remember the southern village where Oki said she was born.

But if she closed her eyes, she could feel the bearded man's surging white steed between her legs, could see him bent over the animal's neck, dark hair knotted over one ear—could smell the leathers he wore.

The weedfisher who had been her father? For all the memory she had of him, he might never have existed.

Had he existed? Catching her breath, Keva peered up at Oki. If Par told stories that were less than the truth, what about Oki? Had Oki told her the truth—any of it? Or had she told her a story full of measured lies?

The sharpness of her gaze cut Oki like a blade, taking her breath.

Oki's stained hands dropped and her face sagged, losing all its dogged certainty. A grey stain spread under the surface of her skin.

Before she could regain her composure, before Keva could follow her own thoughts to their logical conclusion, there was a cry from the farthest trees. Keva turned as other cries followed, conveying the alarm. Oki scrubbed her stained hands on her trousers, the grey of her face deepening. She hesitated for only a moment, mouth twisting, then turned and ran heavily toward the shouting voices.

Keva hesitated, then ran after her. She gathered what had happened as she ran, from the voices that relayed the alarm through the trees. The beetle hunters had been scratching at the loose bark of an ancient grey alder when a spinner had darted from its nest to sink poisoned claws into one of the hunters. The name that was called back through the trees was Lekki's.

Lekki! Keva's breath came hard and her blood beat a protective fury. Lekki, her foster-sister, Lekki with her teasing grin and unruly hair.

The bloating had already begun when Keva and Oki reached the grey alders. Lekki thrashed blindly against every hand, her hair matted with perspiration, her clawed leg grossly swollen. Her eyes were half-open, but there was no teasing light in them now, no awareness at all. Keva caught her breath in a painful sob. She had seen spinner poisoning before, had seen how quickly it worked. Too soon the venom would make Lekki's fingers thick, would swell her eyelids and close her throat, choking her.

Oki had seen spinner poisoning too. She threw herself down, pressing her daughter's thrashing body to the ground. "Be still! You'll make the poison spread."

Reason came briefly to Lekki's glazed eyes. "Mah—?" The half-uttered word was thick.

"Be still." Oki peered around at the gathering fisher-people, agonized. Keva read her thought from her eyes. There was no remedy effective against spinner poisoning except firetips—the shiny tip leaves from the quick-withering vines that grew in soil scorched by a recent lightning strike. Oki had found fresh firetips that morning and hidden them in her cache. But no one could calm Lekki as she could. No one could hold her quiet and keep the poison from rushing through her bloodstream. If she left her to go to her cache—

"I'll go," Keva said, half choking. "I'll bring the leaves. Oki—I'll go."

Keva expected a quick nod, a hurried command. Instead Oki hesitated, holding Lekki's thrashing body to the ground.

"*I'll go,*" Keva insisted, poised to run.

"Yes," Oki said at last, a harsh whisper. "Go."

Keva wasted no time wondering at Oki's reluctance. She pushed through the gathered people and ran, her breath burning in her throat. *Lekki*—her early memories were distorted, disordered, many of them not accessible at all, but she remembered how lost she had been before Lekki was born, before she had had Lekki to bathe and feed and look after. Only as she watched Lekki grow had she begun to feel she was one of the fisher-people, as Oki insisted she was.

But she was not. Crisis made her mind work quickly and revelation came with rushing certainty as she ran through the trees. The bearded man—*could only be her father.* Otherwise why did Oki refuse to talk about him? Why did she insist upon a drowned weed-fisher father whenever Keva mentioned him? Otherwise why was she so like him, with black hair and bronze limbs and arched brows?

She stumbled against a heavily mossed tree and gripped its rough trunk, not wanting to follow her thoughts to their logical conclusion. If the bearded man were her father and if he were kin of the barohnas—

But if she were kin of the barohnas, why had she been left here with the weedfishers? Why had Oki raised her as her own, feeling as she did about the barohnas? Oki had always treated her with a bristling, hovering possessiveness. Could Oki behave so to someone who was kin of the barohnas?

Had Oki even told her the truth about the barohnas, or had she spoken from spite?

There were no answers. Keva's blood ran as swiftly as her thoughts. Reaching the hollow tree, she knelt and tore out plugs of moss. She reached into the dark cavity and pulled out several wrapped bundles of herbs and medicinals. It was easy to tell which were firetips, even without unwrapping the bundles. The feel of the fresh leaves was springy and there was a sharp, distinctive odor.

Catching her breath, Keva jumped up and ran back through the trees. By now someone would have fetched water and pounding tools and someone else would have opened the wound to make it bleed. If the tip leaves were potent enough, if Lekki could stand the bleeding—

Lekki was struggling for breath when Keva returned. The fisher-women worked over her silently, one making a poultice and pressing it to the wound, another occasionally lifting off the poultice to squeeze fresh blood from the gash, Oki stroking Lekki's hair to keep her still. Keva watched, shivering, her throat closed so tightly she could hardly swallow.

When half the afternoon was gone, the swelling eased and Lekki began to breathe freely again. The women carried her to Oki's hut in a makeshift litter and Oki put her to bed, smoothing a fresh poultice on her wound and making her drink a brew of steeped leaves.

Later neighbors brought food but neither Oki nor Keva ate. Both moved around the hut dully, caught in the hard weariness of crisis. It wasn't until Lekki slept and Oki finally sank into slumbrous silence at the foot of her bed that Keva remembered she had not stuffed the moss plugs back into Oki's cache. Keva hesitated, wanting only her own bed, then sighed and moved quietly to the door. Oki shifted and muttered but did not call her back.

Mist was gathering upon the stream again, and in the distance Keva heard the hiss of geysers. The damp smell of early evening was heavy under the trees. Keva tried briefly to recapture the urgency of her earlier thoughts, then relinquished the effort wearily. She found Oki's tree deep in shadow. She knelt, gathering up the scattered medicine bundles and stacking them in the tree's cavity.

Hard—there was something hard buried in the crumbled matter that lined Oki's cache. A stone? And with it something that felt like fabric—as if the stone were wrapped in fabric, a fabric so finely woven Keva's fingertips could not distinguish the individual fibers.

Keva sat back on her heels. A stone and fabric, hidden—*as so many things were hidden.* Keva hesitated a moment longer, then closed her hand around the stone and drew it from the tree's cavity.

She opened her hand slowly, breath held, and unwound a narrow strip of blue cloth. She gazed down, her breath seeping away, her heart thumping softly at her ribs. Par said the women of the mountains—the barohnas—used a black stone called sunstone to capture sunlight. They wore fire-cuffs cut from it and sat upon glowing black thrones. And they used other stones too, which he had not described so vividly. Frowning, she looked down at the stone that had been wrapped in the blue cloth. It was dark blue, many-faceted, and it was mounted in a dull metal setting. Keva rubbed the blue fabric that had wrapped the stone, then stroked the stone itself, cautiously. It was cool to her touch. The fabric was slippery-smooth, the blue of summer sky.

The blue of song. Trembling, Keva smoothed the strip of cloth on the ground and reality shifted from its familiar axis. The strip of fabric was stained and dusty, its edges raveling, but when she touched it she remembered the bluesong as clearly, as achingly, as if she rode behind the bearded man again, clinging to him while their mount carried them—where?

Here? Had they ridden so long only to come here? And had he brought her here only to abandon her? Slowly Keva rose, the sharp sting of tears in her eyes. There was memory, elusive memory, in the touch of blue cloth, and it hurt. *Why* had the bearded man—*her father*—gone and not come back, leaving her only disordered snatches of memory?

Her hand closed on the scrap of cloth, the mounted stone. No one had to tell her these were hers—perhaps the only heritage she would ever have. They were stamped with her father's presence, steeped in it. And Oki had hidden them from her.

Keva's hands trembled. The strip of fabric was just long enough to thread through the stone's metal mounting and tie around her throat. She threaded and tied it and the fabric clung to her throat, blue and cool. Her eyes stung. *Hers*—this was hers, perhaps the only thing she had that was truly hers.

She did not return to Oki's hut immediately. Instead she sat for a while at streamside, watching first moonlight silver the mist that grew on the water. She sat with her knees drawn up, one hand clutching the stone at her throat. She sat until the water was entirely lost in night mist. Her mind worked with cool detachment, her thoughts falling in patterns of geometric symmetry. They were so precisely, so formally structured they hardly seemed to be her own.

At last she stood and returned to the hut. She entered silently and stood looking down at Oki where she slept, heavy, slow, greying. Oki's hair was untidy, her trousers stained. She slept with her mouth open. Lekki slept curled on her side, one plump arm uncovered, her breath faintly rasping. Her eyelids were puffy, not from spinner venom but from the salt of tears.

Keva gazed down at mother and daughter for a long time, her thoughts as remote as they had been at the streamside. Whatever she respected in Oki—her strength, her persistence, her gritty stubbornness—and whatever she loved in Lekki, there was nothing of either of them in her. She was not a weedfisher. She had never been. "I don't belong here, Oki," Keva said with softly stirring anger.

Oki did not respond.

"I don't belong here, Oki," Keva said less softly.

Oki mumbled and moved. Her eyes opened and came to reluctant focus, first upon Keva's face, then upon the stone at her throat. Oki sat, her features registering surprise quickly followed by thick fear. "The stone—"

"I found it in your cache. That's why you were frightened when I saw you this morning. This belonged to my father and you hid it from me."

Oki scrubbed a hand across her eyes and shook her head numbly. "No. Your father—"

"My father left me with you, and he left these things for me. You were to give them to me." That must be how it had been. He had entrusted fabric and stone to Oki for her. They were a message of her heritage, of his love. Perhaps they were even a promise, one he hadn't been able to keep: that he would return for her. "You hid them instead." She didn't try to keep the harshness from her voice.

Oki raised thick-fingered hands to her face. Slowly the fingers closed and she let them fall. "Mountain things," she spat.

So her father *had* come from the mountains. "They belong to me," Keva insisted with muted elation.

Oki thrust herself up from the bed, her eyes taking fire. "Do they?" she demanded, her voice stinging with spite. "And what will you have with them? Ice and stone and fire—that's what you'll find in the mountains. Ice on the ground, stone in your heart, and fire— fire to burn whatever displeases you. Is that the best I've taught you? To make yourself so hard you have stone where your heart should be?"

Keva stared at Oki, the hair at the nape of her neck rising. Ice, stone, fire . . . "I don't know what you're talking about."

"I'm talking about the barohnas. That stone is one of theirs."

Instinctively Keva clutched the smooth-polished stone. "No, the stones they use are black. Par told us. They—"

"Their sunstones are black, the ones they burn with. But they have other stones and this is one of them—just as bad. You have to be stone yourself to use this stone. You have to be as cruel and as hard as stone."

Keva met her vehemence with a tight frown. The stone was a

token from her father. She would not have it any other way. "I'm not cruel," she said stiffly.

Oki swelled with anger. "The worse for you then." Her jaw set so rigidly it jutted. "Because there are two kinds of mountain women: those who learn to be hard and become barohnas—and those who don't. The ones who don't learn it die. Is that so much better than being a fisher-woman? Dying in the mountains trying to find some hardness to save yourself with?"

"I—" Nothing Oki said made sense. How could she answer but by returning the attack? "My father—why did he leave me here? Why didn't he come back for me?"

Oki grunted, her eyes blazing with spite. "He didn't leave you here. He left you in my hut three days south. He was riding and you were sick. He stopped at my hut and I gave you brews and nursed you for seven days. Then he went to take his animal to the forest to breed while you finished healing."

Of course—her father had left her with Oki in the southern fisher village where they had lived before coming here. Her father had left her—and intended to come back. Why hadn't he?

Perhaps he had. Perhaps . . . Keva's fingers tightened on the blue stone. She guessed the truth a moment before Oki admitted it. "Oki—"

Hard satisfaction twisted Oki's face. "He thought he could leave you in my hut and come back and find you still there. Well, he came back. He came riding back, but what he found was an empty hut."

Yes. "Because you took me away."

"I took you into the trees the very day he left. I told my neighbors you died and I was gone to bury you. Then we hid by day and walked by night. We hid and walked while he rode away without you. What made him think I was going to nurse you and then give you back? When my mate was drowned in the storm and none of those vixens in the south would lend me a mate to make a child of my own?"

Keva nodded as another piece of the puzzle fell into place. It hadn't been her parents who had died in the storm. It had been Oki's mate. "The bottomweeds—"

"The bottomweeds took him and I had no one. Until *he* came and left you. What did he expect? Why would I heal you and let you go to become one of them? No, I let him ask my neighbors and I let him search for your grave. Finally he gave it up and rode away. He was that kind of man. I saw it in his face the first day he came, when he thought you would die. He was used to losing what he cared for—just as I was used to being lonely. But I ended that."

Keva shook her head weakly. To let her father search for her grave, to let her wonder, to lie for so many years—

"You're the one who's stone, Oki. *You.*"

The muscles of Oki's jaw bunched. Her eyes darted to the bed where Lekki slept. A moment's baffled anger touched her face. "I had no one," she muttered.

"Did he have someone? After you took me?"

Oki's face quivered. She turned away, heavy shoulders set. "I had no one."

The only sound in the hut was Lekki's sleeping breath. Keva stood like stone for minutes, wondering what she must do. She could not stay here. She was no longer a child, to be stolen and hidden. Nor was she an orphan. She had a father, somewhere. Reluctantly she turned and looked at her sleeping foster-sister. Hard—it would be hard to leave Lekki, and without saying good-bye.

It had been hard for her father to leave her, and then Oki had stolen her from him. He had had no chance to say goodbye either.

Shaking her head, frowning, Keva turned to the hamper where she kept her clothes. She must go, and she must be practical in her going. It was spring now, but it would be cold in the lands beyond the warmstreams. She would need warm quilts and extra clothing. Her hands shook as she bound her heaviest clothing into a bundle and made a second bundle of her bedding.

She refused to turn and meet Oki's eyes. Refused to think of anything but the practicalities of her leavetaking. She would need a few days' ration of food to hold her until she learned to forage in strange terrain. And some extra to carry her through the mountains, where forage would be scant. Silently she stepped across the hut and filled a basket with flatbread and dried berries. Stifling a momentary qualm, she dropped Oki's sharpest digging blade into the basket.

Oki did not speak as Keva slung her possessions over her shoulders and stepped to the door. Keva paused and glanced back, her eyes stinging with regret. She would miss Lekki. Would miss seeing her grow and become a woman. And yes, she would miss Oki too.

But somewhere her father was as lonely as she had been, and he thought she was dead. Turning, she stepped from the hut. Where she would find him she could not guess. Nor could she guess whether he would know her. But she would know him. Even if he had shaved his beard, even if he no longer rode his white steed, she would know him by his searching eyes. She would know her father.

As for what she might learn about her father's kin, about her mother, about the stone—she put those thoughts aside. She was going to find her father. This was not the time for other considerations.

Going, leaving . . . Tears started down her face then, and she knew that inside the hut tears had started down Oki's face too. She could hear the rough, angry sound of her grief.

More clearly she heard the bluesong, calling her to the search. Clasping the stone at her neck, she ran blindly into the hissing darkness.

TWO

DANIOR

It was morning and the diked fields beyond the palace were faintly green with new growth. The air was warm, touched with portents of summer. Danior stood at his window and watched the season's apprentices follow their masters across the plaza, going for their first instruction in the fields, in the weaving sheds, in the breeding pens. His sense of isolation was sharp as he watched them go. Some had been his game-mates just a few years ago, until they had reached their first majority and had been sent to mind herds or carry messages. Now they were fifteen, the age of choice, and they had selected their guilds and gone to take their places.

He had reached the same age, but he had been offered no choice. No one had set his feet to a path that would lead him to a place in the life of the valley. Bleakly he paced away from the window, wondering what the response would be if he went to Juris Pergossa and asked to be apprenticed to a guild. Wondered what silent questions her grey eyes would ask before she recorded his request and dismissed him. Wondered how long it would be before his mother called him to the throneroom to suggest he withdraw his request.

Worse, his mother might not suggest he withdraw it. He might be admitted to a guild, but by an unwilling master. What guild master, after all, had ever been called upon to train a child of the palace? There was no etiquette, no convention for the situation. If a son of the halls failed his apprenticeship, there were guidelines to be followed so that no one need be embarrassed. But if the barohna's son were apprenticed and did not train well—

And what promise did he have that he would train well? That he would ever make a place for himself in one of the guilds—when no one from the palace had ever been inducted into a guild? When no barohna's child had ever come to the age of choice without a clear-cut task waiting?

He pressed his temples, trying to stroke away the sense of empti-ness that had yawned after him all winter, that threatened to swal-low him now. Sometimes this spring he walked across the plaza in bright sunlight and turned quickly to see if he cast a shadow. Other times he stood gazing after hall stewards and kitchen monitors as they went on their errands, wishing he could guess what they saw when they looked at him. Wishing he could tell if the emptiness, the lack of direction, was as apparent to them as it was to him. Occasionally this spring he sat beside his mother's throne while she met with advisers and waited for someone to send him away, as they always had. This year no one did. Because they saw that now he stood as tall as a man? Or because they did not notice him there at all?

His fists closed tight. If they did notice him, who did they see? A dark, tall youth whose presence among them was anomalous? A youth who had no defined place in the social structures of the valley and no path to guide him? Was that why they didn't send him away? Because they had no better idea than he did what was to be done with him?

And if they did not notice him, what did that make him? A product of his own imagination? Thought without substance?

It was at times like that that the restlessness overtook him—as it did today. If he was to have a place, he must find a path. He must build a legend—separate from all the other legends of the valley, of his family. And this was the time to begin to build it. Today. Tensely he turned from the window. His gaze lingered only briefly on the rugged stone wall of his sleeping chamber, hesitated bare moments over the pits and gouges of centuries. He took only pe-ripheral notice of the orange blaze of the stalklamp that grew upon his walls. In his thoughts he was already walking across dike tops to the orchard where the whitemane grazed. He already looked upon its white presence among the trees, promising that if he mounted, if he rode the animal no one but his father had ridden, his legend would be initiated. He would begin to understand who he was and where life might lead him. He had not decided how far or how long he would ride. Just the feel of the whitemane between his legs was what he required.

And if he did not go to the pasture soon, he would think too much and lose nerve. Steeling himself, he slipped from his chamber

and down the stalklit hall. The palace was a place where centuries
lived in the stones, where history paved the floors and soared in the
arched passages. He let none of that touch him today. He deliberately insulated himself against the myths and tales that found permanence in the stones of the palace. It was not his history that lived
here.

Not his at all. But if he rode the whitemane, if he did that one
deed, perhaps he could make it his.

Reaching the lower floor, he paused in the arched entryway to
the throneroom. Light from the mountain lenses blazed from mirrors set high in the walls and made the throne glow. Danior's sisters were curled upon embroidered cushions before the throne, ciphering scrolls. They were younger than he and they were of a
kind, delicately made, with auburn hair that hung straight to their
shoulders and autumn-gold eyes. Sometimes he looked with trepidation at the fine bones of their wrists, at their fingers that appeared
almost too fragile to manipulate eating utensils. Their voices were
laughing wisps.

But they were palace daughters and their fragility was a sham. It
was he who could not find his way, while his sisters only waited for
their chance to take up the sunstone and become barohnas of the
sunthrone.

He stood looking at them silently and they did not notice. Then
he turned and hurried to the plaza door, before he could lose courage.

He needed fittings: halter of finest white leather, intricately
woven reins, an embroidered pad to protect the whitemane's back.
He hurried across the plaza and down stone avenues to the shed
where the animal's things were kept. There he folded halter, reins
and pad into an empty grain bag. He was not surprised to see that
his hands shook. If he rode the whitemane, he would not just initi-
ate his own legend. He would usurp a part of his father's legend as
well. And while he doubted his father would be angry, the presumption frightened him, as if he offered himself for a task that
might prove too large.

He wasted just a moment gazing around at the other fittings,
trying to calm himself. Here was the embroidered collar and coat
the whitemane wore when he paraded in the plaza at Midsummer
Fest. There was the heavy coat that fitted down over his flanks on
Darkmorning to protect him from the cold of the mountains. And

hanging nearby were a black halter and reins of heavy black leather deeply incised with stylized patterns.

His hands still shook. Quickly Danior slipped from the shed and ran down stone paths, across dike tops, away from the palace and its precincts.

It was a clear bright day, cloudless. Lenses flashed from the mountainsides, beaming thick shafts of light to the great mirrors of the throneroom. Danior paused to trace the heavy shafts to their individual mirrors, then hurried on. When people passed with tools and implements, he evaded their greetings. Finally he left the fields behind. The terrain changed, the ground becoming stonier as he neared the flank of the mountain.

It was not yet blooming time in the orchards. The trees were covered with tight-curled buds and fledgling leaves that rattled as Danior passed. The grasses that grew under the trees were tender and stalky. Here and there Danior found the print of hooves, but they did not form a path for him to follow. He could only search randomly. Once he saw the flash of an Arnimi ship in the distant sky. He watched until it was gone, then resumed his search.

The orchards were wide, but it was not long before he sighted the whitemane grazing near a rocky outcropping. He halted, sucking an involuntary breath. The silky texture of the animal's mane, the glistening white hairs of its coat, the pink transparency of its eyes— there was nothing on Brakrath so heart-stopping as the whitemane. It was a legend living, a legend that had given itself to a man: his father. Now he must take some of the legend for himself or go back to the palace empty.

When he moved forward again, the animal heard his step and raised its head, ears pricked. Its lips pulled back to reveal strong white teeth. On its brow was a black, five-fingered blaze—his father's mark. Unconsciously Danior wiped his palms against his trouser leg and swallowed back apprehension. It had been easier to think of riding the whitemane in his chamber than it was here.

He paused again, gathering nerve. His father talked to the animal —when he groomed it, when he fed it, when he rode it. But words deserted Danior and he approached the whitemane in tight-throated silence. The animal had a light, sharp scent and its whiteness was dazzling. Danior halted and pulled a handful of grass. He held it out. "Come," he urged. His voice was softer than he intended, more plea than command. As if he were begging for what the animal could give him.

The animal studied the wad of grass, the pinkness of its eyes deepening. Danior breathed shallowly, poised. When the animal stepped near he would slip halter and reins from their bag and slide them over the animal's head. He had seen his father do the same thing many times. Then he would strap the pad to its back. And finally he would catch his fingers in its mane and pull himself to its back.

That was what he intended. But when the animal stepped forward, when it bent to nuzzle the clump of grass that dropped from his hand, when he pulled harness and reins from the bag, ready, a force like a quickly tightened fist squeezed his heart. He dropped halter and reins and stumbled backward under the dizzy rise of panic. Because a new thought had come to him, one he hadn't considered before.

Touch the whitemane? *What if he marked it?* He knew by heart the story of how his father had come upon the whitemane as a foal in the forest, of how he had been drawn to it and had put his hand to its brow. When he removed his hand, the mark of his fingers had remained, a black blaze.

What if *his* first touch marked the whitemane too? What if he seized its mane and turned the silken hair black? What if he touched its neck and left a permanent discoloration? His chest choked shut at the thought. He had no right to ride the animal. What if the very mark of his calves marred its belly?

It was frightening enough that he had come to usurp a part of his father's legend. But to mar the whitemane's gleaming coat—his hands turned cold. His nails, normally pink against his dark skin, were chalk white. Shakily he tried to bring himself under control. His father was the only person who rode the whitemane—but not the only one to touch it. He let other people groom it and feed it when he could not. Every day children stopped beside its pen to rub its nose and whisper to it.

But Danior was not others. He was neither a child of the stonehalls, sturdy and fair, nor a palace daughter like his sisters. He was a palace son, the only one ever born. He had no place, no history, no future decreed by tradition. Who could tell what stain lay in his fingertips?

Or was that just an excuse to abandon his plan? An excuse not to discover that riding the whitemane would make no difference in who he was or in all the things he wasn't?

The grass he had pulled lay wilting on the ground. The

whitemane nudged it once, then wandered away, browsing. At last Danior folded harness and reins back into the bag and retreated, walking stiffly, his fingers so cold he could not close them. If this had been a test, he knew bleakly, he had failed. He had come away empty.

Later that day, from his chamber window, he saw his father riding the whitemane back to its pen. The black blaze glistened against the animal's unspoiled whiteness. Danior watched with fists closed tight on nothing.

Later still Danior lay staring up at patches of tangled stalklamp and evaluating the sorrowing bitterness that rose in him. Why was he the only one who had no tradition, no place, no way?

Later still, moved by an impulse he recognized as misdirected even as he surrendered to it, he left his bed and went to the stairs. His shadow lost itself in the softer shadows of the stairwell as he descended. If he had no tradition of his own, whose must he live by? If he were a palace daughter, it would be time to stalk his beast and invite the change that came only at the risk of life. Perhaps, he told himself without fully believing it, there was a breeterlik, a cragcharger, a snowminx waiting in the mountains now to test and change him just as his sisters would one day be tested and changed.

It was dinner time and the corridors were empty. Danior's stomach contracted sharply at the smell of roast fowl and fresh-baked bread, but he did not join his family and the palace workers in the dining hall. Instead he turned down the long corridor to the training room.

Despite the scrubbed cleanness of its stone floor, the painstaking cultivation of the stalklamp that grew bright upon its walls, the training room smelled of years of disuse. Danior paused inside the door. There were tumbling mats on the floor. The wall was hung with protective visors, padded vests, staffs, pikes, targets—everything a palace daughter needed to train to take her beast. Everything was clean and waiting.

Danior let the tall stone door close silently behind him. Waiting —the training room was waiting. It had been waiting since his mother and her sisters had trained here. *Alzaja, Mara, Denabar* . . . He frowned. He could not remember the names of all his mother's sisters, though he heard them each year at feast times. He could easily imagine them, palace daughters all, as slight as his sisters, as fragile.

A chill shivered down his spine. Seven sisters—six had failed in their challenge and died on the mountainside; one had survived and changed and taken the throne: his mother. In a few years his own sisters must come here to train. There were only three of them. If none survived, the valley would die when his mother lost the power of the stones. There would be no one to catch the sun's heat and concentrate it where it was needed. No one to warm the fields and orchards and extend the brutally short growing season. No one to insure that there was grain and fruit.

Danior stared around the training room and tried to guess how many palace daughters had trained here over the centuries—and still left the room empty; how many had died for each one who lived and changed.

The room was haunted. Danior looked down at his hands and saw that his nails were white again. Handle the staffs and pikes his sisters must train with? Mark them with his fingers, all the things that had only been used by palace daughters preparing for the test few could survive?

Unconsciously he rubbed his fingers on his trouser legs, relinquishing the impulse that had brought him here. He had not marked the whitemane and he would not mark the sparring tools. What could it possibly prove if he went to the mountains and killed a beast? That there had been a beast waiting to give one of his sisters—Tanse, Aberra, Reyna—the power of the stones and he had killed it instead. Stiffly Danior turned and left the training room.

He felt lost in the corridors. He felt as if he had surrendered what little substance he owned, had become nothing more than a wisp of disconnected thought boiling along the floor. He was surprised to find himself in the empty throneroom, standing before the faintly glowing throne. He didn't reach out for its warmth. He simply stood before it in the dark, his thoughts echoing and empty, then withdrew.

Afterward he didn't remember going through the arched door to the plaza, didn't remember wandering down stone-paved streets and lanes, didn't remember hunching against the wall of the whitemane's pen and falling asleep with his knees drawn up to support his head.

His face chilled and his back turned stiff as he slept. He woke with a mumbled protest and realized that someone shook him by the shoulder. "Danior—Danior!"

He raised his head. His father knelt beside him, calling his name. His father: as dark as he, with a smooth strength in his stride and eyes that sometimes seemed to look far and sometimes were turned penetratingly near. His father, who had seen places no other person on Brakrath could even guess at. Tonight moonlight struck the planes of his face and threw shadow in his eyes. Stiffly Danior pushed himself to his feet, trying to see past the shadow. Had he ever seen fully beyond the obscuring veil of legend, he wondered. If he could press the veil aside, if he could learn whether his father had ever felt as he did, lacking, uncertain, alone . . .

His father stood too. "Aren't you cold?"

Danior shook his head, involuntarily measuring his height against his father's, frowning. It was a painful incongruity, being at once nothing and as tall as legend. And he knew he could not ask what he wanted to know. There were no words for questions that lay so close to the heart. Sighing, he glanced up and saw that the night was half gone.

His father misunderstood his glance. "Chia hasn't risen yet. Tanse is still at her window watching."

Danior bit his lip. He had forgotten that tomorrow—today? was it that late?—was Tanse's host day, the first spring rising of her host star, Chia. Everyone in the valley would hum Chia-songs tomorrow and eat foods harvested or prepared on the day of Chia's last autumn rising. Eggs taken from the nest and put into pickling jars on that day, bread baked from wheat harvested on that day, dried berries and fruits—Danior touched his stomach and felt hollowness: for the dinner he hadn't eaten, for the host stones he had not been offered as an infant because they were never offered to males, for all the traditions that had no place for a palace son.

As if to aggravate the condition, his father said, "Word comes from the orchard tender that you borrowed my halter and reins today."

Danior flinched, embarrassed that he had been seen when he thought he had not, anxious that his father thought the matter important enough to seek him out. "I didn't see anyone in the orchard."

His father shrugged, turning to lean against the wall of the pen. "Does it matter? You may ride Fiirsevrin anytime you wish. Tonight if you want."

Involuntarily Danior shrank from his father's questioning gaze. Ride the whitemane now? Did his father think he could intrude that casually upon legend—the legend of the marking, the legend of a steed ridden by no one but his master, the legend of an unbreakable bonding between steed and master? If he rode the whitemane, it would never be at a whim, easily. "No," he said almost defiantly. "I've never touched Fiirsevrin, and I won't now."

That denial brought his father's gaze to tight focus. For a moment his face was almost severe, the dark eyes sharp beneath the arched brows. "Tell me this, then. Do you want to ride him?"

The question was not an invitation but a query, deliberately probing. Danior drew back instinctively. "No." Despite the panic that rose in his throat, he kept the single syllable flat.

But his father heard beyond word and tone. The focus of his eyes grew sharper still, penetrating. "Ah. You went to ride but changed your mind. I have watched you. I think there are many things you have considered this spring, but I haven't seen you do any of them. What will you do, Danior, now that you've reached the age of choice?"

Danior felt his breath quiver. He could not believe his father had asked it—and as easily as if the question weren't a direct offensive against the most tenderly guarded ramparts of his privacy. What *will* you do? Remain in the palace, isolated and without place? Live at the edges of life, trying to subsist on someone else's traditions, someone else's legend? Or hunt a beast to its den and let the beast make his decisions for him?

What decisions? Danior's fists closed. He had no decisions. If Tanse went at her first majority to hunt a breeterlik or cragcharger, its killing of her or her killing of it would have meaning within the legends of the valley. If he went, neither outcome would have meaning. Because who was he?

A palace son. The only palace son a barohna had ever conceived and brought to live birth. The only palace son who had ever taken first steps in a Brakrathi palace. The only palace son ever to stare out tall windows and wonder what path he must take, how he was to raise the courage to find and follow it.

It seemed to Danior that he had no courage. His father's question only underscored the fact.

His hands hurt from clenching them. He stared at his father and felt pain turning in upon itself and becoming anger. If his mother had chosen a man of Brakrath—a herder, a breeder, a gem master —to father her first child, he would have been born a palace daughter or not at all. Instead she had chosen a man from another world. Danior wondered bitterly if she had given thought to the ultimate result of that union, the birth of a child who stood outside all the traditions of Brakrath. "Maybe I'll do what you do," he said, making the words bite. "Maybe I'll be a consort." A man without trade or tools. A man with neither occupation nor profession. And never mind the legends he bore, the tales built around his arrival and presence here. Never mind the place he had made for himself.

His father frowned faintly at the jibe. "Ah, do you think I'm ashamed to be a consort, Danior? Just because there are no others? In that case I'll tell you now—I'm not. The responsibilities your mother carries are heavy. The decisions she makes determine the life of every person in Valley Terlath. And she chose to abandon tradition and give her loyalty to me rather than to a stone mate. She chose to make me the person she talks to, the person she shares concerns with, the person who remains a constant in her life. I'm not ashamed to be that person. I never have been.

"But you shouldn't plan to follow in my footsteps. There will be no consorts after me. The Council made that clear when it sent my brothers away. The barohnas aren't ready to put aside their pairing stones and take permanent mates. Not from among the men of the halls and not from elsewhere either."

Danior shivered and turned from his father's steady gaze, already ashamed of his jibe. He had never known his father's brothers and he had never dared question him about them. But he thought of them sometimes when people laughed on the plaza beneath his window and his room yawned with emptiness. He knew a few things: that there had been four of them; that they had been so like his father and so like each other people said they might have grown from the same egg; that they had come from the stars just as the Arnimi did; that the Council had sent them back, three of them. The fourth . . . He frowned up at his father. "The Council didn't send all your brothers away. The oldest—"

"No, they didn't send Jhaviir away, though I'm sure they wanted to. We've never discussed any of that, have we—the things that happened before you were born. I've wondered why you didn't ask me."

Danior shifted uneasily. "I thought—I thought you wouldn't want to talk about it." If he had had brothers and lost them—brothers like himself; brothers to understand what he said and to understand all the things he was afraid to say; brothers to go to in the middle of the night when the emptiness was too much—the memory would ache.

His father inclined his head thoughtfully. "There were times when I didn't want to discuss them. It wasn't so hard when the Council requested that the Arnimi send the three youngest to Arnim. Jhaviir was still here. We weren't close, but I felt we would be one day—when we were older, when we had more time to reflect on all the things we had in common."

"Jhaviir was Lihwa Marlath's mate?" Danior probed reluctantly.

"Yes, that's why the Council didn't send him away. The younger three had no ties here. But Jhaviir had already taken Lihwa as his mate, just as I had taken your mother. And she wouldn't peacefully have seen him go—any more than Khira would have seen me leave. That's one of the things that troubled the Council. Barohnas have never taken men as permanent mates. They have always chosen the fathers of their daughters casually, formed a brief liaison—seldom so long as a season—and reserved their loyalties for their stone mates and the other women of the Council. Then we came, my brothers and I, and first your mother and then Lihwa chose to discard old loyalties, old ways. To keep a permanent mate." Absently he reached into his pocket and extricated a worn velvet pouch.

Danior stared at the pouch, at the faceted blue stone his father drew from it. "A pairing stone," he said aloud, surprised.

His father nodded. "Yes. When the gem master heard that Lihwa and Khira had taken their thrones, he cut stones for them. Their mothers had been stone mates, their grandmothers before that. He thought they would be too. He thought they would require stones to link their thoughts, to keep the bond between them strong as they governed their valleys.

"But when he brought this stone to your mother, she wouldn't wear it. We were close, so close she thought it would hurt me to see her hold the stone and share thoughts with Lihwa. She thought I would feel excluded—and angry—every time I saw the stone light."

Danior frowned, wondering how far he dared press his questions. "Would you have felt that way?"

"No. But it's hard to persuade a person who has strong feelings that they aren't common to everyone. She thought I would be hurt and she decided to have the stone destroyed. I felt that someday she would need the stone to share thoughts with someone beside me. Someone who understood better what it is to command the sun-throne: Lihwa. So I asked her to let me hold the stone instead. And she did."

"But Lihwa died," Danior said reluctantly. "And Jhaviir too."

His father gazed down at the stone. He spoke slowly, each word carefully weighed. "I don't know that he did. He rode away, certainly, after Lihwa died, and no one has seen him. No one has heard of him. But there are many places he might have gone where we would not have heard. His training was far more rigorous than mine. He learned to use weapons as a small child. Eventually he learned all the disciplines of a soldier. He was armed when he left and he knew the mountains. He explored them far more intensively than I ever did. At least I tell myself all that when I find myself wondering what became of him. And that's more and more often as I grow older."

So the memory did ache. Knowing, Danior hesitated over his next question. "You were twins," he ventured, "but Jhaviir grew up fighting and you did not." He had never understood why his father and his brothers, so much alike, had been raised differently, by different people.

"No, we were far more than twins. People here called us that because they couldn't accept what we really were. It violated their most closely held feelings about the way life is passed from parent to child, about the sacredness of that process. That, I think, was the second reason the Council voted to send my younger brothers away. They didn't want the institutions of Brakrath and the loyalties of the barohnas to change as rapidly as they appeared to be changing. And they were uncomfortable with what we were, with what they felt when they saw us, so much alike, and knew how we came to be that way. We weren't twins. We were images."

"Images?" Danior glanced up sharply. What could his father mean? An image was a face glimpsed in the looking glass or a sketch quickly drawn with pen and ink. An image—

His father spoke softly, turning the pairing stone in his hand. "We were Rauthimages. Well over a century ago a man named Birnam Rauth left his home world—a planet called Carynon; it lies in the direction of your mother's host star, Adar—to become an explorer. A scientist. He had obtained support to compile a study of little known worlds. Worlds no one had studied or exploited yet. On one of them he encountered several members of a ship-dwelling race, the Benderzic. Without his permission, the Benderzic took cells from Birnam Rauth, placed them in culture, and from each cell they grew a new Rauth. That's what I am, that's what Jhaviir was, that's what all my brothers were, and there were many of them—new Birnam Rauths, identical to the original Birnam Rauth and to each other in every way." His eyes narrowed speculatively at Danior. "Can you accept that? That I'm the rebirth of a man born two centuries ago? His image?"

Danior fought down a bristling reaction at the indignity of the process his father described. "People aren't grown that way."

"But they are, Danior, and in many places. You've seen hall tenders grow stalklamp that way. They break off a piece and place it in a growing medium. After a while it roots and develops and it can be potted to grow on your wall. That's much the way my brothers and I were grown, but in a laboratory on a starship, under far more sophisticated conditions. Then we were left as small children on various worlds, to learn the languages and ways of the people who lived there. In our way, we were explorers too, as Birnam Rauth was."

Stubbornly Danior shook his head. He knew something of starships. He had met the Arnimi who visited the valleys occasionally to record information. They had come to Brakrath by starship and certainly they did not employ children. "No one uses children that way," he said. "They can't be trained. They—"

"But they can be programmed, if you don't care that your techniques leave them little trace of their humanity. And who is a more enthusiastic explorer than a child? Even a child who has been turned into a tool. Who is more curious? Who learns more quickly? That's how we were used, as tools. The Benderzic left us for a few years on one world, then took us to another for a few years. We were used like cultural and environmental recording devices. That's what a child is, after all. A child's job is to learn about his environment, and we did our job very well. Later the information we brought back to the Benderzic was sold to concerns interested in exploiting the worlds that were under study."

"Then—" Reluctantly Danior accepted what his father said.

"That's how Jhaviir came to be different from me, even though we were genetically identical. For some reason, the Benderzic left him for almost fourteen years with the Kri-Nostri, a desert people who lived on a world in the eastern rim of this galaxy. Their environment was harsh, and they were just emerging from a long period of wars. I went to several other worlds, kinder worlds, and then I was sent here. When the ship came to retrieve me and the information I had gathered about Brakrath, it was carrying Jhaviir and three of my younger brothers to new assignments. But it never left here. You've seen the place where it is now."

Danior nodded. The Benderzic ship lay on the plain, crushed under tons of stone. That was part of his father's legend: that his mother had destroyed a starship rather than let him be taken away: that later she had taken him as a permanent mate, over the objections of the Council. He had become her consort and Jhaviir had become Lihwa's; the Council of Bronze had become alarmed and sent the younger three brothers to Arnim; and finally Lihwa had been killed in a snowslide and soon after Jhaviir and their child had ridden away on his whitemane and not been seen again.

"That's why Jhaviir went away," he said slowly, guessing. "He was afraid the Council would send him to Arnim too, after Lihwa died."

"Partly, perhaps. And partly because he was never content to live the palace life. He was an explorer, a Rauthimage. He wanted to see new places, to meet new challenges, to learn new ways. It was in his blood, just as it was in Birnam Rauth's."

Danior's eyes narrowed. Was there wistfulness in his father's voice? He had been created from Birnam Rauth just as Jhaviir had. Was there some restlessness in him too? And if there was, why had he suppressed it? "You—did you ever meet him? Birnam Rauth?"

"No. I heard a recording of his voice once, a long time ago. The Arnimi translated it for me. It was a call for help."

"And did—did someone help him."

Slowly his father shook his head. "I think not. He disappeared over a century ago. No one knows how or where. He had completed his funded studies and gone exploring on his own, in a single-man ship. He resupplied at a small port on Rignar, not so far from his home world, Carynon. But he told no one where he was bound when he left, and he hasn't been seen or heard from since, except for the one message. And that wasn't helpful. It simply said he was being held against his will in a place he could not describe. No one could discover the origin of the message—what world it came from, how he managed to record it. He's dead, I think, and I didn't meet him. But there are many people I've never met. Many places I've never seen."

This time there was no mistaking the regret. Danior pressed his temples, uncomfortable with the knowledge that his father lived with a carefully hidden discontent. "You must have wanted to do the same things Jhaviir did," he said tentatively.

"To ride away and see this world, land by land?" His father's gaze flicked to the distant horizon, lost in darkness. "Yes, I've wanted to do that. I've visited the plain, of course. Khira and I lived with the guardians the summer before she bronzed. But once she took the throne, our scope narrowed. Necessity keeps us in the valley during the warmseason, in the mountain palace during winter. There are other societies on Brakrath but I've never seen how their people live, what customs they've created for themselves, how their thoughts are patterned. I've never seen the lands they live in or the barren lands between."

Danior licked his lips. Did he dare ask? "Why? Why haven't you gone?" His mother could not leave the valley, but his father was not bound to the throne. The life of the valley could continue without him.

His father sighed, rubbing the pairing stone between his fingers, staring down into it. "And leave your mother? Leave you? Leave your sisters? No. When I was very young, the Benderzic left me among a people who called themselves the plain people. They were farmers, people who smelled of the soil. They found me in their fields, an abandoned child who didn't know any human tongue, and they took me in and made me human. Then after four years, the Benderzic came and took me away. They put their helmet on me and drew out all the information I had gathered—the resources of the land, the strengths and weaknesses of the people, their habits and customs. And they took my memory away. They left me empty. After they removed the helmet, I couldn't even remember the face of the man who had called himself my father for four years.

"They set me down empty on another world, this time for five years. A woman found me in the trees and took me home and made me her son. She fed me and clothed me. She taught me to read and write. And she taught me what it is to care for other people, what it means to be a human among humans. I even found a few stray memories of the plain people before the Benderzic came and took me again. And took all my memories away.

"Finally the Benderzic left me here. They left me in the cold of winter in the palace tower. Your mother found me and this time she was the one who made me human. I didn't have language, I didn't have memory, I didn't have a sense of myself as anything but a tool of the Benderzic. Alzaja, Khira's sister, had died that year on the mountain and Khira was lonely. She took me for her companion knowing nothing about me. She fed me, she protected me, she destroyed the Benderzic ship when it returned for me. Everything I am, she made me.

"But it took me many seasons to find my memories again. I've never found them all. I can remember going to the temple to hear the godsvoice with my second mother but I can't recall the words to the chants—although I dream them sometimes. I can remember helping my father among the plain people sow seeds, but I don't remember what grew from them.

"I've left too many people and too many places in my lifetime. I've learned what it is to wish for a face I know, one I won't see again. I've learned how quickly even memories can vanish, how empty it is without them, how hard it is to call them back when they've begun to fade. Much as I want to see other lands, I want more to stay here, where I know the faces, where my memories still live around me.

"And so I will, until I have to leave."

"Until—" Danior drew an anxious breath. "You think the Benderzic will come back for you? After all this time?"

"It hasn't been that long in the scheme of things. Eighteen years. And they know, just by the fact that Khira destroyed their carrier ship, that there is something powerful here. Something worth their attention. I think they'll make another probe, eventually, probably using some other breed of image. We're watching for them—the Council, the guardians, the Arnimi. Between us we'll see that their second attempt to evaluate Brakrath is just as successful as their first."

Danior's tense shoulders loosened slightly. "Then if you don't think the Benderzic will take you—"

"Why would I have to leave?" He turned his face to Nindra, letting her pale light wash it. "Tanse is old enough now to make her challenge. She'll begin training at Midsummer. If she doesn't bronze, Aberra will begin to train in two years time—and three years later Reyna will train. If neither of them bronzes either—"

Danior shivered involuntarily. "Then the valley will die when Mother loses the power of the stones."

His father shook his head. "No. Your mother has only begun her childbearing years. If she had followed the old ways, her children would have come ten, fifteen, even twenty years apart, over a period of a century—or more. And no two by the same father. Instead she chose to space them closely and to take them all from the same father.

"That may have been a misjudgement. It may be that only a man of Brakrath can father a barohna. If that is true, if none of your sisters bronzes, I must leave so your mother can bear other daughters in the old way. Because I know she won't take a Brakrathi mate, even for a season, while I'm here."

Danior drew a sharp breath, understanding. If his father could not father a daughter for the throne, his mother must look to someone else. And she did not expect his father to take it well. "You'll have to leave—because she would expect you to feel angry if she took other mates."

"Yes. Hurt and angry and abandoned. She doesn't feel by half measures. She doesn't expect me to feel that way either."

Danior pressed his temples, his thoughts running rapidly ahead. "Jhaviir's daughter—" If she were living, she was old enough to have gone to the mountain now, old enough to show them whether the daughter of a Rauthimage could take the power of the stones.

His father understood his unspoken question and shook his head. "She wasn't a palace daughter, not in the way your sisters are. She was like you—so much like you people said you might have been twins. So I'm not sure she would have taught us anything." Absently he placed the pairing stone on the broad wall of the pen. Its polished facets glinted darkly. He stroked it with one finger, seeming to search for words.

Danior didn't wait for them. Jhaviir's daughter had been like him—dark and long-limbed, with none of the apparent fragility that marked a palace daughter. The one person who might have shared his isolation was gone. "She was like me. So she wouldn't have been anyone either," he said, and was immediately ashamed of the open bitterness of the words.

His father raised his head sharply. "Either, Danior?"

It took Danior a moment to recognize the rebuke in the question. It took him another moment to choke back the sense of unfairness it roused. He bit his lip angrily. "I have no place here. I'll never go for a beast. I'll never join a guild. I'll never do anything—because there's nothing for me to do."

"Never? Anything?" The very gentleness of his father's words challenged him. "How can you be certain—when it's entirely up to you, Danior? There are many things to be done by a person willing to do them."

"Then what are they?" Danior challenged. Was he to demand to be apprenticed to a guild? Demand to be taught by a master too courteous to say that he was not wanted? Or was he to go to the mountain and try to usurp a bit of his sisters' legend? Neither course had any meaning for a palace son. "I wasn't born to any-thing."

"Only because no one like you has been born here before. That doesn't mean there is nothing for you to do. It only means you must find ways of living your life that are as new as you are. Or you must find new ways to do the old things.

"Think, Danior. Your sisters are caught by tradition, bound by it. Perhaps one day they'll die for it. Your mother is caught by it too, bound to the throne. But she set part of her heritage aside and found a new way to live. And I have no heritage at all. I've had to choose my path step by step.

"Now you must do the same. You must put one foot before the other and create your own path, your own tradition."

Make his own legend? As his father had done after the Benderzic dropped him here? But he had no drama to build upon. He was not the rebirth of a man born on another world. He had not been torn from one world and then another. He had not been left without language or memory in the palace tower. He had not even ridden the whitemane.

His jaws knotted. He was overshadowed by his mother, by his father, by his sisters. They blinded him with their light. And now his father told him he must look past the light to find his path. His eyes flicked to the pairing stone. He felt a surge of bitterness. It was as useless as he was. The gem master had cut it to link his mother and Lihwa, but they had elected not to be joined. They had taken the stones from their throats, and now this one was as dark as he was.

Without thinking, Danior reached for the faceted stone. He closed his fingers around it, punishing the stone for his own confu-sion. Words cluttered his mind, words to wound his father with, words to defend himself by.

The Council should have sent all five brothers to Arnim. Should have sent them before his father had ever become his mother's consort, before they had conceived him. The Council should have sent him when he was born. Should—

"Danior—"

Danior clenched his teeth, shaking his head angrily. There were no words to dissipate the burning helplessness he felt. There were no words so strong.

"*Danior*—" His father's voice was strange, urgent.

Fiercely Danior raised his head, at the same time loosening his fingers. He saw the glow first in his father's eyes, reflected there faintly. Disbelieving, he gazed down. The pairing stone lay in the palm of his hand, a faint light at its depths.

His heart stopped. He forgot to breathe. The pairing stone was alive in his hand. The stone that had been his mother's. The stone that should have lived only at her touch. He felt its warmth. Stunned, he raised his head. The blood had left his father's face. In his father's eyes he saw something he had never seen before, something that struck him with terror.

Find his own path. Create his own tradition. Build his own legend. Those were the things his father urged him to do. Those were the things that could give him the substance and definition of a man. But he couldn't guess how to do them, which step he must take first and in what direction.

He couldn't guess, but in his father's eyes he saw the glow of the stone and the bare beginning of a legend—his own. It lay there like a seed, summoning, and he wasn't ready. He wasn't ready at all. He gazed at the stone and began to tremble.

THREE
DANIOR

It was ten days later when Danior climbed down overgrown mountain trails and descended into the unclouded silence of Valley Marlath. Abandoned trees stood chill-bitten in the orchards, their sparse buds closed against the cold. Dikes waited in stony solitude for repair while weeds bristled in the growing fields. Animal pens stood vacant, rebuking him with their emptiness.

When Danior neared the center of the valley, he found the stonehalls as empty as the animal pens. And he found Lihwa's palace desecrated by the harsh brilliance of overgrown stalklamp. The windows had been left unshuttered when the people deserted the valley after Lihwa's death and stalklamp grew unchecked in every deserted chamber. Its orange light glared from every aperture.

Danior approached the edge of the plaza, wondering briefly why the gem master had insisted they meet in Lihwa's valley. He glanced around uneasily, then stepped across the dark flaggings. The sunstone slab Lihwa had once used to draw sunlight rested at the center of the plaza, its polished surfaces untouched by the debris that littered the flaggings. Danior tensed as he approached it, but the stone remained black. Without a barohna, the sunstone was simply a stone—smooth, inert, dark.

Without a barohna, the pairing stone should have been dark too. Frowning, Danior shoved his hand into his pocket and closed his fingers around the pouch that held the stone. The stone should have been dark, but it was not—not when he held it in the palm of his hand. Then it yielded light and heat, burning enigmatically against the cold of his flesh.

Stiffly Danior drew his hand from his pocket. His father had said he must find his own path. But since he had first touched the pairing stone, his thoughts had become a maze, a series of interconnecting pathways that led nowhere—except back to the pairing stone. Always to the pairing stone. How was he to choose when every path led to the same destination—and all he found there was confusion?

His mother, his father, his sisters had touched the stone and it had remained dark. But for him it lived, and no one in Valley Terlath could say why. Did its response signify that he had some latent touch of his mother's gift of the stones? But that came only in prescribed ways, and he had not done the things a palace daughter must do to become a barohna. He had not trained. He had not gone to the mountain and made a challenge. He had not changed. He was as he had always been, hesitant, shadowed, doubting.

So was the stone's light meaningless? An isolated aberration? Juris Pergossa didn't know. His parents didn't know. Certainly he didn't. But surely the gem master would. His mother had not said so when she suggested he be summoned. His father had not said so when he agreed that it be done. They had said only that the gem master was the best person to evaluate the stone. But if he couldn't say why it lit in Danior's hand, who could?

Danior shivered, rubbing his hands against his trousers, and set out across the plaza.

The palace doors stood open, revealing a garishly overgrown foyer. Streamers of stalklamp dangled from matted walls; creeping runners streaked the flaggings with light. Danior studied the foyer floor. There were disturbances in the dust, but no evidence of human passage.

So the gem master had not come yet. Danior hesitated, then stepped through the great doors and passed under the arched entryway to the throneroom. Vines of light encroached from the corridor, crawling across the floor, casting a spectral half-light against the vaulted emptiness of the throneroom. Danior's boots tapped emptily on the flaggings as he approached the dark throne. Even the mirrors mounted high on the walls were dark, their reflective surfaces furred with dust.

Only the sunstone throne was free of ravage. Danior approached it, trying to imagine its clean fiery light in the days when the throneroom had been the living heart of the valley. The clamor of monitors, messengers and advisers; the sound of booted feet on polished flaggings; the smell of bread baking in distant kitchens—

all the activities of the valley had converged here. And the life of the valley had flowed from here, from the sunthrone.

Yet all that had died with one person. Danior frowned, stepping near the throne, wondering if he dared touch it. No one but a barohna was permitted to touch a throne that held light. But this throne was dark.

A sound from the corridor distracted him, making him freeze momentarily, his heart leaping. When the sound was not repeated, he slipped to the arched entry and saw a small scampering shadow far down the corridor. An animal, probably one of the tiny seed-gatherers that invaded the fields at harvest time. Now it held title to the entire palace. Danior gazed back at the throne again, then stepped down the corridor, escaping temptation.

Cautiously he explored the palace and found walls matted with stalklamp, floors treacherous with luminous runners, and the smells of dampness and food spoiling in open jars. Yet there were no open jars.

There was nothing in the palace but dust, stalklamp, and the droppings of small animals. The people had taken everything, even the shutters that should have protected the windows. Only one set of rooms remained furnished and Danior did not enter there. He peered in from the door, breath held. Dust-hoared bureaus, time-faded coverlets, scrolls that lay where they had been dropped so many years before—Danior retreated, unwilling to trespass upon quarters once shared by Lihwa and Jhaviir.

Soon afternoon waned beyond unshuttered windows and the desolation of the deserted palace sent Danior to the tower to watch for the gem master. He leaned against slippery stonework, trying not to think of the pairing stone in its pouch, trying not to worry at the unanswerable questions it raised. A path, a legend, a place—how was he to wrest any of those from confusion and fear? Set one foot before the other, his father had said. But where was he to put the first foot?

Soon after sunset, a figure in leathers and boots appeared at the edge of the plaza. Danior watched, certain the man who crossed the flaggings could not be the gem master. A gem master should be a man of extraordinary proportions or presence, a giant. A gem master should be as tall as the mountains he searched, as imposing as the powers he gave life when he cut and polished the stones he quarried. And the man below was ordinary.

So ordinary in his worn leathers that he might be a worker re-

turning from the fields or a herder who had just settled his flock for
the night. Danior watched until he passed through the doors below.
Then, the pairing stone heavy in his pocket, a sinking anticipation
of disappointment even heavier in his chest, he descended to meet
him.

The gem master stood gazing up at the dust-furred mirrors, a
stocky man with fair hair and sun-beaten face. Beneath his leather
tunic, he wore the roughspun of the halls. When he turned the only
thing remarkable about him was his eyes. They were vividly blue,
as if he had looked so long at the summer sky that he had captured
a part of it—so blue it hurt when he returned Danior's stare.

He was not ordinary after all. Danior knew that when he tried to
greeᴛ him and his breath rasped ineffectually in his throat.

"Danior Terlath?" the gem master asked.

"Yes," Danior managed finally. "My mother summoned you.
About the stone."

"The pairing stone," the gem master affirmed. "Did you bring
it?" His voice was husky, the voice of a man of the stonehalls, and
the hand he held out was blunt and calloused, with short-bitten
nails. But there was nothing of the stonehalls in his manner. He did
not nod or speak with careful indirection.

Confused, Danior took the pouch from his pocket and tugged
awkwardly at its puckered mouth. "This—this is the stone." It lay
on his palm, its faint light driving the moisture from his mouth, its
warmth burning against the cold of his skin. He licked his lips,
watching for the gem master's reaction.

No expression touched the weathered face. Silently the gem master took the stone from Danior's palm and stepped into the stalklit
corridor to examine it.

Danior followed, uneasily. The gem master had said none of the
things a man of the halls normally says upon meeting. He had not
introduced himself, he had not inquired after the fertility of Valley
Terlath, he had not even repeated Danior's name when he addressed him. And his concentration upon the stone was so total
Danior felt excluded. "Did you—did you cut and polish it yourself?" he ventured. It was difficult to guess whether the gem master
was old enough to have been a master eighteen years before. His
face was as creased as his leather trousers but his eyes held a piercing clarity.

The gem master shook his head and continued to examine the
stone, turning it to let its polished facets catch and reflect stalklight.

At last he straightened and turned his attention just as totally upon Danior. "Tell me what you felt the first time the gem lit for you."

Danior shrank from the vivid eyes, reluctant to share his shock, his elation, his terror. "My hand felt warm."

The gem master nodded as if the answer were not an evasion. As if he had heard what was not said as clearly as what was. "And now? What do you feel when you handle it now?"

Danior hesitated, feeling he might as well try to hide from the sky as from the gem master's gaze. Still he tried. "The—the same thing. My hand feels warm."

"How often do you handle it?"

"Only—only when—" But evasion was no use. The gem master's pupils had contracted to minute apertures—pinholes through which he saw everything. Bracing himself, Danior drew a halting breath and let the words tumble with all the force of his perplexity. "I carry it in my pocket by day. I take it out and put it on my bureau at night. I only touch it when someone wants to see it. I—I don't want to handle it at all. I don't want to touch it. I don't even want to carry it. Not until you tell me—not until—" Until what? What did he want to hear from the gem master? That the light in the pairing stone was a meaningless refraction? That he could build a modest legend upon it without heavier demands being placed upon him later? That he could handle the pairing stone without the fear that someday he would be drawn to touch his mother's throne and see an answering light there too? A light that could destroy if he wielded it without training, without discipline. A light he was little prepared to tame. He shook his head, unable to frame a coherent demand.

Nodding as if he had, the gem master slipped the gem back into its pouch. "There aren't so many things I can tell you, Danior Terlath. The master who taught me cut this stone and its mate. He gave them to the barohnas of valleys Terlath and Marlath. The barohnas gave them to their consorts, and one of those consorts gave this one to you. It responds to your touch. It gives you heat and light. I can't tell you what it will do if you continue to handle it. Perhaps you will learn to reach into the mind of the person who holds the other stone. Perhaps that person will learn to reach into your mind. Perhaps neither of you will ever do more than make the stones glow."

Danior's heart missed a beat. *The person who held the other stone?* He had not thought of the other stone, the one Lihwa had given Jhaviir. The suggestion that someone shared his terrifying miracle made his skin turn cold. Made him curl with possessiveness. And misgiving. "How—how do you know someone has the other stone?" Had Jhaviir carried it when he rode away? Had he dropped it somewhere in his wanderings? Who could have picked it up? Who? Danior pressed his temples, trying to still his thoughts. They tumbled too quickly for him to examine them, to discard those that were meaningless.

The gem master's pupils shimmered, widening. A faint line appeared between his brows. "Perhaps no one does," he conceded. "If you were a barohna, I would say it was impossible for one stone of a pair to live if no one held the other. But you aren't a barohna. You aren't even a palace daughter. Yet the stone burns for you. So the usual course of events has been suspended and I have no answers. Have you had unusual dreams since you first touched the stone? Dreams that you were entering someone else's mind? That's usually the first sign that a link has been established!"

"No." But what, he thought with a sudden chill, if someone were using the second stone to touch him? To sample his thoughts as casually as if he had written them upon a scroll and posted them on the wall? His hands tightened against an impulse to dash the stone from the pouch and crush it on the flaggings. For anyone to know how small he was behind the face he wore, how uncertain—for anyone to know his most private thoughts, his fears—

He pressed his temples again, harder, and fastened on something the gem master had said. Fastened on it as if it would deliver him. "You have no answers. You have no answers at all."

"I have none," the man agreed, his eyes rimming with shadow. "I'm only a craftsman. I go to the mountains and find fresh veins. I quarry them. Then, with my tools, I find the living heart of each stone. I cut and polish until the heart is accessible to the barohna who has commissioned the stone. I cut sunstones. I cut pairing stones. Once I cut an eyestone for a barohna who took me for her season's mate. But it shattered when she had it mounted at her winter palace. And no daughter came of our season together.

"I know where to slice a slab, how to cut and facet a stone. But my master never taught me to understand the skills he gave my hands. I don't know why a finished sunstone holds sunlight—or why it holds sunlight only for a barohna. Any more than I know why a palace daughter must take a beast to become a barohna.

Why her body requires that stimulation to change. And why the change is so swift and so profound.

"I know that once there were no barohnas. There were no sunstones or pairing stones, until one day a man named Lensar realized something lay at the heart of a block of stone that had broken off the mountainside. When he cut and polished it, when he found what he was looking for and captured it in the facets of a gem, the woman who loved him discovered that she knew what to do with the gem. She knew how to concentrate sunlight in it and call it out later."

"She burned him," Danior said flatly. He did not want to dwell on what came of the unpracticed use of a stone.

"Yes, she turned him to ash before she knew what she had done. Before she realized how fiery sunlight can be when it has been stored in a sunstone. And she never understood how she had known that sunlight could be stored in the stone and released again. Any more than your mother understands the process by which she draws sunlight from the mountainsides each spring to thaw the fields for planting. She exploits the process without understanding it. If she waited until she understood, she would die without ever using the stone." He turned the gazing brilliance of his eyes fully upon Danior. "Do you understand what I'm saying?"

Danior studied the vivid eyes, the weathered face. They were like earth and sky, one worn and eroded, the other so clear it hurt to look directly into them. "You can't tell me whether someone has the other pairing stone."

"I can't tell you."

"You can't tell me why this one lights for me."

"I can't."

"You—you can't tell me anything," Danior realized, caught between relief and disappointment. "My mother summoned you to tell me what to do and you can't."

"But I've told you something far more important."

Danior's shoulders stiffened rebelliously. Something more important than what he must do, where he must put his foot? "You haven't told me anything."

"Haven't I, Danior Terlath? I've told you that many of us go ahead with the important work of our lives without answers. We go with only questions, following them from step to step, learning by what we do. Learning the nature of the world, learning our own natures, learning how the two interact to carry us ahead." For the first time the gem master smiled. "Usually the first thing we learn is how much more ignorant we are than we ever thought possible. But we press beyond that. We must if we aren't simply to stand still."

Danior stiffened in instinctive resistance, realizing what the gem master was suggesting. That he use the stone without understanding it. That he stroke light from it without knowing where the light would lead. "No. I won't do that," he said. "If I don't understand, if no one can tell me—"

"If Lensar had refused to cut the first sunstone until he knew he would not be harmed, there would be no barohnas in our valleys, Danior Terlath. If Niabi had waited to use the stone until she was certain of her control, she would never have used it at all."

"But I'm not a barohna. I'm not even a daughter. I—"

"Niabi was not a barohna or a palace daughter either. There were no palaces in her day and the people were hungry because there was no one to bring sunlight into the valleys."

"No." The word carried the force of panic.

Shrugging, the gem master reached for Danior's hand and uncurled the cramping fingers. He dropped the pairing stone into the palm, refusing to let Danior draw back. Slowly reflected light grew in his eyes.

Danior gazed down at the stone, his heart thumping at his ribs, a muffled tocsin. The stone's light, its heat—both were more intense than they had been just a few minutes before.

The gem master's words seemed to come from a distance, a pronouncement. "My master said when your father and his brothers came that nothing would be the same in our valleys again. That we would see things never seen before and children born to make them happen. You are one of those children and this is one of those things—a stone that lives for someone who is not a barohna."

Things never seen before. Danior's palm burned. He closed his hand around the stone, trying to hide the sharpness of his fear behind anger—only half succeeding. "I can't use it. I don't know how."

"If you were a barohna, you would wear it on a chain at your throat. You would touch it many times each day, until you became fully sensitive to it. You would feel your way into it, learning with your fingertips, with your senses, with the flesh of your throat how to use it.

"Understand: this is no magical device. It's a tool—but one only a few people are capable of using. And those people learn to use it only by practicing its use. Just as I learned to use my picks and blades by going to the mountains."

The stone burned in Danior's hand. He shook his head in confusion. He wanted to throw the stone down. He wanted to protest, to rebel. But against whom? He was the one who made the stone light.

"I have a chain," the gem master said.

A chain to suspend the pairing stone from. A chain to hold it against the soft flesh of his throat. Danior's jaws bunched. "With you?" The words were whispered.

"Yes."

But the gem master did not move toward his pocket or his pouch. He would not, Danior realized sinkingly, unless Danior requested it. Danior closed his eyes, trying to clarify his thoughts. Wear the stone without answers to any of his questions? Without knowing where the miracle might lead? Stubbornly he clenched his hands at his sides. But his tongue betrayed him. "Let me have one."

"Of course." The gem master reached into his pouch and extracted a thin metal chain. He placed it in Danior's hand, gazing at him almost as if he enjoyed Danior's agony. Then he turned and stepped toward the plaza doors.

He was leaving, Danior realized, and without making anything clear. *"No!* Wait!" Danior ran after him in alarm. "Wait! You—"

The gem master turned back, smiling. "No fear. I'll hear what you do with the stone, Danior Terlath. I'll hear where it leads you. It will be legend in these mountains very soon after it happens."

Legend. Danior halted, torn. He had wanted to be legend. He had wanted to do mythic things. Now they only looked terrifying. He found himself thinking of finding a path instead, of making his way to some goal he could not name. "You haven't even told me why you wanted to meet me here instead of in my mother's valley," he said desperately. So long as the gem master lingered, he would not be alone with the stone.

"Ah. Because the settled valleys cloud over when the warm air rises from the fields. Here I can see the stars. Have you looked at them? They're like stones in the sky—precious stones polished by a hand no one has ever seen. Some night, when the sky is clear, I'm going to reach out and take one." He raised his hand in salute and stepped away through the great doors to the plaza.

Danior stood frozen as the gem master crossed the plaza and disappeared into the deserted avenues. Then he turned, staring down the stalklit corridor. There was nothing there for him but garish light. Choking, he ran into the plaza. Perhaps the gem master planned to sleep in the valley tonight. Perhaps he had already spread bedding in one of the deserted stonehalls. Perhaps—

Danior caught himself at the edge of the plaza, running after the gem master. Grimly he pulled himself to a halt. He was not a child, afraid to sleep alone.

Nor was he afraid to walk mountain trails by night, he reminded himself, though he carried only a pike.

Or perhaps he was simply less afraid to start back to his mother's valley tonight than to stay here with his thoughts. Briefly he stared down at the chain the gem master had given him. Then he thrust chain and stone into his pocket and ran down stone avenues toward the mountains.

He walked until he could no longer look back and see the stalk-light glow of the palace. Then he sat with his back to a protecting boulder and let his eyes close. His legs ached, his feet hurt, and his spirit was suddenly as bruised as his body. And still the unanswered questions burned. The maze opened and expanded, confounding him. If he wore the stone, would he step into someone else's thoughts—or would someone step into his? Would he open himself to critical eyes, scornful eyes, belittling eyes? And if no one else held the second stone, if it had been discarded long ago, where would the light of his own stone lead him? Grimly he followed tortuous paths until his thoughts exhausted him and he fell asleep huddled against the rock.

He woke to find the sky fierce with stars and the cold of the mountain upon him. He sat for a long time, pressing himself against the boulder, shivering, thinking of legends and paths and things never seen before.

His fingers felt brittle as he took the pairing stone from his pocket and threaded the chain through the loop of the metal setting. He felt the stone's warmth in his palm. His choice was clearcut. Wear the stone or set it aside. Follow where it led or go back to the valley, to the emptiness of his chambers. What other alternatives were there? Groping, he found none.

But how was he to begin to follow where the stone led? He read no clue in its glow. It offered no guidance, no direction.

He sat holding the stone, his fingers white and cold, his breath frosting the air, until a new thought warmed him. Perhaps his great-grandmother could read something from the stone. She had held the throne of Valley Terlath for over a hundred years before she retired to the plain. What hadn't she seen in that span? Even if she could not answer all his questions, perhaps she could suggest where he must put his foot if he was to follow the stone's vagrant light. Perhaps she could tell him where the path began.

He shivered under the dawning sky, examining his decision. Then he returned the stone to its pouch, the pouch to his pack. Standing, he walked the trail until he found a lens tender sleeping beside his lens. He woke the man and instructed him to send a message to his parents that he had gone to the plain, to Kadura. Then, drawing a deep breath of the cold dawn, he set course toward the plain.

FOUR
KEVA

It was night and Keva crouched near the ashes of her cookfire, her fingers tight on the stone at her throat. She had had her choice of camp spots for the night—a cove of rocks in the roughlands from which she had just emerged, a sheltering tree at the verge of the plain, a grassy hollow beside running water. She had rejected them all for this place, where the ground lay flat and open and her view stretched unobstructed in all directions.

Still the feeling that she was watched prickled at the back of her neck and made her hand close around the stone at her throat. She wanted to whip her head around sharply, to confront whoever—or whatever—watched her.

Each time she turned, her eyes met only darkness.

The very openness of the plain made her uneasy. She had grown up beside the warmstream, where moss-grown trees provided a protective screen against the roughlands that lay beyond. And even the roughlands did not stretch in flat monotony to the sky. The ground's surface rolled and tumbled and was broken by rocks, brush and trees.

Here there was nothing as far as she could see—nothing but grass, an occasional tree, and the sky, a tangible presence that hung just beyond finger's reach. Memory of the bluesong had been very much with her today. All she needed was sunlight and the slippery feel of the blue cloth at her neck and the song returned to her in all its clarity.

She clung to the stone at her throat. Other things came to her with clarity too since she had left the warmstream. Her fire dreams were more vivid than she had ever known, because now the fire was nearer—so near she could feel its heat upon her face, so near that sometimes she glimpsed its source, a tall figure standing against a burning mountainside. So near she seemed to hear a grumbling roar, to feel—

Keva shuddered and stood abruptly, the back of her neck drawing tight. The emptiness around her had grown so menacing even her thoughts had taken an ominous turn. Anything could sweep down upon her here. Quickly she gathered her possessions and slung them over her shoulders. Forcing herself to move deliberately when she wanted only to run, she traced a path back toward the grassy hollow she had passed earlier in the evening.

Clouds cloaked the moons in white lace. Shadows moved over the grass, stealthily. Keva was trembling by the time she reached shelter of the shadowed hollow. Water welled from the ground in a spring and pooled in a rocky basin. The grass itself was fine-textured, thick, soft and green.

Keva sank into the shadows of the hollow and wrapped her bedding around her, as if it could hide her from the eyes she still felt upon her back. She knew there were predators on the plain, preying on the herds of redmanes. She particularly remembered Par's stories of gliding, sharp-clawed creatures with amber eyes and bobbing ringlets who liked to game with their prey before striking. Perhaps that was what watched her now, a plains minx, teasing its appetite by a slow stalking of her.

Or had the guardians who tended the redmane herds seen her and set someone to watch her? Keva frowned into the dark. Each summer the guardians drove their herds across the warmstream on their way to the lakelands. Last year, against Oki's instruction, she had watched from the trees and had seen women who stood tall in their umber capes, forbidding and silent. They had spoken to the fisher-people, but distantly, and they had permitted no one to approach the animals they drove.

Had the guardians seen her and decided she had come to steal redmanes? Keva tried to imagine one of those imposing women moving in silent pursuit, watching. That was not so difficult. In their hooded cloaks, the guardians seemed made for stealth. But it was difficult to imagine a guardian effortlessly slipping into invisibility each time Keva turned to peer around.

She was imagining it—imagining eyes upon her. The fisher-people had never forbidden the guardians passage across the warmstream. Why should the guardians deny her passage upon the plain?

And when she met them and told them why she had come, why shouldn't they answer her questions? Had they seen a dark man riding a white animal that looked as if it had been refined from their own animals: tall where the redmanes were stocky, smooth where the redmanes were shaggy, graceful where the redmanes were heavy-footed? Had they seen him years before with a child? Had they seen him since and what direction had he taken?

There was no reason for the guardians to refuse to answer her. And if they could tell her nothing, then she must take her questions to the mountains. Keva shivered at that thought, wishing she knew which of Par's tales were true and which fancy, wishing she could guess how much of what Oki said about the barohnas was fact and how much spite. Wishing too that she knew why she felt such foreboding dread of the mountains. Was it only because of the things Oki had told her?

Keva rubbed her arms and pulled her bedding close. She did not sleep well that night, despite the slow murmur of running water.

The next morning when she found footprints beside the spring, her appetite deserted her too. They had been made by clawed feet almost as large as her own, but with the six toes widely splayed. There were just two sets of impressions, but there was broken glass in other places and Keva did not know if she had trampled it the night before or if the animal that left its prints had done so.

She did know there had not been prints at the spring the night before.

A minx? Frowning, she sorted through her pack and pouch. She found only a few dried berries, a half-crescent of bread, but that was all there had been the night before. Nor had her extra clothes or bedding been disturbed. So whatever creature had left prints had not stolen from her.

She retreated from the spring, trying to remember what she knew of plains predators. All her information came from Par's tales, and she did not know how much of that was fact. Was it true that a minx would not attack unmoving prey? That it would circle, that it would tease with sharp claws, but would not spring unless its prey twitched or flinched or tried to run?

Was that why the animal had not harmed her? Because she had been sleeping? Or simply because it had not finished its stalking game?

And the other plains predators, the fyurries that ran in hungry

packs, the lobbers and wassickers, the things Par said howled when
storm clouds dipped low—

She had come this far without a weapon, but she realized now
that she should not go farther. Glancing around uneasily, she left
the shelter of the rocky hollow.

She had intended to walk into the plain this morning, searching
for sign of the herds and their guardians. Instead she turned to the
west, to a place where the roughlands embraced the plain. She
followed the rolling, tumbled ground as it skirted the plain. When
she found a suitable tree, she broke down a sturdy limb and used
her digging blade to sharpen one end to a point. It was a crude
weapon, but she worked on it ostentatiously, hefting it, testing its
balance. If the minx were watching, if it were as cunning as Par
said, it would recognize that she was armed.

She walked slowly back toward the edge of the roughlands, carrying her pike self-consciously. If it were indeed a minx that stalked
her, she felt its eyes upon her through most of the day, stinging, as
the land changed under her feet, becoming lusher, greener. Despite
the promise of the terrain, forage was scant, the vegetation unfamiliar, and she found no water. She hoarded the water she had drawn
from the spring and saved her bread and berries for later, when she
would be hungrier than now.

It was late afternoon when she stood on a rocky promontory and
looked down over a distant herd—the first she had seen. The animals were little more than a shadow upon the muted green of the
horizon. They were too far for her to distinguish individual animals
or guardians. The afternoon breeze brought her neither sound nor
scent of them.

Keva clutched the stone at her throat, gazing down. She had
come to question the guardians and now they were within a few
hours' walk. Yet her feet were reluctant to carry her. What if she
approached them and learned things she didn't want to know? That
they had not heard of her father. That they had and he was dead.

Stiffly she moved to sit in the shadow of a sheltering rock. *Tonight.* She would go down tonight, while the guardians slept. She
wouldn't have to speak to them until morning. With that decision
made, Keva closed her fingers around her stone and leaned back
against the rock, letting her eyelids fall. The late afternoon sun
warmed her to sleep.

It was dusk when she stood, stiffly, and peered down across the
plain. The herd had retreated over the horizon while she slept. She

could see only an indistinct mottling—scattered animals grazing far in the distance.

Keva's mouth was dry and her stomach cramped with hunger. She turned out her pack and found just what she had found in the morning: a few dried berries and a half-crescent of flatbread. She ate them slowly, then drank the last water from her waterskin, trying not to worry. The green below was promising. There would be forage and water on the plain.

And there would be guardians. She had been afraid to meet them by day. Now she intended to slip among their herds by night?

Quickly, before she could change her mind, she took up her pack and pike and began picking her way down the rocky face of the promontory, moving hurriedly, before decision could desert her.

The climb was treacherous with loose rock and crumbling clumps of soil. She was halfway down the promontory, stumbling, scraping herself against rock, when the familiar prickling touched her. *Someone was watching. Someone . . .* Instinctively she raised her head—and froze.

A wiry form stood two-legged at the top of the promontory, its wispy golden fur gleaming in the dusk. Keva caught her breath as the creature moved, turning its head from the shadow. Golden fur grew in ringlets from its scalp, curling across its black-muzzled face. Its eyes were bright and pale, gloating.

A minx, just as Par had described. Without thinking, Keva clutched at a clump of coarse vegetation. The grass pulled free and rock slid beneath her feet. She twisted, snatching for a second handhold, then froze in alarm. Motionless—she had to be motionless or the minx would spring. But she was falling. Her hand closed around a thorny plant. She gasped as sharp spikes bit her palm and then, with a smothered cry, she tumbled down the incline. Raw stone scraped her face and scarred her arms. Her ankle twisted and, just before her head hit a protruding rock, she felt something pull in her knee.

It could not have been long before she regained consciousness. The sky was a little darker and no moon had risen. She lay at the bottom of the incline, pain in her leg, her cheeks stinging. As soon as she realized where she was, panic began to hammer in her head again. She lay without moving, hardly breathing. If the minx were nearby, watching, waiting for her to move—

Slowly she rolled her eyes, probing the shadows. She saw nothing. She turned her head, then sat. Unconsciously she put her hand

to her cheek and drew it back wet with blood. The other cheek
stung too.

Examining herself with careful fingertips, she found wounds on
either cheek. She wiped away the blood with shaking hands, imagining the minx hunched over her unconscious body, drawing its
claws across her face, trying to tease her into motion.

Perhaps she had only cut and scraped her face on the rocks. At
least the minx was gone. Keva struggled to stand, but the pain in
her right leg was so sharp she sank back, gasping.

If the minx returned—

She tried again to push herself up.

It was useless. She lay back, exploring her injured leg with one
hand. She was relieved to find no evidence of a break in the bone.
Her makeshift pike had fallen beyond reach. Fighting weakness,
Keva dragged herself across the ground to retrieve it. Her pack lay
a short distance beyond. She pushed herself to a sitting position,
then used the pike to maneuver the pack toward her. When she was
able to grasp it, she rested for a moment, then pulled up her trouser
leg. Her knee had already begun to swell.

With fumbling fingers she tore strips of cloth from her bedding
and bound her knee. When that was done, she was able to stand,
stiffly, and take a tottering step forward.

But to walk . . . She hiked herself forward awkwardly and pain
told her she had no decisions to make tonight. Run? Hide? Walk to
meet the guardians? She could do none of those things. She could
only rest and hope to be better tomorrow.

She hunched against a tall boulder, pulling the remnant of her
blanket around her. Soon stars came to the sky and the first moon
rose. Allindra the fisher-people called her, Mist Lady. Keva studied
her silver face with distant interest. Seen from here, Allindra was
pocked and striated with shadow. The fisher-people never saw her
this way because they saw the night sky indistinctly, through the
mists that cloaked the warmstream.

With a peculiar, chill detachment, Keva wondered if Oki looked
up at Allindra tonight.

And her father—did he see Allindra? From his animal's back?
From the mountains? Or from some place she could not imagine?

Later she slept and her father rode through her dreams, his
steed's hooves hardly seeming to touch the ground. Sometimes as
he rode, his steed raised its head and its face became Allindra's,
silver and shadow at once. Other times the animal threw back a

fiercer light and became the sun. When that happened a woman came and spread her arms to the animal and its light fled and became hers. The woman burned brightly, but only for moments. Then she was engulfed by a rushing, grumbling darkness. Just instants before she was lost, something spun away from her, a fading circlet of light.

Keva thrashed restlessly, trying to escape the dream, and pain in her leg jolted her awake. She lay staring up at the sky, frightened without understanding why, fists clenched against sleep.

When she did sleep again, pain became fire—fire raised by a woman who stood tall against the sun. Shadow concealed her face and Keva strained to see the eyes that looked into the sun without being blinded, the lips that did not blister, the flesh that did not burn.

Later, much later, she did see the woman's face and she woke with a breathless cry and within moments pushed away what she had seen. All that remained was memory of fire.

Keva woke again soon after dawn, her mouth crusted and dry, her muscles stiff. Experimentally she pushed herself to her feet. The pain in her leg was just bearable as she took a halting step forward. Thoughtfully she balanced there, thirsty, hungry, remembering the herds she had seen grazing in the distance. Where there were herds, there must be water. And surely there was forage. Par said the guardians drank mare's milk. Perhaps she could learn to do that.

Certainly she couldn't stay here. Unsteadily she hobbled across the rough ground.

Her pace was irregular, governed by pain. She covered the rocky stretch at the base of the roughlands and walked among coarse grasses and occasional clumps of large vegetation. Finally at mid-morning, when she still had not found water, she curled in the grass and fell into an exhausted sleep, her entire body aching.

She woke at the soft exhalation of breath on her cheek. Startled, she froze, biting back a cry.

A redmane stood over her, looking down from age-clouded eyes. It was older than any she had seen on the summer drive, its grey coat patchy, its auburn mane tangled. Shoulders and flanks that should have been muscular were flaccid. The animal—it was a mare—stamped its padded feet, nudging Keva, then turned and padded away to browse nearby.

Keva sat for a moment, fighting the pounding aftermath of panic.

Redmanes were not dangerous. She knew that. This one didn't even seem particularly curious about her. And it was old.

So old it couldn't have wandered here from far, and that meant there must be water nearby. Stiffly Keva took her feet. Perhaps the animal was not part of the herd she had seen on the horizon last night. Perhaps it foraged alone or as part of a smaller group. But if she followed it, surely it would lead her to water.

The animal moved away slowly. Keva had no trouble matching its pace. It paused frequently to nibble at the grass, sometimes turning to gaze at her steadily from milky eyes. After a while it seemed to wander less randomly, moving across the plain as if it had found direction, occasionally even breaking into a heavy trot. Keva hobbled after it, biting her lip when her weight fell too suddenly on her injured leg.

It was mid-afternoon when she saw animals grazing ahead, a loose congregation of adults, foals and yearlings. They raised their heads at her approach and gazed at her incuriously. The mare moved among them with a gentle, snorted greeting. As Keva hesitated, a foal approached, its gait loose-legged, and examined her clothing. She touched its neck, stroking the silver-grey fur, and the foal bobbed its head impatiently and cantered away.

Water—there had to be water where there were so many redmanes. Keva hobbled after the mare.

It led her to a narrow strand of water lacing its way through the grass. Keva drank gratefully and splashed her hands and face, carefully washing away dried blood. Then she filled her waterskin and retreated to dry ground, her trouser legs muddy. The mare watched her, cropping at the grass.

Keva sat for a while in the grass, feeling the ache of every muscle and the hollowness of her stomach. Experimentally, she pulled a clump of grass. The roots were long and stringy. There was no sign of an edible bulb. Keva sighed and patted the clump back into the ground. Perhaps later, when she was hungrier, she would chew the unpromising roots. Would range around searching for other types of vegetation. For now she was more tired than hungry. She stretched out for a few minutes in the sun-warmed grass and fell asleep.

She woke with the mare's breath on her face. The animal stood over her, head lowered, gazing at her with disconcerting steadiness. Keva sat, the first chill of evening on her face. "No," she muttered, more to herself than to the mare. It was pointless to walk now, with night coming. Pointless to try to forage. She stood and stretched stiff muscles, then wrapped herself in her blanket and lay down again, huddled around her grumbling stomach.

The mare sighed heavily and tramped away, then returned, lashing its tangled tail. It bent its head and exhaled heavily upon Keva's shoulder.

Keva studied the restless animal, bemused, as it turned away, then approached again. Did it imagine it had established permanent guardianship of her? Did it think it had found a foal, one obliged to follow wherever it led?

Strange foal she was, hardly able to keep up with an elderly redmane. When the mare returned and breathed upon her for a third time, flaring its nostrils, making its breath vibrate loudly in Keva's ear, Keva gave up, rolled her blanket, and followed.

Again their course was slow and wandering. Wherever the mare intended to lead her, the destination was not urgent. Keva followed with baffled tolerance, the ache of her muscles easing as stars came to the sky, as Allindra rose.

When Allindra rose, the mare began to move more briskly, finally trotting, head low, feet pounding. Keva hobbled after her, caught up in some inexplicable sense of purpose. The plain had changed with the moon's rising. The grasses were silvered, and the shadows in the distance offered silent promise. Even the milky film on the mare's eyes was less obscuring. When the animal gazed into the moon, Keva saw dark pupils and a presence behind them far more vital than the body that housed it.

A presence? In a redmane mare who had adopted a two-legged foal?

After a while, Keva heard a whickering in the distance. The mare halted, raised her head and uttered a shrill cry. Then she padded forward again, grunting loudly. Keva hesitated, hair rising on her arms. The mare turned and slapped her tail against her flank. The message was clear. *Come.*

Keva went. Soon she saw the shadowy shapes of several tens of redmanes. They moved restlessly, grunting and whickering as the mare padded among them, then gathering behind her and following just as Keva followed. The elder mare was a personage among the redmanes, Keva realized. A leader, perhaps. No wonder she had expected Keva to follow her.

The mare trotted briskly now, leading Keva to a place where the stream that wandered across the plain briefly broadened into a wide pool. The grass had been worn away from its banks, leaving a broad apron of bare, pounded soil on either side. The mare approached the pool, but instead of lowering her head to drink, she stepped into the water and splashed across.

Emerging on the other side, she shook herself vigorously, then slapped her tail against her flank.

The demand was clear. *Come.*

Feeling foolish, Keva waded into the shallow pool. Water flooded into her boots and her trousers clung heavily to her legs. When she reached the other side, the mare waited while she squeezed water from her trousers and removed her boots to empty them.

The mare planted her padded feet and stood beside the pool, facing the redmanes who gathered on the other side. Keva watched with surprise as more and more animals gathered from the dark. They grunted softly among themselves, pressing closely together, none offering to cross the water.

After a while the mare lowered her head and directed her milky gaze to the pond's dark surface. On the opposite bank, ranks of redmanes pressed still closer to each other, then quieted and stood as the mare did, heads down, eyes upon the water. Puzzled, Keva sat with wet trousers chilling her legs. After a while, when the cold reached her very bones, she bundled herself in her blanket, her teeth chattering.

There was some purpose to the gathering, but she could not fathom it. None of the animals moved now, none drank from the pool. They sent their warm breath against the brisk night air, a susurrus, and they waited, watching the water.

Allindra continued her slow trek across the sky, and still the animals stood. Finally Allindra's reflection touched the pool's edge, silvering the water, then slowly, slowly slid across the water.

The redmanes sighed and the mare snorted once and let her eyelids fall. Keva stared down at Mist Lady's reflection and had the giddy feeling that she peered through the water's surface into another reality. She could not look away. She could only gaze down, falling deeper and deeper, until a breeze came across the grasslands and fluttered against the water's surface. Gently reality rippled and separated.

Reality opened.

Reality—but not the reality of wet clothing and aching muscles, not the reality of chattering teeth and an empty stomach. Another reality entirely rose from the silvered pool as breeze touched its surface. Numbly Keva reached for the stone at her throat. Zan, the second moon, appeared at the pool's edge, her orb smaller than Allindra's, her light sharper, more intense.

As intense as the song Keva had once heard, that song of sunlight and breeze. Keva's fingers closed around the blue stone, then clutched the narrow strip of blue cloth that held it.

The bluesong—she had heard it and it had left traces deep in her memory. But she had never guessed she could sing it. She did now, staring down into Allindra's silver-pocked face, feeling the breeze of a new reality in her hair. She let her lips part and the bluesong came from her throat, sweet, wordless and silent.

Silent. It was not a song of lips and tongue, not a song of vocal cords, not as she sang it. It was a song that came from some deeper place, heart perhaps, or soul. Keva rocked slowly from side to side, clutching cloth and stone, and let the song reach out from her, let the song twist its magic around the night.

Did the redmanes hear it? Did the mare? They stood in silence. Some gazed into the pond, and Allindra and Zan rode upon the surfaces of their eyes, silvering them. Others had let their eyelids drop and they moved as Keva moved, rocking.

She knew from that that they did hear. And she knew from the heaving of the mare's sides that she heard too. The bluesong moved through them all, weaving some alien magic. It fed on sunlight twice-reflected, first from the moons, then from the water. It fed on breeze. But there was a strangeness to it, a quality that was not entirely of this sun, not of the breeze that scoured this grassy land.

The song belonged to some other land then. It came from some distant place where the sun shone hotter but the breeze was softer.

She lost herself in it so completely that she did not notice at first that the redmanes had become totally still, like animals carved of stone. The mare uttered a throaty warning, her body as rigid as the others.

The bluesong slipped away. Keva raised her head and gazed around at the immobile animals, puzzled. The mare's breath rumbled heavily in her throat again. The milky eyes gazed unwinkingly at the perimeter of the gathered herd.

Keva followed the direction of the mare's gaze and saw a wiry form, wispy-haired, its face shadowed. She froze. *The minx.* She had forgotten the minx. Involuntarily one hand tried to rise to her wounded face. She restrained it, knowing she must not move. She could not see the razor claws, but she suspected she had already sampled their capabilities.

The minx slipped among the immobile animals, black-muzzled, furtively graceful. Deep within the silken ringlets that coiled around its face, Keva saw its eyes, mocking amber glints. Grinning, the animal stopped to drive a single sharp claw into a young mare's tender nose. The mare did not move, did not even blink. The minx rocked on its splayed feet, as if in pleasure, then bounced forward and ripped a buck's ear with finicking precision. The buck did not flinch, did not tremble, did not even roll his eyes. His blood dripped on the pounded soil.

But there were foals in the herd and Keva watched tensely as the minx approached one of them. Although none of the adult animals moved, she sensed their apprehension. The minx bobbed over the silver-furred foal, displaying its claws, chuckling. Keva knew that if what Par said were true, the foal had only to roll its eyes, and the minx would abandon its teasing game and kill.

Keva heard her breath sob in her throat. The sound brought an answering mutter of warning from the mare. Slowly the minx brought its splayed claws down over the foal's head, the two longest claws closing toward the foal's eyes. Keva's eyelids fluttered in spasm.

She could not watch. This was not one of Par's tales. She could feel the foal's fear as sharply as if it were her own and she moved almost without thinking, as if her muscles had life. She scooped up her pike and pushed herself to her feet, ignoring the pain in her injured knee, ignoring the faint voice of reason.

The minx clucked in gleeful response, drawing its claws away from the foal, leaping forward with an elastic bound. Its ringlets shivered and the delight in its eyes was bright, unmistakable. It grimaced across the water at Keva in challenge, waiting for her to move again.

Instinctively she froze, her muscles so rigid they cramped. The minx's reflection fell upon the water, grinning. It chuckled huskily, mocking, and Keva realized that if she did not take the teasing animal, it would choose another victim.

She quaked, her heart turning cold. All she knew of hunting came from Par's tales. She had never stalked anything more threatening than a bark-beetle. She did not even know if she could drive the point of her pike through living flesh.

The minx paced along the streamside on limber legs, not taking its eyes from her, waiting. Impatiently.

Waiting for her to move, waiting for her to signal the next phase of the game. Keva tested her fingers, trying to tighten them on the shaft of the pike. They did not respond. She tried to bend her knees, to flex herself into position to attack. The joints remained rigid.

And then the youngest foal of the herd choked convulsively and began to shudder with the stress of prolonged fear. Keva saw the minx's muscles contract as it turned. This time her reaction came as a result of conscious will. Her muscles knotting, she broke the bonds of paralysis and cried out, splashing into the water. The minx spun, ringlets dancing, amber eyes glinting. It flashed a greedy, sharp-toothed grin of pleasure and sprang for her throat.

Some unsuspected instinct guided Keva's pike. Her thrust caught the animal as it leapt and penetrated the rib cage. The very force of the animal's spring pushed the blunt point through the leathery, resistant skin.

For a moment, Keva thought the minx would not fall, thought it would tear her with upraised claws despite the pike buried in its chest. Then the minx staggered and tipped toward her, uttering a low, angry shriek. Its knees buckled and it sprawled, pressing its black muzzle into the mud.

Keva watched with dry throat as the animal died, writhing angrily, clawing at the pike. For minutes after the death, she was numb. Her first coherent thought was that she must retrieve her pike. But the trembling of her hands, the nausea that nestled in the hollow of her stomach, would not let her approach the dead minx.

If it had not insisted upon its game, she realized, it would be feeding now. Feeding on a foal or one of the feeble older redmanes. If it had not insisted, it could have fed on her the night before.

The gathered redmanes sighed and began to mutter among themselves, the foals shrilling nervously. Grunting, the elderly mare splashed across the water and nuzzled Keva. Numbly Keva turned. The milky eyes regarded her unwinkingly, as if the mare were taking her full measure. Then the mare grunted again and moved through the herd.

Following the elderly mare, the entire herd left the pool and moved upstream, heads low. The sound of their feet was heavy in the dew-damp grass. Keva leaned on the elderly mare, aware again of pain in her injured knee, of the sting of her injured cheeks. And aware of a hard, stony sensation in her chest, as if all the adrenalin that had sung through her bloodstream earlier had begun to crystallize there. She had difficulty breathing around its mass, just as she had difficulty believing what she had done. She had killed a living creature, one that walked on two legs as she did.

But if she had not, she would be looking now at carnage. The herd regrouped a distance upstream. The animals ranged themselves beside the narrow band of water, the elderly mare splashing through the water to face them from across the stream. This time she did not insist that Keva accompany her.

Keva stood lost for a few moments, then settled dully into the grass. Later she didn't even remember pulling her bedding around herself before she sank into a deep sleep.

She dreamed the things she often dreamed: fire, a woman who stood at its center, a face she did not want to see. But tonight she retained a certain waking awareness as she dreamed. Even as images moved and changed, she felt her body press against the soil where she slept. She felt the jarring rhythm of her heart. Felt the breath that rushed and sighed in her throat.

Felt difference. Felt change.

She did not want to change. She tried to put the perception away from herself, but a subliminal awareness remained with her, prickling in the hidden corners of her mind. Exhausted, disturbed, she slept until the mare blew warm breath against her cheek. Moaning, Keva pulled her blanket over her face, but the insistent pressure of the animal's breath reached her through the thick fibers. She rolled to her stomach, hunching her shoulders protectively. If she woke, she had to deal with hunger and the ache of her injured knee. Had to think again of approaching the guardians and perhaps learning things she did not want to know. Had to confront too the strangeness she had felt while she dreamed, a strangeness that did not recognize the barrier of consciousness.

If she woke—

This time the mare nudged her sharply. Moaning, Keva threw back her blanket, reproof on her lips.

She never uttered it. It was mid-morning and the sun shone brightly. The redmanes who had gathered the night before were gone. Only the mare stood beside the stream now.

Only the mare—and the solitary youth who stood on the opposite bank of the stream. Keva caught a sharp breath, her hand closing around the stone at her throat. A youth as old as she gazed across the water at her, gazed with her own eyes, from a face enough like hers to be her own. Except that her face wore an expression of surprise while his wore mute, frozen disbelief. Slowly she stood, wondering from his expression if he would run if she demanded to know who he was and where he had come from. Wondering why he stared as if she were an apparition. Wondering why she had felt change in the night. Wondering.

FIVE
DANIOR

The mountains had always shadowed Danior with doubt. There every moss-grown dike and weathered wall, every crag, every peak, announced that he was beyond the order of things, a person with no place. On the plain the order was broader, more inclusive. The herds, the grasses, the vastness of sky and land made the legends of the valley small. On the plain he walked among the herds by day and sat for the teachings by night. He watched the moons on the water, he heard the voice of the redmanes, and he forgot that he had no place.

Even this time, with the pairing stone at the bottom of his pack and uncertainty his companion, he felt shadows lift when he reached the plain. He spent the first night beside Cnarra's teaching pond, where her herd gathered each clear night for the teaching. Guardians gathered there too, tall in their umber capes, but they did not speak to Danior nor he to them. It was spring, the time when the plains predators had young to feed, and the guardians were listening too closely to their herds to heed anything he might say. After the teaching they went silently to stand among the redmanes, watching, and Danior slept beside the pond.

The second night he sat with a small herd that gathered by a rock-rimmed spring. No guardians came for the teaching, although as he walked southward the next day, he saw them among the herds.

The third night he had intended to spend at Waana's teaching pond. But he stopped in the afternoon to help a pair of guardians attend a difficult foaling and slept in their campment instead.

The next morning when he reached Waana's teaching pond, Waana and her herd were nowhere near. He found only a plains minx impaled upon a crude pike, its dead eyes glaring. He circled the creature, chilling, and realized the pike was nothing more than a tree branch sharpened to a point, not a guardian's weapon at all. He stared down at the stiffened corpse, disbelieving, and tried to imagine standing against a minx with a sharpened stick. Certainly someone had, but he couldn't guess who. After a while he went on, glancing uneasily over his shoulder.

He followed the stream and by mid-morning he began to see members of Waana's herd, grazing. When they recognized him, they raised their heads and muttered low greetings, foals and yearlings running to meet him with gawky grace. He paused and stroked their necks, then walked on, letting the earthen perfume of the grasses, the unchanging sky lull him. And so he was unprepared when he approached a bend in the stream and found Waana standing sentinel over someone who slept.

He was still more unprepared when Waana nudged the sleeper and she woke and stood. He stared across the narrow band of water for moments that seemed to stretch into all time and thought he would not be able to speak. Thought he would never find use of his tongue, his throat, his vocal cords again.

He knew who she was, of course—knew at a glance. Jhaviir's daughter. She was so much like himself, who else could she be? Dark, her hair heavy and smooth, she had the same arched brows he had, the same pink nails against bronze skin. And the stone she wore at her throat, the stone . . . His fingers contracted on the strap of the pack where he carried his own stone.

But much as she was like him, she was also unlike him. She was taller by several fingers' breadth and there was a deepness in her eyes, a darkness, as if she glimpsed something she had not yet permitted herself to see fully. And the proportions of her face were subtly different from his, each feature stronger, more prominent. As if—

He caught his breath sharply. As if the scratches on her face had come from a minx's claws. As if she had taken the animal in challenge—and changed. But not completely. If she had changed completely, she would have been taller. The deepness in her eyes, the strength in her features, would have been pronounced. And her gaze would have been as distant as his mother's. *Eyes that see fire,* valley people called a barohna's eyes.

Instead there was passing uncertainty in her eyes, although she kept it from her voice. "Who are you?" The words were very nearly a challenge. Her fingers pressed the stone at her throat, whitening on it.

The stone did not light at her touch and Danior's shoulders eased. For the first time he noticed her clothes, the long, full trousers, the boots strapped tightly at the ankles, the padded jacket. All were in shades of grey, woven—he realized—of vegetable fiber. He licked his lips, knowing there would never be another moment like this one, distressed that he had so little idea how to respond to it. "I'm Danior Terlath. You've come from the warmstreams," he said finally, surprised that the words sounded so commonplace, that they conveyed so little of the confusion he felt. He had found her, Jhaviir's daughter, and what his father said was true. She was enough like him to be his twin. Yet she was a stranger, startled by his presence, by his appearance. A stranger, and as uncertain as he.

It showed in the way she stiffened, her brows contracting. It showed in the wary challenge in her voice. "How did you know?"

"My great-grandmother has told me how warmstream people dress," he said, his thoughts racing ahead. How had she come to be among the fisher-people? Had she lived with them only long enough to outfit herself? Or much longer? And her father—"She's seen them when she crossed the stream with the herds."

Color washed from her face, but she regathered her composure quickly and shook her head, frowning. "You're not a guardian. There aren't any men among the guardians. They don't bear sons. I know that much."

It was his turn to frown. He had told her he was Danior Terlath. Didn't she even know what his use of the two names in conjunction meant? That he was Danior of the barohnial family of the Valley Terlath?

But if she had lived long beside the warmstream, perhaps she didn't know the conventions of the valleys. It was said the fisher-people were reclusive. That they were seldom seen beyond the geyser streams. "My great-grandmother lives in retirement with the guardians. My grandmother too," he explained. "I spend part of every summer in their campments." If the girl had been living with the fisher-people, he wondered, did her father live there too? His father would like to know, if it were true. His father would like to know that Jhaviir was alive, would like to know what had happened in the years since he had ridden away from Valley Marlath, where he had gone, what he had seen.

Before he could frame questions, Waana waded across the narrow band of water to him. Deserted, the girl took a limping step forward and halted, frowning in pain and hesitation. "You've hurt your leg," Danior realized, forgetting everything else. That, he guessed, must be why the mare had been standing sentinel over her. "Waana must have been waiting to lead you to Tehla's campment when you woke. To be treated."

"Waana?" For a moment confusion showed behind the girl's mask of wary composure.

The mare shook herself and let Danior scratch the patchy fur of her neck. "She's eldest mare of this herd. She teaches to the animals that graze out here. You may have passed her pond. She—" He broke off, remembering what he had found beside Waana's teaching pond just a few hours earlier. He glanced involuntarily at the wounds on the girl's face. "The scratches on your cheeks—"

"I fell," she said quickly, not meeting his eyes. "Night before last. I ran out of food and water. I was climbing down a bluff, trying to reach the plain to forage, and I slipped. She came the next day—the mare—and I thought if I followed her, she would take me to water. And to food."

She hadn't eaten since the day before? At least he knew how to deal with that. Quickly he stepped into the stream. "I have food—plenty of it. And I'll show you how to forage for more." If she was so poorly acquainted with the plain that she had gone to sleep hungry, he had much to teach her. And while he taught her, perhaps he could reach beyond her wariness, her uncertainty—and his own confusion. Perhaps they could learn to be at ease with each other.

The girl stepped back, keeping her distance, but when Danior opened his pack and laid out cheese and bread, glancing up at her anxiously, she joined him and accepted a portion without argument. While she ate, he dug honey-bulbs from beside the stream and peeled them with his knife. "I'll show you how to find stringgrass too," he promised. "And poppers, when the season is right." He sat beside her peeling the honey-bulbs, pleased to share the small ceremony of a meal with her. In the halls people said that to share food was to share much. And it was obvious that they did share much. If he could come to some understanding of what it meant to be so much like someone when he had never been like anyone before—

She was clearly aware of the likeness too. Hungry as she was, the girl glanced at him covertly as they ate. He knew because he glanced at her the same way, fascinated by the familiar proportions of her fingers, by the way she used her hands, by the texture of her skin. It was as if he had found himself in another person, as if he might guess her thoughts without questioning her. He could tell by the tautness of her features, by the tight, contained frown between her eyes, that she did not understand why he so closely resembled her and that she was uncomfortable with the resemblance. But she did not question him, although he could not tell if that was because she thought it would be discourteous or because she simply had no better idea than he how to frame her questions. Perhaps it was simply part of the etiquette of the warmstreams not to question. Almost any inquiry was permitted in the halls, but only if it was presented with careful indirection, so that no one would be embarrassed if no answer was forthcoming. Perhaps she simply didn't know how to speak so.

Not knowing the customs she had been raised by, he couldn't guess what to say to put her at ease. Nor did he feel free to question her, however artfully. They sat eating together as if they did so every day, but he didn't know why she had appeared on the plain wearing warmstream clothes, didn't know where she had been all the years since she had ridden away with her father, didn't even know if the scratches on her cheeks had come from a minx's claws. If the pike that had killed the minx had been hers—He retreated to fill their waterskins from the stream, wondering. Wondering at the implications if it had been.

Finally they finished and the girl tossed the hair off her shoulders and stared down at the ground. She spoke softly, as if apologizing for her slowness to identify herself. "My name is Keva. Keva-by-Oki, but she wasn't really my mother. She—" She glanced up, brushing the hair back from her face, frowning. "She adopted me when I was small. And now I'm trying to find my father. I'm hunting for him."

Danior glanced up in quick surprise. Jhaviir? She was hunting Jhaviir? "You don't know where he is?" He was startled by the sharp sense of dismay he felt. How could he take news of Jhaviir to his father if the girl hadn't seen him either? And if she hadn't, where could he be? How had they become separated?

"No. He's—" She frowned, wrapping her fingers around the stone at her throat. "I haven't seen him since he left me at the warmstream. He—he's dark like I am. Like—" She hesitated, then went on hurriedly. "He was riding a white animal. If you've seen a man who looks like—like me, riding—"

"A whitemane," he said quickly. At least he could tell her that much. "It's called a whitemane. My father has one too."

She drew a sharp breath, looking up at him with sudden, frozen wariness. "Your father?"

He drew his arms around his knees, suddenly uncomfortable with her tense watchfulness. What would she do, he wondered uneasily, if he told her what he knew? That her father and his had been replicated on a starship from cells taken from a man who had disappeared over a hundred years ago? That they had been used as tools by men eager to exploit other worlds? That they had remained on Brakrath only because his mother had destroyed the Benderzic ship with a hail of stones? If she had grown up in the isolation of the warmstream, would she believe him? And if she did—

He frowned at a new thought, one he hadn't considered before. If their fathers were brothers grown from the same tissue, what did that make them? Brother and sister? Cousins? Or were they of some order of kinship that had never been named—because they were the first to share it. And if so, what was the etiquette of that kinship? What were the implications that rose from it?

"Your father has a whitemane?" she probed.

Danior nodded, biting his lip, realizing he didn't know what to tell her. That they were kin? That his father could as well have been hers? That their mothers should have been stone mates; that their grandmothers had been? There was too much to be conveyed and he didn't know how she would accept it, any of it. He didn't know what to ask her either. The minx, and the shadow in her eyes . . . Aware of her gaze, he said cautiously, "He found it in the forest. Years ago, before I was born. He named it Fiirsevrin. It means cold fire." But not in any tongue of the valleys. In a language he had learned on another world.

Kadura. His mind churned desperately. *Kadura would know what to tell her.* Certainly he did not, and the unspoken questions in her eyes only added to his confusion. He stood. "I'll take you to Tehla's campment," he said with quick decision. "It's not far. She'll treat your knee and we can stay the night." And then tomorrow they could go on to Kadura's campment. Kadura would know how to answer her questions. Kadura could guess just from what she read in the girl's face how much of the truth she must have and which portions of it would be too disturbing. And Kadura could help him understand better what their kinship meant, what it meant that they were like each other and strangers at once, that they both held stones.

He half expected the girl to refuse. She studied him, frowning, biting her lip, then glanced across the water at the grazing redmanes and stood. They crossed the stream and Waana joined them. At first Keva refused to ride the younger mare who also elected to accompany them. But after a while her lips grew white with pain and she let Danior help her to the young mare's back.

There was excitement among the herds today, but Danior was too preoccupied to notice. He was aware of all the questions Keva still did not ask, aware of his relief that she withheld them. He was aware of her shrinking tension when they passed the first guardians standing among the herds. Aware that she stiffened when a group of guardian daughters came laughing through the grass, then stopped and stared. Aware that the campment itself, when they reached it in mid-afternoon, was alien to her eyes: a collection of patted mud structures overgrown with grass, narrow lanes winding between them.

Guardian daughters ran ahead of them, laughing with particular shrillness, and by the time they reached Tehla's kefri, she had heard of their arrival and was waiting at the door. She stood head and shoulders taller than either of them, her coarsely streaked hair hanging upon her shoulders. Her face was so creased and weathered she seemed as old as the land, but her heavy brows were still dark. She clasped both Danior's hands, her voice rough, little used. "We thought you wouldn't come to the plain this year, Danior Terlath."

They thought he wouldn't come because he had reached his second majority this year and was no longer a child, to summer on the plain. He wondered momentarily what the guardians had expected him to do instead. Wondered what future they thought awaited him. But there was no time for that. He turned as Keva slid from the young mare's back and leaned stiffly against Waana. "I'm going to visit Kadura. This is Keva. I told her you would treat her leg. She fell." He hesitated, gazing up at Tehla, wondering briefly how much to tell her. When she did not speak, he plunged ahead. "She —she's been trying to find Jhaviir."

Keva raised her head sharply, staring at Danior, then turning to meet the spent power of Tehla's gaze, her voice disbelieving. "You know my father?"

Tehla folded lean brown arms over her chest. Time had marked her features so deeply her expression was unreadable. But Danior knew by the cautious tenor of her words that she had noticed his hesitation. "Many of us knew him on the plain," she said carefully. "He spent his first summer here and he rode here sometimes after he took the whitemane. Let me examine your leg and we will talk."

But Keva did not move. Her lips grew white and her fingers twisted in Waana's mane. "Knew . . . Is he dead?" She glanced quickly from Tehla to Danior, her eyes bright with dismay.

He stiffened at the tension in her voice, at her sudden pallor. His impulse was to reassure her, to tell her that her father was not dead. But how could he say that when he didn't know?

"No one knows," Tehla interceded. Strangely, when her dark brows gathered into a frown, some of the austerity was dispelled from her face. "He's been gone since the drought year. No one has seen him from that time. But there are lands beyond the plain. People live in some of them. And Jhaviir was restless."

"The drought year?"

"Twelve years ago. But this is not the time for discussion. I can see you're almost too tired to stand. Come, let me look at your leg." Tehla turned back to her kefri.

Keva hesitated, then ducked her head to follow. Danior rubbed Waana's neck, then entered the kefri after them.

Keva stood by the door, her eyes taking in the curved mud walls, the hard-packed floor, the implements and tools that hung from ceiling and walls. Beside the fire pit were two platforms with rolled bedding. Stiffly she sat on the stool Tehla placed for her. She licked her lips, gathering courage. "If you knew my father, you knew my mother," she said slowly, as if she were afraid of the answer.

Tehla's hooded eyes flashed. "Oh yes. I took my plow teams to her valley often when she was a child. Before she took the sun-throne. Her mother lived in this campment for three seasons after her retirement. Waana carried her bundles when she and Tiahna moved to Vendana's campment." Tehla's hands were rough, the fingers blunt. They moved briskly as they rolled up Keva's trouser leg and probed the swollen flesh of her knee. "Does it hurt when I press here?"

Keva stared at her, hardly seeming to hear the question. "No." Numbly.

Tehla peered at her face as she probed again. "I can see very well that it does."

Keva met her eyes and shuddered. "It hurts," she admitted tautly. "My mother was a barohna. That's what you're telling me." The words seemed to give her more pain than Tehla's probing.

Tehla weighed her response carefully before answering. "She was, yes. But her valley isn't cultivated now. Our teams don't turn the soil there anymore."

Keva spoke flatly, from stiff lips. "Because she's dead."

"Yes. For many years," Tehla said at length, nodding to herself. "And you have done yourself damage, Keva Marlath. Danior, crush pagnyon berries for tea. We will have that while I soak chatter-leaves for a dressing." The words were almost brusque. Tehla rose from her stool and busied herself with a bundle of dried leaves from her storage net.

Danior hesitated. It didn't seem right to turn his back when all the color had gone from Keva's face, when she looked as if she had taken a heavy blow. But she held her lips tightly pressed and would not meet his eyes. Obviously she did not want to be burdened with his sympathy. Reluctantly he turned and took down the mallet and pounding board.

He was much aware of her tight-lipped silence as he worked. But when he served tea, it came to him that it was not grief for her mother that made her pale. She did not seem so much bereaved as frightened by what she had heard of her mother. She accepted the earthen mug with shaking hands and drank silently while Tehla applied the herbal dressing and bound her knee with clean cloth. Puzzled by her reaction, Danior poured her a second and third cup of pagnyon tea. She drank those too, just as silently, although her color had begun to return.

Then of course she was drowsy, as Tehla had intended. She didn't protest when Tehla unrolled bedding and led her to a sleeping platform. Danior sighed and let the single mug of tea he had taken work at his taut muscles. When Keva's eyes closed, Tehla studied her for some moments, then stooped to leave the kefri. Danior followed.

It was late afternoon and guardians passed silently in the overgrown lanes. Guardian daughters ran and shrieked, auburn hair flying, the gawky grace of foals upon them. Danior frowned, slowly recognizing the special quality of their excitement. He raised his head and sampled the air, trying to catch the scent of pollen. "It's time for the running," he said. He should have guessed from the dancing of the yearlings they had passed on their way to Tehla's kefri, from the shrill laughter of the guardian daughters. But he had been too preoccupied with Keva and with his own thoughts.

Tehla nodded, studying the sky. "Tomorrow. Or the next day. The sky will be clear for tonight's teaching."

The special teaching that prepared the yearlings for the running. But Danior had more urgent concerns. "Tehla, I found a minx. This morning. At Waana's teaching pond. It was dead. Killed."

"With a guardian's weapon?"

"No, with a sharpened limb."

Tehla's eroded features disappeared into the folds of her hood. "The marks on Keva's face are much like claw wounds," she said after a while.

"But she's not a barohna," Danior said, perplexed. At least she was not a barohna like any he had seen before. But of course there had sometimes been barohnas who did not change profoundly, particularly in the early days. And there had sometimes been barohnas with maverick powers, barohnas who used the stones to do things no barohna had done before or since.

The pairing stone had lived in his hand, and he was not a barohna.

But he had not killed a minx. Perhaps if he had, perhaps if he could find courage for that—

Go for a beast? A palace son? He pressed his temples, trying to discipline his thoughts, but they escaped control. Reluctantly he recognized that the day had been long, that he was too tired to deal with the growing disorder of his thoughts. "I'm going to have another cup of tea," he said.

Tehla nodded from the depths of her cape. "Do. But remember to wake yourself for the teaching."

"I will." Danior turned back to the kefri, rubbing his temples, trying to stroke away the ache of confusion. Keva slept quietly, one hand on the stone at her throat. Moving silently, he opened his pack and stared down at the velvet pouch that held the other stone. Then he poured himself a second and third cup of tea. Soon drowsiness loosened his muscles and quelled the disorder of his thoughts so that he could sleep.

When Danior woke, oil lamps burned in the kefri but Tehla was gone. He moved stiffly, throwing off his covers. Had he slept too long? Quickly, he went to the door.

It was dark in the campment. The narrow lanes were deserted, although Nindra barely touched the horizon and Zan had not risen.

Danior rubbed a hand across his mouth. He had not overslept. He even had time to wash and eat before the teaching. And he must wake Keva. He hesitated, reluctant to disturb her. But when he turned, she was already awake. She lay on her platform, watching him with a steady, cold gaze.

"Tehla has bread and cheese if you're hungry," he said uneasily when she did not speak. "And milk pudding. There's always milk pudding in the spring."

Keva sat, pushing her covers aside. "And tea?"

Her inflection made him wary. But why would she be angry? "If you want it. But then you'll be sleepy again and miss the teaching."

She nodded, her gaze narrowing. "You put something in the tea that made me sleep."

"It was pagnyon berry tea," he said, surprised at her accusing tone. "That's why people drink it, to sleep. I drank some too."

"Not as much as you gave me. And you didn't tell me what it would do."

Was that why she was angry? Because she hadn't expected to sleep? "I—I thought you knew. Tehla wanted you to rest. You were upset. It upset you to talk about your mother." He frowned uncertainly. "I think you knew she was dead—before Tehla told you." The query was blunt, but this was not the time for indirection. Not when she looked at him with such cold anger.

Her eyes narrowed. "I guessed it. And you knew too. You knew my mother was dead. And you knew she was a barohna."

He eased across the room, but her gaze followed him. Was that what had disturbed her? Learning that her mother had been a barohna? Or was she angry because he had known and hadn't told her? But how was he to guess what she knew and what she didn't know? He couldn't find the sense of the situation, of her anger. "I— yes, I visited her valley just before I came here. I went—" But he sensed dangerous ground and decided not to mention the pairing stone. Not now. Not until he understood better. He averted his eyes, surprised that someone who had seemed so much like himself could make him so uncomfortable. It was a special kind of alienation, one he wasn't prepared to meet.

"You knew my father's name too," she said with the same core of anger in her voice. "I'd never heard it until you used it this afternoon."

"I—his name is well known. Many people know it."

"But I don't know anything about him. I don't know where he

was born, where he grew up. I don't know who his family was. I don't know if he was a barohna, if—"

He glanced up sharply, frowning. "Men are never barohnas." Didn't she know that?

"Then he wasn't a barohna," she amended quickly. "But he must have been their kin if he lived in the mountains. Because he was dark, and there are only two kinds of people in the mountains. Serfs and barohnas. Oki told me, and so did Par. The serfs are fair. They—"

Danior stiffened, stung that she used the old term, the belittling term. "No one holds serfs now. Not since the Seventeenth Cycle of the Council. The people who live in the halls are called freeworkers. They have guilds and associations. They—"

"But your people treat them as serfs, even if you don't call them that. They do the work and you—the barohnas burn them if they refuse. They—"

"That's not true!" Danior protested, wounded. Where had she heard those things? From the fisher-people? Was that why they were so reclusive? Because they still told the old tales among themselves? "No one has done anything like that since the troubled times. No one even speaks of it anymore. You can't even find the scrolls from those days in the public rack. You have to ask the scroll keeper to bring them from storage if you want to cipher them. And my mother—"

"Your mother is a barohna."

"Yes." But how could he convey what that meant when she had heard the wrong things? How could he make her understand the control a barohna must have, the strength, to use all the power of the sun yet never scorch a single seedling? How could he explain what it meant to the people of the halls that a barohna held the throne? If she could see her mother's valley now, the dikes standing in disrepair, the orchards frost-bitten, the fields rank with useless growth—

"Come to your mother's valley with me," he said impulsively. "I'll show you. The people had to leave when she died. They had to go to other valleys because there was no one to draw the sun. No one can live there now, not until another barohna comes. If you see—"

Her shoulders stiffened. "I'm not looking for my mother. She's dead."

"Your father lived there too, in the palace. I've seen their quarters. The people took everything else when they left, but your parents' quarters are still furnished. If you come, if you let me show you—"

For a moment he thought she would agree, but she shook her head. "No. He doesn't live there now. I won't find him by going there."

"You won't find him anywhere," Danior snapped, and regretted it immediately. Color drained from her face, leaving only anger and pain. He extended a placating hand, but she drew away. "I didn't mean it," he said in an agonized voice, sorry he had not guarded his tongue better.

"Do you know that he's dead?"

"*No.* But no one has seen him, Keva. And he'd be recognized anywhere in the mountains or on the plain."

She raised one hand, pressing her temples. When she spoke again, her voice shook but her decision was clear. "Then if he isn't there, he's gone somewhere else."

To the uncharted lands beyond the plain? To all those places where people had wandered since the first-timers had been stranded on Brakrath? Wherever they had gone, little news had come back. No one knew how many of those people had survived, except for those who had gone to the warmstream and the desert.

If Jhaviir had gone to the warmstream, Keva would know.

If he had gone to the desert—Danior frowned, remembering what he knew about the desert clansmen. Sometimes desert traders wandered into the plain, hungry and sly, to offer worthless objects in trade for cheese and bread. The guardians fed them but would not take their wares. Usually the guardians discovered when they had gone that any unguarded objects—pikes, capes, cooking pots, tools—had gone with them. Lately he had heard that the clansmen came to the forest for the running, to steal redmanes. And he had heard of the clan wars that bloodied the desert, of the angry rivalries and the vendettas. If Jhaviir had gone to the desert, had he survived?

"He's gone somewhere else," Keva repeated.

Danior heard the desperation in her voice. He sighed, conceding the argument. "Somewhere else," he said without conviction. "And if we don't eat, we're going to miss the teaching."

She frowned at his unexpected capitulation, her shoulders still rigid. "The teaching?"

If she had just reached the plain, she probably didn't know. "The herds come to the teaching ponds when the nights are clear and the mares teach them about the plain," he explained. "About how to live. How the herd lives. If you were with Waana's herd last night—"

"They stood beside the water," she said slowly, "but nothing happened. They just stood there."

"You didn't hear because you didn't know how to listen. You have to press the ground with your hands and close your eyes and listen in a particular way. I'll show you. If you're going to travel on the plain, you need to sit to the teachings." Few people beyond the guardians ever heard the voice of the herds. Few people ever learned what the redmanes had to teach. If he could not answer her questions, if he could not give her news of her father, at least he could give her this.

He thought she would refuse. But after a moment's silent resistance, she nodded. He went quickly to fetch bread and cheese, eager to share the teaching with her, eager for her to understand he had not meant to hurt her.

The teaching pond was in an area of hard-pounded soil beyond the campment. It stretched grassless in every direction and sloped gently to a shallow basin filled with spring water. The guardians had already gathered, silent in their heavy nightcloaks. Their daughters laughed and ran, auburn hair flying. The herd gathered on the other side of the pond, the yearlings and foals as eager as the guardian daughters.

"We sit here, at the top of the slope," Danior instructed Keva. "The guardians and their daughters sit nearer the pond."

Keva weighed the situation with a taut frown. Danior thought for an anxious moment she would refuse to sit to the teaching after all. But finally she pulled her cloak tight and sat.

Nindra already touched the edge of the pond. Moments after Keva and Danior arrived, the elder buck appeared from the dark and approached the water, his auburn mane ragged, the coarse hair of his tail tangled. But by Nindra's light his haunches seemed more powerful than fat and he ignored the night wind that tore at his heavy grey coat.

He stood for a while beside the spring, gazing up at the assembled guardians and daughters. When the last shrilling foal, the last restless daughter settled quietly, the buck lowered his head to drink.

"Put your hands to the ground now," Danior whispered.

Keva did so, frowning. "I don't hear anything."

"It hasn't started yet," he assured her. He could see the resistance in her muscles, the tension of all the things she didn't understand: what the redmanes had to teach her, whether the things he had told her were true, where her father had gone. "You have to put your palms against the ground. Don't press hard. Just let them rest there. And let your thoughts go. Take a deep breath, and when you let it go, let your thoughts go with it, so there will be room for the teaching. It isn't hard."

Reluctantly she uncurled her fingers and breathed deeply, but Danior could see from the tense set of her face that she had not emptied herself.

Perhaps she wouldn't be able to do so this time. Perhaps the questions that preoccupied her were too immediate. Perhaps the teaching was too far beyond anything she had known before. He curled his own hands in sympathetic tension. But that would solve nothing. Sighing, he let his palms rest against the soil as Tarla, eldest mare of the herd, padded to the spring to join the buck. She was older than he, but her body held memory of a younger time, of bondings and matings and foals. She moved with pondersome grace. She grunted in answer to the buck's muted greeting, then bent her head to drink. Danior relaxed and released himself to her, grateful to escape his own thoughts for a time.

Behind her all the redmanes of her herd stood with heads lowered, eyelids drooping. The eldest mare raised her head and for a moment seemed to peer directly at Danior. His muscles tightened in a moment's instinctive resistance. Then, almost without his consent, his breath seeped away. His eyelids closed and his head fell forward, the level of his consciousness sinking with each sighing breath. He forgot Keva, forgot the pairing stone, forgot everything as the teaching began.

It came to him like a possessing consciousness, first reaching tentatively into his mind and senses, then dominating them, a welcome force.

Listen, my herd. The peace of our herd is greater than any in this world. It must be preserved in each of you. So mind me, foals. Pondwater smells different when stingmadders nest in the rocks. It smells this way . . . this way . . . When it smells so you must not drink or you will surely be stung and the madness that follows will destroy the peace of the herd.

Listen, my herd. The strength of the herd is greater than any in this world. So mind me, mares. There are years when you must not foal. In those years the egg has formed improperly and your offspring would be so malformed as to hinder you and detract from the strength of the herd. You will know you must not conceive by the tightness of your abdomen when your mate approaches you. It will feel to you . . . this way . . . When this happens, you must turn from your mate and walk alone, for the strength of your offspring is the strength of the herd.

Listen, my herd . . .

The teaching continued, monotonous, soothing. Danior roused himself after a while and saw that Keva had pressed her hands to the soil, that she had bowed her head and closed her eyes, that she appeared to be listening too.

Listen, my foals. We all dwell together in the strength of our herd, which is yours to preserve. Near the end of summer, you must eat certain barks and leaves to balance the nutrients you have taken from the fresh grasses. At those times, there will be a sensation at the back of your throat that will feel to you . . . this way . . . You must learn to heed this signal, for the strength of our herd lies with us all.

Take care, young bucks and mares. Soon will be the time for choosing mates. Our peace is precious, yet there are some who would disrupt it. You will know them by their inattention to the teachings and by their careless behavior as they pass among us. It is not ours to drive them away unless they openly violate our peace, but you must not mate with those careless ones. They will give you foals who carry the same heedless qualities. Our peace lies in the wisdom we share. You must preserve it always.

Heed me, mares . . .

Keva was listening. Danior could tell from the waxen immobility of her eyelids, from the slow measure of her breath. He raised his head and gazed around for a moment, then bowed his head, relieved. Because if the teaching touched her as it always touched him, washing away inner barriers, perhaps the awkwardness, the hesitation that had come between them today would dissolve and they could begin to know each other. Could begin to understand what it meant that they were alike, that they had found each other. That neither of them was alone any longer. He glanced covertly at her, wondering if that could ever mean as much to her as to him—not to be alone. Sighing, he slipped back into the teaching.

SIX

KEVA

The teaching was as it had been the night before. The mare stood stolidly, the redmanes let their shaggy heads droop, and the moons moved upon the water. And Keva did not understand. What was she supposed to hear? What did a redmane mare have to teach her?

That her dreams of fire were only dreams and not a foreshadowing? That nothing irrevocable had happened when she killed the minx? That the sense of change that had come in her sleep was only a product of fatigue and the strangeness of the plain?

That the tales Par had told of barohnial daughters who killed beasts and took their mothers' powers—to draw fire from the sun, to make stones dance—were fantasies, centuries removed from reality?

That she would find her father?

Instead of opening and resting against the soil, Keva's hands knotted. She could feel the haft of her makeshift pike against her palm again, could feel the resistance of the minx's leathery skin. Then the rupture and the plunging entry.

Her mother had been a barohna. Must she become a barohna too? Had she already begun to do so? She shivered, wondering if she had any will in the matter. Wondering what other things she had yet to learn that she did not want to know. All day she had been aware of levels of complexity proliferating just below the surface of her understanding. She had met Danior, she had eaten with him and talked with him and felt that the ground was about to open and reveal a web of relationships and possibilities she had never suspected.

She had felt the web was about to draw her in, that there was nothing she could do to free herself from its adhesive strands.

Danior, Tehla, her mother, the dead valley—

She glanced at Danior. He had drawn up his knees so the soles of his feet pressed the ground, as did the palms of his hands. His eyes were closed, his face still. He seemed to have gone somewhere else entirely.

Keva caught her lip between her teeth, then drew up her own knees and placed her palms to the soil. If there was another place to go, a place where her thoughts might be stilled for a while, then she would follow Danior there. Gazing across the pond, she saw Waana among the redmanes, watching her from cloudy eyes. Sighing, Keva closed her eyes and let her head fall forward. She let her breath seep away, taking thought with it.

At first she heard only a thin, distant stirring. The wind? A voice? It played upon her consciousness, and she breathed more deeply and let the world slip away entirely.

She was aware of memories first, stretching back over time. Memories that had been passed from mare to mare yet were still fresh. Memories of all the warmseasons the herd had ever known. Memories of the sunrises of centuries.

Then the focus of her awareness narrowed and she moved deeper into the teaching mare's consciousness. The mare's senses became hers. She felt the pain of the mare's arthritic joints. She felt the acids that worked in her stomach. She felt the mare's enduring strength.

But beyond that Keva became aware of all the experience the mare had gathered in the years of her life. The mare's memories became hers: the sunlight of her youth, the birth-shrill of her first foal, tens of years of moonlight bondings and matings. Keva let her breath sigh away and she sought out fresh grazing lands with the mare and tasted lush grasses. She chewed pungent barks. She tossed her head and loped across the plain with the herd, her feet making the soil pound like an earthen heart.

She took the mare's wisdom for her own. *Listen, my mares. When it is time for you to deliver, there are leaves you must chew. You will find them growing near the streams and ponds. When your time is near, you must go to the water so that you may feed on them. If foaling time finds you elsewhere, your labor will be hard and your foals will be damaged. And they will detract from the strength of the herd.*

Listen, bucks. Your instinct is to guard the herds. But we have human guardians among us now, as we did not when your instinct was forged. If you see predators stalking, you must not give your lives needlessly. You must shrill the warning abroad. You must broadcast alarm to every mare and every foal, and the guardians will hear it. They will come and the predators will go without taking your foals and without taking you. They will go because they have learned to fear our guardians more than they fear hunger. And you will be preserved for the strength of us all.

Listen, foals—

The teaching continued, enveloping, enfolding, instructing. Giving herself to it, Keva learned how to recognize the best grasses, where to find the barks that provided the necessary acids when the grazing was too sweet, how to discipline a spirited foal. She learned how to distinguish good water from tainted, how to recognize when storm was coming, how to contribute to the peace and strength of the herd. Then the mare's voice faded and Keva was aware of the shuffling of feet, of the shifting of bodies. She was aware of anticipation. Her own? The mare's?

The mare's voice returned, fuller, deeper. *And now, my herd, we have come again to a time that is as old as our herd. You have felt the southwinds today. You have tasted in them pollen from the flowering trees of the forest. Here the days have been cool with light morning rains, but to the south the days have been warm and dry—until now.*

Listen, my herd. Now the spring rains have come to the forest. They have washed the dust from the trees and brought the flowers bursting from their bud-cases. And with the pollen comes the time of the running. We have cherished the yearlings among us. We have protected them and taught them and guided their feet.

Now something else must guide their feet, something older. Now the pollen calls them and they must run to the forest—as we once ran. They must run with pounding feet and bursting lungs. The pollen calls and they must test themselves. They must establish which among them are strong and which weak, which wise and which foolish, which generous and which selfish. Only in the running can they learn their places in the herd.

And you, mothers; you, fathers; you, grandsires and granddams and elder siblings—you must release them to the running. You must let them find their places, even though some you love will find their hearts are not as strong as they must be, even though some you cherish will learn they are not fit to give their herd foals, even though

*some will fall from exhaustion and others will fall to the predators
who are called by the pollen just as our yearlings are.*

*Listen, my herd, the running serves the strength of our herd. We
must make its rule our rule. However we love the weak, we cannot
permit them to be ranked along with the strong. However we cherish
the foolish, we cannot permit them to find mates and bring more
foolish ones among us. We have guardians to stand among us and
watch with us for predators. We have guardians to help us in many
ways, and that is good. We did not always have these women among
us.*

*But even with their guarding presence, we must serve our own
strength. For only in strength will we find peace and only in peace
can we continue as we have these hundreds of centuries.*

Listen, my yearlings—

With effort, Keva withdrew from the teaching, the stone tight in
her hand. *The forest.*

Her father had gone to the forest. Gone to take his whitemane
for mating. Oki had told her so. Now the yearlings were going there
too, running in some kind of test of fitness. She did not know where
the forest lay, except southward, but if she could follow the yearlings . . . She pressed the stone too tightly and it cut her palm.
She released it and pressed her hands to the soil again, reaching for
what she could learn.

When at last the moons passed from the surface of the pond and
the mare's voice faded, Keva emerged slowly from the teaching.
She came as if from a strange land, wondering. She looked up to
find Danior gazing at her.

Gazing expectantly with her own eyes. The serenity of the teaching began to slip away almost immediately. The web opened before
her. All the questions, all the inexplicabilities returned. *Danior.* So
like her he could be her twin. She could read every mood that
passed across his face. The tension of muscles, the tautness of flesh,
the hooding of eyes—she had a sense of what emotion lay behind
each small alteration of expression, just because he was so much
like her.

But she didn't know why he had gazed at her as if at an apparition when they first met. She didn't know why he seemed eager to
tell her certain things, yet withheld others. She didn't know why
they should be so alike.

Ask him? Something prevented her. Perhaps simply a reluctance
to exploit the eagerness she saw in his eyes when she was thinking

of slipping away without him and going to the forest. Of searching for her father there.

"You heard? The teaching?"

She touched probing fingers to her temples, realizing she didn't want to talk. She wanted to think, about the running, about the forest, about what she must do. "Yes," she said shortly and was immediately sorry for the disappointment she saw in his eyes. Would it be a betrayal to slip away, to leave him? What claim did he have, beyond their disturbing resemblance?

The claim of one person who had fed and helped another.

It made her feel no better that he drew back at her tone and didn't press. Didn't even study her as she knew he wanted to do, from the corner of his eyes. Didn't try further to assess her mood and its causes. They joined the guardians who walked silently back toward the campment. Tehla had left an oil lamp burning. She already slept on the platform nearest the fire pit. Danior insisted Keva take the other platform. He unrolled his bedding on the floor near the curved wall.

He soon slept. But Keva lay on the padded platform with eyes open, trying to sort her thoughts. Finally, too restless to lie still, she got up and slipped from the kefri.

The lanes of the campment were deserted. The moons hung low in the sky. As Keva moved away from the kefri, Waana rose from the shadows and followed, snorting softly. Beyond the campment, bucks and mares slept in the grass, their younger foals curled beside them. But the yearlings moved restlessly, running, dancing, feet pounding. Moonlight touched their silver coats, washing away colt-gawkiness, endowing them with fleeting grace.

Keva watched them, shivering when she realized she saw the gleaming coat and restless grace of her father's whitemane in the yearlings tonight. The yearlings could only be distant cousins of the whitemane, if that. But tonight they seemed to offer a promise, one she did not understand. Keva clutched the stone at her throat and let her thoughts take their course. Her father had taken his whitemane to the forest. That had been years ago, but perhaps there was something to be learned in the forest anyway, even now. Perhaps he still returned there sometimes. Perhaps she would find some sign there—or meet someone who had seen him. She caught her lip between her teeth, undecided. Go when there were so many things she didn't understand here? So many unanswered questions?

So many facts she couldn't fit into a coherent whole? Go when she knew Danior would be hurt?

Waana stirred against her. Pensively Keva began to walk again. Eventually her feet led her to the teaching pond. She descended the sloped bank and stood beside the water. Waana bent to drink, and Keva knelt beside her.

She cupped water in her hand, intending to drink, but never raised it to her mouth. Instead she stared down, suddenly unable to move. Her reflection gazed at her from the surface of the pond. Her reflection, but with a difference. Because this was not the face she had glimpsed so often when she bathed in quiet pools. Unbelieving, she leaned over the water and saw a new depth in her eyes, a subtle new proportion to her features. They were bolder, stronger. Her nose was more prominent, her mouth wider. Her eyes were set deeper. Yet the actual physical alteration was so subtle she almost wondered if she imagined it.

She had not imagined she had killed a minx. Had not imagined she felt some change later as she slept. And her mother had been a barohna. She could not argue that when both Tehla and Danior told her it was so.

Those stories Par had told . . .

Disturbed, she retreated from the water. She hugged herself, suddenly cold. Cold and frightened. And decided. Grimly decided.

She couldn't stay here. Reality was slipping away from her here, taking identity with it. Quickly she slipped her fingers through the strip of blue fabric at her neck. Surely when her father had left her with Oki, he had left the stone and the bit of fabric not just as tokens but as a message. And not a message that she was to wander mountains and plain learning things she didn't want to know, changing in ways she didn't understand. A message that she was to find him if he did not come back for her.

Or did she tell herself that because she was afraid of the face she had seen in the pond? Afraid of what might lie behind the altered features?

Danior—but she didn't think he would understand if she told him she was going. He would try to dissuade her. Or perhaps even insist upon accompanying her.

And so she wouldn't tell him. Quietly she slipped back to the kefri and gathered her possessions. Furtively she slipped bread and cheese into her pack. Neither Tehla nor Danior stirred. She paused briefly at the door, looking back. Another leave-taking, this one not so wrenching as the last. Quickly, before she could have second thoughts, she stepped into the lane.

The pad of feet told her Waana followed. Keva paused, wondering how much the old mare understood. The redmanes opened their lives to the guardians through the teachings. Did understanding flow the other way too? Did Waana have any inkling of where she was going or why?

"If you come along, are you strong enough to carry me when my leg hurts?" she asked softly, rubbing the mare's neck. Waana snorted softly and continued to follow.

As they passed beyond the campment, Keva found a pike some guardian daughter had left lying. She took it and walked southward from the campment, anxious to leave the campment as far behind as her feet would take her.

Later, when her knee began to ache and Waana nudged her repeatedly, she climbed onto the mare's back. She rode, tired and aching, until well after dawn. The grass was damp with dew and the sky tinted delicately pink when she pulled the old mare to a halt. Twisting awkwardly, Keva peered back in the direction they had come.

There was no sign that anyone had seen them go, that anyone followed. Guiltily she wondered how long it would take Danior to realize that she had not just wakened early and gone to explore the campment. Would he guess where she had gone? From what clue? Would he try to follow her?

She rode until she couldn't keep her eyes open longer. Then she slid clumsily off the mare's back. "We'd better sleep," she said huskily. Sighing, she spread her bedding in the damp grass.

She slept uneasily, her knee aching, her muscles tender. Her only dream was of tall trees and long shadows. Tossing uneasily, she wondered if the trees were fabrication or memory. Wondered if she had visited the forest as a small child, with her father. She woke at noon, not to the sound of running feet but to their jarring rhythm in the soil. *The running*—She pushed herself up in quick alarm, expecting to see a line of yearlings bearing down upon her.

She saw only Waana standing beside her, dozing. There was no sign of the yearlings, even in the distance. Lowering herself, she pressed her ear to the soil and heard the sound of feet again. The soil, she realized, acted as a giant drum, transmitting distant sounds, making them seem near. Reassured, Keva rolled her bedding, then poured water from the waterskin and splashed her face.

She was extracting bread and cheese from her pack when Waana shuddered awake. The old mare shook herself and flexed her neck, as if the muscles ached. Then she stood with feet planted wide, eyes closed. Keva knew from the quivering of her eyelids that she felt the running too.

Keva walked through the early afternoon, Waana following. She paused and gazed around frequently, studying the horizon in every direction. Sometimes the vibration of the soil grew heavier and she seemed to hear a faint grumble from the distance. Other times the soil carried no sound at all.

And then, to the south, she saw a receding grey line—and she saw another dark line approaching rapidly from the west. She halted, pressing herself apprehensively against Waana, her fingers catching in the mare's auburn mane.

The vibration of the soil became pronounced, pervasive. It reached up through the soles of Keva's boots. She felt it in Waana's prominent hip bones, in the muscle of her haunches. But Waana did not seem alarmed, so Keva forced herself to set aside her own trepidation.

Gradually the dark line from the west resolved into individual animals, yearlings running silver-coated in the afternoon sun, tossing their heads, slapping their tails. They ran eagerly, snorting and squealing and darting at each other, then dodging away.

The yearlings grew from indistinct shadows to individual animals, racing across the grassy plain. Some ran a zigzag course, cutting buoyantly back and forth in front of others. Others ran doggedly, as if the effort were already costing them. Some faltered and choked on their breath. But all ran.

All ran south. Toward the forest, where flowering trees cast pollen on the air. The yearlings lunged past, silver coats gleaming, and then they were gone. They left only trampled vegetation and pounded soil.

Keva was surprised to find that the rhythm of the running persisted in her heartbeat long after the yearlings were gone. She leaned on her pike, using it as a walking stick, and continued in the direction the yearlings had taken. She felt, as she walked, that she partook of a rite, one she comprehended more with heart than mind. Occasionally the earth shuddered and she saw other dark lines on the horizon. Once a wave of yearlings from the direction of Tehla's campment passed. Later there were animals from the more distant regions of the plain. They passed with sweaty flanks and foaming mouths, passed with less and less of the joyousness of the early runners. They had come farther, their reserves were slimmer.

Some will fall . . . A cloud crossed the late afternoon sun and Keva thought of the night shadows of the forest, of the predators that waited there, attracted by the same pollen that called the yearlings. Keva curled her fingers in Waana's mane, beginning to wish she had not brought the elderly mare with her. Wishing she knew how to send her back to her herd.

She wished it more keenly a short time later when she found the first fallen yearling in the trampled grass, padded feet twitching. She hurried to its side, frightened by the way it lay, by the involuntary spasms of its muscles. Its breath was faint, its heartbeat weak when she pressed her ear to its chest. Yet there was no sign of injury.

She cradled the young animal's head in her lap, rubbing its fur, trying to rouse it to drink from the palm of her hand. Instead its legs stiffened in a final spasm and its head lolled, the eyes glazing. Keva stood with angry tears in her eyes, her stone clutched tight in one hand. Soft silver fur, eager feet—if the foal had stayed with its herd, if it had not pressed beyond its strength, running—

Waana nudged her, snorting softly. Keva turned and found something in the mare's eyes she could not understand, some painful understanding. But instead of honoring it, Keva turned on the mare with all the anger she could not loose on the dead yearling. "Go back! I'm not your foal! Go back to your herd!" She didn't want Waana's company if the journey to the forest was too hard for the old mare, if she might fall as the yearling had fallen. Keva stamped her foot. *"Go—get!"* Quickly she turned and hobbled away, tears streaking hotly on her cheeks.

Despite her admonition, the old mare followed, head hung, milky eyes dull again.

At last it was dark and Keva approached a barren tumble of rocks that seemed fury-flung across their path. She paused, leaning heavily on her pike, her knee aching. Two jagged pinnacles of rock stood against the evening-grey sky, their rough contours reflected in a clear pond at their base. Surrounding the pond were hundreds of boulders and jagged rocks, scattered as if someone had thrown them down in anger.

Keva turned and looked around uneasily. Shadow lay heavily behind the tumbled boulders. Anything could inhabit those shadows. Anything . . .

Waana picked her way to the water, shoudlers sagging with fatigue. When finally she raised her head, nostrils quivering, Keva watched tensely, grateful she had not turned back. Waana's eyes were filmed but if there were predators, she surely would smell them and give warning.

The old mare gave no sign of alarm. Shuddering with fatigue, she turned back to the water, dipping her muzzle again. Reluctantly Keva sat beside the water, clutching the stone at her throat. Something about the air of this place disturbed her, some lingering mood. It almost seemed to bear a residual anger, as if something had happened here that could never be undone. She did not want to spend the night here. But her knee ached and Waana was exhausted.

Rousing herself, Keva took food from her pack but found she could not eat. She was too tired, her muscles too painful. Finally, when the sky was as dark as the shadows cast by the tumbled boulders, she unrolled her bedding and stretched out stiffly. Sleep overtook her quickly. She seemed to hear pounding feet in her dreams. Once she heard a shrill scream in the distance and lay with eyes wide, knowing the cry was no dream.

Nor was it a dream later when Waana's voice wakened her. Keva shivered free of her bedding and sat, pressing her hands to the soil. Waana stood by the pond, the light of the risen moons in her eyes. *Hear me, foal. This is the time when I can speak to you. Our herds have been upon the plain for more centuries than any can remember. The peace and strength of our herds are eternal. They are forever.*

They are forever because we have learned how we must preserve them. We have learned what things we must eat, what signs we must watch for, how we must honor one another. More, we have learned to teach our young these things so that our strength lives in each generation as in the last.

And beyond that we have learned that we are one. We walk the plain in separate bodies and those bodies are endowed with different gifts and intelligences. But the spirit that animates us is one, not many. We are not divided. We are joined. The benefit of each is the benefit of all.

So too the weakness of one is the weakness of all. We cannot be strong and weak at once. Nor can we live in peace if we permit weakness among us. And so there are tests and trials to winnow the weak from the strong.

You have watched the running and seen that some will die. Some with weak bodies, some with foolish minds will fall. We send them to fall not because we have no care for them but because they are imperfect receptacles for the spirit of our herd. We cannot achieve strength and peace if our spirit is bound to weak vessels.

The running is for the benefit of all, my foal. It is for the benefit of weak and strong alike, wise and foolish. There are those distinctions among us, but there are no divisions. The interest of an individual cannot be separated from the interest of the herd.

And so you must not be troubled as you continue on and see sad things. You must trouble yourself only with your own safety. Because if you continue as today, there will be dangers for you too. And I have no other foal like you.

No other at all like you . . .

Keva opened her eyes and gazed at the still pond, wanting to respond. If she could speak to Waana as Waana spoke to her, in the silence of her mind . . . Impulsively she pressed her hands to the soil. Rough particles gritted against her palms. For a moment she thought she couldn't do it, thought she couldn't deliberately reach out to Waana.

But Waana had heard her once, when she sang the bluesong. She was sure of it. If she could just project her thoughts, float them upon the water's surface . . .

Her voice, when it came, startled her with its silent clarity. *You're going to leave me. You're going to go back to your herd, Waana.*

I must. The running is for the young, who must test themselves and learn their places. I am old and I will fall another way.

And your herd needs you.

No, that is not why I must leave you. There are others to teach when the moons are on the water. We all carry the same memories, the same lessons. And some among us understand your kind more clearly than I do. I came this far because I wanted to protect you. But now I have become more understanding of you, of what is in you, and I know that I must let you find your own way, your own place. I must leave you, foal.

But if there are predators, Waana, are you strong enough to escape them? If they follow you, if they attack—

No, no, they are hunting tender meat, foal, and I'm stringy. But you must be alert for them as you near the forest. They will not venture far into the trees, not the rock tigers, the dune lobbers, the plains and sand minx. But they will be hunting nearby. And there are men from the desert clans who hunt the forest at running time. You must watch for these men, foal. They live in a hard land and it has made them hard.

I should never have brought you here, Waana. Regretfully.

You didn't bring me. I came. And I will go. But if I can hear you teach again as you taught that night at my pond, before you learned to listen, it will make a lesson to be passed to many generations. A lesson many will enjoy hearing. We have lessons like that, taught only to pass a moonlit night, to please.

She wanted to hear the bluesong again. Keva clasped her stone, uncertain she could teach it at will. It was elusive, a thing of reverie and dreams. *I'll try.*

She took a deep breath and let her pupils widen to accommodate Allindra's silver reflection, hoping the light would touch deep and release the bluesong. For a time nothing changed. Then reality shivered, parted, and the bluesong came. Sunlight and breeze and some other force brought it living to the night. Unconsciously Keva fingered the strip of slippery cloth at her throat and let the song rise from the deep place where it lived.

The bluesong . . . It fed on sunlight twice-reflected. It fed on breeze. It cast its alien spell. Keva lost herself in it, in its silent notes and living colors.

At last she grew tired and the song slipped away. Keva shuddered back to awareness. Her body had grown stiff, her hands cold. Waana's voice came to her lightly. *There are bright things in the song, foal, but there are dark things too—behind the light.*

Keva clasped her stone, pressing one hand to the soil. *Dark things?* What dark things could there be in the bluesong?

Dark things, Waana said, lidding her milky eyes. *But they are not real.*

Keva nodded, not understanding, too tired to think. She stretched out to sleep again.

When mid-morning sunlight woke her, Waana had gone. Keva sat, licking dry lips, feeling very much alone. She rolled her bedding and slung her pack on her back. Leaning on her pike, she picked her way among the tumbled boulders.

She soon realized there was something here she had not seen the night before. Some boulders were strewn randomly across the ground. But many were heaped together, and beneath them, crushed and mangled, she saw the dull glint of a metal body. It was larger than anything she had ever imagined, an elongated shape.

Frowning, touched with sudden chill, she picked her way around its perimeter, climbing precariously from boulder to boulder.

A large metal vessel—many tens of paces long, crushed. She gazed up at the two rocky pinnacles that stood beside the pond, realizing there must have been others once, companion formations. And some force had pulled them apart and flung them at the metal body. She didn't think, from the pattern they took, that the fall had been natural.

Her entire body was cold. Her arms were stiff with gooseflesh. She could not stay here. Too much anger lingered in the air. As quickly as she could, she picked her way clear of the field of boulders. When she reached its edge, she paused, looking back, pressing her stone—wishing there was someone to tell her what had happened.

Perhaps she didn't want to know. Shivering, she turned away.

A shadow lay upon the day. Bright morning sunlight could not dispell it. Nor could the occasional flurry of running yearlings. Because now as she walked, she came across more and more fallen yearlings. Some were still warm, others cold. Twice something had torn their throats and she found tracks around the mutilated corpses. The tracks of a minx.

She began to watch as she walked. And she walked as briskly as her knee would permit. Each time she saw a shadow, a smudge ahead, she thought she would find a fallen yearling, and dread made her chest tight, her breath shallow. A lone runner stumbled past, its mouth foam-flecked. Keva watched it and wanted to call it back, to send it back to its herd. But it could not test itself there.

Late in the afternoon she reached a grove of tall trees. She took their shade gratefully. It was too early to stop for the night. The forest still lay somewhere south. But her knee was throbbing and she was light-headed with hunger and all she had seen. She would rest, then continue by night.

She ate, then found a place where brush formed a protective screen and fallen leaves lay deep and soft. Exhausted, she curled up to sleep.

She slept dreamlessly and the trees darkened around her, throwing their shadows in a broad gridwork. When she woke, it was at a faint sound. She sat, her mouth dry, her heart thundering. Moving cautiously, she peered out through the screening bushes. Moonlight fell through the trees, casting as many shadows as it dispelled.

As she watched, a dark shape detached itself from the trunk of a tree and moved with hunched shoulders to the shelter of another tree. It moved upright, on two feet.

A minx? Perhaps the very one that had savaged the yearlings she had found that afternoon. Keva chilled, straining for a better view of the animal. It was stalking something now, she realized. Something that moved deep in the trees, something that picked its way carefully, its coat gleaming by moonlight.

A yearling. Keva's hand clenched on her stone. A yearling separated from its running mates and wandering in the trees. She did not pause to think. She took her feet, her fingers cramping around the haft of her pike, steeling herself to utter the cry that would turn the minx's attention to her.

The yearling was receding into the trees. Its pursuer slipped after it, moving from shadow to shadow with predatory concentration. Keva hesitated momentarily, then left the brush and stepped silently after predator and prey.

She glimpsed no more of the minx than an indistinct silhouette as it glided from shadow to shadow. She saw the yearling more clearly: the proud carriage of its head, the lanky grace of its stride, the rich glint of its coat. It moved with unexpected delicacy, pausing often to listen. Keva clutched her pike. It didn't matter what Waana had taught. She could not turn away and leave the yearling to the minx. At least she had a pike to defend herself with. The yearling had nothing but delicate hooves.

Her heart stopped. *Yes,* the yearling had stepped into a patch of moonlight and its feet were capped with hooves. For a moment Keva felt slack with shock. *Hooves.* Unbelieving, she crept forward again. The yearling paused in a shaft of moonlight, gazing back the way it had come.

She could see it clearly now. Could see that moonlight did not glint from the silver-grey fur of a redmane yearling. This animal was white, its coat sleek and shining. Even its mane was white, lying like strands of silk upon its graceful neck. Its eyes—she was near enough now to tell—were pink. They had a translucent quality, as if she were not seeing the color of the irises but of the blood vessels behind them.

This animal was a yearling, but not a redmane yearling. It was a whitemane.

And it knew it was followed. Keva saw that in the quivering alertness of its nostrils, in the prick of its ears. Keva glanced toward the shadows where the minx hid and her stomach turned. She had seen what the minx had done to the foals that had fallen in the running.

Her throat tightened. Her hand rose and closed around the stone. She pressed it, trying to find courage to distract the minx.

Before she could move, before she could cry out, the minx stirred, its feet making a barely perceptible shuffling sound. The yearling heard and danced backward, hoofed feet tapping a nervous rhythm, gathering itself to flee. And the predator uttered a piercing cry and lunged.

For a moment all Keva's responses were frozen. She was plunged into vacuum, into timelessness. The pike dropped uselessly from her hand. A dizziness spun into her head, and her respiration slowed, as if her body had suddenly begun to burn some fuel other than oxygen, some fuel manufactured from its own cells.

What came next seemed to Keva to happen more slowly than any event of her life. Later she was only able to remember frozen images: the minx throwing itself at the yearling, body arched; the yearling's eyes glaring with helpless fear; her own body moving forward into the moonlight. The dizziness spread until it consumed her, bending her awareness into new configurations. Then came the shaking of the soil, the rumbling of the earth, the grinding of rocky sublayers against each other. Soil erupted and was flung into the air. The stony strata that lay below the topsoil shook. Rocks and boulders tore free and flew through the air.

Flew at the minx, which forgot its prey and flung itself against a mossy trunk, mouth gaping.

Human mouth gaping. The flying stones did not arc toward a minx but toward a wiry youth scarcely older than Keva. His dark hair was knotted behind one ear. His dark eyes stared, his thin-lipped mouth gaped. He wore clothes like she had never seen before, flapping robes over loose trousers. And at his waist—

At his waist were two colored sashes, one vividly blue, the other red.

Sashes like her father had worn, although coarser, less brilliant. Staring, she saw that they were knotted as her father had knotted his, loosely, so that they hung low over one hip.

Stones hung in the air and then dropped heavily to the ground short of their target. Dark eyes stared into hers, the pupils wide with shock. And it had happened so quickly that the youth's cry still echoed in the trees. As the last stone dropped, Keva saw that he did not hold a weapon. His knife still hung at his waist. He had thrown himself at the whitemane yearling unarmed.

Why? But there was no time for questions. They turned as one and saw the yearling flee, hooves pounding. The youth stared after it for a bare moment, then overcame his paralysis. His face twisting with fear, he ran in the opposite direction.

Keva gazed after first one, then the other. Slowly the tension ebbed from her muscles and she stared around her, trying to ground herself in reality again. Soil was torn from its place and thrown everywhere. Approaching the raw gash in the earth, she peered down numbly. Moonlight did not reach the bottom of the gash from which the rocks had been torn.

The stones . . . she stared at them where they lay. She might have persuaded herself that they had erupted into the air of themselves. But she knew better. She had flung them. Somehow. Something in her had changed when she had killed the minx and something had changed again tonight. And she had opened the earth and the rocks had flown. Not at her command but in execution of her will, of her anger. If she had not seen in time that they flew at a human rather than a minx, the rocks would have crushed the youth.

Keva shook her head, trying to overcome the growing numbness of shock. She had to think. She had to understand. Were Par's tales true? Had she become a barohna when she killed the minx?

Wouldn't Danior have recognized it if she had? Wouldn't he have told her?

But he had not told her he knew her father's name, not intentionally. He had not told her he knew of her mother, not until Tehla spoke of her. And his manner had been halting, cautious. Because he recognized what she was?

Her mind worked numbly. If this was what it meant to be a barohna, would she tear the earth apart again? If she were threatened? If she were startled? Or angry? If someone approached from behind without speaking, might she unwittingly crush him before she had time to deliberate?

Her entire body began to tremble. Weakly she sank to the ground and let her head fall back against a tree trunk. She clutched her stone as talisman against confusion, but confusion reigned free. She sat, her body boneless with shock, her mind staggering. She sat while the stars crossed the sky and woods creatures moved warily around her. She sat and did not cry, although she wanted to. She was afraid the tears would petrify on her cheeks.

"Oki, I'm not hard," she whispered aloud. *"You were wrong about me. I'm not hard at all."* And if she was not hard, how could she be a barohna? She tried to find comfort in the question, but it was lacking.

SEVEN

DANIOR

It was mid-afternoon before Danior admitted what his heart knew—that Keva had gone. He stood at the edge of the campment, feeling the vast openness of the plain like a knot in his stomach, like an ache in his head, like a hungry, nauseous, frightening emptiness. No one had seen her go. No one knew what direction she had taken or when she had taken it. But she had gone and she could be anywhere.

She had gone to continue her search for her father. He was certain of that. She had learned that her father had not been seen in the mountains or in the plain. So she had carried her search elsewhere.

But where? She hardly knew the plain. How did she expect to find her way safely beyond it to other lands?

And what other lands were there? The warmstream, the roughlands, the lakelands, the desert. He licked his lips and rubbed the back of his neck, where the muscles had clenched tight. The roughlands, the lakelands—no one lived there. Did she know? But the desert—would she have gone to the desert? Did she even know where it lay? And had she heard of the clansmen? His fists knotted. If only he had warned her. But how was he to know she would go without telling him, just go and leave him wondering?

Wondering? No, this yawning sense of dread was certainly more than that. Frowning, he groped through the complex tracery of his thoughts. She had not given her knee a chance to heal, so she would travel slowly, even if Waana had accompanied her. He could overtake her if he knew what direction she had taken.

But he did not know. And the plain lay vast in every direction. He gazed around, squinting against the sun. It was quiet in the grazing grounds. The yearlings had gone earlier in the afternoon, shrilling and stamping. Only the adult redmanes and the younger foals remained. The scent of pollen was no more than a subliminal tickle in the air. Why, he wondered with quick bitterness, was it so important to know where she had gone? To be with her?

Obviously she didn't consider it important to be with him. Otherwise she would not have gone—and without a word's parting. So that was the other side of what he felt at her leaving: a hard, lonely anger, like a fist knotted in his chest. Tensely Danior rubbed his temples, trying to bring his thoughts to clearer definition. They had met, they had walked together, he had taught her how to listen to the teaching. And she had gone.

It wasn't enough. They had hardly touched. He had hardly begun to understand what it meant that they were at once so much alike and so different. What it meant that she had killed a minx, that he could make a pairing stone burn, that they had lived so long in ignorance of each other and then met. By chance. Only by chance.

Use the stone? What other way was there, when she could have gone in any direction? How long could he stand here frightened and angry, doing nothing? Still, he hesitated, his head aching with unresolved questions, before he left the grazing ground and returned to the campment.

Tehla had not gone to the herd today. She worked in the milk kef with three other guardians, their lean arms wet to the elbows with creamy milk, tubs of milk pudding steaming around them. Danior went there when he had fetched his bedding and his pike from the kefri. "Thank you for the shelter of your kefri, Tehla," he said formally. "I must go on my way now."

"You won't stay for the night's teaching, Danior Terlath?" asked Mirala, youngest of the four guardians. She had been a guardian daughter a year ago, and much of the laughter was still in her eyes. She teased him with it, showing gleaming teeth.

"No," he said shortly. "I'm going to my great-grandmother." A lie, and he knew from Tehla's impassive nod that they all recognized it. His face reddened. Why couldn't he tell them the simple truth? That Keva had gone and he must find her. That he had things to learn from her, that he intended to learn them. Something kept him from saying any of it. He turned away sharply.

But before they would let him go, he had to stuff cheese and freshly baked bread into his pack. And Mirala told him in laughing tones that she would meet him in the orchard when she brought her first plow team to Valley Terlath next year and his face reddened even more fiercely. Though why it embarrassed him that she suggested he father her first daughter . . . He snapped his pack shut and left the hut hastily, running down the narrow lanes of the campment.

He knew he had no hope of finding Keva's prints in the grass. The yearlings had trampled everywhere before finally going south. But since he had to go in some direction, he chose to go south too. Perhaps it was only the faint musk of pollen that drew him. Perhaps it was instinct.

He did not open his pack until he was well beyond the campment. Did not remove the stone from its velvet pouch until there was no one to see. Then he held the stone in his palm and felt a wracking shudder of doubt. He had seen barohnas wear pairing stones that glowed so brightly the light hurt his eyes. His gave only a small light, as if it could not find the vitality in his touch to burn with full radiance.

Perhaps he could not even learn its use. Perhaps it would never do more than faintly glow. He dropped the chain over his head anyway and placed the stone at his throat, his hands shaking, his throat dry.

Nothing happened. The stone lay against his flesh, faintly warm, and nothing changed. With a moment's surge of nausea, Danior closed his pack. He had only the gem master's words to encourage him. The pairing stone was a tool. If he was to learn to use it, if he was to find Keva with it, he must wear it, stroke it, become sensitive to it. He must find his way to its heart with his fingertips, with the flesh of his palm.

He closed his hand around it and because he had no idea what else to do, he continued walking south. The musk of pollen became perceptibly thicker as he went. Occasionally he saw yearlings running, individually or in groups. After a while, he began to feel like a yearling himself, called to a test. One he didn't understand but could not turn from.

He walked until dark, sometimes holding the stone, sometimes only stroking it. Then he spread his bedding near an outcropping of boulders. He sat for a long time pressing the pairing stone to his palm, trying to find something more in it than faint warmth. When he held it before him, it illuminated his hand, throwing the creases and folds into relief. But nothing more happened. Finally, discouraged, he rolled into his bedding and slept.

His dreams were confused, discolored by the day's events. He searched endlessly for things he could not find, reached for things he could not touch, mouthed words that held no sense. And he clutched the pairing stone. Even as he slept, he felt it grow warm and then hot against his palm. Vaguely he remembered what the gem master had said. That sometimes the link was forged in sleep. With barely focused effort, he tried to reach into the stone, to breach its crystal facets and press through to another place. He tried with all the power of dream.

Then he was not dreaming at all. The flesh at the base of his throat warmed and began to burn. He stirred uneasily and struggled to sit, rubbing his eyes. He shook his head, trying to clear it, trying to understand. He seemed to sit in two places at once. The boulders he leaned against were interpenetrated by others. He gazed up and saw the moons, but they were four, as if he saw Nindra and Zan twice, from differing perspectives. Anxiously he peered around and found the edges of reality blurred, eroded.

From nearby he heard a familiar voice. Waana's voice, he realized—teaching. But where was she? With Keva? Had he linked with Keva? Anxiously, he tried to capture the words of the teaching. They eluded him, distant, wispy. But the smooth succession of visual images—of the herd, the plain, of familiar places—was clear now. He might have been sitting beside the teaching pond.

Instinctively he tightened his clasp on the pairing stone and made a deliberate effort to reach out. The effort made the flesh of his throat burn, as if nerve centers there blazed alive.

He reached but it was not Waana who taught now. Keva's voice came to him instead and was quickly succeeded by another, one he had never heard before—one that made a chill race down his spine.

The voice was not human. And it did not teach with words. It taught with a bright-hued song and with visual images, not sharp-edged but shaded, as if shadow overlay them. Frowning, he attempted to bring them to focus and the breeze of another place moved into his mind. Shadow pulled back and sunlight fell hard and clean from a sun he had never seen. Confused and compelled at once, he realized that he did not see it now, but he felt its power in the song that sang blue.

The song Keva taught was at once energy and substance, light and sound—all those things caught up in an enveloping silkenness.

It wrapped slippery fingers around him, reaching for him. It coiled around him and carried him to another place. He went willingly, barely aware of the burning of the pairing stone in his palm.

Another place. Silently Danior struggled to orient himself. There was land behind the bluesong and there were trees. He saw their reaching white stalks, saw moving shapes on the ground beneath them. Swift, clever shapes. Caught, he fell deeper into the bluesong. He became totally drenched in its light, and a face emerged. Glinting yellow eyes, obliquely set—predator's eyes. Yet the face was not threatening. It was clad in glossy chestnut fur and it smiled toothsomely, its pink tongue flicking out mischievously.

A rock-leopard? No, something gentler, playful. But it didn't play now. Danior brought his attention to tighter focus and saw that the creature had begun to groom itself, pulling its pink tongue over the chestnut fur, lingering until the fur lay clean and damp. Moving closer, Danior saw that the creature rested not upon the ground but in a bower of brilliant silks. They were of many colors: scarlet, amber, noon-yellow—chartreuse, emerald, crimson. And blue, the blue of sky, so brilliant and clear it hurt to see.

But Danior did not withdraw his attention. He thrust himself deeper into the spell, deeper into the realm of color and song.

He thrust himself deeper and then there were the dark things. Nightmare images growling out of nowhere, casting sticky arms around him, tearing him with razor claws. They clutched at his mind, trying to drag him into their nightmare pit. They tangled their claws in his hair, they tugged and tore—

The stone! They reached for him through the stone! Gasping, he tore the chain over his head and threw the stone away from him.

It fell in the grass, but the scream was still in his throat, a raw cry, as he shuddered free of the pit, of the bower, of the strange song Keva taught. He glared around in shock, expecting to see the dark things come boiling after him.

He saw only moonlight and grass. And his pairing stone, fading to darkness.

He wrapped his arms around his drawn-up knees, trembling. He had reached out through the pairing stone. Reached out into some strange place Keva knew. Someplace where there was a yearning blue song and a hot sun and a predator that slept on brilliant silks and groomed itself with a pink tongue.

But the dark things—he tried to summon back the faces of terror, so alien to anything he had ever experienced. The terror did not lie just in the images but in the sense of being caught, of being drawn in.

Into what? He could not formulate a clear answer. The dark things were alien, their threat incomprehensible.

The only recognizable image he salvaged from the episode was of the pinnacles. Keva was spending the night at the place where his mother had torn down the rocks to destroy the Benderzic ship. He rubbed shaking hands across his face. At least he knew that Keva had gone south, that instinct had guided him well.

Numbly he retrieved the pairing stone from the grass and placed it around his neck again. He did not touch the stone with his fingers, did not stroke or clasp it. Shaken, he rolled back into his bedding and stared up at the stars.

It was near dawn before he slept. It was midday when he woke. His mouth was stale, his hands tremulous. The water he splashed on his face felt icy, although the morning was not cold. He could barely bring himself to eat. He sat for a long time staring at the horizon before he got to his feet and began to walk south again.

He walked slowly, stopping often to lean on his pike. He felt as if the stone had drained him of energy, as if it had fed on him. His thoughts ran a slow course, monotonous and undemanding, yet in some way alien to any thoughts he had had before. Because now he had used the stone and he had seen the dark things.

He hardly saw the occasional yearling who passed. He stopped before dusk beside a small pond, knowing it was useless to press on to the pinnacles tonight. He wouldn't find Keva there now. And tomorrow he would travel more quickly. Sighing, he sat and opened his pack. This time the smell of bread and cheese at least teased his appetite, although he found he could not eat much.

He had almost finished his meal when he heard a shuffling sound. Slowly he stood, peering into the gathering shadows. A predator? He closed one hand around his pike, the fingers cramping.

The shuffling neared and, with a surge of relief, Danior recognized Waana. She picked her way through the grass cautiously, her gait hobbling, painful. "Waana," he said softly, not wanting to startle her. Had Keva turned back? He peered anxiously beyond Waana but did not see her.

So it was not to be that easy, finding her.

Waana raised milky eyes, studying him silently as he made his way to her. When he reached her, she bowed her head. Danior studied her more closely, concerned. She stood as if she were not just tired but in pain. Quickly he bent to examine her, raising her padded feet one by one.

Even in the dusk, he could see the gash on her left hind pad. The wound was caked with dirt and dried blood. "You've torn your pad. If you'll let me wash it and bind it—" He hesitated, not certain that she understood speech. Some mares understood well; others understood no better than most valley people understood the silent communication that passed among redmanes.

Waana grunted and moved to the water. Painfully she lowered herself to her side and gazed up at him.

At least she understood he would care for her. Quickly Danior sorted through his pack. He carried little beyond food, a waterskin and a few extra clothes. He selected a roughspun tunic, tore it into strips and wet it in the pond.

Biting his lip, he flushed the wound with water, cleaning out caked dirt. He had nothing to sew shut the gash, but he bound it as tightly as he dared. She had probably cut herself on the jagged rocks of the pinnacles.

"Now if you'll sleep," he urged, "you can walk tomorrow."

The mare grunted and did not attempt to stand. Relieved, glad to have her company, tired, Danior spread his bedding nearby and slept almost immediately.

When he woke later and found the moons on the water and Waana standing beside the pond, he pulled his bedding closer and refused to join her. "You shouldn't put your weight on your foot tonight."

But she continued to stand teaching to no one. Finally, when he could not fall asleep again, he sighed and left his bedding.

She taught as she always taught: how to find the required foods, how to sense the presence of danger, how to treat herdmates, how to live. She taught everything Danior would need to know were he a redmane. He sighed again, more deeply, and released himself to the teaching. Gratefully he felt some of his energy return, moving from his fingertips to his arms, from his arms to the base of his neck, warming him.

She taught at length, until the moons neared the edge of the pond. Then her voice changed. *Listen, valley foal. Sometimes we take lessons from other plains creatures. Sometimes we take lessons from our guardians. Now I have learned a new lesson that is not a lesson at all. All the herds will want to hear it, although it will contribute nothing to their peace and strength, only to their pleasure.*

It is a lesson full of light and shadow, a teaching from a place we don't know.

Instinct told him what Waana wanted to teach. He tensed, his fingertips chilling again. He wanted to raise his head, to break the spell of the teaching. But more he found he wanted to walk under the white-stalked trees again. Wanted to look more closely at that strange place. With only a moment's hesitation, he raised his hand and clasped the stone.

Listen, Waana admonished. *You will hear light things and they will make you glad. And you will hear dark things, but they can't hurt you because they aren't real. Listen, valley foal.*

Then the song came, smooth and silken, and lights moved behind Danior's closed eyelids. They took many colors and many degrees of brightness as Danior watched, as if alien moons shone on changing surfaces. Then there were strands of silken cloth, some free and flowing, others stretched tight into translucent sheets of color. There were trees, their trunks reaching into the surrounding darkness like tall white stalks. There were pink bodies, hunched and fearful, and long sinuous bodies with dark fur. Stalking creatures large and small turned glinting eyes to the light, then fled. Danior reached for it all, the stone burning his fingers, its light stinging his eyes.

The song continued. The many lights fused into one and picked out faces from the backdrop of darkness. Pink fleshy faces, dark-furred faces, yellow-fanged faces—Danior groaned as the faces became feral.

The light narrowed to a searing pinpoint, then widened again and Danior gazed into a dark-furred face with oblique eyes. It was thick-muscled at the jaw, supported by a heavy neck. He recoiled, his heartbeat rising from a distant drumming to an anxious clatter. It was a bestial face, a threatening face, yet there was something about it, something . . .

Curiosity drove him and he reached for more detail. This face was duller than the one he had seen the night before. The eyes were sulphurous, muted. The teeth did not smile. Still, upon closer examination, this animal was much like the other he had seen, grooming itself in its bower. He concentrated on the burning patch at the base of his throat and looked more closely.

Shadow peeled back, light spread, and he saw a heavily muscled body with matted chestnut fur. Saw a pink tongue that hung laxly from between stained teeth. And he saw pain. Saw it clearly.

Was the animal injured? Lost? Danior expelled a long breath and light spread again. The animal stood among tall white trees with veined black leaves. It stood with its matted head raised, gazing far up into the trees.

Danior followed its gaze. High in the trees he saw a bower of brilliant silks. Moonlight shone through them and emerged stained many colors: chartreuse, emerald, crimson—scarlet, amber, noon-yellow. Narrowing his eyes, he saw a shadow against the silk panes. He turned and saw that the heavy-jawed animal on the ground gazed up at the bower in mute pain.

It was the bower he had seen before. And the other animal was there again, grooming itself. Danior frowned, trying to find the sense of the scene. A bower of colored silks in the trees. One animal within it, pulling its tongue through its dark fur. Another animal staring up at the bower with eyes that held no spark, staring up in pain—as if at something it knew well, yet could not attain. Danior watched the brutal face, trying to find something in the dull eyes that would tell him more.

He was afraid to reach too deeply. There were shadows just below the surface of the dull eyes. He was afraid of what might live in the shadows.

Dark things. Images of terror. Incomprehensible terror.

Waana said the dark things were not real.

But the animal that stood looking up at the bower seemed real. Real somewhere. Confusion made Danior's neck draw tight, made his head ache. Confusion and the bare beginnings of panic. He exhaled heavily, trying to breathe away the heat at the base of his throat, where the pairing stone rested. Immediately he found himself moving away from the animal in the trees, from the bower. He exhaled again and shadow flowed among the white-stalked trees. The strange, wordless song Waana taught faded.

Trembling, Danior extricated himself from it entirely. Regained the reality of the plain, of stars that glittered overhead, of solid ground beneath him. He sat for a moment, numbly triumphant. He had that much control. He could reach into that other place, then extricate himself from the terror before it began.

If he could do that . . .

Shakily he stood, running his fingers through his hair, trying to understand. Last night he had worn the stone and it had taken him into Keva's consciousness. That was how the stone had been intended to function, after all. It had been created to link one mind with another.

But how had the images that accompanied the bluesong—the colored silks, the white-stalked trees, the chestnut-furred animals—come to be in Keva's mind? Had she even been aware of them? Or had she only heard the song? And why hadn't the linking of minds been mutual? Why hadn't she been aware of his presence, his thoughts? Did the pairing stones only work for him?

Waana at least had reached past the song to the white-stalked forest. How else could she have warned him that the dark things were not real? And did her warning mean that the other things were real—the trees, the bower? He had no way to ask her. Frowning, he touched the pairing stone with a single fingertip, then drew back when the stone began to glow. A tool, he reminded himself. The stone was simply a tool, one he understood imperfectly. And the only way he could perfect his understanding was through practice. Through reaching down into its heart.

Practice. He must practice. The moons left the water. Waana sighed and lay down in the grass to sleep. Danior sat for a while, staring at the dark water. Then he raised his hand and closed it around the stone again. He reached for its core, for the place where it lived. He knew when he touched it because the stone took light, casting a cloudy blue radiance against the surface of the pond. Reach—he must reach, as he had done the night before while he slept, as he had done tonight, going deeper and deeper into the stone, into the white-stalked forest. Instinctively, he drew a deep breath and held it, pressing his eyes shut. The node of warmth at his throat grew, intensified. He thought of Keva and he reached for her, reached for her heart, for the thoughts that framed her consciousness.

Quietly, almost effortlessly, he stepped into her mind. At first he touched only memory. He smelled the sulphur tang of geysers and felt mud under his toes. Reaching nearer—*reaching,* that was what he must do—he saw the surface of the water. There were yellow-throated plants floating there. Other stalks reached up through the water—to take sunlight, he understood, drawing upon what Keva knew.

He explored the warmstream for a time, then reached into other pockets of memory. And then the warmth at his throat spread and he stepped into present time. It took him moments to recognize it for that because Keva was dreaming. He felt the pressure of her body against the soil where she lay and traced the quick, confusing passage of dream-images: a tall woman who stood against fire, a bright circlet that flew into the grumbling darkness, confusion, fear, uncertainty. Danior stirred uncomfortably, wishing Keva would waken.

But when she woke, it was to see a dim shape stalking a whitemane yearling. Confused, Danior tried to ground himself in her thoughts, tried to reach through her rising alarm to find and define his own response. A minx? Surely she wouldn't go against a minx with just a pike? Surely—

And then, before he could fully orient himself, she was tracking the minx and rocks flew. The earth tore, boulders rose in the air, a frightened face stared—and when the whitemane and the terrified youth had both fled and Keva was alone, Danior was caught in the same shocked numbness Keva experienced.

Jarred by the intensity of the experience, frightened, he pulled his hand free of the stone. Keva's thoughts slipped away and he retreated from the pondside, shaking. She was a barohna. If he had had any doubt before, it was gone now. Keva was a barohna. She had torn up the ground. She had pulled stone from the earth and made it live. Only a barohna could do that.

And the youth who had stalked the whitemane—Danior's thoughts ran rapidly in an unwelcome direction. The youth had been a desert clansman. He knew that from his coloring, from his features, from the robes he wore. But the youth's bright-colored sashes, the way he wore his hair, knotted tightly behind one ear— Danior had never heard of a clansman who dressed so.

But Danior had glimpsed Jhaviir in Keva's dream, and he had worn a colored sash—the bluesong—and he had worn his hair knotted behind one ear. Was the desert youth dressed in imitation of him? But why imitate Jhaviir—if he had not seen him? And recently?

Danior's throat tightened with alarm. Did Keva realize that the youth had been a desert man, a clansman? That his dress, his appearance had been unusual? If she knew anything of the desert people and how they costumed themselves—

Quickly he took up the stone and inhaled deeply. He reached.

Numbness, terror, bewilderment, doubt. A reluctant recognition of what she had done and its significance. With relief, Danior found Keva wasn't thinking of the youth at all. She was thinking only of herself.

But later, when she did think about the youth—Danior released the stone and retreated to his own thoughts—when she did think about the youth, about the details of his appearance, she would recognize the same thing he did. That the youth was dressed in imitation of Jhaviir. That he must have seen Jhaviir. Recently.

And then, if she learned the youth was a clansman—Danior didn't pursue the thought further. There was no time—no time for thought, for question, for doubt. No time for hesitation. He rolled his bedding with trembling hands and left Waana without a word's parting. Quickly he began to travel south, half-running. If Keva learned the youth was a desert clansman, if she decided to go to the desert in search of her father—Danior thought of the stories he had heard of the desert people, of their raids, their wars, their savagery, and he chilled. He ran faster, urgency driving him, knowing he had to reach Keva before she decided to go to the desert. Before she decided to go among the warring clans without even guessing the danger.

EIGHT

KEVA

Keva walked slowly the next day. The herbal dressing Tehla had applied to her knee had lost its potency and her knee swelled against its bindings. The minx wounds on her face itched. But she was so preoccupied that she hardly noticed those things. If she refused to think about what had happened the night before, she told herself, if she refused to hear the grinding of stone upon stone, if she refused to admit the fear that yawned before her like a pit—

But of course she could think of nothing else. She walked numbly, hardly seeing the trampled grass, the occasional trees, the yearlings who ran and fell. Now more than ever, she realized, she must find her father. Danior had kept things from her, for whatever reason. Her father would not. He would tell her why the earth had torn. He would tell her why stones had grumbled in the air. He would tell her how to reverse the changes that had come in her, the differences she had seen in her face, in her eyes, the other differences she had not seen but had felt.

What had Oki told her? That there are two kinds of mountain women: those who learn to be hard and become barohnas. And those who don't—who die.

Keva clutched the haft of her pike. Were those the only choices she had? To be a barohna and hard. Or to die. Couldn't she reject both alternatives and find another course? Or was she helpless against forces she didn't understand? Forces within herself, bred there, developing now toward some inevitable end?

It was no use tormenting herself. She would find her father and he would tell her what she needed to know.

Late in the afternoon she began to pass clumps of trees, thickets of brush, and she knew the forest was near. The smell of pollen was in the air, heavy and musty-sweet.

At last she saw the forest ahead, dark and towering, stretching dimly from horizon to horizon. And she saw a field of grey. Yearlings—hundreds of yearlings sprawled in the grass to rest. As she came near, sentries at the perimeter of the herd snorted softly. Keva picked her way among the sleeping animals and felt the warmth of their gathered bodies. Soon her own eyelids began to droop. Giving in to the heavy weariness that had followed her all day, she spread her bedding and stretched out.

She slept without dreaming, gratefully leaving her preoccupations behind. But when she woke it was dark and the youth she had seen the night before was in her mind again. She had only glimpsed him by moonlight, but she remembered the structure of his face: long, narrow eyes set above high, sharp cheekbones; thin lips; narrow nose with nostrils sharply flared. She remembered his clothing too, the wide, dust-stained robe caught at the waist by bright sashes, the loose trousers. His feet had been bare, the toes long, the nails caked with dirt. He had worn his hair in a knot behind one ear.

He had to be a desert man. Certainly he was not from the mountains, not from the warmstreams, not from the plain. And there were no people living in the roughlands or the lakelands. Hadn't Waana warned her that men from the desert clans hunted near the forest during the running?

But the way he wore his hair, the sashes at his waist—their texture was coarser than the bluesong's. The fabric was harsher, the color duller. But the youth had worn them as her father had worn the bluesong, knotted to hang at one hip. Was that how all men of the desert dressed? Had her father found the bluesong in the desert? Had he taken it from the clansmen?

Or had he been a desert man himself? Slowly Keva opened her eyes, staring at the darkness of the forest. Danior—he was so like her, they might have had the same father. But he had come from the mountains. How was it that her father wore his hair like a desert man, yet had lived in the mountains with her mother, a barohna? Her mother was dead now, but if her father's place had been in the mountains, why had he gone away?

To return to the desert? To his people there?

She shook her head, trying to clear it. Trying to separate the important questions from the irrelevant. It didn't matter where her father had come from or why he had left the mountains. The thing that mattered was that she find him. And if he had not been seen in the mountains, on the plain, at the warmstream, then she must go to the desert.

It didn't matter that she knew nothing about the desert people except that they hunted redmanes at running time. And that the youth she had encountered had been gaunt and dirty. After her days' travel, she was not particularly clean.

The desert. She must go to the desert.

And to find it, she realized, she must continue to the forest and find the desert youth or some other desert person to direct her.

She gazed up at the moon which had slipped higher above the trees. Around her sleeping yearlings began to stir. One shook vigorously and nudged her with a curious nose. She rubbed its soft ears, but it granted her only a moment's attention. The forest musk had grown stronger, sweeter, and the yearling was impatient to go. Anxious to join others who were stirring, awakening, greeting each other with gentle snorts and subdued whickerings.

Keva stood, rolling her bedding, slinging it on her back. Taking up her pike, she picked her way among the yearlings.

By the time she reached the edge of the herd, yearlings danced and shrilled around her, tossing auburn manes, padded feet pounding. She paused briefly to watch, then continued walking.

She had not gone far before yearlings overtook her and the ground jarred with the pounding of their feet. They passed in a long grey wave, celebrating noisily. Then came successive waves, until she walked alone again and the animals ran ahead. Soon she didn't even hear the sound of their voices as they spread and lost themselves in the shadow of the forest.

She came upon the forest gradually. Isolated trees appeared and were succeeded by small stands. Those thickened into taller, denser stands and finally she knew she had entered the forest. The trees stood tall and widely spaced, with broad trunks and sparse limbs. They threw a gridwork of broad shadows. The forest floor was spongy with fallen leaves. It gave silently under her feet, tugging at the butt of her pike when she leaned on it.

And the smell of pollen—Keva coughed at its concentrated musty-sweetness. She paused for a moment, staring up into the trees, and a pale face loomed down at her. She jumped back with a gasp, instinctively thrusting with her pike.

There was no body behind the face. It was a fleshy white blossom. It bent toward her on a rubbery stalk, reaching out for—what? Confused, she backed away and the blossom slowly retracted, drawing back up into the shadows.

She moved ahead cautiously, trying to find some familiarity in the trees, in the texture of their bark, in the dry smell of their leaves. Trying to find some memory. Perhaps she had been here before, with her father. Perhaps they had ridden through the forest together on his whitemane. But tonight she felt only strangeness, and fleshy white blossoms continued to reach down to her, mute faces carrying the choking sweetness of pollen.

Once as she groped through the gridwork of shadows, she heard a scream in the distance. She froze, her fingers whitening on her pike. It was repeated, then shrank away through the trees.

The silence seemed heavier then. She put her feet down carefully, trying not to disturb the silence, and stopped often to listen.

Finally she heard shuffling sounds ahead, heard the faint snort of a redmane. She hesitated, then continued ahead. Redmane yearlings moved in the moonlight, lifting soft noses to the blossoms that groped down from the trees. They pressed their noses deep into the blossoms and drew them out coated with yellow pollen. Keva halted and watched as they progressed from flower to flower. Occasionally one of the yearlings sneezed softly and shook its head. Behind the yearlings, the pollinated blossoms drew back and pulled their pale petals shut. Slowly they retreated back up into the trees.

Insects. The yearlings were doing the work of insects, she realized with slow-dawning surprise. The trees that grew by the warmstream were pollinated by soft-shelled crawlers who carried the yellow grains from tree to tree on their sticky legs. These blossoms used redmanes to carry their pollen. The yearlings moved from tree to tree with none of the shrilling excitement of the earlier evening. Moved docilely, as if this were what they had come for.

Experimentally Keva approached a hovering blossom. She reached into it and found a velvet head. When her fingertips tingled, she drew them back yellow. The blossom pulled away, its petals still open. Not knowing what else to do, she slipped ahead and plunged her fingers into a second blossom, stroking pollen into it. The blossom hovered for moments, then drew back, closing its petals upon her hand.

The caress was cool, satin. Carefully Keva extricated her hand and watched as the blossom furled tight. She moved on with a peculiar satisfaction, moonlight creating dappled avenues before her. She had made the running. She had survived the journey to the forest. And she had fulfilled the imperative of the blossoms.

Now that she was here, she must find someone to direct her to the desert, and she couldn't guess how that was to be done. But something in the pollen, in the soft whicker of the yearlings, put concern from her mind. She spent the early hours of night as the yearlings did, meeting the demand of the blossoms.

By the time the moons passed zenith, the perfume of the forest had grown fainter. Hundreds of pollinated blossoms retracted into the trees and hoarded their scent behind closed petals. The yearlings began to move briskly again, kicking up their feet, nipping at each other's flanks. Keva selected a small group and followed them. The yearlings seemed not to mind her company. Occasionally one or another of them turned and gazed back at her, then darted ahead after its companions.

Keva had almost forgotten to think of predators when the yearlings began to move warily, ears cocked, tails held high. Keva slowed, tightness coming to her chest. The yearlings—there were seven—halted, stamping their feet nervously. Keva saw fear in their bristling manes, in their rolling eyes. Reluctantly she joined them.

Blood spattered the forest floor, its smell thick on the air. Nearby a plug of grey fur was ground into the leaf mold. Keva gripped her pike, her eyes following the dark trail of blood into the trees. One of the yearlings looked up at her anxiously, shrinking against her.

The yearlings lingered a moment, then snorted nervously and altered their course. They drew closer together as they padded through the trees.

After a while they forgot their fright. But Keva continued to watch the shadows until she saw that the trees were thinning, that they approached the edge of the forest. She rubbed her eyes and wondered when the yearlings would stop to sleep, wondered if they would gather by the hundreds as they had before. Wondered how she was going to find the desert youth or one of his kind. Wondered—

She was so preoccupied, she noticed nothing—no sound, no shadow—until suddenly the forest exploded. Loud cries, crouched forms, running feet—Keva was caught at the center of yearlings. She froze, her eyes recording a flurry of images: running men, flying ropes, savage faces. The startled shrills of the yearlings mingled with the harassing cries of the men. The yearlings were pressed in upon themselves. Ropes dropped over their heads and tightened upon their necks. The smell of fear was heavy.

Keva did not regain use of her muscles until she felt a rough noose fall over her shoulders and tighten around her arms, pinning them to her sides. She spun around, caught between shock and anger, a hoarse cry in her throat. Stained teeth gleamed at her from mud-smeared faces. The rope that bound her jerked sharply and she lost her balance, her pike dropping from her hand.

She struggled against the noose as she was pulled across the ground. A panicked yearling lunged and caught her leg with its padded foot. She cried out; her hands opened and closed futilely. She could not raise her arms to push away the rope.

Worse than helplessness was the rising bile in her throat, the dizziness, the sense even as she fought the rope that she was moving into a timeless place, a place where the earth would part at her will and stones would fly.

No! She swallowed back the bile and took a gasping breath, refusing to let control slip away. She heard a burst of guttural speech and a sweating face loomed over her, white teeth flashing. A dark man with narrow eyes and sharp cheekbones pulled her to her feet, swiftly looping his rope around her again and again, binding her tight. He wore soiled robes and loose trousers, his feet bare. His hair was cut bluntly to fall in a heavy black cap around her head. Before she could do more than record a brief impression, he pushed her aside, casually knocking her to her knees, then to her stomach.

Gasping, she rolled over and struggled to sit, pushing herself up against the rough trunk of a tree. The screams of the yearlings were terrible. The men—there were five of them, perhaps six—threw them to their sides and bound their feet. They worked with practiced swiftness, as if they had done this chore times before, as a team.

As if they had hunted redmanes many times before. Desert men —she had found her desert men.

The finding did not reassure her. Keva pushed against the tree trunk, struggling to take her feet, but one of the men felled her with a swift shove and dug his bare toes into her ribs, grunting angrily.

She fought back tears of pain and bit her lip, fighting the dizziness, the whirling sense of timelessness again. And wondering why she did so. If ever there were a time when she needed to be hard, when she needed to be cruel—she clenched her teeth and imagined the earth parting and its rocky foundations grumbling through the air, pounding at the dirty men in their baggy robes. She imagined their screams, their blood.

She choked back the images. She could not question them about her father if she stoned them. And she did not want to see blood, theirs or anyone's. *My father is a desert man,* she would say when they turned from their brutal handling of the yearlings. *I've come to find him. I've come to be with him.* And they would untie her and take her to him.

Watching the callous way they handled the yearlings, she doubted it. She squeezed her eyes shut, trying to escape confusion.

When she opened her eyes again, the seven yearlings lay bound under the trees. The desert men prodded at them, measuring the firmness of their muscles, the girth of their bellies. Keva shuddered. One of the yearlings raised its head and pleaded with its eyes, begging her help.

But what could she do, short of tearing up the earth? The heaviest of the men turned. His eyes narrowed speculatively and he rose and advanced toward her. She cringed involuntarily, unable to speak. He was older than the others. His face fell in deep furrows, the skin weathered by sun and wind. As he approached, she realized there was something in his eyes she had never seen before, not by the warmstreams, not on the plain, not in her nightmares: an angry hunger, directed at her.

Keva stiffened, unwilling to think of him as the same kind of man her father was. He did not wear a sash; his robes were caught at the waist by a rope. He did not wear his hair knotted. The darkness of his skin was different too. It came from years of harsh weathering, not from natural pigmentation.

His hands were calloused and thick. He extended them like weapons he would take pleasure in using. No, she decided desperately, if her father was a desert man, he was not this kind of desert man.

Keva stared at the man's rough hands, licking her lips. She had heard stories of men who used force. Not the laughing force of a playful lover, but angry force, a force that did not admit the humanity of the woman it was directed against. By the warmstreams, if a man debased himself so, he would be sent away, to live and die alone. Keva licked dry lips, understanding how such men must look to their prey. She pressed herself against the tree, trying to make herself small.

But where was it written that her choice was to kill him with stones or to deliver herself to him? Or that if she did deliver herself, she must yield him spirit as well as body? Keva's jaw stiffened. Grunting, she struggled to her feet. Her knee cramped with pain but she bit back her cry. Raising her head, she met the desert man's eyes directly, with a will. She would not stone him—not if she had control. But let him look into her eyes and he would see that she could. Let him look and he would see what was latent in her.

See it, she urged him.

He took another step forward and faltered. The steeliness in his eyes wavered. Then his gaze dropped to the stone at her throat and the pupils narrowed so swiftly they shrank to hard black motes. He uttered a harsh word, not to his mates but to himself.

Test me. But he was staring so intently at the stone, at the strip of blue cloth that held it, that he did not see the challenge in her eyes. Keva frowned in confusion, pressing herself against the tree.

The desert man grunted, then reached with a knotted hand and snatched the stone from around her neck.

But it was not only the stone that drew him, Keva saw immediately. It was the cloth. The desert man rubbed the slippery fabric between thumb and forefinger, his face greying. Then he held the stone to his eye and peered through it. His mouth clamped shut with a snap. He glanced back up at her, appetite dying from his eyes, leaving only dregs—not of cruelty, not of anger, but of fear. He inhaled heavily, then drew back one hand, as if to redeem himself by striking her.

Keva found voice. "Test me," she hissed, challenging him.

He did not meet the challenge. The desert man's hand rose, then fell back to his side. He struggled to break free of her gaze. Jerkily he backed away from her, perspiration suddenly shining on his face.

Keva choked back elation and stood free of the tree, looking past the first man to the others.

They had turned from their work to watch the encounter. The first man stumbled to them, the strip of blue fabric trembling in his hand. He muttered guttural words. The other men examined the stone and fabric and gazed at Keva with dawning wariness. They began to talk rapidly among themselves, gathering close, as if for protection.

From her. They were afraid of her. She was bound and helpless and they feared her so sharply she could smell it. They fingered the cloth. They fingered the stone. And they muttered and grunted and backed away.

What did they take her for? A barohna? Were they as frightened of the barohnas as Oki had been? She released a slow breath, wondering how much she could make of their fear if she could hide her own. "Your ropes are hurting me," she said, keeping her voice firm and clear. "Untie me."

Even those few words heightened their fear. Sharpened it.

"Let me loose," she said, pressing her advantage. "And let my animals go. I won't have them stolen." When they did not respond, except to clutch closer to one another, she took a step forward, careful not to betray herself with a limp. "Untie me."

With a grunt, one of the men slipped a long-bladed knife from his waist. Its blade glinted dully. The other men hissed in alarm, their faces turning the color of ashes. One seized his arm and twisted until the weapon fell from his fingers. He protested, the cords of his neck bulging, but the others stilled him with a series of deep-throated utterances.

The advantage was hers, Keva saw, her heart leaping so hard against her ribs it left her breathless. She would be foolish not to press it. Steeling herself, she stared at the muttering men and stepped toward them again. She said nothing. She simply walked, deliberately, firmly.

Later she marveled that none of them saw that she was as frightened as they were. Marveled at how swiftly they disappeared. She took six even paces and abruptly the men groaned and scattered into the trees. The one who had dropped the knife dodged forward and snatched it up. Glowering at her with a moment's bravado, he snatched up her pack too and ran after the others. She heard the swift pad of bare feet, heard one voice raised, and then she was alone.

Alone with her arms bound and seven yearlings tied at her feet. They hadn't even left her the digging blade from her pack. She hesitated, evaluating her situation with a momentary sense of letdown. She had frightened away the clansmen, but she could not reach the knots that bound her.

The yearlings—if she could bring her hands together in front of her, perhaps she could at least release the yearlings. Frowning, she pressed against the ropes, trying to find some slack, but there was none. She could not slide her arms together. And that meant she could only use one hand at a time.

She must act quickly, she knew, if she was to do anything. Her fingers were growing numb. Soon they would be too clumsy to grapple with the coarsest knot.

Painfully she dropped to her knees beside the nearest yearling. It thrashed and reared its head, trying to gain its feet. "No, no. Lie still. I'll try to untie you," she coaxed. "Lie still."

She could tell by the roll of the yearlings's eyes that he didn't understand her words but was reassured by her tone.

She maneuvered to bring her right hand within reach of the knots that bound his hind legs. Her position was awkward, half-crouched, her hand bound tightly against her side. She could not see what she was doing without arching her neck so sharply her back cramped.

She fumbled at the knots. The rope was loosely woven, and that acted in her favor. When she found the free end, she was able to compress the rope enough to work it through. The effort partially restored circulation to her fingers, but left them sore and quivering. And there were more knots, many more.

Working painstakingly, trying to ignore the pain in her knee, the cramping of her neck and back, the increasing tenderness of her fingertips, she eventually freed the first yearling. It took its feet uncertainly, stumbling a little, and stepped back from its companions. Keva watched with held breath, afraid it would flee into the trees. She did not trust the silence of the forest.

The yearling edged away from the group, then returned, sniffing its companions thoughtfully. It bared its teeth at the ropes that bound them.

If it would chew the ropes—but the yearling turned away and lay down a short distance from the others, obviously troubled and uncertain.

Working with bleeding fingers and cramping muscles, Keva freed the yearlings one by one. None abandoned the group. Even when the last yearling stepped from its ropes, the yearlings remained clustered under the trees, gazing at Keva from solemn eyes. She tried to imagine what they were thinking. Did they understand she could not free herself? Or were they waiting for her to throw off her ropes and lead them out of the forest? They were accustomed to human protection.

She looked around uncertainly. It was not far to the edge of the forest. But Allindra was approaching the horizon and Zan followed. Soon it would be dark. Dark until dawn. And Waana had said that most predators did not venture far into the trees. Better to pass the dark hours deep in the trees than exposed where there was less protection.

Keva pushed herself against a tree trunk and struggled to her feet. Her fingertips were sticky with half-dried blood. "Come," she said. "Come with me." Clumsily she stumbled into the trees. She clutched and unclutched her hands as she walked, trying to keep her fingers from numbing.

The yearlings padded after her, heads hung in weariness.

They could not be more tired than she was. She hardly saw the occasional unpollinated blossom that bent inquiringly as they stumbled through the trees. She walked until her knee began to buckle with every step and the yearlings staggered. Then she selected a place where three young trees grew closely spaced and sank to her knees. Carefully she took a sitting position, her back against the broadest of the three trunks. The yearlings settled nearby, grunting and sighing.

Keva closed her eyes, wanting only to rest until it was light enough to walk again. She knew that if she slept, her fingers would numb completely. She might not be able to restore circulation again.

Despite her intentions, her breath grew thick and she slept, her head sagging.

Her dreams were fleeting, tainted with disturbing snatches of familiarity. She saw Oki's face, she saw the curved walls of Tehla's kefri, she saw Danior at the teaching, his eyelids pressed shut. She saw places she had glimpsed through Waana's teaching, saw red-manes running. Confused, she tried to reach after the disparate images, tried to order them into coherence. Sometimes she thought she stood and walked across a familiar plain, only to have the grasses disappear from underfoot. Sometimes she thought she lay asleep in Tehla's kefri.

Sometimes she thought she didn't dream at all. She thought she had wakened and was about to leave her bedding. She had only to kick off her covers, stand . . .

It was during one of these intervals, when she thought the forest around her was real and not a dream, that the white yearling appeared. Keva gazed into the trees and saw a faint brightness. She groaned, trying to bring her eyes to sharper focus, and the brightness stepped nearer and took form: smooth white flanks, delicate hooves, silver-white mane. It approached, stepping lightly. As it neared, the redmane yearlings stirred and raised their heads, their eyes dull with sleep.

The white yearling extended its neck and pressed its smooth pink nose against Keva's cheek. The flesh was warm, the animal's breath soft. Keva moaned, expecting in her confusion to be free at the animal's touch, expecting the ropes to fall away.

They did not. She remained tied, her hands numb, her arms aching. She tried to reach out to the animal but could not. Keva sank back against the tree, squeezing her eyes shut in disappointment.

When she opened them again, the white yearling had withdrawn into the trees. He stood poised for a moment, then turned and cantered silently away. Keva shut her eyes and passed back into the full confusion of her dreams.

Sometime later a sound brought her swimming awake. She opened her eyes and drew breath sharply. This time she was not dreaming. The image was too clear, too sharply delineated. The desert youth stood over her. She could see the pores of his skin, could trace the line of his hair where it was pulled sharply back, could smell the sweat and dust that stiffened his robes. The knife in his hand was real too. Even without moonlight, she saw the cutting sharpness of its blade.

She saw those things in a fraction of a second and knew, as he bent nearer, that she did not have time to react. She didn't even have time to catch her breath as he brought the knife up and then down in a sure, clean stroke.

It took her a moment to move past shock and realize that the knife had not slashed at her throat, at her chest, at any vital organ. Instead the youth made one swift slash at the ropes that bound her, partially severing them. Then he jumped back, his face white, his eyes glittering.

He hardly seemed to breathe as he watched for Keva's reaction. Clenched muscles stood clearly defined in his forearms and his jaw. After a moment, he lowered the blade. His lips worked stiffly. "See? I would not hurt you. So you will—you will let me untake the ropes." His voice was low, the words wary and boastful at once. When she did not answer, he said, "I speak mountain talk, see? I will unfasten you with ropes."

Keva shook her head dumbly, shock still binding her throat. Surely she imagined him. Or dreamed him. Surely—

"Wrong?" the youth demanded with a subdued flash of anger. "Unfasten you from ropes? Those are the mountain words?"

She did not imagine him. The anger told her that. Keva forced herself to catch a deep breath. "Yes," she said, measuring out the syllables, careful not to betray herself with a hysterical sob of laughter. "Yes, unfasten me from the ropes. Those—those are the words."

"I knew they were," the youth boasted, studying her with frowning intensity. He was as she remembered, wiry, his cheekbones sharp against his wind-burned flesh, his eyes narrow and dark, frowning. Although his robes were soiled, the two strands of fabric at his waist were clean, as if he washed them even when he didn't wash himself.

The youth caught the direction of her gaze and bared his teeth. "You see my sashes. They show I am of the family Magadaw and of the Greater Clan, which is led by the Viir-Nega. So I am both his clan-kin and his soldier. And you are his kin too. I see it in your face. I saw it when you made the stones dance. Your skin is like his, your brows. But your eyes . . ." He frowned. "He told us he had kin in the mountains. Women."

Keva stared at him, trying to read the glinting intensity of his eyes. The Viir-Nega? She was his kin? *Her father?* Her eyes flashed to the youth's bright sashes. Her father *was* a desert man? He called himself the Viir-Nega? This youth was a member of his clan? And the other desert men, the ones who had pulled the stone from her neck and then fled in panic—perhaps they hadn't been frightened because they took her for a barohna. Perhaps they simply took her for her father's daughter.

Certainly the youth seemed impressed by the kinship. Instinctively she spoke sharply, determined to use the awe she saw in his face to best advantage. "Yes, the Viir-Nega is my kin. Untie me now, please."

Although the youth lost color at the sharpness of her words, his voice quickly regained its boasting edge. "I will. And then I will take you to the Viir-Nega and we will see what he says of me for finding you."

Keva had a moment's misgiving. Was she making a mistake, claiming kinship to a man she had never heard of before today? What might be the price of her presumption if he denounced her? Still she managed to say haughtily, "He'll thank you, I'm sure." But would he? Could the Viir-Nega really be her father, or was he someone else entirely? And how much trust should she put in the youth with his knife and his boasting gaze?

But what choice had she? The youth was her only resource, however governable or ungovernable he might be.

The youth darted her a swift glance, eyes glinting. "Yes, I will take you and he will thank me. And to make public his thanks he will give you to me for my marriage. All I have to do is ask. I am that well-regarded among my people. Then I will have a wife who can draw fire and make stones dance and later I will have a sash with voice and a whitemane to ride beside the Viir-Nega's when we parade to clan-call. I will have all those things with you."

Keva glanced up sharply, biting back the impulse to a sharp response. Certainly she had no intention of becoming a part of his ambitious plan but she could make that clear later, when her hands were free. "Untie me," she said with all the authority she could summon and was relieved to see fear brighten in his eyes again at the sharpness of her tone.

NINE

DANIOR

The pounding of his boots against the soil, the surging pressure of his blood against his ear drums—Danior ran across the plain to a rhythm of drumming urgency. He hardly noticed the cramping of his legs, the burning of his lungs. He felt only the need to reach Keva before she placed herself in jeopardy. There were so many things she didn't know, so many stories she hadn't heard, and ignorance made her vulnerable. Even if she could tear the soil and make stones fly, she was vulnerable. And he felt her vulnerability as his own.

He ran until the sun rose, until a tight band closed around his chest and he could run no more. Then he stopped and slept, heavily, his fingers curled around the pairing stone.

When Keva woke he woke too and pushed himself again, trying to narrow the gap between them. He had traveled to the forest before, riding there with the guardian daughters to fetch knots of resin to be melted for caulking. Now he stopped occasionally to press the pairing stone and take his bearings from what he saw through Keva's eyes. He recognized rock formations, small groves and stands of trees, brooks and ponds. By mid-afternoon he realized he could not overtake her before she reached the forest. Several hours still separated them, his thighs were weak and cramping, and his eyes were grainy from lack of sleep.

Still he pressed on until the hour after dark. Then the ache of his legs, the pounding of his temples was too much. He spread his bedding under a clump of trees, promising himself it would be for only an hour.

He tossed uneasily, hardly falling asleep before he was drawn into a series of half-waking dreams. His throat burned and he saw tall trees, Nindra and Zan caught in their reaching arms. Then he was beneath the trees and white-faced blossoms reached down. Redmane yearlings moved through a gridwork of moonlight and shadow and he heard them whicker and shrill. He smelled the soporific sweetness of pollen. He sighed under its influence, slipping back into the full darkness of sleep, only to emerge later, wandering the forest again. Vaguely he realized that he clasped the stone, that its light penetrated his closed eyelids. He realized he wasn't dreaming at all. He tried to rouse himself but failed, the heaviness of exhaustion upon him.

Still later his throat began to burn and for a few moments he was caught in a welter of images: mud-smeared faces, glaring teeth, ropes. He stirred in half-waking alarm and struggled against an unaccountable sense that he was bound, his arms pinioned to his sides. He shuddered, shaking himself fully awake, only to have the dream—if it was a dream—end abruptly with the image of a reaching hand. Danior sat, staring into the dark in confusion. Keva? Had he clasped the stone in his sleep again? Had something happened to Keva? His heart hammered with half-apprehended panic. Anxiously he clutched the pairing stone, but nothing came. Confused, disoriented, he lay down again. Perhaps he had only dreamed. Perhaps . . . His thoughts ran no farther before he fell again into exhausted sleep.

It was first light when he woke, his muscles aching, his mouth dry. Instinctively his hand moved to the pairing stone. He pressed it and felt it warm against his palm. But when he reached tentatively for Keva's thoughts, the stone brought nothing. Troubled, he shrugged off his bedding and gazed around uncertainly.

He reached again when he had eaten and could not raise even the stir of memory. Sleeping. She must be sleeping, too tired to dream. He tried to assure himself that it was so. But he was anxious as he rolled his bedding, snapped shut his pack, and set out.

The morning was clear, the air only faintly scented with pollen. As he walked, Danior met yearlings returning to the plain. Their coats were matted and their eyelids drooped. Their noses were smeared yellow with pollen. They scarcely grunted in passing.

By midday, when his stone lay warm in his palm and he still could not touch Keva's thoughts, he was able to reassure himself no longer. He passed the place where the yearlings had slept the evening before, where Keva had slept. A few yearlings slept there again, but there was no sign that Keva had returned from the forest with them.

Something had happened to her. The thought, repressed through the earlier hours of the day, came to him with grinding clarity. Otherwise he would be able to touch her thoughts, would be able to see what she saw, hear what she heard. Instead there was only silence.

Troubled, he ran toward the trees.

The soil of the forest was trampled. Blossoms hung drunkenly from long stems, furled tight. Danior hesitated, gazing around, wondering what he must do, where he must search. Reluctantly he thought of predators and desert clansmen. Remembered the confusion of dreams from the night before: ropes, mud-smeared faces, a reaching hand. Remembered the unfounded panic that had made his heart pound. Had it been Keva's instead of his own?

Disturbed, he threw off his pack and crouched under the trees. Perhaps he simply had not tried hard enough to reach her. Perhaps he had let fatigue raise barriers between them. Quickly he took the stone in hand and inhaled deeply, putting every other thought away. The stone warmed immediately and he felt the heat of active nerve centers at the base of his throat. He held the stone before him, staring into it, trying to find his way into Keva's thoughts. If he reached deeply enough, if he extended himself fully—

He breathed deeply, investing himself entirely in the stone, in its growing light. Losing himself in it. He let its brilliance fill his eyes. His throat began to burn. He reached.

For long moments he was aware only of the blaze of the stone. Then alien memories began to take form: far stretches of a harsh land, a sun that burned too brightly, empty cooking pots, quenched fires, hunger. Frowning, he reached deeper and had a confused impression of a sweaty body, of crusted fingernails, of brooding anger compounded by fear and a stinging sense of injustice. The forest floor lay underfoot and there were companions nearby, the sweat of fear upon them. And they were angry too, as angry as himself. He could read it in every dark face, in every burning eye. He—

He . . . Danior pulled back, stung to panic. *Where was Keva?* And why had the stone taken him into a stranger's thoughts? Danior swallowed down the sour rise of fear—fear that could only erect further barriers. Disciplining himself, he pressed his eyes shut and forced himself to take several steadying breaths before reaching again. As he reached, he held an image of Keva in mind: her face, the arch of her brows, the deepness of her eyes.

Effort. He was aware of effort, of his throat first cooling and then catching fire. And then the memories came, of hissing waters and coiling weeds and a heavy-limbed woman who hovered possessively. A man sat beside the streambank spinning tales, another man rode a whitemane, a bluesong reached out for sunlight and breeze.

Danior pressed his eyelids tighter, trying to reach past memory to the present.

Suddenly he had a wavering vision of a dark face: narrow eyes, hungry cheekbones, lean jaws—the youth who had leapt at the whitemane yearling and narrowly missed being stoned. Alarmed, Danior let the vision waver. Then, catching himself, he drew a deep breath and held it, clarifying the vision. The youth sat under the trees, a knife buried blade-first in the soil beside him, his hand clenching and unclenching on its handle. He was speaking, but although he strained, Danior could not hear what he said.

Keva—he felt her presence now. She sat near the youth, eating. Bread, cheese—he felt the food on her tongue but could not identify it. Nor could he hear what she said when she spoke or fathom the emotion that lay behind the words. It was the desert youth who came to him most clearly. A complex of emotions played across his lean face: wariness, uncertainty, fear. He tried to hide them behind arrogance and only partially succeeded. He played with the knife constantly, pulling the blade from the ground, then tossing it with a sharp flip of his wrist, burying it again.

They sat, eating, talking, while Danior struggled to bring the scene to clear focus, to hear what they said. Before he was able to do so, Keva and the desert youth stood, packing their possessions, and began to walk.

Danior lost the vision then. He sank back on his heels, his face wet with perspiration, his hands trembling. It was minutes before he was able to stand, quivering with relief.

He had found Keva and she didn't seem to be in immediate danger. Though why had it taken so much more effort to reach her today than ever before? He rubbed his throat, puzzled. The distance that separated them was less now. And he was more practiced.

Perhaps the fact that he was tired and anxious, that she was distracted by the desert youth's presence made it more difficult to reach her. At least now he knew she was in the forest. And from the slant of light through the trees, he knew the direction she traveled.

Toward the southern perimeter of the forest. Toward the roughlands and the desert that lay beyond.

He frowned, remembering the snatch of memory that had come when he first tried to use the stone. A desert man's memory. Had he somehow reached past Keva's thoughts into the desert youth's mind?

No, the person he had reached had had companions—desert men like himself. Angry and seething with injustice.

And they were in the forest too. Quickly Danior slung his pack over his shoulder and took up his pike, a fresh sense of danger fueling his stiff muscles.

He used the stone to guide him. Each time he reached, he found the distance that separated him from Keva and the desert youth less. By late afternoon he began to recognize individual trees she had passed earlier. Once a straggling group of redmane yearlings stumbled past, tossing tangled manes, yellow pollen still clinging to their noses. Eventually Danior found the print of Keva's boots and the desert youth's bare feet and followed their trail.

It was near sunset when Keva and the youth abruptly changed direction, veering eastward. Danior halted, peering at the forest floor, and quickly realized why they had done so.

There were hoofprints in the soil, a single line leading eastward. Danior studied the prints, something that had troubled him suddenly coming clear.

The youth had been tracking a whitemane yearling when Keva first saw him. He had stalked it through the trees and lunged without rope or weapon. Now, staring down at the track of hooves, Danior realized why. He had been trying to mark the whitemane.

Danior frowned, considering that conclusion and its implications. The youth wore his hair knotted as Jhaviir had worn his. He tied colored sashes at his waist—and now he was tracking a whitemane. If the youth were trying to emulate Jhaviir, then Jhaviir must be alive—in the desert. He must have influence. Position. Legend.

Legend to be carried back to his father. Tales of places Jhaviir had ridden, people he had seen. Danior's hand tightened on the haft of his pike. For the first time, he recognized the stirring of Birnam Rauth's blood in himself. He felt it in the rising beat of his pulse, in the fresh eagerness that toned his muscles. He wanted to see strange places and alien people too, wanted to quench his curiosity with them—a curiosity he hadn't even guessed he owned. Quickly he turned to follow the tracks in the soil, hardly noticing this time that his thighs ached and his calves cramped as he ran.

He didn't use the stone again. Soon he was near enough to hear the faint sound of Keva's and the youth's feet, near enough to see them slipping among the trees. They walked single file, the youth leading the way, studying the whitemane's tracks, Keva following with her pack and the youth's bundled possessions. Danior tracked them cautiously, keeping his distance, occasionally moving near enough to reaffirm his impression that Keva accompanied the youth willingly, without constraint.

Eventually the sun slid below the horizon and the forest grew dark. The youth hissed and he and Keva halted and sat to eat. Danior moved nearer, barely able to glimpse them in the shadows. They talked, a low murmur, but Danior was wary of moving close enough to understand. Then their voices fell to nothing and Danior guessed they were napping until the moons rose.

He moved nearer, tensely, wondering if he should try to wake Keva, to let her know he was near. She slept curled against a tree, just a few paces from where the youth slept. If he moved quietly enough, if she didn't cry out when he touched her, when he shook her—

The youth drew a sighing breath and shifted, muttering to himself, and Danior retreated. He would catch her attention later, when she woke. He crouched behind a nearby tree, wondering if she would be relieved to see him, or if she would be angry that he had followed her. Wondering why the stone did not take him deeply enough into her thoughts now to guess her reaction. He hugged himself against evening chill and soon, without intending it, he slept too.

The moons had risen when he woke—woke to a sense of presence. He opened his eyes warily, half expecting to find the desert youth standing over him. Instead he saw a whitemane stallion poised among the trees, moonlight shimmering on its smooth, snowy pelt. Its mane lay like silver upon its arched neck and its eyes were pink transparencies. *Fiirsevrin* . . . but there was no five-fingered flame upon this whitemane's brow. It moved through the trees with unconquered aloofness.

Had it come for him, as Fiirsevrin had once come for his father?

Cautiously Danior took his feet. He held his breath as the animal approached, pleased that it did not seem afraid, that it seemed simply curious. He exhaled gently, standing very still, letting the animal come nearer. If the stories he had heard were true, if the whitemanes were descended from animals the first-timers had turned out because they could not feed them, then perhaps he held as much fascination for the whitemane as it held for him. And if he could touch it, if he could place his mark upon it—

The animal came near enough for him to catch its scent, light and dry. Near enough for him to feel its body heat. Slowly, with a sense of unreality, Danior raised one hand. But before he could extend it, the whitemane pricked its ears and took a wary step back, raising its head sharply.

The desert youth emerged from the shadows of a tall tree. Moonlight touched his staring eyes, silvering them. His prominent cheekbones thrust at the thin flesh of his face. His lips drew back, leaving his teeth unguarded. He seemed not to breathe. Keva stood behind him, her face shadowed.

Danior caught a steadying breath, reluctantly shrinking back into the shadows. If the whitemane had come for anyone, it must be for the desert youth. He was the one who had tracked the animal. He was the one who had faced the hail of stones, yet come back to try again. And he was the one whose eagerness glittered in his eyes, rasped in his throat.

Jerkily the youth extended one hand. Danior was not surprised to see that it trembled as the youth took a single step, then another toward the whitemane. As he slipped closer to the animal, he slowly raised his extended hand. The whitemane retreated nervously and the youth froze. Then the animal stepped forward again and extended its head, nostrils flaring.

The youth's hand trembled so violently Danior was afraid he would frighten the animal away. But the whitemane was curious. It bent to smell the youth's loose trousers. And the youth thrust out one thin, dark hand and pressed the animal's brow.

For moments only the whitemane moved, casually sampling the admixture of odors the desert youth carried on his trousers. Only the whitemane breathed, snorting softly. Danior, the youth, Keva —all stood frozen. Then, slowly, reverently, the youth drew his hand back.

The whitemane's brow remained white. The youth's fingers left no mark.

Danior wished afterward that he had not even glimpsed the youth's face in the moment after that. Wished he had not seen the swift, fiery desolation. The youth took a single step backward, his face drained of color, his lips twisting. Then, the muscles of his jaw knotting, his hand fell and he twisted his knife from his waistband. Startled, the whitemane raised pink eyes to him and retreated a few nervous steps.

Before Danior guessed what he intended, the youth flung himself at the animal, tangling the fingers of one hand in its mane. He caught the blade of his knife between his teeth, freeing the other hand, and with it seized at the whitemane's neck. Grunting, he clawed his way to the animal's back.

The alarmed animal backed away, then began to rear, screaming with fright. Its delicate front hooves thrashed the air. It arched its neck and quivered. Then it arched its back and began to buck and heave, its breath coming in heavy gouts. The desert youth clung, eyes glinting, sashes flying.

Danior pressed himself against a tree trunk, trying to avoid flying hooves. The whitemane rolled its eyes and scraped the youth's legs against the trunk of a rough-barked tree. When he still clung, the animal pounded away through the trees, bucking and rearing, shrilling angrily. Danior gasped, seeing the downward flash of the youth's knife blade as the animal carried him into the trees.

Then the youth flew from the animal's back, arms helter-skelter. He smashed to the ground and lay struggling for breath. The whitemane fled, hooves beating a drum rhythm.

Danior and Keva ran to the desert youth. His eyes stared and his mouth gaped painfully as he fought for breath. A trickle of blood ran from his nose. In one hand he clutched a swatch of the whitemane's mane. Keva bent over him, helping him sit.

"My knife—" he choked when he was able to draw breath.

"Over there. You dropped it."

Following the direction of Keva's glance, Danior retrieved the knife without thinking and placed it in the youth's hand—and realized from the sudden frozen immobility of the youth's features that his attention had been so concentrated on the whitemane that he had not noticed Danior until now.

The youth heaved himself to his feet, the cords of his neck standing out, his fingers white-knuckled on the knife handle. His eyes darted from Danior to Keva and back again. He uttered a sharp demand in a language Danior did not know.

Before Danior could guess how to respond, Keva caught his arm. "Rezni, this is my kinsman, Danior—Danior Terlath. Danior, this is Rezni, the Nathri-Varnitz—Bold Soldier of the Viir-Nega."

Danior's glance flickered to the youth's knife, then back to his rigid face. How could Keva speak so calmly when the youth seemed poised to leap? How could she nod with as much composure as if she had just introduced one friend to another? As he hesitated, her fingers tightened on his arm again. And this time he realized, with a start, what she intended the light pressure to tell him. That he must follow her lead. Must not let the youth see that he was frightened or confused. Must respond as calmly to the introduction as if the youth did not hold a raised knife. Danior steeled himself to offer the traditional welcome to strangers. "My valley warms at your approach, Rezni. I hope you leave yours green."

The youth's eyes narrowed, but the knotted muscles of his jaw relaxed slightly. "You are kinsman of the Flame? What—what degree is this kinship?"

The Flame? Before Danior could let doubt show, Keva squeezed his wrist again. "The Nathri-Varnitz is taking me to meet our kinsman, the Viir-Nega: Savior of the Greater Clan. He has honored me by offering me marriage and a place at his back during the next clan-call. Under the circumstances, you can tell him the degree of our kinship."

Marriage? Danior darted a startled glance at Keva. Surely she had not agreed to marriage with a desert man. Not in the short time since they had been separated. "You haven't—"

"How can I accept when I already have obligations to the throne of Valley Marlath?"

"The Flame of Marlath can burn in my *han-tau* despite all her encumbrances," Rezni interjected fiercely. "There are more places than the mountains for a woman who can make stone live."

So she had not agreed. But something in the flicker of her eyes when she met his startled glance, something in the continued pressure of her fingers on his wrist told Danior he must speak carefully. Told him she followed some considered strategy with the youth. Danior licked dry lips. "Of course there are," he agreed. Was she simply trying to confound the youth, to immobilize his aggressive instincts by impressing him with her importance? Was that why she called herself the Flame of Marlath, why she claimed to hold her mother's throne? He spoke carefully, hoping he guessed her intent correctly. "But the Flame—the Flame has heavy encumbrances.

She has the responsibility for all the people of her valley. For the success of their crops, for all the food they eat. I know because I am —I am her Rauth-brother."

The youth frowned suspiciously, glancing from one to the other of them. He spoke stiffly. "I don't know that kinship."

"It means our fathers were the same man once," Danior said, extemporizing. "Though they are no longer, of course."

The youth stared at him. "Of course," he muttered, as if he understood. But it clearly angered him that he did not. His voice took a hostile edge. His eyes narrowed. "You frightened away my whitemane. You were hidden here and you startled him."

"Danior wasn't hidden at all, Rezni," Keva contradicted him immediately. "I saw him."

"Perhaps you did, but I didn't. And my whitemane ran. If he had stayed, if I had touched him again—"

Danior recoiled at the youth's accusing tone, his thoughts taking an intuitive leap. "No, he—he was too old to be marked," he said with as much authority as if he knew it to be true. His father, after all, had marked Fiirsevrin when he was little more than a foal. Jhaviir, or so legend said, had marked his steed when it was a yearling. But this whitemane had been an adult stallion, too old perhaps to bond himself to a master. "You—you have to find a younger animal, one who hasn't come into his final growth. And you must never frighten a whitemane by riding him before he knows you."

"If I hadn't taken his back, I wouldn't have even his hair to show," the youth retorted bitterly, flourishing the swatch of gleaming white mane. "I would have nothing."

Nothing. For a moment desolation burned in Rezni's eyes again, and Danior realized with quick surprise that he understood the desert youth. Apparently the desert was a place of legends just as the mountains were, and Rezni had none. He had come to the forest hunting a whitemane to mark, but the first animal had eluded him and now the second one had run away. He had offered marriage to Keva and she had spun him a tale of responsibilities in far places. By rights—if Danior correctly understood the mores of the clans from tales he had heard—the youth should simply have taken her, but she had shown herself too dangerous for that. And now Danior had come and spun more confounding words Rezni could not admit he didn't understand.

Rezni had nothing as surely as Danior had had nothing before he touched the pairing stone. And the society of the desert clans must be far less kind to a man who had nothing than the society of the mountains.

"We can track him if you don't believe me," Danior said.

Rezni stared at him suspiciously, licking his lips. Finally he shook his head, hostility abating. "No. I promised the Viir-Nega I would return to Pan-Vi in time for clan-call, even if I found no whitemane. There is no more time left for tracking."

"The call is in three days," Keva explained quickly to Danior. "And of course the Viir-Nega will want to present us to the clan at that time."

Danior hesitated momentarily, then nodded. The Viir-Nega. Pan-Vi. Clan-call. So many things he didn't understand, but apparently Keva did. And apparently she knew some reason why they should accompany Rezni, why they should trust him. Unconsciously his hand rose to his throat. If he could use the pairing stone to touch Keva's thoughts . . . Unconsciously he flicked a glance at her throat.

Her neck was bare. Surprised, Danior glanced toward her pack. Had she hidden her stone from Rezni? Or had the desert youth confiscated it? "Your stone," he said, touching his own lightly, with his fingertips.

Keva rubbed her bare neck, shrugging. "It was stolen. Last night."

"And she refused to raise the earth," Rezni expanded immediately. "She is a barohna from the mountains. She can make stone live. With the right stone, she can call down fire from the sun. But she let men from one of the small-clans tie her and take her jewelry. If she had thrown the same stones at them she threw at me—"

"I don't—I don't do that unless I have to, Rezni."

"Against me? It was necessary to do it against me and not against the small-men? When I'm a soldier of the Viir-Nega?"

Danior recognized an argument that had been aired before. But he had no time to reflect on Rezni's grievance. Keva's stone had been stolen—the night before. Yet he had reached into her thoughts today.

Not easily. Not well. But he had reached them.

He had reached someone else's thoughts too. Those of a desert man with dirt-caked nails and an angry hunger. *The man who had stolen Keva's pairing stone.*

But the stones were not supposed to work that way. He should not have been able to touch anyone's thoughts but Keva's—and hers only when she wore the stone.

He should not have been able to reach behind the bluesong either and see yellow-eyed predators prowling an alien forest. Dizzily he raised a hand to his throat, then realized Rezni had stopped speaking and was staring at the stone. Danior knotted his hand, drawing it away—but not before he felt the first vagrant warmth of the stone. "If we have only three days, we'd better walk before we sleep tonight," he said quickly.

Rezni's attention was not so easily deflected. His narrow eyes contracted to slits. "That stone—it's like the jewel Keva described to me. But you've made it light."

"I—" Danior darted an uncertain glance at Keva. But what guidance could she give him? She had worn the other stone in ignorance, considering it simply a piece of jewelry, a keepsake from her father.

Now she stared at the stone he wore. "You didn't have that the last time I saw you," she said slowly.

"I was carrying it in my pack." If only he could speak to her alone, without Rezni. If only they could spend just a few minutes answering each other's questions—

Rezni's eyes darted from one to the other, his face suddenly darkening with angry comprehension. *"I know that stone.* The Viir-Nega has described stones like that to us. You carry a thought-stone and you thought I would never recognize it—as if I were an ignorant man of the small-clans instead the Nathri-Varnitz, given that title by the Viir-Nega himself." He turned on Keva. "And you told me it was a piece of jewelry the small-clansmen stole. You said it was an ornament you wore on a ribbon. You didn't even raise the earth. You let them take a thought-stone and now they can see everything we do. When we reach Pan-Vi, they will see into the heart of our campment as if—as if they stood there in the flesh. They will hear everything the Viir-Nega plans. They will watch when we go to quarry fire-coals. They will attack when we are most poorly guarded and shatter our panes and let our gardens die."

"No, the other stone is useless to the small-clansmen," Danior assured him quickly. "Keva's the only person who can use it. In anyone else's hands, it's only what she told you—an ornament."

Rezni's eyes narrowed. "You tell me that? In truth?"

"Yes. If you know about the stones—"

"The Viir-Nega has told us everything about the stones," the youth said sharply. "And we have tales of our own about them too. Every clan has tales of the atrocities that drove them out into the hard-lands. There are stones that see far distances—"

"Eyestones," Danior confirmed. "The barohnas used to mount them on their palace towers, to keep watch over the valleys. They're seldom used now. My mother has never commissioned one."

"Stones that hold sunlight and loose it and burn everything."

"Sunstones. They're used to heat the valleys so crops can grow. They were used for—for other things during the troubled times. But no one uses them that way now. No one—"

"Thought-stones," Rezni continued relentlessly, nodding at the pairing stone. "Stones that carry thoughts from person to person."

"But only among certain persons."

"You have one."

"Yes, it was paired to Keva's stone. But the men who stole her stone will never be able to use it. They don't have barohnial blood. The power of the stones is inherited."

Abruptly Rezni relented. He squatted and pegged his knife blade-first into the ground. He watched it quiver there. "They can't spy on our campment with it?"

"No. It's impossible."

"But if the stones are paired—can they spy on you? Since you hold the other stone? Can they use it to enter Pan-Vi through your thoughts if I take you there to present you to the Viir-Nega?"

"No," Danior assured him, distractedly, as something Keva had said earlier struck him. *Our kinsman, the Viir-Nega.* Did she think—

But Rezni reclaimed his attention, drawing his knife blade free and thumping it into the earth again. Small muscles tightened under his eyes. "Can you use your stone to spy on them?"

Danior shuddered, feeling the intensity of his gaze like a blade. "I already have."

"Ah, because you have barohnial blood, as Keva does." He gazed at the stone, his pupils contracting to dark points. "My family-clan, the Magadaw, came from the mountains a long time ago. In the time of atrocities. My father and my father's father have told me what strains our blood carries. Not all the children of the barohnas were raised in palaces, you know. Some were turned out to live with the slaves who worked in the fields."

Danior read the direction of his thoughts immediately, from his words and from the speculative covetousness of his gaze. Anxious to dispell any dangerous misconception, Danior took the chain from his neck and displayed the pairing stone on the palm of his hand. It glowed softly, then became more brilliant, staining his fingers, his wrist, with light—staining Rezni's face when he bent near. "You take it," he said.

Rezni's pupils widened. He took the stone with lean fingers and dropped it to the palm of his hand. It darkened immediately.

"An ornament," Danior said, relieved the stone had not betrayed him. "For me it's a thought-stone. For you it's an ornament."

For a moment disappointment darkened Rezni's lean face. He stared at the stone, trying to will it to life. When it did not respond, he returned it to Danior with a rejecting shrug. "So I will bring the Viir-Nega a barohna from the mountains and a stone that will take us into the camps of our enemies. It's enough. Even the whitemane is a small loss."

A small loss to the legend that would accrue when he returned bringing powerful allies. Danior hung the pairing stone at his neck again and exchanged a long glance with Keva. He found no hint that she was reluctant to be taken to the Viir-Nega as the Bold Soldier's offering. No hint that she wanted to turn back, with or without Danior's help.

Because she thought the Viir-Nega was her father? Could it be? And if it was—

Danior bit his lip, thinking again of the pairing stone. He had accurately described its function to Rezni. What he had not told Rezni was that it was not functioning as a pairing stone should. He should not have been able to use it to reach the clansman who had stolen the other stone. He should not have been able to reach Keva when she did not wear her stone. And the bluesong—

A tool. The pairing stone was a tool, one that behaved differently for him than it would have for another—because he was different from any person who had used a pairing stone before. He told himself that firmly. He had taken the stone in hand, he had practiced its use, and he had learned what he could do with it.

He had taken the stone in hand and it had brought him here. And now it was going to take him to the desert with Keva and Rezni. To a place he had never thought to see, perhaps to Jhaviir as well. He touched the stone and felt a quick surge of anticipation.

As if reading his acceptance, Rezni stood briskly. "You are right, Danior Terlath. We have only three days. There is no time to sleep."

TEN

KEVA

They walked through the hours of moonlight, Rezni setting the pace, pausing anxiously each time Keva or Danior lagged, as if they were precious acquisitions that might slip from his grasp. Twice they heard movement in the trees. Each time Rezni called a halt, pressing a finger to his lips. "Men from one of the small-clans," he announced. "Listen—you can tell from the way they stumble. No man from the Greater Clan walks so heavily, not since the Viir-Nega taught us silent-stalking. We move as silently as moonlight."

Keva listened to the faint brush of bare feet. When the clansmen passed and Rezni took his fingers from his lips, Danior peered into the trees. His voice was low. "How many parties come for the running?"

"Many. They come from most of the fifty-three small-clans—and the three larger clans send several parties."

"And the Greater Clan? Does the Viir-Nega send men to steal redmanes?"

Rezni snorted disdainfully. "The Viir-Nega knows how little redmanes are worth in the hard-lands. He brought one to us once, a mare, and had it talk in our minds, those who could hear it. Now we understand why it is a waste to bring them to the desert. We can't give them the right foods. And they can't live without their herds. They die."

"But the small-clans apparently find some use for them," Danior persisted.

"The small-clans take them so they can brag about how many they have captured," Rezni retorted haughtily. "They try to make them work, but they die too quickly. So all that's left are the hides and the meat. A dishonor to eat that if you have ever heard a redmane teach. But of course the small-clansmen have not because they have no Viir-Nega to teach them to listen."

"The Viir-Nega spent time on the plain when he was younger. He lived with the guardians for a summer when he was a boy," Keva explained, wondering if Danior understood what she was trying to tell him: that she suspected the Viir-Nega was her father. If she could only speak to Danior directly, without tailoring every remark for Rezni's ears—

But it had seemed important earlier to claim long acquaintance. How could Rezni look at the two of them and guess that they had only met once? That she didn't know the actual degree of their kinship, couldn't guess why Danior had followed her here? What Danior had said about their fathers, that they had been the same person once—was that why he had come? Why he had put aside his initial wariness of Rezni to accompany them to the desert? She shook her head, confused. How could their fathers have been both the same person and different persons? Surely that was simply something Danior had thrown out to confound Rezni.

As they resumed their trek, she thought of other things Danior had told Rezni: that the stone the clansmen had stolen had been paired to his stone, that the two stones had been created to link the thoughts of the two people who wore them. Unconsciously her hand rose to her throat. Was that why he had followed her, how he had found her? Because of the stones? But her stone had never glowed as she had seen his do earlier.

Perhaps only Danior had the use of the pairing stone. She shivered and hoped it was so.

They walked until the moons set and there was only starlight to guide them. By that time they neared the edge of the forest and her knee throbbed. The trees were sparse. Thorny bush encroached. "We'll sleep here," Rezni said. "Under the bushes, where none of those stumblers will trip over us."

Danior glanced around doubtfully, some of his earlier wariness returning. "If the small-clansmen did find us—"

"Then they would cut our throats for what we carry. That's how it is among the small-clansmen."

"And among the Greater Clansmen?" Danior spoke softly, probing.

"The Viir-Nega's principles of honor teach that stealing is dishonorable. So if we stumble across small-clansmen hiding out here,

I will cut their throats simply to prevent them from cutting ours, but I will not touch their possessions. Here—don't let the thorns scratch you. They're venomous at this time of year."

Danior paled at the contrast between Rezni's casual callousness and his concern for their comfort. Keva slid under the bushes and squirmed against the soft soil, guessing how doubtful he must be. Because she shared his reservations. But if she did not go with Rezni, she would never know if the man who called himself the Viir-Nega was her father.

She expected, from the tired ache of her muscles, to sleep immediately. But she found herself thinking instead, wondering what she would find when they reached Pan-Vi—the Greater Clan's desert settlement. She stretched stiff muscles, considering all the things Rezni had told her, about himself, about the Viir-Nega, about his own family, wondering how many were true. Wondering to what extent he was even to be trusted. He was boastful, he was suspicious, he was callous, but he had untied her, he had rubbed her limbs to life and fed her, he had ridden the whitemane.

And he was taking her to the Viir-Nega. She shifted, peering through the shadows, hoping to find Rezni's face unguarded in sleep. Instead he watched her as he would watch a treasure he feared would be stolen, his eyes gleaming wakefully. Keva sighed and turned away.

The next day they crossed the roughlands that lay between the forest and the desert, walking silently, alert for sign of small-clansmen. Keva's knee hurt less than it had the day before; she had thrown away the soiled wrappings and it was little swollen. Occasionally they saw redmane droppings in the thorny vegetation. Once they found a dead yearling. Danior knelt beside it but could not say what had caused its death. "Every year the small-clansmen take animals and every year they die," Rezni observed. "They eat too much mutton. It makes their minds as small as their clans."

Later they found three clansmen sprawled in the brush, scowling at the afternoon sun with fierce, dead faces. Their throats had been slashed, their bodies stripped of everything but their loose trousers. Rezni kicked their stiffening legs and studied the ground for prints. "Thieves steal from thieves," he observed this time and walked away.

Keva met Danior's eyes and saw that he was as sickened as she.

But in other ways the journey stirred something in Danior Keva had not seen before. After they left the forest, he questioned Rezni closely about vegetation and land formations, about game animals and water sources. He made Rezni show him the burrows of small seed gatherers, insisted that Rezni point out tracks in the rough ground, and when he learned that Rezni had trained to spar with pikes, Danior cut down a tree limb and engaged him.

Rezni had not been trained to show quarter and Danior emerged from the encounter bruised, with a bleeding lump on his forehead. But in some way Keva did not understand, the episode cemented a comradeship between them that excluded her. Much of the time after that, she walked separately from them and listened to their talk without giving it full attention. She had thoughts of her own to preoccupy her, and Rezni and Danior seemed to have much to discuss.

They reached the desert the next day and Keva quickly learned she did not like the long, harsh-lit distances, the crackling dryness of the sparse vegetation, the hissing of the wind. But Rezni's eyes glinted with pleasure as he dug bare toes into the fine granules that drifted across the ground in many places and piled against the dry vegetation. "Silica sand," he told Danior. "We saw no use for it until the Viir-Nega taught us to melt it to make glass. Now we join our glass panes and make *han-taus,* so we have homes and gardens in one, and you will see how well we live with this sand to help us."

Danior scooped up a handful of sand and watched it trickle between his fingers. "You grow crops? I didn't think there was enough water in the desert for that."

"There is if your *han-tau* is well sealed and if your Viir-Nega has shown you how to dig wells and how to develop forage plants into crop plants. There are methods for everything, uses for everything, once you learn them, and now we have. We mix the soil, we plant the seed, we water them. When the seeds sprout, they take up the water and when they have used it, they exhale it again. It clouds on the panes at night, when the air outside is cold, and drops back to the soil in the morning. That's why we're stronger than the small clansmen, because we know these things. The small-clans live on stringy mutton and forage, but the Viir-Nega has taught us to grow green food all through the year."

Danior nodded thoughtfully. "Has he ever told you where he learned to grow crops under glass?"

"In a place no one on Brakrath knows but him. A place so far away he can never go back. He brought our clan language and the principles of honor from the same place and gave them to us. He can never go back to his rightful people, so he has made us his people."

Keva sharpened to attention. Was that why her father had ridden so far—because he was trying to find his people? And if that were so, who were his people? "But he won't teach the small-clansmen how to make glass and grow gardens?" she said doubtfully. Was that like her father, to hold knowledge so closely, to refuse to share it, whatever its source?

"He'll teach anyone who pledges to the Greater Clan. But the small-clansmen would rather come and break our panes than learn. Just as they rip each other's tents and steal each other's women. Their minds are small. They don't have the Viir-Nega's principles of honor to discipline them."

So it was not the Viir-Nega who was small-minded. Keva gazed around, and decided it was not so surprising the clansmen were brutal, with the silica sands slithering underfoot and the wind hissing from every direction.

It was hot on the third day of their journey. Keva's clothes, heavy-woven to repel streamside mists, clung. The watering spots Rezni showed them were brackish and the forage he found left her mouth sour. When he trapped a small animal and wrung its neck, she shuddered and could not eat. After Danior and Rezni had eaten, she trudged behind them and thought of sweet, cool bulbs harvested from the mud at the bottom of the warmstream, of pungent, juicy root strands, of weed stems dried, salted and braided into chewy ropes.

She kicked at the ground, sweat damping her hair and trickling down her back, and was not aware of much beyond her wandering thoughts when Rezni's lean fingers suddenly closed on her forearm. She started, too surprised to protest as he pulled her down behind a clump of brittle vegetation. Danior already lay on his stomach.

"There—small-clansmen," Rezni hissed. "Don't raise your head. They have redmanes. Walking Adder Spring is just ahead. They're taking them to drink."

Keva stared through dried branches in the direction he indicated. The clansmen were some distance away, indistinct shapes, but she could see that they drove their small herd of yearlings almost directly toward the brush where she, Danior and Rezni lay. "They'll see us," she said in sharp alarm.

"Not if we're still." Rezni squirmed against the sandy soil. "Push yourself down into the sand. Don't raise your arms or legs. Just brush them back and forth until you've made a hollow and the sand trickles in." Quickly he demonstrated, rocking back and forth until the loose grains yielded a hollow for his body and filtered in to cover it.

Danior and Keva followed suit, burrowing into the warm sand. Sharp grains worked between Keva's clothing and her skin, making her itch.

The clansmen neared. Soon she heard their voices, heard the reluctant clump of padded feet. Peering through the dried brush, she watched a dozen yearlings labor through the warm sand, heads hanging, eyes dull. Five clansmen in soiled tunics drove them, beating their flanks with knotted ropes. The clansmen wore their hair loose and long. Their faces were weathered dark, their voices as harsh as the land.

"Gothni," Rezni hissed.

"You know them?" Danior whispered.

"Well." Rezni's lean face drew tight with scorn.

The clansmen were too preoccupied with the march to notice three pairs of eyes watching them from the brush. But as the yearlings drew near, the most alert raised its head and halted, testing the air. The tallest clansman kicked its flanks, muttering angrily, but the yearling refused to move. It shrilled, then cocked its head, listening. Finally it lowered its head and broke free of the group, sniffing the sandy soil.

Rezni muttered angrily as the yearling followed its nose toward the brush, a single clansman yelping after it, flailing with his rope. Keva pressed her face to the sand, but when she heard the clansman's sharp exhalation, she knew they had been seen.

Before she could react, Rezni heaved himself free of the sand, knife in hand. Danior followed suit, shoulders tense, face ashen, one hand closed around the haft of his pike. Uncertainly Keva stood, shaking away sand, remembering all the things Rezni had said of the small-clansmen. Surely he had exaggerated, painting them meaner than they were.

Surely. But the men she had met in the forest—

The single clansman retreated one step in surprise, then flung his rope aside and snatched the knife from his waist. The long blade flashed. His kinsmen froze. Then they too were crouched, blades in hand, advancing warily. Keva stared at their bared teeth, their narrowed eyes, her pulse suddenly racing with remembered fear.

Before she could respond, Rezni seized her arm, addressing the

advancing clansmen sharply in a language of harsh consonants and
sputtering vowels. They halted and looked from Rezni to Keva
uncertainly. The nearer clansman licked his lips nervously, eyes
darting.

"Now!" Rezni hissed into Keva's ear. "Now or it will be too late.
I've told them you are a barohna from the mountains."

"You've told them—" Keva twisted to stare at him, not understanding. The clansmen gaped at her, nervous pulses beating in
their bare throats, the smell of fear on them. Fear, she realized,
because he had told them she was a barohna. She turned, staring at
Rezni's strained face, realizing what he wanted of her.

What Danior wanted too. "Keva—" he urged softly.

They wanted her to tear up the earth. To break loose its stony
foundation and throw it in pieces at the small-clansmen. Rezni
thought he could use her like a weapon, and Danior thought she
must let herself be used so. She shook her head angrily, pulling free
of his grasp.

And the clansmen, seeing her confusion, moved. The tallest uttered a vengeful series of syllables and backed away, seizing the
nearest yearling by the mane. Swiftly he pulled the startled animal's
head back and plunged his knife into its throat.

Immediately the other clansmen retreated, throwing themselves
at the grunting yearlings, knives raised. Keva's heart closed tight in
shock. She stared, unable to move, to understand.

"Now—or they'll kill them all," Rezni hissed. "They'll leave
nothing but carcasses."

"They—" Keva couldn't believe what she saw, what she heard.
It happened too quickly, overwhelming her. The screams of the
yearlings, the stained blades, the blood—it came in a crimson
spray, and suddenly her chest felt heavy, as if she were drowning.
As if her lungs were filling with the yearlings' blood.

No, not blood. It was an agent manufactured deep in her own
cells that filled her lungs, excluding oxygen. An agent that made
her reel dizzily, reaching numb fingers toward her temples. She
groped for control but a floating sense of timelessness overtook her
and she could not even raise her hands to press staying fingers to
her pounding pulses.

Time. It had become a tangible stream. It buoyed her, carrying
her beyond the present moment and its imperatives, beyond anything she understood. She fought helplessly against its current,
against its eddies and undertows, against the vortex she knew lay

ahead. But the struggle was useless. She already felt herself drawn into the black maw. She already heard the grating sound of sand being whirled into the air. Hundreds of sharp granules, thousands, countless millions, lifted and boiled. Before she could call them back, they formed a spinning funnel that reached abrasive arms for the clansmen. It enfolded them, muffling their screams, obscuring their thrashing limbs. It grew, becoming so dense the air seemed solid. Solid and moving at once. Grinding.

At last Keva's reaching fingers found her temples. She pressed, trying to establish control. If she were the one who held the sand in the air—

And she knew she was. Because as she pressed her temples and gasped for breath, as she sucked oxygen into her lungs, the vortex slowed. Grains of sand began to spin free and fall back to the ground. She continued to draw shallow, panting breaths and sand rained from the air. It fell away until the vortex was an ephemeral thing, a spinning scarlet tracery, a veil.

And the things the veil hid—no, it did not hide them. It pulled away and revealed them. Grotesque things that had been men and now were only masses of raw flesh. Keva stared disbelievingly as the last of the blood-stained sand fell from the air.

The yearlings had dropped to their knees, instinctively huddling together against the abrasive sand. Their thick coats had been sheared away, their auburn manes shredded, their ears scrubbed to bloody stubs. They shivered violently, but they were alive, those the clansmen had not killed before the sand rose.

The clansmen were dead, skin and muscle eaten by the whirling sand.

Keva stared at them. This was her work. She had called up the sand. She had made it spin. Now she clutched her throat, trying to hold back nausea. "I—I don't understand," she said when she could speak. "I don't understand why—why they killed the yearlings." That, of all the things she didn't understand, she could articulate. Only that.

Rezni clutched her forearm, his fingers like claws. His dark eyes stared, as if the slaughter left him numb too. "Did you think they would leave them for us? That's the clan way—to destroy property rather than see it fall to the enemy."

Keva swallowed back the acid rise of sickness. Property? The yearlings were property and not living creatures, capable of caring and sharing? "And they—the clansmen were enemies?" Or had their reaction, their swift slaughter of the yearlings, been simply a reflex action, a thoughtless presumption of hostility conditioned by the harshness of the desert?

"All the small-clans are our enemies. They're afraid of us because we have changed our ways. But these—the Gothni—were my special enemies. They came to Pan-Vi two seasons ago when we were gone to fetch fire-coal and broke the panes of my father's *han-tau.* They let the dry air in to kill our gardens. And they took a woman who was kin of mine." He managed a smile of bitter satisfaction. "She's a widow now."

"She—what kin was she?"

He regarded her with brief suspicion, then shrugged. "My sister. The tall one, Parni, the first to sink his knife—he's the one who took her. But he'll never have a child from her now. Not a child to raise as a Gothni. Parni, Ned, Tarlin—there isn't a brother left from Parni's tent. Tethika will return to my father's *han-tau* before ten days pass."

Keva shook her head, not believing any of it. A stolen sister, the dead yearlings, the bloody remnants that had been living clansmen —suddenly she felt cold. Her teeth began to chatter. She hugged herself and stumbled away to vomit.

They agreed, when Keva could talk, that they could not leave the seven surviving yearlings to find their way back to the forest. There would be other small-clansmen traveling the desert. And the yearlings were too disoriented to undertake the journey alone.

"I have a few green things in my *han-tau* for them," Rezni agreed finally. "And our well has water for them. We will slaughter a few sheep to compensate. We need the mutton for clan-call anyway. We can return the redmanes to the forest after clan-call."

Keva acceded numbly and they resumed their journey. She saw that Danior was silent, pale. He glanced behind anxiously as they walked, as if he expected to see a vortex of sand rise in their wake. The redmanes stumbled, the patches of abrasive sand irritating their pads. Even Rezni was subdued, the muscles of his jaw knotting spasmodically with some private tension. Keva was grateful that he didn't talk, didn't boast of her rout of the Gothni, of his part in it.

Instead he watched her solicitously and tailored his pace to hers, occasionally insisting they stop to rest. "The hard-lands make hard people," he offered the third time he called a halt. "You will learn to be hard too, Keva, in time."

Hard. The same word Oki had used. "No," she said without inflection. She would never be hard. Not if hardness meant not caring for the harm she did, not if it meant swallowing back her fear of what she might do next. Today had taught her that.

"But you will. You have the substance. You're a barohna from the mountains."

He was trying to reassure her, she realized—even to console her. Instead his words only underscored the bleakness of her mood. "No," she said and refused to discuss it further.

They lost one of the yearlings in the afternoon. It lay down and refused to move, and after a while it quivered, stiffened and died. Rezni and Danior kicked sand over the corpse, although they had left the bodies of the clansmen exposed. "We want men from the other small-clans to see what became of the Gothni," Rezni explained. "The Zollidar—the men who took your stone—are already boasting by now that they stole a stone from a barohna. When the Gothni are found, it will be apparent that you are not such an easy victim after all. That you must be approached with care by anyone who wants to live. But there's no purpose in leaving his carcass to be seen. It carries no message."

Keva shrugged and walked on in silence.

Then it was sunset. They stood on a low bluff. Rezni touched her arm and pointed toward the southern horizon. "Pan-Vi," he said—without arrogance, without boast. With something Keva had not heard before: reverence.

Danior dropped his pack and bedding and gazed in the direction Rezni indicated. "There, Keva. Beyond the band of thorn bushes. You can see the sun on the panes. If you look closely, you can pick out individual structures."

"Yes, look to the eastern perimeter and you will see my father's *han-tau*. It's the round dome—you can see it beyond the two rectangular *taus*. They belong to Pesta and Frinz, who were Sisserle before they pledged to the Greater Clan. My *tau* is hidden from here, but you will see it later."

Danior nodded. "How large was your family-clan before you joined the Greater Clan?"

"The Magadaw? We brought thirty-seven men and fifty-eight women to the Greater Clan. That was five years ago."

"You were one of the men? You were that old when your clan joined?"

"No, I made my initial vow two years ago, at autumn clan-call.

And tomorrow at clan-call we will all renew our pledge. That is done each season."

Danior gazed toward the distant settlement. "Does anyone ever decide not to renew?"

Rezni snorted. "Every call there is someone who covers his mouth when the pledge is taken. Then the Viir-Nega must give him a private audience and a private pledging."

"They don't ever just go away? Leave?"

"Where would they go? Where could they get panes to build new *han-taus?* The furnaces are here. The glassworkers are here. No one is permitted to remove panes from Pan-Vi. They would only be wasted—broken by the small-clansmen."

"And no one wants to live in a tent again?"

"No one wants to go back to the old ways, no matter how much they complain," Rezni said staunchly.

Keva listened to their talk absently and gazed at the distant structures, wishing she felt more than a pervading numbness. If the Viir-Nega were her father, he lived behind the glass panes that glinted in the distance. She would meet him before she slept again. Her search would be finished.

But if the Viir-Nega were not her father, she would still meet him. And she would learn that she need not have made the journey. Need not have seen blood spray in the air. Need not have made a vortex of sand and scrubbed the living flesh from five screaming clansmen.

Feeling sick, she sat with her head on her knees until Rezni and Danior were ready to walk again.

The air cooled after sunset and she was grateful for her heavy clothes. The yearlings raised their heads and padded more briskly, grunting among themselves. They descended from the bluff and the terrain changed, pockets of sand giving way to hard-baked soil. Soon they reached a solid wall of densely grown vegetation, every branch armed with long thorns. "Our guard maze," Rezni explained. "The small-clansmen burn it, but we water it from our wells and it grows back. And we cut new paths. Walk in my footsteps. The thorns are at their most poisonous at this time of year."

He walked ahead, picking a route through the bristling vegetation. The yearlings entered the maze reluctantly, gazing up balefully at the surrounding walls of vegetation. One tried to sample the oily foilage and was pricked on the nose. He shrilled angrily and

Keva and Danior had to hold him by the shreds of his mane to keep him from blundering blindly through the venomous bushes.

Then they emerged from the maze and moonlight lay on hundreds of glass panes. Keva caught her breath and felt Rezni press her arm. When she glanced up, he was smiling—without bravado or boast, a smile of pure pleasure.

"It's beautiful," she told him, surprised at her answering pleasure. Structures of every conceivable shape and size, formed from thick glass panes, were gathered on the barren soil. Small lamps burned inside them, flickering. The shadows of lush interior foliage patterned the panes. Even by first moonlight, Keva could see that some panes were clear and others tinted. "Beautiful," she repeated.

"Now you see why I boast," Rezni said. "Come—the Viir-Nega will be in his tent."

"I—" Suddenly the anticipation she had not felt earlier caught her, twisting her heart, making her breath catch. Making her suddenly apprehensive of what lay ahead. She stared up at Rezni dumbly, trying to find some excuse to hold back, to delay confronting the Viir-Nega.

But Rezni caught her arm, drawing her quickly ahead. They hurried down lanes of pounded soil, the yearlings grunting with excitement at the smell of moisture. Watchful shapes appeared from lamp-lit structures, then withdrew when Rezni identified himself.

She was dirty, she realized with belated distress, stumbling. Her clothes were caked. She had not combed her hair since morning. And they were going to meet the Viir-Nega. Quickly Keva drew her fingers through her hair, brushed at her face, tried to straighten her clothes. Danior, she saw, was going through the same hurried grooming process. She suspected her efforts were as useless as his.

"Here," Rezni said when they stood before an oblong *han-tau,* the panes so thick they distorted view of the interior. He tugged at a rope and glass chips tingled somewhere inside. "The Nathri-Varnitz comes," he called into the open doorway. "He brings kin of the Viir-Nega."

Shadow shifted behind glass panes. Feet shuffled and a child appeared. Large, dark eyes. Arched brows. Smooth, dark hair. He stood in the doorway like an apparition, staring up at Danior and Keva, then turned and disappeared without word.

Next a woman appeared and studied them from obliquely set eyes. "I bring kin of the Viir-Nega," Rezni said, repeating the salutation in his own language.

If the woman felt any surprise, she didn't betray it. She nodded tersely, summoning them in.

Keva had no time to glance around as they brushed through the hanging panel of an interior door and entered a room where the air was thick with moisture. Because as they entered, a man appeared from another chamber and Keva could only stare.

Raked soil, the earthen smell of growing plants, the dim light of a lantern—she noticed none of those things. Nor did she hear what Rezni said. Not even the tone of his voice registered. She saw only her father, as unbelieving as she, staring at her from eyes she remembered. Dark eyes, searching eyes. But this time it was not the distance they searched but her face, as if it were some half-remembered terrain, one he had not thought to see again. Slowly, disbelievingly, he raised one hand, the nails like hers, pink against bronze skin, and touched her cheek. The bluesong hung at his waist, knotted. The fabric was as slippery, the color as brilliant as she remembered. Her father even smelled as she remembered.

The only thing different was the ingrained lines around his eyes, as if he had peered into the distance so long watchfulness had been etched into his very flesh. And the polished stone wristlet he wore. Keva had not seen that before. "So the woman lied to me," he said finally, the words glad and angry at once.

Keva laughed. What she heard in his voice was so much the same thing she felt: angry that they had been separated, relieved that he was alive, that she had found him. *"Yes*. She told you I was dead but I wasn't," she said, her tongue beginning to work again—too quickly, spilling out words untidily. "She—she just wanted a child. Her mate had drowned and none of the women would let their mates share her mattress. None of the women in that settlement. So she took me to a settlement three days' walk downstream. She—" Tears stung her eyes. "She let you hunt for me. For my grave. She—"

He placed one finger lightly against her lips, stemming the tide. "Stay. We don't need to say everything at once. Some of it we'll never need to say. I can read your face as clearly as I ever could. And the woman—was Oki her name?—must have told you the truth eventually. Or you wouldn't have come here. With my Bold Soldier."

Keva glanced at Rezni and almost laughed at the fierce pride in his eyes. "She told me. I made her. If I hadn't, I would never have known. But—"

"But you do know and it is as well this way," her father said, pulling her to his chest, touching her hair. "It is as well, Keva Marlath, because I rode in hard places after I left the warmstream. I rode in places no child could have survived. I met men who would have quenched you before I knew what they intended. They came close enough to quenching me, before I finally realized I must stop riding and start building instead." He held her at arm's length again. "Do you know how many times I've wished I had learned that lesson before I lost you? Before I pushed through winter storms and made you sick when we could have taken shelter in the valleys, in the plain, in any number of places. But now I haven't lost you at all."

She laughed, inappropriately—she couldn't help it—and felt tears begin to streak freely from her eyes. She wiped them away impatiently. She had arrived. She had found her father and he was as glad of it as she was. This was no time to cry.

Her father didn't seem surprised. He held her until she had wiped away the last of her tears and conquered the weak laughter that kept rising in her throat. Then he glanced beyond her at Danior. "And this?"

Danior started, caught off guard. "Danior Terlath—I'm Danior Terlath."

The Viir-Nega's brows rose. "Of course. Who else could it be? You've brought news of your valley, I hope. News of my Rauth-brother?"

"My father—yes."

"And your mother? And Fiirsevrin?"

"Everything," Danior promised, his gaze flicking briefly to the sash at the Viir-Nega's waist.

The Viir-Nega nodded, glancing at Rezni. "And in addition to news, you have sand in your boots and dirt in your hair, all of you. Keva, Danior—Maiya will take you to the wetroom to wash and she will find clean clothes for you. That will give me time to talk with the Nathri-Varnitz so he can return to his *han-tau*. His wives are beginning to be anxious."

Wives? Keva darted a startled glance at Rezni. He scowled at the floor, a dark stain rising in his cheeks, and refused to meet her eyes. He seemed relieved when the woman who had met them at the door reappeared and gestured for them to follow.

The wetroom was a small chamber, and when Keva glanced up, she saw that its panes stained the stars deeply blue. There was a large round tub half-filled with water recessed into the graveled floor. A species of plant that seemed, by lantern light, to have foliage of the deepest violet grew profusely against the curved glass wall. Maiya silently laid out lengths of absorbent cloth and said, "Clothes—later."

When they were alone, Danior turned and studied the room. Then he glanced back at Keva, apparently uncertain of her mood. "I think we're supposed to sit in the tub," he said finally. "And scrub with leaves from the plants."

Keva studied the violet foliage doubtfully, grateful that at least the tendency to tears and laughter had begun to subside. "Rezni told you that?"

"He told me his wives grow purple star for their wetroom instead of redleaf soap-plant because it isn't so likely to irritate the skin." He bent to unlace his boots, then glanced up uncertainly. "Do you want to bathe alone?"

"No, there's room for two," she assured him. "You knew Rezni had wives?" There at least was a subject that did not threaten her fragile composure.

"He told me. But he thought if he told you that you wouldn't be first-wife, that there were two before you, you would refuse him."

Keva stared at him in amazement. "I refused him the first time he asked. I told him—" Tales—carefully calculated tales. That she was barohna of Valley Marlath. That she was traveling to visit her kinsman, the Viir-Nega. That she must return to her people when she had seen him.

"Yes, he thought that was a good sign. It lessens a woman's worth if she agrees too quickly. His other wives come from very strong family-clans. He's made good alliances by taking them, but he's decided to give them to his younger brother if you accept him. Then of course you would be first-wife."

So Rezni had already plotted her future. She wondered briefly what else she had missed in not listening more closely to Rezni and Danior's talk. She repressed a moment's impulse to laugh, guessing tears would follow. Obviously many things were different here, but she would not think about them tonight. Her mood was too fragile. Tonight she must put everything aside: unanswered questions, unexplained relationships, inexplicabilities—and images of sand whirling in the air.

Sand and blood. She shivered, choking back nausea.

Danior noticed and caught her arm. "Are you all right?"

"I felt cold," she said weakly. Cold and sickened and confused, even though she had found her father's roof and was safely under it. And from what she had seen of the desert, it was clear she had come to an alien place, clear there would be other moments when she felt cold, many of them.

But not tonight. She had completed her search. She had found her father. Tonight she would put away disturbing thoughts.

Tonight.

ELEVEN

DANIOR

Danior had many things to think about as they bathed. The stories Rezni had told him of plundering small-clansmen. What Keva had done that afternoon and the mark it had left on her. Jhaviir: the place he had made for himself among the clansmen, the sunstone wristlet he wore, the bluesong. Danior had a sense of discoveries and events following so quickly upon each other that he had scant time to reflect, to wonder where he must put his foot next. He had taken the first step, and broad avenues had opened to him, drawing him from event to event.

Now they had brought him to a land he had never expected to see, to people he had never expected to know. Had brought him to friendship with Rezni, to reunion with his father's brother. More, they had brought him to an anxious sense that he had come here to be tested. Not in the traditional way of a palace child, by going to the mountain to kill or be killed. But in a more complex way, in a way no one had been tested before. In a way, perhaps, that he would not even understand until the test was done. And the danger, he guessed, was not that he might die, not even that he might fail, but that he might turn away.

He had wanted to today, when the sand fell and he saw what it had done to the Gothni. He had wanted to run—back to the forest, back to the plain, back to the valleys, where the forces of the stones were leashed and harnessed by centuries of tradition.

But Keva could not turn back. She was caught, bound—not by tradition but by the very forces tradition had evolved to guard against. She had no mother to set an example for her. No Council Elder to instruct her. No stone mate to share her bewilderment and her doubt. She had only Danior and her father.

And Danior had a full sense of his own inadequacy. What could he tell her? How could he guide her? He could only stay, offering his presence. Perhaps that was part of the test: accepting his own helplessness.

When they had finished bathing, they pulled on the loose robes and trousers Maiya had brought for them and made their way back to the front of the *han-tau*. There they found a low table spread with food. Cushions were arranged around it and half a dozen children sat cross-legged, waiting. When Keva and Danior entered, they turned and stared with a bold-eyed curiosity that made Danior stiffen self-consciously.

The oldest boy stood and gestured to the vacant cushions, speaking rapidly. Danior sat, Keva beside him, and glanced around cautiously, wondering what to expect. A formal dining; a family meal; a ceremonial? He didn't know the desert etiquette for any of those occasions. But perhaps there was none. The younger children were already picking at the food, snatching tidbits from the serving bowls, protesting loudly when the oldest tried to discipline them. Keva, he saw, barely noticed. She watched the doorway with barely veiled anticipation. Some of the color had returned to her face. Her eyes were brighter than they had been since afternoon.

By the time Jhaviir appeared, the children were openly warring. "My young clansmen," he said deprecatingly, striding into the room. He had dressed in fresh robe and trousers and reknotted the bluesong at his waist, but Danior saw he no longer wore the sunstone wristlet. "They'll quarrel over a shadow on the sand. I've seen them do it. That's the desert way."

Nevertheless Danior noticed that the children jumped to their feet and came to order immediately at his appearance. They only sat again when he selected a cushion beside Keva and crossed his legs.

When the children were quiet, he said, "I've already told the children we will use only mountain language at the table tonight, which will give us some peace since only Tedni and Resha—" he indicated the two older children "—have begun to learn it." He smiled reprovingly at the impatient children and said, "Yes, you may eat now. Here, Keva, Danior—fill your platters quickly or you'll have nothing."

A small melee ensued, from which everyone finally emerged with a filled platter. Danior hesitated at first, then decided that if this was the etiquette, he would observe it rather than go hungry. When he sat again, he tried to identify what he had snatched from the confusion and recognized almost nothing. Fruit, meat, roasted seeds and pods—all unfamiliar except the mutton. But it took him only a few bites to realize how hungry he was.

Keva ate more cautiously, glancing around the table doubtfully. "Doesn't Maiya eat with you?" she asked finally.

Jhaviir's arched brows rose. "No, no, neither Maiya, Ramari nor Kliya. They like peace with their meals, so I eat with the children and they eat with themselves. In fact, Maiya suggested you might prefer the women's table, but I told her that you would not mind eating with us tonight. I wasn't wrong, I hope."

"No. Of course not," Keva said quickly. But Danior noticed that she stared down at her plate, her face flushing. He studied her covertly, realizing she had not guessed her father followed the desert custom. Though why it should make her uncomfortable that he kept three wives . . . Perhaps she held strong feelings, as his mother did, and could not imagine sharing a mate.

Later Danior gathered from the loud protests of the younger children and the frowning annoyance of the eldest that the children were not normally dismissed from their father's presence so early. Tedni, the eldest boy, lingered, arguing, until his sister Resha tugged him away.

When they had gone, Jhaviir excused himself and groped in the vines that grew along the wall for a small flask. "Now we will drink," he announced, pouring amber liquid into hand-blown glasses and seating himself again. The planes of his face gleamed by lantern light. *"Hi-basa,* made from a tuber I discovered in the roughlands and brought here. Drink slowly or you will regret it. In fact, you will probably regret it anyway, but we must observe your arrival with something more than a hasty meal."

Danior accepted a glass, studying Jhaviir, trying to understand how he could be both so much like his father and so different. His facial structure, the proportion of body and limbs, the shape of his hands—all those things were identical. But Jhaviir moved differently, every motion broader, more emphatic, as if he deliberately called attention to himself. And there was something in his eyes, in the way he spoke, that seemed directed to the same end. He carried himself, he spoke like a man who has placed himself upon a stage, who expects to engage every eye. Danior watched him and wondered whether his own father's reserve was cultivated or whether

Jhaviir's more commanding way was a deliberate manner. Carefully Danior raised his glass.

The *hi-basa* had a resinous taste that made his tongue burn. Aware of Jhaviir's weighing gaze, he took several swallows anyway. At the fourth, blood rushed to his head with vengeful speed. He set the glass down with a clatter and was immediately embarrassed by his sudden clumsiness.

"Very slowly," Jhaviir cautioned. "And now, before any more time escapes us, there are things we must learn from each other. Rezni tells me, Keva, that you are barohna of Valley Marlath, that the valley is peopled again and you serve it. But I know that if that were so, your flesh would be burned dark at this season, so soon after the thawing. And I observe that it isn't."

Keva flushed, meeting his gaze reluctantly. "No, I—I don't even remember Valley Marlath. I only heard of it when I met Danior. I left the warmstream—" She glanced at Danior uncertainly. "It was eleven or twelve days ago. I went as soon as Oki told me what she had done. That she had stolen me. I was going to the mountains to find you, but I met Danior and he told me no one had seen you there. So I decided to follow the redmanes to the forest to see if I could learn anything there."

"Ah. And you met Rezni in the forest. And showed him how a barohna makes stone live."

"*No.* I—I don't know what I did. He frightened me. I thought— it just happened." She stared down at the table top, her lips tightly compressed, tears standing at the corners of her eyes. "I don't know how," she whispered. "It just happened."

Jhaviir gazed at her at length, frowning. Then he leaned across the table and took her hands, holding them palm-upward in his. He studied the fingers one by one, as if they could tell him something. He sighed deeply, suddenly seeming neither emphatic nor commanding. Suddenly seeming only tired. "Pardon me for insisting when we should only drink quietly and speak of inconsequentialities. But the things we must discuss are important. Have you thought of going to Valley Marlath and taking the throne? The people have scattered, but they would return. Gladly, I know, if you want it."

Keva pulled her hands back as if he had burned them, color washing from her face. "*No.* I'm—I'm not—*no!*"

Jhaviir studied her pleading face, then took his fingers and gently curled them shut. Again strain showed in the fine lines around his eyes, in the bunching of muscles in his jaws. His words seemed reluctant. "I appreciate that you have just arrived, Keva. I appreciate that you should have time to rest before we talk like this. But you've come at an important time—on the eve of spring clan-call, and at a period when the small-clans are at their most hostile. You are obviously a significant personage—both of you are significant personages. You presented yourself so to Renzi and by now—just in the time it took you to bathe—word has gone around Pan-Vi. So has word of the way you terrorized the Zollidar and left five Gothni dead on the desert. And since you caught the Gothni near Walking Adder Spring, very soon word will be around not just here, but all over the hard-lands. Dozens of parties pass Walking Adder at this time of year. It is one of the places where neutrality has been declared among the small-clans.

"And so I must make a request I realize you won't welcome. No more do I welcome the fact that I must make it. But I must ask that you permit me to present you to the clan tomorrow during the ceremonies both as my daughter and as a barohna—a barohna who has come to ally herself for a while to the cause of the Greater Clan."

Keva raised her head sharply, staring at him. *"No,"* she protested with open horror. "No. *Please.* I only came here to find you. I—"

"I know that," he said, obviously sorry for the pain his request caused. "And I would like to be able to give you the time you need. But you must understand what a fragile social organism I have created here, Keva.

"I don't know how much you remember of the stories I used to tell you of my own childhood. Not a lot, I expect. Some of them, I see now, were only worth forgetting.

"I grew up among a people called the Kri-Nostri. They were a rigidly disciplined people who lived a carefully structured life among harsh circumstances. Their discipline, in fact, was the only thing that saved them from falling victim to recurrent drought and warring neighbors. That and the reputation they built for themselves as soldiers who turned back from nothing. I learned how to be strong from the Kri-Nostri. Just as important, I learned to give the appearance of strength even in my weak moments. And I learned to love adversity. I measured myself against it every day and let it make me stronger. That was the Kri-Nostri way.

"Then I found myself here, a Kri-Nostri soldier plunged into the society of the valleys. Everytime I rode down stone avenues, I felt diminished. Because nothing I had been trained for was of any use in the valleys. There were no enemies, no wars, no need to be strong or vigilant. No need for any of my soldier's discipline. There wasn't even the simple physical hardship of pitting myself against a harsh land. The barohnas have tamed the valleys.

"So I rode out of the valleys to find hardship. And not just that. I rode to find the sense of myself hardship could give. The sense of strength, of control.

"I rode long past the time when I should have learned better. I rode until I realized that hardship was no longer making me strong. It was only making me lonely. I began to recognize that—belatedly —after I lost you, Keva. I recognized that it meant nothing that I rode through the worst weather without flinching, that I pushed myself when I was tired and sick, that I carried the skins of minx and rock-leopard and had brought down breeterlik and crag-chargers. I had no people. I was alone.

"I had passed through the desert several times and seen how the clanspeople lived. Among the Kri-Nostri, it would be said they are like children: without discipline or principle. In truth, even a Kri-Nostri child is better disciplined than most clansmen. Certainly a Kri-Nostri child, left to himself, would devise a better way to live.

"Perhaps that's what decided me. I had just lost a child, or so I thought, and the desert was full of children, hungry and dirty and ignorant—waiting to be shown a better way to live. And hardship —they offered me hardship in full measure. I saw quickly that here I could use everything I had learned among the Kri-Nostri: strength, vigilance, cunning, persistence.

"And so I elected to stop here, to make the clanspeople my family. Because I had finally recognized the need for family and society, for constance. Something that would extend beyond my own lifetime if possible. And the land was familiar. Sometimes at sunset I walk a distance from Pan-Vi and I can imagine that I stand on the silica sands of Grenish again. The colors in the sunset sky are like those I knew there, harsh and red. The heat, the dryness are the same. This place says home to me. And it uses me fully. More than fully sometimes. Certainly it required all my strength and all my bravado to establish myself among the clansmen.

"I won't tell you all the things I went through to make a family of these people. I will tell you that when I came here, the people who now live as the Greater Clan belonged to twelve small-clans and two larger ones. They were nomads, hungry and hostile, living in ragged tents and speaking six different languages. Their women were haggard and beaten. Their children more often died during their first year than not. And their men slaughtered each other upon the pettiest of pretexts.

"I measured myself against them as I once measured myself against physical hardship and I welded them into a social unit. I gave them a common language, a language no one else on Brakrath speaks. I gave them agriculture and technology. I gave them principles and social organization. I fed their self-importance by offering them titles and honors. And I brought them symbols. This for instance." He indicated the bluesong. "This is a magic no one else on the desert commands. Only the Greater Clan has a singing silk. And of course I've given them a leader who holds the silk and has claim to important associations. Myself.

"Now you have come and affirmed my claim to important associations. You are my daughter and you have done things only a barohna can do. But if I don't present you in a suitable manner at clan-call, your presence won't support my position at all. It will undermine it.

"Reticence isn't respected here, Keva. A man—or a woman—who doesn't flaunt his advantage is asking to be dismissed as a weakling. That's simply the way of these people. I'm sure they will seem like braggarts to you. To them, a person who doesn't boast must be hiding weakness. And weakness is no more well-received than reticence. It is a matter for shame. So as their leader, I must proclaim myself more loudly than anyone else. Or lose their confidence. And I dare not lose their confidence.

"What we have built here is still too fragile. We're still raising the first generation of children who will remember no loyalty but to the Greater Clan. If I don't show myself strong, their parents may very well sink back into disorder. And then everything will be lost and the small-clans will overwhelm us. There will be no mark of my work here but broken glass and wilted crops. Do you understand me, Keva?"

It was apparent to Danior that she did, that she understood why he must present her to the clan as a barohna. Her lips had begun to tremble. She spoke in a reluctant whisper, avoiding his eyes. "What do you want me to do?"

Jhaviir sighed deeply, passing one dark hand across his face, pressing his temples in a familiar gesture. Danior studied him, guessing he seldom let anyone see him like this, tired, regretful, subdued. "Nothing difficult, Keva. Ride with me to clan-call. Listen to a lot of rhetoric in a language you don't understand. Conduct yourself as you instinctively did with Rezni, as a person of position. My people will be impressed simply because they want to be impressed. They want to have strong allies."

When Keva continued to stare at the tabletop, saying nothing, Danior said doubtfully, "The small-clansmen—when they find the Gothni, when they realize what happened to them—"

Jhaviir gazed down into his glass, swirling the amber liquid, sighing again. "I have achieved two distinct things in my years here, Danior. I've united a group of quarreling clans into the Greater Clan. And in the process, without intending it at all, I have also partially united many of the other small-clans—simply by offering them a common enemy."

"The Greater Clan," Danior said softly, understanding. The very existence of the Greater Clan had forged tentative bonds between the smaller clans. Not bonds of friendship but bonds of common fear.

"Yes. They have lived in the old way—wandering, fighting, plundering each other's camps—so long that they have no understanding of any other way to live. Nor do they understand that we *have* found another way to live. They see us growing stronger year by year, and they think it is only a matter of time until we move against them. And so every year, they draw closer together. They fight each other less and press us harder. And now—" Jhaviir's eyes flickered to Keva, who still stared at the table, lips tight. Brows arching, he raised his glass in a shrugging gesture.

Now. Danior glanced at Keva and saw she did not realize what Jhaviir had left carefully unsaid: that when the small-clans learned a barohna had joined the Greater Clan, they would feel even more threatened. They would unite even more firmly—more savagely— against their common enemy. "How quickly does news travel on the desert?"

"Very quickly now. The small-clans still fight and steal among themselves, but they have commissioned couriers who are permitted to pass without harassment. By now they are already running."

Carrying the news. Danior touched his pairing stone, troubled by the picture Jhaviir had drawn—of a fragile union, of savage enemies, of people who could easily slip back into chaotic ways. And there seemed nothing he could do. "Do you want me to come to clan-call too?" he asked uncertainly.

Carefully Jhaviir placed his glass on the table. He glanced at Keva, then turned his full attention back to Danior. "As my Rauth-son? Yes, it is important that you come. In fact, I would like you to lead Ranslega, my stallion. Rezni will march with you carrying the songsilk—the first time I've permitted another person to do that. I would like to bestow a ceremonial title upon you—and perhaps another on Rezni, for guiding you here. For your part, all you need do is put on a soldier's face, like a man aware of his own strength."

Like a man with a legend in his own land.

Because that was what Jhaviir was telling him—was telling them both. That legend was important among the desert people, far more important than in the mountains. It was legend that assured strong allies, that provided protection against rapacious neighbors—that insured survival. While he was here, he must behave like a man secure in his own legend. Even if that legend were totally ephemeral. Even if behind it he remained the same person he had always been, doubting and uncertain.

Certainly the fact that Jhaviir had revealed his own vulnerability took some of the sting from Danior's doubts. If Jhaviir, who had ridden in places Danior had never seen, who had welded an unruly people into a small nation, must put on a public face, how could Danior's uncertainties make him small? "I will," he said.

"Good. You understand—and we can turn to lighter matters," Jhaviir said, raising his glass.

Relaxing, they sipped the resinous *hi-basa* and let it dissolve the last barriers of reticence. Gradually Keva's face took color again and she spoke of her life by the warmstream, of Oki, of Lekki, of a young fisherman who teased her from his boat. Danior related what he could of people Jhaviir had known in the valleys: his mother, his father, Juris Pergossa, others. Jhaviir told them of lands he had explored during the early years, while Lihwa was in her winter palace—lands Danior had not guessed existed. And he told them of the morning he heard an alien song and discovered a length of brilliant blue silk caught in the branches of a tree, blown there from the nearby wreckage of a small star-trader.

Danior gazed at the blue sash at Jhaviir's waist and stirred to full attention, casting off the growing fuzziness of drink. "Where—do you know where it came from? What kind of place?" Had Jhaviir seen silken bowers in white-stalked trees and pink-tongued predators too when the silk sang? Or was he the only one?

"No." Jhaviir shook his head regretfully. "I don't know where the ship traveled from or why it wrecked itself there. I suspect it flew by an automatic system that failed. Perhaps it was an accident much like the one that stranded the first-timers on Brakrath—except that I found no sign of a crew. The other cargo it carried—I had no use for it. I left it."

Danior sighed. So he was the only one who had reached beyond the bluesong. The only one who had seen yellow-eyed predators in an alien forest. "You only took the bluesong?"

"Ah, I took songs of other colors too, Danior. But I never showed them to Lihwa. She was unhappy with my restlessness. She wished me to winter with her in her mountain palace, though she understood me too well to insist. So I hid the silks and only wore the bluesong after I left Valley Marlath. Then later, when I was separated from Keva, I went back and retrieved the others. And hid them again when I settled here. The Kri-Nostri call that the principle of *karnikile-karmaka*. The hidden treasure-weapon—a very loose translation. I learned as a boy always to keep something back."

Danior nodded thoughtfully. "Your people—they know about the other songsilks?"

"I've dropped hints—hints that one day I will confer them upon the most diligent as symbols of special recognition. One day when we reach a certain point in our life together." Quickly Jhaviir emptied his glass and turned it upside down. "And now the drinks are enough and you are tired. It is time we slept, daughter, Rauth-son."

Danior wanted to protest, wanted to talk more, but his tongue was growing thick. Jhaviir showed him to a cushion in the chamber where Tedni and his younger brothers slept. Danior stretched out, his mind full of half-formulated questions, half-digested insights. There was much he could learn from Jhaviir, he realized—much no one else could teach him.

More, perhaps, than he could learn from Keva. Perhaps there were even things he could teach her, if she would let him, just as he had taught her to listen to the teaching. Sighing, he clasped the pairing stone, thinking of the couriers who ran between the small-clans. By now word had already gone out that the Greater Clan harbored a barohna. And only he and Jhaviir knew the barohna was untrained and unwilling. He pressed his pairing stone, trying to guess what he could do to help guide Keva past her fear. He remembered too well his first fear of the pairing stone.

But use of the pairing stone was a small gift compared to the power Keva had unleashed. And what could he tell her? To walk the path, to learn from doing seemed dangerous advice, although it might be the only advice he could give. Because if she did not explore her gift, if she did not practice its control, it would rule her.

Uneasily he closed his eyes and sought sleep.

He woke in the morning to find Tedni, Jhaviir's oldest son, standing over him frowning fiercely. And to find that his head throbbed dully. He sat, rubbing his eyes, hoping water would wash the foul taste of the night's drinking from his mouth. Morning sunlight poured through heavy glass panes. The younger boys had gone.

"You slept in your clothes," Tedni said, the words heavily accented, accusing. "Now Maiya will have to get you clean ones and you will have to wash those." Impatiently the boy brushed dark hair back from his sharp-boned cheek. "It was my place to lead Ranslega to clan-call before you came, you know. I lead him every year because I am the Viir-Nega's first and strongest son. Now my father tells everyone you will lead him."

Slowly Danior stood, pressing his palms against his aching temples, trying to comprehend Tedni's grievance. Apparently Danior had usurped a valued ceremonial chore. "Why don't we walk one on either side of Ranslega?" he offered without thinking. "We can share the privilege."

Tedni's pupils contracted sharply and his lips thinned to a narrow line. "If you will walk three paces behind, we will share," he agreed haughtily.

Danior's face colored. "The Viir-Nega didn't ask me to walk behind anyone." It wasn't hard, given the ache of his head and the boy's scowling arrogance, to put a sting in the words.

Tedni drew himself up on the balls of his feet, scowling more fiercely than before. When Danior did not respond, he abruptly bared his teeth in a flashing grin. "I'll speak to my father," he said and dodged away.

Danior looked after him with a shrug, then brushed at his clothes and ventured to the wetroom to splash his face. Either *hi-basa* or fatigue had left his eyes dull and dark-rimmed, his complexion sallow. His muscles felt leaden, his movements poorly coordinated.

He washed and ate with the others, jostling for food, his head throbbing. Jhaviir's edict that mountain language be spoken at the table had apparently applied only to the night before. Today the children squabbled in their own language. No one made any allusion to Danior's rumpled clothing.

When he ventured outside to where Jhaviir was grooming Ranslega, he saw no trace of the night's drinking on Jhaviir. He raised one hand in greeting and said, "I've told Tedni he can walk at Ranslega's left side if he remains five paces behind you and doesn't touch the halter strap. He's old enough this year to walk at the front of the procession."

So Tedni's grievance had been manufactured. "He told me he always leads Ranslega to the clan-call," Danior said without much surprise.

Jhaviir bared teeth in a broad smile. "He would tell you that. And he'll tell you many other things about his importance here if you give him the chance. Keep him in his place if you want to be his friend. Otherwise you'll just be someone he uses. Here—you've probably braided Füirsevrin's mane a hundred times. Do Ranslega's for me."

Danior retreated a step, wanting to refuse, but Jhaviir had already handed him the comb and left him with the animal. Danior hesitated, then laid a cautious hand on the whitemane's shoulder. The animal's flesh was firm and warm. When he raised his hand, it left no mark. Relieved, he began parting and combing the silver-white strands.

Keva joined him after a while, standing silently in the harsh morning sun, her eyes darkly ringed, her face pale. She watched, then took the comb from him when she recognized his total lack of skill.

"Did you eat?" he asked, worried by her pallor, wondering if it came from *hi-basa* or lack of sleep.

"No," she said shortly, deftly working the stallion's mane into plaits.

He could see she didn't want to talk. Withdrawing, he found brushes on the ground nearby and silently began brushing Ranslega's coat. Occasionally he stopped to gaze uneasily around. Jhaviir had erected his paned home at a distance from the others, so that it commanded a view of the desert. Beyond it, the land rolled away to the south in barren hillocks. Brown-dried vegetation stood sentinel. Peering back in the direction they had come the night before, Danior saw the guard maze, its thorny growth incongruously green against the dun of the desert. By daylight, it was not so imposing as he remembered it. It made little better than a half-circle around the gathered structures, leaving the perimeter unguarded in every other direction.

He searched the distance, frowning against morning sunlight. By daylight the Greater Clan's settlement seemed frail shelter against the barrenness of the desert. Glass panes sheltered the gardens and conserved the precious moisture that fed them. Barefoot men and women with sun-hardened faces gathered for clan-call, their children squabbling in the dirt lanes. And beyond lay sand, wind and the small-clans.

Danior darted a glance at Keva and saw that she too peered uneasily toward the desert.

After a while Rezni appeared, padding down the lane barefoot, his robe and trousers blazing white, his hair freshly knotted. He carried both knife and spear. He paused to survey the state of Ranslega's grooming, then said with measured self-importance, "I'll get the riding pad and the halter." When Keva did not look up from her work, he tapped Danior's arm, raising his brows questioningly.

Danior lifted his shoulders in a noncommittal shrug. Certainly he wanted no part in Rezni's suit for Keva.

Soon the whitemane stallion stood braided and saddled, his neck proudly arched. People pressed near, staring at Keva and Danior, muttering in clan-language. Tedni appeared, ducking beneath the whitemane's belly, and addressed Rezni with a long, boastful harangue. Rezni answered him sharply and the boy dodged away, shooting back a rejoinder over one shoulder.

"He wants us to understand that all these people have come to watch him lead off the procession," Rezni remarked. He turned, his eyes sweeping the watching people haughtily. "They have, in fact, come to see me carry the bluesong." He raised his head, baring his teeth. "So?"

"I don't think so," Danior answered but saw from Rezni's darting glance that the boast had been addressed to Keva. When she did not respond, Rezni's eyes sparked with intensified interest. But before he could try again to command her attention, Tedni returned, loosing imperious instructions in every direction. Rezni snapped his bare heels together. "The Viir-Nega comes. I will assist you into the saddle."

Keva met his eyes for the first time, distantly. Deliberately, she put aside the grooming comb, seized the whitemane's mane, and pulled herself to his back. "I don't need help."

Rezni's dark eyes glittered and the watching people sighed as Keva caught the whitemane's reins and raised her chin. She looped the reins in her right hand. Her face was pale, every muscle so tautly controlled she might have been carved from stone.

Danior stepped forward quickly, taking the whitemane's halter strap, trying to assume some of the same poised control. For that was what Jhaviir wanted of him: a manner. He even managed to echo Rezni's haughtiness. "What route must we follow, Nathri-Varnitz?"

Rezni gazed up at Keva, his dark eyes brightly calculating. "I will walk to your left and show you," he said. "And if the brat presses closer than five paces, we will stop and throw him into the thorns. A few scratches will improve his appearance."

The people in the lane began to shout and Jhaviir strode from his *han-tau.* He wore robe and trousers bleached a dazzling white, a braided rope at his waist. More, he wore an air of command that took every eye. His oiled face gleamed. On his outstretched hands, he carried the bluesong, folded. Danior gazed at him and could see no trace of the tired man who had spoken to them the night before.

He raised his arms, addressing the people in clan-language. From their sudden, hooting cry, from the stamping of their feet, Danior guessed his words carried some ritual challenge. Jhaviir met their response with a cry of his own. And then the procession began, Jhaviir and Keva riding, Rezni bearing the bluesong on outstretched hands, Danior leading Ranslega, and Tedni jostling for position, pressing forward so insistently he stepped on Danior's heels. Rezni hissed at him without breaking stride. By the time the procession had wound its way through all the lanes of Pan-Vi, Rezni had taught Danior a number of expletives. Tedni accepted them as tribute, grinning fiercely, and pressed harder, until even Keva had difficulty repressing a pale smile.

By the time the procession reached the edge of the desert settlement, every man, woman and child marched with it. Some wore bleached robes, some only stained and soiled trousers. All wore a blue sash and a sash of another color: scarlet, gold, emerald, violet. There were knives at every waist, spears in every hand. One group of men and women hobbled separately from the others, wearing robes splashed with dried blood. "Those who have taken the enemy blade and lived to tell," Rezni informed Danior. Another group, men, women and children, carried half-burned garments. "Those who have lost a warrior since last clan-call." Their number made Danior chill, since he knew the clan assembled for call each new season.

Finally they emerged from the lanes and stood upon a shallow elevation, looking down over the gathered people. Danior peered around and saw a single small tree, its limbs severely pruned, the soil at its roots damp. There, he guessed, the bluesong would sing.

But first there was rhetoric. Jhaviir began with a long, posturing harangue that made the people mutter and stamp and glower across the barren lands. He was followed by the leader of each affiliated family-clan in turn, by impassioned citizens who simply wanted to speak, even by children who seized the opportunity to posture at the Viir-Nega's side and shout slogans. Once a girl who looked hardly old enough to be a mother urged a toddler forward. The child was so surprised to find herself standing beside the Viir-Nega's stallion that she could only stare in open-mouthed wonder. Finally Tedni coaxed her away and returned her to her mother.

Then Rezni shuffled his feet and thrust back his wiry shoulders and Danior guessed it was time for his part in the ritual. Danior glanced uneasily at the songsilk. Warmth gathered at the base of his throat, where the pairing stone rested.

Control. He drew a deep breath and exhaled it in a series of shallow pants, discharging the heat.

But when the blue sash hung in the tree, when Rezni stepped aside and the breeze caught the shimmering fabric, when the strange song began, Danior's hand rose to the pairing stone and found it warm. Trembling, his fingers closed around it. *Control.* He could dismiss the node of heat that grew in his throat. He could listen to the bluesong as everyone else did, with only his ears. But now, with the strange, bodiless voice in the air, he did not want to listen that way. The bluesong caught sunlight and breeze and created a caressing, wordless melody from them, and Danior did not want to draw back. He wanted to let the heat grow. He wanted to walk under white-limbed trees again. Sighing, he let his eyelids fall shut. The heat in his throat intensified and he extended himself, reaching beyond the robed clansmen, the glaring sun.

It was dark under the white-limbed trees. A single moon hung in the sky and Danior was alone. There was no sleek-furred form with yellow eyes, no coarser form with swollen muscles. There was only soil that yielded softly underfoot and trees. And the bluesong. He listened and it came to him from deep in the trees. It summoned, light and sound inextricably interwoven, softly beckoning. Hesitantly he experimented and found he could move toward the source of the sound.

The song did not grow louder as he approached. It simply grew sweeter, more yearning. And as he moved, Danior had a growing sense of light, although the trees remained dark. Dimly he felt Rezni's fingers dig his forearm, heard the stirring of feet, and then heard another song from the distant trees.

Not blue. This song was not blue. It was another color, brighter, lighter, trilling. Danior drew a deep breath and moved forward again until he stood looking up at a bower of bright silks. A noon-yellow length of silk reached out on the soft night breeze, casting a wordless song against the shadow. Danior stared up, spellbound, until the silk was drawn back, secured, and a dark face peered down at him from the bower.

Oblique yellow eyes, chestnut fur, delicate pink tongue licking nervously at sharp white teeth. Did the animal see him? Danior tried to raise his hand, tried to call out, could not. Somewhere high in the trees a small creature shrilled.

The yellow-eyed creature drew back until he saw only its shadow against the silk panel. It manipulated the silks, releasing a new panel. The silk rippled and sang a crimson song, sweet and brooding, deep-throated.

Caught, Danior stood under the trees and listened to songs of every color. Stood under the trees and tried without effect to raise his voice. Stood under the trees and wondered where his reaching power had brought him, what place, what world, whether it was real or fantasy. Had he reached into some untapped part of his own mind? Or did a forest like this exist somewhere, with songsilks and a creature who released them to sing in the moonlight?

The dark things—they had been unimaginably alien. How could they have come from his own mind? Remembering them, he drew back into the trees.

The dark things did not reach for him tonight. Instead the yellow-eyed creature bound the last of the colored silks to the framework of the bower and then released the single silk that had not sung. It twisted violently in the moonlight, ivory entwining itself with silver, although the breeze was mild.

And it did not sing. It spoke. It caught at moonlight, seized at breeze, and pleaded with Danior in a hard-edged masculine voice.

He didn't understand the words it used. They were of a language he had never heard before. But their pressing need was clear. The voice begged him.

And it was a voice he knew. A voice he had heard from child-hood.

A voice he had heard today.

Confused, Danior caught a deep breath and held it until the kernel of heat in his throat grew so large it threatened to choke him. The effort did not bring him any nearer the white silk. Did not make its pleading words any more comprehensible. Danior stag-gered backward, his entire chest burning. He coughed, trying to clear blocked air passages.

Quickly the forest slipped away. Trees darkened, the moon faded. But still he heard the insistent voice.

Danior shuddered, dispelling the last of the burning mass in his throat. Jhaviir stood with one hand on his shoulder, the fingers digging hard. "What did you see? Danior—what did you see?"

Danior shook his head, too shaken to speak. "I—"

"Our enemies!" Tedni hissed, trying to push between them. "Your stone burned so bright it made your face blue. You saw our enemies!"

"No. I saw—something else," he finally managed, the words painful. "A white silk. A white songsilk." He stared into Jhaviir's startled eyes, begging him to understand, to tell him what it meant, that familiar voice pleading in a foreign tongue. "Is there—do you have a white silk? Hidden?"

Tiny muscles contracted beneath Jhaviir's eyes. "I have one."

"Have you—have you ever listened to it?"

Strain was clear on Jhaviir's face now. He darted a glance at the people of the Greater Clan, who pressed near, hands on their weap-ons. "Yes. Once."

"Did you hear—your own voice?"

Jhaviir frowned, releasing Danior's shoulder. His voice was crisp. "I heard my voice. My brother's voice. Someone lost."

Lost. Distressed. Danior pressed his temples, aware that the Greater Clan watched. What had his father said? That there had been one message from Birnam Rauth since his disappearance over a century ago. A message to the effect that he was being held against his will in a place he could not describe. Danior pressed the pairing stone with testing fingers. Had the message his father heard been recorded in a songsilk? Had his father found a white songsilk

—either here or on some other world? And today—how had he reached beyond the bluesong to hear Birnam Rauth's voice? If it were Birnam Rauth's voice. The pairing stone—

He didn't understand how he had done what he had done. Perhaps he would never understand. And the people of the Greater Clan were beginning to stir, to mutter among themselves. Apparently they thought, like Tedni, that he had used the pairing stone to glimpse their enemies. Danior dropped his hands to his side. "Tell them—tell them their enemies are still sleeping," he instructed Jhaviir. "Tell them I will have to use the stone again when the sluggards have wakened. All I see now are their dreams."

Jhaviir nodded, baring his teeth appreciatively at Danior's quick recovery. "Their cowardly dreams," he amended. "And I'll add further embellishments. And later, when we are done here—"

He didn't have to complete the request. "I'll use the stone to look into their camp," Danior agreed. Surely that could be no more jarring than what he had just heard and seen.

"Yes." Jhaviir strode back to his place and raised his arms. Danior's statement and Jhaviir's embellishments rang grandly across the hard-lands. The Greater Clanspeople closed calloused hands around their weapons and shouted and stamped with derisive pleasure. Tedni beamed up at Danior.

Mercifully the next part of the ritual was a sharing of plenty. Tedni suddenly heeled away to join a group of older children. They returned carrying platters of fruit and meat and jugs of water. Danior sat gratefully and ate. Jhaviir squatted a distance apart while the clanspeople were served, solitary, his oiled face distant, unreadable.

And the sun burned down.

The sun burned down and Jhaviir resumed his oratory. Tedni returned and translated hoarsely. "He's telling them about the barohna now. About how she came all the way from the warmstream searching for him, about how she will stay so long as she is respected here, about the things she might do if we are brave enough, if we are strong enough." Tedni shot Danior a challenging gaze, his lean fingers closing on the knife at his waist. "You have seen that we are very strong here. We are very brave. And we work in our gardens."

"I've seen the gardens in your *tau,*" Danior assured him, watching the intent faces of the Greater Clan.

"Stay and you will see my very own garden. And he is telling them that he thought to give his Rauth-son—you—a token of his esteem, but no token can shine as brightly as the thought-stone." Tedni licked his lips, his gaze falling keenly on the stone. "If I am truly your brother in some degree—"

"I'll let you hold the stone. Some other time."

Tedni's eyes flashed with satisfaction as he continued his half-whispered translation. "But Keva Marlath, Flame of Marlath, has no thought-stone to blaze at her throat. She let the Zollidar steal hers so we could have eyes in the camp of the small-clans. She tricked them and they carried the stone away unsuspecting. So she has no jewel left.

"And so he is pleased to give her something that has been his own all these years, something small that comes from his heart. He gives it with the people's pledge that they will be deserving of her and of any power she chooses to exercise on their behalf. He gives it—" Tedni jerked and stared up at Danior in pain as Danior's fingers bit his forearm. "Brother—" he protested.

Danior loosened his grip, his mouth half-open in protest. Because he knew even before Jhaviir reached into his robes what he would bring forth. What he intended to give Keva, publicly, where she could not refuse it. He should have guessed sooner, but he had been distracted, only half-listening.

Did she know what it was, the carved stone wristlet he had seen on Jhaviir's wrist the night before? Did she know her mother had carried the sun in it? Had melted snow and ice from an entire valley, creating spring flood waters so deep the growing fields had to be diked to prevent the soil from washing away? Did she know the token Jhaviir bestowed upon her was one of the most powerful tools of a barohna?

Instinctively Danior rose to the balls of his feet, but a quick glance at the gathered people froze the warning in his throat. Jhaviir knew the danger as well as he did. But Jhaviir did not show the people any uncertainty. As Danior watched, clinging hard to his own composure, Rezni escorted Keva forward. Jhaviir took her arm, drawing her to him, freezing Danior with a warning glance. *Not here—say nothing here.*

Danior stared at the breathless people. His hands balled tight and his stomach turned to stone as Jhaviir first displayed the wristlet and then slid it over Keva's hand. Miraculously his hand did not even shake. And Jhaviir had lived in Valley Marlath. He knew that no fledgling barohna casually slid wristlets over her wrists for the first time while people stood near. Knew that instead she met the gem master high in the mountains to accept the wristlets he had carved and polished for her, then waited until he was an hour gone before she ever touched finger to them.

Knew that she practiced their use in solitude until she was ready to wear them among people.

Jhaviir knew the same things Danior knew. But the wristlet was in place and he held Keva's arm aloft for all to see. Danior watched in fascination as the sunstone quickly took life. Within moments the dark band became a blazing circlet of light. Keva gazed up at it, her face paling, her body sagging.

Jhaviir slipped off the wristlet and began speaking again, still holding Keva's arm. Tedni nudged Danior. "You—you're going to hold the sunstone for her. You're going to carry it," he hissed, his eyes wide. "He wants you."

Danior was so relieved to see the sunstone darken in Jhaviir's hand that he did not object. He moved forward automatically, without thinking. He hardly noticed Rezni's avid stare, hardly saw the belated tremor of Jhaviir's fingers as Jhaviir slipped the wristlet over Danior's wrist. He stared down at the stone cuff, holding his breath in brief anxiety. If it brightened for him too—

But it did not.

Slowly Danior raised his head, daring to breathe. He met Keva's eyes and saw fear and rebellion—and shocked disbelief. Gradually, through his own confusion, he became aware of a waiting silence. He looked out over the gathered clan and realized they expected him to speak.

Legend. He must be a man with a legend. Because he was Rauthson to the Viir-Nega, holder of the sunstone. Numbly he raised his wrist, exhibiting the sunstone wristlet. Tapping some reserve of nerve, he proclaimed in a carrying voice, "I accept the office of guardian of the sunstone."

Then, although no one understood his words, the people of the Greater Clan began to shout and pound their feet. Danior held his arm stiffly aloft, and hoped no one noticed the perspiration that coursed down his face and damped his robe. Unconsciously he raised his other hand and touched the pairing stone. If there was to be a testing, its time had surely come today. It had surely come now. Because he wanted nothing more, at that moment, than to turn and run. To flee the desert, to flee the fire he had seen in the sunstone, to flee the paths that continued to open before his feet—and Keva's.

TWELVE
KEVA

If her memory had once been disordered and indistinct, there were events seared there now Keva knew time could never soften. She would always remember the silent warning in her father's eyes when he slid the carved stone cuff over her arm. Would always remember her startled terror when the cuff blazed alive, the suffocating sense that she was about to be drawn so far beyond anything she understood that she would never find her way back. Would always remember Danior's bloodless pallor when her father took the band from her wrist and placed it upon his—and the moment when she understood what had so briefly circled her wrist: a barohna's fire-cuff. That was when her knees weakened and she almost fell.

But some instinct had stiffened her and she had played out her role—because what else could she do with all the Greater Clan watching? She had stood with chin high through the rest of the rhetoric, the muscles of her scalp and neck rigid and cramping. Had not even cringed when the ceremonies ended and people surged forward, shouting words she didn't understand.

There were so many other things she didn't understand that words no longer troubled her.

She didn't understand the changes that had come to her. Didn't understand the things she had done—in the forest, on the desert, today. Didn't understand how she could have come to find her father and found a barohna's fire-cuff instead.

That was what hurt most. That her father had placed the fire-cuff on her wrist before hundreds of people without telling her what it was or what he intended. As they rode back through the lanes of the settlement, she seized blindly on that wrong and tried to build a wall of anger to block out the fear and confusion that threatened to engulf her. Anger, at least, was hard and clean. The others were formless, suffocating.

But her anger was as weak as she was. She trembled, wanting only to hide—from the people who pressed around her, from the demands they made, from her own thoughts. When they neared her father's *han-tau* and he pulled Ranslega to a halt, she slid quickly from the whitemane's back before anyone could reach to help her down. "I want to be alone. I don't want to talk to anyone," she said in a half-strangled voice, and ran into the paned structure. Then, because she didn't know where else to go, she ran to the wetroom and threw herself down on the rim of the tub, giving up the effort to hold back tears.

Later, when she could cry no more, she took down a jug and drank, then splashed her face and bathed her hands and arms. Trembling, she studied the brown ring where the fire-cuff had rested against her skin. There was no blistering, no rawness, no pain. The texture of her flesh had not changed. The skin had simply darkened. She rubbed it and felt a last tear streak down her face. Would she ever again be the person she had been? Or must she always live with the feeling that she had become a stranger? The band of dark flesh seemed a stigma, one that set her apart—even from herself.

After a while dusk came. She heard subdued voices from the rest of the *han-tau*. Once the door panel folded aside and Resha peered in. When Keva did not speak, the girl dropped the panel and slipped away.

A little later Keva thought she smelled food. Her stomach contracted hungrily, but before she could decide whether to end her seclusion, the door panel was pulled aside again. A shadowed face peered in.

"You come. Come to the women's table." The words were halting, heavily accented.

Keva stood uncertainly, trying to remember the names of her father's wives. Maiya, Ramari . . . She couldn't remember the name of the third, the one she had not yet met. She hesitated. Anger, fear, confusion—everything was still fresh and painful. But she was hungry too and she couldn't hide herself in the wetroom forever. "Yes," she agreed.

The face withdrew and Keva stepped from the wetroom.

She expected to be led to the front of the *han-tau*, to the room where her father's wives ate. Instead she followed the shadowed woman down a short corridor and out a rear door. When they emerged, the woman turned, looking back uncertainly. "You come," she repeated. "Women's table."

She was little more than a girl, Keva realized, seeing her clearly for the first time. Hardly older than herself. Her face was plump, with round, anxious eyes. And she was pregnant. Keva frowned uncertainly. "Where is the women's table?" Not outside, surely.

"You come."

Keva glanced back, hesitating. Why would her father's wife lead her away from his *han-tau?* Did neighboring women eat together in some other *tau?* And why lead her anywhere so furtively, glancing anxiously back over her shoulder? She discovered quickly that it was no good to ask. The girl seemed to have only a few words of Keva's language, apparently learned by rote, and Keva had none of hers. For a moment Keva thought of turning back. But what harm could this girl offer her? Shrugging, Keva followed.

They threaded dirt lanes and the girl brought her to the back entrance of a domed *han-tau* with vividly colored panes set among the clear to form a bold pattern. Its interior was lit by a solitary lantern. Keva hesitated. The woman enjoined her to come again, then led her through darkened garden rooms to the source of the light.

A low table sat among growing vines, spread with food in glass bowls. Four platters sat at the end of the table. Silently a young woman stood from her cushion on the floor. She was years older than the girl who had led Keva here, her face harder, more weathered. Her eyes were narrow, watching. She stared openly at Keva.

"You are welcome to Rezni's *han-tau,*" a proud voice said, and Keva turned to see Resha, her half-sister, sitting at the far side of the table. "We are to eat first and then it will be time to talk."

Rezni's *han-tau?* Keva's eyes darted around the room. But she did not see Rezni. Only Resha, the pregnant girl, and the hard-faced young woman. "What—why did she bring me here?" she demanded, biting back her first impulse to indignation.

Resha drew herself up importantly. "Women's talk. They brought you for women's talk. There are matters to discuss, and I will make their words into mountain language so you can understand. But first they want to give you food."

Keva's gaze shot back to the two women. They studied her intently, straining for the words they could not understand. Rezni's wives—they could only be Rezni's wives, she realized. The wives he proposed to set aside for her. And they had summoned her here, not Rezni? What did they have to discuss with her? She shifted uneasily, but she could find no anger in their eyes. "I don't know their names," she said, stalling.

Resha flashed bright teeth. "Tinata—this is Tinata, from the family-clan Kranich," she said, presenting the plump-faced younger woman. "And Aeia, from the Baanta. Two strong families."

The two women inclined their heads, still watching intently for her response.

"Did Rezni know they were going to invite me here?"

To her surprise, Resha grinned broadly. "Oh no. He has gone to eat with his brothers. And taken his son. He has had his chance to speak. Now is their chance."

So Rezni had a son. Something else he had not mentioned. Keva sighed, realizing she would only meet prolonged argument if she tried to leave. And she was hungry. "Please tell them I'll be honored to eat here." At least neither young woman appeared angry, although the older studied her so closely it made her uncomfortable. She rubbed her wrist, then realized that Tinata was offering her a cushion. She sat.

The meal was conducted with none of the confusion of the meals she had experienced at her father's table. Tinata, Aeia and Resha served each other and addressed themselves silently to the food, eating methodically. Keva followed their example and found herself hungry for the first time since reaching the desert. As she ate, some of the emotional residue of the day dissolved. She began to feel more relaxed. Began to feel she could deal with strangeness and confusion, at least on this level.

Then the meal was done. Resha piled their platters together at the end of the table and squirmed on her cushion, her eyes flashing with expectation. In a manner that suggested ritual, Tinata and Aeia reached beneath their robes and extricated long-bladed knives. They laid these on the table before them, then turned to Keva with expectation.

The moment extended uncomfortably. "What do they want me to do?" Keva demanded finally.

"Offer your blade," Resha said. "It's part of the talking."

Part of the talking to place weapons on the table? To demonstrate trust? To show that nothing was hidden? The only blade she had ever owned was a digging blade, and that had been stolen in the forest. "I don't carry a blade," she said finally, wondering if it was the wrong thing to say. Would they take her lack of a weapon as a sign of weakness?

Resha quickly translated and to Keva's relief, all eyes turned to her with awe. Aeia spoke rapidly, her sun-chafed face intense.

"You are very strong, to need no blade," Resha translated. "But of course you are a barohna from the mountains. No other woman in these hard-lands would dare go unarmed. Tinata and Aeia are pleased to negotiate with you."

"I—" Keva groped in fresh confusion. "Please—what are we to negotiate?"

Resha's teeth flashed in a quick smile of triumph. "Tinata and Aeia wish to negotiate the matter of the marriage. Rezni came to them last night and told them they must go to his brother so he could make you first-wife of his marriage. No lesser status would be suitable and his brother is a skilled glassworker already, although he is only fifteen. He would make them a good marriage. But Tinata and Aeia have considered this proposal and have prepared a counter-offer, since the obligation cuts with two blades."

Two blades? The two blades on the table? And was Rezni so sure of himself—of her—that he had already discharged his wives? But they didn't appear angry or dispossessed. Keva pressed her temples. One thing was clear, and that was that she did not intend to become Rezni's wife. "Resha, please tell them that I don't intend to—to upset their marriage. I've told Rezni that I don't intend to become anyone's wife. I—"

"But this would be a very good alliance," Resha contended immediately, without direction from Tinata or Aeia. "We have discussed this among us, since I am your eldest sister. I am a year older than Tedni, you know, and he will be twelve this season. Tinata comes from a very strong clan. The Kranich wear the scarlet sash. You saw how many scarlet sashes were worn at clan-call. It is a powerful alliance for you. The Baanta are not so numerous, but they are very cunning. They are hard workers too. Aeia has the gift of soil-working. Everyone knows she is the best gardener in this entire quarter of Pan-Vi. No one will be hungry here. And she has already given a son to the marriage. And Tinata will give a child too, very soon."

"Yes, I see that," Keva said faintly. "I—"

"So the obligation is there, both blades. They cannot leave Rezni, since they have borne him children, and he cannot discharge them for the same reason. Not without their consent. Not even to his brother.

"And so this is what they have decided will be best. They will permit themselves to be discharged to Dari for one night, so that you may have that night to become Rezni's first-wife. Then they will reenter the marriage the following day. You will gain the rank of first-wife and strong alliances, and they will have a marriage stronger than any in the Pan-Vi. And of course there will be a feast like hasn't been seen for many seasons, since you are the Viir-Nega's eldest daughter."

Keva gazed at the two silent women, beginning to understand at last, struggling not to express her surprise in laughter. It wasn't only Rezni who proposed to marry her. Tinata and Aeia were proposing the match too, but with slightly different conditions. And Resha, as her eldest sister, felt competent to advise her. Even, from the self-importance on her lean young face, felt privileged to do so.

Keva's first inclination was to refuse immediately and unequivocally. But she had learned enough of desert ways to guess that a blunt rejection would only make her a more desirable candidate. And so she must find some other way to deal with the proposal, although she couldn't guess what that might be. "Is this the way marriages are always made in the clans?" she asked cautiously.

Resha translated quickly, then said, "This is what the principles of honor prescribe. This is how marriages are made among the Kri-Nostri, who handed down the principles of honor to the Viir-Nega. Among the small-clans the way is to steal a woman from some other clan. Aeia was stolen once, when she was very young—younger than I am—but she put the knife to him."

"She killed him?" Keva glanced uneasily at the older of Rezni's wives.

Resha nodded. "She is a Baanta. Very cunning. And Tinata—" Resha turned to the younger wife and spoke rapidly. Tinata snatched up her knife, narrowing her round eyes, and slashed at the air. Resha bobbed her head emphatically. "Tinata is very brave, even though she is not so strong as Aeia. We have already decided that Tinata will be guard-sister to you until the marriage is agreed upon. I will stay here to take her place and she will go to my father's *tau* with you. She will carry her knife for you to demonstrate the strength that will come with the marriage."

Tinata intended to guard her? When she was little more than a child herself, and clumsy with pregnancy? Keva chose her words carefully, anxious to refuse the offer gently. "Please tell her I appreciate her offer, Resha. And I appreciate the service you have done us all, by making our words clear to each other. But I—I'm used to being the oldest sister. I'm used to being the one who protects the other. I would be uncomfortable if she left her home to—to guard me."

"But it is her obligation. Everyone knows Rezni has asked you to be first-wife and that Tinata and Aeia will be proposing a counteroffer. People will say she has no principle."

"But we all know she does. It—it's obvious even to me, and I've just met her. And she should stay here. Her baby—"

"It is not due for another season."

Keva bowed her head, aware of Tinata's gaze, of Aeia's. "Is this —guarding me—part of the principles of honor?"

"It is an ancient custom the Viir-Nega brought from the Kri-Nostri. It is called the principle of *nishana nishata.* Two against the threat. Tinata will be very ashamed if you refuse her protection."

Keva shook her head, wondering how she had come to this, accepting protection from a pregnant girl? But how could she refuse and make Tinata ashamed? "I haven't even said I will join the marriage," she pointed out. "My father—"

"He will understand when he sees Tinata with you," Resha said with finality. "Everyone will understand that you are considering the marriage. And everyone will tell you the advantages."

Keva tried to argue further, but to no avail. The very fact of her reluctance made Resha argue Tinata and Aeia's proposal with greater insistence. And so Keva found herself in the lane a little later with Tinata at her side, knife ostentatiously drawn, her round young face set in what was apparently intended as an intimidating scowl.

Had it been Aeia, Keva would have shrunk from the glint of the blade. Fortunately Aeia, as first-wife, had to remain to tend the gardens. Keva rubbed her arm, grateful for that. And grateful that she had passed the early part of the evening without thinking of the fire-cuff and all the other things that troubled and confused her.

They followed a route she didn't recognize back toward her father's *han-tau.* The moons had already risen. Their light glinted from hundreds of glass panes. Lanterns glowed and growing plants cast nodding silhouettes. Keva wondered in passing where the redmane yearlings had been quartered, who was feeding them.

Then Tinata held out one arm stiffly, hissing. Keva halted and heard feet pounding in far lanes. Heard the shout of a single voice, then answering cries. Finally heard the pounding of many more feet. She turned to Tinata. "What is it?"

Tinata answered in clan-language, turning and peering down the lanes, listening intently. Then she caught Keva's arm and began to run, dragging her back the way they had come. She hissed a single word. "Yarika!" Keva could not tell, from her blazing eyes, whether she was frightened or excited.

By the time they neared the edge of the settlement, other people ran with them, and Keva heard the same cry. *"Yarika!"*

"Keva!"

Keva turned in confusion. Tedni and Danior materialized from the darkness, the stone at Danior's throat casting a faint blue radiance. "The Yarika are coming," Tedni proclaimed with a fierce grimace. "They're coming with torches to burn our maze, but we're ready for them this time. Because Danior saw them with his stone. They robbed the Zollidar and took the thought-stone, and we're ready for them. We'll cut them to meat."

Keva glanced quickly at Danior, her stomach tightening with quick fear. "You aren't going?" To fight marauding clansmen with knives? When he had no training? She was surprised at the sharpness of her reaction, but she remembered the bruising he had taken when he had challenged Rezni to spar with pikes.

He shook his head briskly. "Only to the edge of the campment."

"So he can tell us what he sees," Tedni declared. "With his stone, he doesn't even have to know the Yarika clan-language. He understands everything without knowing their speech. So he will use his stone to see what the Yarika are doing, to hear what they say among themselves, and I will pass word of what they intend to the others."

Tinata caught Keva's arm. She spoke rapidly, jabbing the air with her knife for emphasis, her round eyes blazing.

"She says that if you go to the fighting, she will go before you," Tedni translated. "She will defend you. She will show you that no one harms a wife of Rezni's *han-tau.*"

"I—"

"That is the strength of Rezni's marriage," Tedni continued. "She is of the Kranich clan, you know. Her people wear the scarlet sash. You saw at clan-call—"

How many wore the scarlet sash. Keva pressed her temples with both hands, trying to bring some order to her thoughts. Did women go to the fighting as well as men? Was she expected to go? To confront the Yarika, who had stolen the pairing stone from the Zollidar? To—but she did not want to think of it. It made gall rise in her throat.

And the excitement she saw in Tinata's flashing eyes, heard in Tedni's boasting words—how much of it was anticipation and how much fear? Her eyes darted to Danior. "My father—"

"He wants you to wait in his *tau,*" he said quickly. "He only wants to turn the Yarika back. They're one of the smallest of the small-clans. If he turns them back, the others will take the thought-stone from them. Then he will have an ear with the larger clans. The ones that are uniting against him."

"But then the others—" Keva frowned, wishing she had listened more closely the night before, when her father had talked of the small-clans.

"He wants you to go back to the *tau,*" Danior repeated.

Keva shoved her fingers through her hair. What choice did she have? Tinata was anxious to prove herself, but Keva was sure that part of the fire in her eyes was fear. For good reason. What chance did she have, clumsy with pregnancy, against skirmishing clans-men? "Tedni, tell Tinata. Tell her we aren't going to the fighting. We have to wait in my father's *tau.*"

Tedni spoke rapidly. Tinata argued briefly, her blade wavering mid-air. Then she put it away with a grumbling show of reluctance.

"She wants you to understand she only goes because the Viir-Nega orders it," Tedni said. "She wants you to know she will al-ways stand between you and the enemy. She—"

"I understand." Impulsively Keva seized Tinata's hand. "I un-derstand."

Tinata's round eyes grew. She squeezed Keva's hand, nodding eagerly. Then she turned and led the way back toward the Viir-Nega's paned hut.

No one remained but the younger children and Maiya. They bombarded Tinata with questions, the children lacerating the air with imaginary knives and taking militant stances, kicking and grunting. Isolated by her lack of common language, Keva sat on a cushion in the room where she had eaten the night before. After a while the children went to bed and the paned structure became quiet. Tinata dozed, curled up on her cushion, her eyelids quivering. Maiya came and spoke a few words Keva did not understand and disappeared.

The single lantern guttered and extinguished itself. Keva let herself fall into a peculiar, drifting state of consciousness, her thoughts wandering and vacant, as if she deliberately put away any thought of the fighting on the desert, as if she were willing to think of anything but that. Eventually those thoughts caught up with her anyway. She shivered, staring up at the stars that shone through the glass panes. Trying to shake a rising anxiety, she padded to the front door and looked out into the lane. She saw no one, heard nothing. There was only moonlight and silence.

She was about to retire again when she thought she heard the faint shrill of a redmane. She hesitated, reluctant to leave Tinata. But there seemed to be no danger here. And she knew she would not sleep. Not until her father and Danior returned. Quickly she slipped down the lane, listening for the shrill to be repeated.

She wandered randomly through the dark settlement, thinking of the desert beyond, of its vastness. Thinking of the vulnerability of glass panes and sleeping children.

Thinking of anything but her father and Rezni fighting in the dark.

The redmane shrilled again, from nearby, and she found her way to the sheep pens where they were quartered. The yearlings whickered and grunted excitedly at her approach, pushing their way through the protesting sheep to the low walls of the pens. Keva pressed their enquiring noses and rubbed their necks, laughing at their eagerness, until a small form materialized from nearby shadows and hissed at her.

She started. A girl of perhaps eight glowered up at her. The child spoke rapidly, pointing to the penned animals, gesturing forcefully. Keva frowned. Was the child telling her that she was caretaker of the yearlings? That she slept here, watching the pen? Or was she spinning some verbal extravagance? Keva nodded as if she understood and the child puffed her chest haughtily but continued to glower possessively.

Sighing, Keva turned back into the lanes. She wandered randomly for a while, until she reached the edge of the settlement and peered across the moonlight desert, her chest tightening again. Suddenly it seemed that the night had become very long, that it had been many hours since she and Tinata had heard the first warning cry. Tedni dismissed the Yarika as one of the smallest small-clans.

But that didn't make the bite of their knives any less deadly. She gazed around uneasily, wishing she knew what was happening on the desert. If she could find Danior and Tedni—

Tedni had said they would be somewhere at the edge of the settlement. Probably, she guessed, near the guard maze. She glanced around, taking her bearings, then began skirting the settlement, calling their names softly until the guard-maze loomed. She peered into its shadows. "Danior?"

No response. But somewhere in the thorny vegetation, she heard a coughing sound, a low voice. She peered into the wall of green. The moons were low now, ready to set. If she could find her way into the maze, if she could see just well enough to pick her way down its venomous corridors—

The voice she had heard before grew louder. She hesitated. "Tedni?"

"Keva?" It was Danior's voice, muffled.

"Here. I'm over here."

It was several minutes before they emerged from the maze, Danior stumbling, his face bone-pale. Tedni tried to support him, but they had hardly emerged from the maze before he fell to his knees, vomiting violently. Tedni held his shoulder, then ran to Keva.

The first thing she could think was that something had happened to her father, that Danior had seen it with his stone. "My father—" she said breathlessly. Had he been injured? Killed?

"No, no—we don't know. They're coming back. They're coming back now," Tedni said. He was as pale as Danior, shadow carving deep hollows in his lean face. "But it was bad. It was bad, sister. Danior—" He turned back, concerned. "Can you walk, brother?"

Danior took his feet shakily, his lips white. For the first time Keva noticed that he didn't wear his stone. Instead Tedni carried it, the chain spilling from one hand. Keva drew back. "What happened?" she demanded, wondering if she wanted to know. Wondering what could be so bad it had driven all the color from Danior's face.

"The man who was wearing the other stone—the man he was seeing through—" Tedni gasped, gazing up at Danior with frightened awe.

"The stone—I was there," Danior said finally in a dry croak. "I was there when they skirmished. When they fought. I was there when his brother was killed. I was there—" His voice choked away.

Keva's stomach squeezed sourly as she understood what he was trying to tell her. "You saw everything," she said in a harsh whisper. The stone had taken him to the heart of the fighting and he had seen it all.

"Everything—but I didn't just see it. I felt it. I *felt* everything." He glanced quickly at Tedni. "Those people, the small-clansmen—"

"They're animals!" Tedni spat.

Danior shook his head. "They're—no, they're not animals, Tedni. They—they know you're here, Keva. They've already heard. They think—they think the Greater Clan will push them off their ranging lands now, the lands they need to feed their sheep. They think the Greater Clan will take their women and kill their children. They—"

"Because I'm here?" Keva shrank back, not wanting to believe.

"Because—*yes*. They don't understand. That's what Jhaviir meant last night. That's what the small-clans would do if they had a barohna. They would drive the other clans off the land. Kill them. Keep only the women to breed with.

"They're hungry. That's how they live—hungry. Every bite they take means someone else has to go hungry. Every bite someone else takes means they go hungry. If they had a barohna, they would use her to drive everyone else away."

"But my father—" Her father wasn't a small-clansman. He had drawn people together, not driven them away. He had taught them to work glass and grow gardens. His people were fed.

Yet involuntarily she remembered something Rezni had said at the beginning of their journey from the forest. That if they met small-clansmen on the trek, he would cut their throats but leave their possessions undisturbed. Because stealing was against the principles of honor.

Was killing an enemy without provocation against the principles of honor? Or was the very existence of an enemy provocation enough?

"No," she said, and realized from Danior's strained look that he didn't follow her thoughts. "My father wouldn't—" He wouldn't kill the small-clansmen if he had the power to do so simply to insure the security of the Greater Clan.

"They fought," Tedni said, glancing back toward the bristling maze. "The Yarika have never fought like that. They're thieves—not soldiers. But my father couldn't drive them back. They threw themselves on his knives."

Hungry. Starving. Driven hard by a hard land. They had thrown themselves on her father's knives because they expected to die anyway. Because the Greater Clan had a barohna.

Her mouth was suddenly dry. Because she had come to find her father, people had died. She had pressed her search and now five Gothni were dead. The Yarika were dead. Probably even the Zollidar, from whom the Yarika had stolen the pairing stone. All because she had come to the Greater Clan's settlement. She licked her lips, knowing her face had grown as pale as Danior's.

And there was only one thing she could do. "When—when will my father return?" she demanded. She felt as brittle as glass in that moment, ready to shatter under the driving assault of emotion: horror, sorrow—and stronger than either of those, anger. Rising anger.

Tedni stared up at her, vertical creases appearing between his eyes. "By dawn. Maybe sooner."

Her father would return by dawn and soon after she would leave. She would go away and try to forget she had ever ridden a whitemane and heard a bluesong, had ever known a dark man with searching eyes. She would go, but not through any decision of her own. Her right to remain with her father had been taken from her. By the Yarika. By the Gothni and the Zollidar. By all the other desert clans.

Because even if her father did not intend to destroy the smallclans, even if he only intended to defend Pan-Vi, people had died because she had come here. And if she remained, more would die. Men and women. Perhaps even children as young as Tedni and Resha.

She turned, bitterness suddenly welling in her throat. "Tell my father I'll be with the redmanes," she said, and ran quickly back toward the paned settlement before Danior and Tedni could see that she cried. Before they could see the blind, burning anger behind her tears—and the helpless confusion it hid. She had come to make a search and the clans had turned it to carnage. They were hungry, they were driven—but they were driving her from her father when she had just found him.

Animals, savages—no, they were neither. And she knew she must not hate them for what they were: flawed human beings who made her responsible for their lives and their deaths. But she was flawed too, and in those moments she did hate them.

THIRTEEN

KEVA

"Keva! Keva!" Moaning, Keva groped through a barrier of fire toward her father's voice, then shuddered and tried to turn back. She didn't want to wake, even from her dreams of burning mountains. She didn't want to grapple again with everything that had happened the night before. She pressed her hands to her eyelids, resisting, but her father touched her forearm and everything came spilling back anyway. The Yarika. What Danior had seen with his stone. The people who had thrown themselves on the Greater Clan's knives. Her anger.

"Keva, you've slept on the ground. Your arms are cold as the mountain. Come—get up and I'll have Maiya warm the tub."

Sobbing, she opened her eyes. It was early morning, barely past dawn. Her father crouched beside her, barefoot. He was freshly scrubbed, dressed in spotless robe and trousers. But looking up, she saw something in his face that water could never wash away. A stain: blood. And he wore a bandage on one arm.

She pushed herself up stiffly, surprised to find Tinata curled against her, her white robe soiled. Keva dislodged her carefully and glanced around in confusion. Reluctantly she remembered coming here, to the pen where the redmanes were confined, hoping to find some reassurance in their familiar presence. Just as reluctantly she remembered she had found none. Quickly she put away the last confusion of sleep. "You're hurt."

"I have a few cuts. Some bruises. We had a hard fight."

He spoke with full gravity, and she recognized almost unwillingly that the stain in his eyes was not blood but pain. "Did you lose many from the Greater Clan?" People she had seen at clan-call yesterday, shouting and triumphant—how many were dead now?

"A few. Most of the dead were from the Yarika."

Yes, because the Yarika had come expecting to die, quickly by knife and spear or slowly, driven from their grazing lands. Her fists clenched. She turned away and caught a deep breath, trying to find strength in it. "I'm leaving," she said—quickly, because telling him that was the hardest thing she could imagine. Everything beyond would be easy. Painless.

He rocked back on his heels, his arched brows contracting with surprise. "No." The protest seemed involuntary, something that escaped despite his better judgement.

And that made it that much harder for her to go on. "Yes. I only came to find you. To find if you were alive, to tell you I was. To tell you Oki lied. And now we—we both know and I have to go. If I stay—" She shook her head, not wanting to cry again, not wanting him to see her anger, her fear, her confusion.

He laid a staying hand on her arm, but before he could argue, Tinata's round eyes flew open. Gasping, she sat and groped in the dirt. She snatched up her knife, speaking rapidly, pleadingly, to Jhaviir.

He nodded, quieting her. "Please—she wants me to tell you how ashamed she is that she guarded you so poorly," he explained. "She should never have fallen asleep and it will not happen again. Her knife will protect you even through the hours of night. She—"

"Oh, please—tell her no one else could have guarded me as well," Keva protested, wondering guiltily when Tinata had found her, how long she had slept curled uncomfortably on the bare ground. "She needs to sleep."

"She needs to bathe and eat and sleep, all those things," he agreed immediately. "And she won't do any of them without you. Come back to the *han-tau* and let us fill the tub. You can both bathe. And then we can talk, quietly. Privately."

Keva wanted to argue. But her father was already helping her to her feet, brushing at her clothes. Tinata's fingers were blue with cold. And people were gathering, men with bandaged arms, women with spears and bleak faces. This was not the time or place to talk.

She held her tongue while she and Tinata bathed, while they ate —quietly, from the women's table—while Tinata was persuaded to sleep. Then she returned to the room where they had eaten the night she arrived. Danior sat cross-legged on a cushion, the thought-stone on the table before him, the fire-cuff on one wrist. Keva hesitated, then sat beside him, surprised to see how old he looked. Years older than the youth she had met at the teaching pond just a few days ago, his face ashen, a distracted frown gouging creases between his brows.

Her father joined them soon, taking a cushion opposite them. Early morning sunlight fell through glass panes, scoring fine lines in his face, revealing a bruise near his left ear she had not noticed earlier. He studied Keva silently, rubbing his neck, as if he could stroke away fatigue. Finally he said, "I believe Danior and Tedni told you in better detail than I did about the fight we had last night."

Keva drew a deep breath, wishing she had gathered her possessions and gone the night before. Wishing she hadn't prolonged her leavetaking. Because all the things she had tried to put back were returning, rising to the surface. Her voice shook with them. "Yes. And they told me why the Yarika fought so hard. Because they thought the Greater Clan would drive them off their lands. That's —that's why I'm leaving. Because if I stay—" She stopped, catching a tremulous breath. Surely she didn't have to say more. He already knew as well as she did what would happen if she stayed. Slaughter.

His pupils narrowed. Small muscles tightened, pulling his features taut. He spoke sharply. "You're leaving because the Yarika, who have been invited to pledge themselves to the Greater Clan many times, chose the old ways instead? Because they were so frightened by the stories they heard that they used our knives to kill themselves with? They could have joined us anytime. They could have built *han-taus* among ours and taken the seed we offered them. They could have come to clan-call yesterday and shared the plenty with us."

Keva shrank, not wanting to hear him speak so harshly of the dead. "But they didn't."

"No. Because they didn't choose to live by the principles that apply here. That we don't steal. That we don't fight among ourselves. That women aren't stolen and children aren't beaten. The Yarika chose the old ways instead.

"Not because they were evil. Just because they had lived too long by the old ways to trust anyone but their own clan-mates.

"And now they have died with their clan-mates, by the old ways. They chose the time and they chose the weapons. And it has nothing to do with you. What happened last night was not your decision or mine. It was theirs."

Theirs, but a decision they would not have made under different circumstances. Keva stared at the fire-cuff on Danior's arm and felt angry tears rise in her eyes. She should have gone the night before, before he had a chance to argue with her, to confuse her further.

Her father leaned across the table, catching her hands in his, pressing them until she met his eyes. "Do you remember your mother, Keva?"

"I—I think so," she said, stiffening at the abrupt change of topic. "I remember a woman standing against fire. And not burning. I remember—" She shuddered and her voice hardened. "Oki told me about the barohnas. About the things they did when the fisher-people still lived in the mountains. About the burnings, about—" She stopped, the words drying in her throat. The anger she had felt the night before, against the Yarika, the Gothni, the other small-clans—was that what warring barohnas had felt when they unleashed their fire?

They were driving her away—the small-clans were driving her away before she even had a chance to know her father. Her hands closed to fists. She bit her lower lip.

"Oh yes, there was a period when the barohnas abused their powers. But it was very brief, Keva. Less than three centuries. And there have been twenty-three centuries of peace since. I don't think you can hold the actions of a few confused women against hundreds of women who have lived only for their people's benefit."

Confused? *She* was confused—and wherever she looked for answers, she found only more questions. Keva shook her head helplessly, trying to draw her hands from his. He would not release them. Nor would he release her eyes. "You don't understand," she said. Didn't understand the caustic anger she had felt last night, still felt today. Didn't understand how heavily the deaths of the Yarika and the Gothni weighed on her. Didn't understand how those deaths had already poisoned the desert for her. The small-clans were ready to kill because a barohna had come to the desert, yet she knew she could never be as Oki said a barohna must be. She shook her head angrily. "I'm not like a barohna. I'm not hard."

"Hard?" His brows rose sharply. "What do you mean—hard?"

"I—what happened to the Gothni. I can't stop thinking about it. I dreamed about it, last night, this morning. I remember it when—when I'm eating, when I'm bathing. I—"

Her father pressed her fingers, forcing her to meet his gaze again. "If you felt any other way, I wouldn't want you here among my people, Keva. In the mountains the people say a barohna is stone where she lives. Rock. But understand—that doesn't mean a barohna is uncaring. Unfeeling. It means that she is strong enough to hold steady against her own impulses. Strong enough never to use her power lightly, without thinking. A barohna must be hard in just that one way. She must be as firm as a rock in her control."

Keva shook her head stubbornly, remembering Par's stories of the power of the sunstone. "I—I don't think anyone has so much control." Certainly she did not.

He shrugged, releasing her hands, leaning back. He pressed one hand to his eyes and looked briefly inward. "Keva, has anyone told you how your mother died?"

"No." Hoarsely. No one had told her, she hadn't asked, and she didn't want to hear it now. Because that wasn't what they were discussing. That—

But he ignored the rebellion that crossed her face. "Then it's my privilege to tell you. There aren't so many people who know the whole story.

"Lihwa was already a barohna when I met her. A girl of fifteen trying to meet a woman's responsibilities, beginning to regret that she had assumed them so many years sooner than she need have. She went to the mountains to take her beast early, the very day she reached her first majority, and her mother lost the power of the stones almost immediately. So Lihwa had hardly two hands of days to return to the mountains and practice the use of her cuffs. Then the valley was hers to maintain, hers to govern. It became her responsibility to draw sunlight late in winter and use it to thaw the growing fields for early planting. Her responsibility to make cold summers warm. Her responsibility to hold back the frost in autumn until the crops were done. Her responsibility to make all the decisions expected of a barohna.

"The responsibility sat heavily. She began to wonder why she had gone to her beast so soon. Why she had pressed to become a barohna when she could have been a palace daughter for years longer.

"I met her in the first summer she governed the valley, the first summer I spent on Brakrath. A warm day. She wasn't needed in the valley so she went to the mountains. I had been living in the plain with the guardians, but I left and went exploring, trying to find my way in this new world. I was angry and a little lost because I wanted to return to the Kri-Nostri and it was impossible.

"I regretted a lost people, a lost culture. She regretted a lost time —the youth she had put behind too soon. That created a bond between us very quickly. We traveled together for two days, and when she went back to the valley, I went with her.

"I soon found the people of Valley Marlath weren't the Kri-Nostri, any more than the guardians had been. They were disciplined, but in an entirely different way. They had no need for a Kri-Nostri soldier and I wasn't prepared for the life they did offer. I felt that if I could not be a soldier, I was no one. I stayed for a few hands of days and left. But the bond with Lihwa had been created and I returned. I soon became her consort—her wandering consort.

"In the winter when Lihwa went to her winter palace in the peaks, I spent some of the cold-time with her. I spent more of it traveling across Brakrath, measuring myself against this world— never taking what I wanted from it because I wanted the wrong things.

"You were born in the second of the four years we had together. After your birth, Lihwa made me wear her pairing stone and take one of her wristlets each time I left, thinking they would bring me back to her. It isn't usual for a barohna to retain a mate beyond one season. But what we had was different from what most barohnas have with their mates. A permanent bond rather than a passing liaison. I wish I had honored the bond better, but I didn't know how.

"She wore the second cuff herself. It was enough for her use. She could store enough sunlight in a single cuff to do all she needed.

"We reached late winter of our fourth year. I had marked Rans-lega the year before, in the forest, and that winter I returned to the mountains with him. Lihwa had kept you with her, and the three of us spent several hands of days together in the winter palace. I was less restless than usual. It was a good time—for all of us, I think. I remember I envied my brother Iahn—Danior's father—then because he never seemed to be torn between the need to go and the desire to stay. But of course his experience before coming to Brakrath had been very different from mine.

"Then one morning we saw the smudge-pot burning in the palace plaza, signalling that the people had wakened from wintersleep. It was time for Lihwa to go for the spring thawing.

"That afternoon we walked together to Misana's Cropping, a rocky overlook two-thirds of the way down the mountain. From there Lihwa walked alone, so she could let her wristlet blaze and the people would see she was coming. The Spring Coming is one of the large celebrations in the valley. Everyone gathers on the plaza. Parents pile their children on their shoulders so they can see the barohna as she walks down the mountain, her cuffs blazing. So they can see the long cold time is over again.

"I waited on the cropping with you. The people waited in the plaza. The sun set and Lihwa walked in the dark, her wristlet blazing—blazing so brightly she seemed to walk at the center of the sun. Perhaps that's what you remember—your mother walking down the mountain that day."

Keva frowned, trying to draw the scene fully into memory. A figure silhouetted against fire, the mountain—but there was more. She remembered a cracking, grumbling sound, a shaking. And fear. Did she remember fear? "I—don't know," she said, her muscles tensing. In anticipation of what her father would tell her next? Or in memory?

Jhaviir nodded, sitting back on his cushion, seeming to withdraw into time. "I remember—every detail. The way the rocks of the cropping ground under my boots. The glint of moonlight on the snow. Ranslega's restlessness. Perhaps he felt what was coming. The mountains that cup the cultivated valleys are stable. Occasionally there are rock slides, but not often. Snow slides are far more common, particularly at that time of year. While we watched from the cropping, a mass began to move on the upper mountain. It swept down to the east of us. Swept down directly toward Lihwa."

Keva drew back, memory becoming sharper. The ground shuddering underfoot. A sense that the darkness of the mountain itself was tearing apart, that it was bearing down. And fear—yes, sharp, breathless.

"She had just fractions of a second to recognize what was happening and to decide what she must do. Just fractions of a second to find and weigh alternatives. To realize that she had enough energy stored in her cuff to turn the snow to steam. To boil it away—and scald the people waiting on the plaza. The slide was so heavy, it had caught her so near the bottom of the mountain, and there was no time for the people on the plaza to flee. And no place to flee to.

"I didn't appreciate all this at the time. I only understood later, when I had time to think. At the time I heard the avalanche, I looked up and saw moonlight on a moving mass of snow, I looked down and saw Lihwa staring up. She was too far away for me to see what was in her face. But I saw what she did. She pulled off her wristlet and threw it away. And then the snow swept down and crushed her. She must have died instantly."

"She—" Keva saw the scene so clearly it took her breath. The snow grumbling down the mountainside, the lone figure, the dying brightness of the fire-cuff. A dream . . . memory . . . reality. Something wrenched in her chest, bringing tears to her throat. "She threw it away so she wouldn't use it," she whispered.

"Yes. She was afraid that if she kept it, she would forget herself at the last instant. She would lose the control she had spent four years building and save herself."

And scald the people waiting on the plaza. Keva pressed trembling fingers to her temples, not knowing what to say. Not even sure she could speak.

Her father sat erect again, addressing her with a weighing gaze. "You know, the first night, when you came looking for me, I hoped to hear you had come looking for your mother too. I'm sorry you didn't."

Keva stared down at the table top, sorry too. Sorry she had been so eager to dissociate herself from the person she feared her mother to have been, so afraid of what she might learn that she had not troubled to ask anyone—Tehla, Danior, her father—who her mother had in truth been. A woman who ruled with fire, cruelly, or a girl just a few years older than herself, with responsibilities she had never imagined. She glanced at the fire-cuff on Danior's wrist and tried to accept what she had learned, tried to accept without guilt the fact that she had not asked sooner.

But knowing who her mother had been, how she had died, did not change what had happened since she had come to the desert. Reluctantly her thoughts turned back to the Gothni. "The men I killed—"

"There were other ways you could have dispersed them. But you had no way of knowing. And you had no one to guide you." Reaching across the table, he slipped the fire-cuff from Danior's wrist. He toyed with it, dark fingers rubbing its polished surfaces. "The man who cut this for your mother was one of the most accomplished gem masters on Brakrath. When he presented it to her, he told her it was a tool, simply a tool. One she must learn to use just as he had learned to use his stone-cutting tools. She must learn what she was capable of doing with it, must learn how to control herself in the use of it, how to use it without harming the people around her.

"All the gifts of the stones are like that. They are tools you must learn to use. But you didn't have a chance to learn before you met the Gothni. You suddenly found yourself with an ability you didn't know you possessed. An ability you had never witnessed or experienced in anyone else. It's not surprising that you didn't use it as well as you might have."

Keva sighed, gazing reluctantly at the fire-cuff. Would she ever dare touch it again? Ever dare intentionally draw the sun with it? Ever dare try to make controlled use of that and the other gifts of the stones? "I—I don't even know how the stones work," she said. "I don't understand how anyone can catch the sun in a stone."

Jhaviir nodded. Reaching into the growing beds behind him, he broke a single leaf from the vines. He placed it on the palm of his hand. "Tell me how this plant takes sunlight and water and turns them to green plant tissue. Tell me how Lihwa and I danced and laughed together in our quarters after Midsummer Fest and here you are sixteen years later, a person in your own right. Separate from either of us, although if we hadn't come together that night, you would never have existed."

"I don't know," Keva admitted. She couldn't explain any of those things.

"Neither do I know. But there is order to life and there are rules that govern its processes—and the processes of the stones as well. Someday we will understand them. The fact that we don't understand them now doesn't mean that the rules don't exist. That we can't explore them and benefit from the processes."

Danior roused himself. "You have to practice," he said. "To learn about the stones, you have to use them. If you don't, you won't learn—anything."

Keva nodded, remembering how she had called back the stones she had hurled at Rezni without knowing how she did it. How later she had managed to bring the sandstorm under control too.

But she had brought it under control too late. The Gothni were dead.

And Danior—he had used the thought-stone the night before. What had it taught him? How fear felt when it coursed through another man's body? The shadow of what he had learned was still in his eyes. She frowned, remembering Tedni's awe, his solicitude. "The man who carried the other stone—" she said impulsively, frowning.

Danior's lips twitched. He refused to meet her eyes. "He—died."

A cold hand closed on her heart. He had died while Danior held the stone that linked them. And he need not have. If she hadn't come here—

But it had been the Yarika's choice not to join the Greater Clan. His choice to live in the old way. His choice to join in the attack on her father's people.

Keva bit her lip, her thoughts running confused in every direction. If she stayed, other people would die as the Yarika had, for the same reasons. Because they knew—wrongly—that if they didn't destroy the Greater Clan, they would be driven from their lands, extinguished.

But if she didn't stay, if she left and the small-clans learned she had gone, knew there was no longer a barohna in Pan-Vi—

"If I leave," she said, groping, "what will the small-clans do?"

Her father frowned, stroking the fire-cuff absently. "Keva, the small-clans have pressed us from the beginning. They have stolen women, they have stolen goods, they have destroyed our *han-tau*— they have killed our children. If you stay, they will almost certainly join against us. Soon, I think—maybe very soon—hoping to destroy us, and you, before we grow any stronger."

"But if I leave—"

"Then they will press us too. I don't know how quickly or how hard. But they will press. They always have."

Keva touched anxious fingertips to her temples, trying to find some relief from the disorder of her thoughts. Her decision to leave the warmstream and find her father had been so simple. Her decision last night to leave the desert had been equally simple. Now it had become so complex she didn't think she could deal with it.

"Danior—what will you do?" Strangely, she realized for the first time that she didn't even know why he had come to the desert. She had accepted his presence, his company, without question. Not even wondering.

He stroked the thought-stone with one fingertip, then carefully coiled the chain around it, creating a nest of metal links. "I don't know," he said. He looked up at her and shrugged helplessly. "I don't know. I thought I would stay. But now I have to think again. Last night—"

Last night he had become old. Last night he had died in another man's mind. Keva nodded. They sat for a long time without speaking. From other parts of the *han-tau* Keva heard children's voices, smelled food cooking. Beyond the glass panes, the sun cut a slow arc. Looking up, she saw that the fine lines around her father's eyes seemed more deeply etched than they had been just a few minutes earlier. As if he contemplated a hardship more severe than any he had met before. He frowned, rubbing the back of his neck.

Finally he turned his hand palm up and rapped the table once, a gesture that seemed almost ceremonial. "Keva, we have an institution we call *tarnitse*. I won't even attempt to translate it for you. I brought it from the Kri-Nostri. When there is a decision to be made, a new project to be undertaken, and our thoughts are frayed, we go to *tarnitse* to bind the strands together again."

Something that would help her sort through confusion and deal with everything she had learned? Was it a rite—or a place? "Where would we have to go? Does it happen here—in Pan-Vi?"

"No, we've built our *tarnitse* hut south of here, over a spring. We go there and fast and take silence. The only voice allowed to speak in the hut is the voice of the water. After a while, if you listen carefully, the *tarnitse* water can tell you things you would never guess otherwise."

Keva pushed her fingers back through her hair and thought of the times she had gone to streamside to think when she was young. Certainly she needed to think now. Needed to send confusion away on the moving waters. "I'd like to go," she said.

Danior shifted and took up his pairing stone. With a decisive gesture, he placed the chain around his neck. The glowing stone nestled against his throat. "I'd like to go too."

"Of course. The traditional time to begin the journey is two hours after dawn. It's too late today, but Tedni will be honored to guide you there tomorrow. He'll know what you need and pack it." He rubbed a tired hand across his face. "And now I think we all need to sleep. Danior?"

Danior nodded and rose. Keva stood too, realizing from the ache of her muscles how little she had slept the night before, how tired she was. She accepted a handclasp from her father, then made her way to the room where Tinata slept. Her mind was brimming with images—of flying sand, of grumbling snow, of a woman who stood against fire, arms extended, reaching back to be remembered. But she had been eager to forget rather than remember. Tears wetting her eyes, she found a cushion and curled up, hoping to sleep without dreaming.

FOURTEEN
DANIOR

Danior stirred in his sleep, trying to shield his eyes from the sun that glinted off the sand. The cushion where he slept shifted against his belly as he crawled forward, one fist knotted so tightly on the handle of his knife the knuckles ached.

No. His fingers were closed around his pairing stone; he had clasped it in his sleep. Someone else's fingers ached against the bone handle of a knife. Someone he recognized as little older than himself but leaner, harder, someone whose thoughts came to him as clearly as his own even though they did not share a common language. Garrid was his name and bravado and curiosity drove him forward, crawling flat on his belly.

He wanted to run. Wanted to put the Yarika and their dead, staring eyes far behind. Uneasily he raised his head and glanced back to where their sprawled bodies lay, blood blackening the sand. His throat closed against the acid rise of fear.

But he had not come so far out of his way to turn back now. And the pendant he had taken from the dead Yarika—that would protect him. He was sure of it. He had hesitated over taking it. But the cut and polish of the stone was so shining, the workmanship of the chain so intricate, it had to be more than a simple ornament. And while it had not protected the Yarika, certainly it would protect him.

He was not a Yarika, after all, dirty and hungry and ignorant. He was a Fon-Delar, member of the largest clan on the desert and the most prosperous.

Largest, most prosperous and strongest—except for the clan that had pitched its glass tents below. The clan that had slaughtered the Yarika.

A thrill of envy made him shiver in the hot sunlight. His uncle, Kanir, was headsman of the Fon-Delar. But Kanir wasn't half so well known as the Viir-Nega—headsman of the deadliest fighters, the most skilled knifesmen on the desert! Even the women of the Viir-Nega's clan carried knives, and that doubled the clan's fighting strength. Certainly no one among the Fon-Delar would trust a woman with a weapon.

Garrid squirmed forward, remembering the night the woman his brother Pelar had stolen from the Vernica had snatched a knife and slashed Pelar's scalp, slicing off his ear. And that only because Pelar had ducked before she could drive the blade into his throat. Garrid had decided that same night that he would never steal a wife from the Vernica. Some other clan, perhaps, less savage.

And now that the time for establishing his own tent came nearer, he even toyed with the idea of arranging a ritual stealing. That would diminish his stature, certainly, but he wouldn't have to constantly guard his back. He had a few sheep of his own. He could offer those for the bride and perhaps his uncle would sponsor a wedding feast. A rich wedding feast commanded almost as much respect as a good stealing.

He had reached the thorn-maze, crawling on his belly. Cautiously Garrid took his feet and studied the thorny wall. When he found the entrance, he made his way down narrow paths cut through the woody vegetation. It would be simpler just to skirt the edges of the maze and look down on the campment from another perspective, but the dense leaves offered him cover. And there would be sentries mounted at the perimeters of the campment today, so soon after the engagement with the Yarika.

Eventually only one thickness of thorny vegetation separated him from view of the glass-paned structures of the Viir-Nega's campment. He peered through the oily leaves as he had so often before. It seemed strange to him, planting permanent tents in one place, instead of following the sheep across their ranging lands. It seemed strange, growing food plants instead of subsisting on mutton, game and forage. It seemed strange, making all the promises one had to make to live as the people of the Greater Clan lived. Promises not to go armed against each other, not to steal women, not to take from each other. Although as youngest brother, he felt a certain sympathy with that stricture, since he was always the one things were taken from.

Yes, many things seemed strange, but the glint of glass panes by sunlight fascinated him—as it always did when he detoured in this direction. The notion of burying seeds and watering them and watching brilliant green plants spring from the soil fascinated him. Unconsciously he touched the stone he had taken from the dead Yarika. That fascinated him too. He stared into it and tried to decide, from its flawless clarity, if it could be glass instead of stone, made by the craftsmen below. Craftsmen who had once been ordinary clansmen. It would be all the more valuable if that were so because then it was a token of what men could do if they just knew how.

So many things fascinated him. Sometimes when he passed this way, he stood in the maze and thought of walking into the Greater Clan's settlement with his hands in the air, signaling that he would not touch his knife, and talking with the people who lived this new way. Often he gazed down and wondered what it would be like to watch sunlight from inside one of those glass tents, to see it stained by colored panes. He wondered what it would be like to stitch a new robe and not have to surrender it to Pelar, only to get it back two seasons later torn and stained. He wondered what it would be like to wear the pendant he had found openly, with no fear it would be stolen.

New ways. But his thoughts were tinged with fear. There was no enemy so bitter as a brother abandoned. And all the men of Fon-Delar were his brothers, although the strength of the blood-tie varied. He stepped back into the maze, frowning with a new thought. Did his uncle know the Yarika were dead? Garrid frowned, wondering why they had committed themselves to an assault to the death, why they had died when they could have skirmished and run. Everyone knew the Greater Clan seldom pursued its enemies. It simply fought them back and returned to its glass campment. Weakness, Pelar said, but Garrid suspected the Greater Clan behaved so because they had found more important things to do than fight.

Creating glass from sand could be more important, once you learned the secret.

Planting seeds could be more important too.

But he dared not suggest those things to Pelar.

And the Yarika were dead. Perhaps there was something he didn't know. Something new. He had been gone for seventeen days, scouting for new range lands. He had spoken to no one but a mes-

senger for the Hensi, and that fourteen days ago. Perhaps there was
a new war he hadn't heard of.

He turned and picked his way back through the maze, concerned
now. Anxious to reach camp and learn what had happened in his
absence. He put disloyal thoughts—dangerous thoughts—behind.
But as he emerged from the maze again, he tucked the stone pendant under his robes, where no one would see it. Especially Pelar.

As Garrid started back across the desert, Danior pulled his hand
from the pairing stone and sat, pressing his temples to dispel a
momentary confusion. The Fon-Delar—one of the two large-clans
on the desert, their men respected for their bravado with knife and
spear. Rezni had told him that much. But Garrid's thoughts had
been so much less fiery than the Yarika's. He had not been filled
with hysterical fear, with the vengeful need to sink his knife.

Perhaps that would change when he heard of the barohna. And
he would hear soon if messengers were already running.

Danior found Jhaviir in one of the growing rooms, cultivating
seedlings, working with such concentration that he might have
been observing a solemn rite. He looked up at Danior's approach,
then stood when he saw Danior's expression. "Yes?"

Danior gave the news reluctantly. "Someone else has taken the
stone."

Jhaviir's fingers closed on the tined tool he used. Tension scored
vertical lines between his brows. "Tell me."

Wishing he did not have to, Danior told him what he had seen,
what he knew. When he finished, Jhaviir rocked back on his heels,
nodding thoughtfully. "A nephew of Kanir. Garrid, Pelar . . . I
don't recognize the names. But close to Kanir. So my decision to
leave the stone on the neck of the Yarika who wore it was well-
taken. We will have a well-placed ear in the camp of the Fon-Delar
when this young clansman reaches home. Tomorrow, probably, late
in the day."

Danior nodded, feeling neither triumph nor elation. How could
he when they intended to use Garrid's fascination with the glass-
working skills of the Greater Clan against his people? He pressed
his temples, wishing he could learn to use the pairing stones without developing rapport with the wearer of the other stone. Wishing
he could step coldly, impersonally into another mind and emerge
untouched. He frowned, a new thought striking him. "Do you want
me to stay here tomorrow? When Keva goes to the desert?"

"When she goes to *tarnitse?*" Jhaviir stood, brushing his hands on his robes. He paced away, picking his way thoughtfully among the seedlings. Finally he shook his head. "No. You will be traveling south and any attack that comes within the next day or two will come from the north or east. So you will be in no immediate danger. I will ask you to break *tarnitse* occasionally to monitor the stone. If there is urgent news, send Tedni with the message immediately. And follow with Keva and Tinata."

"Tinata?"

Jhaviir shrugged. "Tinata has pledged her knife to Keva."

Yes, and Danior had seen how enthusiastically Tinata's protection had been accepted. "Does Keva know she's coming?"

"She's probably guessed by now. And you—have you eaten? No? And you haven't had much chance to explore Pan-Vi either. You'll want to see the furnaces and the special nurseries where we're hybridizing seeds. Find Tedni and tell him it's time he showed you around. Then even if you never leave Brakrath, you'll have seen a bit of another world. A bit of the Kri-Nostri culture."

A bit of Kri-Nostri culture surrounded by sand and wind and hostile clansmen. But of course the Kri-Nostri culture had evolved in just such a place. Danior touched his stone and for a moment ran across the hard-lands with Garrid, hurrying to reach his people. A worm of fear grew in Garrid's stomach as he ran. Danior released the stone, feeling the same worm grow in his own stomach. But he was not afraid for his safety but for Garrid's. And there was nothing he could do. If only he could use the stone to project a plea to Garrid, to call him back to the Greater Clan's campment . . .

Fleetingly he wondered if he would be able to speak to Garrid in his own language if they met face to face. Could he use the pairing stone to tap Garrid's sense of the Fon-Delar tongue, to learn how individual words and phrases felt in his throat, on his tongue, to learn what images accompanied the sounds? If he could teach himself to speak the Fon-Delar language simply by monitoring the pairing stone—

Distracted, he went to find Tedni, who was pleased to show him how the furnace turned desert sand and its impurities to glass of many colors. Later Danior saw the carts used for hauling fire-coals from quarries located far to the west and saw the special nurseries where common desert plants were culled and bred to produce the most desirable seeds for cultivation. Tedni plunged so enthusiastically into his duties as guide that he scarcely noticed Danior's preoccupation.

Danior touched the pairing stone at intervals through the day, searching Garrid's memory for clues to the spoken language of the Fon-Delar, mouthing the words and phrases he found there. He clutched the stone when he slept, making Garrid's dreams his own. And he touched the stone again the next morning when Tedni woke him shortly after dawn. Garrid was traveling south again, running, the worm in his stomach a coiled serpent now because of what he had learned from the messenger he met at dawn. A barohna in the hard-lands, housed in the glass campment he had looked down upon yesterday. A barohna, woman fire-warrior from the mountains. His few sheep—he imagined them reduced to blackened bones and terror made his heart race. There would be no arranged stealing if he had no sheep. There would be no wedding feast. If he had no sheep, there would be nothing.

Fire-warrior. He imagined her laughing as she threw bolts of sunlight at his sheep and he ran faster.

Danior had expected some argument when Keva learned that Tinata was to go with them to the *tarnitse* hut. But she simply shrugged, accepting Tinata's company, and Danior realized she was as preoccupied as he.

They ate and made farewells and then they stepped upon the desert, Tedni leading the way, Tinata following, her dagger ostentatiously at the ready. Occasionally as they walked, Danior caught an anxious glint in her eyes, but she did not abandon her protective pose.

The *tarnitse* hut was located two hours' walk south of Pan-Vi, a small structure of dried grasses tied to a framework of sturdy poles erected directly over a small spring. A trickle of water cut a channel beneath one wall of the hut and ran briefly into the desert, a tracery of green marking its path. Danior studied the structure dubiously, wondering what he could learn here. Not to touch so deeply when he read from the stones? Not to care? Perhaps he could learn nothing. Perhaps it was impossible to use the stones and remain untouched.

"My father has instructed you what to do here," Tedni said importantly. "You are to eat now and then go into the hut when the sun is at its highest to begin the fast. Tinata and I have the office of guarding you while you listen to the water."

"Yes, he instructed us," Danior said absently. Perhaps it was impossible.

Tedni nodded with satisfaction and made a show of setting out the customary seeds and dried fruits and mutton strips.

Then the sun stood high and Danior and Keva approached the *tarnitse* hut. Danior peered through the narrow doorway. Needles of sunlight pierced the loosely thatched roof and glinted on the water that bubbled from the center of the floor. There were no furnishings, no implements or tools, no embellishments of any kind. There was only the bare floor and the slowly bubbling water.

Self-consciously Danior entered and lowered himself beside the tiny spring. Someone had pressed shards of glass into the damp soil that surrounded it, creating a tiny, jeweled basin. Keva avoided his eyes, guarding her thoughts. But he did not need the stones to guess what they were or to know the pain they brought. Was she to go or stay? There would be bloodshed either way. Bloodshed because she had come—because they had come. Sighing, he gazed around, letting his eyes grow accustomed to the dimness, trying not to feel stifled by the sense of enclosure.

He sat as Jhaviir had instructed them, cross-legged, one hand lying palm-down on each knee. He closed his eyes and let his head drop forward, making a conscious effort to empty himself, as he would have for a teaching. He breathed evenly, trying to send one troubling thought away with each measured exhalation.

But there was no teaching voice in the *tarnitse* hut. There was no voice at all. There was only the ache of his legs and the faint sound of water. And gathering heat. The early afternoon sun beat down on the hut. After a while, when his thoughts continued to drum anxiously at his awareness, Danior knelt and drank from the spring. The water was cool, faintly sweet.

But it told him nothing. Sweat ran down his back and made his skin itch. His calves and thighs began to cramp. His thoughts, he found, ran in chains, each successive thought leading to others, none new, none helpful. Remain in Pan-Vi? Hold the pairing stone through skirmish after skirmish? Follow more frightened, hungry men into death? He pressed his eyelids shut, feeling nausea rise in his throat.

Go then? Leave Jhaviir, Rezni, Tedni, the others to fight their battles unaided. Battles more fierce for the fact that he and Keva had come. Could he do that?

If only there were some alternate course, some third path. But he found none.

After a while he remembered he had promised to monitor Garrid's thoughts. Anxious to break the monotonous chain of his own thoughts, he clasped the stone and reached out. Immediately the ache of his legs changed, becoming harsher.

Garrid had run so hard he thought he would cry out from the cramps in his calves. And he saw as he limped into the campment that he need not have pushed himself. He saw that news of the barohna had already come. He knew that immediately from the air of barely repressed hysteria among the tents. Men stalked grim-faced on hurried errands, fingering their knives, thoughts of starved sheep and rent tents clear in their faces. Women gathered posses-sions and supplies, packing to flee. Children stared with hollow eyes, as frightened by the adults' fear as by what they heard of the barohna.

Garrid ran seeking his uncle, but no one could tell him where Kanir had gone. Messengers had come, and then Giddon and Sonkar of the Tyuna had come into camp with hands raised. Later delegates had come from the Pazniki and the Ternar clans too. And they had all retreated, leaders of rival clans plotting together as if they were long allies. Because—did he know?—a barohna had burned the Yarika. Had left their seared bones scattered on the desert in a pool of melted sand. Fortina and Simar—and others in the campment too—had seen the moons dim when she did it. They had been wakened by a sudden screaming darkness in the middle of the night and had known immediately that disaster was upon them all.

Disaster: a barohna serving the Greater Clan. A barohna come to drive them deeper and deeper into the hard-lands, where there was no forage—where there were only alkali beds and the skulls of wandering beasts. Garrid listened to the stories and before he reached Pelar's tent almost believed he had seen the burned bones of the Yarika himself, instead of men dead by knife and spear. Almost believed he had seen a pool of melted sand instead of glass-paned structures sitting peacefully under the midday sun.

Finally, when there were no more stories to be heard, Garrid went to Pelar's tent to scrub away the worst of the grime and to change to clean robes. Instead he lay down for a moment and fell heavily asleep, oblivious to the chaos in the campment and the ache of tortured muscles.

Danior sighed, slipping free of Garrid's mind. Certainly there were no answers there. He flexed his legs briefly, searching for a more comfortable position, and tried again to let the voice of the spring speak to him.

Nothing. Stray thoughts darted through his mind. Impressions of places and people he had never seen. Garrid's fear. His own. Unconsciously he mouthed words from Garrid's clan-language, wondering if they would be comprehensible to a Fon-Delar.

Afternoon passed and the light in the *tarnitse* hut faded with the sun. Keva passed into shadow, head bowed, eyes closed. Danior gazed at her restively, at the pinched set of her eyelids, at the tension in her jaws, and realized that she might have been in another land, for all he could guess of her thoughts. What did she hear in the water? Was she finding answers? Or was she simply hungry and stiff, as he was? He wondered a while longer, feeling empty and alone, cast out. It seemed an invasion to reach for her thoughts with the stone. But after a while he did it anyway.

Dry throat, aching back—and irresolution. Keva tried again and again to center her awareness upon the sound of the spring. Instead her thoughts scattered to every quarter and took her feelings with them. Guilt at what had happened simply because she had come to the desert. Anger when she thought of leaving her father. Fear of the fire-cuff and of her own anger. Wishful memory of a time when everything had been simpler. Danior sighed and released the stone, realizing she had found no more direction than he had.

Perhaps if he tried harder, perhaps if he reached for the voice of the water as he had reached for Keva's thoughts . . . Certainly he had nothing to lose by the effort. He bowed his head and tried again to set aside the chatter of conflicting thoughts. Deliberately he loosened tight muscles and let his head fall forward loosely. He reached out for the faint sound of the water. Reached as it bubbled its incomprehensible tongue, speaking to the earth in a language all its own.

Language. The pairing stone had taught him a language more potent than any individual tongue. He had linked his thoughts with the Yarika, he had linked them with Garrid, he had linked them with Keva, and he had learned that they all felt the same things: fear, confusion, uncertainty, anger. He had learned that those things were universal, that they drove everyone—palace son, barohna or clansman.

But what could he do with that understanding? It was useless if he sat here while the clans gathered for war. But if he went to the small-clans . . .

Startled by that half-formed thought, he pulled his head erect, staring at the darkened walls of the *tarnitse* hut. If he went to the small-clans, he could do nothing. What could he tell them when he didn't speak their tongues? But if he went to the Fon-Delar—

If he went to Garrid's clan, perhaps he could make himself understood. Perhaps he could tell them what he knew: that their fears were baseless; that Keva had not come to drive them off the desert; that the old ways and the new could live side by side. Not happily, perhaps, but bloodshed wasn't necessary.

Quickly he bowed his head again, wondering. Could he do it? With Garrid's awareness to guide him, could he coax the Fon-Delar language from his untrained tongue and throat? Could he speak to the Fon-Delar?

If he could . . . The Fon-Delar was the largest of the small-clans. They were respected—feared. If he could talk to Kanir, their headsman . . .

He rubbed his temples, trying to think clearly. By now the desert would be teeming with clansmen and messengers. But he had learned things—tricks and ploys—from the Yarika and from Garrid that would help him make his way unnoticed.

And what options did he have? To wait for the clansmen to converge on Jhaviir's settlement? Frowning, he clasped the stone again, hoping to find Garrid still sleeping.

Instead Garrid was stumbling across the desert again, trying to keep pace with his clan-brothers, his legs trembling with fatigue. The shouts of his clan-brothers were in his ears, and the shouts of the Pazniki, the Ternar, the Widebolt and the Kessermin too. Five clans, running together, their knives pledged to each other against the Viir-Nega and the barohna. Five clans—

But the things they shouted—maybe what they said of how the Gothni had died was true. But he had seen the Yarika; they had not been burned. And he had been walking on the desert at the time they died, and he had not seen the moons dim.

What if there was no barohna? What if they were running to smash the Viir-Nega's campment for no reason? What if—

Garrid stumbled and Pelar bellowed at him angrily. Quickly Garrid pulled himself up, fighting the cramping pain of his calves. How could he drop back, even if there was no barohna in the Viir-Nega's glass campment? How could he lessen himself in the eyes of his clan-brothers when he must rely upon them each day for protection, for support against the hard-lands? He seized desperately at images of burned sheep. There was no other way he could keep running.

Burned sheep, burned sheep, burned sheep . . . He synchronized the pounding of his feet to the terrifying syllables. The others synchronized their feet to different syllables. Angrier syllables. *Kill the barohna, kill the barohna, kill the barohna* . . . Garrid gasped for breath as he ran. If the tales he had heard of barohnas were true, he couldn't guess how they would accomplish that. He couldn't guess how anyone could kill a barohna. But he ran anyway to the rhythm of his own private chant, his heart bursting.

Danior broke the link, trembling, but the rhythm of running feet persisted. It pounded in his heart, heavily. And he knew he could not sit here any longer. Could not sit here waiting. He must try to reach the Fon-Delar. Try to turn them back. A hopeless cause, perhaps, but he could think of no other.

Keva had not opened her eyes. Cautiously Danior stood and moved to the door of the hut. Outside it had grown dark. He saw only the light of the first stars. Tedni and Tinata were talking in low voices. He listened until their conversation became more desultory and finally tapered to nothing.

He peered out. Tedni slept sitting upright, propped against the side of the structure. Tinata had curled up a short distance away, her knife falling loosely from her hand. He hesitated for a moment, then stepped silently from the structure.

The night air was cool. His stomach growled irritably and he was thirsty. But he decided not to risk trying to extricate food from Tedni's pouch. And he did not pause to drink. He must try to reach the Fon-Delar, try to turn them back. Try to tell them in their own tongue that their offensive against the Greater Clan was misconceived. He pressed the stone and looked at the rising stars through Garrid's eyes and took bearings. Then he began to run.

FIFTEEN
KEVA

Once or twice, as she sat in the early evening shadows of the *tarnitse* hut, Keva thought she was about to hear some soft insight, some quietly spoken direction. Once, after it had grown dark in the hut, she saw her mother's face, young, laughing. She clung to the smiling image and tried to understand how her mother could have been so many things in such a short time: a caring mate, a loving mother, a barohna—and a girl who had taken responsibility too soon and suffered its weight.

Keva was just a few years younger than Lihwa had been, but she had neither lover, child nor people. And she was afraid to touch the fire-cuff.

Worse, she couldn't even guess if courage lay in taking the fire-cuff and using it against the small-clansmen—frightened men fighting for survival—or in turning her back while her father's people fought the small-clansmen. How could she justify that kind of courage if her father died? If Rezni were wounded? If Tedni or Resha were scarred or crippled?

She sighed. She had brought her dilemma to the *tarnitse* spring and the water told her nothing.

Nor, apparently, did it speak to Danior. She opened her eyes at a faint sound and saw he had moved to the door. Surprised, she watched as he peered out for long minutes, then slipped from the hut. She hesitated, expecting to hear him speak to Tedni. When he did not, she stood stiffly and moved to the door too.

Tedni and Tinata slept. And, dimly, she saw Danior disappearing into the dark, running. She caught a startled breath. Had he learned something from the thought-stone? Was he going back to Pan-Vi to warn her father?

But if he was going to Pan-Vi, why did he run to the east, deeper into the desert, instead of south? And why was he going himself, instead of sending Tedni? Keva hesitated, watching him. He didn't move like someone simply stretching cramped muscles. He moved purposefully. And quickly. Soon she would not be able to see him at all.

She turned, gazing back toward the spring. But she had already learned there were no answers there. And it made her apprehensive to see Danior disappearing into the dark. There were clansmen on the desert and Danior carried no weapon. All he carried was the thought-stone. Deciding, she slipped from the hut and followed him.

The air was cool, the sky dusted with stars. Keva's stiff muscles welcomed activity as she ran in the direction Danior had taken. Once she thought she had lost him, but a few minutes later, stopping to catch her breath, she saw his thought-stone glow a short distance ahead.

She hesitated, wondering momentarily if she had been right to follow him. He had left secretly. He might not be pleased to her.

But if the stone had told him something, she must know too. Instinctively she called his name softly, as if the desert had ears. "Danior!"

He turned slowly, the stone fading. "Keva? You followed me."

He wasn't angry. He was dismayed. "Yes. You left without me. Where are you going?" When he shook his head and avoided her eyes, refusing to answer, she caught his arm. "Where, Danior?" What had he learned? And why keep it secret from her? Surely they could share everything now.

He licked his lips, obviously reluctant to confide. But his reluctance only made her more determined, and she refused to release his arm. Finally he drew a sighing breath and said in such a low voice she hardly understood, "To the Fon-Delar."

"The—" She stared at him, momentarily confused. The young clansman who had taken her thought-stone from the Yarika—he was a Fon-Delar. Her father had said the Fon-Delar was one of the largest clans on the desert.

She understood that much. "But—why? You don't even know where to find them. And if you did—" What did he intend? To walk into their camp unarmed? Offering what? Saying what? "You'll be killed."

He shrank from her gaze. "No. I'm going to talk to them. I can take my bearings from the stars. From the moons when they rise. I'll find Garrid and make his uncle—his uncle is headsman of the Fon-Delar—understand that they don't have to attack Pan-Vi. That you don't intend to drive them off their grazing lands. That you won't harm their flocks."

She stared at him incredulously, wishing suddenly that she had the other thought-stone, that she knew how to use it. Perhaps then she would know if he believed what he was saying. If he believed he could talk to the Fon-Delar. "You don't know their language," she protested. "You—"

"I've heard Garrid use it. I know how the words sound, how they feel on his tongue, what they mean. I—"

She drew back. He couldn't believe what he was saying: that he had learned the Fon-Delar language through the thought-stone. He had been linked with Garrid for less than two days. Had he even heard the Fon-Delar clan-language spoken aloud in that time? And to go to their camp—"They'll kill you! If you go into their camp—"

"They're not in their camp. They—Kanir had gathered four other clans. They're coming."

Coming—Keva's mouth went dry. She felt her hands begin to tremble. "Coming to attack Pan-Vi," she breathed.

"Yes. Five clans."

Including the Fon-Delar, which was almost as large as the Greater Clan. And they stood here talking. "We have to tell my father," she said quickly. "We—"

Danior frowned, hesitating. "I didn't want to wake Tedni. I was afraid he would follow me. But if you'll go back to Pan-Vi—"

Go—and leave him alone on the desert? *"No.* You're the one who has the thought-stone. You're—"

He shook his head violently. *"No!* Keva, there's no time. It took Garrid a full day to travel from Pan-Vi to the Fon-Delar camp. By the time he got there, his uncle had already heard about you. About the Yarika. The clans left the Fon-Delar campment at dusk. They'll reach Pan-Vi by dusk tomorrow. But I can catch them halfway if I travel fast enough. I can intercept them early tomorrow."

And make some doomed effort to speak to them? Using a language he had never spoken? Telling them things they would never believe? Because if the Fon-Delar had a barohna, would they want simply to live as before—quietly, without disturbing their neighbors?

No.

Then why should they believe that the Greater Clan chose to live that way?

But if she went with Danior, if she met the Fon-Delar on the desert and showed them she intended none of the things they thought—reluctantly she followed that line of thought. They would never believe Danior if he told them her father did not intend to drive the small-clans from their lands. But if she confronted them and let them return to their camps unharmed—she hesitated. There was so much she didn't understand. So many things that were unclear. Some she hadn't even thought of until these last few days. "I —I don't even know why you came to the desert," she said haltingly.

"Why?" Danior pressed his thought-stone and blue light briefly stained his fingers. "Because you were coming. You were looking for Jhaviir and you didn't know about the clans. I was afraid you would be hurt."

"And you never stopped to think you might be hurt too?"

He stared down at the ground, as if reluctant to admit a weakness. "I thought about it."

"But you came anyway." Why? If she could at least understand that—

He was long in answering. When he did speak, the words seemed to challenge her. "I wanted to learn something from you. Something—" He met her gaze and shrugged helplessly.

He had come to the desert to keep her from harm. And to learn something he couldn't name. That, she realized when he didn't go on, was the best he could tell her. "I'm coming with you," she said, knowing there was nothing else she could do.

Danior looked up at her sharply. "No. They'll try to kill you."

"That's why they're coming to Pan-Vi—to kill me."

He licked his lips anxiously. "Yes," he agreed finally, reluctantly.

"Then I'll meet them on the desert. With you." And if they would not listen to Danior, if he could not speak to them as he thought he could . . . She combed her fingers back through her hair, putting those thoughts aside. "If you won't come back to Pan-Vi, then I'm going with you."

"Your knee—" he protested.

"It's healed. I won't slow you. I'm coming, Danior." He had, after all, come with her: to protect her, to learn from her. Perhaps she had something to learn from him. Certainly it would be better than sitting beside the *tarnitse* spring, listening for a voice that never came.

He sighed heavily, accepting her company with open reluctance. He paused to take bearings again, and then they ran together. As they ran the moons rose, silvering the desert, and the air grew chill. After a while they slowed to a steady half-run. Gratefully Keva let the pounding rhythm of their feet anesthetize her against thought.

They had traveled for perhaps an hour when Danior faltered and called a halt. "Keva, there—" he said, pointing to the west.

Keva pressed one hand to her chest, gulping for breath, and peered to the west. A small arc of the horizon was tinged orange. Above it, a heavy cloud blotted out the stars. Keva's heart jumped against her ribs. "The maze." One of the small-clans had set fire to the guard-maze.

Danior's eyes glistened in the dark. "Rezni said the small-clans burn the maze every spring. It grows back."

And there was nothing they could do now if this was more than a torching of the thorn bushes. Her father had assigned sentries to the perimeter of Pan-Vi. Everyone had carried weapons this morning, even the children. If one of the small-clans had mounted an offensive, they would be turned back.

But if it were an aggregate group, several clans united—

It was useless to speculate. They ran again, covering ground so swiftly by moonlight that they seemed to glide across sand and soil. After a while Keva ran without looking at the ground, trusting instinct to keep her from stumbling. The growing ache of her muscles seemed unimportant, someone else's pain.

Later, when they stopped to rest, her legs trembled and her hands shook. She gulped dryly for breath, wishing for water. Water in any quantity, tepid, stagnant, stale. She squeezed her eyes shut and imagined food spread before her. The effort brought only a small trickle of saliva. But when Danior had monitored the stone and was ready to run again, she ran too.

The moons stood halfway up the sky when they reached a small spring, little more than an ooze of water that disappeared quickly into the soil. Kneeling, cupping their hands, they caught enough to quench their thirst and to splash their hands and faces. Then they sat back, laughing with relief. "If any of this is edible—" Keva speculated, studying the green vegetation that surrounded the spring.

Danior studied a cluster of thick stalks and uprooted one. "This is," he said, rinsing a fat white bulb in the spring. "Rezni told me about it. Peel the outer skin first." He passed the bulb to her and pulled another for himself. "And that—the grassy stuff. It stings your gums, but you can eat it. The leaves. The roots. Everything."

They made a small feast, drank again, and when they took their feet, Keva ran almost light-heartedly.

Her mood fell again when the moons set. They paused, Danior losing himself in the stone. When he released it, he was frowning. "Garrid is sleeping."

"The others—"

"I don't know if everyone has stopped for the night, or if he dropped behind." He gazed up at the darkened sky. "It's hard to plot our course without the moons. We're so close we see the stars from almost the same perspective."

That close. Unconsciously Keva raised her hand to her throat. "Danior, when we meet them—" What did he plan?

Danior rubbed an anxious hand over his forehead. "I've been practicing as we ran. He hasn't spoken much while I've been linked, but I can touch his memory. I've—I've found all the words I need there."

Words he could reproduce intelligibly? Keva remembered how Tinata had laughed when she had tried to speak a few words of the Greater Clan's language. A simple error of inflection could alter the meaning of an entire conversation. And what could Danior have learned of inflection when he had never heard the Fon-Delar langauge spoken aloud?

But it was too late to turn back. Keva studied Danior's set face and guessed it had been too late from the moment he had slipped from the *tarnitse* hut. "We may as well sleep too," she said. "Until Garrid wakes."

Danior nodded distractedly and they burrowed into the shallow drift of sand beneath a clump of dried vegetation. Danior closed his eyes, but Keva saw that the light of the thought-stone seeped from between his fingers. Was he dreaming Garrid's dreams?

Had he once dreamed hers? She wondered if it need disturb her if he had. Wondered how it felt to walk through another person's mind.

Surely it felt less lonely than living with no thoughts but her own. Tired, uneasy, she closed her own eyes and eventually slept, sand gritting against her skin.

She dreamed with haunting intensity, dreamed scenes, emotions, exchanges she realized must be long-repressed memories. Her mother climbing a rocky trail, stopping to curl snow into a ball and throw it, laughing. Another occasion: her mother's voice, raised, and her own anxiety that she had displeased her. Jealousy when her father came riding a tall animal and went to greet her mother first. Terror when the snow grumbled down the mountainside. The wordless fear that somehow she had made it fall, with her jealousy.

And incomprehension when her mother failed to brush the snow aside and continue to walk down the mountain. Incomprehension and growing fear of the silent mountains that stood witness to what she had done.

But she had not called down the snow. That was simply a child's misapprehension, one she had never realized she harbored. Until now. A *misapprehension*. Sleeping, dreaming, she examined it, saw the damage she had done herself with it, and absolved herself.

She woke at dawn, choking on unshed tears. Woke with the feeling that decisions had been reached while she slept, corners turned, changes accepted. Sitting, she glanced around. Danior was curled in the sand, his eyes pressed shut, the stone tightly clasped. She stood and brushed away sand and looked up into the rising sun. The same sun that had always looked down on this land.

The same sun barohnas had always drawn their fire from. Licking dry lips, she knelt beside Danior and studied the fire-cuff. She wondered what he would think if he could read what she was thinking now: that it was time she wore the cuff.

After a while he woke, drawing a deep breath, his eyes opening. "He's awake. Garrid's awake," he said.

"And the others?" Her voice didn't seem her own. She had made a final rapprochment with herself while she slept. Had accepted her innocence in her mother's death. Had recognized that to be angry did not mean to destroy. And in so doing, she had stepped out of herself and into some new phase of life, some new readiness. She wondered, in her new detachment, what that readiness would bring.

"They're waking too, the other Fon-Delar." Danior sat, scrubbing his face with one hand. He gazed at the sun and briefly clasped the stone again. "They're near," he said when he released it.

Near. But the clansmen had been near since the night she had killed the minx. They had been waiting unglimpsed on the horizon of her life since then. Perhaps even before. "I want the cuff," she said.

She spoke with such lack of emphasis he didn't understand at first. "They're—what?"

"I want the cuff." She wanted to wear it and feel the sun blaze at her wrist. Wear it and do what she had to do. Because that was what barohnas had always done—what they had to do. Her mother had had to throw her cuff away. Now she had to assume hers.

Danior's pupils contracted to points. His lips whitened. "You—you don't know how to use it."

Of course she didn't know how to use it. She had scarcely touched it. She permitted one fingertip to hover over its polished surface, surprised at the sense of detachment she felt. Fear, confusion, anger—all those things had dropped away, leaving only certainty. "Today I will learn to use it."

"No. I'm—I'm going to talk to them. I've learned the words I need to know. I know how to tell them that we don't intend to burn their sheep. I know—if you use the sunstone—"

She met his anguished gaze with distant surprise. After the things he and her father had told her, after the assurances they had given her, did he expect her to take the cuff and burn the Fon-Delar? Before he even made his attempt to speak with them? She frowned with a weary, detached patience. "Did you and my father lie to me? In all the things you told me about barohnas?"

He shook his head numbly. "No."

"Then I want the cuff."

He shook his head again, mouth working, but whatever argument he tried to muster would not come. She wondered abstractedly what it might be, even as she silently disallowed it. She extended her hand and let him see that she would not be denied. He licked his lips and then, with fingers that suddenly seemed very stiff, he slipped the cuff off his wrist.

It glided over Keva's fingers and seated itself on her wrist with an almost sensual coolness. Keva touched the polished surfaces with her fingertips and with catching breath felt them begin to warm. Within moments the stone cuff took fire. She held out her arm, caught by the brilliance of sunlight captured in stone. If she gazed long enough into the blaze of the stone, she realized, she might gain a vantage point from which she could look back over all her lifetime, over the lifetimes of all the women who had preceded her.

"It—it takes in light by itself," Danior said. "You don't have to do anything but wear it and it gathers in the sun, although if you want, you can make it draw faster. But to discharge the energy—"

"Yes?" His voice seemed to come from a distance. She gazed into the fiery stone and saw the world in broken images, as if she looked at many different worlds at once. The world of her mother, of her grandmother, of her great-grandmother, of the first barohna who had ever drawn the sun's fire. She wondered who that woman had been, what she had felt the first day she had captured the sun.

"You have to learn to discharge the light without burning anyone. You have to practice. You—"

Something in his tone, some agitation, briefly caught her attention. She nodded, remembering what her father had said. That her mother had had barely two hands of days to go to the mountains and practice the use of her cuffs before taking the throne from her own mother.

She did not have any days to go to the mountains. Not now. Was that why Danior kept licking his lips, why his face was so ashen? Was he afraid she would use the sunstone carelessly?

Not a baseless fear when she had no one to tell her how to take care with the sun.

Uncomfortable time passed between them, Danior frowning, biting his lip, she absently stroking the bracelet with her fingertips. Finally Danior said, "We'd better walk." His voice was pitched high with unsuccessfully repressed fright.

They walked, stopping once at a tiny spring, drinking sparingly. Danior touched the thought-stone often, frowning, muttering to himself in what Keva realized must be the Fon-Delar tongue. She wondered if he knew what he was saying or if he was just echoing something Garrid said.

The sun rose in the sky, separating itself from the horizon, becoming round and rosy-gold. They walked farther and the hair stirred at the back of her neck. She caught Danior's arm, pulling him to a halt. The western horizon was no longer a stable, dark line marking the separation of earth and sky. Instead it moved, as if in a series of slow muscular contractions. "The Fon-Delar," she said, pointing.

Danior stiffened, clasping his stone. After a moment he released it. "Yes. Keva—"

"Yes?" She asked—unnecessarily. She already knew what he was going to say.

"Don't use the cuff."

"Not unless I have to," she agreed—and saw by his face that he knew better than to ask more.

They saw after a few minutes that they needn't continue walking, that the Fon-Delar were traveling directly toward them. They halted, Danior holding himself stiffly, his features blanched, Keva gazing at him dispassionately, wondering if he would be able to speak the Fon-Delar language, wondering if he would even have the chance to do so. The fire-cuff blazed at her wrist, rivaling the newly risen sun. Looking down, she saw that the band of brown flesh had widened.

The detachment that had brought her this far began to slip when the Fon-Delar came nearer and she saw individual figures: lean men with dark hair, running. With a warning twinge, she remembered the Zollidar, who had caught and bound her before she could react, the Gothni, who had slashed the yearlings before she had realized what they intended. These men were of the same stock, hardened by a hard land. And their intent was to kill her. Could it be done? If they acted quickly enough, before she guessed they had the courage to try?

The Fon-Delar did not run in an organized phalanx. They simply surged across the sand in a wave, long knives at their waists, spears in hand. And there were hundreds of them, she saw, carried forward by the momentum of rage.

"Danior—" Involuntarily she recoiled, her voice losing body. Could the Fon-Delar stop to listen even if they wanted? If the men in the front ranks tried to halt, they would simply be pushed forward by all the hundreds behind them. And she began to see individuals now, none of them with the look of men who would stop to listen to anyone.

Yet she had to stop them. Her mind worked dizzily. She hesitated, reluctant to call the sand into the air. But was there another way?

She didn't have time to devise one. The first Fon-Delar had seen her and instead of slowing had begun to shout hoarsely. Quickly she pressed her eyes shut and caught her breath. She had only to think of a blood-mist rising in the air and the result was swift. Her throat closed, cutting off oxygen, and her lungs began to fill with that other substance. That intoxicant that drove her quickly beyond the bounds of time. She became aware of the slow surge of blood in her veins. It drummed at her ears and eddied in the large vessels of her abdomen. The running Fon-Delar slowed to a peculiar, fluid crawl.

Danior shouted something that she did not hear. Because now sand rose in a tall column. It peeled from the desert floor in sheets and spun into a towering, glistening vortex, the sharp-edged granules catching the early morning sun, glinting with its rosy light.

Keva distinguished faces among the front-runners now, dumbstruck. Sun-hardened flesh turned pasty, fiery eyes stared in startled shock, mouths gaped. Quickly Keva seized for full control of the sand and sent tendrils reaching lazily for the astonished clansmen. She set the sand upon them with calm deliberation. Because if they knew what had happened to the Gothni, if they understood the warning in the sting of sand—

Lightly. She scoured them so lightly she drew only threads of blood from sun-beaten cheeks. The nearer clansmen threw their arms before their eyes, shouting in terror.

But they kept running, driven by the men behind them, driven by their own momentum. Running with spears raised, shouting in ragged unison now. Shouting—she could not understand the words, but she knew they were directed at her.

And they did not stop running. Clansmen—they were clansmen. She would have been stopped by less than this, but what was she? A warmstream fisher-woman. She had never been hardened by hardlands and hard ways, not as these men had. "Stop!" she cried, knowing it was useless. She and Danior had miscalculated. They had come to reason with men who were beyond reason.

The first bone-tipped spear flew so close she felt its breeze on her arm. It quivered into the ground close behind her. The second skimmed her leg and Keva felt her blood rise dizzily, singing shrilly in her ears. Her first angry instinct was to call up every grain of sand within reach and scour the flesh from the men who raised spears against her. *Savages. Animals.* But she heard Danior shouting—screaming—in Fon-Delar, saw him clutching the thoughtstone, and knew she must not. She must be hard too, in a barohna's way. She must be stone where she lived—proof against her own intemperate instincts.

"Run!" she screamed to Danior, but he only stumbled a few steps backward. *"Run!"*

How could he run when spears came cutting through the glistening vortex of sand, when they buried themselves in the ground everywhere—when one buried itself in his shoulder? Keva stared, momentarily unbelieving, thinking irrationally of the small animal he and Rezni had snared when they crossed the desert. Danior's face didn't register pain or surprise. He simply staggered backward, his eyes staring in shock. His mouth worked, but she could not read the words.

Perhaps he was telling her now what he had wanted to learn from her. Why he had come here.

Perhaps he had come simply to join the loneliness of his confusion to the loneliness of hers. She spun around angrily, instinctively raising her arm to the early morning sun. It was red-gold, light and fire. It sat fat upon the horizon. Fat with the very fuel she needed.

The very fuel she must not use.

She sucked a harsh breath and drew the sun into her fire-cuff anyway. Drew it without knowing how she did so. Her heart leapt against her rib cage. Her lungs caught fire, and the cuff blazed so brightly she could hardly see the storming sand, the clansmen. Could hardly see Danior where he had fallen, blood on his robes. If he died, she would never learn to share thoughts with him. Would never escape the lonely bonds of her own mind.

She caught a second breath and held it, and her sense of time became so distorted that she looked down at Danior and saw him do a slow, writhing dance in the sand. His body rolled. His hands rose. They grappled with the spear, uselessly. His legs beat the sand —but slowly, so slowly. He stared helplessly at the fiery blaze of her fire-cuff. Then, still more slowly, he rolled to his side and pressed his face to the sand.

She spent precious moments gazing down and wondering why he tried to bury himself. After a while she guessed it was because of the blaze of her cuff. He had seen her rage and he thought it would spill over him in flames.

She knew she must not spill rage upon him. Must not spill it upon the clansmen. *Stone. She must be stone where she lived.* Almost casually she turned back and released fire at the spears that hung in the air. They burst into flames and fell in ashes. One among the front rank of clansmen burst afire too. His scream erupted slowly, a bass growl. She shuddered as the smell of burning flesh reached her and for a moment felt trapped in the very temporal distortion she had created. She had so much time here to feel the weight of her obligation. So much time to realize that she was the only one who could save the situation—and that she no more knew how to do that then she had a few minutes before.

And the clansmen kept running. Slowly, their faces torn with raw panic. Kept running because they didn't know how to save the situation either. Didn't know how to destroy the woman who burned their spears. Didn't know how to retreat. Didn't know how to do anything but continue to run, staring at the burning spears and at the gobbets of molten glass that had begun to rain around them. Because each time Keva threw fire at a spear, her fire caught the suspended sand too and melted it and liquid glass fell from the air.

She almost laughed at that. Of course! Rezni had told her, Tedni had told her, her father had told her—the panes of Pan-Vi were made from molten sand and its impurities. Now she made glass too. It rained upon the ground, and as it fell more and more heavily, the first screaming clansmen finally began to turn in flight.

Glass. Even as some clansmen fled, others took their place, bone-tipped spears drawn back to fly. *Glass.* So easily formed. The first globules were already cooling on the ground. Was there an answer in glass? If so, she must find it quickly, because Danior was bleeding. Quickly because more spears were raised.

Quickly. She caught a deep breath and let the fire-cuff blaze as she pulled sand from everywhere. Drew it into the air in thick sheets and turned her fire upon it. Turned so much fire upon so much sand that sheets of molten glass hung in the air where there had been sand. Hung fiery and bright and so hot that she felt her lips sear.

She held the sheets in place for as long as she could maintain their weight. Spears sank into them and were embedded or caught fire. A clansman who could not turn back quickly enough threw out his hands and the flesh was burned from them. Another lost his balance and toppled into the molten sheet and died in scalded silence. Others turned and ran, their robes scorched, their hair smoking.

Slowly she let the molten curtains of glass drop, folding in upon themselves until they became a thickly pleated wall. A wall to separate her from the clansmen. A wall to stop their spears, to muffle their cries. Keva exhaled and realized giddily that she had routed the clansmen. They were running, scattering back in the direction they had come. Running in total disorder.

Keva held the molten wall in place until its pleated folds began to solidify. Then she drew a deep breath and turned, uncertain what she would find.

Danior lay half-sprawled on the denuded soil, one hand pressed to his shoulder, staring at her from unbelieving eyes. His robes had fallen away in ashes. His flesh was burned dark. Even his hair seemed burned. But he stood, pushing himself to his feet, with no apparent pain.

Her flesh was burned dark too, but there was no pain and no blistering. Her hair—she raised an anxious hand to touch it, but it did not fall away in ashes. It had taken a new texture, had become coarser and duller, but it was not burned. "My hair—" she said in surprise, as if everything else—the glass wall, the vanquished clansmen—was expected, but this was not. And why did it seem that she stood taller? That her arms and legs had lengthened, that her shoulders had become broader—that even the contours of her face had altered? She raised a cautious hand and found that the lines of her face were bolder, stronger. Her eyes were more deeply set, her jaw more pronounced.

Danior watched her cautious probings and managed a half-choked laugh. "Has—has anyone ever told you the legend of Lensar and Niabi?"

"Lensar?" She did not know the name. And why did he ask her now? "No."

"The first gem master and the first barohna. I'll tell you some-day," Danior promised, his voice shaky. Experimentally he drew his hand from his shoulder. "The heat—the spear burned in my arm and sealed the wound."

She stared at the puckered wound, at the blackened flesh around it. "I don't understand," she said, suddenly light-headed. Had she really done it? Really called down the sun and turned back hundreds of screaming clansmen? She could not believe so. But the wall stood before her. She felt its heat on her arms. If only she had the other thought-stone now, if only they could portion out Danior's shock and her disbelief between them . . . She touched Danior's arm, satisfying herself that he was not blistered, not burned, that he was not at all harmed. No more than she. "Why didn't you burn? Why—why didn't I?"

"Barohnas don't burn," Danior said. "But I thought I would." He examined the dark glint of his unburned flesh, laughing with relief, then gazed the length of the wall she had created. It was striated with color, its texture rough. In places it slumped shape-lessly. "If you can do that again, when we return to Pan-Vi—"

Build a wall around the Greater Clan's settlement? To hold back the small-clansmen until the clans could come to some understanding? Until they could learn to live in peace? "I can do it," she said, imagining the wall she would make, tall and shining. A wall so long, a wall so tall. She gazed the length of the wall she had already built and she began to laugh too. She had made peace with her mother, she had made peace with herself. Now she wore a barohna's face and she could stay with her father as long as she wished. She could take all the time she needed to close the gap of years. She could take time to know her father and herself better. Time to learn how a barohna might live if she elected to remain in the hard-lands. Time. She turned back to Danior, wishing she could share her joy with him fully. Instead she could only say, "Can you walk?"

"Yes," he said, and gazed long at her, as if he understood her thoughts without even touching the stone that hung at his throat.

SIXTEEN

DANIOR

Sometimes, forgetting, Danior wore the pairing stone to bed and stepped into Keva's dreams, moving through the unfolding succession of images she used to teach herself what it meant to be a barohna. He saw sunlight fall in heavy waves, breaking and cresting and then being directed into carefully defined channels, all the wildness tamed and controlled. He watched reality melt under the blaze of the sunstone and saw how carefully, how painstakingly Keva recreated it, so that nothing was ultimately lost. He clutched the pairing stone in his sleep and shared the effort and the joy.

More often he remembered to remove the stone before he slept, just as he disciplined himself during the day to wear the stone but not to clasp it. Because there was no mutuality when he used the stone. He could hold it and move into Keva's thoughts. He could see what she saw, hear what she heard, learn what she learned. He could follow the entire complex tracery of her emotions. And he suspected that she guessed sometimes that he did so.

But he could not share with her. All the things he heard and saw during his days in Pan-Vi, all the things he learned stopped with him. He had only words to convey them to Keva. Clumsy words.

He wondered sometimes what had become of the other pairing stone. He had not touched Garrid's mind since the morning Keva had called down the sun. Danior didn't know if he had remained among the Fon-Delar or if he was among the tens of men and women who had pledged themselves to the Greater Clan after Keva routed the Fon-Delar. Didn't know if he had discarded the stone or if he kept it hidden, seldom handling it.

So he was left alone with his thoughts, and it was time to return to the valley. Time to let his parents know he had survived the first seasons of adulthood. If he left now, he could reach the valley before they left for the winter palace.

If he left now . . . But he put back thought of what else he could do when he reached the valley. Because he had not yet summoned the words to ask Keva.

Tonight. He must ask her tonight, before he left. Or not ask her at all.

"Danior?"

Sighing, he sat from the cushion where he had been napping. Tedni squatted before him, his eyes bright, anxious. Unwillingly Danior steeled himself for some demand. "Is the meal set?" He had told Jhaviir he would leave immediately after eating and walk through the night, to avoid the heat of day.

"Soon. Danior—"

Danior waited, bemused by Tedni's momentary diffidence. It wasn't like Tedni to hesitate. Certainly it wasn't like him to ask instead of cavalierly demanding. "What can I give you?" Danior said, when the demand was not forthcoming.

Tedni momentarily hooded his avid eyes. When he looked up again, he had taken on some semblance of his father's easy authority. "There is a principle among the Kri-Nostri called—called the *baldoca-baldat*. The teaching of brothers," he said. "It prescribes that if there are brothers, they teach each other and show each other what they know. If one knows a place he shows the other, as I have shown you Pan-Vi and the desert. And better than anyone else could have shown you because we are Rauth-brothers. And of course because I am my father's oldest and strongest son. Then if the other prepares to travel, if he prepares to go to places the first brother has not seen, it is his turn to teach. To show. It is an obligation of brothers."

Only the watchful narrowing of Tedni's gaze told Danior that he had described a non-existent principle. Carefully Danior sat back on the cushion. Was it so surprising Tedni wanted to come with him? Wanted a brother to show him the way across strange lands— lands he might never visit otherwise? Certainly Danior had yearned for brothers to show him across other, inner lands. "Why are you asking me so courteously?" he demanded. He had learned that he could speak to Tedni as sharply as he liked and draw little more than appreciative laughter.

But Tedni didn't laugh this time. He squirmed forward on his knees, his eyes narrowing still more intently. "To show you how much I have already learned," he said promptly. "I have heard my father say that people don't speak and behave in the same way in all the lands of Brakrath. I have heard him say he had to learn to speak and behave like a desert man before he could live here.

"So I have watched you and I have watched him during his private times, and now I have decided to show you that I can master the way of other places. Of course it shouldn't surprise you that I can learn a manner when I am eldest son of the Viir-Nega and one of his best workers and strongest soldiers."

So he had already begun trying to tailor his manner for the trip. "Of course you still have a few things to learn," Danior observed, just because it needed saying.

This time Tedni did laugh, sharply. "Of course I have things to learn. And it is your obligation to teach me, since you are my Rauth-brother. I have already packed my possessions. I want you to look at them and tell me if I have forgotten anything."

"I wonder—have you perhaps forgotten to ask your father if you can go?"

"Have you perhaps forgotten that I am twelve now," Tedni demanded promptly. "So where I go is not a matter for my father to decide. Although I am sure he will want to give me his best knife and chopping blade to carry."

He was so sure, Danior reflected, that he had probably already packed them. And he wanted to see the world: the forest, the roughlands, the plain, the mountains. Wanted to learn new manners, new ways. Wanted to grow and find his own path.

It took Danior only a moment's reflection to recognize that he wanted to show him. Wanted to teach him, brother to brother. Perhaps there were even things he could learn from Tedni. "Bring me your things," he said. "I'll see if you have forgotten anything."

Tedni jumped up and returned shortly with his pouch and pack. Examining them, Danior found he had forgotten nothing. He had not even forgotten the knife and blade he was certain his father would want him to have. And by the time he repeated their conversation to Jhaviir at the table a short time later, it had become substantially altered, with Danior waking Tedni from a sound sleep and begging him to accompany him on the long journey, with Tedni packing hastily because he saw his brother did not want to travel without him. Perhaps, in his hurry, he had even forgetfully packed some things that were not his own.

Jhaviir nodded at his tale and said only, "It is as well you packed them, first-son, because of course I want you to have them." He turned to Danior. "And there is something I want you to have before you go. Resha—bring me the chest I showed you earlier." When she jumped up and disappeared, Jhaviir cast a warning eye over the younger children, who had begun to push and squirm, then turned back to Danior again. "I wonder if Tedni expected me to be surprised, when my knife and blade and best boots disappeared into his pack two days ago. If you would rather he not accompany you—"

"No, I'll be glad of his company," Danior assured him quickly.

"Good. He's eager to broaden his understanding, and you will be a good guide. Just see that he doesn't broaden himself at anyone else's expense. And now I have a request: that when you reach Valley Terlath, you give news of me to my brother."

"Of course," Danior said. News of where Jhaviir's search had finally led him. News of a people who had learned to make the desert green. News of warring small-clans who were slowly making the first uneasy steps toward peace. He glanced at Keva, at the sunstone cuff that glowed on her wrist. He would even carry back news of a barohna living in the desert—a barohna whose father was a Rauthimage. That news held hope for his sisters.

"And will you tell him that I would welcome a visit from him?" Jhaviir continued. "We didn't have much chance to become acquainted when we were younger. The Benderzic helmet took so much of his memory that he was still trying to find his way during those first years. I managed to retain my memories, but they drove me—drove me away from the valleys. Now I think we would find much to say to each other."

"I'll tell him," Danior said, wondering if his father would leave the valley, where his memories lived around him, to visit a brother who was also part of his memory. Perhaps he would, for a season.

Perhaps one day he would have to leave, for longer.

"I'll tell him," he repeated.

Then Resha came with a metal chest, scratched and battered, alien markings on its sides. The younger children fell momentarily silent, leaning forward with flaring eyes. Jhaviir raised a warning hand against the eruption of questions and demands and opened the lid. "You must select the one you want," he said.

Danior caught his breath. The chest was filled with songsilks, a rainbow of them nestled together: azure, chartreuse, crimson, emerald, lilac.

And white. Folded among the others was a white silk like the one he had seen when he clasped his pairing stone at clan-call. A white silk he knew would speak with a familiar voice.

His father's voice. Jhaviir's voice.

Birnam Rauth's voice.

He hesitated, meeting Jhaviir's gaze. All the tempting colors, all the bright songs—could he bear to wear the white silk and hear its pleading voice instead? Could he bear to carry Birnam Rauth's message with him wherever he went?

Could he bear to leave it here, unheard? For a moment, as he hesitated, it almost seemed that Jhaviir questioned him with arched brows. Asked him silently whether he had the courage to wear the white silk—or the courage to leave it.

What if he wore it for years and never learned its secret? Never learned where Birnam Rauth was being held or by whom? Never even learned if he was still living?

But he had seen the white-stalked forest and its inhabitants. He had glimpsed the configuration of the stars through the trees. Given those details, the Arnimi might be able to consult their datafiles and tell him what world Birnam Rauth was being held on. Then, if there were a way to reach that world—

Danior considered all those things and reached his decision. He drew the white silk from the chest.

It lay smooth and cool in his hands. He licked his lips, aware of the children staring, ready to erupt into clamor. Jhaviir silenced them with a frown, watching as he unfolded the silk with trembling fingers and carefully tied it at his waist.

There was no breeze in the room, so the silk did not speak. But later, when he went on the desert, its voice would follow him. Pleading. Speaking of isolation and imprisonment in an alien tongue.

He was able to eat little, though even the youngest children urged tidbits on him from their own platters. He was too aware of the silk at his waist and of the journey before him. And too aware that he must speak to Keva soon or not at all.

He found no opportunity through the meal. He found no opportunity when he and Tedni gathered their possessions and strapped them to their backs. He found no opportunity as they walked through the lanes of Pan-Vi, with all the clanspeople carrying torches behind them. He knew then, heavily, that he should have spoken to her sooner.

They approached the great glass-wall and Jhaviir called the clanspeople to a halt. He marked the parting with a handclasp, first taking both Danior's hands in his, then taking both Tedni's. "Come back with spring, both of you," he urged. "We need good workers and strong soldiers."

Tedni, Danior saw, was suddenly overawed by the step he was taking. He turned and looked up at Danior with stricken eyes and Danior knew they must leave immediately, before he lost nerve. Danior darted an anxious glance at Keva, wishing he could speak his question here. But it was a private question and people pressed near on every side.

Apparently Keva read something from his glance. She turned to her father and said quickly, "I'm going to walk a few minutes with them. Don't wait for me."

Relieved, Danior ducked through the portal. Keva and Tedni followed. When Danior glanced back, the torches of the clan glowed through the thick, wrinkled glass of the wall, making it wink with light. Tedni turned and stared back with awe.

"Danior?" Keva urged, touching his arm.

Tensely he met her eyes. They were a barohna's eyes, far-seeing and deep. The flesh of her face and arms was burned dark from the fire she had drawn to build the glass-wall that marked the perimeter of Pan-Vi. But he had grown over the summer and stood as tall as she. And the work of the gardens had left him well-muscled. Nothing, he guessed, would ever make him feel small again.

Still he felt hesitant—as, he had learned, everyone did sometimes, even Jhaviir. Uncertain, anxious, even frightened. Perhaps he and Keva were something never seen before on Brakrath, but no new emotions had been born with them and no old ones lost. "Keva—" Unconsciously he clasped the pairing stone that hung dark at his throat. "Keva, if I ask the gem master to cut new pairing stones when I reach the valley, one for each of us—will you wear one?"

He ventured a lot with that question, he knew. He was not asking her to wear an ornament or to share an occasional thought with him. He was asking her to go where he went, to see what he saw, and to let him go always with her. He was offering to open himself to her in a way that just a short time ago had terrified him. And he was asking her to open herself in the same way.

She drew back and for a heart-stopping moment he thought she would refuse. Her hand touched her throat. She frowned. "Do you think I could use the thought-stones?"

Was that her only reluctance? Doubt? "Yes," he said. "I know you could, now. Before you didn't know your stone was anything more than a keepsake. And you wanted no part of the power of the stones. You only wanted to find your father. But now—now you've learned to use the stones. You're not afraid of them."

She nodded, slowly. "I'm not," she said.

She wasn't afraid at all, not since the night she had routed the Fon-Delar. She had learned that she could use the sun without burning, could use the stones without harming.

And apparently she wasn't afraid to share thoughts with him either. "I'll ask him then, when I reach Valley Terlath. I'll send a message by courier. He can have the stones ready next spring."

"Yes."

So the question he had hesitated over for days was that easily resolved. Danior felt a quick surge of elation. He was returning to the valley with a brother, with a stone mate, with word from his father's missing brother, and more—with a sure sense of himself. He had learned how little he needed legend. He had learned that tradition had no more meaning than he was willing to give it. He had learned to place his foot squarely on the path and to take one step after another. He had even learned not to fear where his feet would lead him.

Tonight they would lead him into the desert. Quickly he clasped Keva's hands. "Next spring," he said. "I'll come back next spring with the stones." And then neither of them would be alone again.

IAHN RAUTH-SEVEN

Word passed quickly, as it did in the valley. Two young men had been seen coming down the trail from the mountains, one of them the palace son. Two young men had been seen walking in the orchard, pausing to feed clumps of grass to the whitemane. Two young men had been seen climbing to the animal's back and riding it across the dike tops toward the stone avenues, toward the palace.

Two young men, one of them his son. Of course no one ran to meet them. That would embarrass the travelers. No one called out, but a few people looked up from their work and nodded a greeting. And Iahn went to the edge of the plaza to watch for their arrival.

His son—at first he thought the slighter one who rode behind the other was his son and he didn't recognize the tall, assured figure who pressed gently at the animal's neck to guide it. Then they came nearer and he did recognize his son—and saw from his face who he had become in the two seasons since he had gone.

Someone who knew his way and was not afraid to follow it. Someone who had come back to the valley but not to stay. Someone who had made the world his home.

And the way he wore his hair, knotted behind one ear, the sash at his waist—

The white sash that seemed to reach for the breeze—

Iahn caught his breath, recognizing the sash. He had seen one like it, years before, on another world. He had snatched it from the wreckage of an unmanned trader ship and hung it in a tree to hear it sing.

It had spoken instead, with a voice he later recognized as his own.

As Birnam Rauth's.

Later still, when he remembered the words the silk had spoken, he had gone to the Arnimi and they had translated them for him. The words . . .

"Danior," he said in greeting as Danior pulled the whitemane to a halt and dismounted. He succeeded in keeping the concern from his voice. But that meant that some of the pleasure was missing too. He sounded far more distant than he intended, far less pleased than he felt. "I'm glad you've come. We're leaving for the winter palace in two hands of days."

Danior caught his hand in a quick clasp. "I thought you would be going soon. That's why I came. This—this is my Rauth-brother, Tedni. Jhaviir's son. We're going to winter in the palace so I can teach him to cipher scrolls, and in the spring we're going back to the desert."

Jhaviir's son. His attention quickened as he glanced at the boy who slid down Firrsevrin's flank, his dark eyes glinting with barely repressed excitement. "So you have news of my brother," he said quickly.

"Yes. And his daughter. And many things."

Good news. He could tell from his tone. Danior had returned safely and he had brought good news. "Come and tell me," he said, and this time he put everything he felt into the words.

Still, as they walked toward the palace, the younger boy boasting about the exploits of the journey and about the whitemane they would mark in the forest on their return journey, he was aware of the white silk at Danior's waist. Aware of the faint sound of its voice when the breeze caught it. Aware of the words it said in its unfamiliar tongue.

I am held here, I don't know how. They keep me bound and they feed me strange substances. I can't speak, but the thoughts that leave me go somewhere. Somewhere, and I think they are recorded. If you hear them, come for me. Let me go. Set me free.

My name is Birnam Rauth and my thoughts are recorded. If you hear them, come for me.

Come for me.

Iahn frowned. Someone would have to go.

Someday someone would have to go.

STARSILK

For my own sithi,
past, present, future . . .

ONE
TSUUKA

When Tsuuka had soothed her weanlings to sleep and seen that her cubs were curled in their bower, warm in their bedding silks, she descended to the lower limbs of her tree to her solitary bower. It was the third night since she had taken song-dreams, and the barriers her mind set against the nightmares were crumbling. Dark images pressed against her eyelids, making them heavy. Painfully she stretched out on the silent-silks piled on the floor of her bower, letting the cool swaths slither across her furred limbs, and permitted herself to slip briefly into a light, dreamless sleep. Even as she dozed, she monitored the depth of her sleep, not permitting awareness to escape her entirely. Because to do so was to give herself to the nightmares that hovered at the raw edges of her fatigue.

When the moon rose and shone against the brilliant swaths that formed the walls of her bower, she shivered alert again. Rising, she pushed aside first the scarlet swath, then the amber, and stretched. Her brief sleep lingered in her limbs, a faint warmth, but fatigue still tugged at the rest of her body and the nightmares still pressed near, dark-clawed and insistent. Growling softly, she curled back into the silent-silks and groomed herself, drawing a rough tongue through her glossy chestnut fur. Carefully she cleansed away the dusty residue of the day. Moonlight made jewels of the dampness her tongue left behind.

But she could no more groom away fatigue than she had napped it away earlier. When her fur dried, the need for sleep tugged at her again, irresistibly, and she knew that this time it would not be light and dreamless. The peculiar tension that drew at her muscles was unmistakable. She knew she must take song-dreams before she slept again or she would slip into the pit of nightmare. And she hadn't even a bower-sibling to hold her as she thrashed against its black walls.

Shivering, reluctant, she rose from her bed. She slid the scarlet and amber swaths back into place, shutting out the inquiring moon, and loosened the azure songswath that was drawn tight against the framework of the bower. This was her skyswath, her bower companion, the silk she had chosen to share her closest thoughts.

The swath reached immediately for moonlight, trilling brightly, tuning its song. At the same time it uttered its ritual question, speaking softly within Tsuuka's mind. *Tsuuka? Are you Tsuuka, daughter of Mirala, sibling of Maiilin? Are you Tsuuka, mother of Dariim and Falett, Paalan and Kaliir?*

Tsuuka stretched her aching muscles, arching her fingers and toes until the black claws snicked free. *I am Tsuuka!* she cried in silent response.

Breeze caught the sky-blue swath and made it flutter, bringing rising brilliance to its audible song. Even its silent voice became more distinct. *Are you Tsuuka, hunter of the forest and the clearings? Tsuuka, who stalks so skillfully, who pounces so lightly, whose cubs and weanlings are always fat and sleek?*

I am Tsuuka! she cried again, again silently, caught between the swimming need to let her eyelids close, to let her breath grow thick and regular in her throat, and some residual resistance to the swath's induction ritual. The silk's voice was supple and sweet; it promised her what she must have. But she did not want to deliver herself to song-dreams tonight, nor any night. She did not want the helplessness they brought, however briefly.

Still what choice had she? Breeze rippled at the azure songswath, producing a softly accusing note. *If you are Tsuuka, why are my sister-silks silent? Why do you hold their harmony captive?*

At this plaint, Tsuuka's lips curled in a predator's grimace, sharp with gleaming teeth. *Why would you sing when I only want to sleep, silk? My weanlings and my cubs are in their swathings. The forest is still. Why must I free your voices when I want to rest?*

Because you know what dark things are loose among the trees, clamoring for your attention. To us they are only the thoughts that join us to the spinners and to the unseen. But to you the images they bear are nightmares, and when you grow tired they draw close around you. You must take song-dreams to rebuild the barriers of your mind.

Dark things that were only thoughts: it was the same answer she always heard, no more satisfactory tonight than on any other occasion. Irritably Tsuuka drew black claws across the captive swath. *Hear me, silk. I am Tsuuka who stretched you here, Tsuuka who can free your voice or bind it silent against the poles. Why are your thoughts nightmares to me? Why do they draw me into the pit? Why is there no way to escape but through song-dreaming? Tell me quickly, silk, before I bind you tight again.*

The silk rippled softly. *Why is the moon in the sky, my Tsuuka? Why is the wind in the trees? Do you know? Then why do our two kinds live together in the forest, you guarding the spinners from grass-pups and prickle-hides and other predators who would harm them, the spinners protecting you from the insect flyers that would sap your blood—and we delivering you from nightmares? How would you live without us? How would we live without you? This is the way of our life, as it has long been—as we have long lived it.*

The way of their life. As always there was evasion in what the silk said. There were questions left unanswered. But Tsuuka drew in her claws, reluctantly admitting the inevitability of the swath's argument. There were sithi who did not live in forest, sithi who hunted in the grasslands that stretched beyond the tall trees. They were wretched things, their bodies welted from the feeding-stings of flying insects, their coats patchy, their cubs ill-fed because the flyers so weakened them that they hunted poorly. But in the forest the spinners climbed to the flyers' high nests, where the sithi could not reach, and fed on their larvae before they could hatch. *I would not live without you and be fed upon,* she acknowledged. *I would not raise my cubs that way.*

And don't you like our songs, Tsuuka? The silk's voice had grown smug, self-satisfied. *We will sing everything that pleases you. We will sing you songs as silken as the meadows by moonlight, as majestic as the trees standing against the stars. We will sing you songs as piquant as the faces of your cubs, as soft as the fur of your weanlings. We will sing you songs to drown out the cry of your sibling as she wanders the forest.*

Tsuuka quivered unwillingly at this reminder. *My sibling doesn't live in this quarter of the forest, silk. It has been seasons since I last heard her cry in the trees. It has been seasons since I last saw her empty face and met her empty eyes.* In fact, no one but the skyswath spoke of Maiilin now. The other sithi kept silence, as if they had forgotten her name, as if they had forgotten everything about her that first day Tsuuka returned from the deep trees, crying and alone.

But Tsuuka thought of her sibling often, with aching heart. Did Maiilin listen to the silks now as she wandered the distant quarters of the forest? Did their song torment her damaged mind with loosely tethered memories of their cub days, when they had been sleek chestnut shadows darting through the meadow, laughing together, both as bright and swift and free as only Tsuuka was now? *My sibling has gone, and none of my young will be like her. All my cubs will be sleek and free,* Tsuuka protested with the insistence of fear. Because what guarantee did she have that it was true? *Sleek and free like me.*

I am sorry you grieve for your sibling still, when she bears the chains of her damaged mind in total ignorance, the silk murmured silkenly. *But we love our freedom too, Tsuuka, hunter. Hear how bright my voice is, now that you let me reach out for the light I love? Free my sisters and we will all sing for you. You are tired. The barriers of your mind have begun to crumble. We will sing songs to rebuild them, to banish the images that join us and draw you to the nightmare pit.*

Tsuuka sank back to her bed, retracting her claws. Her furred body was long, sinuous with predator grace, and her head was delicately formed, set with eyes that gleamed like yellow jewels. In them were reflected all the brilliant hues of the songswaths stretched taut upon the framework of her bower. She drew a furred hand across her eyes, acknowledging that there was no other way. She must either take song-dreams or face the nightmare pit.

Reluctantly she made her choice, the choice she always made. Then she rose and loosened the songswaths, first the scarlet and amber swaths, then the lilac and noon-yellow ones, finally the chartreuse, crimson and emerald swaths. Their voices sighed through the bower, murmuring to each other. *Sing!* she commanded, throwing herself down on the silent-silks. She closed her eyes and let her breath slowly thicken.

For a time there was only the gossiping murmur of the freed fabric, wordless, faint. Then the breeze came again, rippling at the moonwashed rainbow, and the lilac silk uttered a soft trill. The sound rose joyously, drawing response first from the yellow, then from the amber swaths. The chartreuse joined its ringing voice to theirs, and finally the darker silks, the scarlet, emerald and crimson, added their deep, clear tones.

Their sound was silken, sweet, their harmony pure. But Tsuuka snicked her claws free and drove the sharp tips into her flesh, determined to cling to some vestige of alertness. Kaliir had been restless today, her eyes too bright. She could well wake in the night. And the time was near when Dariim and Falett must choose their own tree and build their first bower. She could see encroaching maturity in the new, hard shine of their fur, in the lengthening of their limbs. Sometimes Dariim thrashed at her bedding, briefly caught in a cubdream, faint parody of the swirling night-vortices that drew in adult sithi. If Tsuuka could not respond to her young . . .

But it was already too late. The rising voices had taken possession of her. Numbness began at the base of her skull and spread along nerve passageways across her shoulders and down her back, reaching for her limbs. As the paralysis touched her arms, her claws retracted involuntarily and her hands fell. With a whimper she rolled to her back. One glossy-furred leg remained flexed. The other stretched straight. Her breath came in shallow pants. Her yellow eyes remained open and staring.

The songs the rippling swaths sang her were as promised: of forest meadows and tall trees, of hot sun by day and cool breeze by night, of the distant sound of cubs playing and the nearer sound of spinners tittering over their work. The songs were of all things Tsuuka celebrated. There was no hint of discord, no lapse of harmony.

Yet as the swaths sang, Tsuuka was aware of a single, high note that was sustained through the entire chorus. It was penetrating, barely perceptible, yet insistent, inescapable. She tried to roll her head to pinpoint its source. But paralysis was complete. She could neither focus her staring eyes nor close her sagging jaw.

Did the note come from the azure swath? From the yellow? Perhaps it came from more than one. It continued, penetrating, painful, frightening in its rapidly increasing intensity. Soon it became more than sound. It became something near-tangible that flowed into the tips of her fingers and burned along the pathways of her nervous system, twisting her body in convulsions. She uttered a helpless whimper, her arms and legs thrashing, as a sudden rush of nightmare images flashed into her awareness, the contents of a hundred torturing dreams exploding into her consciousness in a single instant.

Before they could unfold, before they could scour her raw, the penetrating note flared from the realm of sound into visibility. A thin strand of intense yellow light, it laced itself through the exploding nightmare images, brilliantly illuminating them. Then the strand blossomed with visible energy, becoming so fiercely luminescent that everything else was lost in its glare. With a silent scream, Tsuuka surrendered consciousness to the song-dream.

She slept long after that. When she woke, she sprawled gracelessly across her bed-silks, her fur still matted with perspiration. Her limbs were flaccid. But the penetrating note was gone, as were the tension and fatigue of the past few days. And the nightmares which had beckoned were gone too, banished back across the renewed barriers of her mind. As she dragged herself to a sitting position, the song of the swaths caressed her, their lyric wordless, yearning and sweet, as it had always been.

As always. And yet . . .

But she did not want to think now of evasions, of unanswered questions, of half-glimpsed realities she could never bring to full definition. Tenderly, carefully Tsuuka groomed herself in the waning moonlight. She drew her pink tongue through her wet fur, unconscious of everything but the rainbow voices. Peace infused her as she smoothed the last rumpled patch of fur back into place.

By then the moon was setting and the voices of the swaths fell to a chorus of whispers. *You are Tsuuka,* the azure swath murmured as the others ebbed into silence.

I am Tsuuka, yes.

The moon leaves and our voices dim, my Tsuuka. Did you find our song all we promised? Did it take the nightmares from your mind?

It was everything, Tsuuka responded. *I will loose you again when next the moon comes. I will listen again. As always.*

We will sing again, the swath replied. *You are Tsuuka.*

Then their voices were gone. Tsuuka rose from her bed-silks and made her way around the circular bower, drawing the silks taut against the framework of poles. When they were secure, she pushed aside the lilac and yellow swaths to watch the moon set behind the trees.

When its last rays were gone, Tsuuka paced around the bower. Her senses possessed a ringing clarity and her muscles rippled smoothly beneath the freshly groomed fur. She was primed for the day that lay ahead, a day of hunt, of play, a day of sunning herself in the clearing when her belly was full and her cubs fed. But it was not yet dawn. It was too early to leave her tree. And there were questions in her mind that she did not want to confront.

She peered around the bower restlessly, looking for occupation, and her gaze touched the one swath she had not loosened. Stretched mute against the bower poles, it was of white silk and it shone softly even without the illumination of the moon. She never released the starswath when the other swaths sang. It could not blend its voice harmoniously with theirs. She had only to loosen it and the others fell into resentful silence, refusing to continue their song.

Yet this swath did not require moonlight to sing. The light of a single star was sufficient to tune its strange voice. And the questions it raised in her mind were enough to distract her from the other, more troubling questions that sometimes disturbed her nights. Tsuuka drew her fingers down its shimmering length. The silk seemed to respond, straining at the poles to feed on the warmth of her hand.

"Do you love your freedom, silk?" Tsuuka asked aloud. This of all the silks was deaf to her thoughts. Nor could it whisper in her mind. In fact it seldom spoke in any way she understood.

Drawn taut against the poles, the swath could make no reply.

"Do you love your freedom?" Tsuuka repeated, slowly easing the tension on the white swath.

Breeze slapped at the slackened silk, whipping a wordless note, high and trembling, from the swath. At the same time the swath spoke in a second voice which fell into a lower register. The words it uttered were incomprehensible, spoken in some alien tongue, sharply articulated, crackling with urgency.

Her eyes narrowing, Tsuuka touched the pole again, giving the swath more slack. Immediately it caught the breeze and billowed, both its voices rising, one singing wordlessly, the other speaking with a strange, crackling insistence.

"You are very poorly modulated," Tsuuka suggested, running the back of her hand down the rippling silk.

Disregarding her comment, the silk sang and spoke, its words sharp-edged, cutting in their force. Occasionally the voice uttered a spate of words Tsuuka found very nearly comprehensible, as if it spoke her own language, but with faulty emphasis, the words molded too crisply, too precisely separated into individual units. Once or twice she even caught the term "sithi-hunter," the name of her kind.

Frowning, she lounged back against her silks. The starswath was a puzzle. Its song could scarcely be so called. It held no power to soothe; its power to relieve was nonexistent. Yet she had heard the copy-master speaking by the stream one night when the spinners had tied it there to air and had wished to have one of its copies for her own. Few other sithi owned them. Their voices were too harsh, the words they spoke meaningless. But Tsuuka's nights were lonely without a sibling, and the starsilk would offer distraction.

The spinners had created the silk at her request, whispering over their stick-looms, extruding the sticky substance that formed in the special glands of their throats, joining and smoothing it into a mute, glossy sheet. When the swath was completed, they hurried away to their nests carrying the mute swath and the copy-master, securely rolled, with them. What occurred there was secret. No sithi had ever seen, but Tsuuka knew it involved moonlight and breeze and a second substance produced by the spinners' throat glands, not sticky this time but watery and acrid-smelling.

Later that night the spinners had washed the new silk in the stream and hung it to dry. Its voice had filled the moon-dappled clearing beneath the trees with an incomprehensible tension, as if the developing process had wakened some slumbering spirit who protested the wrongs of a previous existence. The new silk had spoken almost as vehemently, sung almost as harshly as the copy-master, although it had not twisted so angrily against the pole, had not strained so fiercely at the knots that bound it.

Tension—there was tension in the starvoice, impatience, a frustrated desire to communicate. And the frustration was emphasized when occasionally a few words emerged in the sithi tongue, as now. *"From beyond your sun, sithi, so far beyond your sun . . ."*

How had a silk learned to speak the sithi tongue? And what did it mean, from far beyond her sun? It was another puzzle that could not be resolved. She would never know why the starswath spoke both in the sithi language and in a foreign tongue. She would never guess what it wanted to tell her so urgently.

There were many things she did not understand, among them what had happened to Maiilin that day so long ago in the heart of the trees. Tsuuka growled softly to herself, wishing that memory did not press so insistently at her mind. Despite the years that had passed, she had never been able to relegate the events of that day to forgetfulness.

The day had been warm, the air a caress against their cub-fur, and there had been something in the breeze that had challenged them, something that had reminded them they would not be cubs much longer. Maiilin had wanted to go into the grasslands that day, to hunt in the brush as their most distant ancestors had. She had wanted to run in the deep grasses, she had wanted to climb the twisted, lonely trees, she had wanted to do reckless things while the wine of spring was in their veins.

Tsuuka, always the more cautious sibling, had found a dozen reasons not to do any of those things. There were flyers in the grasslands, and she did not want to be stung. Game was sparse. And what landmarks could there be in the stretching grasses? How would they find their way back if they ran too far? And what if they met the few sithi who still lived there? Would they be hostile? Perhaps they even carried disease. She had heard they were sickly and ill-fed—and too ignorant to know they would be neither if they made their home in the forest instead of the grasslands.

Finally she had prevailed. She had persuaded Maiilin not to go to the grasslands. But she had not coaxed the restlessness from Maiilin's mood. And so she had let Maiilin tease her into venturing into the heart of the forest instead, where the trees grew so densely that sunlight hardly touched the ground. There the tree trunks were not white and dry-barked but dark and mossy. Maiilin had been there alone many times, or so she said, although their mother had warned them against it. Was Tsuuka afraid to go even once? Was Tsuuka still a milk-cub, clinging to her mother, afraid to see the mysterious things Maiilin had seen? Was Tsuuka afraid to climb the oldest trees? Afraid to look into the secret places deep in their cavernous trunks, where there were things Tsuuka could not even imagine—strange, growing things with blind eyes and half-formed limbs?

Tsuuka didn't believe everything Maiilin said. She didn't believe Maiilin had done and seen everything she claimed. Certainly she had no desire to do and see those things herself. Half-formed, growing things—she shuddered, their mother's warning clear in her mind. And although she weakened eventually and went with Maiilin, she seemed to hear her mother's admonition more distinctly with every step.

"When you go to search for your own tree, cubs, you must not go near the heart of the forest. Nor must you go there in play. Listen to me. There are things no sithi must see, and that is where they live."

Things no sithi must see? Even then, before she was old enough to hear the silks' silent-talk, Tsuuka had understood that the spinners and the songsilks joined thoughts with something called the unseen. That in fact the unseen directed the activities of the spinners and decided which silks were to be created and when. Was that what no sithi must ever see—the unseen? And if so, what was it—a blind, growing thing? Why did it hide in the heart of the trees, and why must no sithi see it?

One thing was certain. If there was something she must not see, she did not want to see it. And so when they neared the place where the trees stood tallest, Tsuuka hung back, hoping Maiilin would be cowed by her own daring. Because there was something ominous in the quiet of the deep trees. There were no bright sithi bowers here. They had left those far behind. There were no sounds of activity, although several times as they made their way farther into the shadows, Tsuuka thought she heard scurrying sounds nearby. She listened anxiously, realizing she didn't even know what game lived this deep in the trees. She had heard that spinners came here. But would spinners rattle furtively in the brush, hiding from them, when the sithi were their protectors?

Finally apprehension overcame her and she refused to go farther, despite Maiilin's chuckling scorn. She hunched down and made herself small in the shadows, leaving Maiilin to go alone to the secret places she insisted she knew.

And Maiilin did go. Tsuuka shivered miserably as her footsteps faded into the trees.

It wasn't long before Tsuuka began to hear sounds—sounds she had not heard before. Rustlings, shiftings, creakings. Did she imagine them? Did she hear them only because she was alone and frightened? Or was something moving in the shadows—in the same shadows where Maiilin had disappeared? Did the very darkness move, as if it were about to rise up and reach for her?

Suddenly Tsuuka did not want to be alone. And she did not want Maiilin to be alone, no matter how boldly she had ventured into the deepness of the trees. Because there was something there. Something . . .

But before Tsuuka could summon courage to leave her hiding place, before she could make her reluctant limbs work, she heard a sudden, shrill scream that seemed to come from many throats. Terror-struck, she shrank deeper into hiding, trembling at the thrashing sounds that came after the scream—then paralyzed by a hoarser scream that was followed in turn by the longest silence she had ever known.

She cowered, hardly able to breathe, listening with every quivering nerve for another sound, terrified for her sibling. Because although she had not recognized the first volley of screams, it seemed to her that the second scream had been Maiilin's. And now there was only silence, ominous and long. She measured it by the frightened throbbings of her heart.

Finally, when there was no sound—when there was no sound at all—she crept from hiding and picked her way through the trees in the direction Maiilin had taken. Her heart leapt so wildly she could scarcely breathe. The shadows seemed to writhe lazily behind her, half-animate.

She still remembered how small Maiilin looked, silk-bound on the carpet of leaves. She still remembered how still Maiilin lay, with the sticky strands coiled around her. They seemed to have dampened her consciousness, as if they were permeated with something that paralyzed wit and will. Tsuuka approached in open-mouthed shock. Who could have bound her sibling this way, with strings of fresh silk? Certainly not the spinners. They looked to the sithi for protection. And this silk did not smell like any silk spit by spinners. It had a pungent odor.

She would never forget the awful moments when Maiilin began to stir. Because when her sibling wakened, she did not recognize Tsuuka. Her eyes were glazed, her tongue thick, her muscles slack. And she was able to answer none of Tsuuka's questions. She only looked at Tsuuka with blank lack of recognition.

Maiilin had been able to say nothing. Quick, curious Maiilin had been silenced. Tsuuka tore the drying strands of silk with her claws, careful not to let it touch her flesh. She pleaded with Maiilin to tell her where the silk had come from, why there was a swelling wound in her left flank. But when she was freed, Maiilin only took her feet and staggered away into the stuporous shadows, groaning.

There had been something agonized in that utterance, something pleading. But Tsuuka had been able to do nothing because she had not known what was to be done. She had not even been able to coax Maiilin to come back to her. And when she had run to fetch her mother and the other adult sithi, they had refused to come. They had even refused to tell Tsuuka what was happening.

Tsuuka had not learned until later that her sibling had turned into a growler. She had not even known such a thing could happen.

She had thought the few growlers who wandered the forest were misborn, like Pitha's cubs, whose legs were twisted, or Manoo's weanlings, born blind. She had never learned otherwise because the sithi did not speak of the growlers. On that topic, a dread silence reigned.

And so she was solitary now, except for her cubs, deprived of the bower-sibling who should have shared her life, who should have hunted with her and sunned with her and raised cubs in kinship with hers. Tsuuka's jeweled eyes dulled, reflecting her growing sense of disturbance.

As if to emphasize her mood, a growler cried deep in the trees. The hoarse voice resonated ominously.

Tsuuka's ears came erect. She ran to the silken wall and pulled aside the noon-yellow swath. But did she want to see the growler? Did she want to see the coarseness of its features, the emptiness of its eyes? With a low growl, she stepped away, sliding the yellow swath back into place. Quickly she pulled the starswath taut, then loosened the azure songswath, her fingers trembling.

The swath caught the breeze immediately. Its voice drifted wispily into the chamber, light-starved. *Are you Tsuuka?*

I am Tsuuka and I am torn, she cried silently. *Sing, swath! Sing me glad again!*

For a moment there was only a silken fluttering. Then the breathy voice returned, faintly. *If you are Tsuuka . . .*

Tsuuka projected her demand forcefully the second time, urgent as the growler roared again from the trees. *I am Tsuuka and I command you to sing!*

But my sisters, the swath persisted, its voice plaintive. *My sisters are pulled mute, Tsuuka.*

Mine is a growler, lost in the far quarters of the forest! Tsuuka retorted fiercely. *And you know your sisters cannot sing when the moon is set. But there is light enough for you, skyswath. The moon has retreated beneath the horizon but there are high clouds to cast back the last of its light. So sing to me, soothe me, or I will tear you down and throw you away.*

The swath quivered. *I am no voiceless rag, to be thrown down and forgotten. I am your soul-silk.*

It will happen if you refuse me my song! There are nightmares making in my mind again, swath.

A light breeze sighed against the reluctant swath. *They are not the nightmares that stalked you earlier. These nightmares come from your thoughts, not ours. But loose me from my pole and I will sing to you, Tsuuka, my hunter.*

Tsuuka hesitated momentarily, then set her trembling hand to the pole.

The silken cloth furled free, its loose end fluttering away on the breeze. As the fabric danced, now dipping, now twisting, shadow played along its length in ever-changing patterns. The song it sang was sweet and subtle, a reflection of the light it gathered. When the growler cried again, Tsuuka scarcely heard.

Later, when she realized from the increasingly jubilant note of the swath's song that the sun lay just below the horizon, Tsuuka reeled in the swath, secured it and stretched out on her silent-silks to groom herself for the day.

Yet the troubling questions were still there, nibbling at the edges of consciousness. Why had Maiilin turned to a growler? Had she seen what no sithi was intended to see? What could that be, and what was the unseen? Tsuuka was an adult now, yet she knew little more than she had as a cub. The time was near when Dariim and Falett must leave her tree and find their own. If Maiilin had become a growler for no reason, why should not Dariim, who was much as Maiilin had been, be taken the same way? For no reason. And if there was no reason for that most fundamental event, was there a reason for anything? Or did the world unfold purposelessly around her? Was life no more than a randomly woven net of event, created without plan or care?

Tsuuka had never thought in that vein before, and she did not want to do so now, yet the questions were there. And so she was relieved when she heard Paalan and Kaliir waking, when they came tumbling into her bower to roll in her silent-silks with her, growling and feinting, distracting her from her thoughts for a while. She would be alone again, but not while the sun shone and her cubs demanded attention from her.

TWO

REYNA

It was early when Reyna woke, but the narrow slot of sky visible from her window was vivid with sunlight and there was already laughter on the plaza below. Reyna lay staring at her ceiling, trying to warm herself to the day. In a few hours the first feast of the new season would begin, and at dusk it would be wood-smoke time. The women had already built pyramids of logs on the plaza, and the children were bringing sticks and twigs to add to them. Reyna could hear their shrieks when occasionally a pyre swayed or tottered under their ministrations. She could smell the festival breads too, baking in the kitchens, and she knew that in the stonehalls, her agemates were crouched over their work tables, stitching with anxious fingers. This was the year and season of their second majority, of full adulthood. Today they were permitted to add their first stitches to the family gowns, and tonight was their first night to dance while wood-fires burned.

Reluctantly Reyna pushed aside her coverlet and went to the window, leaning bare arms on the rough stone sill. Last year she and Aberra had watched the dancing together from the shadows of the plaza. They had tasted the husky fragrance of the smoke and watched their parents as they moved among the other gowned dancers, firelight glancing off the dark planes of their faces. Danior had danced too, a third tall, dark figure among the sturdy, white-haired people of the halls.

That had been last year. This year everything had changed. Danior, their brother, had gone away soon after wood-smoke night last year, and they had heard nothing from him until he returned at harvest time with a mate, a lean-limbed desert woman who wore a double-edged blade at her waist even when she sat to eat. They had stayed just long enough for Reyna to guess she would never learn to bear Tiva's black-eyed gaze easily. Then they had ridden back to the desert.

More disturbing, when Danior and Tiva had gone, her father had gone with them—and for no apparent reason. Reyna knew that he and her mother had argued. She had heard words from the chamber they shared, late at night. And there had been silences at the dining table, while they sat staring at their plates and eating little. Reyna had found it unsettling to have tension between them when each had guarded the other's interests so vigilantly for so long. Reyna had wondered uneasily if they would find some resolution to their disagreement or if they must go to Juris Minossa for mediation.

They had done neither of those things. Instead one day her father had announced that he intended to ride with Danior to visit his brother Jhaviir in the desert. He wanted to see the glass-paned city the desert people were building there, he said, where so recently there had been little but sand and scorched brush. He wanted to know more about the customs and languages of the desert clans. He wanted to see the changes his brother was bringing to the region. He would record what he saw and send messages to Reyna and Aberra often. And one day, when he had seen enough, he would return to Valley Terlath.

Those were the things he had said. But there had been something different behind his words, something he had tried carefully to conceal. Reyna had glimpsed it briefly before he rode away: some injury, some grief. Uneasily she had tried to guess its origin, without success. And since she didn't know why her father had gone, she couldn't guess when he would return. Sometimes when she glanced over the two brief messages he had sent, she thought perhaps he would not.

And if that weren't enough—

But she didn't want to think about Aberra now. The morning was warm, and it was wood-smoke day—time to put away grief. Turning quickly, Reyna pulled on her shift and hurried from the chamber.

There was no mistaking the excitement in the corridors. Sweepers wielded their brooms carelessly, laughing and jostling. Apprentices scampered aimlessly. A crew of stalklamp trimmers had left their barrow unattended. It was heaped with glowing vines. The mingled smells of festival foods baking floated in the air. Reyna nodded briefly to Nivan, her mother's personal runner, and hurried to the stairs, suddenly hungry.

She had hoped to find people in the dining hall, still breakfasting at the long tables. The empty chairs at her own table disturbed her less when other chairs were full. But this morning the hall was empty except for a clutch of herders. They addressed themselves silently to their morning meal, their faces ruddy from the sun. Reyna filled her platter from the serving table and sat watching them, her appetite slowly slipping away. Because her thoughts followed an inevitable course as she gazed at the herders.

They went to the mountain just as Aberra had gone. They went striding up its rocky flanks each spring with their herds, carrying a pike and a pack—the same things Aberra had carried. Through the grazing season, they met all the perils of the mountain. Sometimes they even met its beasts, although not intentionally. They did not seek out the breeterlik, the crag-charger, the minx, as Aberra had gone to do.

Sometimes they met them anyway. But the herders had come back for wood-smoke night. And Aberra—

Aberra had not come back. Quickly Reyna pushed back her chair, unable to sit longer at the empty table. She wasn't crying. She had finished with that days ago. But her stomach had turned sour and there was a lump in her throat—familiar manifestations. If only she could eat without looking at Aberra's empty chair, if only she could climb to the tower without listening for Aberra's footstep behind her, if only she could cipher without expecting to glance up at the sound of Aberra's voice, if only she could learn to do those things—

She had not learned yet and Aberra had been gone for nineteen days. Reyna stood, clumsily, almost spilling her drink, and bolted from the dining hall. She moved blindly through the corridors, wondering how long would it be before she could turn and not expect to see Aberra beside her? How long before she could speak and not expect Aberra to answer? And why hadn't she guessed, that morning when Aberra had failed to join her in the scribing room, that she was going to the mountain? Why hadn't she guessed, after the winter's clumsy sparring matches, after the spring evenings when Aberra had left her dinner untouched and bolted herself into her chambers, after the mornings when she had emerged looking as if she had not slept, that she was preparing herself to go? That she was preparing herself to track down one of the great beasts of the mountain and confront it with only a pike, hoping to kill it and return to the valley with all the changes of a barohna upon her?

Certainly Reyna had recognized Aberra's fear. And she had recognized the sparse preparations Aberra made for her challenge. But she had never thought ahead to the day when Aberra would conquer her fear and go.

Or had she conquered it? Perhaps it was fear that had finally driven her to go. Certainly she had left the dining table and, with no word to anyone, taken up her pike and pack, and gone. Simply gone, walking pale and remote down stone avenues, through the orchard, up the flank of the mountain. Word came swiftly back, carried by breathless orchard monitors, that the eldest daughter was going to meet her challenge. Reyna had heard and run after her, cold, disbelieving, first the stone pavement, then the soil of the orchards unreal beneath her pounding boots. Aberra had gone—without making her formal parting from their mother. Without asking Reyna to walk to the trees with her. Without imparting the things an older daughter traditionally imparted to a younger one when she left to make her challenge. Aberra had gone, abrogating every tradition of a palace daughter's leave-taking.

Reyna could not believe it. But when she reached the orchard, the children who had come to pollinate the blossoms stood staring up the flank of the mountain, their pollen brushes forgotten. Reyna looked where they looked, and far above she saw a speck of white: Aberra's shift.

Then she believed it, although at first she nourished the closely guarded hope that she was mistaken, that Aberra had not gone so abruptly, so poorly prepared, to make her challenge. That she had gone for a day's walk, not to meet her beast.

But Aberra had not returned that night or the next morning. No one had heard of her since.

Afraid of the fear, the old people had said, and Reyna recognized that it was true. Aberra had never been bold. Her spirit had been as fragile as her body. She had never liked rough games or frightening tales. Because she was afraid, she had waited seasons past the time when a palace daughter normally went to make her challenge. Finally, Reyna guessed, she had grown so oppressed by the daily terror of waking and realizing that her challenge still lay ahead that she had simply gone, impulsively, without preparation or ceremony, before she could renege.

Reyna halted, suddenly cold with a thought she had not examined before. When her time came, would the fear be the same?

When her time came? She shivered, drawing a hissing breath. She was fifteen now. This was the season of her second majority. Within a year, within two, her agemates in the stonehalls would bear their first children. When her mother was fifteen, she had held the sunthrone for two years.

Shaken, Reyna realized she had let confusion and grief blind her to one clear fact: with this year, her time had come, unless she intended to wait as Aberra had. And what would she gain from that? Turning, Reyna looked around at the people who hurried through the corridor. A few nodded to her. A few spoke. But what were they thinking? Did they already wonder among themselves when she would follow her sister? Did they ask each other what her chances were, whether she would be the next barohna of Valley Terlath?

Or did they see a lack in her? A lack as glaring as the lack she had seen in Aberra? Was that why she sometimes surprised a shadow in Juris Minossa's eyes? Because she was the only palace daughter remaining and Juris Minossa saw no strength in her? Was that why her mother had been more distant than ever since Aberra had gone?

Did she have the strength to become a barohna? Could she take stone into her heart and make herself hard with it? If she trained, could she kill her beast and return walking as tall as her mother, all the changes of a barohna upon her? Or would she die as Tanse had died, as Aberra had died? She had wondered these things before, but abstractly, with no sense of urgency.

Today they struck her with full force, and she tried to find answers. Sometimes, she realized, she felt as strong as the mountain. But other times she felt fragile, as if she would shatter in the breeze. If there were some way to know which in truth she was, weak or strong—

But there was not. No palace daughter had ever gone to the mountain knowing whether she would return. And what would it serve her to know? If she had some choice, if she could decide to spend her life differently, to serve her valley in some other way—

She could not. A palace daughter's choice was to go to the mountain and survive—or go to the mountain and die. A palace daughter had no other purpose in life and no other service to offer.

And these were not thoughts for a festival day. Reyna glanced around, suddenly oppressed by the mood of celebration around her. The contrast painted her own mood darker.

A bough for the fire—she and Aberra had always gone to the plaza before the dancing began and added boughs to the pyres. This year she must fetch boughs for them both—and one for Tanse as well.

She seized desperately at that excuse to desert the palace. She must have been pale as she hurried down stone corridors toward the plaza. Palace workers paused to glance after her. Once one of her agemates, apprenticed to the bakers, called her name, concerned. Reyna walked faster, pretending not to hear, her boots striking the flagged floor sharply.

If she had a choice, if Aberra had had a choice, if Tanse had had one—But for a palace daughter, there were no choices. By the time she reached the plaza, Reyna was running. She hardly noticed when she reached the avenues. She hardly saw the stonehalls, the sheds and storage buildings, the diked fields. She ran, not acknowledging the people she passed, not even slowing to welcome the bright sun.

She didn't slow until she reached the orchards. There she threw herself into the grass, breathless. Tiny fruits hung upon the trees, drinking sunlight and turning it to sugar. New leaves spun a lacy canopy overhead. They rustled in the morning breeze, speaking with a hundred green voices. *Aberra, Tanse*—

Reyna quickly realized she had come to the wrong place to cast off grief. The orchard held too many associations. When Tanse had gone to make her challenge, this was where she and Aberra had paused while she told Aberra all the things an older daughter traditionally passed on to her younger sister. And when Aberra had gone, this was where Reyna had stood with the children, helplessly watching.

Blinking back tears, Reyna glanced up the flank of the mountain, to the spot where she had seen Aberra's white shift that morning. If she could call that moment back, if she could reel time backward and draw Aberra back to the orchard—

Reyna caught her breath. For a moment it seemed time did flow backward. Because there was someone on the lower flank of the mountain, following the trail downward. Rigidly Reyna rose to her feet, staring up the mountain, her chest tight.

She had not been mistaken. Someone climbed down the mountain. *Aberra?* Her heart began to pound rapidly. It had been nineteen days. Had it simply taken Aberra that long to track her beast, to take it? Was she coming back now, changed, ready to harness the sun and capture its heat in the sunthrone? Was she coming back to serve as the next barohna of Valley Terlath?

Reyna did not move voluntarily through the trees toward the first rise of the mountain's flank. Her feet carried her forward without instruction. She continued to gaze up, magnetized by the figure that moved among the rocks. If it were Aberra, if she had survived—

Hardly glancing down at the uneven ground, Reyna left the orchard. She moved toward the rocky trail, holding her breath— hoping.

And then, with sharp disappointment, she saw that it was neither a barohna nor a palace daughter climbing down the mountain trail. The figure was male. He carried a bulky load on his back. And when he came nearer, she saw that he was dressed in furs, that he carried a pike in one hand.

Reyna sagged to a flat stone at the foot of the trail, tremulous with disappointment. A hunter. It was a hunter who came down the mountain, probably drawn to the valley by the prospect of feasting and dancing. She could see now that he wore a vest of breeterlik hide, that he wore both cap and trousers sewn from rock-leopard fur. He appeared young, no older than her brother Danior, and he was lean and sun-hardened. His hair flashed white by sunlight.

As he came nearer, he seemed not to notice her sitting on the stone, her knees drawn up, her eyes wet now with unshed tears. There was a distance in his gaze, as if he were so occupied with his own purposes that he didn't even notice the trail beneath his feet.

Reyna frowned, watching him with reluctant interest. He was near enough that she could see his face now and he didn't look like a man coming to the valley to celebrate. His lips were set, his brow deeply creased. He moved in an envelope of isolation, as if he were totally alone in the world, as if it held no one else but him.

He moved as if he were as alone as she felt at that moment.

Perhaps that was what it meant to be a hunter: to be alone. Or perhaps—her heart closed tight, a fist in her chest—perhaps he had come bringing news of Aberra. Perhaps he knew what beast had taken her, how it had happened. Perhaps that was why he frowned into the sun with such somber purpose.

She stood without thinking as he reached the end of the trail.

"My sister—" she said, then halted, afraid she had spoken too suddenly.

But she hadn't startled him. He must have been aware of her all along, although he had given no sign. He turned slowly, examining her with guarded grey eyes. He seemed not to comprehend her half-spoken question. He seemed not to know how to respond to it. He touched his lips with his tongue and said, "Your sister?" His voice was husky, as if he had not used it for many days.

Reyna sighed, dropping back to the stone. "I thought perhaps you had seen my sister, Aberra. I thought perhaps you had news of her." When he did not respond, she said, "She went to her challenge four hands ago. No one has seen her since." It seemed to her, as he continued to study her, that he held himself carefully in her presence, as if he expected some injury from her.

What injury did he think she had to offer? And if he hadn't come to dance at the festival, if he hadn't brought news of Aberra, why had he come? Not just for the company of people, surely. Everyone knew what hunters were: aloof, solitary, self-governed.

Perhaps he had come simply to sell his furs. Carefully he set his load to the ground. "I don't know of your sister," he said.

Again Reyna noticed the unused quality of his voice. Was that why his manner was strange: stiff, guarded, and distant? Simply because he spent too much time alone? Was that why he seemed wary, as if he expected a rebuff?

"I don't suppose you've stopped to talk to any of the herders on the other slopes?" she probed. "Or to the lens tenders?"

"I haven't stopped to talk to anyone."

She nodded, bowing her head, letting go her brief hope that Aberra might still return. When she glanced up again, the hunter was peering down over the valley, studying its distant structures with the same guarded attention he had given her face a moment ago. She sighed. "Tonight is wood-smoke night," she said. Perhaps he didn't know.

Perhaps he didn't care. He didn't nod, didn't acknowledge her words. "You're the daughter of the palace below?" he asked finally, turning back to her.

"Of course." He didn't have to ask that. Her slightness, her fragility, the auburn of her hair and the amber of her eyes told him that. Who but a palace daughter looked as she did?

"And below is Valley Terlath?"

"Yes."

"Your barohna then is Khira."

"Khira is my mother." Why did he ask?

A distracted nod. "And the Arnimi quarter here. They fly their ships from here."

Reyna stiffened. The Arnimi had quartered in the western wing of the palace since her grandmother's reign. They came and went unobtrusively, observing without mingling, recording without interfering. No one had any complaint against them. But if the throne were hers, she would send them to some other valley—or back to their own distant world. And quickly, because she had never learned to like them.

"They fly from here," she said shortly. And why did that matter to a hunter? She stood again. "I must go down. If you've come for the festival, you can walk back with me." It was only civil to offer that. And, reluctantly, she was curious. She had never met a hunter before. Were they all so guarded? Were they all so tense? Or were they so only in the presence of strangers?

Who was not a stranger to a hunter? Certainly he glanced sharply at her, as if her courtesy were suspect. Abruptly he squatted and with the tip of his pike drew a random figure in the hard soil. "I'm not going down until tomorrow."

She shrugged, disowning any show of disappointment. "We will see you then," she said formally and turned to go.

She had not taken many steps before he spoke again. "Wait."

She turned, surprised. The word sounded more a plea than a request, and when she turned back, he seemed momentarily disconcerted, whether with himself for calling after her or with her for responding, Reyna couldn't guess. Quickly he bent over the load he had deposited on the ground. "I found nigh-berries this morning. And yesterday I dried fairyflowers. I have dried meat too, in my pack."

He wanted her to eat with him? She hesitated, surprised that he asked—equally surprised to find that she wanted to accept. Despite his manner, there was something in his eyes that spoke to her, although she could not name it. Perhaps it was only a kindred loneliness. "I brought nothing," she said slowly.

He frowned, his white brows drawing together sharply. "I asked for nothing."

Had she offended him so easily, just by suggesting she did not want to be entirely his guest? When they were strangers, just met? "No. You didn't," she said carefully, sinking back to the flat stone.

Perhaps she would understand him better if she ate with him, although she could not think why it mattered that she understand him. "I would be pleased to share your food. I'm Reyna Terlath," she offered.

"I'm Juaren."

"And your valley?"

It was a natural question, but it brought a glint to his eyes and made his lips draw tight. "I have no valley. I'm alone."

Alone. He was just as alone as he appeared, although she could not guess why that must be. Surely a hunter was not required to renounce his valley entirely. Surely there was some hall he considered home, even if he did not go there to take wintersleep.

Reyna felt alone too as they ate. Juaren served her from his pack, laying out foods silently, making no attempt to talk with her. Occasionally she felt his glance upon her, but when she looked up, he turned quickly away, frowning and tense, as if he felt awkward in her presence.

She sat silently for a time after they had eaten, wondering if they didn't have something to say to each other—wondering what it might be. He reloaded his pack and sat staring down at the ground, drawing figures with the tip of his pike. If he wanted to talk, she decided finally, he didn't know how to do it. He didn't know how to begin. Or he was afraid to begin.

Neither did she know how to begin, when she knew so little of him. What could she say to a man who claimed no valley? A man who seemed so uneasy in her presence? A man who must have spoken to no one for days? Finally she stood. "I have to go down now. I'm taking boughs to the wood-fire."

He nodded.

"Tomorrow then."

"Tomorrow," he agreed, remotely.

But again when she had gone a distance, he called her back. "Reyna Terlath," he said.

She turned. "Yes?"

He frowned, hesitating. When he went on, the words seemed to cost him effort. "I lost my guild master when Coquel had his seventh winter rising. I have walked alone since then."

"That—that's a long time," she said, awed. She could not imagine walking half the winter alone in the mountains, while people took wintersleep in the valleys below. Certainly if she had done so, she wouldn't fall into easy conversation with the first stranger she met. It would take her many hands of days to rediscover the habits of company. "It's a very long time."

He nodded and squatted again, occupying himself over his pack. When she did not turn away immediately, he said distantly, "Tomorrow."

"Yes," she agreed, and turned back toward the orchard.

She did not glance back until she reached the trees. Then she saw that he peered intently at the sky, shielding his eyes with one hand. Puzzled, she followed the direction of his gaze and saw an Arnimi aircar spiraling over the valley, glinting in the sun. Her lips tightened and she turned away to find boughs for the fire.

That occupied only a few minutes of her time. She had the entire walk back to think of their meeting, to wonder if Juaren had come only to sell furs or for some other reason. To wonder why he seemed afraid that she would slight him. Why expect her to be arrogant just because she was a palace daughter? No one else expected it. She wondered too how he had wintered alone in the mountains, with no one to speak to, no one to share thoughts with, and survived. If she had a choice, she would never choose a hunter's life, not if it meant she must walk alone.

If she had a choice . . . but she had no more choice than Tanse had had, than Aberra had had—than her mother had once had. She shook her head impatiently and began to run.

She did not see Juaren again until night. By then tables had been set, pyres had been lit, and wood smoke floated over the plaza. Reyna hovered in the shadows, watching as her agemates appeared in their gowns, generations of embroidery weighing down the antique fabric. Tima, Maffi, Pili—she remembered when she had run down stone avenues with them, laughing. She remembered when they had watched together while spring lambs were born. She remembered the day they had tossed rocks into the drinking well and Juris Minossa had learned of it and called them to her chambers.

Bittersweet memories, because tonight Tima and Maffi and Pili danced and Reyna did not. She stood in the shadows, watching gowned figures move through the veiling smoke, smelling the sweetness of the fire, listening to the crackle of logs. Finally, when the laughter became too loud, the celebration too joyous, she slipped away into the palace.

Empty corridors, lit by the orange glow of stalklamp. Flagged floors that echoed with the sound of her boots. Tables of food, ravaged now. Empty platters and mugs everywhere, even on the floor.

Her feet led her down long corridors to the throneroom. There she hesitated under the tall arches, gazing at her mother's throne. By day, when Khira sat on the throne, the mirrors mounted high on the throneroom walls captured sunlight broadcast from the mountainside lenses and focused it upon the throne. If the barohna were upon the throne, it caught light and glowed.

Tonight the sunthrone was dark. Khira was in her chambers, or perhaps she watched the dancing from the shadowed verges of the plaza. Reyna knew she would not dance this year. Reyna's father was in the desert, and a barohna did not dance with any man who was not to be her mate, for whatever term.

But if her father didn't intend to return—Reyna gazed at the throne uneasily, then slipped away, not wanting to explore that thought.

She wandered the corridors until eventually she found herself on the plaza again, listening to the beat of drums, to the flutter of flutes, watching the ceaseless changing of partners. There would be talk of the dancing for many days. Tomorrow the elder women would begin to study genealogies, and soon there would be the pledging of mates, some for the season, some for the year, a few for even longer terms.

Reyna had never felt so alone on wood-smoke night. She had never felt so alone at all.

Then she saw Juaren near the edge of the plaza. Firelight touched his face and made his white hair gleam. He still wore his hide vest, his fur cap and trousers, and he looked as alone as she. He looked as if he walked in the high mountains, with no one near. He didn't glance at the dancers as he walked among them. He didn't pause to listen to the music, to study the gowns with their heavy embroidery. He didn't acknowledge the glances the younger women directed at him or the unspoken question of the men.

Reyna was surprised at the sharpness of her reaction. Perhaps the spice of wood smoke touched her more than she guessed. Or perhaps it was the beat of the drums. Suddenly her mouth was dry, her heart pounded, her face burned. Why had he come, when he had said he would not? Had he heard the music drifting through the trees? Had he seen the light of the fires? Had he realized, sitting alone at the foot of the trail, that he wanted to speak with her again? They had said so little the first time, but she thought that was because he had not known how to speak, because he had been alone too long. And he was walking directly toward her now and he knew no one else in Valley Terlath.

Did he know that palace daughters didn't dance? Surely he saw how she was dressed. She wore the same shift she had worn that morning, roughspun, unadorned.

He paused, finally meeting her eyes. His face was guarded, but something that might have been a question flickered in his eyes. And how many questions were there to be asked on wood-smoke night?

Only one. Reyna's stomach clutched. She didn't know whether to nod acceptance or turn away in refusal. If he were only passing through Valley Terlath, why shouldn't he dance with a palace daughter? He was no more interested than she in choosing a mate, in making a pledge. But the drum beat was throbbing and wood smoke was sweet, and they were the only two young people not dancing. Perhaps—

He had stopped. That was all she noticed at first. He had halted, his face stiffening, his hands slowly closing at his sides. Not even his eyes moved. Suddenly they were directed toward the center of the plaza, flat and unreadable.

Slowly Reyna realized that the dancing pairs had drawn back, gazing in the same direction. The older people who gossiped at the edges of the plaza had become still. Even the music missed a beat, as if the drummers were momentarily distracted. Reyna peered from the shadows, puzzled.

Then she saw. Her mother was moving across the plaza, tall and dark in her festival gown, her hair falling dark upon her shoulders. Firelight played upon her face, upon her barohnial features—wide mouth, strong nose and brows, commanding eyes. She moved with a slow inevitability, her face telling nothing of her thoughts. Her sunstone cuffs glowed at her wrists, rings of fire.

Reyna licked her lips, recognizing that her mother moved as Juaren had moved a few moments earlier, as if she were alone, as if she saw none of the people who clustered on the flaggings. But she saw Juaren. She gazed at him and deep-buried pain flickered in her eyes.

Reyna drew a harsh breath. Why did sight of Juaren pain her mother? Reyna could not imagine. He had never visited Valley Terlath before.

But the pain was clear now. It tugged at Khira's mouth. It darkened her eyes. It showed in the set of her shoulders and the rise of her chin when finally she stood before Juaren and held out her hands.

He took an involuntary step back, white-lipped, stunned. It took him moments to find his voice. "You are—you are Khira Terlath," he said. The words were husky.

Khira's voice was clear. "I am Khira Terlath, and I will dance with you."

The words echoed, and color ebbed from Juaren's face. He grew rigid, his eyes fixed. He groped for words—words he did not find.

"I will dance with you," Khira repeated, extending her hands.

Reyna caught a stunned breath and held it, reluctantly understanding what she saw, what she heard. Khira had asked Juaren to dance and he could not refuse. No man refused the barohna. Not because she held some dreaded authority, although hers was the final word in most matters. Not because she was feared, although with her glowing cuffs she could burn any person to ash. But because she honored the man she invited to dance.

She honored him publicly, offering him the hospitality of her chambers—offering him the honor of becoming her mate, however briefly, of fathering her next daughter.

But Khira had a daughter, a daughter who stood frozen at the edge of the plaza as Juaren stepped stiffly forward and accepted Khira's hands. Khira had a daughter who watched white-faced, speechless, hardly even aware of the people who turned to glance covertly at her. She stared as Juaren and Khira fell into the familiar steps, understanding with crushing clarity what she saw.

A hunter had come from the mountains. Her mother had seen him and had invited him to be her mate—perhaps just for this one night, perhaps for the season. She had invited him to share quarters with her and to father a daughter.

Because—what other reason could she have?—she saw some lack in the daughter she already had. Because she had decided that although Reyna would go to the mountain—what choice had a palace daughter?—she would not return.

Because she feared that if she did not bear another child, there would be no barohna to warm the valley and make it live?

Yes, those were the things she thought. Her actions spoke them aloud for everyone to hear. Slowly Reyna's hand crept to her throat. There was a cry of hurt and protest lodged there. It choked off her breath. Her mother had so little faith in her that she had summoned a stranger to her chambers. She had so little faith that she intended to share her bed with a man she had not seen before tonight.

No wonder there was pain in her eyes. Khira was the only barohna on all of Brakrath to take a permanent mate. She was the only barohna to bear four children in succession to the same man. But one of those children—Danior—was male and could not assume the throne. And the other three had been lacking. So she must take another mate. She must take a stranger, as other barohnas did.

Reyna struggled for breath, groping unwillingly for the full dimension of the situation. Was that why her father had gone to the desert? Because her mother must take a new mate and he did not want to see it? Because he did not want to see her dancing on woodsmoke night with another man?

Reyna did not want to see it either. She wanted to protest. She wanted to cry out. She wanted to tell her mother, here, now, before everyone, that she needed no new daughter. That she had one who recognized her obligation, however belatedly.

But what good would that do? Reyna drew her hand from her throat and made a fist of it. Her mother had a clear duty to the people of the valley, and she had chosen tonight to fulfill it. She could not yield to words.

Instead Reyna must offer action. She must demonstrate that she was fully aware of her obligation—and fully aware that the time had come to meet it. She must choose the date for her challenge. She must announce it, and then she must train to meet it. She must work until her body was hard and her spirit unflinching. She must train until she was as strong, as hard as she sometimes felt she was. She must take stone into her heart and prepare to best any beast the mountain could offer.

How long would that take? It didn't matter. She was of age now, and she had a duty, just as her mother did. The mountain had always been her future, her choice. This was the season when she must go. She had already taken too long to waken to that.

Dancers moved across the flaggings again, her mother and Juaren among them. Wood smoke curled around them, obscuring their faces, hiding expression. Trembling, pale, Reyna turned from the plaza and fled down palace corridors to her chambers. She saw clearly what she must do, and she had to believe that the doing was possible, that she could find the stone to harden herself with. But as she threw herself across her bed, the knot in her throat was not an unuttered protest. Nor was it unshed tears. It was fear, hard and choking. It was fear, the beast she must live with day and night until she went to meet her challenge.

THREE

REYNA

The beast drove her hard over the next hands of days. Reyna trained, sometimes in the solitude of the training room, with torches casting long shadows, sometimes on the plaza, sometimes in the fields and the orchards. She did everything she knew to harden herself. She ran, she tumbled, she climbed and jumped. She called upon the fair-haired youths of the halls to spar with her and to wear the beast masks for her. She wove targets and drove her pike into them. She did things neither of her sisters had done, things she had found written in scrolls, things she had heard told in tales.

She pushed herself hard and slept the same way, tumbling into dreamless oblivion each night, forgetting everything, even the ache of her muscles. Often, as her training progressed, she woke feeling strong. She woke feeling certain, her mind clear, her body elastic, and she knew she could face her beast and win. Even so, she could not bring herself to announce the date she had set for her challenge. Because on other days her confidence ebbed and she did not feel strong at all, not even in the first quiet moments of the day.

That disturbed her because she was much aware of what went on around her. Her mother had pledged Juaren for the warmseason. He slept in her chambers, and sometimes Reyna heard them talking in low voices in the evening. Their conversations seemed passionless, formal, empty. Occasionally they danced on the plaza late at night. Reyna watched from her window and thought from the way they held themselves that neither danced with the other. They both danced alone, even when their hands touched.

They seemed alone at the dinner table too, sitting silently, hardly glancing at each other. At first Juaren looked up whenever Reyna joined them and she saw the same momentary question in his eyes she had seen on the plaza on wood-smoke night. But no matter what she understood of the way other barohnas lived, taking mates in casual succession, she could not meet Juaren's eyes when he sat in her father's chair. Nor could she bring herself to acknowledge him when she met him outside the dining hall. Not only had he taken her father's place, his very presence was public testimony to her mother's lack of faith in her. Each time she saw him, she became smaller in her own eyes. The pain of that was real, almost physical. If only her mother had spoken to her first, if only her mother had trusted her to prepare, to be strong . . .

Soon he no longer glanced up when she entered the dining hall. Soon he learned not to see her, at the table, in the corridors, on the plaza. Nor did he seek acquaintance among the people of the valley. He carried the isolation of the mountains with him wherever he went, a barrier, a protective shield.

Against what, Reyna wondered. Did he expect rebuff from the people of the halls too? Her father had been loved in the valley. Had Juaren heard? Did he expect everyone to feel as Reyna did?

Or did he expect to be received without welcome for some private reason? Had he been received that way elsewhere? He ate in the dining hall less and less often as the warmseason progressed. He ate alone on the plaza instead, kneeling on the flaggings, untouched by the glances of the people who passed. And he spent much time sitting cross-legged on the wall that overlooked the western plaza, watching Arnimi aircars come and go. He studied the cars with frowning attention, as if he intended to catalogue every detail of their construction, as if the people who flew them held more interest for him than anyone else in the valley.

Reyna could not blame him if he were bitter or angry, although he seemed neither. There were courtesies normally shown a guest in the valley, and she had shown him none of those. And her mother —it must be belittling to be pledged to a woman who scarcely acknowledged his presence. It must seem to him that he had emerged from the isolation of the mountains to an isolation far more grievous.

Occasionally Reyna paused in her training and took herself to task for her own conduct. On the day they met, Juaren had seemed wary that she would slight him. Now she had done so, not once but many times, and he accepted her behavior as if it were only what he had expected, as if it were exactly what he had guarded himself against.

Why? Why had he expected to be treated no better than he was treated in Valley Terlath this warmseason? And why didn't it anger him?

Perhaps it did. Or perhaps it injured him, despite his effort to remain aloof. Because occasionally she glimpsed him at a distance and realized how stiffly he held himself, how tightly he wore his lips, how carefully guarded his glance had become—even more guarded than on the first day they met. Perhaps the situation made him feel as small as it made her feel.

Reyna did not have as much time as she would have liked to think of it. Her training demanded her close attention. That and the beast-fear that chased her. *Stone.* She must have stone in her heart. That was how a palace daughter became a barohna—by having the gritty substance for it. By making herself as hard as the sunstones a barohna used to warm her valley.

Still it seemed to Reyna that her mother had not made herself so hard. The people of the valley looked to her for a successor, and she had undertaken to provide one. But each day she became more silent, more distant, more withdrawn. She moved about her public functions like a woman half-blind, speaking distractedly when she must sit to hear disputes, ruling indifferently when her word was solicited.

And Reyna knew that if she did not make her challenge on the date she had chosen, if she did not succeed in it, Juaren would be only the first of a succession of temporary mates. There would be other men living in Khira's chambers, other men for whom the honor of being a barohna's mate would turn to ashes, other men who would find themselves dancing at night with a woman who might as well have been stone.

A woman who was not stone. If she were, why did the passing days paint such a dark mood upon her?

And all needlessly.

It had to be needlessly. Reyna told herself that each day as she went to the training room. The discipline she imposed upon herself would not be wasted. She would not even consider that possibility. By the date she had chosen, she would be strong enough for any beast, and Khira would need no other daughter. Juaren could return to the cleaner loneliness of the mountains and her father could return from the desert.

Reyna repeated that vow to herself as she completed the set of calisthenics she had prescribed for herself that day and began to run around the perimeter of the training room. But what use were vows, she wondered, when she could not find courage to announce her date? Her very silence was an admission of doubt. Her mother, Juris Minossa, everyone in the valley must recognize it as such.

Troubled, she completed the circuits she had set herself, washed from the bucket and pulled on a fresh shift for dinner. The smell of roast fowl and fresh-baked bread met her when she stepped into the corridor, but the clutching in her stomach was not hunger. The date—she must announce the date.

Tonight? Could she find courage tonight? The words were so simple. All she had to do was catch her mother's attention and utter them.

If Juaren were not at the table, perhaps she would do it tonight. Perhaps she would find courage tonight. Silently she pledged herself to that as she walked down the corridor.

She held her breath when she entered the hall. Palace workers already ate at the long tables, talking quietly among themselves, laughing. Juaren was not there.

Tonight then. She shivered as her appetite deserted her.

No one looked up as she made her way to her mother's side. Sitting, Reyna studied Khira covertly, measuring her mother's strength against her own apparent fragility. Her mother's hands were long and strongly built, her own were delicate and pale. Her mother's features were prominent, her own slight. Her mother's hair was burned black by the sunlight she caught in her sunstone and dispersed across the valley. Reyna's was auburn silk. And her mother's eyes—

Eyes that see fire, valley people called a barohna's eyes, deep and distant and far-seeing. Tonight they turned upon Reyna and Reyna caught a moment's unguarded pain in them. She recoiled, startled.

"Fresh eggs, daughter?" the serving monitor asked, bending near.

"*No,*" Reyna protested without thinking. Did it hurt her mother so much to look at her? Did she think so little of the preparation she was making for her challenge? Instinctively Reyna pressed her hands to her thighs, feeling the new strength of muscle there, trying to find reassurance in it. She was slight, but so was every palace daughter. Khira had been slight once too, before she had met her challenge.

"My mother—" she said quickly. She must give her the date now, before she lost courage.

Her mother sighed deeply and pushed back her half-eaten dinner, hardly recognizing that Reyna had spoken. "My daughter, we must have words. Come to the throneroom when you have eaten."

"Come? Yes, I will come," Reyna said slowly, her voice trailing away. What could she say when her mother had risen and was already striding away? Reyna looked after her with the same baffled foreboding she had felt when she watched Aberra walk up the mountainside. First the hurt in her mother's eyes, then the abrupt summons. What did it mean? Did her mother think she was training poorly? Did she think she had already delayed her going for too long?

"Fowl, daughter?" The serving monitor bent near again, eager to fill Reyna's empty platter.

Reyna had no appetite. "Nothing," she whispered, sliding from her chair.

There were places in the palace where she went when she was troubled: the small, enclosed northern plaza, the scribing room, the weaving chambers. Time lived in all those places, legend and reality fusing. Tonight she chose the tower. She climbed the stone stairs slowly, her face bathed in the orange glow of the stalklamp that grew upon the damp walls. When she reached the windows, she leaned on the rough stone sills, gazing out over the valley.

There was little enough to see, so soon after sunset. Moisture from the fields her mother had warmed that day rose and clouded the stars. The moons had not yet risen. The only sources of light were the sunstone slab on the plaza and the winking beacon the Arnimi had mounted on their wing of the palace.

Reyna watched it for a while, wondering distantly why Juaren watched the Arnimi with such close interest. Then, the weariness of the day's training aching in her shoulders, she descended and went to the throneroom.

She had expected to find her mother alone in the great vaulted chamber, only the darkened mirrors for company. Instead Juaren sat on the dais to the left of the throne, stitching a pelt. He raised his head as she entered and addressed her with a guarded gaze.

Stiffening, Reyna approached the throne. When she felt its warmth on her face, she said formally, "You asked me to come, my mother." At least her voice did not shake.

Her mother sighed deeply, as she had done before, and nodded.

"I asked you to come. Juaren, would you send a runner for Verra? Tell her my daughter has come and ask her to join us now."

Silently Juaren put aside pelt and needles and left the throne-room. Reyna looked after him, confused. Verra? The one Arnimi her mother called friend? What had an Arnimi to do with what they must discuss? "My mother, I have set the date for my challenge," she said quickly. If they could discuss it before Juaren returned—

Something in her mother's eyes stopped her. Her mother's lips hardened. "No, my daughter, you will not go." Khira's fingers pressed the glowing arms of the throne. "That is why I have sent for Verra. To tell you why you will not go."

Not go? The words were so unexpected Reyna stared at her mother blankly. How could she not go to make her challenge? Every palace daughter did that. How else were the valley thrones to be filled, the fields warmed, the seasons tempered? No matter how many died, each sister went in turn until one returned a barohna.

And Verra—Verra was to tell her why she must not go? Reyna knew how little her mother liked the Arnimi. It surprised her that she permitted them to maintain quarters in the palace. Did she allow it just because Verra was her friend?

But her mother had done other things that were surprising too, things that made her a legend in far valleys. Not only had she met her challenge before she came of age, she had taken a starship instead of a mountain beast as her bronzing prey. She had done that, Reyna knew, because the starship had threatened to take her father from Brakrath. And later she had broken with tradition by refusing to wear the pairing stone that would have linked her to a stone mate, another barohna like herself. Instead she had taken Reyna's father as her confidant and as her permanent mate, in defiance of all custom. And he was not even Brakrathi.

He was not Brakrathi, and he no longer lived in the palace, Reyna reminded herself dully. Reyna's hands tightened as Juaren stepped back into the room. He walked lightly, as if he wished to leave no print on the polished floor, and sat beside the throne again, picking up his work without word. But she saw some stiffness in him, some guarded quality, and knew he was as aware of her presence as she was of his.

"Mother—"

"We will talk when Verra comes."

Reyna frowned, subsiding unwillingly. "We will talk then," she agreed.

Verra was not long in arriving. She entered quietly, her boots tapping lightly on the flaggings. She was a woman in her middle years, her hair greying, fine lines webbing her eyes. Reyna was relieved to see that at least she had brought none of the other Arnimi. Reyna did not want to be in their presence tonight. There was something cold in their prominent eyes, something arrogant in the thrust of their padded bellies, something affected in their plucked eyebrows and black-painted eyelids. They had come before Khira was born and had spent the years observing Brakrathi society, just as their parties were observing other societies scattered through the galaxies. Their intent, she knew, was to compile a history of all the races of humanity, detailing their development since Earthexodus, the period when the stars had been settled. Brakrath held particular interest because its settlers had never reached their intended destination but had been stranded here instead, cut off from outside influence for tens of centuries before their whereabouts was discovered.

Reyna could appreciate the value of the history the Arnimi proposed. She could not appreciate their methods of gathering information. It seemed as cold as their eyes, as arrogant as their bellies. Even tonight Verra wore her meters and instruments strapped to her black uniform belt, ready to ply them. Reyna glanced at them and bristled. What could they tell the Arnimi that their senses could not? It seemed to Reyna that their constant use of instruments was nothing more than an admission that their faculties were dull.

An attitude she had taken from her mother, she knew. Still Verra was not as objectionable as the others. The years had left traces of understanding upon her features and there was an animation in her eyes none of the other Arnimi had. She inclined her head formally. "Barohna."

"Friend," Reyna's mother responded. "You know why I summoned you."

Verra's gaze shifted briefly to Reyna. "The matter we spoke of three nights ago, when you called me to your quarters."

"That matter. My daughter has been training to make her challenge. I have just told her that she is not to go."

Reyna shrank as all three gazes turned upon her, her mother's distant, Verra's frowning, Juaren's guarded but probing. Her shoulders tightened. "My mother—" What could Khira mean, that she was not to go?

Her mother raised one hand, refusing to hear her objection. "You are not to go. I know it startles you that I tell you so, but there is a very good reason why you must not. I disregarded it in the case of your sisters. Now I have decided that I must not disregard it again. That's why I've called Verra here." Frowning, she stood and descended from the dais, going to stand beneath the mirrors mounted high on the walls. She gazed up for a time—but not, Reyna realized, at her own reflection. She was looking at something beyond that, something that brought pain back to her eyes. She turned sharply. "I know how little use you have for the Arnimi and their methods, daughter. You learned that from me, just as I learned it from my own mother. They go about our valleys watching and recording, using their instruments as if they were better than ears and eyes. They study all of Brakrath the same way. Recently they have even dared go to the desert and approach the clansmen.

"The Council's first impulse, when the Arnimi arrived on our world, was to send them away. But they promised to make themselves unobtrusive. And what harm could they offer, so long as they did not interfere in the governing of our valleys? So they were permitted to stay and to conduct their investigations, although they had to agree to many conditions and many restrictions.

"Seven years ago, the year after Danior first went to the desert to visit his uncle, Verra came to me and told me the Arnimi had learned to tell with their instruments which palace daughters had the substance to become barohnas—and which did not."

Reyna stared up at her mother, drawing breath sharply. The Arnimi could tell that with instruments? It was a statement that went against everything she knew. She darted a disbelieving glance at the meters Verra wore at her waist. "No," she said. "There is no way anyone can tell that." No one could guess which daughter would return from the mountain a barohna until it happened. No one had ever known, through all the centuries. Some daughters trained until they were strong and hard and died anyway. Others went carelessly and came back changed. There was no pattern, no clue. For the Arnimi to say that there was—

"I understand your disbelief," her mother said, pulling her embroidered gown close as she strode back to her throne. She looked down briefly at Juaren, who had put down his stitching and listened without expression. "I did not believe either at first, when Verra told me. Not even when she showed me the log the Arnimi had made of their study over the past fifteen years and I saw that they had predicted correctly in every case. We have always believed that there is some presence in the heart of the palace daughter who is destined to become a barohna. That there is some hardness of spirit, some governing control dormant in her. We call it stone, and we have always believed that if she trains well, the crystals will form to their full substance and guide her—in taking her beast, in learning to use the barohnial stones, in finding the wisdom she requires to govern her valley. We have believed that it is the final crystallizing of the inborn stone that causes a palace daughter to change so dramatically when she kills her beast. We have believed this is what makes her grow, body and spirit, overnight.

"But the Arnimi have discovered that what makes a barohna is a tiny cellular mass, a bundle of fibers—located not in the heart but in the brain. It lies there dormant until the adrenal stimulation of the challenge, of near-death, causes it to undergo a rapid alteration, and that produces an accompanying maturation in the entire body. The Arnimi have learned to detect the small electrical aberration that announces its presence even in its dormant state."

Reyna stepped back from the throne, instinctively rejecting what she heard. "They've discovered this with their meters, I suppose," she said in a hard voice. The Arnimi thought they had learned something centuries of barohnas had never guessed—not by using their senses or their reason but by using their instruments.

"Yes," her mother said without embellishment.

It was an answer more effective than any argument. Reyna stared at Khira for long moments, not wanting to believe, caught between confusion and the beginnings of anger as she felt herself wavering. She turned sharply to the Arnimi. "And did you bring your instrument with you tonight?" Was that what her mother had called her here for? To be examined like a head of livestock? The thought made her face burn.

Verra did not respond to the challenge in Reyna's voice, only to her words. "I have it here," she said evenly, taking a small unit from its holder at her belt. "Of course you must understand that the actual analysis of electrical activity is not a function of this particular instrument. It only serves to transmit raw data to our banks, where it is analyzed and charted. Then the appropriate response is transmitted back to the hand unit. In our initial metering of you some years ago—"

Reyna stiffened. "You've never metered me with this instrument. I've never seen it before." But she was not entirely certain that was true. She had never been able to avoid the Arnimi and their meters entirely. And the Arnimi meters were much like one another, shiny cases, dialed faces, pinpoints of vivid light—

"No, I'm sure you have not. We performed the initial metering in our quarters seven years ago, as part of a general physical examination. We used a broader range instrument at that time, since there were so many different functions to be examined. I'm sure you remember the occasion."

Reyna frowned, wishing she could deny that she did. But she had entered the Arnimi quarters only once, when she, Tanse and Aberra had been sent there by their mother. Reyna remembered clearly the smell of cold metal and the chill eyes of the Arnimi personnel who had swept sensor-wands over their bodies. "You told us we were being examined for our health," she said sharply to her mother.

"Yes, and if I had heeded what Verra told me, your sisters would be alive today. They would never have gone to their challenges. Because it was useless. There was no stone in their hearts to give them command of the sunthrone. Not the smallest crystal."

"Or to use our terms of reference, Reyna," Verra said, "the activating mass was not present in their brain tissue. There was nothing there to be stimulated to growth by the adrenal rush of the challenge. Nothing to spur change and rapid maturation. Nothing to enable them to use the sunstone, the pairing stones, any of the stones a barohna must use. Had one of your sisters by chance taken her bronzing prey, she would not have returned to the valley a barohna. She would have remained a palace daughter, never growing, never changing."

Reyna shook her head stubbornly. "No. No." Surely if what Verra said were true, there had been palace daughters who had taken their beasts and not changed. What had happened to them?

But she knew without asking. She knew what she would do if she killed her beast and found herself unchanged. She would look for another—and another after that, until finally one of them ended her quest with its claws.

But remain a palace daughter to her death? That was what her mother was suggesting. That was what her mother insisted upon, in fact, by forbidding her to go to her challenge. Reyna shrank from the suggestion, her face paling. Remain always small and fragile, with the stature of a child? Grow old that way? Uselessly, unable to command the stones—unable to fulfill any function within the structure of valley life?

Slowly she turned to stare at her mother. Was that what she was suggesting? That she simply remain in the palace, without function, without office? That she spend her life that way, while the people questioned her silently with their eyes? Her voice faltered. "If I take my prey—"

"If you take your prey," Verra said gently, "it will mean nothing, Reyna. Except that you had the courage and agility to do it. Here—" Lightly, before Reyna could draw back, she pressed her instruments to the flesh of Reyna's temple. When she withdrew it, a small amber light glowed on its dial. "If you had the potential to become a barohna, the indicator would show red. But it does not. You can see that clearly."

Reyna glanced from her mother to the Arnimi and back again, her thoughts running so rapidly she could hardly apprehend them. *Clearly?* She could see many things clearly. There was a throne to be held. There were seasons to be tempered, fields to be warmed, a valley to be governed. Without a barohna to capture the sunlight from the barren mountainsides and store it in her stones, without a barohna to release it as it was needed, none of those things could happen. The valley would grow cold and die. "I can see that you believe an instrument before you believe me, my mother," she said with anger so tremulous she was afraid she would melt to tears. "I have done what I could for you. I have trained as Tanse did not, as Aberra did not—"

Muscles hardened in her mother's jaw and emotion flashed from the deepness of her eyes. "Yes, you have trained, and I have watched you, knowing I let your sisters die needlessly. Because I refused to believe what the Arnimi told me, although your father urged me to. Because I refused to break with the old ways in this one thing, although I have broken with them in others. Now I do believe what Verra tells me. Now I intend to do what your father begged me. I forbid you to make your challenge.

"How many daughters must I lose before I trust my friend not to lie to me?"

Reyna shrank from the hard passion of her mother's words. So Khira believed she had no stone, no hardness. No crystalline substance to call response from the barohnial stones. Why then did she feel as if her entire heart had turned to rock?

Or had it turned to ice? She felt cold as she thought of doing what her mother intended her to do: nothing. There were palace daughters who never made their challenge, of course. They lived out their lives in their mothers' palaces, child-like wraiths without place or purpose. But she could not live like that. Better to go as Aberra had gone. As Tanse had gone.

Or so her thoughts ran. At the same time her hands clenched painfully and her heart beat to a frightened rhythm. She felt as if it would leap from her chest.

Was this what Aberra had felt, she wondered, going to the mountain with her pike in hand, knowing that she would not survive whatever encounter chance brought her? Reyna wondered distractedly what beast had killed Aberra. A lumbering breeterlik, spraying acid from its belly sphincter? A minx, pink-eyed gamester that walked on two feet? Or had Aberra crawled into a sheltering cavern and died slowly, of exposure? Perhaps someday someone would find some sign of her. Then they would know. As for herself—

"If you won't let me try," she said, making her voice hard, "who is going to take the throne when you leave it?" She had never, she realized, spoken to her mother so coldly—or with such challenge. She had never dared. But tonight she had nothing to lose from it. Tonight she could speak anything.

Her mother's fingers tightened briefly on the arms of her throne. "Your sister will take the throne," she said.

Her sister? "I have no sisters."

"You have one. She will be born late next winter. She is already well enough developed that Verra can tell me that she will be the next barohna of Valley Terlath."

Reyna took a single step back, feeling time grow thick around her, binding her. It had been fewer than forty days since woodsmoke night. Her mother had already conceived? And Verra had already used her instrument on the unborn child? Reyna's thoughts, her reactions were suddenly so slowed by shock that she seemed hardly able to speak. *Her sister*—Juaren's child. Juaren's child already lived in her mother's womb, taking her place, her purpose, her life.

Because that was what she saw slipping away now: both purpose and life. Before tonight she had recognized that she might die on the mountain. Now they told her that not only must she die, her death would be for nothing. She must go without even the chance of returning.

Or she must stay and not make her challenge at all. Reyna stared helplessly at them all, her mother, Verra, Juaren. In her mother's eyes, in Verra's, she saw pain. She did not comprehend what she saw in Juaren's gaze. For one disquieting moment, it seemed almost like understanding. As if he understood better than either of the others what she felt. But why should he understand? She could find no reason.

Gradually the initial shock ebbed and her mind began to work at normal speed again, considering the possibilities that faced her. There were not many. Examining them, she fixed upon the only one she found tolerable. Did none of them understand, she wondered, that although her mother could forbid her to go to the mountain, she could not stop her? Did she propose to put a guard at her chamber door? To confine her by force?

Reyna was sure she did not. Valley Terlath was not governed that way. Her mother relied upon authority to restrain her. Just as Verra, she realized, relied upon rationality.

But authority had no power over her now. And rationality could not sustain her when everything had shattered around her. Slowly she looked down at herself, at her slight figure, at the fragility of her hands and wrists. She was slight and small, little taller than a child. How long could she live this way? A hundred years? Two hundred, trapped in an immature shell of flesh?

She answered her own question. She would live this way no longer than the day after Midsummer Fest. Then she would test the accuracy of Verra's instrument in her own way. She had already made her plans, and what had she left but those?

Certainly not hope.

Deliberately she let her eyes sweep over the three of them, Juaren, Verra, her mother. Softly she said, "I have selected the date when I will go to the mountain, my mother. And that is the date when I will go." She was surprised how little her voice shook.

She was equally surprised at the composure she mustered as she turned and withdrew from the throneroom, her boots snapping against the polished flaggings. But of course that was only external. Internally she had already begun to shake as she reached the corridor. Her legs already felt weak, her head light. Forcing herself, she continued along the corridor, spine stiff, boots striking the stone flaggings smartly.

She did not waver until she reached the upper corridor and neared her own chambers. Then she sagged against the stalk-grown wall, her throat thick with unshed tears.

"Daughter—" The hall monitor approached and spoke diffidently, his wizened face concerned.

"Nothing. It's nothing," she said, drawing herself up and entering her chambers. She stood at the center of the floor for a long time, staring at the same stone walls so many palace daughters had stared at before her. She could guess the fear they had known after announcing the dates of their challenges. Surely that was the same from generation to generation. But at least they had been spared the futile anger, the helpless bitterness she felt tonight. She lay down on her bed, tears beginning to burn hot tracks down her cheeks.

Nothing. Verra had made her nothing with her meter. Her mother had made her nothing with her command. Juaren had made her nothing by fathering the next barohna of Valley Terlath. Now it only remained for some mountain beast to make nothing of the little that remained. She would go to the mountain on the day she had chosen.

FOUR
REYNA

"**D**aughter! Daughter, the barohna asks for you. She has things to speak to you."

Moaning, Reyna tried to escape the insistently whispered words, the fingers that tapped at her shoulder. Her mother had things to speak? Hadn't her mother already spoken enough tonight? Reyna rolled away, squeezing her eyes shut. "No." The protest was muffled by her bedcovers.

Nivan, her mother's runner, sighed regretfully and tapped at her shoulder again. "Daughter, she has told me to bring you."

"No," Reyna repeated, but she knew it was useless. If she didn't go with Nivan, her mother would send a second runner and a third. Reyna rolled out of her covers. "It's still dark, Nivan," she said, glancing toward the window.

Nivan nodded apologetically. "Kimira's night will be here soon."

Yes, Kimira's night, the interval after both moons had set, when darkness was total; the time when once a young girl of the stonehalls had dreamed herself lost and wandering in the fields. She had awakened in her own bed, but at dawn the field workers had found the frozen droplets of her tears shining on the ground—or so it was said in the halls. Some of the people of the halls still believed their spirits deserted their bodies during Kimira's night and wandered through an elusive dimension that had neither time nor place.

Certainly Reyna's spirit felt dislocated. Shivering, she put feet to the floor and went to her window. Starlight held a special hurting brilliance tonight, when it should have been dulled by what she knew. "Tell my mother I will be with her when I have dressed."

Her fingers were stiff as she pulled on trousers and laced into boots. She stared at them as if they belonged to someone else, their very clumsiness reminding her of the choice she faced: to remain a palace daughter or to die uselessly.

Because despite her angry declaration earlier in the evening, if she went to the mountain, what use would her death be? It would not bring a moment's warmth to the valley. The sunthrone would not light because she had gone. The fruit of the orchards would not be sweeter. Grain would not grow taller in the fields.

But if she remained . . .

Another chill shuddered through her body. Standing, she rubbed her swollen eyelids. Then she stepped into the stalklit corridor.

She had not visited her mother's chambers since her father had gone. The room seemed more austere than she remembered. Hadn't there been small figurines on the bureau? Woven hangings on the walls? Those things were gone now. And her mother had let the stalklamp grow so thickly across the ceiling that its runners threw a bright, harsh light against the bare walls.

Her mother's face, seen by the gaudy orange light of overgrown stalks, seemed as hard-used as the walls. Beneath the stone-burn, her features were pallid. And there were clusters of deep wrinkles in the fabric of her gown, as if she had bunched it spasmodically in her fists. Juaren sat on the windowsill, his face shadowed, frowning. Looking at them, Reyna guessed neither had slept. And there was something in the atmosphere of the chamber that made her wary, a sense of words spoken in her absence, words that concerned her. She hesitated, then met her mother's gaze with a quiver of doubt. "You wanted to speak with me."

Her mother frowned, seeming to reach past some reluctance. "Yes. We must talk again. Our conversation earlier was cut short."

Her brief hesitation steeled Reyna. "No. I left without being dismissed, but there was nothing more to be said." Nothing at all.

"It was cut short," Khira repeated, finally finding conviction in the words. She swept at her hair with a strong-fingered hand. "You know custom as well as I do. I told you tonight that you are to have a sister. There were things that you should have said to me in turn, things that are traditionally said upon this occasion. You left without saying them. I've thought about it and I've decided I must hear them now."

Reyna stared at her mother disbelievingly. Was that why she had been called back at this hour? Was that why her mother had not slept? Did she really expect her to make the customary pledges—to care for and to teach a sister she would never see? A sister who would be born seasons after she died? "I can't pledge anything to this sister," she said. "You know I have already set a date for my challenge."

Khira's eyes narrowed. "And will you keep it with no thought for your sister?" she demanded. "Perhaps you don't have a full sense of the obligations of an older sister to a younger one. Aberra was too close to you in age to fulfill the usual responsibilities. But this child will be sixteen years your junior, and you are needed to tend and teach her. You are needed to supervise her through the winters, when I go to my mountain palace. You are needed to tell her the legends of our valley and to see that she learns to cipher scrolls and to conduct herself well. So long as there is an older sister, those are her obligations. Most sisters consider them privileges."

Reyna caught a sharp breath, realizing belatedly why her mother pressed the issue, angry that she did so. Did her mother think she could be so easily dissuaded from making her challenge? Did she think she would welcome any excuse to forget the date she had set? That she would seize upon this one? "I would have considered it a privilege too if you had given me this sister five years ago, when my father still shared your chambers."

For a moment she thought she had gone too far. Khira lowered her head, a frown darkening across her face. But when she spoke again, it was softly, in reluctant concession. "I knew you would answer me that way. I knew before I even spoke. I've seen myself in you since you were small, and you've given the same response I would have given. Even your tone is the same: angry."

Khira had seen herself in her? Reyna shrank from the words, wondering if Khira intended to mock her with them. "If what you and Verra say is true, I will never be like you."

Slowly Khira shook her head. "Never mind what Verra's instrument says. You know what I am. Impatient. Strong-minded. Possessive. And all too tender in certain places. You are much the same. So much so that I thought you would be the one to take the throne from me, even after what Verra reported to me seven years ago."

Reyna looked up sharply, surprised. "You thought that?" Her mother had found her impatient? Strong-minded? Possessive? From childhood? It didn't seem to her that she was any of those things, not to a significant degree. In fact it occurred to her, studying her

mother's face, that if her mother had indeed seen those things in
her, it had been from the simple need to see herself mirrored in one
of her young. And Reyna had been the only one who could bear the
reflection without wavering.

"Yes. When Tanse left, I knew she would not come back. For
many years, I did not think Aberra would even find the courage to
go. When she did, I knew she would not return. I knew it as well as
you knew it. But you—"

"You thought that I would go—and return?" Reyna wanted to
believe that much at least: that her mother had seen some strength
in her. Because if her mother had seen it, despite what the Arnimi's
instrument said—

"I felt you would. But I've learned from the Arnimi that my
feelings can be mistaken. That they often are."

"Perhaps this time they are not," Reyna said slowly. If her
mother believed that she could go to the mountain and return a
barohna, despite what Verra said—

"If I go—"

Her mother's gaze shuttered. She turned abruptly and stared at
the pitted stone wall. "You will not go. I have already told you
that."

Reyna caught a baffled breath, anger returning. "And I have
already told you that I will, on the date I have selected." But the
words did not hold the same conviction they had held earlier. They
were flavored with hesitation. Because if the Arnimi were indeed
right and her mother wrong—

"You will not go," Khira repeated. She turned back, her eyes
suddenly as hard as Reyna had ever seen them. "Because if you do,
your father will never return to Valley Terlath. And I have already
told you what I am: strong-minded and possessive—and tender in
certain places. Your father is one of the places where I am tender. I
won't spend the rest of my reign without him."

Reyna retreated involuntarily from the blaze of her mother's
eyes, confused. Her father would not return? She licked her lips.
"What—what has my father to do with whether or not I make my
challenge?" He had never even spoken to her on the subject. Not
once, and she had been far closer to her father than to her mother.
In fact, she realized, the few times she had tried to speak of her
challenge with him, he had turned away and begun speaking—too
hurriedly—of other things.

"Do you want him to make his home in the desert permanently?"

"No." That, at least, didn't require deliberation. "But why should he? Why—"

"He has already told me that if I let you make your challenge, that if you die, he will never return to Valley Terlath. Even if you do stay he may not return, because I didn't stop Aberra. I didn't tell her. I waited too long and she went."

And her mother blamed herself for that? "Palace daughters have always gone," Reyna protested. Palace daughters had been born to that expectation from the day Niabi first drew fire from the sunstone.

Khira shook her head. "You and I understand that. We are Brakrathi. But your father is not. He honored my decision not to tell you the results of the first Arnimi examination. He honored my decision to let Tanse go.

"But her death put a distance between us. Perhaps it was only grief at first—his grief. A barohna learns to hold her daughters lightly, to keep a distance from them, no matter how deeply she cares for them. Life in the valley can't stop each time a palace daughter goes to seek her beast.

"But your father never learned to keep that distance. Finally, last year, he came to me and told me that unless I instructed Aberra to set aside any thought of making a challenge, that unless I instructed you in the same way, he could not stay. When I refused, he went to the desert. It was not his place to speak to Aberra or to you. The tradition was not his to set aside. It was yours, mine, Aberra's, but never his. All he could do was leave."

So that was why they had argued late at night. That was why they had been silent at the dinner table. Because her father had not wanted to sacrifice his daughters to tradition. And since it had not been his place to intervene, he had done the only thing he could do. He had gone.

Reyna frowned. Could she go now, knowing it meant her father would not return? Knowing it meant her mother must live alone or take a succession of mates? Torn, Reyna glanced up and saw that the hardness had gone from her mother's eyes. They were shadowed. "The Council—does the Council know about the Arnimi's tests?"

"Yes. They have elected, at least for now, to speak of them to no one."

"They know and they're doing nothing?" Reyna said incredulously.

Khira shrugged. "The matter isn't as simple as it appears, I suppose, although it appears simple enough to me. The Council feels it isn't just a matter of deciding which daughters are permitted to make their challenge and which are forbidden. The Council wants time to consider the entire fabric of our society. Time to decide how much change can be permitted without damaging that fabric—and everyone who depends upon it."

Reyna shuddered at that argument. Their own daughters—and the Council chose not to tell them. Chose to let them die as they always had, winnowing themselves in that brutal way, when the same thing could be accomplished so much more cleanly, so much more easily with a tiny instrument.

But what would the Arnimi's instrument leave those who had been turned away from the challenge? Life—but on what terms? How many would want to live out their lives as palace daughters, with no place and no pride—not even the pride of a bravely chosen death?

Confused, she raised one hand to her temple, trying to stroke her thoughts to order. What was life without pride and purpose?

What were pride and purpose without life?

"You told me," she said finally.

"Yes," her mother agreed, and said no more.

And Juaren sat on the sill listening to it all with silent attention. Reyna's hand quivered against her temple as she weighed diverse factors: tradition, her father's wishes, her mother's, the expectations of the people, her own long-held expectations. "I have to go," she said finally, knowing there had never been any other answer. To renege would rob Tanse's death, Aberra's death of all meaning. She could never think of them without guilt if she acceded to her mother's wishes. And to remain in the palace, the people questioning her silently with their eyes—

There was always the chance that the Arnimi were wrong. They had dissected and studied most Brakrathi lifeforms, but they had never dissected a barohna. And how many palace daughters had gone to their challenge since the Arnimi had begun their study? The number could not be large. There was room for error. "I have to go," she repeated, more strongly.

Juaren turned away sharply at her declaration, frowning out the window, lips tight. Her mother sighed deeply, her hands bunching her gown. Slowly she paced to the window and stared out too. "It is Kimira's night," she observed distantly.

"The moons have set," Reyna agreed. It seemed appropriate that they were gone. What did not seem appropriate was the bright, clean fire of the stars.

"And you must have your challenge."

"I must," Reyna agreed again, despite the sudden pressure of tears against her eyelids and the tightening of fear at her chest.

Her mother lingered longer at the window. Then, as if reluctantly, she turned and approached the bureau. Bending, she drew open a lower drawer and took out a carefully folded length of white fabric. She unfolded it, letting it spill through her fingers. "You know what this is."

Reyna gazed at the silken length uncertainly, frowning. It resembled a mourning sash, but the fabric slipped so smoothly, so sinuously through her mother's fingers it might have been alive. "The starsilk," she said, puzzled. "Danior brought it when he came back from the desert the first time he visited our uncle. It—it has a voice." She knew little beyond that. Danior had seldom worn the silk in the valley, although Reyna had heard that he sometimes wore it when he rode alone in the mountains. And the voice it spoke with, if what she had heard were true—but that could not be. That, surely, was a tale. Valley Terlath was full of tales.

"Here. Listen to it speak." Her mother stepped to the window and shook the silken fabric loose into the night breeze. It reached out sinuously, twisting like something alive, starlight painting it white against the darkness.

Reyna's breath caught in her throat as the silk began to speak. Its voice was the voice she had been told the silk used—her father's. But the words were alien, sharp and pleading at once, jagged with urgency. Reyna chilled, trying to understand why her mother held the silk to the wind, why it spoke with such wrenching distress. She knew her father had come from beyond Brakrath as a child. Was this his voice speaking some language he had known before coming here? But the silk didn't speak with a child's voice. Its voice was a man's.

Reyna glanced at Juaren and saw that he had come stiffly alert. He listened to the silk with full attention, his face for once unguarded. "It's—my father's voice," she said.

Slowly Khira drew the silk in the window and coiled it. "It is— but Iahn doesn't speak this language and he never uttered these words. You've heard the term Rauthimage, haven't you? You've heard it whispered in the halls. You've heard the name Birnam Rauth?"

Reyna stiffened. "I've heard certain things," she said. They were not things she cared to give credence. "I know that my father came here in a starship as a child, that you destroyed another starship when it came to take him away, that people say he is enough like his brother Jhaviir that they might have been born to the same season." But the other things she had heard—

"Yes, Iahn and Jhaviir are alike because both are Rauthimages."

Reluctantly Reyna nodded. "I've heard the term. But what it means—"

"I'm sure you've heard what it means as well, but you refused to believe. Most valley people find it hard to accept. They understand so little of the ways of the universe beyond Brakrath, of the peoples who live there." Khira bowed her head and stroked the silken fabric. "One of the peoples is the Benderzic, a ship race. They don't inhabit a world or a land. They make their home in a series of ships that orbit a small yellow sun near Pernida's Crown. They are different from us—and from the Arnimi—in a number of ways. More ways, I'm sure, than either of us could comprehend. One of those ways is the manner in which they reproduce. They don't take mates as we do and have children as a result of the mating.

"Instead they take cell scrapings from individuals selected to be parents and grow offspring from those cells. The scrapings are placed in a growing medium and through various techniques eventually an infant, genetically identical to the parent, is formed from them." She paused, studying Reyna closely. "I'm sure you find that as repugnant as I do."

Reyna hugged herself in distaste. "I do." Repugnant and incredible at once, not something she would believe if anyone but her mother told her of it.

Her mother shrugged, unconsciously touching her abdomen. "The process is something like the one by which we propagate stalklamp from cuttings, or so the Arnimi tell me. But of course humans are not cuttings. And even more repugnant is the way the Benderzic maintain their economy. They select individuals from outside their own race and take scrapings from them, without their permission. Then they sell the offspring—the images—or exploit them in other ways.

"Well over a century ago the Benderzic encountered an explorer and scientist named Birnam Rauth. They took tissue from him without permission. Later they propagated offspring—images—from his tissue and trained and programmed them to gather certain types of data. They made them into information-gathering tools, little more than human instruments, and then set them down on various worlds. Their function was to learn about the resources of these worlds, about the dangers, about the customs and limitations of the people already living there. After a while, the Rauthimages were retrieved and the information they had gathered was sold to anyone willing to bid for it.

"Perhaps Birnam Rauth would have protested what the Benderzic did, when he learned of it. But he disappeared shortly after his encounter with them. He was traveling alone. No one knows what world he was bound for or if he reached it. He resupplied at a small port on Rignar, not far from his home world, Carynon, and was not heard from again.

"Iahn was a Rauthimage, of course, as was his brother Jhaviir—your uncle. Iahn was left here as a child, to gather information to be bid away to anyone who wanted to exploit our world. And when the Benderzic ship came to retrieve him, I did not permit it to do so."

"You made the ship your bronzing prey," Reyna said. That part of the story at least was familiar.

"Yes. I was too young to go for my challenge. I had just begun my initial training. But this challenge came to me, and I had no choice. I was a child when I went to the plain for the summer. The Benderzic ship came, I destroyed it, and I returned to the valley a barohna. And I took Iahn as my permanent mate, even though the Council disapproved."

"But the silk—" Reyna said, puzzled. Where was the tale leading them? She saw that Juaren listened closely, wondering too.

"Before Iahn came here, he lived for a short time on several other worlds. On the last of them, a star-trader crashed shortly before the Benderzic took him away. After the crash, the people he lived with looted the trader. Part of the cargo was silks similar to this one. He held one briefly in his hands and heard it speak. He didn't identify the voice as his own at that time because the silk spoke with a man's voice and he was still a child.

"Later a similar star-trader crashed on Brakrath. These ships are apparently without any sentient crew. The Arnimi think they may not even be traders, despite the goods they carry. They may be uncrewed spy ships, masquerading as traders in order to trace the movements of the Benderzic drop-ships.

"At any rate, Jhaviir found the second trader many years later and retrieved the silks it carried. He recognized the voice this one carries at once, because by then he was a man and it was his voice too. He kept the silk, as well as others that carry no human voice, and eventually gave this one to Danior. The Arnimi used their language files to translate the words it speaks.

"It carries one message, repeated over and over. *I am held here, I don't know how. They keep me bound and they feed me strange substances. I can't speak, but the thoughts that leave me go somewhere. Somewhere, and I think they are recorded. If you hear them, come for me. Let me go. Set me free.*

"*My name is Birnam Rauth and my thoughts are recorded. If you hear them, come for me.*

"*Come for me.*"

Reyna caught her breath sharply. So the silk carried a distress call—from the man her father had been taken from. "Where is he?" she demanded. "Is he still alive? Could he be?" She knew that different strains of humans had different life expectancies. And she had heard that some, on some worlds, had learned to extend their lives far beyond the span even a barohna could anticipate.

"He could be. The Carynese—and of course your father and Jhaviir are genetically Carynese, even though they've never seen Carynon—come from what Verra calls evolved stock. They live for as much as four centuries under normal circumstances."

And so Birnam Rauth might still be alive. Although why it concerned her, when she could do nothing . . . "Where is he being held? Do you know?"

Her mother stroked the silken fabric. "I do. You know, Reyna, that Danior is able to use a pairing stone, even though he has none of the other powers of the stones."

Reyna drew her gaze from the shimmering fabric. "Yes." Her brother was an anomaly, the first son ever brought to live birth by a barohna, the first male ever to use any of the barohnial stones, although his abilities were few and sharply limited.

"He and Keva, Jhaviir's daughter, wear paired stones. Through his, he is able to reach not only into Keva's mind but into the world the silks came from. When they sing—this is the only one that speaks; the others sing in a voice that is not human at all—he can walk on the world where the silks originated. Not physically of course, but with his senses. He's seen the surroundings, the inhabitants. He's seen the configuration of stars in the sky, and from that the Arnimi are able to calculate the location of the world."

The world where Birnam Rauth was being held? "They know—they know where the message came from?" Never mind that she could do nothing. Impulsively Reyna took the coiled silk from her mother's hand. She went to the window and spilled the silk out to capture the wind. The sharp urgency of its voice made her draw it back immediately. "And no one has gone to see what happened? To see if he's alive?" How could anyone hear the message and not want to investigate? Certainly she wanted to know what had happened, and she had hardly heard Birnam Rauth's name before tonight.

"To our knowledge, no one has. It's been over a century since he disappeared. The Arnimi relayed this new information to the Co-Signators, but they declined to investigate. They consider the chances that he is still alive very slim. And the world the silk comes from has never been explored—except, of course, by Birnam Rauth. The only person who wants to go, who wants to see if he can learn what happened is your father."

Reyna looked up at her in surprise. But why be surprised that the urgency of the message affected her father as it affected her, especially when it was spoken in his own voice, by a man who could be called his father? She frowned at a sudden stab of apprehension. "He's not—he hasn't—" Had her father lied when he said he was going to the desert? Had he gone somewhere else instead—to search for Birnam Rauth?

"No. The Council has forbidden him to go. He still carries a Benderzic tracer."

"A tracer?" Reyna glanced at Juaren and saw that he was listening as he had before, with full attention, eyes narrowed, face unguarded.

"When the Benderzic dispatch a Rauthimage, they implant a tracer deep in his heart muscle. It enables them to locate him over great distances when they return for him. If Iahn were to leave Brakrath and encounter the Benderzic—"

Reyna felt herself suddenly breathless. "What would they do?"

"The same thing they would have done if they had taken him when they first came for him. They don't consider a Rauthimage human. They consider him a tool, to be used. And they have very specialized means of using him. They would very easily learn things we don't want known about Brakrath. Iahn has lived among us too long now to leave. We can't have what he knows auctioned away."

"Then he can't go," Reyna said, relieved. Distractedly she glanced at Juaren and saw that his thoughts had raced ahead of hers.

For the first time he left the windowsill, standing, the glint of stalklamp bright on his white hair. "Do I understand you, barohna? Iahn can't go—but other people can. Other people can go to learn what happened?" His eyes were narrowed, intent.

Reyna stared at him, startled by the suggestion behind his words. *Other people can go?* What other people were there? What other people cared what had happened to Birnam Rauth?

There was herself.

She examined that thought, stunned by it. The Council would not permit her father to leave Brakrath to investigate Birnam Rauth's distress call. The CoSignators, the alliance the Arnimi were pledged to, had declined to make a search. One man, lost for over a century, was of no urgent concern to them.

But this was not any man. This was the man her father had been taken from. In some essential way this man *was* her father. And she had touched the silk, she had heard its plea. She had wanted to respond.

She still wanted to, no matter how incredible the possibility.

And why, she wondered suddenly, had her mother told her any of these things? Why had she brought out the silk and let it sing? Reyna drew a careful breath, wondering if the answer that occurred to her could possibly be the correct one.

Hesitantly she tested it. "If someone—if a person decided to go to learn what happened, how would she get there? And the world—what is it like? Do you know?" Surely she was wrong. Surely her mother did not intend that she go.

But Khira did not rebuff her query. Instead she answered it with careful deliberation, as if she were picking her way through some critical negotiation—as if she were indeed proposing what Reyna thought. "Danior has seen it of course. He tells me there are beasts there, beasts as imposing as any you will find on the slopes of Terlath."

And so it was true. Her mother had brought out the silk and made it sing, she had told Birnam Rauth's story—all for one reason: to offer Reyna an alternative to going to the mountain. To offer her a choice no palace daughter had ever had. "So I could make my challenge there," she said slowly, hardly believing she spoke the words. Would she go so far? Would she place herself at risk to search for a man who was probably long dead? Only because she had heard his voice? And because her mother did not want her to go to the mountain?

She had already sworn to go to Terlath, and to no purpose. If she could not bronze, she would bring nothing from the mountain even if she took her beast.

But if she went to the place where Birnam Rauth was held, even failure would have some meaning. And if she were successful, if she found him or learned what had become of him, if she brought that news to her father—

"How could I travel there?" Would her mother have suggested the journey if there were no way she could make it?

Would she really make the journey if there were a way she could do so? The prospect was incredible. But she had wanted a choice. She had wanted a way to prove herself, to serve, without dying uselessly.

She had proposed to go to the mountain, knowing she would not return.

Khira stared briefly out the window, catching her gown in her hands, crushing it. "If you choose to go," she said finally, "the Arnimi will give you a small ship and see that you know how to use it. Or they will send someone to pilot it for you."

"You've already spoken to them?" Had she planned that far ahead?

"Only to Verra, and she has no authority. But they will do what I ask. It is little enough after all the years I have permitted them to quarter in my palace."

Reyna studied her with a sense of unreality. Her mother forbade her to go to Terlath—but she would permit a journey of this magnitude? And she would ask the Arnimi to give her a ship and teach her to use it?

She would do those things. Her tension as she waited for Reyna's response was testimony to that.

Reyna touched her lips with a dry tongue, finally realizing why Khira's mood had been so dark these past days. Not because she had taken a stranger into her chambers. Not because she would bear a daughter by him. She had chosen a hunter, after all. After this warmseason she need never see Juaren again. And her liaison with him was a matter of duty.

Her mood had grown from Reyna's activities instead. Each day she had watched her train and known it was for nothing. How had Khira described herself? Impatient, strong-minded, possessive—and tender in certain places. She had learned, as barohnas did, to keep her distance from her daughters. But she had never kept her distance from Iahn. He was her consort, her confidant, her counselor, the person she held closest. Each time she had looked out and seen Reyna training for her challenge, she had seen Iahn's self-imposed exile extending into permanence.

She had tried to turn Reyna from her challenge with reason, with command, with diversion. And finally she had offered her a choice, a challenge of another kind, one from which she could return, not as a barohna, but perhaps with some measure of pride. One which offered purpose.

The very essence of a choice, Reyna realized, watching her mother torture the fabric of her gown, was that it must be made. She must accept or decline it. And how much time did she need to weigh alternatives?

Very little. Surprisingly little. "I'll go." Although the words were bold and her decision firm, her voice wavered.

Her mother gazed at her blankly for a moment, then glanced quickly down and smoothed her gown against her thighs. "I thought you would," she said. It was hard to tell if her voice held regret or relief. Perhaps there was some measure of each. "You will need to train for this, just as you have trained for your challenge. I will speak to the Arnimi and make the other arrangements. If you do well, we will welcome you back to our valley before too many seasons." The words had the air of ceremony. With them she put a distance between them again.

"I will train," Reyna affirmed, respecting the distance. Certainly she would need to be strong to meet the challenge of a strange world, a world where silks spoke and sang, a world no one had seen except through a pairing stone. Her mind worked quickly. Plans—she must make plans. She had committed herself to an unthinkable journey. Now she must decide how to make it successful.

She must train harder and longer, of course. Then she must go to Wollar, if there were time, and ask him to teach her to track. That would be a useful skill anywhere. Although—she glanced at Juaren. He could teach her to track as well as Wollar, perhaps better, if he would—if he could overlook the slight she had given him since he had pledged himself to her mother.

Any thought of asking that service of him died when she saw his expression. If his face had been unguarded before, it was naked now —naked and white. Even his lips were pale. He touched them with the tip of his tongue and stepped forward. He looked like a man who had glimpsed an opportunity, only to see it snatched away. "Barohna, I will go too," he said.

Reyna drew a sharp breath. Juaren's eyes flickered from Khira to her, and she saw immediately that he mistook her surprise for objection. His features hardened defensively and a pulse leaped in his temple. "I will go," he repeated, a hard edge to his voice.

Khira concealed her surprise no better than Reyna had. She raised her head sharply, her pupils narrowing to pinpoints, her shoulders stiffening. "You?" she said. "Why? Why would you go, Juaren?" This certainly had been no part of her plan.

Reyna echoed her mother's question silently. Why did he want to accompany her on this journey? Birnam Rauth was no one to him, and the voyage could be perilous. But one of the first things he had asked her the day they met had concerned the Arnimi. And he had spent long hours this warmseason sitting on the wall overlooking the western plaza, watching their aircars come and go. She remembered how intently he had watched, remembered the concentrated attention he had directed at the Arnimi.

Was that what drove him? His interest in the Arnimi? But what did that stem from? What was its origin?

He drew a long breath, looking from one to the other of them. For an unguarded moment he seemed about to offer some explanation. But he quickly thought better of it, shook his head, and said stiffly, "I am a hunter, barohna, and we set prices for our goods. You knew that when I offered you my furs. You knew that when you asked me to stitch them into garments for you. You knew I would ask something in return. Now I am asking it."

Khira ran a long-fingered hand through her dark hair, frowning. "It seems a large price for a bale of furs, Juaren." It was more question than statement. And strangely, Reyna saw, she seemed injured by his words. As if she really cared that he proposed to leave.

Juaren steeled himself against her frown. "Any one of those furs could have cost my life, barohna. I showed you the scar I took from the minx's claws. I told you the course of the infection that followed."

"You told me," Khira agreed slowly. "And I was concerned and asked you to remain with me until you could find an apprentice. I even asked you to come with me to my winter palace at the end of the warmseason. But you gave me no answer."

"I didn't," he said reluctantly.

"My mother—" Reyna said, startled by the direction the discussion took.

Khira raised one hand, silencing her. She spoke carefully, as if she wanted to be fully understood, as if it mattered to her. "Juaren, we have danced together, we have talked together, we have made a child together. You have had my heart for the season. I offered it for the next as well. But you ask a price instead."

Juaren's lips briefly froze. Pain touched his eyes. "I ask the price for my furs, barohna," he said. "Not for anything else. And your heart—"

Reyna glanced quickly from one to the other. Had her mother really given him her heart? She had seen no evidence of it. And neither of them had thought to ask if she wanted company on her trip.

That was as well, because she didn't know. She hadn't had time to think the question through. It was too unexpected.

"Your heart—" Juaren said again, softly. "Perhaps you think you've offered me that. But I don't believe you have it to offer. Not now. Not while your mate is in the desert. And certainly not if he returns."

Khira sighed, nodding in reluctant recognition of the truth. "Then I suppose it doesn't seem I've offered you much at all."

"An honor," he said. "And your company sometimes, when your responsibilities were not too heavy. And concern."

Khira shrugged, accepting what he said. "Then indulge my concern and tell me why you want to go on this journey. You don't have Reyna's reasons. Birnam Rauth means nothing to you. And there clearly is danger."

This time it seemed to cost him more to evade her query. Juaren stared down at the floor, biting his lip. Finally he shook his head and said simply, "I'm a hunter, barohna."

Khira's brows rose. "Then what is your prey? What do you expect to find on a strange world that you can't find here?"

"I'm a hunter," he repeated.

"And you won't tell me more than that? You ask to go with my daughter but you won't tell me why?"

"I ask the price for my furs."

They had reached an impasse. He was pale, tight-lipped, tense, and Khira was hurt, although she tried to hide it. They both turned to Reyna. "Daughter, this decision clearly isn't mine. It has to be yours," Khira said.

Hers, and she was hardly ready to make it. "I think I should go alone," she said, but without conviction. Whatever Juaren's need, it seemed as compelling as hers. And she remembered well that moment on wood-smoke night when he had walked across the plaza toward her and she had thought they might dance. She remembered the question in his eyes. She remembered the meal they had shared earlier in the day.

She remembered too the slight she had offered him since then—the unwarranted slight she had never had courage to rectify. Impulsively she said, "Juaren, on wood-smoke night—" She let the question trail away, wondering if he would guess what it had been.

"I know that palace daughters don't dance," he said, meeting her eyes squarely. His were grey, unsmiling. In their depths was the same question she had seen before. "But I thought that perhaps if we danced in the shadows, where no one would see—"

Reyna sighed, cherishing the intention as much as she might have cherished the experience. Yes, they might have danced in the shadows. But everyone would have seen and wondered what it meant. There would have been whispers and stories for days.

But of course a palace daughter was always the subject of whispers and tales. If she went on this journey, the stories would not end in Valley Terlath, and they would span years rather than days.

If she went on this journey with a hunter, a man from the mountains, the stories would be even more eagerly told. But was that her concern tonight? Reyna bowed her head. When she raised it again, she had weighed all the factors and she had decided. "Come with me," she said. There had been a question in his eyes from the beginning. She didn't know that she could answer it. Perhaps he was too wary to fully divulge it. Perhaps she didn't have the answer. But at least she could make amends for her behavior. And she would not be going to a strange world completely alone. "Come with me."

FIVE

DARIIM

Dariim and Falett clawed open a nest of sharp-snouted bark-shredders that morning and feasted in the bright mid-day sunlight, grinning at each other with gleaming eyes and sharp teeth. Later, while Falett napped with their mother, Dariim heard a telltale scratching near the roots of a nearby tree and cornered a fat brown treemole. Chuckling, she carried it back to share with her sibling. And later still, their mother caught a heedless grass-puppy that came tumbling right under her nose, and they all feasted again. And so Dariim curled next to her sibling that night with no thought of midnight frights. She fell asleep thinking of nothing but the day's prowess, her full stomach, and the time when she would be the swiftest and the best hunter in the woodlands, as her mother was now.

At first she slept with light contentment, her muzzle buried in Falett's fur. Then, slowly, her sleep deepened until even the moon-light that fell across her eyelids dimmed. Soon she retained only a shadowy awareness—until, abruptly, she shuddered awake at the sound of her own voice raised in a hoarse, moaning growl.

Her hands and feet twitched and her claws were working blindly at her bedding. Startled, she drew them in and stared around in waking confusion. Her heart throbbed against her chest wall, but as on every other night when she had awakened this way, her dis-tended eyes found nothing to explain her fright. She was in her bower, Falett curled asleep beside her, the moon shining upon them both. And they were alone.

Tremulously Dariim pressed the back of one dark-furred hand to her sibling's muzzle. Falett stirred and curled tighter, baring her teeth in a grin of sleeping satisfaction. Dariim gazed down at her, trying to find reassurance in her slow, deep breath. Why had she thought there was something here, some dark, cloying presence, when there was only Falett?

Had it been a nightmare? At that thought, the hair at the back of her neck rose, an instinctive response. Briefly she was tempted to nudge Falett's shoulder, to wake her sibling to share her unease. Dariim and Falett had suckled and tumbled together from birth; they had stalked their first treemoles together and shared their first kill. They carried the same scent; the smell of Falett's fur was the smell of her own, familiar and comforting.

But what comfort could Falett offer against the nightmares, if that was what had come in her sleep? And if the nightmares had begun coming to her, why not to Falett?

Why should there even be nightmares, when the night was warm and the hunting good? Only because the spinners and the songsilks and some creature no sithi had ever seen sent silent thoughts in the air? Why should those thoughts throw such long shadows? There were many questions in Dariim's life. Sometimes they flashed through her mind so brightly they might have been sugar-darters skimming at the flowers of the clearing, the sun iridescent on their wings. She could not catch them no matter how stealthily she approached or how fluidly she leapt. They always whisked away from her grasping claws, then came taunting back at her.

Now apparently there were to be questions. She curled back into her silks, considering them, wishing Falett shared her free-ranging curiosity. She had learned to tell from the distracted way her mother carried herself, from the puffiness of her eyelids and the twitch of her nose, when the nightmares stalked her. She had slipped to her mother's bower on those nights and seen her lying in the thrall of the swaths, head thrown back, teeth bared. Song-dreaming that was called, when the swaths reached out bright arms of silk and turned moonlight and breeze to song—song that drove away the nightmares.

But how did the songs drive away the nightmares? Or was it the swaths' silent-talk that did that? How would she know until she had a silk of her own, until she had heard for herself what the silks said in their silent tongue while they sang? Dariim pulled her tongue absently through her fur, wondering as she slowly groomed herself back into drowsiness.

When sleep came, drawing at her eyelids, making her breath soft and slow, a shiver of fright quickly brought her awake again. She sat, an involuntary tremor running through her body. Finally, when the cold sense of fear did not pass with the minutes, she slipped from her silent-silks and, ashamed, crept down the trunk to her mother's bower.

Tsuuka lay curled as peacefully as Falett. Her songsilks were stretched tight upon their poles: scarlet, amber, azure; lilac, yellow, emerald; crimson and chartreuse. Moonlight touched them and fell across the bower floor in a muted rainbow. Dariim padded across the bower and fingered the silks. They were slippery-smooth, cool to her touch. Just stroking them made her wonder again, and more keenly, about the songs they sang and the things they did.

But wondering would not sharpen her senses for the hunt. Only sleep would do that, and Dariim did not intend to go hungry. She curled up beside her mother, forcing her mind to be quiet. The scent of her mother's fur was distinctive, reassuring. Soon Dariim slept again.

But again moonlight dimmed and she had the sense of a dark presence. It tugged at her, trying to pull her into some spinning, whining, ill-defined blackness. She whimpered, her muscles stiffening, and struggled to drag herself away. Slowly a growl of terror grew in her throat.

The sound of her own voice woke her again. She shuddered from the silks, her fur damp with perspiration. Shaken, she blinked unhappily at her mother, wishing she could waken her and nuzzle next to her to be comforted like a weanling.

But she wasn't a weanling. She was a cub in her seventh summer. In a few seasons, she and Falett would select their own tree and choose their own silks. For Falett there would be lilac, amber and yellow, because Falett did not like bright colors and bright sounds. For Dariim there would be emerald, crimson and azure, and perhaps she would have a starswath as well, as her mother did. But she would not listen to it often. Its voice was so sharp-edged, so urgent, it made the hair rise at the back of her neck.

The thought of sleeping again made her hair rise too. Disturbed, she slipped from her mother's bed and padded to stroke the songsilks. If she had a silk of her own, she wouldn't have to fear sleeping. If she had a silk, it would chase the nightmares away, although she shivered when she remembered how her mother's arms and legs twitched when she took song-dreams.

But after song-dreaming her mother slept, and the next day no game in the woodlands was safe from her. Dariim thought of her mother's prowess and her eyes glinted. She drew her fingers across the crimson swath, counting the game she might take if she tuned her muscles well. Bark-shredders, treemoles, the tiny, juicy squabblers that hid under the fallen leaves . . . Her eyes darted around the bower. Did she dare loosen the swaths with her mother sleeping so near?

She knew she did not. But after a moment her eyes brightened and then gleamed with a hopeful thought. The spinners had been working beside the stream today, making new silks. There would be songsilks there now, drying.

Dariim toyed with this new idea and its manifold possibilities, licking distractedly at her fur. There would be no one to see if she took a silk from the streamside. The sithi slept in their bowers and the spinners had scrambled to their nests hours ago, giggling and chattering. And there were places in the woodland where she could take a silk to listen to its song.

She thought longer, her interest sharpening. She had so many questions. How was she to know if these were nightmares if she didn't try to turn them to song-dreams? If they were nightmares, was she ready to speak to the silks now, silently, as her mother did? She tried to imagine a smooth, cool azure voice sounding in her mind, tried to imagine herself speaking back to it. What would her own silent voice sound like? Would it be like her spoken voice, husky, sometimes growling? Or would it be different?

Finally it was curiosity that drove her down the tree. She was a hunter, not prey. If she could not sleep, at least she could stalk the answers to her questions, just as the dark dreams were stalking her.

The white trunks of the trees gleamed by moonlight. As Dariim darted through the grove, she heard a silken voice from somewhere overhead and peered up. A single silk curled from Misaad's bower, reaching eagerly into the moonlight. Dariim caught its amber light on the yellow surfaces of her eyes. Her tongue darted at her lips, small and pink, suddenly eager. Then she ran on.

She heard the seductive murmur of voices before she reached the stream, a rainbow chorus, some voices trilling sweet and high, others falling into a lower register. Their song was without words, without perceptible meaning. Yet it made Dariim's heart beat faster. Her mind growled with the same cub-hunger that sometimes gripped her stomach.

Hunger, even this one, challenged her, making her aware of the inborn cunning of her muscles, of the razor keenness of her senses.

She was a sithi-hunter, daughter of Tsuuka, sister of Falett. She was sleek and silent, a shadow with teeth. She chuckled to herself as she ran through the grove and then slipped among the streamside trees. Reaching the water, she stared up at her prey with eager eyes.

She saw silks of every color, singing in the breeze. Their bright hues danced across the surfaces of her eyes. Drinking their brightness, she felt an involuntary stirring of the flesh of her neck, a quivering alertness.

There was no one watching. She slipped forward. Her fingers sampled individual swaths, searching for the brightest, the smoothest, the one with the sweetest song.

She had thought she wanted an azure swath like her mother's. Instead it was a clear red one that caught her attention. The song it sang was like molten sunlight, like a dancing band of energy, like a piece of her own spirit given color and substance.

The song it sang was red, and sweeter and more piercing than any other song. The red silk reached for the moon with rippling impatience, as if it intended to snatch all the silver light for itself. It was tied differently from the others, Dariim saw, wound tightly around the pole and secured with knots like none she had ever seen before. Seeing it, hearing it, she didn't hesitate. Quickly Dariim flexed to her toes and worked at the intricate knots.

The chore proved easier than expected. When she had undone the first two knots, the silk itself seemed to do the work, the slippery fabric twisting and wriggling until it shed the remaining knots. No sooner was the last knot loose than the silk twisted in Dariim's grasp, thrashing wildly. Her claws snicked free in instant response. "You have a song for me," she muttered hoarsely, clutching the slippery fabric. "You're going to sing to my dreams." Despite the gruff words, she felt a flash of alarm at the swath's unexpected strength, at the way it writhed, trying to escape her grasp. None of her mother's silks fought. Nor did any of them sing with such fire.

Quickly, before the swath could wriggle free, she tied it around her waist, using three hard knots, and tucked the free ends under. Then, with a burst of exhilaration, she dropped to all fours and ran into the trees. She kicked up her feet as she ran. She slashed the air with her claws, cutting a crooked, capering course. The silk clung to her waist like a band of hot energy.

She knew she must take it far from the bower of any sithi before she let it sing. She was a cub with no tree of her own. She hadn't yet taken her first grass-puppy, and no spinner had ever made a song-silk for a cub.

Especially not a silk so strange as this one. Even with its ends tucked securely under, it hummed impatiently every time she crossed a patch of moonlight. And when she paused and touched it, it writhed under her fingertips. Certainly none of her mother's silks behaved so.

Had she taken it from the stream too soon? The spinners extruded the silks during daylight hours, giggling over their stick-looms, drawing long strands of silk from their throat glands and coloring them with the juice of their tongues. Then they carried them to their nests during the first hours of night to let them take voice from the copy-masters they kept hidden there. Finally they washed them by moonlight in stream water and hung them to dry. Was there a final process she knew nothing about, some juice or spittle they applied to make the silks tame?

If so, she had taken her red silk before it was done. It wriggled at her waist like a thing with a will of its own.

That only made her blood beat faster with excitement. She had not stalked her first grass-puppy, but she had a songsilk like no other sithi had. And she would be the only one to hear its wild song.

There were many parts of the woodlands where no sithi claimed trees. One was deep in the heart of the grove, where the oldest trees stood. Another was at the southern reaches of this quarter, where fire had mysteriously found a footing and turned the trees to torches. That had happened years before her birth. Now brush and white-stalked saplings competed for space and sunlight, and there was no tree sturdy enough to house a bower.

Bounding, growling, chuckling, Dariim raced toward the southern arm of the grove.

By the time brush caught at her fur and scratched at her eyes, she had forgotten her nightmare. She had forgotten the questions that had sent her slipping down her mother's tree. She had forgotten everything but the exhilarating energy of the red silk at her waist.

She dodged into the scrubby bushes, searching for a sapling strong enough to resist the tug of the silk. By then the ends of the silk had already wriggled free and flapped noisily against her furred flanks.

She found one sapling taller than the others, its trunk sturdier.

Biting at her lip, Dariim untied the swath from her waist, careful
not to let it writhe away from her. It raised its voice as she worked,
singing its red song, making her fingers clumsy with its energy.

It struggled as she secured it to the sapling, snapping angrily at
her, stinging her arms. But when she pulled the triple knots tight
and jumped back, the red silk reached for the moon, its voice
brightening.

Dariim backed away from the sapling and sat, wrapping her
arms around her drawn-up legs. *Hear me, silk,* she said silently,
willing the words to reach the silk through the bright clamor of its
song. *I am Dariim, daughter of Tsuuka, sister of Falett. I am the
swiftest and the sleekest cub-hunter in the forest and I would speak
with you.*

The silk rustled, twisting back upon itself briefly, but Dariim
heard no reply.

*Listen to me, red swath. You are my silk now. I want to sleep
without any dreams but song-dreams. Today I took for prey a nest of
bark-shredders and a treemole. Tomorrow I'll stalk a grass-puppy, so
my muscles must be strong and my senses clear. I need your song-
dreams.*

If the swath heard, it gave no clue.

Frustrated, Dariim scooted forward, moonlight glinting fiercely
from her oblique yellow eyes. *I want song-dreams from you, silk.*

Still there was no response. Dariim flicked her claws free and
drove them angrily into the palms of her hands. She bared her teeth
in thought. Was there a trick to silent-speaking, one she didn't
know? Or was the silk not ready? Had she taken it too soon?

Perhaps it was improperly made. Perhaps if she had left it by the
stream, the spinners would have seen its imperfection and dumped
it into their melting vat.

No. She could not hear it sing, so much more brightly, so much
more strongly than any silk she had heard before, and think there
was an imperfection. If there was any imperfection, it was in her.
She was too young, just a cub. She was not ready for silent-speaking
and song-dreaming. Perhaps the darkness that stalked her sleep
was not a nightmare at all. Perhaps it was something else entirely.

Her claws dug deeper at her palms. Now that she took time to
think, she knew she should return the silk to the stream. She knew
better than to snatch any other sithi's game. But some other sithi
had asked the spinners to make this silk, and she had stolen it. She
growled to herself miserably, rocking back and forth while the silk

sang its electrifying song, yearning for the moon. Slowly, caught, Dariim drew in her claws and became quiet, listening.

The red silk spun tales she could not comprehend, its song wordless and compelling. Behind the song Dariim heard feelings alien to any she knew, feelings colored with an intelligence she did not understand. It was an old intelligence, one tempered by more years than she could imagine. But it was impatient too, vigorous and insistent and resentful.

Dariim became so lost in the strange song she did not notice that the swath had gradually worked loose from the knots she had tied. She did not realize what had happened until the silk billowed wide and fluttered away from the sapling, gliding and twisting away on waves of moonlight. Then she was so startled she could only stare, her mouth gaping. Shock fluttered uselessly in her throat and emerged as a meek growl of surprise.

Gathering wit, she drew her tongue back into her mouth and jumped up, loping after the silken fugitive. It seemed to be celebrating its freedom, swirling and spinning in the silver light, rippling back upon itself, then stretching itself full length and gliding.

It flirted through the charred area and led Dariim back to where the trees stood tall. It was like a streak of midnight sun rippling past the reaching white trunks of the trees. Dariim galloped after it, still too surprised to feel anything but a first baffled intimation of loss. Her silk—she couldn't catch her silk. It moved too quickly, too fluidly. Her legs wouldn't carry her fast enough, she couldn't leap high enough.

And it was fleeing into the deepest heart of the grove, where the trees grew so old and tall they made the air dark with shadow—the deepest heart of the grove, where her mother had told her never to go. She knew that spinners came and went here, tottering awkwardly on short pink legs, their eyes large and witless, their tiny bodies soft and vulnerable. But no sithi made bowers or hunted here. Because there was something here . . .

Dariim ran among the thick-trunked trees with faltering steps. The very darkness was cloying, familiar.

The very darkness was like her nightmare, black, insubstantial, smothering. Reluctantly, the hair rising along her spine, she cantered to a halt, staring after the fluttering red silk. All her muscles twisted with the pain of watching it go, until finally she could stand it no longer and dropped to fours, pursuing it again.

The sound of her running feet was sponged up by the soft

ground. She ran in silence, hardly even aware of the rush of her breath and the soft flutter of her heart. As she ran, her body fell into the rhythm of the chase. Her weight rocked easily, her stride lengthened, she found new depths to her lungs.

And then she was in the darkest heart of the trees, and the silk floated buoyantly higher, higher, until it was obscured in the limbs of a moss-trunked tree larger than any Dariim had ever seen. She rocked to a halt, settling back on her haunches to stare up. Far above, where moonlight reached through the dense foliage, she could see the silk. It had tangled itself in the upper branches of the tree.

Dariim hesitated only a moment. Claws were for many things, and one of them was climbing. She unsheathed hers with a snick and leapt at the moss-furred trunk, never taking her eye from the silk.

She had climbed barely three times her own length when a sudden shrilling cry rang down from the tree. It seemed to come from dozens of throats, a sharp, penetrating screech of anger. Dariim froze, clinging to the trunk, and stared up.

Spinners lined the lower branches of the tree, their witless faces drawn with fury. They flailed their tiny arms and screamed down at her, glaring with so many fiery eyes Dariim shrank back. She had never seen spinners like this before, furious and threatening. It surprised her that anything a spinner did could frighten her. But her heart was fluttering wildly at her chest wall and her skin crawled with the instinctive desire to turn tail and run.

Why were they here, in the heart of the grove? What was in the tree that made them so angry that she trespassed? Had they come for the silk she had stolen? But how had they known it would lodge in this tree, the oldest, the tallest, the mossiest in the grove?

Why did they come and go here so much in the first place? She had never wondered before. She had never thought about the spinners at all, in fact.

She thought about them now, clinging to the damp bark, the muscles of her thighs cramping. For the first time it seemed strange to her that these tiny, reclusive creatures could create the bright silks that sang by night in the forest. It seemed strange that she could not understand the chatter that passed among the spinners but that the silks they created could speak silently to sithi in the sithi tongue. It even seemed strange that she had never wondered about any of these things before. She felt as if a new and perplexing realm of questions had opened to her.

She also felt reluctant to climb higher in the face of the shrilling spinners. Muttering to herself, she released her claws and dropped to the ground, landing on all fours. She peered up the tree again, then turned and stalked away, the spinners screaming after her, turning the shadowy air dense with their anger.

She didn't surrender her carefully assumed dignity until she was beyond sight of the tree where the spinners shrilled. Then she sat on her haunches and looked back, suddenly dejected. She was Dariim, daughter of Tsuuka. She was sleek and fast and strong. One day she would be the best hunter in this quarter of the forest. But tonight she had run as fleetly as her ancestors and she had not taken her prey. It still clung to the upper branches of the tree. She could hear its song above the fading shrill of the spinners.

Her silk. She was a cub too young to speak with a silk, and it was a silk too wild to be tamed. But it was her silk.

First, though, there were many questions to be answered, and she had nowhere to take them. Slowly she turned back in the direction of her mother's bower. After she had walked a distance, she no longer heard the shrill of the spinners or the wild song of the silk. She heard only the sound of her feet on the soft ground, and somewhere in the distance the baleful cry of a growler. Shivering, she began to run.

SIX

REYNA

There were many things Reyna had expected to feel when Brakrath fell away through the port of the shuttle, when the palace grew small and the growing fields tiny, when the workers became no more than toiling insects—when at last the clouds grew thin and the mountains became snow-capped nonentities, stripped by distance of power and legend.

Wonder at seeing Brakrath as none of her people had seen it before. Gratitude that the Arnimi had agreed to her mother's request to arrange transportation. Relief that the Council had not forbidden the journey and that it was Verra and not some other Arnimi who had been designated to accompany them. Curiosity about where Juaren had gone the day after their meeting in Khira's chambers. He had left with no word to anyone. The Arnimi had brought him back only two days before they were to leave, lean, brown, and even more a stranger than he had been the first day she had met him.

Instead of those things she stared out the port at the rapidly shrinking face of Brakrath and felt an emptiness so profound it was more like nausea. The orchards she had roamed since childhood, the mountain paths her feet knew, the familiar sky—as Brakrath diminished below, Reyna had a sudden, aching regret for all those things. She wished she had gone away too, just to feel the land beneath her feet before she left it.

In the valley every sensory clue had meaning for her: the way the shadow of the clouds moved across stone avenues; the texture of the air at Darkmorning when the first snows fell; the familiar smells of the cannery, of the kitchens, of the fields and pens. She had learned to sift and evaluate all those clues without pausing to deliberate. She knew when it was time for the children to go to the orchards with brushes to pollinate the trees. She knew when the women of the halls would release the kestries they incubated from eggs each year and let them fly over the fields to assure a successful planting. She knew when there had been drinking in the halls and when there would be singing and story-telling. She had tuned herself so finely to the ways of the valley that she gave no second thought to the customs and formalities of communal life.

Now the motion of the craft told her that everything she knew had become meaningless. Reyna shivered and clutched the arms of the couch Verra had strapped her to. The smells of the cabin were foreign, the air so dry it parched her throat. She had no way to evaluate the sounds and vibrations of the craft. She had only the sense of humming, droning disturbances just below the threshold of sound. And when they reached the carrier ship and went among the people who crewed it and who traveled upon it—and Verra had told her there would be many—she would not know how to speak to them. Even if she understood their language, what were the proper things to say? What were the courtesies? How would they respond if she inadvertently violated them?

And how many of these questions were troubling Juaren? She had tried to catch his eye, had tried to find some acknowledgement there, but his manner was distant, distracted. Was he as overwhelmed as she by the step they were taking? Or was it just a hunter's nature to become a stranger again after every parting? Was that why he had become a hunter—because of some natural aloofness that could never be entirely breached?

Reyna shivered. She had taken breakfast an hour ago in the familiar confines of the palace dining hall. Now she might never see Valley Terlath again. Bleakly she wondered how her mother had ever thought her strong-minded. She felt only cold and afraid.

"Reyna?"

She glanced toward the couch where Verra reclined. Her voice sounded lost in the small cabin. "Yes?"

"There are drugs I can give you if you're nauseated."

Reyna looked at her blankly, her words not fully registering. Nauseated? But that was only a part of the fear, a fear harsher and more consuming than any she had known before. And all the sharper because she could do nothing about the causes of it. Involuntarily she glanced at Juaren. He lay with eyes closed, his face grey. Did he feel as ill as she did? "I don't need anything," she said.

But Verra had already unstrapped and bent over her, studying her with a frown. "I think you should let me give you a derm. If your stomach is upset, you might not retain an oral."

"I'm—"

"In fact, I'm going to give you both derms. Neither one of you has ever been off the ground before. I don't want to dock aboard *Narsid* with the two of you spewing."

Reyna wanted to refuse, but when Verra returned from the tiny comfort cabin, Juaren extended his wrist silently. Reluctantly Reyna accepted the cold spray too. To her surprise, the nausea ebbed away within moments, taking the worst of her fear with it. She lay back against the couch briefly puzzled. She had thought she was nauseated because she was afraid. Could it have been the other way? Then, seeing that Juaren had unstrapped, she unbuckled her own straps and sat, carefully.

Juaren had already moved to the large viewport before she dared take her feet. She stepped across the cabin after him gingerly, half expecting her weight to disturb the balance of the small craft.

Brakrath had shrunk to a compact, cloud-swept globe below. Like a child's ball carelessly suspended in the air, it looked as if the slightest force could bounce it beyond reach forever. Reyna stared down, licking dry lips.

"It—it looks so small," she said, as much to herself as to Juaren.

Their eyes met briefly, and in his Reyna recognized a flash of her own feeling, a wish that their home looked more imposing. He nodded tensely, stepping away. "You said you would show me how the ship is operated," he reminded Verra.

The Arnimi nodded. "I did. We have an hour before we berth aboard the *Narsid*. Then perhaps three ship-days before we're placed in stasis for the long-range pod. I'll show you as much as you can see in that time." She smiled, her eyes bright with enthusiasm—something Reyna had rarely seen in an Arnimi. "But it won't be enough. It never is."

She was wrong. They saw far too much in the next few hours. Reyna had barely begun to understand what Verra told them about the operating principles of the small craft when they reached the *Narsid*. It swallowed their tiny shuttle and they stepped out into the silver-brightness of its metal belly, a place of towering shadows and echoing catwalks. Before Reyna had time to sort her impressions of that, a courier met them and guided them from the docking deck into the corridors of the carrier. There strange-suited people surged past them, their scent alien, their look barely human.

Tall people with oddly-jointed limbs and cavernous faces. Short people with glistening ebony skin. An occasional somber Arnimi, prominent eyes bulging, padded belly quivering. People who wore suits of fur and people whose fur was their own. Once a group of men and women in brilliant yellow suits ran by, laughing, their dark eyes flashing from strikingly proportioned faces. Reyna turned and stared after them, so startled she couldn't frame a question.

Verra touched her arm. "Tathem-eds," she said. "They look very much like your own people, don't they?"

Reyna nodded numbly. They were like a race of barohnas, tall, bronzed, handsome. But the mark of the sunstone wasn't upon them. Their faces were mobile, their eyes bright and laughing. And there were men among them, men dark and tall as men never were on Brakrath, except for her father and his brother. "What do they do? Are they part of the crew?"

"Oh yes. They've crewed aboard CoSignatory ships since Tathem signed the Conventions, three centuries ago. And they perform as well. You'll see them dance later in the lounges, if you want. First we have to log in and get our cabin assignments."

Logging in: a procedure conducted in a language Reyna didn't understand, involving formalities that had no apparent meaning. She learned several things from it. One was that she was to be identified while aboard the carrier by the print of her right thumb. Another was that in certain sections of the ship, where few people passed or paused, every natural scent was swept from the air by invisible equipment, leaving only a chill emptiness. Finally was that Juaren was no more at ease aboard the *Narsid* than she. She saw that in the tense set of his shoulders, in the perspiration that beaded his upper lip despite the sterile chill of the air, in the wariness of his gaze as they left the administrative section and made their way through the ship again.

Everyone seemed to have purpose in the busy corridors. Everyone seemed to understand the fast-clipped words that crackled from the walls. Everyone seemed to walk with brisk certitude, seldom pausing to nod or speak to anyone else.

By the time their blue-suited guide had conducted them to their cabins and abandoned them there, Reyna's head rang with a muffled sense of confusion, the muscles of Juaren's jaw twitched with tension, and Verra's smile had become strained. They had been assigned a suite of rooms, three small cells with beds and comfort cubicles opening off a larger room furnished with angular metal chairs and tables. Glancing around, she saw that her pack was half-hidden beneath one uncomfortable-looking chair, Verra's case and Juaren's pack piled against it.

There was no window. There was only a wall painted with a tangle of green stems, a sullen orange sun rising from one corner. Reyna stepped back and licked her lips involuntarily. Was the rendering intended to make the room seem spacious? It only made her feel that she was about to be devoured, either by green tendrils or orange sun. "Verra, the people we saw in the corridors—the people who work this ship—"

"The crew is taken entirely from the CoSignatory worlds. We try to have permanent representatives of each world aboard each ship of this class. It helps us understand each other. We consider *Narsid* and its sisters vehicles for cultural exchange." Verra confronted the angry painted sun, drawing one hand back through her hair distractedly, a faint frown settling at the corners of her mouth. "Later, if you want, I'll tell you which people originated from which worlds. And there are tapes to tell you about their cultures, if you want to screen them. Although you may prefer to screen technical tapes or entertainment tapes. You can learn almost as much about a people from their art and technology as through a more formal approach."

Where they came from, how they manufactured trade items— Reyna shook her head impatiently. That wasn't what she wanted to know about the people she had seen, although perhaps that was what an Arnimi would consider significant. She wanted to know how they reconciled themselves to the arid air of the carrier, to the false color of the walls, to the constant crackle of disembodied voices. "How long must they stay here? On the ship?"

The question seemed to touch some sensitive spot. Verra's frown deepened. "Many of them spend their entire adult lives on board. They raise their families here, in cultural enclaves set aside in the private corridors of the ship." Abruptly she turned from the muraled wall. "And I've been away from all this for a long time. It's beginning to seem almost as strange to me as it must seem to you. Perhaps Commander Bullens is right. Perhaps I've begun to assimilate to a greater extent than I've been willing to recognize."

Reyna studied the Arnimi woman, puzzled by her reference to the commander of the Arnimi party on Brakrath. Then she frowned. One of the conditions the Council of Bronze had set the Arnimi was that those who came to study Brakrath must remain until the study was completed. Communications with Arnim or any of the CoSignators were severely limited and monitored by Council members. So Verra had lived for almost thirty years on Brakrath, isolated from her own people and her own world except for the other members of the Arnimi study group. "My mother asked the Council to permit you to return to Arnim," she said impulsively. She had overheard talk of her mother's request after the Council session which had reluctantly endorsed her own trip.

"Yes, when I return you to Brakrath, I will be permitted to visit Arnim. To meet my children." Verra spoke distractedly, as if the words had little meaning for her.

"Your children?" Reyna said and was immediately sorry for the surprise that sounded so sharply in her voice. The Arnimi study group had arrived on Brakrath thirty years before. But Verra could have been little more than twenty at the time, too young to have borne children and seen them grown. Had she left them on Arnim for someone else to raise?

"My children," Verra repeated with a shrug. "I made arrangements for them before I left Arnim. I was able to give birth to the first one personally, shortly before we departed." Slowly her frown darkened, becoming something else, more painful. Abruptly she turned away. "We're all tired, Reyna. I'll request an alarm in an hour. Then we can go to the dining room and after we've eaten, we'll explore the ship." Before Reyna or Juaren could respond, she slipped into one of the cubicles and slid the door shut.

Reyna stared at the glossy-painted door, trying to make sense of what Verra had said. She had given birth to one of her children personally? How had she given birth to the others? Did the Arnimi reproduce in the same impersonal way the Benderzic did? How old were Verra's children now? Apparently at least the first was already an adult.

And after she had escorted Reyna and Juaren back to Brakrath, she would meet them. Yet she didn't seem eager. The flatness of her words, the darkening of her eyes before she turned away—

Reyna had never considered before how little she knew about the Arnimi. She knew they came from a world they had restructured to resemble Old Earth, where all humans had once lived. But considering how long the Arnimi study group had spent on Brakrath, considering how intensively they had surveyed the land and the people, very little information had passed in the other direction. Reyna's father had commented once that the Arnimi deliberately held themselves aloof to preserve their objectivity, to prevent their personal response to the Brakrath culture from coloring their observations.

It would be easier to think they remained aloof from simple natural arrogance. Of the several dozen Arnimi Reyna knew by sight, only Verra ever paused to exchange courtesies. Only Verra ever smiled. Only Verra was friend to a barohna or to anyone of Brakrath.

Gradually Reyna became aware that Juaren was watching her, grey-eyed, somehow wary. Tired, confused, she couldn't bring herself to meet his eyes. "I'm tired," she said, as abruptly as Verra, and slid the painted metal door into the middle cell.

The bed was hard. There was no bedding and she could find no way to dim the harsh white light that glared from the ceiling. She lay rigidly for long minutes, every muscle tense, as if she could brake the *Narsid* with her own scant muscular strength.

Finally, when the light continued to glare through her closed eyelids and her muscles refused to loosen, she retrieved her pack from the main room. She set it beside her on the bed and opened it. Familiar tools, personal possessions, extra clothing—the starsilk. Sighing, she pulled out the silk and let it slip through her fingers. It gleamed softly against the roughspun of her shift.

But when she stood and held it full-length, it did not speak. There was no movement of air in the cubicle and the only light was artificial.

Holding the silk reassured her anyway. It reminded her that she had not left Brakrath casually, upon a whim. Even if she did not return from her search, she had gone for a good purpose.

Briefly she crushed the white silk in her fingers. Then she folded the silk and put it aside and lay down again. She slept immediately.

Her dreams were swift and confusing, played out against a backdrop of painted walls. She followed them to strange places, struggling to make sense of the increasingly incoherent images. She was relieved when a soft rapping at her door broke the flow.

"Reyna?" Verra's voice was muffled.

Reyna opened her door and stared at Verra in surprise. The Arnimi woman had discarded her severe black uniform. In its place she wore a richly embroidered festival gown, its soft blue folds coiling around her feet. The patterns worked upon it were intricate, finely done, incorporating many of the same symbols and devices Khira wore. But Khira's festival gowns were old, handed down over the centuries, the softly aged fabric heavy with generations of needlework. This gown had been created by a single hand.

Verra saw her confusion. "Your mother wanted to give me a gift, years ago. I asked for this," she explained. "But of course I've never been permitted to wear it. We're required to maintain uniform on-site."

To maintain uniform for thirty years? "The sun in spring," Reyna said softly. Surely that small acknowledgement of Verra's transformation was appropriate after thirty years. The lines of the gown concealed the Arnimi woman's protruding abdomen, and its color made the shades of her hair richer. To complete the effect, she had wiped the black lines from under her eyes and drawn in a delicate blue webwork.

Verra colored, obviously pleased. "The autumn sun, I'm afraid," she said. "Now—I overslept the alarm and Juaren has already gone to look around. Are you hungry?"

Juaren had gone alone? Set out into the maze of corridors and passageways with no guide? But of course he hunted the mountains that way, winter and summer—alone. And Reyna was surprised to find that she was hungry. "Yes. Do we have to call back the guide?"

"I think we can find our way. I've looked over the directory and the corridor maps. Most of the basic public units are located centrally, just as I remember from our original journey. And we'll know immediately if we wander too near the peripheral units—the enclaves and the support areas. Those zones are posted."

Posted? "The people who crew the ship—" Reyna said uncertainly.

"They don't like casual travelers wandering through their residential corridors." She glanced at Reyna's shift. "Why don't you wear your emerald coverall? It makes you look just a little taller."

It was Reyna's turn to blush. Without thinking she had undertaken the journey in a coarse-spun shift, like a girl of the stonehalls going to tend her family's sheep. Certainly she had seen no one else in the corridors that morning who looked as much the child as she did. "I'll change," she said, embarrassed.

"Wait—please don't misunderstand," Verra said quickly, touching her arm. "I'm the only person on ship who has seen a Brakrathi before today. The other passengers, the crew—they'll be curious. They'll be looking. We want to give them something to remember."

Reyna hesitated. "They—they know we're here?" No one they had passed in the corridors earlier had given any sign of interest.

"By now they do, yes. Word has passed that the Brakrathi party is aboard."

"And I look like a child."

Verra frowned at the bitterness of the words. "No. You look like a young woman—one who doesn't require physical stature to be imposing. But why detract from the effect by wearing the same clothes you would wear to the training room or to the fields? A lot of people will be watching while you're aboard *Narsid*. A lot of people wonder why the Council of Bronze has refused to permit trade between Brakrath and the CoSignators. A lot of people wonder why no intercultural exchange has been allowed, why the Council has refused even to hear a presentation of the Conventions. They wonder why there is no Brakrathi enclave on any ship of the fleet, despite the invitations that have been extended."

Reyna stiffened, her gaze flickering momentarily to the painted orange sun. Her people had been offered a place aboard the ships? They had been offered trade and exchange? But what had they to gain from those things? "Why would we want to leave Brakrath?"

"For any number of reasons," Verra said gently. "To learn more about the other races of humankind. To find new ways of doing things. To form alliances against the hostile races who prey on us all. To gain new perspectives."

Reyna frowned up at the Arnimi woman. What was she suggesting? That the Council was wrong to exclude trade from Brakrath? That the exclusion suggested they were concealing some weakness? She remembered what her mother had said about the fabric of society and all the people who depended upon it. The people of the halls were finely tuned to life in the valleys. What did other races have to offer that would serve rather than disrupt? Could they turn back the winter? Could they make the summers warm? Only the barohnas could do that. "We aren't ready to change. We don't need to change."

"No, Reyna, but you may not always have free choice in the matter. Your people lived for tens of centuries in isolation. But now the CoSignators know Brakrath is inhabited. The Benderzic know it is inhabited and they've surely guessed that it has desirable resources. And there will be others. Ignorance won't be a defense against any of them. Neither will isolation.

"But I'm not asking you to abrogate the Council's position on exchange. I'm not asking you to do more than to understand what the Revanids, the Teyites, the Koyus, all the others will be thinking, will be wondering, when they see you in the public units of the *Narsid.*"

Reluctantly Reyna nodded. The Revanids, the Teyites, the others —whoever they might be—would be wondering if the Brakrathi were reclusive because they hid some weakness. Because they were afraid of contact. Because they were ashamed. It was her place to show them that none of those suppositions was true.

She could not do that looking like a child. "I'll change," she said again.

"And let me do your eyes."

The emerald coverall had been patterned after a coverall Reyna's father wore when he first arrived on Brakrath. It was cut from the finest spun fabric and tailored to fit sleekly. It was completely free of decoration except for a vertical stripe that ran its length on either side, lending her the illusion of height. Reyna pulled it on and smoothed the fabric against her body.

When she was dressed, Verra brushed her auburn hair and secured it in an intricately convoluted roll at the crown of her head. "I wore my hair this way when I was young," she said softly, studying the effect. "And I wore these on my ears." From a small container she took a pair of clear, faceted stones. "Here—let me put them on you."

She clamped them to Reyna's earlobes and Reyna gazed at them in the tiny mirror, catching her breath. The stones caught light and shivered it into hundreds of dancing motes. Their clarity, their brilliance surpassed that of any stone from a gem master's bench. "What—what do they do?" she asked. She couldn't guess the use of such stones in the right hands.

Verra laughed, stepping back to study the effect. "Absolutely nothing, Reyna. All you can do with these stones is look like a young woman of wealth."

Gingerly Reyna touched one brilliant stone. A woman of wealth? Was that the illusion Verra was trying to create? Was that what she had been before coming to Brakrath? "When you wore them, Verra—"

"Yes. I was a woman of wealth. Or at least the daughter of people of wealth. Not in one of the larger cities, but in a rural province, where the social lines were much more clearly drawn. That's why I'm a rebel, I suppose. Because I was reared so differently from my shipmates. They grew up in certificated nurseries, but my parents took me into their home and raised me themselves, along with my brothers and sisters—a process almost guaranteed to produce deviants of one kind or another, at least on Arnim."

Verra a deviant? A rebel? Because she had learned the simple gift of friendship? Because she had set aside the arrogance of the other Arnimi?

"But I'm not a woman of wealth any longer. I decided that experience would make me richer than anything my family had to offer. And perhaps it has. I don't know—perhaps it has." She paused, frowning at the doubt she heard in her own voice. "And now the eyes. I have a green pen that should do the job. Close your eyes, Reyna."

Reluctantly Reyna obeyed. A few minutes later she stared in surprise at the effect Verra had created. She had drawn an intricate pattern of asymmetrical whorls on Reyna's lower lids, then carried it scrolling upward in a sharp sweep to her temples. Reyna gazed at herself in the mirror, hair upswept, jewels flashing from her earlobes, her eyes peering enigmatically from their carefully rendered mask, and almost believed she was as much a woman as she looked at that moment.

No one stared as they made their way through the busy corridors. No one pointed or whispered or tried to detain them. But it was clear now that word had passed that they were aboard. As she followed Verra toward the public dining area, Reyna was aware of the quick flicker of dozens of eyes, of sharpened attention and swiftly focused gazes. And thanks to Verra's tutelage, she was aware of the questions behind the glances and the gazes.

She was instinctively aware of the responses she must make. She had learned from her mother to hold a steady gaze. When they met, the people of the halls averted their eyes and nodded formally to each other, but her mother never dropped her gaze. Even though she uttered the same ceremonial observations that the people of the halls did, she spoke the words with raised chin and unwavering eyes.

Reyna did not have a barohna's eyes, but she steeled herself as she accompanied Verra down the busy corridors and held every eye that met hers.

Dark eyes, pale eyes, narrow eyes; eyes with specialized lenses and eyes with oddly shaped lids; eyes so large and dark they seemed to have no pupil; eyes so pink and squinting it hurt to see them. She held her head erect and met them all, trying to appear as strong-minded as her mother had told her she was.

But when they reached the dining hall, she was able to eat only a few bites from the platter Verra fetched her. Then she sat so stiffly her muscles ached. She didn't even know, she realized, what meal they ate. Had they slept through the afternoon? Was this their evening meal? Or was it only midday? The harsh lights that illuminated the dining area told her nothing.

"Do you know the hour?" she asked finally, when Verra pushed back her own platter.

"Early afternoon ship time. Midafternoon our own time." Verra glanced around. "Why don't we go visit the public growing rooms? Perhaps we'll find Juaren there—or in the zoological section."

"Yes," Reyna agreed. Juaren at least would be familiar. And Juaren, of all the people on the ship, would not try to guess the mood and worth of an entire people simply from the way she carried herself.

But they did not encounter Juaren until much later. By then Reyna had almost convinced herself with her own pose. She had walked tall through so many corridors, she had met so many eyes, she had become aware of so many people who turned and glanced after her covertly, that she began to feel that she was what Verra said she was. She had almost begun to believe that she was not just a child in a woman's guise.

They visited the planting rooms and she saw vines that swayed to music and flowers that grew from seed to blossom while they watched. They visited the zoological area and she saw creatures as various as the worlds they had come from, some alert and pacing, others held in stasis except for specified hours each day. In the late afternoon they watched the Tathem-eds dance in the forward lounge, their lean, handsome bodies speaking a language even Reyna could understand. Other groups appeared after them, offering their own entertainment to passengers so various Reyna could not remember the names of all the worlds Verra told her they had come from.

So gradually she hardly recognized at first what was happening, assurance deserted her. She looked around, beginning to feel lost among the strange peoples who sat together in the lounge. Was she the only one to whom all this was new, dazzling—overwhelming? Was she the only one who found the mingling of so many scents confusing? Was she the only one whose eyes ached from the harsh-ness of the lights?

Was she the only one who wanted only to retreat to her chamber, to her bed, to try to assimilate everything she had seen and heard?

But she had no chamber on the *Narsid*. She had only a cell. And she didn't think she could assimilate everything in just a few hours. It would take much longer.

Verra touched her arm. "It's enough, isn't it?"

Reyna nodded reluctantly. It was enough. She ached to escape the people, their scent, the lights. But she didn't want to be closed in tight quarters with the painted sun. "Is there someplace we can go that's—" What word did she want? Quiet? Private? Their quar-ters were quiet and private.

"There's a place I haven't shown you yet. It will be less crowded than this, especially at this hour." Verra stood.

She led the way through long corridors, quieter now than they had been earlier. Even the voices that spoke from the walls did so more quietly, with less of an emphatic crackle. Reyna followed, pressing her fingertips to her burning eyelids, trying to cool them.

Then Verra guided her through an arched portal and the entire universe pressed against her eyelids. They had stepped through a curtain of plastic chain into a large chamber with smoothly curving transparent walls. Beyond the walls lay the stars, nothing to ob-struct view of them but the narrow black railing that fit itself to the contour of the transparent walls. Reyna caught her breath, startled by the brilliant display. A few steps into the chamber, even the floor fell away into transparency. She stared down, suddenly dizzy, knowing that if she stepped forward she would lose her balance and spiral weightlessly down toward—

Toward what? What world lay below the *Narsid*? If she lost her balance, if the floor opened under her feet, how long would she tumble before she touched soil again? Or would she fall among the stars forever? Had anyone ever fallen from a ship like the *Narsid*? She tried to imagine what legends might be told of the person who had.

She tried to imagine what legends would be told in the valleys of Brakrath if she were the first to fall.

"Do you want to hold the railing?" Verra suggested.

"No." Her answer was unequivocal. Because to hold the railing, she must cross the floor. She must walk on the stars. Surely no one would voluntarily take that first step.

But there were other people at the railing. She realized that gradually as she grew accustomed to the fire of the stars. A tall, spindle-limbed woman with clawed hands. A lantern-jawed man even taller. Two people garmented entirely in black, only their eyes visible. And Juaren was there, dressed in hides and furs. He turned at the sound of their voices. A momentary flicker of his eyes suggested he was as relieved to see a known face as Reyna was. But he quickly veiled the betraying emotion, watching Reyna with guarded eyes.

She realized after a moment that he recognized her disorientation and was waiting to see what she would do. He was waiting to see if she had the courage to walk on the stars.

"You would feel much steadier at the railing, Reyna," Verra urged.

She knew she would not. But Juaren had set foot upon the void. How could she do less? Steeling herself, she crossed the brief distance gingerly, as if she trespassed upon an unstable ledge, as if she expected rock to crumble and spill her down the mountainside at any moment.

Then she gripped the railing. Instinctively she stared out, not down, and she did feel steadier. Carefully she drew a deep breath. When the ship did not rock, she loosened her painful grip on the rail and turned to Juaren. She saw with surprise that he gripped the railing even more tightly than she did, his fingers white upon it. He gazed slightly upward and to his left, his features pale, carved into stony stillness. Frowning, Reyna followed his gaze.

Intuition told her what he looked at. Her own hands tightened on the rail again. "Our sun—"

He nodded tightly, his lips pale. "There was an attendant here earlier. He pointed it out to me. If you look, you can see the shape of one triangle within another. Our sun is at the apex of the inner figure."

She studied the sky. "There?" she said uncertainly. "Near the red star? Is that Adar?" Adar was her mother's host-star, only visible from Brakrath during the darkest days of winter.

"I don't know which star is Adar. I can't tell from here. But our sun is the small one. The pale one. If you describe a line between the red star and that smaller yellow one—" He tapped at the transparent substance that separated them from the stars. "—if you draw a line, our sun lies just below it. *There.*"

That was their sun? So dim? So pale? She could barely distinguish its light. "Are you sure? The attendant—how did the attendant know what star you were looking for?"

"He knew who I was. What else would I be looking for?" He spoke sharply, as if she had challenged him. And his hands, she saw, had closed even tighter on the rail. Obviously the shrinking paleness of their sun made him as anxious as it made her.

"I thought—I thought it would be larger," she said. And brighter. More prominent in the company of stars. But if this scant brilliance was all that was required to nurture the people of Brakrath, to warm their summers and bring their crops to harvest . . .

She frowned, an unwelcome thought stirring at the back of her mind. *If* this was all that was required? But if their sun was sufficient, why must her mother draw sunlight from the barren mountainsides into the valley to support the crops? Why must palace daughters offer themselves to die on the mountain? If this was all that was required, why had her sisters died? Why had her father left the valley? Why did her mother carry Juaren's child?

Was this what Verra meant by gaining new perspectives? Seeing their life-giving sun for what it was—a star pale among its brighter companions? Reyna began to feel empty again, as empty as she had that morning, when Brakrath first fell away through the port. Her chest tightened painfully. Her hands grew cold on the railing.

Something of what she felt must have shown in her face, because Verra and Juaren stared at her, Verra concerned, Juaren tight-lipped, his own face unexpectedly bleak. She recoiled from their gazes, wanting to turn away, to retreat to her cubicle. Their sun was a pale star—and what was she? A child who had put pebbles in her ears, drawn a mask upon her face, and called herself a woman. She stared out at the stars and felt herself shrinking within her emerald coverall.

She couldn't stay here. At least in her cubicle there would be no one to watch her grow small.

But some gritty pride gripped her. She drew a sharp breath, angry at her own weakness. "You've never told me why you came," she said. "My mother asked twice and you didn't answer."

"Why?" Apparently she had asked the wrong question. He was suddenly both more tense and more distant than before. "Because I made a promise. And because I'm a hunter."

What kind of answer was that? And why was he reluctant to trust her with his reasons? Because she had shown him discourtesy after he pledged to her mother? Or was there some other strain in him? She looked down at his hands, white-knuckled on the rail. It almost seemed, from the way he held himself, that he guarded some closely-held vulnerability from her. "You've come to take prey then?" she probed. It seemed important to know, to understand at least that much.

"I've come because I made a promise," he said again, his voice low, strained.

"To your master? The master of your guild?" she guessed. "But why would he send you to another world to hunt? Aren't there furs enough on Brakrath? Furs enough for all the members of your guild?"

He turned sharply, his eyes glinting. "You know nothing about my guild," he said. "You know nothing about the things my master taught me."

She shrank, confused. Had she made him angry so easily? How? Did he think she had somehow slighted his guild with her questions? "I can guess what he taught you," she said. "To track, to stalk—"

Juaren's face had grown taut, the flesh pulling tight across the bones. "Those are the least of the things a hunter learns. Why do you think there are so few of us? My master trained only me, just as his master trained only him. There aren't so many who are willing to live as a hunter does. We ask a price for our furs, but we pay a price too, you know."

She drew back, the stony bleakness of his eyes making her wonder what price he had paid, how many winters he had spent stalking prey in the mountains while the people slept below.

Just as they slept below the *Narsid* tonight. Reyna pressed her temples, her hands beginning to shake—like a child's. She tried to seize control of the reaction and could not. There was a reason for that: what else was she but a child? Why dress herself like a woman and stand trying to understand Juaren when she hardly understood herself tonight? No wonder they could only talk at cross purposes. They had traveled too far today. They had taken too long a step, from their home to the stars. He must be as anxious as she was, though perhaps for different reasons. "I'm tired," she said, bowing her head, touching her temples.

For a moment it seemed her gesture touched him. Almost involuntarily he extended one hand. But at the last moment he drew it back. "I'm tired too," he said stiffly and turned away, hurrying across the transparent floor and out the arched door. The plastic chain curtain thrashed briefly behind him and then hung still again.

Reyna looked after him in dull incomprehension. They hadn't argued, but she almost wished they had. Then perhaps he would have betrayed himself. Perhaps he would have revealed himself. How could she even guess where his tender places lay if he wouldn't let her step near? If he considered every probe something to be guarded against?

Tired, confused, she turned back to the window. But she could not look out at the blaze of stars without seeing again how small their world was, how dim their sun. Slowly the corners of her eyes filled with tears. She brushed them away angrily. "I want to go to bed," she said.

"Of course," Verra agreed. "The day has been long."

And there would be longer ones still, Reyna guessed. She had come far from home. Many long days lay between her and her return. Wiping her eyes again, she turned and followed Verra from the chamber.

SEVEN

REYNA

Reyna woke when her stomach told her it was morning and lay staring at the walls of her cubicle. She gathered nothing more from them today than she had the night before. Certainly they suggested no way she might learn to talk with Juaren. Perhaps she was wrong to think she could. She was a palace daughter, after all, raised to think only of Valley Terlath, of the service it might require of her one day. He was a hunter. He had chosen a life outside the valleys, a life of isolation. Perhaps she would never understand him. Perhaps he would never trust her.

Given that, what were they to do now? Simply maintain their distance? But they had left Brakrath together bound for the same destination. Soon they would enter stasis on the same small vessel. And soon after that they would set foot together on an unknown world. If they could only talk first, if they could only reach some understanding . . .

Perhaps if she insisted, they could talk this morning. But when Reyna stepped into the lounge they shared, Juaren's door stood open and his cubicle was vacant.

Reyna hesitated, glancing around the lounge—painted sun, coiling vines, walls that pressed relentlessly near. Wherever Juaren had gone, she didn't want to wait for him here.

Briefly she examined herself in the tiny mirror, taking her own measure. Yesterday she had dressed to answer the question of a thousand eyes and had ended by feeling small. Today her mood was different. Today, she decided, she would dress to answer her own questions.

Quickly she stepped into her shift. Then, working briskly, she pulled her hair back and fastened it into a loose braid like she sometimes wore when she trained. She examined herself again in the tiny mirror, then rubbed away the faint remnant of green ink with a damp cloth. Finally she took down the white songsilk and tied it at her waist.

She paused then, exhaling softly, letting the cool fabric spill through her fingers. There was a silken spell in the white cloth even when it was silent. It seemed to melt against her waist, to warm itself from her stroking fingers. And it reminded her that she had not come aboard the *Narsid* to be seen. She had not come to answer the unspoken questions of strangers, no matter what Verra's evaluation of the situation. She had come with one purpose: to take passage to the world the silk had come from. If there were questions to be answered aboard the *Narsid,* they were hers. And if the people in the corridors looked at her and saw a child, then that was what they saw. Surely they had seen children before.

The momentum of decision carried her forward, out the door of the suite. She did not pause when she heard Verra's door open, when she heard the Arnimi woman's surprised query.

There were many places on the *Narsid* where Verra had not taken her. Reyna discovered that by following her feet through the branching corridors. There were several small dining areas she had not seen before, the smells that came from their adjoining kitchens so cloying she didn't pause to see what was served at the tables. People ate here, she suspected, whose foods were so repugnant that other people aboard did not want to see or smell them.

There were small garden rooms, some of them cold and dry, others oppressively damp and warm. She paused in each one and sampled the air, wondering what worlds were simulated there. Later she discovered a large room lit by blazing orange lamps. Long-limbed people lay on thin mattresses on the floor, soaking up the heat, their dark skin gleaming as if freshly burnished. Once she found a room that was filled entirely with steam. She entered the first of double doors, then retreated in panic when she saw dark, moving shapes in the steam. She hurried away, embarrassed, before anyone could see how frightened she was. But perhaps other people had those nightmares too.

Twice, in remote corridors, she was challenged by blue-uniformed guards. Once, from the far end of the corridor, she heard children's voices. She turned back reluctantly, realizing that she had approached a crew enclave, wishing she could see at close quarters how the people who worked the *Narsid* lived.

At last, when the harsh lights were beginning to burn her eyes and the dry air made her throat hurt, she found a dim room where dozens of small screens were recessed into the walls. People sat before the individual screens while rapidly changing scenes appeared upon the screens. Reyna slipped quietly into the room and watched. After a while she realized that the people selected which scenes they would see by going to a central console and punching at colored buttons there.

Were these the tapes Verra had mentioned? After watching for a while longer, Reyna approached the console and casually punched a sequence upon the colored buttons. A moment later a small, opaque cube slid from a narrow chute into her hand. She looked around quickly to see if anyone were watching. But the others were too preoccupied with their own screens to notice her uncertainty. Shrugging, she approached a vacant chair and did as she had seen the others do, dropped the cube into a small chute in the chair's padded arm.

Her screen filled with color and light and a feminine voice murmured incomprehensibly near her ear. Reyna jerked, startled, but forced herself to remain seated. For a time she could not resolve what she saw into coherent patterns. Then she realized she looked at tiny flakes of living color which swam through an underwater environment. The webbed water plants they swam among were delicate, their long, trailing leaves veined with color. Periodically they seemed to be sucked erect by some force and briefly held there, immobile. Then, released, they began to dance and sway in the turbulence of the water, until finally the water was still again and the plants drooped into a second immobility.

She watched the strange dance and the swimming flecks in fascination until she realized that the tape had begun to repeat itself, and not for the first time. She had seen the same configuration of swimming flecks at least twice before, caught for a moment in a framing circle of leaves. She frowned and gazed around the room until one of her neighbors tapped at his chair arm and his screen became dark. Experimentally Reyna explored the arm of her own chair and found a control. She tapped it and her screen too immediately darkened. Then she went to the central console for a fresh tape.

She remained in the room, progressively more lost in the scenes the cubes called up for her, until she heard her name spoken behind her.

Surprised, she half-rose and looked around. There was no one behind her, but before she could sit again, her name was repeated. "Reyna Terlath. Attention, Reyna Terlath. Please proceed to the nearest ID station and identify yourself. Reyna Terlath—"

The ship's com was speaking her name from the walls, instructing her in her own language, however poorly spoken. She drew away from the chair guiltily, wondering what she had done wrong. Her first impulse, as the message was repeated, was to flee to the suite. If someone wanted to speak to her, let him approach her there. And in person, not in the form of a disembodied voice.

But she had kept no mental chart of the corridors she had followed in her odyssey through the *Narsid*. She had simply walked, relying on chance to take her back to some familiar area eventually. And so far it had not. Now, she realized, she didn't know how to return to their suite.

Nor was she entirely certain how to locate the nearest ID station. Were those the inconspicuous metal plates that appeared in the walls of the corridors at irregular intervals? She had seen other people press their hands to them.

"Reyna Terlath—"

She looked around self-consciously and was relieved that no one seemed to notice her name crackling from the walls. Quickly she deserted the screening room.

She blinked uncertainly in the brightly lit corridor and walked until she located one of the metal plates. Looking around again, catching no more than a few sidelong glances, she pressed her hand to it.

Nothing startling occurred, except that the summons from the ship's com abruptly ceased and the usual incomprehensible string of communication resumed. Reyna hesitated, looking up and down the corridor. What would happen now that she had done as instructed? Or had she? How was she to know if the metal plate was actually an ID station? She waited for a few moments beside it, then turned uncertainly back toward the screening room.

But the fascination was broken. She stood for a few moments scanning the panoply of bright scenes, then withdrew, wandering down the corridor aimlessly.

From somewhere nearby, she soon smelled food cooking. She quickened her pace and found herself at the entrance to the dining area where she and Verra had eaten the day before. As then, the area was crowded. Reyna paused, glancing around the room. She saw people she had seen before, or others very like them, but she did not see Verra or Juaren.

However there were many people eating alone. Surely she could learn how to obtain food from the tall consoles at back of the hall, just as she had learned how to screen tapes.

But before she could enter the dining hall, a blue-uniformed woman approached, holding out one hand in injunction. "Reyna Terlath, come," she said, stiffly, as if the Brakrathi syllables were strange in her mouth. "Come with me."

Reyna hesitated. Was this why she had been instructed to press the ID panel? To indicate where on the ship she was to be found? Unconsciously she stroked the songsilk, smoothing it against her leg. "Where do you want me to go?" she demanded, suspecting there would be no explanation, suspecting the woman had only learned to parrot those few words of Brakrathi.

"Come with me," the woman repeated. "Reyna Terlath, come with me."

Shrugging, Reyna went.

The woman led her past a uniformed guard and down corridors she had not seen before. The walls were painted with a geometric design of dazzling brilliance. Yet each time Reyna glanced through an open door, she saw people hunched over desks and consoles with no brightness in their eyes.

At last the woman indicated that she was to enter a door to their right. Reyna did so and found herself in a small, cluttered room furnished with shelves, table and chairs. Paper was strewn liberally in deep piles and the walls were hung with printed documents she could not read. Not knowing what else to do, she sat down and looked around. Something about the room was familiar, but she couldn't say exactly what. Its close dimensions? Its untidiness, as if the urgent press of work precluded order?

She turned at the sound of the door, then colored as Juaren stepped into the room. He glanced at her in quick surprise, hesitating before taking the chair farthest from hers. He nodded to her, then stared down at his hands tensely, saying nothing.

Nor did she find anything to say, although the situation had become even more familiar—two people shown into a small, cluttered room and left there alone. She squirmed in her chair and glanced at his guarded face. Surely he recognized what she did in the situation. He must have lived in a settled valley before going to the mountains. He knew how disagreements were mediated, how misunderstandings were rectified. Surely he saw that they had been brought here to talk.

But what were they to say? How were they to begin? "I think," she said, her voice sounding tentative, "I think that if we don't speak, Verra will come and mediate for us. She's probably already here, somewhere." In another room nearby or in the corridor, waiting to step in and assume the role of the juris if they could not talk without her.

Juaren nodded, still staring at his hands. The knuckles had grown very white. When she said nothing more, he spoke, the words low, difficult, as if they were spoken against resistance. "I don't know what we have to say to each other. It's been many days since we met."

She was not surprised at the bitter edge his words held. It had been many days—many days of silence. They had eaten at the same table but she had never offered him bread or accepted food from his hand. They had passed in the corridors but she had never spoken. She had recognized from the first that he was wary of slights, but she had offered him nothing else.

And now she demanded that they talk. "I just thought that if we could talk, if we could understand each other—" She paused, and when he made no response, she plunged ahead, letting some of her own frustration show. "All right, this is what I have to say. You know very well why I came. But when I asked why you came, you wouldn't tell me. And when I tried to learn about your guild, you answered me as if I were a child. You made me feel ignorant." That much was true, even if it did place the blame for their strained relationship on the wrong shoulders.

He shifted in his chair, glancing down at his hands again, uncomfortably. "Everyone is ignorant in something," he said finally, his voice neutral.

So at least he had put aside bitterness. But he had given her an observation, not an answer. "Of course."

He shifted again, a muscle in his jaw jumping. For a time he seemed to struggle against his own reluctance. Finally he raised his head and met her gaze directly, as if he had forced himself to a decision. As if he had forced himself to put aside doubt and trust her. "Everyone is ignorant of my guild. You think that because I call myself a hunter, I only hunt. You think that's all I've ever done. You think the crafts of hunting are all I learned from my master. And you think I do it for the price it brings."

"I—I thought so," she admitted. "But last night I heard you say that you pay a price too." Isolation. Danger. The loneliness of the mountains in winter. How must it feel to stand on the mountainside, cold and wakeful, while the people took wintersleep below? Because women of barohnial blood did not take wintersleep either, she knew what it was to wander through the halls of an empty palace during the long cold season. She knew how empty the vacant chambers were. She knew how little taste food had when she sat alone at the table. But at least she had shelter, food, and a library to read from.

He sighed deeply. With effort, he opened his hands, letting them lie palm-up on the table. His nails had bitten crescents into the skin. "I paid a price before I ever joined the guild," he said. "I was a winter-child."

The unexpected self-revelation made Reyna chill. She drew a painful breath and stared at his bleeding palms, at the sudden, unguarded bleakness of his face, and wished she hadn't heard what he said. But she was the one who had insisted he talk. She was the one who had demanded he take down the barriers he must have set around those bitter words. And—just from those few words—she understood much about him that she had not understood before. She understood why he had preferred the isolation of the mountains to life in his home valley. She understood why he guarded himself so carefully, why he withheld trust. She understood why he met slight as if he expected nothing more. "How—how did it happen?"

"How?" His voice took a hard edge. "Komas, my master, had an explanation for it. Some people, he told me, are intended to be born. There is a power—in the mountains, in the sky, perhaps in the sun itself—that intends their birth. So their two parents are drawn together. They dance at Midsummer. The tides rise, the woman drinks the ovulant, and the power has its way."

"A child is born," Reyna said softly. It was a familiar ritual and a familiar tale, time-hallowed. Most of the children of the halls could count Midsummer Fest as the date of their conception. But a winter-child was not born as a result of the Midsummer dancing. Children conceived at Midsummer were not born until late the following spring, after their mothers had wakened from wintersleep and had had time to replenish their sleep-depleted nutritional reserves. A winter-child was conceived earlier in the year, whether intentionally or by mischance. And a winter-child was born in the winter, while his mother still slept. "Was it intentional?" she asked. She knew that occasionally a woman slipped the ovulant from the storage room shelf and drank it out of season. Usually that only happened when she was in the grip of some unresolved conflict—with herself, with her mate, with her family. What she had done was quickly enough detected and the birth prevented.

"No," he said. "It was spontaneous. Some power intended me born—or so Komas insisted—and so my mother ovulated out of season. She ovulated spontaneously, without even knowing it had happened. My father had no more way of knowing than she did. And when she realized she had conceived, she concealed it. Maybe she believed in the same power Komas did. Perhaps she was only frightened of a termination. Or perhaps she was embarrassed to ask for it. Maybe she thought no one would believe the ovulation had been accidental.

"Whatever her reason, instead of going to the midwife and requesting a termination, she put on heavier skirts and laughed at the dining table about the extra reserves she was putting on for winter. No one guessed it was anything else—not until waking days, when they found me beside her. She must have wakened for the birth, because I was wrapped in the blankets with her. But she was dead and I was alive. Alive and warm."

Reyna shuddered. Alive and warm because he had passed wintersleep in his mother's womb, fattening on her reserves while she slowly starved. "If she hadn't taken the sleepleaf, if she had petitioned to be excused from wintersleep—" she said.

"Then she would have lived. Or if she had conceived me even a month later, she might have lived. It was the last month that killed her."

Yes, during the last month the unborn child went through its swiftest growth, drawing most heavily upon its mother's resources. Then the mother needed to be awake, able to feed herself, or the child would take everything, draining her. "Your father—"

Juaren shrugged. "They had pledged for a single year. By the time I was born, the year was done. He turned me back to her family and moved to another hall. When I was ten, I petitioned Juris Karnissa to call him to her chambers so we could speak. I thought—" His eyes narrowed and he knotted his hands again. "I thought there was something to be said between us, though he had never spoken to me or even nodded. I thought that if we sat together in Juris Karnissa's chambers, we would find something. I didn't have any idea what, just that it was important that it be said —and soon, or we might never speak." He shrugged again. "Of course that was what he wanted. That we never speak. He declined the petition."

And never spoke with his son. Reyna felt the same cold claw of anguish at her heart that Juaren must have felt.

But he had been born to that anguish. Not much was spoken aloud of winter births, but there were whispered tales, passed with shivers and dread. Every girl of the halls grew up with the secret fear that in some winter of her womanhood, a cold, ground-dwelling spirit would reach into her unguarded womb and leave an unnatural child there to drain away the fat she had stored for the long sleep. Every girl of the halls entertained the secret fear that some spring her family might find her pale and cold in her bed, with a rosy, fat child beside her.

To be that rosy child, to grow up with tales whispered around you, tales suggesting that you were the product of a supernatural violation, to be set apart forever, an intruder who had come without invitation, without welcome . . . how could he have lived that way and learned to trust? How could he have lived that way and learned to expect acceptance?

Reyna hugged herself miserably. "And I treated you just as your father did. I refused to speak."

"Yes." He frowned down at the table top. "After my petition was refused, I went to the mountains and never returned. I had no place in the valley. I never did have, even with my mother's people. They whispered the same stories everyone else did, no matter what they said aloud. I had only lived with them thinking one day I could earn a place. Finally I recognized that I could not." His voice fell. "And now you are in the same position. You have no place in your valley either."

She looked up sharply to see if he spoke with satisfaction. But she had never met spite from him, and she didn't meet it now.

And he was right. She had no place. Even if she found Birnam Rauth alive and brought him back to Valley Terlath, what place would she have? She would still be a palace daughter who could never become a barohna, who could never attain any semblance of womanhood. That was why, she realized, when her mother had first told her that she must not make her challenge, she had seen understanding in Juaren's eyes. He had recognized from his own experience what she was feeling.

"Neither of us has a place," she said. Restlessly, she released her hair from its braid and drew it through her fingers. "But you still haven't told me why you wanted to come."

He shrugged, trusting her now. "It was what Komas wanted."

"Your guild master? The man who taught you to hunt?"

"The man who taught me what hunters once were, in the first days," he said. "Even the hunters have forgotten, most of them, and there aren't many left now. We've been called hunters so long . . ."

"In the first days after the stranding?" she probed when he did not go on. That was how the first timers had come to Brakrath so many tens of centuries ago. They had ridden a starship that fell, stranding them.

"In the first days after the stranding. In the first years. In the first centuries," he said softly. "We were sentries then, not hunters. We stood outside the valleys and watched."

He had stopped speaking again. He seemed to be looking back, perhaps trying to picture those first settlements, before the people had adapted to Brakrath's harsh conditions. There had been no barohnas then. There had been neither stonehalls nor palaces. Sleepleaf had not been discovered. There had been only poorly prepared people struggling against the long, harsh winters and the short, inhospitable growing seasons. There had been only people starving.

And hoping. "They watched for ships," Reyna said, remembering the things she had read in the palace library. "The people thought they would be missed. They thought ships would come to find them, to take them to the world they had been bound for when their ship fell. And so they sent men to stand sentry."

"At first they thought ships would come to find them, yes. Later they feared other ships would come—to destroy them. There were rival groups leaving Earth during that time. Earthexodus they called it. Sometimes people from the different groups tried to claim the same world, and there were wars. So the first timers realized after a while that they might as readily be found by unfriendly ships as by their own."

"I don't remember that," she said slowly. But she hadn't read all the scrolls. She didn't know all the stories.

"It's true. Komas told me, just as his master told him. And there was another consideration as well. The first timers had learned that there were other races traveling among the stars too, not even human. If any of them sent down ships—"

Reyna remembered dark shapes moving in the steam and shuddered. "They wanted sentries to stand watch against that too."

"Yes, even though they might be able to do nothing to protect themselves. Sometimes when I'm in the mountains I think of that: a few thousand people, stranded, barely able to care for themselves—and the sky."

Reyna shivered. The sky, from which anything could come. She shut her eyes and saw their sun as she had seen it the night before, frail among its thousands of brighter sisters. The people of Valley Terlath had never seen what she saw or felt what she felt. They had never guessed how obscure their world was. But the first timers had known and they must have recognized that their own strength was as insubstantial as their sun's.

"Sometimes when I'm in the mountains, I like to think I'm standing sentry for one of the early settlements, taking a few furs just to occupy myself, to have something to offer for my keep when I visit the valleys. Our pledge comes from that time. Komas was the last hunter living who could repeat it in the old words—except for me." Softly Juaren recited a rhythmic strand of words.

He spoke them so softly Reyna could hear the loneliness in them—and the love. She pressed her temples, for a moment confused by that—the love. The people of the valleys had made him an outcast with their whispers and their superstition. Why should he have any tenderness for them?

But why should she care what became of the people of Valley Terlath? Her sisters had died for them and received nothing but a small place in the legends of the valley in return. She would have received nothing more for her own death. Her eyelids trembled and she pressed them tight against unwelcome tears. "What—what does it mean in modern tongue?" she demanded.

"Just that I will stand watching through every storm. That if I see danger I will approach and study it. And that then I will wake the people, so they can prepare." Again he opened his hands, frowning down at the crescent-shaped wounds in the palms. "And that is why I came."

She looked up at him, frowning. He seemed to think he had made himself clear, and in fact he had explained many things. But the critical point eluded her. "You came because—"

"The ships have come. First they brought the Arnimi. Then they brought the Benderzic. Finally they brought the starsilk. Komas saw them all, and so did I. We saw Arnimi aircars flying over the land. We visited the place where Khira stoned the Benderzic ship. We learned where your uncle found the trader and we went there.

"Komas thought at first that when we had seen all the ships, we would have fulfilled the second condition of the pledge. We would have studied the danger. But we realized when we had seen the last —the trader—that it wasn't the ships that were the danger. It was the people who sent them. They were the ones we must study."

Reyna frowned, carefully following the line of his reasoning. He had taken a pledge to watch for ships and to study them if they came. But when he had seen the ships, when he had examined them, he had realized they were no more than shells. The danger lay with the people who flew them. "The Arnimi. The Benderzic. And whoever sent the trader," Reyna said slowly. "They're the ones you must study." And he had studied the Arnimi, sitting long hours upon the plaza wall.

"Yes, but not only them. We thought about it more and realized it was the climate beyond Brakrath we must evaluate. We must learn how our strengths measure against the strengths of other peoples. We must learn what our weaknesses are. We must learn—" He sighed. "We must learn the danger. And then we must waken the people."

He said the words as if he had said them to himself hundreds of times, trying to plumb their full meaning. *Waken the people.* Something in his voice made her shiver again. "What—what do you mean—waken the people?"

"They're sleeping," he said. "They have no interest in anything beyond Brakrath. They see the Arnimi aircars but they hardly wonder about them. They know what your mother did to the Benderzic ship, but they do no more than make tales of it. They heard the starsilk speak when your brother wore it but they don't ask themselves why it speaks. They simply shrug the question away and make more tales. They don't feel compelled to look beyond their own valleys for anything."

"Everything they need is there," Reyna protested. Yet just the night before she had wondered if it were.

"Then what if someone else—some other race—wants what we have? The Benderzic—"

Reyna drew back in her chair, frowning. *The hostile races who prey on us all,* Verra had said. There must be many such races if the

Benderzic had come to gather information about Brakrath to bid away, if the Arnimi and the other CoSignators felt obliged to band together for mutual protection.

Brakrath had no such protection, beyond the strength of the barohnas. And what, she wondered uneasily, was that? Three hundred women scattered widely through the mountains, communicating only through pairing stones and messengers. The pairing stones were cut in sets of two, so that the two women who wore them could communicate with one another. But if either wanted to communicate with any other barohna, she must send a messenger on foot.

Was that good enough? And how did the sun-wielding power of the barohnas measure against the technological strength of other races? Reyna caught at the starsilk, crushing it between her fingers, and realized she didn't know. She knew nothing of the strength of other races. She only knew that they were many in numbers and various in form. She couldn't even begin to count how many different kinds of humans she had seen since she had come aboard the *Narsid.* She hadn't thought to ask Verra if the ship transported non-humans too. Nor had she thought to ask how many races of non-humans existed, how widely spread they were, what they were like in their habits and temperaments.

Juaren was right. The people of Brakrath were sleeping. And she had been sleeping too. The Arnimi had been quartered in Valley Terlath since before her birth. Yet she had never tried to learn from them the things they knew about the universe beyond Brakrath. She had had too much scorn for them to do that.

And what was her scorn based upon? Upon the fact that the Arnimi used instruments she didn't understand to measure things she considered unimportant? Or simply upon the fact that they were strange, unattractive and distant, with no place in the legends of Valley Terlath?

She had other questions too, as unwelcome as those. How, for instance, were the people to be wakened if they didn't want to wake? If the Council of Bronze didn't want them wakened? Her mother had gone against the Council in telling her she must not make her challenge. Would she go against the Council again—not just once, but time and again?

Was the Council sleeping too? Certainly they were reluctant to see change. Was that a reasoned reluctance or one no more rationally based than her own scorn for the Arnimi? The fabric of valley life—how easily might it disintegrate? And if it did disintegrate, what had they to put in its place? The people lived well now. But there had been many times in their history when they had not, when they had lived at the bare edge of survival. There had been times of disorder and hunger.

Given the intransigence of the environment, the two traveled in company—disorder and hunger. Reyna combed her fingers back through her hair, wishing she knew where to turn for answers. "Your master, Komas—" she said. "He died in the winter."

Juaren rubbed his forehead, as if stroking at some remembered pain. He spoke without expression. "We decided last winter to come to Valley Terlath to study the Arnimi. We wanted to observe them while everyone else slept, when they would not be expecting it. And we thought that after the thawing, we would speak to Khira. We thought that she would hear our warning with more attention than anyone. She's had most of her life to observe the Arnimi, and she lives differently than other barohnas. She has learned to look beyond tradition—in some things at least.

"But we were caught in a storm as we crossed the upper pass from Valley Pentilath. Komas slipped—he fell, and I couldn't reach him. The drop was too sheer. He had fallen too far." Juaren shrugged. "I called and he didn't answer. He didn't move. I waited. The snow fell. The wind blew. It began to get dark. Finally I knew there was nothing I could do except roll rocks down to cover him and hope he was dead when I did it." He raised his head, his voice growing hard. "I could do nothing for him then, but I won't fail him now. When I knew that we would be permitted to go, I went back to where I left him and I pledged him that. There are only a handful of hunters left, and most of them have forgotten everything but taking skins. I'm the only one left who knows the old words. I'm the only one who knows what must be done."

So that was where he had gone in the days before their journey. To renew his pledge to his guild master. His loss was clear in the bleakness of his words. The one person who had accepted him, who had given him place and purpose, was gone. Now he was the only one who remembered that the people must be wakened.

But how? And to what effect? Reyna caught one end of the starsilk and rubbed it against her cheek. He had answered her question, but in doing so he had raised many more. "I'm sorry you lost your master," she said finally, inadequately. "Do you have some idea how to waken the people, if—if we must be the ones to do that?"

"I intended to speak to Khira, but this wasn't the season. She's had too many concerns and she has asked too many concessions from the Council recently. And beyond that, no. I have no idea at all."

Nor did she. None. "You didn't even want to tell me," she said.

He glanced away, frowning. "I wanted to tell you," he said slowly. "Some things become more real when you speak of them. But other things become less real. Particularly—"

Particularly if the person he confided in belittled them. And she had given him little reason to expect a fair hearing. Reyna sighed. "But at least—at least we can talk to each other now," she said tentatively.

"Yes," he said, his head still bowed.

Yet they did not. They sat in silence, each following the direction of his own thoughts, until the door opened. Verra paused in the doorway, studying them in their silence, disappointment touched her features. "I brought you here to talk," she said finally. "I spoke to Commander Cezari just a short time ago. We are going into stasis tomorrow morning, soon after waking time. I know you haven't argued. There is no open dispute between you. But if you can't talk with each other—"

"We have talked," Juaren interposed, rising, nodding as formally as he would have nodded to a juris in her chambers.

Reyna rose too and joined him in the formality of his greeting. "And we have resolved our differences, Verra," she said. "You have our gratitude for bringing us together."

Verra looked from one to the other of them and suddenly flushed with poorly contained pleasure. "You've talked? I thought perhaps I had driven you farther apart, trying to serve as juris."

"No," Reyna assured her. "You've given us each other." At least for the space of the journey she had. Reyna glanced at Juaren, confident he would not contradict her. "If ever I have a valley of my own, I will establish you in offices there." Verra had even found the right setting for their confrontation, a cluttered office much like the chambers from which valley jurises administered their halls. Reyna doubted she herself could ever bring the same sensitivity to resolving a problem between two Arnimi.

The brightness in Verra's cheeks mounted. She patted nervously at her hair, an Arnimi gesture that had always irritated Reyna. "I'll remember that, Reyna Terlath," she said. "I won't forget the offer of an office in your palace. And now, if you have managed to reconcile yourselves, perhaps you would like a tour of the stasis chamber. I'm sure you'll be more comfortable with the process if you understand it."

"Of course," Reyna agreed, amused by the brightness she had brought to Verra's cheeks, when they both knew she would never have a palace of her own or an office to offer. For the first time since she had learned that she could not be a barohna, the bitterness was gone. She had found other concerns, necessary concerns. There was a danger—many dangers—to be studied and a people to be wakened—and Birnam Rauth still to be found, if he was living. She didn't know any better than she had a few minutes ago how they were to achieve any of those things. She didn't even know that they could be achieved. But she no longer felt alone, without purpose or place.

She glanced at Juaren and for the first time saw him smile. She answered with a smile of her own, tentative at first, then certain. Perhaps they neither had a place in Valley Terlath—or any valley. Perhaps he would always be a winter-child and she a palace daughter. But they had a place together, at least for a while.

EIGHT

TSUUKA

Tsuuka stretched in the grass of the clearing grooming herself while Paalan and Kaliir tumbled and growled nearby, baby teeth gnashing. Occasionally she roused herself to slap playfully at one of them or to soothe the other when their sparring became too rough. The grass was warm, the sun bright, and they were fed, all of them, cubs, weanlings and herself. Tsuuka should have had no concern beyond cleansing herself and letting the midday sun dry her fur.

But her languor was as much feigned as the weanlings' ferocity. There was a harsh note in Dariim's chuckling growl today and a half-concealed brightness in her eyes. Not the brightness of mischief or pleasure but of something secretive, something that made her bound recklessly through the trees, frightening away game and shredding white-barked trunks with restless claws. And whatever the secret, Falett didn't share it. That was clear from the way she peered after her sibling, head cocked, teeth bared in an anxious grin.

Restlessly Tsuuka roused herself and called to her weanlings. They gave up their sparring reluctantly, but when Tsuuka had groomed them, they settled down to nap readily enough. She rose and looked over them with distracted eyes, waiting until their breath was soft and regular before she padded away. Their stomachs were full and they had tired themselves. They would sleep now until mid-afternoon, when the shadows of the trees lengthened and reached out to cool the grass.

So she had that long, but for what she didn't know. She paced into the trees. Dariim had darted away again, Falett running after her. Tsuuka dropped to fours and picked up their scent from the soil.

It didn't take long to find them. They were hunched under the brush near the streamside, watching the spinners as they washed freshly spun silent-silks in the running water. Tsuuka saw immediately from the aloof set of Dariim's shoulders, from the half-concealed glint in her eyes that she did not want to be there, sitting quietly. She held herself rigidly, her shoulder not touching her sibling's, and her claws were extended, restlessly shredding the soft soil.

Tsuuka watched them a moment longer, studying the hard shine of their coats, the set of their ears, the new lankiness of their limbs. Dariim was crafty in her stalking already, daring in her attack, and Falett was learning, although more slowly. They would not live much longer under her silks.

But the most perilous days were ahead, the days when the last, keen energy of cubhood drove their maturing bodies and challenge gleamed more brightly than judgment or caution. Falett would not be drawn far from safety. Tsuuka knew that because Falett was much as she herself had been. But Dariim . . .

Tsuuka's eyes narrowed to yellow slits. Dariim had already been drawn away. Today's restlessness told Tsuuka that. Something had blazed its mark in her eyes, and Tsuuka did not even know when it had happened.

She did know her own heart. She had never relished the fact that she felt something for Dariim she did not feel for the others. But today she knew it was true. She did not know what had happened to Maiilin in the heart of the trees so many years ago. She could not guess what had stolen her wit and left an empty husk. But if she herself had been bolder, if she herself had been braver, perhaps it need not have happened.

But she had hidden, and now her only recompense was that her second-born carried Maiilin's spirit. How could she let that rebirth be threatened?

Yet how could she counter the threat when she couldn't even guess its source? Tsuuka lingered in the shadows, wondering, until she heard a shrill of alarm from the other side of the water. She responded automatically. Without thinking, she splashed through the stream and bounded into the trees that lined its bank.

A prickle-hide had emerged from a fresh tunnel. The soil it had thrown aside rose nearby in a cone, still damp. It slowly circled a screaming spinner. The little creature's witless eyes were wide, glazed, as the predator described its slowly narrowing circle. The prickle-hide had already raised its venom-quill. Tsuuka could see the deadly amber drops glistening on its tip.

That gave her pause for only a moment. The prickle-hide had seen her and its venom was deadly, but experience told her the prickle-hide would require precious seconds to renounce the prospect of game and deploy its quill for defense instead. Tsuuka did not grant it those seconds. She sprang immediately, muscles moving fluidly, the fur at the back of her neck softly erect. With practiced claws, she dealt the startled prickle-hide a glancing blow that bowled it to its side. The animal squealed, legs flailing, and tried to regain its feet, but Tsuuka already tore at its vulnerable underbelly. Before the spinner could cease its mindless squealing, the predator was dead.

Dariim and Falett appeared in the next instant, quivering with alertness. Tsuuka broke off the poisoned quill and plunged it into the earth. Then she raised her bleeding prey and shook it. "For you, cubs," she said, the words hissing softly. "Find the sun and make your meal." The unexpected feast would occupy them for a while and give her time to study Dariim's mood.

Falett chuckled happily and, when Dariim held back, took the game herself. Although there was no relish in Dariim's response, she followed as her sibling carried the prickle-hide in search of a sunny spot. When Tsuuka had cleaned her claws, she followed them both.

She always found pleasure in watching her young feed. But today Dariim had little enthusiasm for the unexpected feast. She tore at the meat, but without her usual hoarse mutter of appreciation. And there remained something secret in her eyes, some boldness that was veiled but not dampened.

Tsuuka stretched out nearby, watching. It was plain that Dariim no more wanted to be here than she had wanted to watch the spinners work. It was also plain that her drooping eyelids hid furtiveness as she licked her lips and stretched out in feigned satiety. Falett dispatched the last of the prickle-hide and presented herself to be groomed, grinning and sated. Tsuuka pulled a lazy tongue through the cub's fur and let her own eyes narrow to drowsy slits.

Dariim smoothed her coat perfunctorily, then sank down in apparent sleep. But through her narrowed eyelids, Tsuuka saw the telltale rigidity of her muscles, the quivering of her eyelids. When

Falett dozed, Tsuuka tucked her own chin into her fur and let her breath rasp thickly in her throat, but she remained alert beneath the guise of sleep.

She did not need to open her eyes to know when Dariim rose and padded away. Some sixth sense told her that. She waited for moments, then opened her eyes.

Falett slept soundly, the sun warm on her fur. There was no sign of Dariim.

So she had gone to pursue whatever had blazed the mark in her eyes. Growling softly, Tsuuka rose and took her cub's scent.

She remembered some of Maiilin's cubhood ploys, remembered how cleverly Maiilin had outwitted their mother when she had wanted to pursue mischief. There were the feigned sleeps followed by the secret disappearances. There were the abrupt, galloping bursts of speed after game no one else could see. There were the meandering rambles that seemed to lead directly away from her actual destination. There were the long scampers down streambeds, where the running water washed away her scent.

Dariim exercised none of those ploys today beyond the first. Her trail led directly through the trees and toward the heart of the woods. Following, Tsuuka realized with sinking heart that that was no accident. Dariim had found something in the deep trees, just as Maiilin had so many years before. And despite all Tsuuka's warnings, she was pursuing it.

Things no sithi must see. But what could there be in the heart of the trees that was never to be glimpsed? Tsuuka followed Dariim's scent, her thoughts darting without order or reason. The unseen—what was the unseen? It joined thoughts with the spinners and the silks, it directed their activities, but why was it never seen? Was it the thing in the deep trees her mother had warned her about? Or was the unseen something else entirely?

She knew so little. Sometimes questions came to her, but she batted them away unexamined. Because she was afraid of them? Because Maiilin had had questions and had screamed and become a growler? Or simply because questioning brought back memory of Maiilin and with it a burdening sense of her own failure? If she had not hidden that day, if she had gone with Maiilin . . .

Tsuuka ran through the trees, letting the questions come now. And they were many. How were the spinners, witless and vulnerable, able to create the silks, which spoke so cleverly, so silently in her mind? Did the silks' cleverness come from something the spinners wove into them? Or did they mirror some hidden cleverness of the spinners themselves? And why did the thoughts that joined the spinners, the silks and the unseen become nightmares when they touched sithi minds? Just because sithi were sithi and not spinners or silks? Just because the images that carried information to one mind touched a different mind more darkly?

And what had happened to Maiilin? Could spinners have done that to her? Tsuuka knew that spinners came and went in the heart of the trees. But why would spinners have trussed Maiilin in strings of foul-smelling silk? And how could spinners have quenched her wit? And why? The mysterious things Maiilin had claimed she saw in the cavernous trees, blind, half-formed growing things—perhaps it was true. Perhaps she had seen those things. But what were they?

Tsuuka growled miserably as she ran. If she had gone with Maiilin, perhaps she would know what those things were.

Or perhaps—a sudden chill rippled down her back, raising the fur—perhaps if she had gone with Maiilin, she would be a growler now too. Perhaps both of them would be wandering the verges of the forest, crying when the silks sang.

Black claws closed around her heart. It had happened to Maiilin. It could well have happened to her. But it must not happen to Dariim. Tsuuka ran faster, letting her muscles work to their own rhythm. She was grateful that her heart pumped swiftly with the effort. Otherwise she would have known the beat of its fear.

The trees around her became denser, taller, their trunks stained now with moss and fungus growths. Even the smell of the air became different—damper, closer, heavier. Beneath layers of decomposed leaves, the soil was wet, as if the sun never reached here to dry it. And there was a silence that was as heavy as the air. Here there were no spinners chattering, no sithi chuckling or growling, no scamper of small game. Here there was only stillness.

But the stillness was not absolute. For as Tsuuka ran farther into the trees, she heard a voice in the distance. Her feet missed a beat, making her lurch awkwardly. A silk singing so deep in the trees? There were no bowers here. Although spinners came and went, they did not carry silks with them—not here.

But the song was unmistakable, vivid and clear—and wild. Because this silk sang by sunlight. It tuned its voice on the sun's bright energy and cried out with a feeling she had seldom heard in a silk. Here was no sweetness. Here was no subtlety. Here was no trilling pleasure. Here was protest and triumph and mockery.

Tsuuka slowed, baffled. Dariim's scent was stronger here. She traced it until she reached a place where it led in several directions at once. There she stopped, growling. Obviously Dariim had circled, leaving crossing trails. If she knew which to follow—Tsuuka raised her head and gazed into the trees.

Her throat closed with alarm. A chestnut shadow clung to the heavily mossed trunk of one of the tallest trees. Dariim was scrambling up the tree, claws tearing at the heavy bark, ears laid back. And above her, tangled in the highest branches, was a red silk. It clung to the tree and stretched out for the sun, its song throbbing as if it were sunlight given voice.

A copy-master—someone had set a copy-silk free. Tsuuka recognized the special quality of its voice now. For most of the time, copy-silks were kept hidden, starved of light and breeze and freedom. But sometimes the spinners tied them briefly beside the stream to air after they had used them to make songsilks. There was a special plaint to their song, as if there were memories caught in their silken strands that protested imprisonment.

Tsuuka could not guess why that should be, or why master-silks were not permitted to sing in the moonlight like the songsilks that were made from them.

But now someone had set a copy-silk free and Dariim was stalking it, clawing her way up the moss-flanked tree. When she crept near, making her way precariously from trunk to branch and from branch to still more fragile branch, the silk freed itself and rippled away, singing its scornful song.

Tsuuka caught her breath as narrow branches bowed under Dariim's weight. Thwarted, Dariim picked her way back to safety and peered toward the silk's new perch. Even from the ground, Tsuuka could see the hungry intensity of her gaze, could see the quiver of straining muscles.

She bounded forward, raising her voice angrily, when Dariim bounced to the ground. "What have I told you, what have I said—" The words came in a hissing rush, the same words her mother might have uttered years before, words driven by angry terror. "Have I told you that you are not to come here? Have I told you why? Yet here I find you. Here—"

Dariim spun and faced her with wide-eyed startlement. Momentarily the pupils of her yellow eyes were fixed. She grunted with surprise.

But neither surprise nor her mother's anger penetrated the spell that gripped her. Before Tsuuka could say more, Dariim darted past her and set claws to the tree where the silk clung now.

Impotently Tsuuka watched as she scurried up the slippery trunk. Helplessly she caught her breath as the silk teased her, singing its fiery song from the tip of the most fragile branch, then billowing away as Dariim crept out the swaying branch, claws extended. Agony streaked Tsuuka's thoughts. What must she do when her cub would not listen to her? What must she do when her cub was ensorcelled by a copy-silk? Capture the silk herself?

Another time she would have shrunk from that suggestion. No sithi kept a copy-silk. And no sithi was welcome this deep in the trees. She could feel the unwelcome in the air. There was a secret here that must not be discovered.

But she would not have Dariim's wit quenched as Maiilin's had been. She would not carry that grief.

Growling to give herself courage, she bounded toward the tree where the silk had entangled itself this time, the tallest, the oldest of the trees. She dug angry claws into its bark and felt the slime of moss against her belly as she climbed. There was a foreign odor to this tree. It didn't have the clean, dry smell of the tree where she made her bower. Some secret mustiness breathed from its hollow interior, as if something lived there.

But what could live inside a tree? Something blind? Something half-formed?

There was no time to wonder. The copy-silk rippled from limb to limb, singing a taunting song. Glancing down, Tsuuka saw that Dariim hesitated at the base of the tree. Fleetingly she wondered why her errant cub had not already set claws to bark. Certainly she had not hesitated before.

Then from inside the tree, from the hollow cavern of its interior —from inside the tree came sound and motion. First Tsuuka heard the rising shrill of voices, a sound so concentrated it made her ears ring. Then she felt a boiling resonance, as if tens of bodies swarmed over one another in mindless excitement. She froze, her thoughts ringing wildly, intensifying her confusion. What *could* live inside a tree? Shock loosened her claws and she slid an arm's length down the slippery trunk before anchoring herself again.

By then spinners had begun to boil from the interior of the tree and line themselves along its broad-stretching branches. They were not the fully matured spinners who spun beside the stream. These were frailer, their tiny limbs underdeveloped, their pink flesh transparent. Tsuuka could see blood vessels branching beneath the translucent flesh, could see the shadow of internal organs. She could even see the folds of tiny brains through the thinness of their skulls.

And in some of them she could see something that made her cold, a curving, sharp-pointed organ that grew where the tongue should have been. And their sacs, the sacs of their necks—She stared, her pupils fixed in shock, as her claws loosened and she slipped down the mossy trunk. The spinners continued to shrill. The sound rose and fell, piercing in its intensity, making something deep in her ears flutter as if it were struggling to escape.

When Tsuuka's feet touched ground, she jumped back from the tree, still staring up, mouth open in shock. *Stingers.* Some of the spinners had stingers instead of tongues. And their neck sacs were taut with sulphurous fluid. She could see its color through the transparent flesh.

Stingers and venom—for what purpose? Her mind darted. Were these the spinners that had bound Maiilin? Had they stung her as well? Tsuuka was peripherally aware of Dariim crouched nearby. She bared her sharp cub's teeth in a defiant grimace, her claws kneading the air in a reflex gesture. As Tsuuka stumbled back from the tree, Dariim took a single crouching step forward.

Tsuuka's reaction was spontaneous. Whipping around, she dealt Dariim a blow that knocked her to the ground. Before the cub could bounce up again, Tsuuka flew at her, slapping and growling. Anger, fear, shock—she put them all into the blows she rained on Dariim's startled body. She cuffed and bit until Dariim wriggled away, scrambled to her feet, and fled.

Tsuuka loped after her, howling angrily—howling so loudly she drowned out the shrilling of the spinners and the mocking song of the silk. Running on all fours, she swatted at the heels of the fleeing cub, not troubling herself that the rebukes she uttered were little more than strangled cries.

She chased the cub until Dariim dodged into a marshy growth of brush and eluded her. Tsuuka searched for her, nettled branches tearing at her coat. And Tsuuka listened for her. All she heard was the heaving of her own breath, the splash of her own feet. She could not catch Dariim's scent on the marshy ground, although the smell of fear was distinct beneath the brush.

Perhaps it was her own. At last she gave up. She groped free of the brush and threw herself down, laboring for breath.

When she took her feet again, her mouth was sour and the long muscles of her legs quivered. She longed for the balm of sunlight and she was worried for Paalan and Kaliir, left alone longer than they had ever been alone before. Yet she was reluctant to go back to the clearing when she could not find Dariim. She hesitated, weighing her fear for Dariim against the needs of her other offspring. She had little concern for Falett. When she woke, she would accept her mother's absence with equanimity. But Paalan and Kaliir had seldom been alone. They would cry when they woke and did not find her there to tend them.

Torn, Tsuuka paced through the trees, trying to order her thoughts. She did not like to leave her weanlings to waken alone. But if they cried and Falett heard, she would go to them. And if she did not, there were other adult sithi who would take a moment to comfort them, however distractedly. Riifika, perhaps, who had given birth to stillborns just a few days ago, who had neither cubs nor weanlings of her own.

There was no one else to return to the heart of the trees and see that Dariim did not try again to retrieve the red silk.

And so Tsuuka returned to the shadowy depths of the grove, stealthily, silently—reluctantly—her ears alert to every sound.

There were scuff marks in the rotted leaves beneath the tall trees. Her scent and Dariim's still clung to the soil. But there was no sign of the spinners who had boiled from inside the eldest tree. There was no sign of the red silk; apparently it had flirted away. And there was no sign that Dariim had returned.

Cautiously Tsuuka eased herself to her haunches in the shadows. She veiled the brightness of her eyes and settled down to watch.

Occasionally she heard the red silk singing in the distance, its voice heralding the sun. Twice she saw it flutter among the trees and briefly entangle itself. She laid back her ears, trying to shut out its song. There was something mocking in its bright tones, yet angry too—and lost, as if it searched for something it could not find.

Yet what could a silk have lost, even a copy-silk? She knew so little. There were so many questions she had never asked. And so many others she had asked but had never heard answers for. She thought fleetingly of her skysilk, with its evasive ways and its distracting song.

The spinners did not emerge from the tree again. Tsuuka crouched, waiting, until the air cooled and darkness began to come. Then she rose, stiffly, and padded away.

She did not find her weanlings crying where she had left them. She did not find Falett searching for her in confusion. When she reached her tree, she found all four of her offspring in their bowers. The weanlings slept quietly, with no sign of disturbance. Falett and Dariim were curled in their silks. Only Dariim opened her eyes when Tsuuka looked in upon them. They gleamed in the dark.

Tsuuka tried to read their expression. Was it abject? Was it defiant? Or was it both at once? Tsuuka held Dariim's gaze, her own stern, until the cub dropped her head and hid her muzzle beneath the silks. Then Tsuuka silently retreated to her own bower, taking with her no illusions. Dariim was not cowed either by the day's experience or by her mother's displeasure. She was only temporarily dampened.

But tomorrow, the next day—

Tomorrow or the next day she would slip away again. She would resume her stalking of the red silk. Nothing Tsuuka told her, no promise Tsuuka extracted from her would long hold her. Dariim wasn't of an age for caution. She was of an age for testing, and the same qualities that made her a promising fledgling hunter—boldness, curiosity, persistence—would draw her back to the heart of the trees.

Tsuuka stretched out on her silent-silks, cold with that understanding and the helplessness that accompanied it. Only time and wisdom could dissuade Dariim, and she had no way to force those things upon her. All she could do was tell her again that she must not go where she had gone, must not see what she would look for anyway, must not question the very things she would question.

Briefly Tsuuka's eyes lingered upon her own silks. Then she hooded her gaze, sinking deep into thought.

She did not emerge when the moon rose. She did not emerge when she heard Petria's amber silk begin to sing from the trees, when her own silks rippled wistfully in the passing breeze. She did not even emerge from her thoughts when a moving star brightened to brilliance in the sky and discharged a spark that swept sharply downward, a deep sound accompanying its descent.

She only escaped her troubling thoughts when finally she slept. It was an uneasy sleep, haunted by a mocking red song, the shrill of angry voices, and fear. Because she knew that there was only one way to prevent Dariim from going back to the heart of the trees. That was to go there herself, to take the red silk before Dariim could return for it. And she was afraid.

NINE

REYNA

A forest of white-stalked trees. Chestnut-furred animals with oblique yellow eyes. Bright silks singing in the branches. Those were the things Danior had seen with the pairing stone when Jhaviir's blue silk sang. But Reyna didn't see any of them tonight as she gazed out the open hatch of the Arnimi ship, the starsilk folded under one arm. Instead she saw the moon—there was just one—waning over a featureless plain. She saw a single tree, misshapen. And she saw stars that seemed muted after the brilliance of those she had seen from the *Narsid*.

Undecided, she glanced back at Juaren and Verra. They slept on their couches, Verra pale, cramped, as if her stomach hurt, Juaren frowning in his sleep, shielding his eyes against the ship's dim interior lights. It would be hours before they woke again. The sedative they had taken to counter the discomforts of the transition from stasis assured that. But Reyna's afterdose sat untouched in its sealed cup. She had wakened from stasis with nothing more than a dull ache at her temples and a sense of disorientation.

She could deal with neither of those by pacing the small ship's interior. Memory insisted she had entered stasis only that morning. She could still see the cold pallor of the technician's face as he bent over her. She could still hear his disinterested voice as her consciousness slipped away in carefully measured stages. She even imagined she could hear first the hatch of the Arnimi ship, then the much heavier hatch of the warp-pod thump shut, although she knew she had slipped into stasis before either ship had been sealed.

She knew tens of days had passed since those events, days during which they had crossed broad gaps between stars that weren't even visible from Brakrath. But how could she grasp the reality of the transition by gazing out ports and hatches? And how could she hear the starsilk speak?

Surely she had watched here, surely she had listened here long enough to be confident there was nothing waiting outside the ship. Glancing back again, deciding, she let down the metal ramp and stepped out, easing the ship's outer hatch shut behind her.

Moonlight showed her a broad, flat expanse of terrain grown with low brush, grass, and an occasional discouraged tree. The air touched her face softly, warmer than she expected and heavy with flavors and nuances completely alien. She paused for a moment, doubtfully, testing and weighing. But the ship's hatch would not have opened if there were any element in the air inimical to the human metabolism. Verra had assured her of that.

She picked her way carefully through the ragged grass, stopping to listen with every stop. When she reached the misshapen tree, she stood for moments without moving, testing the night for any unexpected sound. A tiny shadow moved in the air and brushed at her cheek. She jumped back, catching her breath in surprise. An insect that flew? There were none like that on Brakrath. If it were poisonous—

But she wouldn't be driven back to the ship now. She had been confined long enough, and the starsilk couldn't speak to her there. When the tiny shadow returned, she fanned it away and unfolded the starsilk. Stroking it, she shook it out and fed it to the breeze.

It raised its voice immediately, speaking the familiar words. *I can't speak, but the thoughts that leave me go somewhere. Somewhere, and I think they are recorded. If you hear them, come for me. Let me go. Set me free.*

My name is Birnam Rauth and my thoughts are recorded. Come for me.

She didn't need Verra's translator to understand that much. Before leaving Brakrath, she had listened to the silk until she knew every sharp-edged syllable. But tonight, as the breeze rose, the silk raised a second voice too, one that did not speak but sang.

Startled, Reyna caught the silken fabric, silencing it. She peered around, breath held, hair rising.

She was alone, just as she had been before. There was no sign of any living creature. But in those bare moments, the silk's unexpected song had raised some inexplicable sense of presence. She felt as if someone stood behind her, as if he might touch her, might put his hand on her shoulder.

Her father's voice—her father's voice as well as Birnam Rauth's spoke from the silk. She had expected that. But the silk had never sung before, and briefly she stood as if frozen. Then carefully, she tied the silk to the lowest branch of the malformed tree and stepped back.

The silk raised its voices again. As she stood there, Birnam Rauth spoke his message to the night breeze time and again, the words, their inflection, always the same. At the same time he sang, but Reyna heard no repetition in his wordless song. It was seamless, without stanza or verse, rhyme or meaning.

Even so it spoke things to her, things that stirred deeply. She listened as the moon slowly sank and the breeze grew fitful. Tiny shadows flew before her face. Sometimes she thought she felt the flutter of wings. Once an insect landed on her shoulder and she brushed at it carelessly, preoccupied. Birnam Rauth's song made her think of lonely winters and empty corridors. It made her think of the forces that had driven her here: pride, stubbornness, pain. And it made her realize, shivering, what things she owned beyond consciousness and breath, made her think of the bright legends that lived in her, of the memories she held and of others she might one day hold, whether dark or shining.

After a while, unbidden, a song of her own rose. It was silent, it was inner, it was a song much like the starsilk's—a song of questioning and loneliness. Caught, she sang until the moon sank beneath the horizon. Then, slowly, dazed, she emerged from her trance—and realized with a sharply indrawn breath that she was no longer alone. Eyes watched her from the brush.

Reyna froze, staring directly into them. They were yellow, the pupils vertical and elongated. Their elevation told her their owner stood at least as tall as she did. Reyna stood pillared in ice for the space of a dozen shallow breaths. Then, haltingly, she began to think. Her pike was in the cargo hold and she was not wearing her hunting blade. If the creature that watched was a predator—

But it only watched, eyes unwinking, coming no nearer. Perhaps if she backed toward the ship, slowly, without offering provocation—

But the silk still sang from the tree. She could not leave it. Drawing a deep breath, steeling herself, she stepped forward. She did not fan at the shadowy insects that fluttered at her face in a new flurry. One moved along her arm, tickling her, but she ignored it. With stiff fingers she untied the starsilk.

She did not take time to fold it. She pulled it from the tree, crumpled it under one arm, and stepped back.

She had intended a careful retreat, every motion measured. Instead she felt a pain in her shoulder so sharp, so stinging that she cried out and spun around, slapping wildly. Before she realized what she had done, the creature that watched her took alarm and fled, crashing from the brush and bounding away on four feet.

Stunned, Reyna cupped her stinging shoulder and stared after the fleeing creature. She saw little more than a running shadow. Slowly she dropped her hand. In the palm, crushed, was the insect that had stung her. She stared at it first blankly, then with deepening apprehension. On Brakrath most insects were harmless. But of the few that did sting, several were deadly.

She forgot the creature that had watched from the brush. Numbly, cradling the dead insect in one palm, she stumbled back to the ship. When the hatch closed behind her, she carried the insect to the light and examined it, turning it with cold fingers, not knowing what she looked for. Fragile, jointed legs, filmy wings veined with color—

It was the stinger that made it ugly. Only the stinger. "Verra?" Reyna said weakly, dropping the crushed insect, kneeling beside the couch where the Arnimi woman slept. The starsilk spilled to the floor, unnoticed. "Verra?" A poultice—would a poultice help? But they had brought only Arnimi medicinals, and she didn't know how to use those.

And Verra did not waken. Nor did Juaren when she called to him. He only turned away, pressing his forearm to his eyes as if they hurt. Trembling, Reyna dropped to her own couch. Her shoulder itched violently and her blood raced, drumming in her ears. Her heart jumped so hard at her ribs she felt each beat as a separate blow.

But she could not help herself if she panicked. She closed her eyes and forced herself to draw a series of deep breaths. Then, gingerly, she touched her wrist, measuring her pulse. Surprisingly, it beat little faster than its usual pace.

Unsteadily she reexamined the situation. Perhaps there had been no poison in the sting. She closed her eyes again and forced herself to be completely still for several minutes. Then she stood, carefully, and gazed around the cabin. Juaren slept on his stomach now, his face hidden in the crook of one arm. Verra still huddled as if her stomach hurt. The starsilk was tumbled on the floor, the crushed insect near it.

Carefully Reyna retrieved the weightless body and dropped it in the disposer. The motion did not make her dizzy. Nor was she feverish or nauseated. If there had been poison in the sting, apparently it had affected her only momentarily.

And the creature that had watched her from the brush had not tried to harm her. Nor had she done it harm in turn. But neither Juaren nor Verra would wake, and beyond the ship lay an entire world she didn't know. A world she had journeyed to without even wondering how its strangeness would touch her. Bleakly she lay down again, blinking up at the harsh lights. After a few minutes, when her head began to ache, she unsealed her sedative dose and swallowed it. Then she slept too.

Time passed in slow measure. After a while someone shook her. Someone called her name and tried to force hot brew between her lips. It was the smell of unfiltered air that finally roused her. Juaren bent over her and the ship's hatch stood open. Struggling, she sat. "Verra?" she said numbly.

"She's gone outside to look around. How do you feel?"

"I feel—" But before she could test the stiffness of her muscles, the thickness of her tongue, a more urgent concern came to mind. "Juaren, there's something out there. Outside. I saw it last night."

The pupils of his grey eyes contracted sharply. He straightened, frowning. "You were outside?"

"Yes, while you were asleep. And there was an animal—" She stopped herself. An animal? What did that mean? She had seen watching eyes, then a running form. But she had seen creatures aboard the *Narsid* she would have called animals just a season ago, and Verra had called them human. "I took the starsilk out to sing," she said more slowly. "It—whatever it was—was watching me from the brush. I startled it when—"

Her disjointed account was interrupted by a cry from outside the ship. Reyna stared dumbly as Juaren jumped up and disappeared down the ramp. She sat and forced herself to her feet.

By the time she reached the door, Juaren and Verra were stepping up the ramp, Verra cradling a familiar object in her palm. Her face was pale, her hand trembling.

"It's not poisonous," Reyna assured her quickly. "One of them stung me last night. Here—" She pushed up the sleeve of her tunic and looked with surprise at the red welt on her shoulder. The flesh was tender and hot. At the center of the welt was a core of infection. She touched it gingerly. "It wasn't so bad last night," she said lamely.

Juaren examined the welt. "This is the same kind of insect that stung you?"

Reyna nodded. "I didn't have anything to put on the sting. I thought—I thought it would be all right." At least she had thought that after her initial panic.

Some of the color returned to Verra's face. She stepped to the pharmaceutical cabinet and dropped the dead insect on the counter surface, laughing unsteadily. "I've been too long on Brakrath. I saw the nest in the tree, and I saw insects crawling near it, but it didn't occur to me that they could fly. I'd better treat us both right away."

When she had dabbed Reyna's wound and her own and they had made a quick meal, Verra sat down briefly at her console. "The air analysis was complete before the auto-lock released the door, of course. But there is some additional information the an-system logged in before we were wakened—"

"This place doesn't look anything like what Danior saw when he used the pairing stone," Reyna said doubtfully, gazing out the ship's door. There were no tall trees, no bright silks, only broad expanses of brush and grass.

Verra nodded, tapping at the console, glancing quickly at the data that flickered across the screen. "Danior described the night sky in just enough detail that our ship's system was able to calculate the location of the forested area he described. It used its own discretion in setting us down half a day's walk from there. If we were using the skimmer, we could cover that distance in a matter of minutes. In fact, if we were to break out the lift-packs—"

Reyna frowned, wondering if her reluctance to use Arnimi equipment in her search for Birnam Rauth was simply a part of her prejudice. "We can walk that far," she said.

"Easily," Juaren confirmed. "And we'll learn more on foot."

Verra capitulated without argument. "The lift-packs are fine on unfamiliar terrain if you're using sensory instrumentation to gather basic data. Since you prefer not to use instrumentation—" She ran a hand back through her hair. "I do want to take the translator so we'll have the ability to communicate in Birnam Rauth's dominant tongue."

Reyna glanced at her sharply, wondering if she heard some lack of conviction in the words. Did Verra doubt they would find Birnam Rauth? Did she doubt they would even learn what had happened to him here? Quickly Reyna glanced at Juaren, wondering for the first time what his expectations were.

And her own? What were her own expectations? She found she did not want to examine them. Not today. Not with the sense of presence the silk's song had raised so fresh and haunting.

It was late morning when they locked the ship behind them and made a wide circle around the misshapen tree. By daylight they could see papery insect warrens in its spindly upper branches. Reyna clutched her pike and tried to ignore the crawling of her skin. Her pack weighed lightly on her back. Verra had persuaded them to bring a single lift-pack as insurance against emergency. They had bundled their foodstocks, spare clothing and other necessities together and strapped the load to the lift-pack. It floated behind them, programmed to follow.

The midday sun was yellow-bright. As they walked, Reyna could smell the warmth it gave the soil and vegetation. The grass was thick and darkly green, but the trees they passed were twisted and spindly, infested with flying insects.

They walked single-file through the grass and brush. Reyna wore the starsilk at her waist, ends tucked in. She had to discipline herself not to rub the itching welt on her shoulder. She had to discipline herself against apprehension too. The land was so broad, so empty.

Juaren at least was at ease, more so than she had seen him before, although he moved watchfully. And lightly. Reyna looked for the print of his boots on the soil and couldn't find it. She found her own prints though, and she found Verra's.

Juaren was the one who sighted the small stream cutting its way between brush and tree-grown banks. He called a halt and they studied the glint of water from a judicious distance.

"I'd like to test it, to see if it's drinkable," Verra said doubtfully.

Juaren narrowed grey eyes at the trees that lined the banks. Their frail upper limbs were bowed with insect nests. There was the bright iridescence of wings in the air. He frowned, endorsing Verra's doubt. "What do you think, Reyna?"

Reyna's hand tightened on the pike and her shoulder began to itch again. "If our supplies run out and we don't find water anywhere else—"

"Then we'll take the chance," Verra agreed. She rubbed her arm distractedly.

By mutual consent, they avoided the strand of tree-shaded water that laced across the plain and gave wide berth to the scattered trees. In the early afternoon, when they stopped to eat, Juaren wandered away and returned frowning and distracted. Studying him, Reyna found her own appetite shrinking. If Juaren was disturbed, there must be something here to be wary of. But she saw nothing. And the unfamiliar brightness of the sun, the emptiness of the terrain made her increasingly uneasy. Boarding the *Narsid,* she had worried that she didn't know the language, the customs, the ordinary courtesies of the people she would encounter there.

Here, beyond last night's fleeting glimpse of a running form, there was no sign of habitation. There was only a profound emptiness. as if they had come to a land without legend or history, a land that had no one to articulate the drama of its seasons and give story to its natural features.

Was that why Juaren had grown so silent? Because he felt the emptiness of the land as she did? Reyna studied him uneasily as they resumed their trek. He took the lead, walking briskly, not glancing back. His gaze flickered everywhere, and although there had been desultory conversation earlier, he no longer spoke. He no longer pointed out plant specimens or responded when Reyna or Verra did. Soon they fell into silence too.

Later that afternoon the twisted trees grew in clumps and small groves. Once the wind rose from a clear sky, sweeping a cloud of flying insects toward them. They swatted and fanned until the insects were dispersed.

Soon after that they saw the shadow of the forest on the horizon. Juaren halted abruptly, without word. He gazed toward the tall trees, then studied the horizon in every direction. "I'll go ahead alone," he said finally. The words were distracted, as if they relayed a decision he had made much earlier. "That animal you saw last night, Reyna, and the tracks I've seen today—"

That jarred her. "Tracks?" Was that why he had been so distant? But she had not seen tracks.

He didn't seem to notice her surprise. "There are traces of small game, of course. But the others—they're large, almost as heavy as we are. They move on two limbs some of the time, on four other times. I wouldn't call the print of the front extremities footprints. They're smaller, better articulated, and they have opposing thumbs." He shielded his eyes against the sun, seeming to notice her frown for the first time. "The only animals on Brakrath that have opposed thumbs are humans and minx."

Reyna chilled. She had never encountered a minx, but she had heard tales of their deadly intelligence, of the way they gamed with their prey before striking. Had the creature last night been waiting to play some obscure game with her?

If so, it had not. Instead it had run. "I—I didn't see tracks," she said. "And I don't see why you should go into the trees alone. I—"

"Here—" Without asking, he took the pike from her hand. "Tell me how many signs of game you see from here. Turn a full circle and tell me."

She wanted to argue. This was no fair test; she was not a hunter. Instead she acquiesced, turning completely around, studying the ground intently. She saw nothing.

"That's why I want to go first, alone," he said. Extending her pike, he began to point out disturbed soil, bent grass, a crushed insect imbedded in the dry thatch beneath a clump of brush, all signs so minute she had difficulty seeing them. "I've trained myself to see these things, and I've trained myself to go places where you can't go—not if you want to pass unnoticed. Not if you want to observe without disturbing."

She frowned, knowing what he said was true—and still not liking it. Not liking him to go alone either, to a place they knew so little about. "How long will you be gone?" she asked finally.

"I'll try to be back by moonrise. It may be longer."

"We'll wait here," Verra said, touching Reyna's arm in a reassuring gesture that made Reyna stiffen again.

They both watched as he continued on alone, walking even more briskly than before. At first his path took him nearer the stream. Then he veered away, and soon they could see him no longer. They could only see the shadowy smudge of the forest on the horizon.

Moonrise. How many hours would that be? Juaren had taken the trouble to provide himself with information from the data console before leaving the ship. "How long will he be gone?" Reyna said finally, sorry she had not paid better attention in the last hours before stasis, when Verra had instructed them both in the function of the data console and the use of the translator that made filed information accessible verbally in their own language.

"Five or six hours, I think. It will be dark in two. Are you tired?"

"A little," Reyna admitted.

"Sleep if you want and I'll watch. Then I can catch a nap while you watch."

Reyna hesitated, not wanting to be deferred to. "If you want to sleep first—"

"No, I just want to sit quietly for a while and think my thoughts." Verra touched the controls of the hovering lift-pack and it dropped their possessions gently to the ground.

Understanding, Reyna unpacked bedding and lay down in the grass. She had thoughts to think too. Closing her eyes, she tried to sort the various strands of her mood: doubt, uncertainty, mistrust —of herself, of her own judgment. What if she had brought Juaren and Verra here to no purpose? What if they found no sign of Birnam Rauth? What if they could not learn what had happened to him or how his voice had come to speak from the starsilk? She rolled over, pressing her face to the warm grass, and tried to find some conviction that he was here, perhaps even alive. As she fell asleep, she seemed to hear his song again, lonely and questioning.

Finally she slept. When she woke, it was dark and she knew immediately that she was alone. She sat and drew a shallow breath, listening over the beat of her heart to the darkness that surrounded her. "Verra?"

There was no answer. Shakily she stood, her heart racing now. "Verra?" The sky was clear, bright with stars, but their light was not sufficient to banish the shadows of the plain. Distractedly she stroked the starsilk, pulling one end free. It murmured as it caught the breeze. "Verra?" she called again, more loudly.

"Reyna—here." The answer was faint, cautious.

Relieved, Reyna picked her way toward the sound. Verra crouched near a clump of brush, bending over a dark shape stretched in the grass. Reyna halted. "What—what is it?" As she stared down, the shape began to take form: a long emaciated body, four limbs, a head thrown sharply back, eyes—she couldn't tell their color—staring and blank. Reluctantly she knelt and touched dark fur. The flesh beneath it hadn't yet begun to cool into rigidity.

"I don't know. But apparently she gave birth recently. She's mammalian, and the milk sacs are engorged. I heard a sound—" Gently Verra picked up one limp limb and stroked the foot.

But it was more hand than foot, Reyna saw, long-fingered, black-clawed, with an oddly jointed thumb. Looking more closely, Reyna saw that the arm was sparsely furred, bare in spots. And there were familiar looking welts, larger than the one on her shoulder, far more angrily infected, some of them abscessed. Carefully she pressed the flesh of the arm. There was no fatty layer. The muscle was wasted. She looked down into the shadowy face. "Is she—could she be human?" There had been humans aboard the *Narsid* who were furred, humans she would not have recognized as such if she had met them on a mountain trail instead of in a ship's corridor.

Verra shook her head. "No. She's not from our family. She's far more like *Chatnus Maior.*"

Reyna hesitated, hoping Verra would explain. "Like what?"

"Just a classification. I doubt if it means anything here, unless this is an introduced species. There were strains of *Chatnus—Maior and Minor—*exported at the time of Earthexodus. I suppose it's possible this was one of the worlds they were resettled to. I think it's more likely this is a completely independent form." Slowly Verra stood. "She's not long dead, but I don't think it was her voice I heard."

"Her—her child?" Reyna suggested. "If we're quiet—"

They stood for a while in silence, listening. Once Reyna thought she heard the crackle of brush from the direction of the stream. The sound was not repeated, nor was there any other beyond the sounds that came with the breeze. Finally Verra sighed and said, "Nothing. I'd better sleep if we're to walk any farther after Juaren returns."

"I'll watch," Reyna agreed.

Together they covered the body with dried brush and returned to where they had left their bundles. Verra wrapped herself in her bedding and Reyna sat in the grass, arms around her drawn up knees, more aware than ever of the emptiness of the land. She was able to escape a sharp sense of oppression only by listening—listening intently for a lost voice.

It did not come until long after Verra slept, and then it was so faint Reyna thought at first she had imagined it. Wispy, plaintive—she caught the starsilk in one hand and stood, waiting with held breath for the sound to come again. She heard only the rustle of the grass.

Then, in the distance, she heard the voice again, weakly. Sparing a single glance for Verra, she slipped away, choosing her direction by instinct.

She moved soft-footed in the direction of the stream, and when the plaint came again, it seemed nearer. Reyna hesitated, wanting to answer it, wanting to call out some reassurance. But what could she say to reassure a child who was not human? If she spoke, she might frighten it into total silence.

And if it were not a child, if it were something else, an animal of prey, calling softly—

She refused to consider that. The voice was lost and small. She continued picking her way toward it.

She continued picking her way until she realized that the plaint came from a cluster of trees growing near the stream. She hesitated, imagining the flutter of lacy wings against her face, imagining other things even less benign. She did not know what might live in the shadows. Certainly she did not know that if she met another like the animal that had died, it would recognize her good intentions.

If this were an infant, perhaps it wasn't even the dead animal's offspring. Perhaps it had parents of its own, ready to defend it.

She considered that possibility as her feet carried her forward again. She considered it as she entered the shadow of the trees and fanned at the insects that fluttered softly against her face. She considered it when the whimpering became suddenly very near and she found herself kneeling over not one but two tiny forms. They wriggled helplessly at her feet, pressing weakly against her, apparently drawn to her warmth. She could not see them clearly in the dark, but her probing fingers told her they were smaller than human infants, that they wore coats of soft fur, and that they were pitifully frail. They carried little more spare flesh than the animal Verra had found dead, and their skins were savagely welted.

Reyna fanned angrily at the insects that clouded around her, stifling a cry as one stung her neck. There was no time to wonder if these were orphans or if they had a parent who might return. Quickly she scooped up the tiny creatures and dodged from beneath the trees.

The insects followed her a short distance, stinging again at her neck and arms and at the tiny creatures she carried. When she escaped them, she paused briefly to cradle the tiny creatures more securely. One of them snuggled against her willingly. The other struggled weakly, scratching at her with feeble claws, suddenly coughing as if it would choke. It felt warmer than the other, fever-hot, and its limbs were more frail.

When she reached the place where Verra slept, Reyna knelt and laid the two little creatures on her bedding. Starlight was brighter here, where there were no trees to obstruct it. She examined the creatures, stroking their small limbs, their tiny heads. They were clearly of the same kind as the creature she and Verra had buried under dried brush. And they were surely very young, perhaps only days old. What was she to do with them? What did they need? The smaller one choked again, its tiny limbs drawing up in spasms, and Reyna had the helpless feeling that she could never give it what it needed. She touched the other and it caught her finger in its mouth and began to suck.

Verra woke as she fumbled through the supply bags. "What is it?" Her voice was thick with sleep.

"I found them," Reyna said distractedly. "But I don't know what to do. I don't know what to give them." Medicines? Food? Could they digest human food? Did she dare use the same ointment on their insect bites that she and Verra had used on their own? She rubbed at her fresh bites, wishing she knew.

"You found them?" Verra sat, her voice alert now. She made her way quickly to Reyna's bedding and bent over the two creatures, examining them. "One healthy, or relatively so, one sick," she said. "I think we should separate them. Here—we have some extra blankets. We'd better wrap the smallest and set it aside."

"And not take care of it?" Reyna demanded in alarm. As if she knew how to care for the helpless creature.

"I don't think it can eat, Reyna. And I doubt that we have any medicines that would be helpful. I don't know that we can do much beyond keeping it warm."

"And the other one? I can thicken some water with starch concentrate. Or I can use the protein granules—"

Verra had taken an extra blanket from their bundles and was wrapping the smaller creature in it. "Cubs, I think. On Arnim, these would be cubs."

"You *have* seen animals like them?" Reyna demanded sharply. She watched tensely as the smaller creature began choking again, its tiny body caught in spasms.

"I've seen chatni. A species we imported from Old Earth. There are points of similarity to these creatures." She cradled the creature as it stopped choking and began a gasping struggle for breath. "Why don't you try plain water first. See if it can take it from a spoon or your fingertip. I'll see if this one can take a few drops."

Reyna found her cub could take water from a spoon and licked eagerly at her finger when she first dampened it, then dipped it in protein granules. It seemed to wink up at her from slitted yellow eyes as it sucked her fingertip. And despite its frailty, she thought she caught a sharp-toothed grin on its face when it first tasted starch concentrate.

She became so absorbed in its care that she didn't notice when the air grew cool, when the moon rose. She didn't notice when Verra set aside the smaller cub and briefly bowed her head. Only when her own cub lapsed abruptly into satisfied sleep did she realize that the smaller cub lay still in the same way its mother had earlier.

Verra shrugged, but moonlight caught the glint of tears in her eyes. "There was nothing we could do."

Nothing they could do—and, Reyna realized abruptly, the moon was in the sky. She stood and peered across the silver-lit plain. "Juaren hasn't come back."

"No," Verra said.

Was there nothing they could do about that either? Reyna found her lips suddenly dry. "Do you think one of us should go to find him? If something has happened—"

"I think we should wait right here, as we said we would," Verra said quietly. "He's found his way across the peaks in winter. He'll find his way back here."

"Of course," Reyna echoed, but the words were faint and there was a tremor in her hands as she stroked the sleeping cub. Because if Juaren didn't find his way back, if something happened to him before they had the chance to talk again, if something happened to him on this search she had initiated—

This unwise search? This ill-considered search? Reyna choked back sudden fear. She had known from the beginning that something might happen to her, that she might never find her way back to Brakrath. But if something happened to Juaren or Verra simply because they had accompanied her—

"I thought it would be simple," she said, more to herself than to Verra. "We'd come here, we'd find—whatever there is to find—"

Her voice trailed away. Nothing had been simple at all. They had come and she had listened to Birnam Rauth's song, but she had no idea how to begin her search. She had no idea how to find him. Now Juaren had gone to the forest and hadn't come back, and she held a sleeping cub in her arms, a responsibility she didn't know how to meet. And she didn't even know which of the stars she saw tonight shone on Brakrath or whether it was morning or night in Valley Terlath. She shook her head mutely.

"It's never simple," Verra assured her. "Never. But Juaren will find his way back, and so will we."

Words. Easy to speak, suddenly painfully difficult to believe. Reyna touched the silk at her waist and understood better some of the things she had heard in Birnam Rauth's song the night before. Her own song was beginning to rise again, silently, full of the same things: doubt, solitude, fear. She listened to it as she cradled the sleeping cub and prayed for Juaren to find his way back.

TEN
REYNA

Later Reyna didn't remember when she abandoned her vigil and fell asleep. The cub woke twice as she sat watching and whimpered until she fed it. The first time it quickly fell asleep again. The second time it squirmed restlessly in her arms, its slit eyes gleaming with some incomprehensible reproach. Instinctively she tucked it closer to the warmth of her body, wondering if its untrained senses told it what strangers their two kinds were. Or was it wakeful simply because she had failed, in all ignorance, to provide something it needed?

How could she guess what it required? Perhaps she had fed it too much, perhaps too little; perhaps the things she had given it were wrong. She wondered—had its mother comforted it by rocking? By petting? By crooning? She tried all those things, jiggling the tiny creature and whispering night-songs to its furred ear. It only squirmed with increased irritability, and Verra shifted in her bedding and muttered a sleepy query.

"It's all right. I'm just trying to get it to sleep."

Verra rose on one elbow, rubbing her eyes. "Maybe it's nocturnal. Do you want me to take it for a while?"

Nocturnal? Was that why the tiny eyes seemed to grow brighter and more fretful with the moon? "No. I'll wake you later, if I need to." At least the cub's squirming kept her occupied, kept her from glancing toward the forest every time the grass rustled.

Finally the cub fell into an unwilling sleep, abandoning itself in her arms. Reyna cradled it until her shoulders began to ache. Then she laid it down in her bedding and stretched out beside it. She knew she would not sleep, but she did not want the cub to be cold. It had probably never slept alone before.

Nor did it sleep alone that night. Reyna closed her eyes, trying to ease the anxious frown that made her scalp hurt. And she slept, as abruptly, as totally, as unwillingly as the cub.

Later she realized vaguely that she had abandoned her watch and she fought the drowning-depth of sleep, trying to raise feeble eyelids against it. The effort was beyond her. At some point she was aware of quiet movement in the dark, of the sound of whispered words. Someone threw covers over her bare arms. She tried to burrow into them but her body refused to cooperate even to that small degree.

Later still she realized that a chill dawn lay beyond her closed eyelids and that someone lay close beside her. She roused herself enough to roll over, dragging her covers with her. Juaren slept beside her, cocooned in his own bedding, his hair the only brightness in the grey morning. Relieved, Reyna slept again.

It was almost mid-morning before she roused enough to realize that there was no small, furred body warm beside her. Alarmed, she came fully awake and sat, rubbing her eyes.

The cub was gone. And Verra was gone too, as well as the lift-pack. All that remained were herself, Juaren, and the untidy clutter of their possessions. "Juaren?" Her voice held sleep and panic.

He woke in a way she had never seen anyone wake before. He was soundly asleep when she called. A moment later he was sitting beside her, fully awake, not the faintest cloud of sleep in his eyes. "What is it?"

She didn't know whether to be reassured or alarmed by his immediate alertness. "Verra's gone."

He looked at her uncomprehendingly, then frowned, running his fingers through his hair. "Don't you remember? She told you she was going."

"She told me?" What had Verra told her? When?

"She told you she was lifting back to the ship with the cub. She wants to run a few samples through bioanalysis to get some idea of what its dietary requirements are, which of our foods it can use. She woke you and told you. It was just after dawn. You opened your eyes. You nodded."

"I—I don't remember," Reyna said, alarm turning to a feeling of foolishness. "I didn't even know you had come back. I was—" But did she want to tell him that—that she had been anxious for him? Did she want to tell him she had stared for hours into the dark, willing him to emerge? That there had been a frightening emptiness just below her heart when he had not?

Would he believe those things when he had returned to find her curled in her bedding asleep? Embarrassed, she stared down at her feet. "I was tired," she said.

He nodded, but a moment's distracted frown suggested he caught the discrepancy between words and expression. He hesitated briefly, rubbing his jaw, then stood and cast his bedding aside. "Are you hungry?"

"Yes," she agreed, relieved to change the subject. "Juaren, when you went to the forest—" She smoothed the starsilk against her waist, not certain how to begin. She had so many questions, some of them barely formed. "When you went there—"

Juaren glanced toward the distant trees, his eyes catching light from the mid-morning sun. "It was just as your brother told you. The trees, the silks, the moon—you'll see."

"And the—animals?" Could she call them that? Danior had. But she had seen the slender fingers, the jointed thumb the night before. And she imagined she had seen more than animal cunning in the cub's glinting yellow eyes.

"They're there. In the trees." Juaren brushed at his shining white hair and said again, "You'll see."

So he didn't want to tell her. He wanted her to see with her own eyes. Biting her lip, Reyna bent and rolled her bedding. "Will you tell me, at least—did you hear anything like the starsilk?"

He shrugged, folding his bedding into a compact bundle. "I saw white silks, two of them, but neither of them spoke."

Reyna bit her lip. Was that enough to refresh her doubts? Just the fact that he had not heard Birnam Rauth's voice in the trees? She turned and gazed around, taking the measure of the day. The land did not seem so empty this morning. She heard occasional music in the rustle of the grass, in the rattle of dry brush. The smell of the soil was less foreign. Her eyes had even grown accustomed to the yellow-brightness of the sun. It seemed less harsh than the day before. It seemed warm—welcoming.

Or perhaps it was this opportunity to be alone with Juaren she welcomed. Flushing, Reyna secured her bedding and threw it into the pile of their possessions. "I *am* hungry," she said. "There was that package of food Verra said was special—"

Juaren nodded in quick complicity, apparently sharing her sense of occasion. "Let's open it. Let's see what an Arnimi delicacy tastes like."

They dug through the supplies until they found the carton of colorfully wrapped containers that had been processed on Verra's home-world. There was something unexpected in the bright figures that decorated the wrappings and in the artistry of the food itself, in the contrasting delicacy and piquancy of flavors. "I wonder what the Arnimi do when they eat these things?" Reyna mused as they sampled their way through the carton. Did they smile? Did they laugh and sing? She couldn't imagine a group of Arnimi gathered around a festive table, joined in a celebratory mood. Perhaps only wealthy deviants—as Verra had called herself—knew how to enjoy these foods.

Certainly Reyna and Juaren knew. They sampled every container, making a game of trying to decipher the markings on the packages. Soon they were talking about other meals—about delicacies Juaren and Komas had foraged for in the mountains, about festival foods Reyna had helped prepare in the palace kitchen, about meals taken when they were so hungry even the coarsest food tasted as if it had been prepared for the festival board.

But eventually the meal was done, the carton was repacked, and they both knew the time for laughing was past. They sat in the grass and Reyna glanced toward the dark line that was the forest and said, "I want to learn to track. Like you do." Yesterday had taught her that. She did not want to walk blind again, through this world or any other. She wanted to learn to read the ground, she wanted to learn to use the Arnimi data console, she wanted to learn whatever might be necessary.

Juaren's white brows drew together and he spoke sharply. "Why?"

"I want to see what you see," she said, surprised at his reaction. "I want to know what has passed, the way you did yesterday." She didn't want to feel foolish again—or small, or unprepared.

But he did not seem pleased. He gazed at her with guarded eyes, then glanced away and rubbed his lips with the back of one hand. "You can always ask me. I told you what I saw yesterday, didn't I?"

"Yes, but there are things I need to know for myself. I intended to learn them anyway, before I made my challenge, some of them." Every palace daughter learned to read the prints of the mountain predators from the soil. In the last weeks before she made her challenge, every palace daughter learned to track a breeterlik to its den or a crag-charger to its lair.

"You intended to learn them from shepherds and lens tenders. Not from a hunter."

"Of course. We hardly ever see hunters in the valley. But Wollar would have taken me to Terlath and taught me. He taught Aberra and Tanse."

"Wollar is a herder."

"Then you can teach me better," Reyna said, puzzled. The meal, the laughter, the confidences they had shared seemed forgotten. He held himself stiffly, his gaze remote and unsmiling. She didn't understand his reaction at all. Did he think she was incapable of learning? Did he think a crippled herder, too old to follow the herds, was the best teacher she could ask? She glanced at his set face, confusion turning to baffled anger. "Am I asking you to share secrets of some kind?" she demanded. "Is that why you don't want to teach me?"

Abruptly Juaren stared down at the ground, evading her angry gaze. His forefinger traced an obscure figure in the dirt. He stared at it, lips tight, and finally said, "I didn't say I wouldn't teach you. But—" He frowned, seeming to seek passage around some verbal barrier. Quickly, as if he must hurry the words or not speak them at all, he looked up. "Are you willing to apprentice yourself to me for a full turn of seasons? That's what a master hunter demands of any apprentice. When we go back, when we do whatever things we have to do, will you go to the mountains with me for a year?"

"You—you won't teach me otherwise?" she demanded, as confused by his manner as by his words. "You won't teach me how to read the ground if I won't pledge myself to you as an apprentice?" Was that some rule of his guild? And why was it suddenly so difficult for him to speak?

Juaren shifted uncomfortably, staring down again. "I didn't say that."

Then what *had* he said? Reyna didn't try to hide her exasperation. *"You did.* That's what you did say."

"I didn't say I wouldn't teach you," he insisted, the words abrupt, almost angry. "I only asked if you would go with me for a year when we return to Brakrath." He held himself stiffly, returning her angry stare with a challenging frown, a frown of hard intensity. "I've lived in your palace. I've eaten food from your table. I'm asking if you will live in my palace and eat from my table. For a year."

How could he insist he had not said exactly what she had heard him say? How—And then she understood. Suddenly she understood exactly what he asked and why he asked it so clumsily, and she laughed with surprise. He was asking her to pledge herself to him for a year—not as an apprentice but as a year's mate. And he was distant, he was abrupt because he thought she would refuse. "Tell me," she said quickly, because she saw that her laughter had deepened his frown, "would you have asked me to go with you anyway, even if I hadn't asked you to teach me to track?"

"Yes," he said finally, stiffly aloof, obviously wary of her shift of mood. "I decided that a long time ago."

"That you would ask me?"

"That I wanted to ask you."

Perhaps he had even decided it on wood-smoke night, when they had almost danced together. "And is there a price?" she demanded.

His taut features relaxed slightly. "If so, it's your place to ask it. Not mine."

Her place to ask a price from a hunter. That pleased her. "Then I already have. If you will teach me, I'll—I'll live a year in your palace." The mountains. She needed no time to deliberate. She had never thought of taking a mate. That had always been a consideration for the future, more a duty than a fulfillment. But she could taste the cold air already. She could hear the crackle of their cook-fire and smell the savor of the things they would cook. They would talk every day as they had talked today, laughing, learning all the things they held in common. Learning their differences too. Perhaps at the end of the year, they would decide to take another year together. Or perhaps they would separate. And if her mother objected, if her mother was hurt—

"My mother—" she said unwillingly.

He shook his head. "She'll understand."

Slowly Reyna nodded. She would. Her heart had never been with Juaren, not for more than a few moments, and then only because Iahn was in the desert. If they brought back news of Birnam Rauth, if her father returned to the palace, Juaren would mean no more to Khira than any other man of the halls. Reyna recognized that and glanced up quickly. "So I've told you my price."

He smiled with obvious relief. "It's exactly the price I had to offer." He gazed back in the direction of the ship. "I'll begin paying it now if you're ready to pledge yourself as my apprentice."

"I'm ready."

He hesitated, frowning. "There are obligations. You must commit the old words to memory. And you must listen to me in everything."

"Oh? Am I obliged to obey?" She spoke teasingly.

He didn't respond to her manner, only to her words. "No, you're only obliged to listen—but closely."

"I'll listen," she promised, laughing at his seriousness.

He relaxed and, ranging in a circle from their campsite, they studied the ground together. Juaren used Reyna's pike to point out minute signs and she tried to guess what they meant. All too often she could not even see them until she knelt and frowned hard at the ground. Juaren waited silently, as if she were a blind person trying to find her way—as if she must be permitted to find it without intrusive assistance. "I don't understand how you saw anything yesterday," she said finally, brushing dirt from her knees. "We were walking so fast."

"When you cipher scrolls, do you stop and study each stroke of every figure individually?"

"No," she said. "But—"

"It's harder to find the meaning of the text that way. I know because I read that way before Komas taught me to use my eyes quickly, to let them be a window to let things in quickly, so my brain can find the patterns and report them to me. At first you must stop and study every small sign individually. You must suggest to your brain how to interpret it. But later you must walk quickly, you must look quickly—so you can see things whole, not in parts."

See things whole. She frowned, wondering if that weren't the most important part of the lesson. Wondering when she might begin to put it into practice. Quickly her thoughts veered away in a troubling direction. "Juaren—" He had been to the forest. He had seen the silks in the trees. What did he think of their chances of finding Birnam Rauth alive? Of learning anything about him at all?

But he had turned away, gazing toward the horizon. "Verra's coming."

"I don't see anything."

"You're looking too high. She's traveling near the ground."

Verra joined them within minutes, settling gently to the ground and shrugging out of the lift-pack harness. Reyna was momentarily surprised at the brightness of her eyes, at the flush in her cheeks, as if she had found some welcome freedom in flight. She had devised a sling to hold the cub. It curled against her body, leaving her hands free.

"Is it—is he all right?" she asked quickly. "Did you learn what to feed him?"

Verra nodded briskly, rubbing the tiny creature's back. "More. More of everything we're already giving him. Or her. That's a little inconclusive. But he's metabolizing our food well enough for now. There are some trace elements he'll require in higher concentration, but we have a few days' leeway in providing those. Perhaps we'll be able to foster him out when we reach the forest."

Foster him to one of the creatures who lived in the bowers? Reyna nodded, relieved at that suggestion. Such a tiny creature, yet responsibility for him weighed heavily.

And the cub had begun to squirm again. "Hungry," Verra pronounced. "So am I. Have you eaten?"

"Earlier," Reyna said guiltily. "But there's plenty left." At least she and Juaren had left enough of the special Arnimi delicacies for one person to feast on. "I'll feed him while you eat."

"And then you're both going to learn to use the lift-pack," Verra pronounced. "I decided that on my flight back. It won't do us much good to have emergency transportation if I'm the only one who can use it."

Reyna felt herself stiffen, but Juaren responded by retrieving the pack and studying the controls with unqualified interest. "How long will it take to learn?"

"A few minutes ground-training. Then some practice time. I suppose I should have brought another from the ship so I could air-coach you. But you'll catch on quickly enough. And maybe when you've tried it, you'll want to go back to the ship and issue yourselves packs."

"No," Reyna said automatically. But the suggestion was not so unwelcome as it had been the day before. They would be able to move more quickly, they would be able to see the land better if they used the lift-packs. And it was foolish to reject any device just because it was Arnimi. Not if it would help them find Birnam Rauth.

Or not, she admitted reluctantly, if it would help them exhaust the possibilities of the search more quickly. She took the wriggling cub from Verra and stroked its ears. It immediately caught her finger and began to suck.

They sat in a circle in the grass, she dabbing a mixture of water and concentrate powders into the cub's demanding mouth, Verra poking unsmilingly through her small store of delicacies, Juaren watching them both with silent composure. Finally Verra put the last container aside with a small frown of dissatisfaction.

"I'm sorry we ate so much," Reyna said quickly. "We—we should have left more."

"No," Verra said. She smoothed one of the brightly printed wrappers across her thigh, frowning at it. "You should have saved me some laughter. I'm sure you two laughed when you ate these things."

Reyna stiffened. Did Verra think they had mocked the foods she had gone to such trouble to obtain from the *Narsid*'s stores? "They were good. We tried to guess what would be in the packages before we opened them."

"Without much luck, I imagine. I have one more carton in the hold. When we get back to the ship, we'll dine Arnimi style. Then you'll understand. You're not supposed to enjoy these foods. You're supposed to use them to demonstrate how well you've disciplined your palate."

Reyna frowned, not sure she understood. "How—how would we do that?"

"By not laughing, first of all. By sitting severely, by addressing your entire attention to each bite. By speaking to no one except to find fault with the food."

"But there wasn't anything wrong with the food."

Verra laughed sharply. "Of course there was, although my tongue has gone so stale—or I've spent so much time in the wrong company—that I enjoyed it too. Even the spondiloni, which was overcooked and far too aggressively seasoned."

"Is that what an Arnimi feast is like?" Reyna demanded incredulously. "Do the people come to find what's wrong with the food?" Not for the warmth, not for the companionship, not for the laughing and telling of tales? But to criticize each bite, finding minute fault with it?

Verra laughed. "Let's not call it a feast. Such a good word. We shouldn't contaminate it. And it looks like our small friend has finished his feast. Or hers."

Reyna looked down. The cub had fallen abruptly asleep again. It lay in a posture of abandon in her arms, wearing a sticky mustache, legs sprawling. "You'd better teach Juaren to use the lift-pack first," Reyna suggested.

"Yes. Our ward will wake thinking of his stomach if we move him too soon," Verra agreed.

Whatever her concerns, Reyna found it peaceful to sit in the sun with the cub sleeping in her arms while Juaren glided over the grasslands. Reyna tensed the first time he lifted. But he waved as he swept past and she saw pleasure and concentration in his face and knew Verra had won her point.

It was early afternoon by the time Reyna's turn came. She learned the lift-pack controls easily and then, breathless with fright and anticipation, she looked down and watched her boots slowly lift from the ground. At first, when she hung in the air, she thought she would forget how to use the controls and drift helplessly away. But Verra was calling to her—laughing and waving, running after her—and she managed to manipulate the controls as she had been instructed. Soon she was gliding over the grasslands with the same exhilaration she had seen in Juaren's face.

She practiced until mid-afternoon, occasionally taking turns with Juaren. Then they all gathered again to lay plans. "Moonrise is the best time to go into the trees," Juaren said. He had taken a turn feeding the cub. Now he cradled it, rubbing its ears absently. "We can look around then without disturbing the—what did you call them, Verra?"

"Chatni. It suits them even if it isn't accurate—even if they're something else entirely."

"Yes. We can look around without disturbing the chatni then. They'll be in their bowers. And we'll be able to find our way by moonlight."

"The—the chatni aren't nocturnal?" Reyna demanded.

"Not that I noticed."

So perhaps the cub had been wakeful the night before only because he was hungry. "And the insects—" Unconsciously Reyna rubbed the unhealed welt on her shoulder.

"I saw no sign of them in the forest." Juaren's glance flicked to the lift-pack. "I'll make the run back to the ship this time, Verra. Are there enough packs in the hold for each of us to use one and keep this one for our bedding and supplies?"

"We were issued five." At his questioning look, she went on,

"One for utility purposes, one for each of us, one for Birnam Rauth. If we find him."

If. Reyna didn't miss the qualification. But what had she expected? She smoothed the starsilk against her waist and glanced at Juaren, wondering what qualifications he set against the possibility of finding Birnam Rauth—or even of learning what had become of him. His face told her nothing beyond the fact that he was eager to fly again.

She and Verra passed the rest of the afternoon in desultory activity, Verra studying plant specimens, Reyna discovering that the cub could eat more than she had imagined he could hold and that he liked to have his bulging stomach rubbed. When she indulged him, his eyes narrowed to sleepy slits and he grunted with pleasure. Reyna laughed each time he produced the throaty sound.

They ate again when Juaren returned and then, at his advice, napped briefly. Finally it was moonrise and they buckled into the lift-packs, Verra carrying the cub in the sling she had devised. They rose gently from the ground, their shadows trailing behind.

They flew low, skimming grass and brush, avoiding the spindly trees. At first the trees appeared more frequently, growing in clusters and small groves, lining the winding stream. Then as abruptly as if a line had been drawn across the grasslands, the vegetation changed. Both brush and trees disappeared. The stream emerged naked and ran through the grass—and into the shadow of the forest. Into the shadow of tall white trees that grew in straight ranks, the moon sending down silver shafts among them. Their shadows striped the ground, which was deep with leaf mold. The smell under the tall trees was sharp, fresh. Their arching limbs carried sparse dark foliage.

Reyna, Verra and Juaren settled to the ground within the perimeter of the trees. Reyna peered around in awe. She had not expected them to be so tall, she had not expected them to be so straight. She had not expected them to grow in even ranks, as if they were about to march. The moon seemed to shine more brightly here than it had in the grasslands, creating a gridwork of shadows. Following Juaren's lead, she switched off her lift-pack.

"On foot from here," he whispered, and it seemed appropriate that he did not raise his voice.

Because there was something here she had not found in the grasslands. This, she realized, was a place where legends might live —bright, strange legends like none told in the halls of Brakrath.

This was a place where the shadows knew tales and the breeze spoke a new, more sibilant tongue.

They had entered a living forest. She knew that despite the silence around them. She knew that despite the unmoving shadows. Juaren and Verra knew it too. Reyna could tell from the careful way Verra set down her feet, from the wary glint of Juaren's eyes when he glanced back at her. The cub had wakened and for once did not squirm and mewl. He peered silently from his sling, his eyes wider than Reyna had ever seen them, his nostrils damply flared. The evening breeze played with them all, wrapping fingers in their hair and soughing through the trees.

Juaren led the way, walking with a light-footed step, as if he knew exactly where he took them. Reyna followed and soon lost all sense of direction. Only the position of the moon told her they walked deeper into the trees rather than skirting the edges of the forest. Occasionally the stream laced across their path and they waded through it. Once they paused for silent moments in a grassy dell. There were no insects in the air and no sign of their papery nests in the trees.

They heard the singing long before they saw the silks in the trees. It reached them faintly at first, a single voice that shone through the trees like light given voice. They halted, pressing close together, and a tingling chill passed up Reyna's spine. Silently she slipped her hand into Juaren's. The warmth of his fingers was welcome as they continued on, following the sound.

It grew sweeter as they neared it, clearer and less lonely. And the first voice was joined by others, some near, some distant, all singing wordlessly, each voice separate and distinctive. Hearing them, Reyna had a sense of brightness and color, as if she listened to a rainbow given voice. And she had an increasing sense of unreality. Her footsteps seemed to fall away soundlessly, as if she walked without touching the ground, as if the lift-pack still buoyed her.

They pressed farther. They crossed a wide clearing, deep-grown in grass. Early dew dampened Reyna's boots and chilled her feet. She didn't notice because Juaren's hand tightened on hers and with a floating sense of detachment she looked up and saw bowers blossoming in the white-trunked trees beyond the clearing. Their walls were made of tight-stretched silks of every color: amber, yellow, lilac; scarlet, emerald, gold; azure, chartreuse, red. Moonlight fell through the silks and made their colors luminous, living.

Reyna caught her breath, staring up. There were silks in the trees and their colors were so vivid, her sense of reality so distorted that she felt she could rise weightlessly and touch them. She felt she could float among the silks, singing her own song, a song of wordless joy. But Juaren held her hand, anchoring her, and they walked on.

Cautiously they made their way through the singing forest, no one raising any cry against their intrusion. They stopped often to watch the silks ripple against the breeze, fluttering and twisting in the moonlight. Occasionally Reyna saw a long-limbed shadow silhouetted against the silken walls of a bower. From some bowers two or three silks fluttered loose, raising their wordless song. From others none sang. Narrowing her eyes, gazing up, Reyna saw that there were smaller bowers in the upper branches of the trees. The silks that formed their walls were duller than those that enclosed the lower bowers and none of them reached for the breeze. None of them sang.

The trees seemed to grow in broad avenues. They made Reyna think of the stone avenues of Valley Terlath, wide and empty except when the people were coming home from the fields or when the herders drove their flocks to pasture. Juaren guided them from shadow to shadow. Reyna emulated his light-footed step—not difficult when she felt she might easily rise upon the current of silken voices. Verra followed them both, holding the cub close against her chest, one finger tucked into its mouth to quiet it.

Several times as they moved from shadow to shadow they heard the rustle of brush nearby. Once Reyna glanced down and saw winking black eyes peering from a burrow. When her shadow fell across the mouth of the burrow, its inhabitant vanished, throwing back dirt to close the aperture in the ground.

Then two things happened at once, two things that banished Reyna's enchantment and made her skin draw tight. At some sign she did not perceive, Juaren halted, gripping her hand tightly, and pulled her deep into the shadows. She caught her breath, suppressing a startled question, and followed his pointing finger.

A dark-furred creature stood peering down from its bower, moonlight haloing it with light. As clearly as if it were daylight, Reyna saw the creature: oblique yellow eyes, small sharp teeth, pointed ears, and gleaming black claws. And she saw more. She saw the muscle that rippled smoothly beneath the chestnut fur. She saw the acuteness of the eyes, the flare of the nostrils, the prick of the ears—and her thoughts took an instinctive leap.

A hunter—this was not some enchanted creature. This was not a creature that lived on song and light. This was a creature that tore flesh—a predator. That was clear in the sinuous way it moved as it released an amber silk to sing. That was clear in the set of the graceful, compactly formed head upon the long, slender neck, in the gleam of teeth and claws. This was a hunting animal, and it gazed directly at her.

Before Reyna realized that the creature did not see her, did not see any of them, so deeply were they submerged in shadow, the second thing happened. A starsilk raised its voice from the distant trees, singing the lonely song she knew so well—and speaking the words she knew just as well. She froze into breathless immobility as the familiar syllables called through the trees.

Come for me. Let me go. Set me free.

My name is Birnam Rauth and my thoughts are recorded. If you hear them, come for me.

Come for me.

Caught, she listened to the voice that had called her across the stars. She listened to the words that had brought her here—to the words she had not been able to forget or disregard.

Come for me.

Set me free.

She listened and the hair at the back of her neck rose. Her spine chilled and her heart became stone in her chest, crowding out breath. For the first time she felt the full reality of what she heard—felt it in the hollows of her heart, in the pit of her stomach, in the tingling tips of her fingers and toes.

More than a century ago, a man named Birnam Rauth had walked here, down these same tree-grown avenues. A man named Birnam Rauth had left his heelmarks upon this soil. A man named Birnam Rauth, whose voice was her father's voice, whose face, whose eyes were her father's too. Birnam Rauth had stood under these very trees, looking up at the dark-furred hunters in their bowers, listening to the song of the silks. Perhaps he had felt the same floating sense of enchantment she felt now.

If so, his wonder had turned to something else. And now his voice pleaded through the moonlit trees. *I'm held here. I don't know how.*

Set me free.

Reyna drew an aching breath, feeling Birnam Rauth's plea as a pain in her chest. Whatever had befallen him had befallen him here.

He had come here to explore. He had been drawn to the forest by the magic of the silks—and he had been trapped, imprisoned . . . held. Perhaps by dark-furred hunters like the one they stared up at. Perhaps by something else that lived in the forest, something they had not glimpsed yet. Tensely Reyna glanced at the cub. Its yellow eyes were open wide. Did she see something feral in its gaze? Its claws—so tiny, so sharp. It had only milk-teeth, but she knew now what its adult teeth would look like. They would be white and gleaming, tearing-sharp.

Birnam Rauth—his blood ran in her veins, his voice pleaded from the trees. Something had happened to him here. He had come and never returned. And now she, Juaren and Verra walked under the same trees. She, Juaren and Verra opened themselves to the same danger, seen or unseen. The bright colors, the silken songs— they didn't make her senses float now. They made her heart shrink and her breath grow tight in her chest.

ELEVEN

TSUUKA

Tsuuka never toyed with game. When she took prey, she dispatched it quickly, with a clean blow of her claws or a hard shake of her head. Nor did she ever tease her young. She never hid from them and watched to see them cry. She never dangled fresh meat before their noses and then withdrew it, making them leap and bat hungry claws for it. Nor had she ever torn a neighbor's silk or spoken gruffly to a neighbor's cub or exercised any other form of spite. But tonight she tortured the azure silk—the silk she had chosen to share her most intimate thoughts with—deliberately, knowingly, with calculated cruelty. And she did so without remorse, because any distress she visited upon the silk was small compared to her own.

Stingers . . . She had gone to the heart of the trees again the night before, moving as a shadow did at moonrise, stretching herself silently across the ground. She met neither sithi nor spinner as she went. Nor did she see any sign of the red master-silk as she took up watch in the dense shadows at the base of a moss-trunked giant. For a long while she crouched there, hearing only the slow rush of her own blood and the woody creaking of heavy branches. Sometimes the shadows seemed to shift and she glanced around uneasily but saw nothing.

Then clouds cleared from the moon and the red silk billowed from some hidden place and flirted through the trees. Tsuuka stared up, breath held, every muscle quivering. The silk rippled through the trees like a streak of fugitive sunlight, too restless to stay long in any one place. Sometimes it clung to distant upper branches. Other times it descended and brushed against mossed trunks, its fiery song deepening to a moan. Tsuuka crouched, aching with sustained alertness, until finally the silk fluttered low and tangled itself in the lower branches of the very tree she hid beneath.

Tsuuka didn't waste the barest fraction of a second in deliberation. She had come to take the silk. Every nerve was primed, every muscle ready. And so she sprang, digging sharp claws into the mossy trunk, bolting up the tree.

Swift as she was, the silk was swifter. Tsuuka's fingertips brushed it, her claws snagged it, but the silk tore itself away, its voice rising angrily. Then, before Tsuuka could pursue it up the tree, wood resonated under her claws and spinners boiled not just from the tree she clung to but from other trees as well. She stared around in shock. She had come so silently. She had waited in such shadowed stillness. She had not moved except in the split seconds of her spring. But spinners shrilled at her from a dozen branches, their witless eyes wide with fury. And among them were the ones she had seen before—spinners with stingers.

Spinners with stingers—and they had matured visibly since the afternoon before. Their tiny limbs were sturdier, their flesh denser. Their stingers had acquired a layer of horn, making the point crueler. Their voices held a new, more vehement warning, mindless and shrill.

Tsuuka stared for bare moments into their depthless eyes. Then instinct moved her and she skidded down the tree, dropped to fours and plunged away. Fear—atavistic fear—drove her so hard she didn't consider where she was running or why. The blood of terror pounded in her ears.

But even as she ran she was aware of the burn of the red mastersilk upon her fingertips. She had touched the silk. Her claws had torn it. If she had been an instant swifter—Her thoughts stopped there and swiftly changed course. If she had caught the red silk, would she be running free now? Or would the spinners have spit sticky silk at her, binding her, paralyzing her?

Spinners with stingers. It was so wrong her mind rebelled. Spinners were witless creatures, without guile or defense. They fed on insects and tree-boils, those hard-shelled nodules of sap that formed on tree trunks wherever bark-borers did their work. They had neither claws nor teeth—nor any other defense. Confronted with danger, all they could do was scream until some sithi heard and came to repel the aggressor.

At least that was the reality Tsuuka had always known. Spinners were weak and sithi strong, spinners helpless, sithi their protectors. But now she had run in terror from spinners—not once but twice.

Who could tell her why? She considered that as she climbed back to her own bower and dropped to her silent-silks to groom away the lingering smell of fear. No matter which of the older sithi she went to, she would hear the same rote warning: she must never go to the heart of the trees; there was something there no sithi must glimpse. That was how her mother had admonished her, and that was how she had admonished her own cubs in turn, understanding the warning no better than her mother had.

But her azure silk, her skysilk—she gazed up at it stretched tight among its sisters. Her silk was born of the spinners. It shared thoughts with them and with the unseen. If there was any agency in the forest that could give her answers, it was the silk.

If it would. If it would listen to her questions and not try to trill them away on the breeze. She growled softly, smoothing down her rumpled fur. She knew what she could expect if she approached it with the usual ceremony in the familiar confines of her bower. She had asked it questions before, and it had evaded them—sweetly, softly, reasonably, leaving her placated but vaguely unsatisfied. But if she took it to some unfamiliar place, if she let it feel her claws—

Because she would not be evaded this time. Nor would she be lulled by silent whispers or meaningless melodies. Ignorance and fear had robbed her of Maiilin; they would not rob her of Dariim as well.

She considered the matter the next day as she watched her cubs play and she laid her plans. That night—*this night*—she approached the azure silk silently at moonrise. She loosed it from the bower poles, refusing to identify herself, ignoring its increasingly agitated queries. The silk knew well enough who she was. It was only her uncharacteristic silence that made it shiver with doubt. That and the fact that she had loosened both its ends, as she had never done before. All around her, its sister silks knew something was amiss and they strained at their poles, trying to find slack to tune their anxious voices. She hardened herself against their silent confusion.

The skyswath bundled under one arm, Tsuuka glanced cursorily into Paalan and Kaliir's bower. They snored softly in a tangle of furred limbs. She peered in upon Dariim and Falett, silencing their evening-whispers with a meaningful growl. Then she slipped to the ground and carried the swath through the forest, speaking silently as she went. *You are going to tell me things tonight, skyswath. I have been ignorant long enough. Now I will learn. You will teach me tonight.*

She could scarcely number the things she must know. Each time she reckoned up a roster of her questions, she discovered others beyond them and upbraided herself. How could she have lived so long in the forest and remained so ignorant? Why had she never looked beyond the lazy routine of hunting and sunning and training her cubs? Why hadn't she shared Maiilin's curiosity?

But Maiilin was a growler now, wit and memory dead. Tsuuka shivered with sudden cold, digging black claws into the skyswath.

She carried the swath to a place she knew where six young trees grew in a closely spaced circle. The forest was silent there. No bowers blossomed for a wide distance around. Tsuuka stepped into the enclosure of trees and shook the azure silk free. Then, before the breeze could take it, she lashed it to the strongest of the six white trunks. She caught its ends, wrapping one around either hand and pulling them tight. *You are going to answer my questions, skyswath,* she said. *Because if you do not, I will leave you here, tied like this. I will leave you alone in this deserted place, without your sisters, with no company but your own.*

Or if your response displeases me, I will do more. I will untie you and throw you on the ground. You are no master-silk. You can rise little higher than the breeze will carry you. If you don't answer me, I'll throw you down and let you crawl on your belly until a barkshredder or a grass-pup finds you and takes you to line its den. There will be no one here to hear you cry.

There will be no one here to save you and restore you to the trees, silk. Just as no one can restore my sibling's wit.

Just as no one can restore my ignorance, now that I have begun to ask questions.

She felt the silk throb in her hand; she heard the whisper of a plea in her mind. Slowly, slowly she eased the pressure on the taut ends, giving the silk carefully measured slack. *Tell me why there are spinners with stingers in the heart of the trees, silk.*

The silken voice came softly, diffidently, disregarding her question. *Tsuuka? Are you Tsuuka, daughter of Mirala, sibling of Maiilin?*

You know well who I am, silk, Tsuuka said without patience, snapping at the silk, briefly pulling it taut again.

Yes—yes, you are Tsuuka, hunter of the forest, the silk said anxiously when she let it speak again. *You are Tsuuka, who stalks so skillfully, Tsuuka who pounces so lightly. You are—*

Tsuuka snapped again at the silk, this time holding it taut for a longer time. *Silk, I have asked a question, the first of many. And I have told you what I will do if you do not answer. Why do you waste time making talk that amounts to nothing?*

The silk seemed to recoil. *Tsuuka, hunter, tell me please—what other talk do you expect of me? I am not a master-silk with thought and will of its own, drawn from the life-silk of the preserved. I am only a songsilk, little better than a silent-silk.*

You have never called yourself little better than a silent-silk before.

But I speak truly now, Tsuuka, because you have asked and you are the hunter of my bower. You are the one who commanded the spinners to give me life. You are the one who ordered that I have voice. You are the one for whom I sing.

Then use your voice and sing answers for me! Releasing her claws, Tsuuka flexed them, scratching at the slippery fabric. *You have just said something I have never heard before: that the master-silks draw thought and will from the life-silk of the preserved.*

They do, the silk responded wispily. *Tsuuka, they do. That is why they must be secured so carefully. Because they are precious and rare and their making is difficult. The spinners must find special substances to feed themselves with before they can create a master-silk. Then the work is painstaking and long. And when it is done the swath must be mated for three days and three nights with the life-silk of the preserved selected to give it awareness and thought.*

But once all this is done, once the master-silk is created, it has a will of its own characteristic to its kind and separate from the will of the preserved selected to animate it. And its will is to fly in the trees ripping itself on high branches and scarring its filaments by taking too much sun. Left to its own, it soon becomes so worn it carries only a garbled memory of what it took from the life-silk.

You are confusing me, skyswath. What is a life-silk? What is the preserved? Is it a living thing? Is it the thing you call the unseen? I know none of these things. Why have you never spoken of them to me?

The silk shuddered lightly. *How can I answer so many questions, Tsuuka? I am only a songsilk. You have taken me from my sisters, and I must hear their voices. I must sing my song. That is what I was made for—to soothe and please you, not to trouble you with these things.*

Tonight this is your song. What is the preserved? What is the unseen? You've told me so little, silk, that I don't even know how spinners are born. I don't know if they have young they hide in their nests until they are grown. I don't know if they have weanlings they suckle. Among the sithi, there was an estrus cycle. When the season came, those sithi who were ready to bear young chose mates from among their neighbors and petted and coddled them until their bodies underwent the mating change and produced the fertilizing agent. Tsuuka had never observed any such behavior among the spinners. Nor had she ever seen a spinner who appeared immature —before she had climbed the mossy tree.

She growled, suddenly full of chagrin. She who called herself the swiftest and the best, she who boasted the keenness of her senses— there were so many things she had failed to observe, just as there were so many things she had failed to question.

We are the spinners' only offspring, the silk said with soft regret. *My sister silks and I are the children of their glands. They have no young but us.*

How could that be? Tsuuka's forebrow creased, drawing her ears erect. The spinners created the silks—she had seen that. But to call the silks their offspring, to say they had no others—

Tsuuka's grip on the silk tightened. *Are you telling me tales, silk? If the spinners have no offspring but you, why are there always spinners working by the streamside and feeding in the trees? Where do they come from?* ˋ

Do you insist upon knowing, Tsuuka?

I insist, silk. With a growl.

The silk murmured a self-effacing plaint. *You are a hunter, as swift as the best, yet you concern yourself with these small matters. Matters so insignificant . . .*

Tell me these small matters!

The silk sighed. *If you must know, Tsuuka. The spinners hatch from the bulb-well. The unseen seeds them there and feeds and tends them until their membranes rupture. Then they take their final feeding from her and they go into the forest to live and to bring food to her in turn. Because they are her offspring and that is the way of it. The spinners feed the unseen and the unseen feeds the new bulbs as they grow.*

So the spinners were the offspring of the unseen. But what was the unseen? Who was the unseen? Tsuuka growled in perplexity. So many questions to be asked. Which were the right ones? *I have seen spinners coming and going in the heart of the trees, silk—where I thought nothing lived.* It was a question, even though she didn't express it so.

The silk recognized it readily enough. *Must you know these things, Tsuuka? We keep them secret because they are so insignificant. They are so uninteresting to a sithi hunter.*

I must know, silk. Be certain of that.

The silk writhed with poorly concealed distress. *Then I will tell you. You are correct. The unseen lives there where the oldest trees grow. The bulb-wells are found in the hollows of the trees. The spinners come and go because they must carry digest to the unseen in their feeding sacs. They nourish her so that she can nourish those who depend upon her.*

The new hatching of spinners. *Then the unseen—the unseen is what no sithi must ever glimpse.*

No sithi must see her, the silk agreed.

And my sibling—Maiilin—

I know it hurts you to speak of your sibling, Tsuuka, the silk said softly.

It hurts me, and I must know. You will tell me. Because if she did not learn what had happened to Maiilin, how could she prevent the same thing from happening to Dariim?

The silk's voice fell to a bare whisper. *I was not spun then, Tsuuka. You had not commanded the spinners to give me life because you were no more than a cub. If I had had voice then, if I had had words to warn you with—*

But you did not.

I did not. And your sibling did not listen to the warning your mother gave her. She thought no harm would come to her because she had gone to the deep trees before without harm. She had looked into the bulb-well.

Let me tell you, Tsuuka—there are times when a cub can run and climb and hunt there. There are even times—brief times—when she can look down into the bulb-well and see the bulbs rooted to its walls —because at those times the unseen is sheltered in her pulp-bed at the bottom of the well, safe from sight.

But there are other times when no sithi must walk near those trees, and that was the time your sibling chose to go there.

And so it was spinners who turned her to a growler, Tsuuka said. *Spinners with stingers.*

The silk throbbed silently against the chill air. When she spoke, her voice was wispy, apologetic. *They are called escorts—because they escort the unseen and her successor when they leave the bulb-well. They escort them at times like the one when your sibling chose to visit the deep forest. And you have guessed right. It was their sting that made her a growler, although it was not intended to do that. It was only intended to protect the unseen.*

Against Maiilin? Tsuuka demanded with a growl of anger. *Maiilin didn't go there to do harm. She only went there—*

She only went there because youth and thirst for adventure drove her. You know our nature, silk. We are deadly to game but never to the spinners. Never to you.

You are the protectors of our kind. You make the forest safe so the spinners can go freely and gather food for the unseen, the silk acknowledged meekly. *But there is only one unseen. In this entire quarter of the forest, which stretches so far, there is only one, and only she can seed the bulb-well. Only she can create a successor when she feels her seed sacs begin to dry. Only she can join all our thoughts and direct our lives. And she is not a spinner, my hunter. Not in nature, not in appearance. We dare not rely upon chance and the judgment of a cub—or of any other creature—when she must leave her well. We trust her protection to the instinct of the escorts. They have but one instinct and only she can moderate it, if she is strong enough to do so. Often when the unseen nears the end of her time, she is too weak to do more than trust to the escorts to fulfill their protective function.*

To sting. To paralyze. To deaden—the body for minutes, the mind forever. Tsuuka bowed her head, releasing the skyswath, leaning slack-limbed against a white-trunked tree and letting the weight of responsibility slip from her shoulders. Maiilin's destruction had been only chance. Because only chance had taken them to the deep trees on that day, at that time. She could not have saved her sibling. If she had been brave, if she had not hidden, she would be a growler too.

Slowly Tsuuka raised her head. Moonlight fell silver-bright beyond the circle of trees, but the azure silk did not catch the breeze and reach for it. It hung abjectly. *Silk,* Tsuuka said, realizing she could not stop with her own vindication, realizing what else she must ask next, *tell me one thing more. How can I capture the red master-silk and save my cub from being turned to a growler?*

The silk caught enough breeze to shiver violently. *Tsuuka, my hunter, you cannot. No sithi can own a master-silk. It draws life directly from the life-silk. It carries the full memory of the preserved from which it was drawn—all her joys, all her fears, all the things she learned in the seasons of her life. You cannot tie a master-silk to your bower poles and bid it to sing in harmony with my sister silks and me. It will not. Its voice is no more harmonious than the star-silk's voice. It—*

Silk, I don't care now for harmony, Tsuuka interrupted impatiently. Nor did she care that the silk spoke again of things she didn't understand: the life-silk, the preserved. *If I do not take the master-silk, my cub will go for it again—and again and again. Can you promise me that no harm will come to her in the hunt?*

Tsuuka, hunter—I am just a songsilk. I cannot raise my arms without the help of the breeze. I cannot speak without moonlight. My voice and my awareness come from the master-silk I was bathed with but I carry only the faint voice of thought. I am less than any other creature of my kind except the silent-silks.

Can you promise me? Tsuuka insisted.

I can promise you that if your cub goes to hunt the silk she will meet the escorts. And it will be sooner rather than later. Because the unseen has already remarked the drying of her seed sacs and she has given her successor her last feeding, the one that rouses her from dormancy and stimulates her to maturity. Soon the successor will be ready. Then she must make the pilgrimage from the bulb-well where she hatched to the one where she will seed her own bulbs. And the unseen must emerge to spin her life-silk before her awareness can be preserved in it. That can't be done in the darkness of the well. At both those times, no creature—sithi or other—must go to the heart of the trees. Because the escorts have only one instinct, Tsuuka—to protect the unseen and her successor, and through them all our species.

Apprehension sank black claws into the soft tissue of Tsuuka's heart. Successor, life-silk, unseen . . . She could not guess the nature of any of them. She could not imagine how they looked or what scent they carried. But she had seen the stingered escorts, and she had seen what they could do. *When—when will these things happen, silk?* Her fingers were cold, her inner voice faltering.

Soon is all I can tell you, Tsuuka, the silk said abjectly. *The time is soon.*

And so Tsuuka knew, as she had known before, that there was only one thing to do. She must capture the red silk herself.

Tonight? Must she go for it tonight? She stroked her fur, trying to find courage. What if she went and did not return? What was to become of her weanlings? Falett and Dariim could look after themselves. Paalan and Kaliir could not. She must provide against the possibility that she might not return.

Bleakly Tsuuka thought of Riifika, whose cubs had been stillborn so recently. If she was to hunt the red silk, she must wake Riifika and ask her to care for Paalan and Kaliir in the event she did not return: to feed and groom them, to discipline and train them, to see them safely to their own tree.

Because if she did not come back from the heart of the trees, she would not sun herself with her offspring again. She would not watch them tear meat, she would not hear their chuckles and growls, she would not monitor their cub games and sparring bouts.

Silk—she said weakly. But she could not ask the skyswath for courage. She had to find that herself.

Tsuuka? Are you Tsuuka?

Yes, I am Tsuuka, and I must go again to the heart of the trees. She said it more to herself than to the silk. Then, before the silk could object, she untied it and folded it beneath one arm.

Her senses seemed overcharged as she made her way back through the trees, as if the energy she dared not invest in thought concentrated in her senses instead. She saw every dark-veined leaf and every white-limned trunk separately, the shattered components of a larger reality. Each scuff of the soil, each animal scent made the hair rise at the back of her neck. She detected the distinctive odor of a grass-puppy and followed its trail to a cluster of bushes. She found the spoor of a bark-shredder and saw a disturbance of the earth where a prickle-hide had dragged some tiny prey to its burrow. Every sensory clue impinged upon her, demanding its brief moment of attention.

Her thoughts were so scattered, her awareness so fragmented that she was unprepared for what occurred next. As she neared the stream, she caught an unfamiliar scent on the soil—sharp, alien, distinctive. Tsuuka froze, nostrils flaring, mouth open. Looking down, she saw the print of feet—but feet like none she had seen before. There were three pairs of them, as long as her own feet and broader. None of them bore the mark of toes. None bore any sign of claws. Stunned, she stared down at them, quelling her first irrational alarm, reassuring herself that this was not the deep forest. These were not the prints of the unseen. There were no escorts waiting here to quench her wit.

But something had passed this way, something that had never entered this quarter of the forest before.

And before she could decide what she must do, she heard its voice nearby—low, controlled, the syllables sharp and unfamiliar. She listened, struck by recognition, paralyzed by it.

The starvoice—The syllables were unfamiliar. The voice itself was different in timbre, in pitch. But this was unmistakably the same kind of voice that spoke from the starsilk.

Slowly Tsuuka's frozen wits thawed and she began to think coherently. There were strangers in the forest, strangers of the same breed as the stranger who spoke from the starsilk. Why? How had they come here? Her blood surged with alarm. Her weanlings, her cubs—

Her mind urged caution, but alarm was stronger and it drove her forward. The murmur of voices and the mark of feet guided her until she found the intruders clustered beside the stream, two standing, the third sitting, bending over a small bundle. Tsuuka stiffened as she slipped near, concealing herself in shadow, and heard a familiar whimper—the whimper of a newborn.

Her pupils flared so sharply she felt the pull of tiny muscles. Three intruders, at once alike and different from one another. One bulkier, more muscular than the others. One—the one who sat—as slight as an adolescent cub, with glossy fur that streamed over her shoulders and down her back. Their features were strange and bare. Their claws were broad, blunt and pink. By moonlight she saw the flash of equally blunt teeth.

Cold gripped her, the cold of uncertainty and fear. What kind of prey did they tear with those teeth? How did they sharpen such awkwardly shaped claws and what use did they make of them? *Why were they here—and why did they have a sithi cub?*

More perplexing still, what must she do? Slip away and rouse her neighbors? Send her own cubs to hide? Who had the intruders stolen the newborn from? Why did it whimper so irritably? Had it been one of her own, she would have called it a milk-cry. But perhaps the intruders had injured it. With one hand she kneaded the skyswath, wishing she could call up its familiar voice for counsel.

Then Tsuuka stiffened as the creature who sat holding the newborn stood. She turned, moonlight falling full upon her, and Tsuuka saw two things. The cub she held was frail and welted with insect stings; it had come from the grasslands, where nightflyers fed. And the slightest intruder wore a familiar band of white at her waist.

Tsuuka bared her teeth in a startled grimace. The intruders had come from the grasslands and they had a starsilk. Where had they obtained it? Who had they taken it from? None of the sithi who lived in the grasslands had silks. No spinners lived there to spin them. And the newborn—

Before she could find answers to any of those perplexities, Tsuuka realized that some unspoken communication had passed among the intruders. At a signal from one of them, all three raised their heads and peered into the shadows where she stood. None spoke, none moved, as strange, round-pupiled eyes found hers. A slow breath rasping in her throat, Tsuuka measured the tension of their limbs against hers. Moonlight glanced off the unfurred surfaces of their faces and exposed a stiffness that could only be fear.

She tried to tear her eyes from theirs and could not. Nor could they evade her staring gaze. Tense, silent, they stared at each other over the short space that separated them. Then the slightest intruder did something entirely unexpected. She stepped forward, her eyes never wavering from Tsuuka's, and extended the frail newborn with both hands. When the newborn caught Tsuuka's scent, its slit eyes widened and it began to squirm.

It wasn't courage that made Tsuuka step forward to take the wriggling cub. It was simple instinct. The cub was squirming so vigorously Tsuuka thought the creature would drop it. She took it only to keep it from harm.

She had not thought either of offering the blue silk in exchange for the newborn. But one of the hands she extended for the cub held the silk and the intruder misunderstood. She relinquished the cub, hesitated, and then with trembling fingers slipped the silk from Tsuuka's grasp. She stepped back quickly, stroking the silk, still watching Tsuuka tensely.

Tsuuka felt a warning growl rise in her throat. But the intruder's round-eyed fear dampened it. That and some quality she saw in the intruder's eyes, some kinship of intelligence. Their two gazes held for moments longer. Then Tsuuka took a single step back into the shadows. The intruder followed suit, retreating swiftly without turning her back. When she stood beside her companions again, all three disappeared quickly into the streamside shadows.

Tsuuka stared for a long time at the place where they had stood, ignoring the hungry whimper of the newborn. She gazed at the print of their feet and tried to understand what had happened, what it meant. She had given the intruder her skysilk, however unwillingly. Just as unwillingly she had taken custody of a grassland cub. She stood listening, wondering if she heard the skysilk calling her, wondering if she heard its anxious voice.

But that was illusion, and she must harden herself against it. She must not let this diversion distract her. There were intruders in the forest but they had not offered harm. The master-silk did, and she must capture it. She must not hesitate and lose courage.

She pulled the squirming newborn close, hissing so loudly in its ear that it twitched, and set out toward Riifika's bower, her heart as heavy as an orphaned cub's.

TWELVE
REYNA

An hour's walk upstream from the spot where they had encountered the chatni, the stream broadened and became shallow, cutting its way between towering trees. The air was heavy with shadow and the smell of dampness. There was no sign of bowers in the trees. Juaren examined the ground by moonlight and found only the prints of small animals. "The chatni don't come here. This looks like the best place for us to sleep."

Reyna sank gratefully into her bedding, her mind ringing with impressions: Birnam Rauth's voice calling through the trees, the creature they had met beside the stream, the glint of its eyes and the tearing-sharpness of its teeth—and balanced against those, something in its gaze that went beyond a predator's shrewdness. Something that suggested a creature that reasoned, however alien its thought processes might be.

The fact that the creature had offered her the blue songsilk in exchange for the cub supported her feeling that she had seen intelligence in its eyes—but an intelligence bounded by different perimeters than her own, an intelligence that must be measured against different standards. And what did that mean? That the chatni offered no danger? Or that she, Juaren and Verra must be doubly wary now that the creatures knew they were in the forest?

Reyna slept uneasily, rousing herself often to listen to the silence of the trees. She kept her hunting blade and her pike beside her.

Light seeped dimly through the tall trees when a scuffling sound nearby woke her. She caught a sharp breath and rose to one elbow, closing anxious fingers around her pike, then blinked in surprise. A tiny, pink-faced creature had emerged from the brush and stared at her with the immobility of shock. Startled, she returned its stare.

From a distance, she might have mistaken it for an undersized human infant: pink and bare, with chubby limbs and round face. It stood on two dimpled legs, its bald head tottering unsteadily on its fat neck.

But the resemblance did not bear close examination. The creature's skin was strangely textured, its mouth broad and lipless, and what appeared to be rolls of fat on the neck and abdomen were instead bulging sacs.

Filled with what? Reyna could not guess. It was the creature's eyes that held her, round and dark and vacant, as if they accepted images without comprehending them. "Juaren," she said softly. He slept with his covers pulled over his head. "Juaren!" Carefully, moving deliberately, she turned back her bedding.

She got no farther before the creature reacted. Its eyes widened, its tiny, three-fingered fists clutched, and it emitted a shrill scream, feet firmly planted.

Verra and Juaren woke immediately, snatching at their own weapons. When their initial shock passed, they lowered weapons, glancing at one another in bewilderment. "Where did it come from?" Juaren demanded when the creature continued to shrill.

"I woke up and found it here. It just—I think it just stumbled across us." Reyna had to shout over the creature's din. The sound was like an alarm, strident and penetrating.

Juaren grunted with irritation. "I'm ready for it to stumble away." He rose to his knees, looming over the creature, and clapped his hands.

The creature's eyes flared, becoming still larger, still darker, still more witless. It started so violently it almost toppled backward. For a moment its voice faltered. When Juaren clapped again, it emitted a brief yelping cry. Then, shrilling, it turned and fled, tottering awkwardly on fat pink legs.

Reyna listened to the fading scream, hearing no answering cry from the brush or the trees. Reluctantly, rubbing her eyes, she left the warmth of her bedding and studied the tiny creature's tracks. They were three-toed—familiar. "I don't see others like it here," she said. "But last night, downstream—"

"The ground was covered with tracks like this in the area where we met the chatni. They apparently congregate near the water—but not this far upstream." Juaren joined her, searching the ground in a widening circle. "A few old tracks," he concluded finally. "They don't come here often or in numbers. And they're obviously not dangerous."

That much seemed clear. In fact the tottering pink creature might have amused her if it hadn't screamed with such mindless stridence. Reyna rubbed her arms, trying to warm them. The morning was chill and grey, uninviting. Verra shivered in her blankets, looking no more eager for the day than Reyna felt. Her teeth chattering, Reyna sat and thrust her bare feet back into her bedding to warm them.

But Juaren didn't seem to notice the grey light or the morning chill. He brushed a brisk hand through his white hair. "I want to look a little farther into the trees. I won't be long."

Reyna glanced up in alarm. "Do you think—" Did he think he should go alone? At this hour?

Apparently he did. "I won't be long," he repeated.

Reyna nodded reluctantly. When he had slipped away into the trees, she followed Verra's example, sliding all the way back into her bedding. She curled up, still trying to rub warmth into her arms, but found neither sleep nor comfort. Some vagrant sense of responsibility prodded her. They knew almost nothing about the forest. They didn't know that the chatni were friendly or that there were no other predators. Yet she had let Juaren go into the trees alone, without even his lift-pack.

Perhaps he didn't need the doubtful protection of her company. Perhaps he wouldn't welcome her if she followed him. She knew she could not walk as lightly or watch as quietly as he could. Perhaps she would never train herself to that degree. But finally, hardening herself against the morning chill, she crawled out of her bedding. She splashed her face from the stream, shuddered, and pulled on a clean shift. In deference to the cold, she added a pair of trousers, tucking them into her boots with stiff fingers. Then she gathered up the two lift-packs and shook Verra awake. "Juaren forgot his lift-pack. I'm taking it to him."

The Arnimi woman nodded sleepily and burrowed deeper into her covers.

Wearing one lift-pack, carrying the other, Reyna pressed her fledgling tracking skills into service. The trail Juaren left as he moved downstream was faint, uneven. Sometimes, for short distances, it disappeared entirely. When that happened, Reyna paused and glanced back in the direction she had come, relieved that she had the stream to guide herself by, relieved that there was no wind to make brush rustle and branches sigh, relieved that the forest was still. If she encountered a chatni or if she lost herself trying to find Juaren—

Eventually, of course, she did. She followed the faint track of his boots away from the stream, into the trees, and lost it entirely. Dismayed, she turned a full circle, peering at undisturbed layers of leaf mold. There was no mark, no disturbance, nothing to guide her —nothing to suggest which direction he had taken from this point. She stared at the ground helplessly, as if it had betrayed her.

What must she do? Return to the campsite? Wait for Juaren there? An unattractive option. Surely if she searched in a broad radius from his last discernible print, she would pick up his trail again. Or so she told herself. And if not, at least she would be no more lost than she was now.

Purposefully, decided, she drew a large X in the soil with the toe of her boot. She walked one broad circle around it, then another, studying the soil.

She found nothing. But she continued to search, refusing to admit for a long time that her third and broadest circle had become loose and wandering, that she had lost her own mark as well as Juaren's trail.

Finally, discouraged, beginning to be frightened, she halted and gazed up. The sky was uniformly grey—no help. Nor could she guide herself by the slope of morning shadows. Without sun or moon, there were only vaguely defined pools of grey beneath the trees. And as she stood counseling herself against the first shrill promptings of panic, she realized that somehow all the trees had changed. They had become alike. She stood among endless ranks of identical, sparsely leafed white shafts.

She fingered the controls of her lift-pack, gazing around in growing fright, trying to decide what she must do next. To activate the pack and glide rapidly, randomly through the trees searching for the stream was to admit that she had lost herself.

To fail to do so when she had indeed lost herself was foolish.

Still, stubbornly, she stumbled on, trying to complete her circle —until the moment when Juaren materialized soundlessly from the early morning shadows, making her start with surprise. He pressed one finger to his lips. "Over here."

Reyna sighed with relief but he seemed not to notice. Gratefully, she followed him.

He led her back to the stream, to a point where it had contracted to a narrow strand and looped back upon itself, creating a narrow peninsula. White-trunked saplings grew there and pink creatures like the one that had run from them earlier swarmed up the slender trees, chattering noisily.

"Feeding," Juaren whispered. "There are bubbles of sap on the trunks—you've seen them. They have a brittle shell. If you pierce it, they're full of liquid. Here—" He turned, surveying the trees behind them, finding one of the amber-shelled nodules. He drove the point of his knife through the shell and amber liquid ran down the tree's trunk. "Sticky," he said. "It will seal itself in just a moment. As nearly as I can tell, they lick until the shell dissolves and then fill the sacs at their necks with the fluid."

"Can we go nearer? Without frightening them?"

"We can try. Here—"

They slipped forward cautiously, hiding themselves in the shadows a short distance from the streambank. The creatures shinnied up and down the smooth trunks readily, hugging them with plump pink limbs. They fed until their sacs bulged. Then they tottered away, chattering among themselves, occasionally uttering small shrills.

Reyna didn't become aware until the tittering voices died in the trees that Juaren's shoulder touched hers, that her hand had found its way to his. She pulled away immediately, unaccountably embarrassed, and he dropped her hand with a surprised frown. "I—I thought you might need your lift-pack," she said quickly, wishing she knew some way to turn back the warm tide that rose to her face. It made her feel awkward, as if she had something to hide. "I brought it."

Juaren found his poise more quickly than she found hers. "Good. I want to go up to the treetops. Come with me?"

She gazed up uncertainly, wondering whether he invited her to accompany him in a reconnaissance of the forest or in something else. Did it matter when she had already agreed to go to the mountains with him? She spoke crisply to hide confusion. "Of course."

He strapped into his pack without further comment, then stood for a moment listening to the forest. "Slowly. We don't want to get tangled in the trees."

Reyna nodded, and when he touched his controls, she lifted from the ground after him. They rose side by side, the lift-packs making an almost inaudible rushing sound. They wove between wide-reaching branches, pushing aside foliage, until finally they hovered above the canopy of trees. Reyna glanced down and quelled a moment's dizzy disorientation. Trees stretched below them as far as she could see. The clouds had begun to lift and the sky was faintly stained with color. She wheeled around, peering through the screening foliage. Far below, she saw the glint of water. "If we follow the stream—"

"Our camp isn't far, just a few minutes to the north." Juaren nodded, indicating the direction. "And our ship—"

"Where is it?" she said quickly, realizing that they had drifted together again, and his hand had found hers. Before he could answer, she said, "I—I was lost this morning. A few minutes ago." She frowned, immediately annoyed with herself, wondering what impulse made her tell him that. Was she trying to place some claim of helplessness on him? Or was she only trying to explain, in some circuitous way, why she didn't withdraw her hand? But why withdraw her hand when she had already promised to be his year's mate when they returned to Brakrath?

Perhaps because Brakrath lay stars away and she had never considered taking even a season's mate until yesterday.

Self-consciously she realized that he studied her, guessing at each mood as it played across her face—saying nothing. Abruptly she kicked her legs and touched her controls, drawing him swiftly after her above the treetops. Air rushed at them, tugging at their hair. The quick, decisive motion gave her courage to ask the question she hadn't asked before, the central question of their presence here. "Do you think he's here? Do you think we'll find him?"

Juaren tapped at the controls of his pack, reversing their direction, spinning her around. He pulled her swiftly through the air after him, legs trailing, then drifted to a halt. "Birnam Rauth?"

"Yes," she said breathlessly. Her hair swirled around her shoulders. Strands of it veiled her face. She pushed it aside, not daring to look down. The trees must be spinning. "Do you think we'll learn what happened to him?" she pressed.

Juaren's grey eyes held hers, offering her nothing more telling than her own reflection. "I knew you were lost," he said finally. "I thought if I left you alone, you would find your way again."

But she hadn't. And he hadn't answered her question, an evasion that was clearly deliberate. She sighed, knowing it was no use insisting. What could he tell her except that he did not expect to find Birnam Rauth? That he had come for his own reasons—to learn what lay beyond Brakrath—and that pressing the search for Birnam Rauth was the price he paid for his passage. "I'm—I'm glad you didn't laugh at me," she said softly.

His fingers played at the lift-pack controls again. They swung in a wide arc, then turned sharply and spun back again. When they glided to a halt, his eyes glinted. "Then you won't laugh at me, will you?"

"About what?" The words were faint. Something squeezed tight in her chest, something leaped in her stomach as he swung her again, sharply, without warning. Was he deliberately trying to frighten her? To prevent her from laughing? At what? She brushed the hair from her face with clumsy fingers.

His eyes narrowed and took a hard intensity. "You won't laugh when I ask you to teach me to cipher."

She looked at him in surprise, catching her breath. "To cipher? You already know how to cipher." Every child of the halls learned to do that in his eighth year.

"I know how to read simple-stroke," he said. "I learned that much before I apprenticed myself to Komas. So I can read the breeding records, the harvest rolls, the seed charts. But that's not what I want to read."

"That's all anyone reads," she protested. "Except the barohna and her daughters and the history keepers. And the juris, of course." The people of the halls had no need to consult the library scrolls. The histories recorded there were kept alive by word of mouth in the halls. They were chanted and sung at the festival table. They were whispered to the youngest children as bedtime tales. Everyone knew them—the old stories, the new ones.

"That's not all I want to read," he persisted, and she saw from the hardening lines around his eyes that he had thought long about what he said next. "Do you remember what you told me when I asked why you wanted to learn to track? I want the same thing you want. I want to know what has passed. And I don't want to know it just from tales and songs. I want to hold the earliest scrolls in my hands. I want to touch the parchment and smell the ink and understand the figures—and everything behind them. I want to know what kind of hands wrote them. And then I want to write histories of my own. No hunter has written his story since the early days. I want to write mine and Komas'. And whatever price you want to set—"

Price? She winced under the pressure of his hand, not wanting to talk about prices. Because she understood now what he wanted. He wanted to look behind the familiar tales. He wanted to touch the past, to grasp its scent and its texture. He wanted to track the legendary figures from flesh to the place where myth claimed them. Because what was sung and whispered in the halls was legend. Only the scrolls exposed the human flesh behind it. *Kirsa, who had discovered that dreams hatched from broken shells. Tima, who had realized that the early timers would find humanity only in change. Noa, first of the guardians to stand watch over the redmanes. Niabi, the first barohna, who had found her power only to see her lover fall in ashes at her feet.*

"I'll teach you," she said. "I'll teach you everything I know."

"And the price?" His hand still gripped hers, tightly.

She gazed into the rising sun, then pivoted and said as lightly as she could. "You'll probably have to apprentice yourself to me for a winter. You'll probably have to pledge to spend a full winter in my palace." Where else, after all, was he to find parchment and pens and tables to spread them upon?

"Only a winter?" he demanded, responding to the teasing tone of her voice.

"Maybe longer. Can you stay away from the mountains in winter?"

"If I can't, we'll pack writing tools in our packs and go find the snow."

"We'll go," she laughed. "And you can write your story in the snow pack with a pike." But they could do none of those things until they had fulfilled his promise to Komas, she realized, her mood changing with the thought. They could do nothing until they found a way to waken the people.

And they could not do that until they had returned safely from their search. Reyna gazed down over the forest, the momentary lightness of her mood slipping away. The trees below stretched so far they might be endless. And Juaren believed their search was futile. Reyna touched her temples, wondering if her belief was any stronger than his. "I left Verra sleeping. We'd better get back."

They followed the stream north and settled through the trees to their campsite. Packs and supplies lay where they had dropped them the night before. All three rolls of bedding had been neatly bundled and stacked beside the supplies and Verra was gone. They found a few carefully incised figures in the damp soil of the streambank.

Reyna ciphered them aloud. "She wants us to wait here. She's gone to follow the stream farther north." She gazed upstream, frowning. "She took her lift-pack."

Juaren nodded, unworried. "Did you eat yet?"

"No."

Another time they might have laughed and talked while they made their meal. But a shadow had come between them since they had returned to the ground. Perhaps it was the specter of Birnam Rauth. Perhaps it was the unspoken recognition of the things they must accomplish before she could teach Juaren to cipher the library scrolls, before they could go to the mountains together.

Reyna ate slowly, not tasting the food. When she finished, she stared down at her empty bowl and realized she had not even taken time this morning to tie the starsilk at her waist. Frowning, she rinsed her bowl in the stream and went to her pack.

The blue silk was folded with the white, forgotten. She stroked it thoughtfully, then took it to where Juaren sat. "Do you want to wear this?"

His eyes flickered with interest. "Let's hear it first." Setting aside his bowl, he tied the blue silk to the slender trunk of a sapling.

The breeze was a long time coming. Then it moved gently among the trees, tossing their branches lightly. The blue silk shivered and reached out feebly, raising silken hands to the dappled morning sunlight. The song it sang was brief and disturbing, a sound that made Reyna think of unshed tears. She listened and was suddenly cold. "I—I think we should give it back," she faltered, turning to Juaren. "Back to the chatni." Did he hear the same bereavement in the silk's song that she did?

Apparently he did. He nodded slowly. "Yes." He stood and untied the blue silk. "I'll put it in the pack until we find a way."

They sat silently for a while, waiting for Verra, listening to the silence of the forest and the sporadic morning breeze. Occasionally Reyna thought of the song the blue silk sang and shivered. Finally, when Verra did not appear, Juaren rose and walked along the streambank, gazing down into the shallow water. He picked up a twig and incised random figures in the damp soil.

Eventually Reyna roused herself and joined him. They found tiny creatures in the shallow water and insects that hid beneath the occasional rocks. They examined plant specimens, trying to decide what conditions each required to grow. Once they found a tiny blue flower blooming from a cavity in the trunk of a tree. They studied it breathlessly, as if it might wither under their scrutiny.

When Reyna heard the light rush of Verra's lift-pack, she was surprised to look up and see that it was mid-morning. Verra settled through the trees and touched ground in a flurry of white silks. She wore several starsilks at her waist, their silken arms fluttering. She also wore an emerald silk coiffed into a turban, concealing her greying hair. Its clear, vivid tone made the sparkle of her eyes and the color in her cheeks brighter. "Did you think I had deserted you?" she demanded and then went on without waiting for an answer. "I went up for a quick reconnaissance and flew a little farther than I intended. Have you two taken a good look over the forest?"

"We—we went up for a while. Where did you find those? Did you take them from the chatni?"

Verra caught the white silks and wound them loosely around one hand. "No, but someone did. Did you see the burned area to the southeast? I don't know enough about local growth cycles to guess when it happened, but the trees are just beginning to reestablish themselves. They're fighting their way up through a heavy growth of brush."

Juaren was immediately interested. "We didn't go that far."

"I've realized all along that commerce ships of some kind—perhaps only shuttles; perhaps larger craft—must have made groundfall here to gather the silks the trader ship brought to Brakrath. After I managed to wake myself this morning, I decided to use instrumentation to see if I could find some unexplained radiation that might indicate where they had landed." She tapped her waist, where an instrument pouch bulged beneath the silks, and said quickly. "You'll be pleased, Reyna. I never took it out of the case. When I sighted the burn area, I took one quick float over it and spotted what caused the ignition: a craft substantially smaller than the one that came down on Brakrath but similar in certain other details. I doubt it had independent warp capabilities. It was probably a surface shuttle, and apparently it was loaded and prepared to return to the mother-ship when it failed in lift-off, fell and ignited. The wreckage is pretty sketchy. I couldn't find any sign of a crew. If they survived the crash, they were probably retrieved by another shuttle.

"The only sign of cargo was one fire-resistant carton that had been thrown clear of the wreckage and not retrieved. I pried it open and found silks. These. And this—" Quickly she lifted the emerald turban from her head and unwound it. She stepped into a patch of dappled sunlight and drew the emerald silk back and forth through the air.

There was nothing sad in its fluttering song. The emerald silk raised a clear, bright voice—as clear, as bright as Verra's eyes as she listened to it. She swept it back and forth briefly, intent upon its song, then tied it around her forehead, letting the ends hang free. The effect was rakish, at odds with the austerity of the black uniform she wore. "I want to pick up other colors later. Perhaps for my children. Although—" She caught the emerald streamers in one hand, frowning.

"Don't you think they would like them?" Reyna probed when the Arnimi woman didn't go on. She had difficulty imagining any other Arnimi winding a silk around her head and taking its brightness into her eyes.

Verra didn't respond for several moments. Then she spoke briskly, untying the white silks at her waist. "We'd better give some thought to how we want to structure the day. What we want to do with it."

"I'd like to see the wreckage," Juaren said quickly. "And if we can observe the chatni without disturbing them—" He hesitated, frowning with a new thought. "The instrument you were going to use to find where the trade ships made groundfall—would it help us find Birnam Rauth's ship?"

"Mmmmm. Questionable, after this length of time. But I brought another instrument that could be helpful. I doubt he set down in the forest, since he didn't have a ground party to clear a landing site for him. We'll probably have to scout the less heavily wooded areas around the perimeters of the forest. And it's possible he made landing at a substantial distance, as we did. In that case, a visual search could be quite time-consuming. But with this instrument, we could survey entire blocks of area at a time." She raised a questioning eyebrow. "Reyna?"

Reyna frowned down at the ground, realizing that both Verra and Juaren expected her to object to using an Arnimi instrument in the search. Realizing too that they had given much more thought to the mechanics of the search than she had. Reluctantly she said, "How—how would your instrument find the ship?"

"It's a metal locator. A very basic instrument. If you wish, I'll let you carry it yourself. I can teach you how to read it in just a few moments. In a place like this, where there are no metal products in use aside from what we're carrying ourselves, we can set the ranging parameters wide. We can eliminate days of search."

And perhaps days of danger. Reyna frowned, looking beyond her reluctance, surprised at what she found there: sharp unease at the prospect of finding Birnam Rauth's ship, of learning from it what had become of him. She stroked the starsilk, wondering suddenly if she could bear to listen to its song once she knew why Birnam Rauth had never come back from this land. Wondering if she could bear to wear the silk or even to keep it then.

Wondering too if, in fact, she would ever know what had happened to him.

And Verra was handing her the other starsilks, the ones she had retrieved from the wrecked trader. They shimmered in the Arnimi woman's hands, alive in some way Reyna didn't understand, needing only light and breeze to tune their urgent voices.

"Juaren—" she said and was immediately ashamed of the weakness in her voice. But she could not take the starsilks, could not touch them. It was enough that she wear this one—on the day when they might find what was left of Birnam Rauth's ship.

"I'll wear one," Juaren said quickly. "I'll carry the others in my pack. Unless you want one, Verra."

"No. Reyna?"

Reyna looked up and realized with surprise that neither of them saw her assent—her capitulation—in her face. They had to ask. She studied them both, then nodded, forcing crispness to her voice. "Yes, show me how to use the instrument."

THIRTEEN
REYNA

The Arnimi instrument was an unwelcome weight on Reyna's wrist, but she listened carefully to Verra's instructions and repeated them to herself as they lifted above the trees. Verra's green silk sang in the sunlight, its loose ends fluttering. Juaren wore his starsilk as Reyna wore hers, tied at his waist, ends tucked in. Trees passed below, tall shafts supporting broad platforms of branches. Occasionally they glimpsed the brightness of silk in the lower branches. Sometimes they saw small clearings far below, carpeted in green. Once Reyna saw chatni sunning themselves and she gazed down, wondering if they would look up. They did not.

She watched the lazy way her shadow trailed over the treetops, sometimes following her, sometimes running ahead as they changed direction. Then the trees grew patchy and gave way to ragged brush, and her shadow plummeted.

"Here—" Verra said, descending. "We're entering the burn area. Make this a practice run, Reyna. See if you can lead us to the trader without making a visual scan. We'll go in low. Remember what I told you—press the blue pane for a broad radius reading, then narrow the scan radius as we get closer."

Reyna followed Verra's instructions, and the instrument's indicator screen glowed. Frowning, Reyna studied the visual display—a series of concentric circles, a flickering red brightness shimmering in one quadrant of the outermost circle.

"There—you have it already," Verra said, hovering near.

"That?" The flickering light? She had expected something more substantial, something that hinted more closely at the solidity of the mass of the fallen trade ship.

"That's it. Change your direction of flight—make small corrections, no abrupt changes—as you have to until it stands still. When that happens, continue straight on course and narrow the radius. We won't be able to center the mass until you've set the final radius."

Reyna nodded distractedly. The flickering light had already begun to move, retreating around the screen. Staring down at the display, Reyna made a slight change of direction, leading the way just above the tops of the scattered white-trunked saplings that fought the heavy brush for light and space. The flickering brightness continued to shift. Reyna watched the indicator screen with increasing concentration, becoming only peripherally aware of Juaren and Verra flanking her, matching speed and direction to hers as she methodically altered her course. If she could find the correct course, if she could make the elusive red light stand still . . . She glanced up, taking her direction from the sun, and altered course again.

"When you have the mass centered in the display, Reyna—"

When she had the mass centered, she had only to glance down at the ground. The wrecked ship would be there. Reyna nodded distractedly, realizing that the flickering brightness had not shifted for several seconds, for half a minute, for a full minute—that she had found the correct course. She pressed the next colored pane in sequence, narrowing the scan radius. The flickering light began to shift again, but more slowly. A series of small corrections and it stood still again.

Finally the flickering brightness settled at the center of the indicator. After a moment's blank surprise, Reyna looked down and saw a twisted metal shape glinting dully from the brush. She laughed aloud, surprising herself.

"*Cantro ci!*" Verra said, settling toward the ground.

Reyna eased herself out of the air, avoiding a tangle of brush. "What?"

"*Cantro ci!* One of the least favored expletives in the Arnimi language. It means I'm trying to find some fault with the way you handled that and I can't—to my great annoyance." Verra touched ground, the green silk settling upon her shoulders.

Reyna laughed again. "You can't find anything wrong with the way I did the job, so you're angry with me instead?"

Verra shrugged, catching at the tails of her silk. "Sounds that way, doesn't it? Do you want to look inside the ship? It's pretty well burned out."

A passing glance at the charred interior was enough for Reyna. She had no desire to prod burned controls and charred furnishings. She withdrew, catching a deep breath and gazing up into the brightness of the sun. Then, while Verra and Juaren examined the wreckage, she looked around for sign of the container of silks.

She found it several hundred paces from the wreckage, a trunk of some tough material she didn't recognize, its lid ajar. Inside were silks of every color—cool and slippery against her fingertips. They were crushed tightly together, but when she selected a sunny yellow one and shook it free, it was smooth and uncreased. Standing, she tied it to a slender sapling and let its ends hang free.

When the breeze caught it, the silk sang in a high, sweet voice. Unconsciously Reyna stroked the starsilk, sorry it could not sing a song as brightly, as mindlessly joyous as this one. When she turned and saw Verra and Juaren approaching, deep in discussion, she took the yellow silk from the tree and tied it at her waist, letting the ends float free.

Before they left the wreckage of the trader, Verra chose a rainbow of silks and slipped them into the small pouch she carried. Juaren sorted through the container and selected an icy blue swath. Reyna wondered briefly what he saw in it as he tied it at his waist. The winter sky? The face of the glacier that ground its way through the mountains far to the north of Valley Terlath? But the swath's song, when they flew again, was neither cold nor implacable. It trilled brightly in the sunlight, joining its voice harmoniously with the voices of the green and yellow silks.

Reyna listened to the three fluttering voices and wished she could sing with them, wished she could sing away the gathering tension of her mood. Because she had used the Arnimi instrument successfully. She had located the fallen trader. And now they were flying in search of Birnam Rauth's ship. She activated the instrument as they left the burn area, watching the small screen for some sign of a second metal mass.

At Verra's advice, they flew above the trees to the perimeter of the forest. By the time she saw the grasslands ahead, Reyna realized that a hesitant light flickered at the edge of the small indicator screen. But Verra shook her head. "Our own ship. If you want to home on it for practice—"

Reyna did not. Another practice run would not resolve the tension that made her frown down at the screen and then peer narrowly at the sun, trying to decide which way she must lead the search first. It would not release the tautness of muscles that already made her scalp ache. She hovered briefly, one hand winding the yellow songsilk tight, and then chose to fly northward along the edge of the forest.

In places the boundary of the forest was sharply defined. Tall white trees grew to a certain point and abruptly stopped, giving way to scrub and grass. In other places the trees straggled out into the grasslands, sometimes standing solitary among marshy reeds, sometimes marching in distinct lines toward the eastern horizon. Occasionally they intergrew with the twisted trees of the grasslands. Once Reyna looked down and saw a tattered silk clinging to the branches of a white-trunked sapling. The sun had washed it pale. She circled the tree and saw that the silk had not been tied there, that the wind had tangled it in the branches.

So it was a clue to nothing. No one had hung it there as a sign.

No one had left a sign of any kind, in fact. The land seemed as empty today as it had when she first saw it. Grass, brush, trees—they existed only for themselves.

Yet each time they touched ground, Juaren pointed out the prints of small animals. Occasionally they found the distinctive track of a chatni. And they flew on, silks singing at their waists, songs that grew wilder and sweeter in the warm early afternoon sunlight.

They ate at mid-afternoon, quickly rifling the small pouches they carried. Juaren wandered away when he had eaten and eventually returned with a small frown of dissatisfaction.

Reyna felt the same dissatisfaction. There had been no flicker of the Arnimi instrument, and soon they would have to turn back to the stream, where they had left their bedding and supplies, or to their own ship. She frowned into the eastern sky, frustrated by its emptiness. "Maybe we're searching too close to the trees," she said slowly, thinking aloud. Their own ship had shown as a hesitant flicker at the outer edge of the indicator screen that morning. If Birnam Rauth's ship lay much farther from the edge of the forest than their own, the instrument would not have picked it up.

Juaren nodded, carefully gathering the scraps of his meal and burying them. "If we fly back the way we came, but to the east, perhaps as far to the east as our own ship lies—"

"Then we'll have the start of a grid pattern," Verra agreed. "And if we find nothing today, at least we'll be in position to build upon the pattern tomorrow."

But they had not flown long into the east before Reyna knew

they would not have to search the next day—not for Birnam Rauth's ship. A flicker of red had appeared on the instrument screen, and even as she stared down at it, licking suddenly dry lips, it became brighter, like a beacon. Without thinking, she caught the ends of the yellow silk and tucked them in, silencing the silk's trilling voice. Then, quickly, she took her bearings from the sun, prepared to begin making gradual alterations of course.

Only two small alterations were necessary. After that the red flicker did not shift. She narrowed the scan radius twice, three times, and maintained course.

It was almost anticlimactic when the mass centered and Reyna looked down at the craft that stood in the tall grass below. It was larger than their own ship, its finish duller, its lines heavier. It sat at the center of a ring of solitude, closed against weather and time. Except for the grasses that grew high against its hull, it might have landed the morning before. Reyna glanced quickly at Juaren, at Verra, and saw they waited for her to touch ground first.

She dropped, extending booted toes, and settled in the shadow of the craft. She felt no laughing triumph this time as she deactivated the Arnimi instrument. She felt only disbelief. "This—this is the one? This is the ship?" An empty question. What other ship could it be?

"It's the correct model, it carries the correct markings," Verra assured her.

Birnam Rauth's ship. Reyna stepped forward and placed her fingertips against the sun-warmed metal of its hull. Birnam Rauth's ship—and she felt nothing but distant bewilderment. This was the shell that had brought him here. But what could it tell her now, a century later? And why had that century left no mark on its metal hull? Why did the ship wait here so matter of factly, as if Birnam Rauth might come walking back across the grasslands at dusk? Frowning, she shrugged out of her lift-pack and circled the craft.

The hatch did not open easily. It had been closed too long. Seals had aged. But it yielded eventually and Verra and Juaren stood aside while Reyna ventured first into the ship's interior.

A yielding surface underfoot, the stale smell of air trapped too long in an enclosed space—and lights. They glowed alive when Reyna stepped through the interior hatchway. At the same time a familiar voice spoke. But her heart missed no more than a beat. Her trip aboard the *Narsid* had taught her that walls could speak. And she recognized the tone of the words that came from the recessed speakers, if not their meaning. Her father had welcomed her to the dining table often enough in much the same tone.

Still she hesitated, wondering. Were these words Birnam Rauth had recorded to welcome himself? Or had he expected someone else to step aboard his ship?

Who could have stepped aboard his ship here?

And why hadn't he come back? Back to his empty couch, back to the papers and miscellaneous possessions that were strewn around the interior of the craft. Back to all the things she recognized and the others she couldn't put a name to. Reyna turned a slow circle, taking a cursory inventory: a loosely bound volume, its open pages covered with finely lined sketches; eating utensils, a clean platter, and two knives with metal blades; a tumbled pile of silks, their colors dull, muted; a mug that might have held water; several articles of clothing, tossed casually on the floor; implements, tools, instruments—Birnam Rauth hadn't shared her father's penchant for order.

Or perhaps he had cultivated some other, less obvious form of order. Reyna pressed her temples and stared around, feeling suddenly helpless. She had found Birnam Rauth's ship but what did it have to tell her? That he had been here, that he was here no longer. But could it tell her where he had gone? Why he hadn't come back to resume the commonplaces of his life? Why he wouldn't walk back across the grasslands tonight?

Juaren and Verra lingered at the inner hatch, watching her. With a flash of irritation at her own helplessness, Reyna stepped to the work-counter and flipped the pages of the volume Birnam Rauth had left open.

Chatni—he had filled the loosely bound pages with sketches of chatni. They gazed down from their bowers with the predator alertness she had seen the night before. They stalked small woods creatures. They sunned themselves in the grass. They groomed each other, they played, they fed their cubs. Birnam Rauth had captured grace, humor, and a languid intelligence with his sketching tool. And she realized, studying his work, that he had not done so by keeping a cautious distance between himself and his subjects. His sketches were filled with detail, with characterization. Flipping through the volume, she began to recognize individuals. Near the end of the book, she found a birth sequence and knew that he had been there, that he had witnessed the birth. Perhaps he had even assisted at it.

Also near the end of the book she found a self-portrait—a deft caricature of a man who hovered at the transition point between human and chatni. Birnam Rauth grinned up at her with sharp white teeth, his ears pointed and lightly furred. She stared into the laughing eyes, then laughed herself, until she turned the page and found a chatni gazing up at her with human eyes. This time there was no humor, no laughter. The chatni tilted its sleek head and seemed about to speak, about to ask some question that could never be answered.

Whose question had Birnam Rauth captured in those eyes—the chatni's or his own? Disturbed, Reyna closed the volume. Without thinking, she loosed the starsilk's ends and let them hang free. Slowly she turned. Verra and Juaren still watched from the hatchway, as if they required her permission to trespass upon Birnam Rauth's domain.

"There's another sketch book there, on the floor beside his couch," Verra said softly, nodding. "And voy-caps on the work-counter. His equipment is Ptachidarki—the same capping equipment my mother used for her genealogical studies when I was young. If it's still functional, I'll be able to show you how to operate it."

Reyna turned distractedly. A second loosely bound sketch volume was half lost beneath tumbled bedding. She retrieved it, flipping through it absently. Forest scenes. Small animals. Creatures like the one that had screamed at them that morning—climbing, feeding, washing silks in the stream. "Voy-caps?"

"For oral recording. He probably kept note of his studies on caps. But I don't see any sign of a portable capping unit. Only the player and the stationary capper. If he had a portable capper, he may have been carrying it when—when he left here."

For the last time.

"Do you want me to show you how to use the equipment?"

A tactful probe. And Verra still stood carefully in the hatchway, not intruding. Reyna held the sketch volume close and tried to understand why Verra's diplomatic suggestion rankled—why she didn't want to listen to Birnam Rauth's recordings, why she didn't want to open cabinets and inventory his possessions, why she only wanted to go back to the stream and listen to the trees.

It was too much. The ship sitting untouched in the grasslands, the casual disorder of the cabin, the sketch book lying open on the work-counter—Birnam Rauth's environment was alive. It waited for him. And standing in the cabin where he had eaten, where he had slept, Reyna's bewilderment was turning to loss.

She needed time—time to accept what she found here: Birnam Rauth's humanity. His kinship. All the other things that had been only abstractions until now, although she had thought she felt their full weight from the beginning.

"Why—why don't you go ahead and listen to the recordings, Verra," she said carefully, aware of the sudden fragility of her composure. "I want to look through his sketch books."

"Of course." More tactful words. And Verra stood aside and carefully did not see Reyna's painfully contained agitation.

Reyna found a place in the grass where brush partially obscured her view of Birnam Rauth's ship. She sat, dropping the sketch books beside her, and put her head on her knees. The sun warmed her back. It pressed against her flesh like a weight. But she did not cry, and after a while, distractedly, she began to wonder why.

Because the time was not right? Because they had only found an empty ship? Or because what her mother called strong-mindedness would not let her. The search was only half begun; this was not the moment for weakness. Sighing, she took up the second sketch book and flipped its pages.

The forest passed before her eyes, all its secret places recorded: empty clearings carpeted with flowers, streamside caves, individual trees, some white and smooth-trunked, others mossy, somber, as if the deepest of all the secrets of the forest lived among them. They stood like giants, the caverns in their trunks as impenetrably shadowed as the rock caverns Birnam Rauth had found beside the stream. Reyna passed her fingertips lightly over the loose pages, wishing she could feel what Birnam Rauth had felt when he probed these secrets, when he recorded them. If she had scroll and pen—

But what good would it do her to sketch the empty ship, the living disorder of its interior? Those were the secrets she must probe, and she must use means more potent than a pen.

And what good would it do her to sit here, thinking thoughts that led nowhere?

Finally she stood, heavily, and returned to the ship.

She did not understand immediately what she heard when she stepped through the inner hatch. Two voices came from the wall speakers, one Birnam Rauth's but speaking in a hissing tongue she knew immediately was not Carynese. The other voice was softer, airier. Listening to it—to the utterly alien quality of it—Reyna felt herself stiffen and chill. She realized belatedly that Verra sat with her translator on her knees but did not use it.

Juaren glanced up distractedly as Reyna settled beside him on the couch. "Chatni," he said softly at her questioning look. "He's talking with a chatni."

"He learned their language?" But that was obvious, because surely the tongue that came from the wall speakers had not originated with any human race. Reyna couldn't imagine herself speaking it. And as she listened, she was not certain that Birnam Rauth spoke it well. His words had a different, sharper rhythm than the chatni's. When the chatni spoke, the sounds rushed together with an airy lack of definition. Nor could he reproduce some of the sibilants or the occasional punctuating growls.

They listened silently, absorbed, until abruptly the two voices stopped speaking. Verra stood from her stool, briskly, and popped a small metal capsule from an unimposing box that sat on the work-counter. "His own Class Five," she said softly. "He found his own Class Five." Seeing Reyna's questioning look, she explained. "A classification—a non-human race corresponding closely enough to ours in intelligence, physiology and psychology that verbal communication is possible. And I don't know which would be more remarkable—if we were to prove that the chatni were descended from exported Terran *Chatnus* or if we were to prove that they were not."

Reyna frowned, disturbed by the speculative brightness of Verra's eyes. "We're not here to prove either of those things."

For a moment Verra didn't seem to understand her sharpness. Then she nodded distractedly. "No, of course not." She turned back to the counter. "He's numbered some of his caps. Others he apparently generated without ever putting them into any particular order. Shall we listen to the random recordings first? Or would you prefer to audit the sequential recordings now and leave the others for later?"

Reyna approached the work-counter and studied the three tall transparent capsule containers unenthusiastically. "How long will it take to listen to all of these?"

"Days."

Days of listening, when there was a search to be made? Reyna frowned, dissatisfied with the prospect. "Do we have to stay here? Can we listen to these somewhere else?"

"Mmmmm. The player is fully portable. It's operating on ship's power now, but it should function on standard wafers. Were you thinking of going back to our own ship?"

"No—to the forest," Reyna said. "To the place where we stayed last night." She felt as much at home there as anywhere. And she did not want to eat here, to sleep here. The couch, the work-counter, all the cabin's mute furnishings—everything here was waiting for Birnam Rauth. They were intruders.

"Of course," Verra said. "Give me a few minutes to disconnect the unit and see if he has a travel case for it."

"We won't damage it, moving it?"

"Not unless we're careless. And I don't intend to be."

And in fact they were careful. Verra, the most experienced flyer, carried the case holding the cap player when they lifted away from the grasslands. Juaren carried the containers of capsules, and Reyna brought Birnam Rauth's sketch books. She let the yellow silk flutter as they flew, but the bright pleasure of its song did not touch her.

Days of sitting, days of listening—but how else were they to know where to search next? She stroked the starsilk, discouraged.

Shadows were settling under the trees when they reached the streamside. Their supplies and bedding waited, undisturbed. Verra extricated a portable cooking unit from one of her packs, but Juaren gathered wood and made a fire instead. They gathered close to it while they ate, shoulders almost touching, yet isolated within their thoughts.

Finally Verra spoke. "If you don't want to listen to the caps, Reyna, if you want to look in some other direction—"

Reyna glanced up at the Arnimi woman, surprised that she had read her thoughts so clearly. "If I knew another direction to take, if we had some trail to follow—" she said softly. The print of boots, broken branches, crushed blades of grass—

But of course broken branches and crushed blades had healed by now. The print of boots had faded. Reyna took up the first sketch book and opened it to Birnam Rauth's self-portrait. She gazed down at it, trying to see with his eyes. She had come here to meet her challenge, and he was her prey. And Juaren had told her yesterday, when he instructed her in the first rules of tracking, that she must learn her prey's mind. That she must learn its habits, its appetites, its vagaries and whims. Because only then could she successfully find and follow its trail.

Was there no way to learn about Birnam Rauth except by listening to the recorded capsules? She stroked the starsilk again, freeing its ends, drawing them through her fingers, and found an answer.

The starsilk had touched her with a sense of Birnam Rauth's presence the first night they had spent here. Now she needed to touch his presence again, not—she realized—by a methodical auditing of the capsules but by listening again to his song, by losing herself in it—by stepping outside her own mind and into his. Slowly she stood, tucking the sketch books under one arm. "Why don't you listen to the caps, Verra? And tell me if you hear something you think might be important. I—I need to be alone. I need to be my myself for a while."

She saw concern in Verra's face, sudden guarded stiffness in Juaren's. Impulsively she touched his arm. "I won't be far," she said. "I won't be long."

But she wasn't sure he understood as she hurried away into the trees. She found a grassy hollow near the stream and sat for a while, frowning and undecided, wanting to go back, wanting to explain that her sudden need to be alone wasn't a rejection. But surely he understood that. Finally, unhappily, she rose and tied the starsilk to a branch.

The silk hung dim and white in the deepening shadows, catching at the occasional breeze. Its song was as muted as the dusk, and the smoky quality of its voice, the growing gloom of early night settled upon Reyna like a trance. She let herself sink into it, let herself be drawn away from the concerns of daylight and reason.

The silk sang and she sang her own song, silently—a song that held much the same loneliness, much the same want, much the same occasional baffled anger. She sang, and while she did so, she listened to herself with silent detachment, trying to understand what she heard. Because the things she felt were kin to the things Birnam Rauth had felt, and they would lead her to an understanding of him.

She sang until the moon rose and the silk's voice brightened. Then, letting her own voice die, she looked down at her lap. She held the sketch volumes there, her fingers resting lightly upon their covers. Nodding as if she had received an instruction, she opened them, keeping the first on her lap, spreading the second on the ground beside her. Idly, without direction, her fingers began to turn the pages.

The starsilk sang and her fingers sought both volumes randomly, yet she always came back to the same scene: a dark-mossed tree that stood somewhere in the forest, mystery in its cavernous hollows.

Was this the mystery that had compelled Birnam Rauth? Was this the mystery that had made a prisoner of him? Was this where he wanted her to go to learn what had happened to him?

She sat looking down at the shadowy sketch and listening to the silk's song. Now she felt that Birnam Rauth stood near. Now she felt that his hand touched her shoulder. Was he summoning her? Or did he only want her to listen tonight? Did he only want her to begin to understand, however poorly?

She listened until the moon had crossed half the sky, until the trees held it in upraised arms and her eyelids were heavy. Then, nodding as if she had posed herself a question, as if she had found its answer, she stood. Carefully she untied the starsilk and fastened it around her waist again, ends tucked under. She took up the sketch books and walked back through the moonlit forest. The shadows of the trees fell in broad grids, guiding her.

When she reached the place where she had left Juaren and Verra, she saw that Verra was already rolled in her bedding asleep. Juaren sat cross-legged on the ground a distance away, head bowed, white hair shining in the moonlight. He had tied his own starsilk to a tree and it spoke and sang to him. Reyna hesitated briefly, watching, listening. Slowly she realized that the silk spoke different words than the one she wore at her waist, although its song was the same, restless, poignant, sometimes thwarted and angry. When she stepped nearer, she saw that Juaren wore Verra's translator plugged into his ears. He sat with eyes closed, intent upon what he heard.

She dropped to the ground beside him, and after a while she knew that he guessed that she was there. He didn't open his eyes, he didn't speak, but the tension of his body changed. It altered to accommodate her presence.

Finally he took the plugs from his ears and set the translator aside. His face was without expression—carefully without expression, as if he had deliberately purged his features of whatever he felt. Standing, he took the starsilk from the tree and tied it at his waist. Then he extended one hand, wordlessly helping Reyna to her feet.

"Juaren," she said hesitantly, worried that he hadn't spoken, worried at the distance in his eyes, "earlier—this evening—"

He nodded absently. "I know."

She frowned, beginning to be disturbed by the way he held himself, by the careful impassivity of his features. Why wouldn't he look at her? Why did he still seem to listen to the silk, even though he had tied it at his waist and carefully tucked the ends under? What had he heard in the silk's song, or in its words? "I had to be alone," she said, pressing his hand, trying to cross the distance his distraction set between them. "It wasn't—I didn't go because I didn't want to be with you. I didn't—"

"You went because you needed to be alone," he said, still looking past her. At what? What did he see beyond her shoulder? "And I worried because I didn't want you to be alone—not here, not in the dark. But I understood. I have to be alone sometimes too."

He understood. But why did he speak with such detachment? Reyna drew a hand across her eyes, suddenly tired. The day had been long. Her back ached and her eyelids were heavy. She did not want to ask Juaren now what the starsilk had said. She did not want to tell him about the hollow tree and its shadowed mystery. This was not the time to tell him she thought they would learn there what had happened to Birnam Rauth. This was the time to sleep. "Aren't you tired?" she said.

He turned and finally he met her eyes. His gaze was mirror-like, reflective—betraying nothing. But his voice was gentle. "Aren't you?"

"Yes," she said shakily, relieved at what she heard in his tone. "I'm very tired."

"Then we should go to bed."

Go to bed and rehearse the things she would ask him in the morning, the things she would tell him. Juaren pulled his bedding near hers, and soon she thought, from the quietness of his breath, from the still shadows the moon painted on his face, that he slept. Relaxing, she surrendered her own concerns and slept too.

But briefly. Perhaps Juaren made some sound as he rose, created some involuntary disturbance of twig or stone as he moved away into the dark. Reyna turned restlessly, pulling her bedding close—and woke to the certain realization that she was alone. Verra still slept a distance away, but Juaren had abandoned his bedding. He was gone.

She stared for long moments at the emptiness beside her, trying to reach past alarm to put some order to her thoughts. Where had he gone? The moon was waning and he had said he was tired. Why had he lulled her into thinking that he slept and then left her? If he needed to be alone now, tonight, why hadn't he told her, as she had told him? Was he afraid she would worry, as he had? She sat, rubbing her eyes. The starsilk—she remembered how intently he had listened to the starsilk. She remembered the guarded stiffness of his face afterward. Was that why he had slipped away? Because of something he had heard from the starsilk?

If she knew what the starsilk had said to him . . . Its message had been different than the one her silk carried. She knew that much. If he had not taken it with him—

But he had. She slumped back to her bedding, hugging herself against the cold. What must she do? Let him go, as he had earlier let her go? Track him—when the moon was setting and shadows were deepening under the trees? Crawl back into her bedding and wait, anxiously?

She crouched there, undecided, her arms growing cold, until she remembered that Verra had brought several starsilks back from the wrecked trader. Juaren had taken one and folded the others into his pack. If he had left his pack—Quickly Reyna extricated herself from her bedding and padded across the campsite.

Juaren's pack was piled with the supplies, and the other silks, three of them, were folded inside it. Hands shaking, Reyna slipped them from the pack. She paused to pull on her boots. Then she slipped into the trees, leaving Verra sleeping.

The breeze was sporadic, but its first burst told her that two of the silks carried the same message hers did. The third one spoke differently, its tone calmer, the words distant, almost disinterested. Quickly Reyna folded the first two silks away and slipped back to camp to search for the translator. If she could teach herself to use it, if she could learn what Birnam Rauth had said on this second silk—

But she did not find the translator. Juaren had left his pack but taken the lift-pack and translator with him.

Why? Where had he gone? Leadenly, mechanically, Reyna returned to where the silk hung. She sat and waited until the breeze came again, until the silk repeated its incomprehensible words. At the same time it sang, its song touching her with Birnam Rauth's presence as her own silk had. She bowed her head and he stood beside her. She could not understand the words he said. But they touched her with something deeper, something crueler than the cold of night. They touched her with a cold that bruised her, making her body stiffen and her bones ache. Because they touched her with a growing conviction.

Juaren had not slipped away in the dark because he wanted to be alone. He had slipped away because the silk had directed him somewhere—and he had chosen to go alone.

He had chosen to go alone because there was danger and he thought he was better equipped to deal with it than she was.

He had gone alone to learn what had happened to Birnam Rauth. But if Birnam Rauth had died—where? in the dark heart of the forest? among the cavernous trees?—Juaren could die too, no matter how lightly he walked, no matter how carefully he watched, no matter how closely he listened.

Slowly, frightened, Reyna stood. She could hesitate no longer. Juaren had gone alone, and no matter how carefully considered his reasons, she could not permit it. Because he could as readily die as she. And who would write his story and Komas' then? Who would winter with her in the mountains? Who would cut figures on streambanks and spin above the trees?

She paused only to tuck away the extra starsilks and, on impulse, to find the azure silk and tie it at her waist. Then she took up her pike, shrugged into her lift-pack, and slipped away into the trees.

FOURTEEN
TSUUKA

Tsuuka groomed her wean-lings with special attention that night, and they stretched themselves luxuriantly under her tongue and grunted with drowsy pleasure, suspecting nothing. But when she went to Falett and Dariim, they lay wide-eyed in their silks watching for her, Falett anxiously, Dariim with guarded wariness. And Tsuuka knew they guessed she was leaving them. They had guessed it sometime during the day.

She growled softly, realizing with sinking heart that she should not have waited. She should have returned to the heart of the trees that dawn, while her cubs still slept. But Riifika had wanted the day to lie with the grassland cub, accustoming herself. So Tsuuka had stolen the opportunity to sun herself with her cubs and wean-lings again, to feed and groom them a last time before going back to the heart of the trees.

Shadows lay ahead. She had wanted that last brightness. Now she saw it reflected in Dariim's eyes, mocking her.

"My cubs—" she said, but what had she to say beyond that? She didn't know the words for parting, and a last admonition would not find its mark. Falett would listen with anxious attention, but Dariim had already armored herself against wise words. The blaze of the red silk was in her eyes. Tsuuka gazed at her with a helplessness that approached anger. That she should care so much for one cub when they all needed her—

Impulsively she bent to smooth Falett's fur and said softly in her ear, "Tall trees and a full stomach, my good cub." What more could she wish her firstborn when she could not love her as fiercely as she loved her sibling?

And perhaps she would capture the red silk tonight without

harm. Perhaps tomorrow she would watch her weanlings tumble in the grass just as she had today. Perhaps one day she would see Falett take her first grass-pup and choose a tree to share with her sibling.

Perhaps—a taunting word. Tsuuka's eyes shimmered and she turned from the bower before tears could spill over. She took no parting from Dariim. How could she part sweetly from a cub who wore rebellion in her eyes, never guessing its price? Climbing down her tree, Tsuuka dropped to the ground and padded away into the dark.

Shadows followed her. It had been too many nights since she had taken song-dreams. Nightmares clawed at the weakened barriers of her mind. But she had no time to take song-dreams now, nor did she have her skysilk to guide her. The other silks—scarlet, amber, lilac, yellow; chartreuse, crimson, emerald—none of them could lead her into the song-dreams as the azure silk could. She who was so sleek, she who was so swift—tonight she was prey.

Thoughts—the nightmares were only the shadows of thoughts that passed in the air. Tsuuka reminded herself of that as she padded through the trees, trying to find comfort in it. Had she been insensitive to the nightmares, she could never have shared thoughts with a songsilk.

Had she been insensitive to the nightmares, she would not feel the hair rising at the back of her neck now. She would not imagine that she heard ghost-feet on the forest floor. She would not see insubstantial bodies curling in the air before her, vanishing when she raised irritable claws to tear them. She shook her head, annoyed with her own weakness. The nightmares could not catch her unless she slept. And tonight she would not sleep.

Yet she had no plan for what she would do. She had tried before to catch the red silk and failed. Now, the azure silk said, a dangerous time was coming, a time when the unseen and her successor must leave their hidden places. The escorts were alert, poised against any intrusion. How was she to capture the elusive red silk without being stung? Could it hear her thoughts as the songsilks did? Could she plead with it to give up its freedom to her?

But no sithi had ever kept a master-silk. And why should this one surrender to her? If she could impress it with her need, it would already be in her hands.

Would she know any better what to do if she understood the things the skysilk had said: that the master-silk carried the memory of the preserved, drawn directly from its life-silk? She clawed bitterly at the soil. She did not understand and she could ask the skysilk no more questions. She had traded it, however unintentionally, for a grassland cub. It would take her precious nights to build rapport with another silk.

And to even think of building rapport with a master-silk—she shook herself impatiently.

She drank briefly at the stream, then sat with her eyes halflidded, thinking—and while she thought, drifting across the hazy boundary into somnolence. The forest was silent. The moon had not risen. No silks sang. There was no sound but her own heartbeat —*and the nearly inaudible scuff of feet in the brush behind her.* But when she jumped up and spun around, heart racing, there was nothing there. Not a treemole. Not a bark-shredder.

Not Dariim, following her.

But her fur was damp. Her breath was shallow and quick. Her eyes darted nervously, as if they had a life of their own. The shadows—

The shadows were taking form. They were rising from beneath the trees, spreading wings of black silk, wings that reached to enfold her, *wings*—

Tsuuka shook herself, uttering an angry growl. Nightmares—she had let herself doze and the nightmares had overtaken her. Instinctively she threw herself into the cold-running stream. The shock made her gasp, made her eyes start. It also brought her fully awake again and the black wings retreated and spread themselves back under the trees.

It took her time after that to groom herself dry. She monitored the state of her wakefulness carefully as she did so. She had slept so little the night before. Fatigue ached so heavily in her limbs. It would be easy to slip back into a half-waking state.

Instead, as the moon rose, she found herself moving into a state of heightened awareness, as if her senses had sharpened to compensate for her fatigue. When she was dry she stood and listened to the distant song of silks. Their early evening chorus seemed to glow through the trees, light given voice. She stood and gazed into the trees, expecting to see a shining brilliance.

But the forest was dark.

And time had passed, precious time . . . Goading herself, Tsuuka fell to all fours to cover ground more quickly.

Her senses trembled with alertness as she ran. The forest floor was littered with scents. They lay like fallen leaves, cluttering her path. Here a treemole had paused to urinate. There a groundfowl had escorted her young from one clump of brush to another. A bark-shredder had paused here and touched this trunk with saliva, testing the acidity of the bark. Spinners had left their scent too. And the intruders—

Encountering the sharpness of their day-old scent, she came to an unwilling halt and sniffed the ground. Her nose had not been so keen the night before. She had not differentiated the scent of one intruder from another then. But tonight she found that there were three individual trails, interwoven. She paused, inhaling through nose and mouth at once, then hissing involuntarily at the offensive sharpness of the mingled scents. Questions rose unbidden. Had the starvoice walked on two feet once just as the intruders did, leaving a scent on the forest floor? If so, where had he come from? Where had the intruders come from? Would they be starvoices too one day? She had never heard a whisper of creatures like them in the forest. Why were they here now?

Tsuuka came erect, a new thought making her grunt. The intruders had living bodies much like her own. She had seen them. She had felt the heat of the smallest intruder's fingertips. Their individual scents were in her nostrils now. Had the starvoice had just such a body once too—fleshly, real, as precious to him as her body was to her? And if he had and yet had been captured in silk, to sing from her bower poles—

Then the unseen had a living body too.

She shook herself, letting that thought settle into place. Wasn't that what the azure silk had tried to tell her? That the unseen lived for a time and then was somehow preserved and captured in silk so that master-silks could be made from her life-silk—and songsilks from the master-silks? Yet she had not fully understood, not as she found herself understanding now. She had imagined the unseen to be a shadowy presence—a presence somehow mysteriously threatening.

But the escorts had not been created to guard a dangerous insubstantiality. There was no need to guard the invulnerable. A prickle-hide didn't carry quills because his body was tough-armored but because his flesh was tender. A sithi did not stand guard over her newborns because her newborns were dangerous to her older cubs —but because her newborns were helpless against their heedless older siblings.

And the unseen, she realized with the scent of the intruders in her nostrils, was not only flesh. She was a progenitor of songsilks, or would be when she had been preserved. Someday silks would carry something of her awareness, something of her vitality, but twice removed.

This was what her silk had tried to tell her the night before. That the escorts guarded the unseen because she was made of tender flesh—and because there was no other in this quarter of the forest who could seed the bulbs from which the spinners hatched. If the unseen was harmed, there would be no spinners to spin silks and no silks for sithi bowers. And insects would nest in the forest as they did in the grasslands.

Tsuuka stared up at the moon, putting those thoughts in order, examining the new perspective they gave her. Their lives were interwoven. The sithi protected the spinners from predators. The spinners protected the sithi from insect wounds and in turn nourished the unseen so that there could be more spinners and more silks. And the silks brought song into the lives of the sithi and protected them from nightmares—which were no more than thoughts that threw shadows upon their uncomprehending minds.

But there was more. Her skysilk had saved her from nightmares, but surely she had given something in return. Her silks could not run, could not play, could not taste cold water and fresh meat—not for themselves. But they did those things through her each night when she went to her bower and shared the events of her day with them. They walked the forest upon her feet. They saw the trees with her eyes. They stretched in the grass at their ease and felt the warm sun on her fur.

Was that why they sang in the moonlight? Because they tasted the joy of life through her senses? How else were they to taste it, after all, bound as they were to the poles? How was the unseen to taste it, hidden in her bulb-well, toiling over her unhatched spinners?

And the thoughts that passed between the silks and the unseen—whose were those thoughts? Surely many of them were simply sithi thoughts, sithi experiences, but translated into the silent idiom that joined silks, spinners and the unseen. What else had a silk to tell the unseen but the tales told it by its sithi companion?

What would a nightmare be if she met it waking? Perhaps she would discover that it was nothing more than her own thoughts and experiences, but translated into some other system of images—

the system of images by which the silks and the unseen spoke to one another.

Slowly Tsuuka dropped to fours again, absorbed by her thoughts, wondering what she had gained from thinking them.

At least the nightmares seemed less pressing as she continued through the trees. They were little more than mist in the air. And she was no longer distracted by the over-keenness of her senses.

She did not permit those things to make her careless as she approached the heart of the trees. When she entered the place where the trees stood tallest, where their trunks were most thickly hoared with moss, she moved with deliberation, watching, listening with every step.

There was a special, waiting silence under the tallest trees tonight. She felt it immediately, felt its weight. And, yes, there were nightmares here, shadowy thoughts spreading like dormant wings under the trees. They were concentrated here, she guessed, because this was the realm of the unseen. This was the place toward which the silks' thoughts were directed. This was the heart of the trees.

But many of these are my thoughts, she reminded herself. *Many of these are my own thoughts and the thoughts of other sithi I know. These are the events of our day. The silks have put them into another form and addressed them here to the unseen so she can understand all the business of the forest, so she can better direct the spinners in their feeding and spinning.*

But Tsuuka knew there must be alien thoughts here too, thoughts that had never originated with any sithi—thoughts that originated with the unseen instead and were addressed by her to the spinners and the silks. And Tsuuka still could not imagine the true nature of the unseen. To toil for a lifetime in the musty hollow of a tree, never glimpsing sunlight, never tasting the breeze . . .

Yet what harm could the unseen's thoughts hold for her? She occupied a necessary place in the scheme of their mutual life. She was a hunter, protector of spinners, master of silks. There would be no thoughts inimical to her here—only thoughts alien in their form.

And if she could address her thoughts directly to the unseen, if she could plead to have the red silk . . . Hadn't her skysilk told her the unseen could temper the activity of the escorts? Perhaps she could do other things too. Perhaps she could direct the red silk to give itself to her. Tsuuka closed her eyes and tried to address herself to the unseen, tried to project what she felt to the fleshly creature hidden here in the heart of the trees. Her emotions were of an aching intensity. She focused upon the loss she had experienced years ago, upon the loss she could experience again. She tried to show the unseen the brightness of her cub's eyes—the brightness that must not be quenched. She thought of the streaking red silk and its taunting song. She offered the unseen all the reasons why she must have the silk to carry back to her bower.

She put the full force of feeling behind her thoughts, but there was no answering change in the air. The winged shadows did not lighten. They continued to lie black and heavy under the trees. And the red silk did not appear, delivering itself to her.

Finally she hunched against the nearest tree, hugging herself against the sting of her own helplessness. How could she speak with the unseen without her skysilk? Even if she could find the right form for her thoughts, what guarantee did she have that the unseen had time or strength to care for her troubles—or that the unseen was capable of persuading the red silk to give itself into captivity?

Tsuuka sat that way, hunched and helpless, until she began to be angry with herself. Then she drove sharp claws into her arms and raised her head, forcing herself to consider what she must do next. The moon looked down upon silence. The red silk was not to be seen.

It remained in its hiding place then, and she did not know where that could be, except that it was near. Near enough that she would hear it sing when it emerged, near enough that she could try again to stalk and capture it.

Yet she was tired. Her muscles ached with the need for sleep. They would betray her if she didn't have it. She dug thoughtful claws into the soil, wondering. Now that she fully understood the nightmares, could she sleep without being torn by them?

She could only try. Experimentally Tsuuka hunched herself small again, losing herself in the shadow of a clump of brush, and closed her eyes. Deliberately she let alertness slip away, let the nightmare images draw near. They touched her, darkly, and she drew a slow breath and instructed her heart not to race. Slowly, carefully, she released herself into their slow-moving vortex, letting herself spin without resistance among them. Soon she slept, only peripherally aware of the occasional twitch of her limbs or grunt of her breath.

It was not a sound that woke her later, when the moon had set and the first bare hint of dawn touched the sky. It was not a movement. It was simply the pressure of two agonized eyes. They peered at her from the nearby shadows, wide with terror—Dariim's eyes.

Tsuuka shook herself alert, her breath catching, making her heart race. She had guessed Dariim would not stay in her silks. She had expected her to come here, tonight or some other night. But what had she found that had put terror in her eyes? And Falett—

The silence under the trees was so carefully poised, Tsuuka was reluctant to break it by taking her feet, by padding across the forest floor to where Dariim crouched. She did so expecting the trees to shrill with alarm. But there was only the soft sound of her own feet. And then her own voice. "Where have you left your sibling, cub?"

Dariim looked up stiffly, as if the muscles of her neck had cramped with fear. Her fur was damp, her pupils small and quivering. She licked her lips. "Back—she went back. She wouldn't come here."

"But you would. I told you not to come, but you did. For a silk you know you cannot own." Tsuuka saw that for once she had the advantage over this headstrong cub, because Dariim was afraid while she was not.

"My silk—it's my silk." The words were faint but stubborn. They brought a rising gleam to Dariim's yellow eyes.

"It is a master-silk. No sithi can own a master-silk. They're kept hidden except when they're needed to give voice to songsilks." Tsuuka reached to touch her, to stroke her ears, but Dariim drew back, rigid and trembling. "Don't you know that?"

"It's my silk," Dariim repeated. The muscles of her back and shoulders had begun to twitch. She shook herself with angry impatience. "Mine."

Tsuuka gazed at her, slowly understanding what she saw, slowly understanding the rigidity and the terror. "You came for the silk, but you've found nightmares, my cub," she said softly. Tsuuka understood about the nightmares now. She understood that if she threw herself unresisting into their pit, she could float there, unharmed, while she slept. But tonight Dariim felt darkness clawing for her and she understood nothing.

"Here—they're here," Dariim said, shaking herself again. Her fur was matted, her eyes drowning. "I can see them. I can see them moving in the shadows. But I can't catch them. You're the swiftest hunter in the forest and I'm your cub, but I can't catch them."

Tsuuka grunted. It was like Dariim to try to catch a nightmare. Another time she could tell her about them, about what they were and why they lay so heavily under the trees here. But Dariim would not understand any of those things tonight, no matter how carefully they were explained to her. Tsuuka saw that in the constriction of her pupils, in the convulsive shudder of her limbs.

Tonight she must either give herself to the full terror of the nightmares or she must take song-dreams. There was no other way.

Yet there was no silk to give her song-dreams. She had chosen the red silk, but it was hiding in the trees. To find another, to establish rapport with a silk that did not know her temperament or her mind, when the nightmares already held her in terror—

But there was a silk that knew those things. Tsuuka grunted softly, realizing that. The azure silk knew Dariim—through her. The azure silk had caught glimpses of Dariim from birth. The azure silk had watched the development of her character, the trend of her temperament. And the azure silk knew Tsuuka's concern for her secondborn.

If she could find the intruders, if she could take back her skysilk from them—

It was a possibility that made Tsuuka's eyes gleam and her ears rise erect. She had caught the intruders' scent earlier. If she could follow it to them—

This time Tsuuka did not let Dariim draw away from her. She held her firmly by the shoulders and said to her with all the conviction she could muster, "You are ready for your first song-dreams, my cub. But you can't take them here. Your silk has hidden itself and won't be found. So you must come with me. You must help me search out my skysilk and when we find it, it will give you song-dreams."

Dariim tried to pull away, shaking her head stubbornly. "My own silk—" she insisted.

"You will never capture your silk if you aren't strong. And how can you be strong with the nightmares clawing at you, pulling your muscles tight, making them tremble? You must take song-dreams first. Then you will be ready to hunt your silk again."

That was deception of course. When Dariim had taken her first song-dreams, she would only be ready to sleep. And while she slept, Tsuuka would return to the heart of the trees alone. "We must find my skysilk, cub, and your nose is even keener than mine. There is a scent in the forest tonight, a new scent, a strange scent. I think it will lead us to my silk."

It took her minutes longer to persuade the cub, even though

Dariim was confused and trembling with a fear she did not understand. When she was persuaded, she wandered unevenly through the trees, distracted by every scent. Tsuuka tried to direct her back toward the stream, where she had found the scent of the intruders earlier. But Dariim circled feverishly, twitching, grunting, sometimes poking her nose into the shadows, then starting violently and leaping away. Tsuuka followed, resigning herself to a long search. At least she had persuaded Dariim from the heart of the trees. At least they had left the worst danger behind.

Yet their wandering course had not led them far from the deep trees when Dariim stiffened and stared down at the forest floor in astonishment. She bared her teeth, inhaling through both nose and mouth, then raised her head, eyes shimmering dizzily. "Here," she said. "Here there is something strange."

The scent of the intruders, and it was fresh. Tsuuka joined her cub, studying it. Two of them had passed this way, the small one who had given her the grassland cub—the small one who had taken her skysilk—and one other, she couldn't guess which. "You are a hunter, cub," Tsuuka said softly—and was surprised to feel her heart leap expectantly. Her blue silk, she was hungry for the song of her blue silk. Now perhaps she would have it.

They followed the trail, pausing often to watch, to listen. In the end, it was their ears that found the intruders first. Tsuuka heard the first hard edge of their voices when she raised her head from examining a cluster of brush. She caught Dariim's arm, pulling her down. The sky was chill grey with impending dawn. "Do you hear?" she hissed. "Do you hear the starvoices?"

Dariim cocked her head, her eyes glistening and intent. "There— I hear them there."

Tsuuka nodded, but her gaze lingered briefly upon her cub and wariness made the flesh at the back of her neck draw tight. With every step they took from the heart of the trees, Dariim was less troubled by the nightmares. Her eyes were brighter, her muscles less rigid. Perspiration was slowly drying from her fur, leaving it glossy again. If the fear fell away entirely and she decided to return for her prey—

"Lead me to them, cub, and we will find my skysilk," Tsuuka said softly. "But quietly. You have never seen anything like them. Watch and you will see how strange they are."

The intruders stood together in a small clearing, their heads bent together. The sound of their voices was urgent, impatient—or did starvoices always sound that way? Tsuuka and Dariim approached silently and peered from the shadows. Dariim's pupils danced giddily at the sight of the intruders. "Do you see, cub, how strange they are?"

Dariim's lower jaw sagged, exposing her teeth in all their cubsharpness. "They have never been here before."

"But you have heard a voice like theirs when my starsilk sings," Tsuuka reminded her. "And there—there is my skysilk." The smaller intruder, who was little taller, little heavier than Dariim, wore it at her waist. "There is the silk you will take your first songdreams from. And then you will be swift and strong when you return to hunt your firesilk."

Dariim dabbed at her lips with a delicate tongue. "Their teeth are so strange," she whispered, clutching Tsuuka's arms. "And their claws—"

"Their claws are blunt. We have nothing to fear from those. But the sharpened stick the smaller one carries, we must be wary of that. And if you will look at the larger one—he carries a single tooth at his waist. See how it gleams." Tsuuka did not find it hard to imagine what damage the intruder could do with that sharpbladed tooth. Her own mother had carried such a tooth, but chipped from stone, in her elder years, when her own teeth had failed her.

Dariim had begun to tremble again, but this time with eagerness. "You are the best hunter in the forest, but you have never taken game so large as this," she hissed.

Tsuuka stiffened. "We are not taking game now, cub. We are only taking the skysilk. And how we will do that—" She didn't know. That was the baffling truth. Spring from the shadows and bowl the intruders over with a swift swipe of their claws? It seemed wrong when she remembered that the intruders had carried a helpless cub from the grasslands and entrusted it to her. It seemed wrong when she remembered the kinship she had glimpsed in the smaller intruder's eyes the night before. It seemed wrong when she remembered how many empty nights the starsilk had filled for her.

Step from the shadows and ask for her silk then? Ask as she would ask another sithi? But she did not speak the starvoice language. She did not think she could make her tongue do the things theirs did. She didn't have blunt teeth to collect words behind. Her teeth were sharp; they cut her words into hisses.

She growled softly with frustration. Would the intruders understand if she demanded the silk in her own language? Sometimes the starsilk used a few words of sithi. Perhaps the intruders knew her language.

The one thing she could not do was turn back, not with Dariim watching fervidly to see what she would do. Tsuuka considered alternatives again, swiftly, then stood, decided. "Come, we will do the boldest thing we have ever done, cub. We will walk up to these intruders and ask them for what we want."

That took Dariim's breath, but only momentarily. Then she was all eagerness.

Tsuuka deliberately rattled brush to warn the intruders of their approach. She knew they had heard when their voices abruptly died. They presented her with a tensely waiting silence when she stepped forward, Dariim her shadow.

They were as they had been the night before, the two of them. One tall and muscular, with shining white fur that he wore in a cap, the other slight, her darker fur streaming down her back. Both their faces were stiff with surprise and the remnant of whatever argument they had with each other—if indeed it was an argument. They seemed to require precious moments to believe what they saw. But the larger did not take his shining tooth from his waist, and the smaller did not wield her sharpened stick in any threatening way.

Tsuuka spoke softly at first, not wanting to frighten them. "Starvoices, I have given you my skysilk in error. Its sisters cry. Their song has an emptiness. I must restore the skysilk to my bower." She glanced from one to the other, alert for some sign that they understood.

She was startled when they did—when the smaller intruder immediately laid aside her stick, untied the skysilk from her waist, and offered it on her extended hands. The intruder's face was tense, her eyes round. She seemed to hold her breath. The larger intruder's hand fell but hovered clear of the hilt of his tooth. Tsuuka hesitated for a moment, evaluating the danger, then touched Dariim's shoulder. "Take it, cub." If Dariim wanted to do bold deeds, here was one—one she would not guess was entirely safe. Because who would suppose that creatures like these would understand her request and honor it so readily?

Dariim's eyes glinted and Tsuuka felt the tension of her muscles beneath the shining fur. Her first step was hesitant. Then she sprang forward boldly and snatched the skysilk, whipping it in the air as she jumped back with it.

The intruders drew back instinctively. For a moment they stared at each other and no one made a sound. Then the smaller intruder said something that sounded almost questioning.

But she did not say it in sithi. Tsuuka took the skysilk from Dariim's clutching fingers. She pressed it against her face, eager for its cool touch. "You have restored the harmony of my bower," she said in a grateful whisper. Then she drew Dariim back into the shadows with her.

She waited tensely, clutching Dariim's arm, to see if the intruders would follow. But they did not. They stared after her, then slipped away just as they had the night before, their faces becoming pale ovals against the darkness, then disappearing.

Tsuuka tied the silk at her waist, wearing it as the intruder had. Then she slipped forward and briefly took up the intruders' scent. Their trail led now in the direction of the heart of the trees. She peered in the direction they had taken, puzzled, momentarily touched by an uneasiness she could not name.

But she had no time to examine that unformed apprehension. Dariim bobbed with excitement, chuckling under her breath. Tsuuka saw unwillingly that there was no sign of nightmare upon her now. And soon the sun would rise. Dariim must be safely sleeping by then or she would not sleep at all.

The heart of the trees . . . The intruders were going to the heart of the trees.

"My cub, come," she said, frowning. "We must choose a tree so you can learn what song-dreams are and how strong and alert they can make you."

Dariim chuckled aloud at that, giddy with the success of her brave deed. "But mother, see now—see what I've done. I'm already strong. The nightmares are gone."

"No," Tsuuka said firmly. "They are paler here. But if you go back to the heart of the trees, they will be heavy and dark. Because that is the place where they are most concentrated. Someday I will tell you why. Tonight you must obey me because I know what is best." All spoken with a quiet certainty she did not feel, because she was not at all confident Dariim would obey. Not with the giddiness of her exploit upon her and the terror of the nightmares fading. "Come, cub."

Dariim's resistance showed itself in her trailing footsteps, in the defiant brightness of her eyes as she gazed back toward the heart of the trees. But occasionally as they scampered back through the forest, she touched the azure silk. Then the brightness of her eyes became different, both anticipatory and anxious.

So she was cowed by the prospect of this new experience. That made it easier to insist that she come. She would never willingly betray her fear with open reluctance.

Tsuuka looked for a tree in its prime, one that stood tall and broad but would not creak and wake Dariim when she slipped away later. "Here," she said when she found one that satisfied her. "You must choose the branch. It must be high so the skysilk can find light from below the horizon."

"And you will stay with me?" Dariim probed, gazing up the tall stalk of the tree.

"How else will I be able to instruct my silk to give you song-dreams?" Tsuuka said and was relieved to see no sign that Dariim detected her evasion. Now if only she could set aside the unease she had felt since parting with the intruders—

It refused to be forgotten. It forced itself to her attention again, taking explicit form this time. The intruders were going to the heart of the trees—where the unseen lived. The unseen, who was vulnerable flesh—the unseen without whom there would be no spinners and no silks in this quarter of the forest. Tsuuka's hand closed on her skysilk, so cool, so slippery. Did the intruders know that the unseen was fragile? That she must not be injured? Or did they go there hunting her with their sharpened stick and polished tooth?

Chill stiffened Tsuuka's muscles. She had wondered what prey the intruders might seek with their blunt teeth and dull claws. If the unseen were as fragile as she feared—and who could tell her whether the escorts' stings would deter the intruders? She shuddered, gazing up at Dariim, who already clawed her way up the tree. She wanted to go after the intruders, wanted to be certain of their intent.

Surely there was time to see her cub sleeping. Surely—

But there was no time at all. Because as Tsuuka put reluctant claws to the bark, a dim, fiery song rose from the direction the intruders had taken. Tsuuka stiffened, recognizing it immediately despite the distance. It was the song of the red silk. She glanced up, alarmed, and saw Dariim staring into the darkness, teeth bared. Then, with no warning, Dariim's body streaked past her, dropping toward the ground.

Her own response was almost as swift. The red silk had come from hiding. It sang its taunting song again and Dariim was galloping after it, not even pausing to glance back. Tsuuka dropped to the ground too, fell to all fours, and surged after Dariim.

The red silk, the unseen, the intruders—Tsuuka's heart drummed against her rib cage; her blood pulsed to a dizzy rhythm. She didn't know what use her claws would find tonight. She didn't know who they must defend, the unseen, her cub, or herself. But the jarring leap of her heart, the choking shortness of her breath told her she soon would know.

FIFTEEN
REYNA

It was easier to find Juaren that night than it had been in the morning. Easier in the dark forest than it had been in the daylight one. Not because Reyna had become so much more expert in tracking; she stumbled through the trees almost blindly, guided more by instinct than by the occasional bootmark she found on the soil. But because she blundered loudly, not trying to hide the fact that she was lost—begging him to hear her and to turn back. She tripped on a swollen root, she rattled through a patch of brush, she clambered over a fallen tree—and Juaren stood on a small rise, as still as moonlight, looking down at her.

She halted, catching her breath involuntarily, frozen by the expression in his eyes. Was it displeasure? Unwelcome? Or something else—consternation? Certainly he was not pleased to see her. For a moment she could not speak. "You forgot to tell me you were going," she said finally. "I heard something. I woke up and you were gone."

His face changed, but only to become more masklike. "I thought you were tired. I thought you needed to sleep."

"No," she said, disturbed by the contrast between words and expression, the one concerned, the other unrevealing. "You *waited* until I was asleep. Then you slipped away. Because you wanted to go alone."

Juaren sighed deeply, his hands closing to fists, his face changing again—the mask falling away to reveal the concern behind it. "I wanted to go alone," he said. "Yes. Because the place where I'm going—is dangerous. I may go there and come back. I may not. I don't understand completely. I won't understand until I've seen. And I won't fail you as I've failed the others."

"Fail me?" She stared at him blankly, unprepared for those words, for the hard edge they brought to his voice, the pain they brought to his face. And his hands—she did not want to look at his hands. If his nails were cutting crescents in the flesh, she did not want to see.

"I failed my mother by being born while she took wintersleep. I failed Komas by not pulling him back up the mountain—"

"You couldn't reach him," she said, surprised. How could he blame himself for that? Or for his own birth?

"I failed him. But I won't fail you. If only one of us is to go back to Brakrath, it will be you."

"No—" she said involuntarily. A thought she had never considered. One she would not consider now.

"Yes. No one on Brakrath cares that I've gone. And no one will listen when I go back, not if I go alone. I'm a winter-child and a hunter, not a person to be listened to.

"But you are a barohna's daughter. Your mother, your father, all the people of Valley Terlath are waiting for you to come back. And when you do, they will listen to you. They will listen when you tell them what you've seen, what you know, what you've learned.

"I've made you my apprentice. I've given you the old words. Now you must treat them as your pledge. You must accept my guidance as your guild master and let me go alone."

"You call yourself my master?" she said in surprise, not certain if she was more bewildered or frightened by the things he said. *If only one of them was to go back . . .*

"You asked to become my apprentice. You agreed to certain obligations. One of them is to listen to me."

Yes, she had apprenticed herself to him, and he had warned her that there were obligations—and she had laughed. Now she raised a shaky hand to her temples, realizing she should never have laughed. Not when Juaren spoke of his guild. He had made his guild his family, his valley, his life—because for too many years he had had nothing else.

Slowly she released a long breath, trying to find an answer he would understand. "All right. I have listened," she said finally. "But you've made a palace daughter your apprentice, Juaren. Just a palace daughter. I came here to meet my challenge, and if I don't, I'll always be a palace daughter. I'll never be more, no matter how many pledges I take."

"You're more already," he said without hesitation.

"Maybe you see more. Maybe Verra does. But I don't," she insisted. "If I don't meet my challenge, if I hide in my bed while you go to learn what happened to Birnam Rauth, I'll be a child for the rest of my life. I'll never tell anyone about the things we've seen. I'll never raise my voice. I'll never waken anyone. It won't be my place to do that. Because I will be no one—as surely as if I had never left my mother's palace. And then—then you will have failed me truly." She said the last words reluctantly, as if she were putting her knife to him. Because she understood him better tonight than she ever had before. She understood how deeply he pledged his loyalty when once he pledged it—and how concerned he was not to fail in the pledge.

"No."

"Yes. You want to protect me. But how can I be anything but a child if I let you do it? I want to know what your silk told you. I want to know where you're going. And I want to go with you." Strong words, words that made her tremble. She had to go with him, for all the reasons she had given him. But she knew she could not move as unobtrusively as he could. She knew her reactions were not as swift as his. She knew she might distract him at the wrong moment. She knew she might place his life at risk—more at risk than if he went alone.

But she hadn't come here to wait in her bed. "There's a tree—a hollow tree—" she began.

Juaren's eyes flashed. One hand fell to the silk at his waist. Huskily he said, "How do you know that?"

"Birnam Rauth is my kin," she said. "I guessed it from listening to his silk."

His eyes narrowed. "No. I've heard the message your silk carries—"

"I guessed it from the song—and from something I saw in one of his sketch books." And from Birnam Rauth himself, standing at her shoulder in the dark. Could she tell Juaren that? "There's a tree he sketched several times. It—it attracted him."

"Yes," he said slowly, waiting for her to go on.

But she had nothing more to tell. "Let me hear the silk," she said.

His hand touched the starsilk, almost protectively. He stared down at the forest floor, then looked up, capturing her gaze, refusing to release it. "Reyna, there were times when Komas went alone into the ice caverns and I waited outside. That was my part of the hunt—to be ready if he blundered into a breeterlik, if he needed help or had wounds to be treated."

She caught his arm and pressed it, almost tenderly. "I won't wait outside, Juaren."

His lips tightened. He stared down at the ground again, describing a slow pattern with the toe of one boot. Finally he said, "I'll show you how to use the translator."

He carried it at his waist, concealed beneath the starsilk. He tied the starsilk to a tree and had Reyna sit, the translator in her lap, earplugs in her ears. When the breeze caught the silk, fluttering its loose ends, a genderless voice spoke in her ear.

". . . clearer now. I was disoriented at first, but I've begun to remember details now. I've begun to remember why I went there. Or came here. It's hard to believe I have a physical location, something that could be marked on a chart of the forest. I have no sense of my body—and I think I know the reason for that. But I still have my thoughts, and if I understand correctly what's happened, some of them are being recorded, in some form. Maybe someday someone will hear them, someone who can decipher them—someone who will be interested in what I've found here.

"It's not unique, I suppose. I can find parallels to other species. But this is my own discovery, so I have a certain proprietorial pride —especially since I won't make any discoveries after this one."

Reyna shifted, struck by the dispassionate choice of words, struck too by the methodical way he laid out his observations so that she could understand them.

She could understand them, but she could not believe them. Not immediately, not as she listened in the darkened forest. Sithi—that was the name Birnam Rauth gave the chatni. And the details Birnam Rauth had gathered so carefully through the sithi, through the silks they shared thoughts with, through observation—she found it hard to believe that the silks that sang so eloquently in the trees had been spun by the chattering creatures she and Juaren had watched feeding that morning. She found it hard to believe that the songsilks derived at least a part of their consciousness from other creatures who were years or even decades dead—the preserved. She found it hard to believe that Birnam Rauth had dared go to the deep trees to try to glimpse something his sithi companion and her silk had told him must never be seen.

Something fragile. Something dangerous. Something born wise— the unseen, Birnam Rauth called it—that saw the light of day only twice in the year of its life: once when it made its way from the tree where it had hatched to the tree where it would perform its life work, and later when it made its way from that tree to spin its life-silk and to die.

Life-silks, master-silks, songsilks; spinners, escorts, the unseen and the preserved—and all of them of a single family. But the preserved were no more than the living wills of the creatures whose consciousness was lodged in the life-silks. And there were countless life-silks hidden here in the forest—as many as there had been years since the beginning of their time. Some of them were long forgotten, their filaments intergrown with the wood fibers of the trees where they hid. Some had slipped away into the soil and dissociated into individual filaments. Others were fresher, newer, and these were still used, through the agency of the master-silks, to lend awareness to the songsilks.

No, she believed none of it. But when Birnam Rauth's narrative ended abruptly mid-word, then began to repeat itself, Reyna looked up and thought she saw filmy silks swirling from the white-barked trees. She shook her head sharply, dismissing that perception, and reached with numb hands to remove the earplugs.

"He's here. Hidden. In one of the trees," she said unwillingly. But could she say that Birnam Rauth was alive? Was that a fair description of his state? Birnam Rauth had eventually guessed himself what had happened. The unseen had studied him—his mind, his thoughts, his physiology—through the sithi and the silks. She had found a uniqueness in him that was at once precious, perplexing and threatening, a challenge to her inbred wisdom. So when he had come to the deep woods, when he had intruded upon this most closely held inviolability, when he had tried to see what was not to be seen, she had directed the escorts to capture him. He didn't remember how it had happened; he thought he had exercised more than reasonable care. But the escorts had taken him, and then, because the unseen had not wanted to destroy him, she had spun a life-silk to cradle his awareness and his will.

No, she had not killed him. Not in her view. Because hers was a wisdom far different than human wisdom. She had simply preserved him and hidden him away for her successors to study, to try to understand. She and her kind were vulnerable, a vulnerability that fed their secretiveness and their vigilance. If there were more like Birnam Rauth, they must be prepared to deal with them.

"He's here," Reyna repeated. "Somewhere."

"Yes," Juaren agreed. "When we were flying over the forest today, I noticed a place where the trees were taller, older. The heart of the trees, he called it. The place where the forest lives. He's there."

And they were near that place now. If she closed her eyes, Reyna could feel it beat, that heart of wood. She could feel its rhythm in her bones. For a moment she entertained a craven thought: now we know what happened to him; now we can go back.

But of course they couldn't. Somewhere there was a silk that contained the remnant of Birnam Rauth's consciousness. They could not turn back until they found it. Slowly she stood and took Juaren's starsilk from the tree. "Do you know how to find the heart of the trees?"

"We've taken the right direction. Look—you can see that the trees are older here than they were beside the stream."

The trees were older, taller, darker. Reyna gazed around, seeing that, wondering if these trees sheltered life-silks. There were some with open hollows, some with healed wounds, a few standing dead and empty. But were they empty? Shivering, she remembered the escorts, the stingered spinners Birnam Rauth had described. Remembered what they could do to any creature who became too curious. How would they know which trees they could search, which they dared not?

"If you want to sleep, then come back tomorrow—" Juaren said.

"No." If she left now, how would she find the courage to return? "Which—which direction must we take? To the oldest trees?"

"This way."

She followed, trying to walk as lightly as he did—trying to walk as if the soil were alive and could feel her step. The moon had set, leaving the forest dark except for the distant sparkle of sunlight. Reyna saw it sometimes between wide branches when she glanced up.

The trees became older as they walked. She saw that in their size and in the roughness of their bark. Moss and fungus padded their massive trunks. Their foliage was sparse, carried on branches that reached tall against the sky, and there were wounds in their trunks where lower branches had torn away.

Briefly they paused and talked. When they went on, Reyna felt the presence of life in the trees—life both fragile and timeless. The dark-mossed trunks, the soil underfoot—they seemed strung with living filaments, filaments informed with an awareness that had survived from a time so ancient she could not imagine it. She could almost hear silent songs in the air. She could almost hear—

But the crackle of brush was not a sound from some ancient time. Reyna caught Juaren's arm and together they stared in the direction of the sound.

Two sithi stepped from the shadows, one adult, one younger, no taller, no heavier than Reyna. Reyna stared blankly at their approach. She had given no thought to encountering sithi tonight. She had been too preoccupied. Anxiously she saw that the adult had unsheathed her claws, although she didn't brandish them. The younger hung behind the older, half-crouched, and from the glint of her eyes she was both frightened and excited. Reyna stared in fascination at the sharpness of her teeth, at the smooth motion of muscles beneath her chestnut fur.

She had no time to wonder what they would do. The older stepped forward. Could it be the sithi they had encountered the night before, the one they had traded the grassland cub to? She seemed to recognize them. And she spoke in the hissing, growling language Reyna had heard Birnam Rauth try to speak.

She spoke, but what did she say? The sithi's yellow glance flickered to the blue silk Reyna had tied at her waist. She wet her lips, tentatively. Her ears stood erect. Her brow was deeply creased, making her expression almost quizzical.

Did she want the silk? Had she regretted trading it away? Remembering the sad song the silk had sung, Reyna trusted to instinct. Quickly she untied the silk and offered it.

She knew she had guessed correctly immediately. The adult sithi's pupils shimmered wide and she spoke softly to the younger. The cub took a single hesitant step forward, then snatched at the silk and sprang back. The adult sithi took the silk from her, touching it almost reverently, then spoke again, softly, in a whisper.

"You gave your silk to me and then you missed it," Reyna said, knowing it was true—and knowing the sithi could not possibly understand her words. Then Juaren touched her arm and drew her back into the shadows, and she was surprised to find that she was shaking.

The reaction passed quickly, although Reyna glanced back over her shoulder often as they continued through the trees. And she listened for the pad of feet.

Soon the shadows grew increasingly dense and the trees crowded together, their trunks broad, deep with increasingly cavernous hollows. The air smelled different, damper, mustier, as if the cleansing breeze could not move among the close-grown trees.

"Your pike—may I have it?"

They had not spoken since encountering the sithi. Reyna hesitated, yielding the weapon doubtfully. "What are you going to do?"

For answer Juaren began to tap lightly at hollow trunks as they picked their way among the forest giants. "If there's something here—"

"Juaren—" she said apprehensively, then bit back the protest. If there was something here, they must find it. Somehow. And did she have any better idea than his?

And there was something. Something near. As Juaren tapped at the trees, Reyna held her breath and felt its presence. She felt the beating of its heart in the very heaviness of the air. She felt the waiting quality of the shadows. She felt anticipation. "It's almost dawn," she said. Almost imperceptibly the sky had begun to lighten.

"Soon."

A creature that saw daylight only twice . . . When would the unseen emerge from its bulb-well to spin its life-silk and die? When would the successor it had carefully nourished leave to enter the tree where it would make its own well? Was this the season? Had Birnam Rauth said? Reyna couldn't remember.

"Juaren—" But before she could ask, Juaren tapped lightly at one of the aged giants—and jumped back, pulling her with him, as an indistinguishable shape billowed from the tree's interior and rippled through the air. Briefly it swirled around them, slapping them with silken arms, as if it were angry. Then it rushed away, and as it rose through the trees, it began to sing, loudly, almost fiercely.

Reyna fell back against a moss-cushioned trunk, startled. A life-silk? Had they frightened a life-silk from hiding? How would they know? Birnam Rauth had seen only master-silks and songsilks and the duller silks that lay silently in sithi bowers. She knew a songsilk could not rush through the air as this silk did, returning again to flutter angrily at their faces, then disappearing high into the branches. And she had never heard a songsilk sing so loudly or so impatiently. She stared up. It was impossible to tell if the silk had color, but its voice was like an angry splash of red against the silence of the forest.

The silence of the forest? Reyna had no time to shed her startlement gradually. Because Juaren had caught her arm again, pulling her back against the trunk of the nearest tree. And there were running feet and the rattle of brush. Reyna turned and stared as the two sithi came bolting through the trees, running on all fours, their stride long, rocking, muscular. The adult wore the blue silk tied at her waist, ends flying. It warbled weakly as she ran.

Seeing Reyna and Juaren, the cub jumped aside skittishly and hissed before running on. The adult briefly broke stride, baring her teeth in an unmistakable snarl. Reyna's fingers bit so hard into the bark of the tree that she felt moss pack beneath her nails. Only the lift-pack she wore on her back kept her from pressing herself flat against the tree.

The lift-pack—at least they had lift-packs. How high could the sithi jump? She touched the lift-pack controls strapped to her left wrist. "Juaren—"

"The silk." He had released her. He stared briefly after the sithi and the silk. Then he was running. "They're trying to catch the silk."

"Wait!" she cried, panic-stricken. But the sithi were gone, bounding into the pre-dawn shadows. And abruptly, with no explanation, Juaren was gone too. Reyna stood frozen, trying to understand. There was a silk loose in the trees, singing an angry song. The sithi were pursuing it and Juaren had gone after them. And she stood here alone, as if she had lost command of her legs.

She touched the starsilk at her waist. She touched the controls of her lift-pack. Slowly, not understanding what was happening, she moved away from the tree that shadowed her and took herself in the direction the others had taken. The darkness of night had become the grey of earliest morning. The strange half-light, the looming trees and the deep shadows that attended them gave Reyna a sense of unreality as she pushed her way through the forest. She felt as if she groped her way through a dream, trying to find its symbols and their meanings while she still slept. "Juaren!" It hardly seemed her own voice. "Juaren!"

Then there were other voices, drowning hers. Shrill voices, angry voices—Reyna froze again, momentarily immobilized by shock. The creature that had discovered them sleeping that morning, the spinner—she heard tens of them screaming from the trees. And the sound came from the direction Juaren had taken. Had the sithi alarmed the spinners? Had Juaren?

Or were these the voices of spinners at all? Did the escorts scream too? Birnam Rauth had said they were nothing more than spinners with stingers.

Reyna ran then. Ran into the unreal pallor of early morning. Ran through the ancient trees, the musty smell of them making her choke for breath. Ran until she found herself in a place where the trees stood so ancient, so moss-choked, their hollows so cavernous, that she felt she had made her way into a nightmare.

Perhaps it was a nightmare. Because now she saw the creatures that screamed, and they were not spinners. They were no larger than spinners. They were no less plump, no less infantile. But they wagged horny stingers in the air, their limbs pumping and straining with anger, their eyes depthless and virulent at once. She could barely hear the taunting song of the silk over their voices.

She could barely hear the scream of the adult sithi. But the sithi was indeed screaming. Reyna rocked to a halt, staring around with half-seeing eyes, trying to find the sense of the scene.

The runaway silk—she could see it more clearly now; it was as red as its song—clung to the withered lower branch of one of the ancient trees. The sithi cub plunged up the tree's trunk, eyes glinting, ears laid flat against its skull, teeth bared in a covetous grin. Escorts boiled from the hollow of the tree, from the hollows of neighboring trees, and shrilled, brandishing their stingers. And the adult sithi crouched on the forest floor, screaming with an anguish more punishing than any Reyna had ever seen. Remembering what Birnam Rauth had said the sting of an escort could do to a bright-eyed cub, Reyna understood the older sithi's anguish. It touched her too, making her breath short, making her stomach tight.

She didn't know why the red silk flew free or why the cub hunted it. But she knew immediately that she couldn't stand here and watch the cub stung. And she couldn't stand here and watch the older sithi sacrifice herself trying to defend the cub. Almost without thinking Reyna touched the controls of her lift-pack. It wasn't until she drifted into the air that she realized Juaren already floated in the shadows nearby, pike raised, fending back escorts that scrambled across the wide branches toward the silk. The tiny creatures flailed their stingers in rage, three-fingered fists knotted, toes clinging to the heavily mossed branches. Juaren extended the pike, keeping a safe distance from their wagging stingers, prodding their chubby legs, driving them back.

But only temporarily. Reyna could see that. Tens more of the creatures pressed behind the nearest ones, pushing at them. When one of the creatures lost its grip on the slippery moss and fell, the others seemed not to notice. They drove forward, clutching after the pike now with three-fingered hands.

There was no way Reyna could shout to Juaren, no way to make herself heard. And what had she to say, with the adult sithi suddenly springing and clawing her way up the tree, her fur damp, her eyes slitted, her ears laid flat? Juaren was safe. Even if he could not hold the escorts back, he had only to maneuver away from reach of their stingers. But the sithi had no lift-packs. Watching them claw their way up the tree, Reyna acted upon impulse, without thinking. She fingered her controls and ascended rapidly to the branch where the silk clung.

The silk had tangled itself in a cluster of dried twigs, singing defiantly. It required only a fraction of a second to sense Reyna's presence, to guess her intention as she snatched for it. Too late, it struggled, trying to extricate itself from pointed twigs and streak away. In its fury it caught and tore instead.

And Reyna captured it. She closed fingers around the silk and was immediately startled by the strength she felt in it, the will. It writhed in her grasp, slapping silken arms at her, as she tugged it free of the branch. Instinctively she held it at arm's length, clutching it tight in one fist, afraid it would try to wrap strangling arms around her neck.

The sithi cub blinked up in startled disbelief. Reyna dropped quickly, giving the cub no time to decide she intended to steal its prize and to mount a second offensive. Keeping careful range from the cub's razor claws, she held the struggling silk within reach.

Yellow eyes drew to distrustful slits. Facial muscles slackened, then stretched taut. Then, so swiftly Reyna didn't have time to flinch, clawed fingers snatched the silk. The cub turned and scrambled down the tree, clutching the silk, leaping to the ground at the same time that the older sithi sprang down from the tree.

At first Reyna thought the cry she heard was the older sithi's. The sithi spun when she touched ground, her anguish turning to fury. She slapped the startled cub's face and, when the cub fled, raced after it, swatting and biting. Muscles bunching under her sweat-dampened coat, she chased the cub away into the trees.

And the cry continued, then abruptly ceased. Reyna's feet touched ground and she turned and looked up. Her breath choked away at what she saw. Juaren had not followed her. He still hung in the air. The pike had fallen from his hands and he was thrashing helplessly against white strings that tangled around his arms and legs.

White strings spat by the shrilling escorts. They ejected the sticky strands at him from every direction, and with the involuntary thrashing of his limbs, he wrapped the strands around him. Reyna stared up, paralyzed, capable of only one useless thought. *Birnam Rauth hadn't warned them of this.*

But Birnam Rauth had remembered so little of what happened to him in the heart of the trees. He had not remembered being immobilized by strings of sticky silk. He had not remembered struggling and then slumping into unconsciousness. He had not remembered being reeled in by the escorts and swiftly lashed to the trunk of a mossy tree, head sagging, arms hanging limp. As Reyna watched helplessly, all those things happened to Juaren.

And when they had happened, when he hung immobile, the shrilling chorus of the escorts died. The heart of the woods was suddenly silent again as many tens of depthless eyes turned to Reyna. She stared up. Her hands had closed to painful fists. Her mouth was parchment-dry. Her breath came in painful gulps, as if silken strands bound her too. But the escorts made no motion toward her. They stood with their tiny hands fisted, their eyes unwinking.

As if they had been ordered to watch her. As if they had been ordered to record her image. Reyna licked her lips, to no effect. Her tongue was dry too, cottony. The unseen—Birnam Rauth said the unseen directed the activities of the spinners and to some extent the activities of the escorts too. Now, for some reason, she had directed them to stare at Reyna, to record her movements.

Reyna laughed, a half-hysterical sound, entirely involuntary. What did the unseen see through all those unwinking eyes? A strange and frightened creature, with all the wildness of despair in her eyes? Or simply a creature so alien the unseen could read nothing from its face, from its posture? Nothing but a momentarily leashed threat.

Reyna shuddered, trying to bring herself under control. She could not yield to hysteria now. Juaren was helpless. She was the only person who could help him.

But when she tried to think what to do, what she *could* do that would have any effect, she thought of nothing. Experimentally she stepped forward, reaching for the pike Juaren had dropped.

The escorts responded immediately, crouching and screaming,

stingers wagging. Reyna caught a sharp breath and took an involuntary step back. Obviously she wasn't to be permitted to retrieve the pike. And what could she do if she did retrieve it? It hadn't saved Juaren. He had wielded the pike, and now he hung helpless in the tree.

Briefly Reyna squeezed her eyes shut, pressing her temples with trembling fingers, trying to force some thought to the surface. She didn't dare take even a single step forward. And she didn't dare use her lift-pack to lift toward the tree where Juaren hung in silken bonds. Because if the escorts spat their paralyzing web at her too, if she found herself as helpless as Juaren already was, then there would be no help for either of them.

Go back to the stream? Wake Verra? She pressed harder at her temples, wondering what Verra could do. And what if she ran back to the stream to fetch Verra and returned to find that Juaren had been hidden away in her absence, tucked out of reach in some musty hollow?

There were tens of them large enough to hold him. Tens of them large enough to conceal him while the unseen did whatever she chose to do. Would she spin a life-silk to contain his thoughts, as she had done with Birnam Rauth? Was she curious about him? Did she consider him precious and rare enough to preserve? Reyna shuddered violently, wondering what had become of Birnam Rauth's body. Had it died slowly in a clinging net of silk after the unseen spun his life-silk? Had he been permitted to starve, unconscious and helpless?

She was going to fail Juaren. She was going to fail him in just the way he thought he had failed his mother and his guild master. She was going to stand helplessly while he died. The certainty was like a blow. It took her breath. It left her tearful and stunned.

And depthless eyes continued to stare. *The unseen—the unseen was watching her through the eyes of the escorts.* That certainty came slowly, coldly, making her dizzy with helpless anger. She raised her head and glared up at the tiny creatures that lined the trees.

What do you expect to see? she demanded silently, fiercely. *What do you expect me to do? Just walk away? Didn't you learn anything from Birnam Rauth? Didn't you learn anything about us from him? Didn't you learn that we cherish our bodies? And each other?*

But how could she vent her anger at something she couldn't see? Something whose nature and dimensions she couldn't even imagine? The unseen was here, hidden somewhere nearby. Poised, waiting, watching through tens of eyes. Did her heart, if she had one, beat with the same fear that Reyna's did? Was she hurting with fear? How must this encounter look to her?

It must look as if strange creatures had come thrusting into the most vulnerable heart of her sanctuary. It must look as if their presence threatened not just her but the entire web of life that depended upon her. It must look as if her choices were to destroy those creatures or to risk being destroyed herself, with all her offspring and all her kind.

But we didn't come here for that, Reyna found herself pleading silently, as if the unseen could hear her thoughts, as if she could understand them. *We didn't come here to harm you. We didn't come here to hurt you. Let my mate go and we'll leave. We'll leave now.*

The trees gave no sign that anyone heard. The escorts continued to stare down at her. They crouched on their limbs, as if they had settled into place for a long vigil.

What else did they have to do but to maintain this vigil? That was their entire function—to protect the unseen. *Let my mate go and we'll never tell anyone about this place. We'll never tell anyone that you live here.* Foolish—it was foolish and useless to try to talk to a creature she couldn't see, a creature whose nature she couldn't comprehend. Still, with aching-cold fingers, Reyna untied the starsilk from her waist and held it free. *Listen—you know this voice. This man is my kin, and by now you know he wouldn't have harmed you—no more than we will harm you.*

Reyna felt certain of that. Birnam Rauth had come to the heart of the trees to observe the unseen, never to harm her. And surely, if the unseen and all her predecessors had studied him, they recognized that—with whatever alien wisdom they used to recognize any truth.

The starsilk clung to her fingers and sang with the passing breeze. It sang a song the unseen must have heard before. But there was no sign that the song tore at the unseen, that it even touched her. Slowly Reyna lowered her head. The bitterness of tears rose to her eyes and spilled over onto her cheeks. They were acid, etching their paths in her flesh. Her mood changed.

There were weapons and implements in their ship. Verra had shown her them. Flame-throwers, chopping blades, weapons that cast projectiles through the air so swiftly no one could dodge them. And other, more obscure weapons. Vengefully Reyna thought of those things. If she left Juaren here and went for them, she might never see him again. She might never find where the escorts hid him in her absence. But she could do the very things the unseen must fear most. She could cut the escorts down. She could burn them where they perched. She could torch the heart of the trees. She could make the unseen feel her grief, if not her need.

She could destroy something as rare, as precious as Juaren himself. She could denude the forest. She could quench its spirit and its song.

She shuddered with those thoughts and knew she would never obey them. Was sorry she had even briefly entertained them.

She was too preoccupied to hear the sithi approach. Nor did she notice when the creature's shadow fell at her feet. When the sithi touched her arm, closing slender fingers upon it, Reyna started violently and uttered a half-strangled scream.

She spun, staring into the sleekly furred face, expecting to see bared teeth, finding instead something she didn't believe at first: comprehension.

That startled her more than hostility or aggression. The sithi saw what had happened and understood what Reyna felt. It understood that Juaren was caught and that she was grieving and angry and helpless—entirely helpless. Reyna shivered, trying to put her thoughts in order. How did the sithi understand those things? Did their dissimilarity hide some basic likeness? Were they more of a kind than she had thought?

There were things she and Juaren had understood too. They had understood that the sithi cub intended to have the red silk. They had understood the danger of its quest. They had understood the older sithi's helpless anguish. Had they not understood those things, Juaren would be free now.

Did the sithi understand that too? The creature had released her arm. With a tentative hand, it stroked the starsilk. Its brows drew together, as if it wanted to question her.

Reyna scrubbed the back of one hand across her face, not knowing any way to answer that unasked question. Not knowing any way to speak with this creature who observed her helplessness with obvious sympathy.

Except perhaps in song. And was that such a foolish thought? Reyna knew from what Birnam Rauth had said that the sithi shared some silent communication with the silks. If she sang like a silk, sang her own song—

What else did she have to do? It wasn't as if she had alternatives. Trembling, Reyna held the starsilk to the breeze again. When it began to sing, she sang too, but aloud, as she never had before. She sang all the things she wanted the sithi to understand. She sang of her own world, where the mysteries that lived in the forest were different from the mysteries that lived here. She sang of people she had cared for and land she loved. She sang of the sun shining from her mother's sunthrone. She sang of the mountains, where she had intended to walk with Juaren. She sang of the stories he could not write if he died here, of the children he could not father, of the apprentices he could not teach. She sang of the pain of failing—in her quest for the throne, in her challenge, in her need to save Juaren from death.

She sang promises too. Pledges and vows, these directed more at the unseen than the sithi. Pledges that if Juaren were allowed to go free, she would search no more for Birnam Rauth. That they would leave and forget his lonely song. That if Juaren were freed, they would turn from the heart of the trees and never try to see what must not be seen. That they would return to their ship and to their own world.

She sang pledges that hurt. Pledges that burned as she gave them voice. Because she knew that if Juaren were freed, if they were permitted to go, Birnam Rauth's song would always torment her. She could fold the starsilk and hide it in the most obscure corner of the palace. She could bury it or burn it, and she would still hear its song. For all the days of her life.

Yet she offered Birnam Rauth for Juaren. She offered to leave him entombed forever if Juaren could be freed. And she didn't even know the use of her song. She didn't know if the sithi understood. She didn't know if the unseen even heard it.

Those things comprised the conscious stanzas of her song. Her song spoke from another level too, from a deeper level. Her song spoke from the place where pain lived, where loneliness lived, where duty and hope and trust struggled daily for life.

After a while she realized that the sithi's blue silk sang along with the starsilk. That the sithi stood with her head thrown back, her eyes pressed shut, as if she somehow sang through her silk. Reyna wondered—could the sithi speak to the unseen through her silk? Could she plead Reyna's cause as she understood it?

How did she understand it? The sithi stood with hands rigidly outstretched, claws digging at the air. Her brow was creased, her ears erect, quivering. Reyna drew a tremulous breath, pressed her eyes shut, and resumed her own song.

Slowly, after a while, she realized that something had changed. There was a shifting, a rustling, a stirring. And then there was a return of stillness. She bit at her lip, afraid to open her eyes, afraid of what the stillness meant, afraid of what she would see.

At last she did look, the hardest thing she had yet done, because all her hope lay in the first reluctant glance.

She saw what she hadn't dare believe she would ever see. The escorts had withdrawn. The branches were bare. It was fully daylight and Juaren looked down at her with dazed eyes.

She felt nothing in that moment. There was no time for it, no time to let the intensity of her emotions unfold. And there was no time to hesitate. No time to wonder if the escorts would emerge from hiding again if she lifted to where Juaren hung, slipped his knife from his belt, and sawed with trembling hands at the strands of silk that held him prisoner. She simply did those things, feeling nothing, but laughing while tears streamed down her face.

"Can you manage your controls?" she demanded when Juaren hung by just two strands of silk. He hadn't spoken, but he looked at her with recognition.

He nodded stiffly, as if he were uncertain of his strength. "Yes." It was more question than answer.

"What can you do?" she probed, praying that he had not been left witless like a too-curious sithi cub, stung by escorts—but he had not been stung. He had only been swaddled in sticky silk. And now she had cut the dried strands away, frowning at their lingering odor.

For a moment he gazed at her blankly. "I can use my pack controls," he said finally, with forced distinctness. "I can press the buttons."

"Which buttons will you press to go to the ground?" she insisted.

Again he was briefly blank. "The—the button nearest my palm."

"Yes." Relieved, she brushed the tears from her eyes and severed the last strands of silk.

When they reached the ground, the sithi had slipped away into the trees, leaving them alone. Alone where the trees held musty shadows, alone where life-silks hid. Alone in a place that waited for them to go.

They used their packs to make their way back through the forest. They drifted just above the ground, and sometimes she had to guide

Juaren when he seemed lost or confused. Sometimes he forgot where they were and let his eyelids fall shut and then she woke him. But at other times he knew her and spoke sense to her.

Verra was awake when they returned. She looked up with quick concern, then guided them to their beds. "Sleep. You need sleep, both of you," she said. "Tell me about it later. Whatever it was." Kind words. Rational words. Only the deep crease of her brow admitted to all the questions she wanted to ask.

The reaction didn't come until Reyna shed her pack and slipped into her bedding. Then her teeth began to chatter and her entire body to shake. Quickly Verra fetched her own bedding and swaddled her in it. She prepared hot brew and forced her to drink it. Even so it took time for Reyna to throw off the helpless shivering. She hugged herself, aware that Juaren watched her from his own bed, still trying to understand what had happened.

"Birnam Rauth?" he said huskily.

Reyna shuddered, wishing she did not have to look down into the hollow pit of her grief, however briefly. "We had to leave him," she said as matter of factly as she could. "We had to leave him there. And I promised not to go back."

Drawing a trembling breath, she stretched both hands out before her. They were slender, fragile, the hands of a palace daughter. She had not changed. She had met her challenge, and she had both succeeded and failed in it. She had brought Juaren safely from the heart of the woods, but she had left Birnam Rauth. And none of it had changed her.

Quickly she slipped down into her bedding, hiding herself there from all the things she still held in abeyance: a relief so profound she didn't think her soul could hold it, a grief of the same magnitude. Tomorrow. Tomorrow was time enough to examine those feelings. Tomorrow was time enough to touch them and to let them touch her. Perhaps by then she could accept both her success and her failure. Perhaps by then she could place them in perspective and accept the fact that she could not have had the one without the other.

She pressed her eyes shut and willed herself to sleep.

SIXTEEN

REYNA

Reyna slept without dreaming, as if all thought, all experience had fallen away, leaving her empty even of sorrow. It was midday when Verra shook her. "Reyna."

"No." Reyna turned away, burrowing deeper into her bedding, not ready to wake. Sleep had not even begun to heal her. Her body still ached, her eyes still burned, and the wound of her failure would be raw for a long time, perhaps for all her life. Juaren had not died, but she had left Birnam Rauth somewhere in the heart of the trees and she was pledged not to return for him. "No."

But Verra was insistent. "Reyna—there's someone here for you. I'm sure it's you he wants, from the way he stares at you."

Reyna caught a sobbing breath and pushed irritably at her bedding. Someone to see her? She sat, pulling one hand through her hair, prepared to be angry—with Verra for wakening her with a ruse, with herself for responding.

She sat and she saw who had come to see her. A spinner stood beside the stream. It gazed at her stolidly as if it had been instructed to wait there until she woke. Its round eyes were vacant. Its chubby legs were bowed. It held a parcel almost as large as itself. When it realized that Reyna had wakened, it dropped the parcel and waddled rapidly away, shrilling once in retreat.

Surprised, still half-sleeping, Reyna stared at the parcel it had dropped. The outer wrapper was of ivory silk, stained by time and rain. "Verra—" she said uncertainly. How had the spinner found her here? And what had it brought?

"You don't have your boots on. Let me get it for you." The Arnimi woman stepped quickly to the streambank and retrieved the bundle, placing it in Reyna's hands.

It was not heavy. Its contents compressed easily under her probing fingers. And it appeared to have been hidden away for a very long time. Reyna stared down at it, biting her lip, her fingertips tingling with a first stunning intimation of what the parcel might contain.

Juaren had wakened and was sitting cross-legged on his bedding, watching with an intent frown. Verra bent near. Reyna looked at them both, licking dry lips. Then, afraid to wait, afraid to build expectations that might only crumble, she pulled the wrappings from the bundle.

She caught her breath, realizing with her first glimpse of the contents that she had guessed correctly. Realizing with her first glimpse how well the unseen had understood her song. Or how well the sithi had understood and translated it through her blue songsilk.

Hesitantly, as if her nails might tear it, Reyna drew a sheer white silk from the bundle. It was longer than her starsilk, wider, and it appeared infinitely more delicate. But she saw immediately that there were tough filaments woven through it, and she guessed from the first touch that this was no fragile silk. This was a silk that would endure through many centuries—and many legends.

Standing, she shook out the silk, hoping it would not struggle as the red silk had, hoping it would not try to escape her. Could she bear it if she had found Birnam Rauth and he only wanted to be free? Only wanted to flirt away through the trees as the red silk had?

He did not. The silk moved of its own accord in the light breeze, first swirling around her, then lacing itself loosely around her shoulders and one arm, clinging there lightly. She could feel its life and its will in its silken touch. She could almost feel the processes of its thought as it spoke in the voice she already knew so well.

Verra quickly fetched the translator and it repeated Birnam Rauth's first words for them in its own genderless voice. "Who are you? I can tell you're human. Who are you?"

Reyna drew a long breath, catching her lower lip in her teeth, her eyes suddenly burning with tears of joy. She touched the silk with wondering fingertips. It was hard to believe this had happened. It was hard to believe this was real. She had made a choice. She had renounced her search. But through the agency of the sithi and the unseen, Birnam Rauth was here, speaking to her. She had understood the sithi's anguish and the unseen's vulnerability, and they in turn had understood her.

They had done more than understand. They had reached out, both of them. She had traveled across the stars on her quest, and it had been fulfilled not because she had used wit, not because she had used force, but because she had made herself understood to two alien creatures.

She laughed aloud, giddily. Lessons. There were lessons in this. She had learned some of them last night. She was learning some of them now. And there were many others she must yet consider. But this wasn't the time. Quickly she took the translator from Verra and adjusted it. "I'm Reyna Terlath," she said. "I'm daughter of your son, and I came here because you called."

"Daughter? Of my son? You heard my call?"

"I heard it," she said. And now she was ready to hear many things, to see many things, to do many things—some she had never even considered before.

But there were matters more urgent than that today. She felt the warmth of Juaren's shoulder against hers. She felt the heat of the midday sun on her hair. She felt the pleasure of Verra's smile. And she felt the first stirring of Birnam Rauth's comprehension—that he was free, that he was among kin, that someone had come for him. Quickly she tried to guess the full state of his mind. She tried to guess what things he would want most to taste today, with his first freedom.

Warmth. Light. Breeze. The touch of human hands. Quickly she rose and walked barefoot to a place where sunlight fell unobstructed through the trees, to a place where the breeze could curl easy fingers around them. She summoned Juaren to her side. "Here —hold your arm here, so he can touch you."

The sharing of warmth; the sharing of joy; the sharing of freedom—and later, when those things had been done, they would have stories to tell each other and a journey to make.

Many stories.

A long journey.

SEVENTEEN

REYNA

The first thing Reyna saw when she woke was Juaren. He had framed himself in the window casement, and he sat with knees drawn up, arms wrapped around them, watching her without expression. Midmorning sunlight touched his hair. Reyna sat, pulling her covers with her, briefly confused. Pitted stone walls, time-faded hangings, the friendly disorder of piled scrolls, a forgotten inkstand—

Home. They had reached home, arriving in the darkest hours of Kimira's night. The Arnimi had met their ship and delivered them to the plaza in their aircar. Servants had met them there, solemnly, awed, and conducted them to Reyna's chambers, offering food and drink and someone to chant in the corridor while they found sleep. But Reyna had looked up and seen her mother silhouetted at the window of the watchtower. And she had asked simply that they be left to sleep.

Because there was much business to be conducted the next day. Greetings, reconciliations, requests—intentions to be stated and defended. And changes to be met. It seemed to Reyna that their journey had occupied only a portion of a season, even though they had spent a full double hand of days aboard the *Pitric* on their return journey. But each of the servants who met them was visibly changed. Nivan's shoulders were more stooped. Neddica's eyes squinted from a deeper web-work of wrinkles. And Ondic, who had been a year short of her first majority when they left, now wore the blue-embroidered headband of a second-year apprentice.

Changes. Reyna lay for a moment, meeting Juaren's waiting gaze, and wondered what things had not changed in their absence. Then she got up, shrugged into the clean shift that lay across the back of her chair—she wondered idly how long it had been waiting there—and went to the door.

"Daughter? Are you ready for your meal?" It was Nivan, and she knew from the absence of the specially carved pendant he wore when engaged upon the barohna's business that he had stationed himself there as a friend rather than as her mother's runner. A very old friend, one who had seen Reyna and her sisters through childhood and smiled benignly even on the rare occasions when they had run wild in the corridors.

She turned back. "Juaren—do you want to eat before we meet with my mother?"

Juaren unfolded from the window casement, shaking his head.

Reyna nodded agreement. They had many things to discuss with Khira. Their first meal would taste sweeter with that behind. "Nivan, would you tell my mother we would like to speak with her before we eat? We have—news."

"She is already waiting in the throneroom. She has said she will see no petitioners and no guild monitors until she has first spoken with you."

"And with my year's mate. Would you run for me then and tell her we're coming?"

Nivan went immediately, walking more stiffly than she remembered. Reyna turned back, aware of rising tension—tension Juaren clearly shared. He stroked his ice-blue songsilk and then stepped to the bureau drawer where they had left the bundled life-silk.

Birnam Rauth spoke immediately when they roused him. "Did you sleep well, granddaughter? Juaren?"

Only a faint touch of irony marred his already carefully-trained Brakrathi—irony Reyna guessed he used to mask his occasional unease with his dependence upon her senses and Juaren's. Because while he heard, while within certain limits he felt, he did not see or taste or smell—except through them. And the situation was new enough to him, and to them, that sometimes it stung. "Very well, my grandfather," she replied, meeting his irony with a generous portion of her own. "Will you be worn or will you be carried when you meet my mother?"

"I'll be carried if you can pack me back into my wrappings without crushing my old grey beard."

"You know we're always careful of your beard," she said dryly. "And your tired bones. A man of your years—"

"A man of my years—" he echoed with an invisible smile, wry and deprecating.

She felt as if she had known him for a very long time. She felt as if she had known him all her life. Carefully Reyna folded his silk and rewrapped it. Then she took the hand Juaren offered her and they stepped into the hall.

There were a surprising number of servants in the upper corridors this morning, all assiduously sweeping and trimming, careful not to glance up too obviously as Reyna and Juaren passed. There were monitors too and people from every possible guild and occupation. The trenchers were here, the canners, the weavers, the scribers. There were shepherds and cooks. Creche workers had somehow found errands to bring them to the palace, all their charges trailing behind them, eyes wide. Altogether it was surprising how many people had found business in the palace corridors on the very morning of Reyna's return.

Of course none stared or pointed. None spoke. None did more than smile and offer an unobtrusive nod. Reyna returned their carefully restrained greetings, wondering what they would say among themselves later about the palace daughter who had gone so far to meet her challenge—and returned still only a palace daughter. She guessed there were legends building already.

With her mother's help, she and Juaren must use those legends, just as they must use the ones they intended to build more directly. These people, so innocently smiling, with eyes that had never looked beyond their own isolated world, these people, who didn't even guess they were sleeping—

But she followed those thoughts no further. Because they had descended the staircase and they approached the throneroom. And there, standing a little apart from the others, was her father.

Reyna caught Juaren's arm, for a moment not believing. They had arrived in the dark hours of night. How had her father ridden here from the desert so quickly? But that was impossible. It took a message days to travel to her uncle's glass-paned city. Yet here was her father—like an act of magic, he was here.

Apparently it seemed an act of magic to him that she was here. He gazed at her for long moments, blankly, as if he did not entirely trust his eyes. Then his brows rose and he was smiling, hurrying toward her with arms extended.

He smelled the way he always had. He felt the way he always had. And she came no farther up his shoulder than she ever had.

"How long have you been here?" she demanded breathlessly when he released her. "Did you just come? Did you hear—" But what could he have heard except that they were due to arrive? They had sent ahead no other news.

"I've been here all along—since the season after you left."

She gazed up at him disbelievingly. "You came—"

He shrugged, as wryly as Birnam Rauth might have. "How long did you think I could leave your mother here alone? No matter what I told her when I left. No matter what I told myself. The palace is a lonely place when your kin have scattered. Too lonely for a barohna with all the responsibilities of the throne and the people." He shrugged again. "And my brother's clan-kin kept offering me wives—more wives than I've ever wanted. Some of them were offered rather—forcefully."

Black-eyed wives who wore double-edged knives even to the dining table? Reyna blinked in momentary surprise, wondering how forcefully Danior's mate had been offered. "So you told your brother goodbye."

"And I came home. Just in time to welcome Sonel." He glanced briefly at Juaren, as if evaluating him, then turned and bent. When he straightened he held a fragile two-year-old with auburn hair and glinting amber eyes. "I suppose now that you've traveled, Reyna, you've had time to think about some of our customs. About the fact that you're one of the few palace daughters ever to know her father, ever to pull his hair or spit food on his shoulder. Others seldom even learn their father's name. Of course that is the custom."

"I—" But Reyna saw he didn't really address his observations to her. It was to Juaren that he spoke. And it was into Juaren's arms that he placed the child.

So this was her sister, Juaren's child—the next barohna of Valley Terlath. Father and child studied each other with well-matched reserve and Reyna felt unexpected tears sting her eyelids. "So this is the sister we will teach next winter while you and my mother go to the winter palace," she said, touching the child's fragile hand. This was the sister she and Juaren would tend and tell stories to while everyone else in the valley slept. This was the sister they must prepare to assume the sunthrone. The sister who must one day understand all the things they had learned about Brakrath and the universe.

"The very one," her father agreed, smiling, suddenly embracing her again. "Reyna, you're the first of my daughters I've known as an adult, and you've become the person I hoped."

Heady praise. Praise so unexpected, so disconcerting Reyna hardly noticed when he drew them into the throneroom, hardly noticed when the tall doors closed, shutting out all the people who had watched their reunion. Reyna stood briefly dazed by the brightness of mirrors and throne, by the dark figure caught at the center of their light. It took her moments to realize that Khira was not alone and that Khira was not as she and Juaren had left her: lonely and drawn. Instead she talked animatedly with Verra, glancing up from their conversation with a welcoming smile as they approached.

"My daughter—" She stepped down from the throne, away from the focused light of the mirrors. The hands she extended to Reyna were warm, strong. "I hear from my friend that you have come back well. And I have just had the pleasure of granting a wish for her."

Reyna glanced quickly at Verra as Khira took the throne again. "You're going back to Arnim now? To see your children?"

Verra caught at the tail of the green songsilk she wore as a headband, twisting it around her fingers. "No, no. I'm taking an office in the palace—that same office you offered me once. I'm going to be an adviser to the throne. I'm sure there will be questions I can answer, even if I have to pose them myself." She smiled at Reyna's obvious surprise. "Didn't I tell you I was a rebel? What properly taught Arnimi would ever have thought of traveling all the way back across the stars just to see her children? When she's contributed nothing to the shaping of them except a few body cells? I've decided to do the kind thing and not embarrass them with my interest."

Reyna found she was not entirely surprised. Verra's eyes had seldom brightened when she spoke of her children. Instead they had darkened. And her status as a member of the Arnimi party— did she intend to renounce that as well? Certainly she had hinted often enough of her dissatisfaction. "Your commander—"

"My commander is going to tell me when I discard my uniform this afternoon that I can only make a fool of myself, never a Brakrathi."

So she did intend to renounce her people. "And you'll tell him—"

"I'll tell him that I'm continuing the unfortunate work my parents undertook. I'm making a human of myself. He won't understand, of course. But he has accepted the hospitality of Khira's palace for a number of years. He won't dare take the prescribed disciplinary measures."

Reyna nodded, deciding she didn't even want to know what those measures might be. Perhaps they involved eating day after day from a silent dinner table, flanked by dour companions. Perhaps they involved wearing an austere uniform for thirty years longer. Perhaps they involved never listening to the land and the people, only to instruments. Without the assistance of the Arnimi and their equipment, she and Juaren could never have found Birnam Rauth. But she guessed she would never feel anything more for them than strained tolerance. "Remind me and I'll make ink for your stand, Verra," she said. "I have a formula—one of my own."

"Do it," Verra said, clasping her hand.

Then they could put it off no longer. They must speak to her mother. They must place their intentions before her. Reyna glanced quickly at Juaren. He had set the child down. He addressed a tense glance at Reyna.

"My mother—" she said.

But she didn't have her mother's attention. The child did. She was climbing to Khira's lap, tugging at her gown, pressing her bare limbs against the inviolable stone of the throne. And Khira, instead of reminding her that she must stand beside the throne and never leave the print of her hands upon it, only pulled her up and cradled her and stroked her hair.

Because of course, Reyna realized, Sonel was the one daughter her mother could give her heart to. Sonel was the one daughter whom she need not hold lightly. When Sonel went to the mountain, she would return.

"My mother—" she said again, when the child was settled in Khira's lap. "There are things we have seen, things we must discuss with you and later with all the people of the valleys. I don't know if you know the hunter's pledge, I don't know if you have any idea how many peoples live beyond Brakrath, I don't know if you understand how poorly we're prepared to meet them—"

She stopped, for a moment uncertain. Much depended upon her mother's support. If she and Juaren went from valley to valley to tell the story of their journey, if they took Birnam Rauth to tell his stories as well, and the Council of Bronze forbade the people to listen—

They required her mother's support. She was the only one of them who could speak to the Council, who could present their case and present it strongly. But Reyna could not read her expression. It had grown remote, thoughtful. "My mother—" she began again.

But Khira silenced her with a raised hand. "The child," she said to Iahn. "She's hidden herself in the alcove again. Would you bring her?"

Another child? Whose? Reyna bit her lip, disturbed by the interruption, wondering if she should try to override it. The Council must permit the people to hear Birnam Rauth's stories of all the people and places that lay beyond Brakrath. His was the voice that could rouse them, his the tales that could wake them.

"A moment, my daughter," Khira said. "There is a child—"

Reyna's father went quickly to the alcove off the throneroom, where scrolls were stored. They heard him speak coaxingly. Finally he emerged leading a child by the hand.

Reyna knew immediately that this was no Brakrathi child. She was not fragile and auburn-haired like a palace daughter. Nor was she blonde and sturdy like a daughter of the halls. She was slender and pale with hair so light it was almost like silver. Her face was thin, as if she had been starved, and her eyes were huge—huge and dark and frightened. She looked around at them all with a shrinking gaze and spoke incomprehensibly to Iahn.

"Who—who is she?" Reyna demanded. But she had already half-guessed, remembering the stories she had heard of the winter her father had come to Brakrath.

"The Arnimi tell us she's named Cilka Fynn—or the woman she was imaged from was named that, a long time ago. The field monitors found her three days ago, wandering in the fields, crying and hungry."

Reyna tongued dry lips. "The Benderzic—"

"The Benderzic left her to study our land. Just as they left Iahn once."

The Benderzic had left this child—was she properly called a Fynnimage?—to probe their society, to learn their language, their customs, to discover their resources, their strengths and weaknesses. Because the Benderzic expected that information to be valuable one day. "She's so small," Reyna protested. The child could not be five.

"Who observes more closely or learns more quickly than a child? And who is less likely to be considered a threat? The Benderzic have left this one, and one day they will return for her. Even if they aren't able to take her from us, their attention is upon us. They will find ways to evaluate us, eventually. So my daughter—" Now it was Khira who hesitated, who seemed uncertain. "My daughter, you and Juaren have seen things no other Brakrathi have seen. You know better than any of us—except Verra—what waits out there, beyond our skies. The Council doesn't know of this child yet. I will tell them when session is called at season's end. And I will tell them something else too. The people must know. The people must begin to understand that the universe doesn't end here, that they cannot sleep while the Benderzic gather information to bid away. The people—"

"The people must be wakened," Juaren said softly. "They've been sleeping. They've been dreaming. Now they must wake and see what the morning brings."

"Yes," Khira said, looking at him directly for the first time, obviously relieved that he understood. "And you—you are the people to waken them."

Reyna laughed softly, touching Juaren's arm, feeling the tension ebb from him. So her mother wanted them to do the very thing they had intended to do. She formally requested them to do it. She would defend the necessity of it to the Council.

It was the end of a long journey and the beginning of another. Silently Reyna numbered some of the lessons she had learned: that it didn't matter who held the sunthrone of Valley Terlath, so long as someone did. That with understanding, she became as tall as her mother, as ageless as the throne, as resilient as the silk she held in her hand—and all with no apparent change. That with understanding, she became a woman with a place—in the mountains, in the valley, in her own eyes. And the more she increased her understanding, the more secure she would be in all those things.

So there were many more lessons to be learned and now was the time to begin learning them. Smiling, she offered the bundle that held the life-silk to Juaren, so he could remove the wrappings.

"My mother, my father, my sister, there is someone you must meet."

BIRNAM RAUTH

And so he was free again. He ate light and drank breeze, taking strength from them both. He sang when he wanted, sometimes silently, sometimes aloud. He bathed himself in sunlight by day and starlight by night. He eavesdropped with less and less compunction upon the thoughts of anyone who stepped near. Sometimes when they did not step near enough, he went to them and lightly wrapped silken arms around them so he could use all the complex structures of their bodies to remember more clearly what it was to be human. They never seemed to be frightened by him when he did that. Some of them considered themselves honored.

He had learned many things from this last, long exploration. He had learned to find humanity in alien creatures. He had discovered the alien in himself. And he had learned that sometimes the alien and the human are so far separated by perception and experience that it is difficult to speak across the gap.

He had also learned that being imprisoned for a century in the hollow of a tree had not made him a sage. It had only helped him learn to accept solitude and loss. But at least in the loss of his body, he had acquired the ability to move freely from human mind to human mind, gathering impressions and information he could never have gathered by more clumsy means. So perhaps one day he would be a sage after all.

It was not an ambition he had ever aspired to. To see, to probe, to give his curiosity full reign, yes. To speak with an ancient's wisdom, when he still felt young and hungry for understanding—no.

But when he traveled with Reyna and Juaren, when he spoke to the awed people who gathered to hear the tales of his star journeys —to hear of the strange, benign peoples and creatures he had known, to hear of other peoples and creatures who were not benign at all—he put on a sage's manner. Like Reyna, like Juaren, he knew the need to spur these people to look beyond their own fields and halls, to begin to think of their strengths and weaknesses.

He knew because he had reached into Iahn's mind. He had reached deeply, far past that day when Iahn had stood as a boy on a strange world and wondered why a white silk spoke with a familiar voice. In looking, he had looked into the very face of the Benderzic. He had reached into Cilka's mind too and looked into that same face. And somewhere, scattered across tens and hundreds of little-known worlds, there were others like the child Iahn had been, like the child Cilka was—tools the Benderzic used with no more feeling than if they were made of wood or metal.

The Benderzic would have just as much feeling for the trusting people of Brakrath and for their rich world.

So when Birnam Rauth spoke to those people he put on a sage's manner, he plundered their open minds for every clue to their understanding, and he vowed to shake them until they woke, blinking and confused, to the world that lay beyond their own skies.